Eighth Emperor

By Simon Jimenez

The Vanished Birds

The Spear Cuts Through Water

THE SPEAR CUTS THROUGH WATER

THE
SPEAR CUTS
THROUGH
WATER

—

SIMON JIMENEZ

NEW YORK

Copyright © 2022 by Simon Jimenez

Published in the United States by Del Rey, an imprint of Random House,
a division of Penguin Random House LLC, New York.

DEL REY and the CIRCLE colophon are registered trademarks of
Penguin Random House LLC.

Title-page art: © istock.com/barsrsind

Library of Congress Cataloging-in-Publication Data
Names: Jimenez, Simon, 1989– author.
Title: The spear cuts through water / Simon Jimenez.
Description: First edition. | New York: Del Rey, [2022]
Identifiers: LCCN 2021047263 (print) | LCCN 2021047264 (ebook) |
ISBN 9780593156599 (hardcover; acid-free paper) | ISBN 9780593156605 (ebook)
Subjects: LCGFT: Novels.
Classification: LCC PS3610.I54 S64 2022 (print) | LCC PS3610.I54 (ebook) |
DDC 813/.6—dc23
LC record available at https://lccn.loc.gov/2021047263
LC ebook record available at https://lccn.loc.gov/2021047264

Printed in Canada on acid-free paper

randomhousebooks.com

2 4 6 8 9 7 5 3 1

First Edition

Book design by Edwin Vazquez

This one's for me

The Schedule of His Holy Pilgrimage

———

BEFORE

I

Before you arrive,

you remember your lola, smoking. You remember the smell of her dried tobacco, like hay after a storm. The soft crinkle of the rolling paper. The zip of the matchstick, which she'd sometimes strike against the lizard-rough skin of her leg, to impress you. You remember the ritual of it. Her mouth was too dry to lick the paper shut so she had you do it, the twiggy pieces of tobacco sticking to your tongue like bugs' legs as you wetted the edges. She told you it was an exchange. Your spit for her stories. Tales of the Old Country; of ruined kingdoms and tragic betrayals and old trees that drank the blood of foxes foolish enough to sleep amongst their sharp roots; any tale that could be told in the span of one quickly burning cigarette. "It was all so very different back then," she'd begin, and you'd watch the paper curl and burn between her fingers as she described the one hundred wolves who hunted the runaway sun, and the mighty sword Jidero, so thin it could cut open the space between seconds. Her words forever married to the musk of her cigarette and her bone-rattling laughter; so much so that whenever you think of that place, long ago and far away, you cannot help but think of smoke, and death.

When did she first tell you of the Inverted Theater?

You were thirteen, you think; it was around that age that she often seemed startled by you, offended even, her lip curling whenever you came into the room, as if an untoward stranger had just tripped into her on the street. You thought her distaste was because of your body odor, your oily skin, your shy hunch, but the truth was she was just surprised by how quickly time had passed. Your youth wounded her. It made her want to protect you, and to kick you out the door.

"Sit," she said, when she saw you passing the kitchen. "Listen. I have a tale to tell."

The warm, breeze-blown night came in through the propped-open window, playing at the sheer curtains and the smoke from your lola's fingers, as she told you of the theater that stood between worlds.

"Once, the Moon and the Water were in love." She lingered on that word, love, just as the smoke lingered in the air. "You can imagine it was not the most convenient affair. One was trapped in the heavens, the other the earth. One was stillness itself, the other made only of waves and tempests. But they were happy for a time. The Moon would bathe the Water in its radiance, and the Water would dance, with its ebb and flow, to the Moon's suggestion. And though they occupied different spheres, they were able to visit one another through less direct means, for there is no barrier in this life that love cannot overcome. The Water would send up to the skies plump storm clouds, swollen with its essence, its cool mist and salty breath kissing the Moon's dry and cracked surface. And the Moon, when it wished to visit the Water, would cast its reflection into the Water's surface, and in the Inverted World that lies suspended below our own, in glass and still water, they would meet, and dance, and make love." Your lola paused, and stared at you from between curls of smoke, in study of your expression. There was a time when you would be squeamish at the mere hint of intimacy in her tales, but not this time; this time you simply sat in rapt attention—a sign of maturity that both heartened and depressed her. "Anyway," she said, after a rasped inhalation. "It was in that world of reflection where they built the theater that is the locus of our tale.

"Being the patron gods of artists and dancers, the Moon and the Water both loved the stage, which is why they created their own: a pagoda so tall its height cuts through the heavenly bands, within which the performances of the ages would be hosted. The telling of tales beyond even my knowing." She coughed. "Even after the Moon and the Water parted ways, the theater remained, run by their love-child, a being of immense beauty who took to inviting even mortals such as us to come visit their arena."

You asked her how mortals could reach such a place.

"Through dreams," she said, the cigarette butt ash in her hand. "A deep sleep, in waters deeper than your dreaming spirit has ever swum before. That's all. Dreams, and luck. And when you arrive, you are told a tale of the Old Country; the right tale at the right time. And when you leave—when your body comes up from that deep slumber—you will feel satisfied, whole, though you will not remember why, the memory of your visit forgotten, slipped from the mind like soapy water, the way any good dream might the more one tries to recall it. You will try to remember it. With great effort." She smiled, wistful. "But you will fail."

Your lola began rolling another cigarette.

"Perhaps before the end," she said, "I'll finally remember my own time there."

There was giggling from the other room. As your lola worked the tobacco through the rolling paper, you leaned back in your chair to better look at your brothers, who were listening to the radio in the living room. All nine of them were crowded around the radio like stray cats at a butcher's shop—a leg draped over the arm of the couch—a head lolling off the side of the love seat—chins propped on fists on the coffee table as the weekly serial neared its climax—*all of the inquisitor's men aiming their rifles at the church windows, ready to shoot Captain Domingo dead, wondering as they aimed down their sights why the jackal dared to smile at the hour of his death—the reason clear, once the good captain revealed with a wink the detonator in his gloved hand*—and as you looked at your brothers, you felt both envious that you were not sitting with them and also glad that you were apart from them. That you could see them all from your chair in the kitchen. That you could hold them all in your eye and keep them there.

"We might try to go back," your lola said, staring out the window with her large, wet eyes, "but we only get one turn. One invite. So do not waste it. If nothing else, remember that."

The night air came in through the small kitchen window. A horn from an old car blared down the road. Your father would be home soon with the day heavy on his shoulders. The table still needed to be made. But your lola was unconcerned with time, her drags deep and unhurried. "You will not know the Inverted Theater has called for you until you are already there," she said as she let the paper burn, and the years burn with it. "It is a place you cannot plan for." The shutters trembled against the coastal breeze. "And when you arrive, dream-tripped and unexpectedly, in that amphitheater, the best thing you can do is sit, and watch, and listen, for you are not there by accident."

She sucked on the paper, the tip now an orange rose. The cigarette was just about finished when the front door slammed open. Your brothers scattering from the radio as your father came inside with his mood and all the outside world—your lola gripping your wrist, before you too could go to greet him.

"The tale is for you," she said.

The tobacco burning in her lungs.

"So let the dreaming body go."

She exhaled.

And the smoke, blown in from the dark, envelops you until all you can see are the curls of gray matter swirling around you, the thick fog seeming to lift you, to cradle you, bearing you gently downward until you light upon a smooth, hard surface, and the smoke clears—the memory of your lola in the kitchen fading as day does to dusk, before you find yourself standing before the very place she had once spoken of, all those years ago.

Welcome to the Inverted Theater.

You step out of the smoke and you see it: the towering pagoda on a still lake at night, its reflection in the water perfect, its many levels at once rising high above you and, in its watery likeness, falling endlessly below. Lanterns hang off its curved eaves like earrings, lighting up its ornate facade against the darkness of the black-carpet sky. The structure looms, made up of an infinite stack of balconies, each one painted a different color. From a purple balcony high up a herald leans over and shouts that the performance is soon to begin, to please enter and take your seat.

A stone path begs you to cross the dark water. As you begin your crossing, you realize you do not walk alone. You walk amongst a river of other dreaming shades, who pass through you like gusts of wind, their thoughts coming in and out like radio signals. They are thinking about work. About lost loves. The hours they wasted in rooms darkly lit by stubbed tallow candles. *I was keeping the books for a madman. I knew I needed a new job, but I couldn't risk the downtime—who can risk the downtime?* Some you understand, others are beyond you. They speak in languages you do not recognize, or in terms that, stripped of context, mean nothing. *Thread-ripping down the runner of stars, was in the midst of my third weft, fast a-tumble in my sleeper's mitt, when my dreaming self was coaxed here, to this dark lake shore.* Shades of people from everywhere and everywhen. Faceless, out of focus, loud. And as you cross this lake, their noise comes all at once and overwhelmingly, sounding like nothing less than the vast ocean's roar—a collective hum, breathed out by the mouths of thousands, indistinct and infinite. An infinity in which you now sit.

Eighth row, dead center.

You blink, and you are here—in this many-pewed theater space, lush in drapes and blackwood flooring. The theater is styled from an era long past and almost forgotten. You are seated on a bench that has been reserved for you. You knew this was your seat before you even laid eyes on it. Called to it. Certain of your destination.

You are less certain about other things. As the others find their own seats and the attendants run up and down the aisles with lit candles floating behind them, the tall shade sitting beside you leans over and asks you where you are from.

You struggle to answer.

This moonlit body comes to your aid. With a gentle nudge of the toe, it unfurls the parchment of your people's history, this toe running along the battles and the treaties, the dispersals and the reunions, until it finds you here: in the time of trains and steamships, when cathedral radios crackled from the open windows of the dockside town in which you lived.

There is a war, you tell the shade.

The shade nods in grim understanding.

You are from a time of posters and propaganda. When news of the war effort fluttered down the painted walls of crooked alleys. Sun-draped and salt-scented ocean views disrupted by the silhouettes of warships in the blue distance. Wounded soldiers sometimes boated into town. The war is everywhere, but if you were awake tonight—this night, now—and you turned the dial of your radio, you would not hear the staticky voice of a slick man sharing news of the front but instead the crooning warble of Dorrado "Chilo" Semina, whose voice has captured the hearts of most lovesick listeners across the Unioned Continent—but alas! Tomorrow morning, when you wake, you will have to lie to your compatriots when they ask you if you stayed up to listen to his new single, and you will have to pretend to sing along with their delighted chorus, mouthing the words you shamefully have yet to commit to memory, because right here, right now, as the people of your town swoon to the pop signal, your body lies in deep slumber in a room once shared by you and your nine brothers.

That is you. A merchant's child. But one of many. How old you are outside this dream is irrelevant; in this theater you are as you feel—a youth, deep in your adolescence, and, like all youths, lonely in your own unnameable way. Fearful of your father and hounded by your lola, who was uninterested in the developments of your body, or your roaming interests, as she sucked smoke from a wrinkled cigarette and explained to you the land your family had come from and the tales that had come with them. "There is no preparing for the Inverted Theater," she had said. "It greets you when it chooses."

All of this you say to the shade, and it nods, satisfied, before it turns away to other business. You wonder if you should ask it where it is from, but the shade seems very much done with you, so instead you look about this Inverted Theater with a lost expression, your awe for your surroundings mixed with a deep longing, and unanswerable confusion, as you try to divine for what reason you might have been summoned here.

"There is always a reason."

You begin to suspect it might have to do with the object you only now realize you are holding in your hands.

This spear.

You know it well; the blood-red tint of the wood; the red tassel that chokes the gleaming and deadly point; the strange grooves and etchings that travel the length of the weapon in esoteric patterns. Ever since you can remember, this weapon has dutifully hung on the family room mantel, ignored by all in your house as but part of the scenery, for it was too expensive, too ancient, and too useless to interact with. You and your brothers once caught holy hell for playing with it in the courtyard when you were very young. One of the housekeepers informed your father, and your father, who never hit you but knew other ways to make you feel small, spoke to you and your brothers, one by one, in his office, and never again did you touch the weapon, much less look at it, which is why you feel an illicit thrill to hold it now, whether it be the real thing or merely a dream of it.

"It has traveled far to get here," your lola liked to say, "with farther yet to go."

You notice the other members of the audience, the other shades, stealing furtive glances at your weapon. *We were wondering why this shadow was armed.* And they are wondering why the weapon looks so familiar. Why you have brought it with you to this sacred place. And if you intended to use it.

But such questions would have to wait.

For it begins.

The performance that you have been called to witness. You hear the beat of a drum. A polished wooden stick rapping against taut, oiled skin. Thrum. The drum punches through this dark space. Thrum. It strikes you, right there, the middle of your chest. Thrum. *It made us shiver to hear it.* You listen to the heartbeat of this building. Thrum. The swelled, anticipatory breath of the people around you. Thrum. And you lower the family spear, you let it rest at a slant against your side, forgotten for now, while you and the other audience members all turn to the stage with not a breath released, your unblinking eyes watching the drapes begin their soft and silent lift up into the rafters, revealing, like parted wings, the stage.

Thrum.

This moonlit body stands before you. And though this is your first meeting, all of you recognize this body immediately. *We had seen the renditions, the statues, the friezes.* The depictions of a figure of broad back and narrow hip, with skin the color of a blue summer sky and eyes that shine like light on silver. You have seen the artists' dreams of this moonlit body, with its sea-green hair that sways as if underwater, and as you see this body now, bowing at the head of the stage, you realize that all of the dreams of its beauty were true. Somewhere in your memory, your lola is sighing in a yearning way as she looks up through the small kitchen window at the star-rich swirl of night. "And should you one day find yourself sitting in that theater, lucky enough to watch those curtains rise, it is the child of the Moon and the Water who will greet you. That creature born of the dance between the lunar wane and ebbing tide, now cast in their role as the eternal performer of the Sleeping Sea. Forever imbued with the strength and grace of the most accomplished of dancers."

She smiles.

"A beautiful, moonlit body."

And you look upon this moonlit body with surprise as it breathes in through its nose so deeply its belly distends, pregnant with wind. This body's feet braced on the boards of the stage before it releases in one long exhale all that it has taken in, the gust from its pursed lips blowing out all the braziers in this theater, whipping the fire into smoke until the room votes in favor of the dark and all that is visible to your eyes is the last of the lit braziers onstage—your pupils narrowing on this ancient and raging flame, as this moonlit body stands before it and, like a magician at some unholy font, conjures from its crackling hearth the voices of the ancient and the dead, *our tale soon to be told—of that week of blood, that week of chaos,* the rush of whispers filling the theater, for some tales are too large to be told by one voice alone.

This is the tale of your land,
And the spear that cut through it.

You hear a charge of horses pouring over some distant hill as dancers now swarm the stage, their footsteps a chaotic syncopation. The flames leap, the walls blasted with light and shadow, and in this dreaming theater you swear that you can see the scene as it is, as this moonlit body's movements, and those of the dancers, carve out of the air that land far away and long ago—a place once known to you only through your lola's descriptions, now springing to life in the deep root of you, as if it had always been there. The deep valleys and old forests, the staggering black mountains that cut the clouds, and the carpets of mist that rise from the gulches between sheer cliffs. *This is the land where we lived, and where we died.* The Old Country, your lola called it, but there were other names too. Names etched in runes and woven in tongues long lost to your history. Tonight it is the Land of the Moonless Night. Tonight it is the land that sweats under the Endless Summer—and as the fires of this theater rage, you feel the unblinking sun on your back. You smell the dried grass. You see the dead brooks and the curling fingers of roadside corpses thick with flies that scatter as the riders gallop heedlessly past this parched landscape bearing the banner of their emperor.

This is where our tale begins, with a band of warriors performing a royal inspection of the country, the dancers' feet stamping into the boards of the stage as might a brigade of fearsome riders across a dust-beaten land, and you see with clarity the rider at the head of this royal charge—a man who lifts his laughing face into the air and breathes deep the smells of the country, his birthright, while he leads his warrior-sons west.

"Listen," your lola would say as she lit her cigarette.

Listen, this moonlit body says as the bloodied sun lifts into the parchment sky to the bone-snap of drums.

Listen to the Brigade of the Red Peacock.

The sound of distant thunder in the bright and cloudless day. Thunder between the ache of the rolling hills and the green burst of forests. Thunder that scared the animals into their burrows. The people turning their worried ears to the sky. *We heard them before we saw them.* The thunder of the royal stampede.

The villagers put away their scythes and turned over the feed buckets as the pebbles danced and the terra-cotta eaves trembled. The children held close as the horses crested the nearby rise, two score in number, their riders garbed in red; a gash on the noon horizon. Warriors vicious and without mercy, their faces tattooed with their namesake, their sharp cheeks and hungry eyes framed by red beak and feather; a sight feared by any wise traveler, by anyone who heard the stories, for of the many brigades and bands and gangs that haunted the valleys in those days, it was the Red Peacocks who were deadliest, led as they were by one of the princes of the Throne, a man who had well earned his title of the First Terror.

Across the land, the people lined up to greet them. It was the eve of the Emperor's Holy Pilgrimage, and the brigade was charged with the sacred duty of preparing the land for His Smiling Sun's arrival.

They did so with great pleasure.

"Soon," the First Terror said to the weavers and the quarry workers, the fishermen and the farmers, "in but a matter of days, He will arrive, and in His generosity of spirit, He will visit you all over the course of His five-day journey to the eastern coast. You will present Him with the finest offerings of your craft or your harvest. Your pearls of rice grain, your fresh salted fish. Your richest tapestries. The spirit of your hard work. And He will take these offerings with Him, and He will cherish them, as He disembarks to visit our colonies across the Great and Unending Sea. His visitation, the greatest honor of your life. In later years, you will recall it to the children at your bedside. Squander this moment at your peril." During these speeches the Peacocks slapped open doors and rummaged through dressers and kicked at loose floorboards, searching for evidence of dissent. Chickens were chased out of coops. Sharp knives taken to grain sacks, to linen sheets. The people listened to the ransacking of their homes *but we did not dare turn to look, for we all knew the consequence of turning away from a prince.* "When His caravan passes through this way, you will hear a drum heralding His arrival. You will line up, like so, across the entrance to your village, facing the road; every man, woman, and child. And you will bow. You will bow low, so He cannot see your face. Every head that does not bow for our Smiling Sun will be added to our collection," he said, pointing at the fly-strewn cloth sacks that hung from the horse saddles, the cloth black with dried blood.

In one of the villages, there was a loud clatter—a crying girl dragged out of a small house.

"This rat was hiding under the boards, Father!" the Peacock shouted.

The villagers took in a collective breath. *And we glared at the girl's parents, who in spoiling this child had doomed us all.* The girl's bare feet trenched the hot dirt as she was brought to the prince for judgment.

One of her parents fought against those restraining her.

"She was scared!" the mother cried. "Forgive us! She was scared!"

The father quiet, his head bowed low.

The First Terror drummed his fingers against his waist. He lifted the shivering girl to her feet *and then he looked into her eyes, and we could feel the wind begin to whip and rise and we were certain that this was our end, that the prince would not forgive this rudeness and all of us would be tossed into the pit of Joyrock. That we were spared that day was a fortune beyond measure.* What feeling of grace prompted the Terror to send the girl gently into the crowd, into the trembling arms of her parents, would remain to them forever a mystery. The unnatural wind dying down. An easy smile on his lips. "Let it not be said that the Throne is without its mercy," he said. "But on the day of His caravan's arrival, should any transgress beyond their station, do not expect such forgiveness."

Then they left. The horses rearing not long after the Terror finished his address, the people left in stunned silence, a few of them coughing in the stampede's dust wake. The mother clutching the girl to her breast as the father looked on them helplessly, having given up his daughter for dead. *And never would my wife let me forget the shame of that day. Never again could I meet my daughter's eyes.*

Never would we understand why we were spared.

The reason was a simple one. It was the same reason that the First Terror was in such high spirits during the tedium of his tasks, in those weeks of his inspections. Why he spurred his horse at a quickened pace, so eager to return to the palace without delay or incident. A reason that came vividly to his mind when he looked into that little girl's eyes and saw they were the same color as that of his beloved son.

Of Jun.

"For six months I have been parted from his company. He serves the Throne with pride; I recognize this. And I recognize the importance of his mission. But I cannot help but wish he did not have to perform his duty. That he was riding by my side this day. It has been a great difficulty, waiting for him to be returned to us."

The commander of Badger Gate, a small man with a smudge of hair on his chin, poured tea for the Terror, as was protocol, *doing my utmost to not show the tremble in my hands; my utmost not to soil myself.*

"You are a caring father," he said with a servant's smile, placing the polished-clean teacup before the royal prince. "May all the sons of this country be so blessed, to have a parent like you."

Sycophantic words, nonetheless true. The First Terror wept with his sons and he laughed with them, *and in turn we gave him our unwavering devotion, riding with him to the ends of the country, killing anyone who needed to be killed.* But he had a favorite. And he was not shy about who that favorite was.

"To Jun," the commander said, raising his cup, hoping to please his guest, a social tactic that played excellently, as the Terror toasted him with moist eyes.

"To Jun."

Their cups clapped to Jun Ossa, the twenty-fifth Peacock, who had for six months been guarding the fabled Wolf Door beneath the palace mountains, the sole protector of the empress. The Terror wiped his eyes, moved by this imagined scene: Jun's six-month rotation, spent alone in the cold and the dark of that deep mountain cavern with nothing but one's blade, and one's thoughts, and a locked door to protect, to keep one company. This image weighed on him for the rest of the day, until later, at camp, his other sons placed hands on him in comfort, *and we told him it wouldn't be long now,* the prince then smiling at his boys, grateful for all of them.

Horse spurred onward, they journeyed west and completed their assignment, uncommon mercies spared for those they passed, the Terror's mind split between duty and family. As he made his inspections, as he flipped through poorly kept records and questioned an endless parade of perspiring commanders, he thought of his son. Of Jun the Beautiful Knife, who slit his first throat at eight years of age. Jun the Red Shadow, who alone had tracked the infamous Dorogo Bandit Clan into the vagrant woods after their raid of Lady Panjet's sacred vaults, none of the bandits aware they were being hunted that night, not even as they were bled dry in the dark, one by one, throughout their premature celebrations. Jun the Torchbearer, who lit swaths of grain fields on fire in search of the traitorous dogs who had ambushed the Swan Road patrols. *From our houses we watched our harvests burn and the men we hid burn with them as that little demon lobbed his torches.* Jun the Many Titled, these honorifics bestowed upon him by his doting father.

"I remember the last time I passed this way," he said at Eagle Gate to a quiet crowd of sentries, "some seasons ago . . . my son Jun noted that there was an unacceptable level of indolence amongst your sentries. A disorderly mess hall, an unkempt barracks. Jun is quite adept at such judgments. He rightly shamed you for your lack of discipline, and at the time you had promised to tighten the loose threads of your command. We believed you." His finger sliding all the while across the wall of the barracks, holding up to the sweating creatures who awaited his judgment a print of dirt and dust. He did not have to say anything. The sentries and even their commander fell on their knees and polished every inch of the barracks and he smiled, for though the emperor would not care about the dust, much less see it, it was good to see that the people were still well under control despite rumor of the growing rebellion.

This was how he made the last stretch to the capital; with news for his father that the land was well groomed and tamed for his journey, and with the anticipation for the long-awaited reunion with his prized son. The sun burst from behind a dark cloud. The western mountains known as the Jaw rose ever higher to meet them. And the First Terror howled into the air, and his Peacocks howled with him when the city gates unfolded to their arrival. But whatever triumphant return the Terror might have been expecting come his riding through the steep roads of the Palace City, those expectations were not met, the mood subdued and tense. An unusual alertness to the guards posted along the mountain road—so distracted these men were they took no notice of the bags of severed heads the Peacocks had brought home that day. *We were less concerned with those coming up than we were those coming down—there was a culprit in our midst, readying their escape.*

The Terror sniffed the cold, high-altitude air. He detected a sourness, like rotten lemons, and he knew his father was in a bad mood.

When they had crested the last rise, one of the attendant generals rode up in greeting, and it was from him the prince learned why the mood of the Jaw was so grim. The general wore the painted mask of a tusked boar, for it was the custom of the court to cover one's face entirely when in the emperor's presence—the boar's eyes appropriately wide and panicked as he breathlessly explained the situation.

This is the tale of the end of the Moon Throne.

And it began here.

With the theft of a bird.

It happened, the general said, before the purpling of sunrise, when even the dawn watchtower guards had yet to change shift. Someone had stolen into His royal apartment—impossibly—and thieved the emperor's pet bird right from its redwood cage. And the emperor was not taking this trespass well.

"None of us can reach Him," the attendant general said. "He refuses to entertain any talk of tomorrow's pilgrimage until the bird is found and the culprit justly punished."

"Did He move the bridges?" the Terror asked.

"He did, my lord."

The Terror rubbed his eyes.

Your lola made a cat's cradle out of red thread.

"From peak to peak, the pagodas of the palace stood on the tips of the Westward Mountains," she said. Her fingers shut and then opened again, the pattern of the thread rearranged. "A dozen bridges of finely hewn stone spanned these peaks, connecting these pagodas in a marvelous web. Bridges that turned on giant axes, like the hands of a clock. By the emperor's whim, and the power of his god gifts, the bridges moved, and the layout of the palace would change." Her fingers kept closing and reopening, the pattern of the thread born anew, the connections shifting. You asked her what purpose moveable bridges were on a mountaintop. "Defense," she said. "Throughout the entirety of the royal line there had been attempts of assassination and infiltration. In an emergency, the emperor could command these bridges be directed anywhere He wished. He could, in an instant, isolate His royal apartments from the entire world, and strand His enemies on the disconnected peaks."

She was looking across the courtyard at the windowed corridor down which your father stomped.

"It was the last of the emperors who made the most of those bridges. It is said that He changed their orientation more often than any of His predecessors. And do you know why?" When you shook your head, she said, in an almost joyful whisper, "Because He was afraid." Somewhere, you heard a door slam shut. A motorcar, roiling to life. As your father drove away, the red thread unraveled from your lola's limp fingers onto your palm, and she closed your fingers over it. "He was afraid of death."

"All of the bridges are disconnected," the general said. "The apartments are inaccessible, and half of our workers are stuck on the other pagodas with no way to return."

"This will not do," the Terror said. "We leave tomorrow. We have no time for tantrums." He smiled at the general in a way that made the man take a step back. "I trust that you are presenting me not only a problem but also a solution."

The general nodded after a moment of hesitation. *I could smell the rotting heads that hung from his sons' saddles. Behind my mask my eyes were tearing.* "Yes, my prince. There is a solution. And with your permission, we will carry it through."

Permission was given. Within the hour, the First Terror sat in court amongst the other powerful lords in attendance, surrounding a man they had chosen to take the fall for the crime, with the hope that once someone, anyone, was punished, the emperor's temper would be eased, and the bridges returned to their proper stations.

They chose me. The accused stood in the middle of the room, on the elevated petitioner's pulpit, like a man on a raft about to be pushed out to sea. He was an older man, with a back-bent body, his terrified face covered by the painted mask of a smiling gecko. *For thirty-three years I had polished the porcelain vases and watered the evenlight lilies in the hanging gardens. I worked quietly, I kept to my own business, and unlike my fellow attendants I engaged in no rumor or speculation about the emperor's behavior in the last few months. For thirty-three years I woke up before the first crowing and I went to sleep long after the last candle died in His royal window. I gave my body and my heart to the diligent cleaning of the drapery and the laying out of delicate foods on finely carved trays. I surrendered my opportunities for love or profit because my parents had taught me that nothing was more important in this world than loyalty. And then—and then—*the false charges were read to him by the five Wise Men at the long table on the other end of the room, in cold and detailed order, while in the back the First Terror paid little attention, speaking quietly to another lord about other matters of state. The man was accused of stealing his way into the royal salon, of thieving the emperor's pet bird, and of snapping the neck of the emperor's pet bird out of malice before tossing it over the railing into the chasm, thus preventing anyone from returning the corpse to its rightful owner. The First of the Wise Men made theater of the moment. "For thirty-three years you had served this throne," he spat.

And then, one day, I was finished. The man wept so loudly the lords in the court shifted uncomfortably. *And how could I not weep, as my fellow attendants, and the lords I had served, each approached the Wise Men and gave them the evidence they needed to condemn me? On the memories of their lolas they swore they had not seen me all morning. That for too long I had been complaining about my station. That I had motive.* All of this theater for the benefit of the creature perched on the high chair.

The tortoise's gaze was set on the First Terror. "The Smiling Sun wishes to know your thoughts," the mad creature giggled. "From all the evidence laid before you, to what side of the line does your heart lean?"

The Terror looked up at his father's surrogate and then down at the wet dog of a man in the center of the room. *Thirty-three years.* And without a further moment of consideration, he said, "My Smiling Sun, this man is guilty."

The accused deflated.

For what? I asked.

For what?

"The Smiling Sun wishes to let you know that He remembers you," the tortoise said to the accused. "That while His own father was in court, you used to give Him sweets behind His nanny's back."

The guilty man in the pulpit said this was true. *I gave him little rolls of sugared rice, wrapped in oiled banana leaf. He was the emperor's son, but he was also a child who was bored and lonely.* "I did so gladly, My Smiling Sun!" he shouted.

"Which makes it all the more shameful, that your heart has grown so sick." The tortoise turned away. It let out a plaintive giggle. "May you find peace in the Sleeping Sea."

A guard withdrew his blade. The man stood up—*I would beg, I would offer anything*—his hands reaching up to remove his mask, to beseech the court with his tear-stained eyes, but his shout was clipped by his swift and sudden beheading.

A string of blood slashed across the blackwood floor. The head stopped rolling a few paces from the line of lords. The gecko mask smiled emptily at a man who pressed a handkerchief to his nose, at the brink of fainting. And when the red fountain guttered out, the body fell in a limp sprawl. The last bits of life leaving through the twitch of his right index finger.

"We are finished," the tortoise said.

The lords of the court kissed the floor with their foreheads.

The palace trembled.

As the bridges rumbled back into place, the dead man was dragged by his feet through the open door, *my body thrown over the bridge railing into the nameless chasm, without marker or prayer,* while the Terror made his way across the span to the apartments without even waiting for the bridge to finish its groaning rotation. Midstride he fitted a finely hewn Peacock mask onto his head, for not even princes were exempt from the emperor's edict, and he entered through the whispering doors into the royal salon, taking a moment to rediscover his patience before he announced his presence—to no response.

He excused himself loudly and entered. He took note of the waxed low tables, the parchment rolls slotted neatly into their diamond-shaped cubbies, the extravagant Induun curtains beaten and free of wrinkles, thinking that one would be hard-pressed to believe there had been a burglary, but for the empty birdcage that hung uselessly in the corner of the room.

"Nowhere is safe, it seems," a hoarse voice said. "Not even my home."

Magaam Ossa, Eighth Emperor of the Moon Throne and Father of the Three Terrors, sulked in the dark in his favorite chair.

"It is good to see you, Father," the Terror said. He knelt, and pressed the beak of his mask to his father's skeletal hand.

"Is it?" the emperor asked.

He looked down at his son with his small and lifeless eyes, daring him to answer. His hand, still in the prince's own, was thick with veins, like dead snakes on a still river. The Terror wanted to both crush this weak hand and cradle it.

"I know that today has been trying," he said, "but I come bearing good news about your journey tomorrow. The people—"

His father's hand slipped away. He watched as the Eighth Emperor, dressed in His blackest robe, approached the balcony window like a widowed mourner.

"I was sorry to hear about your bird," the Terror ventured to say. "I have been away for too long, it seems. I did not know you had a new pet."

"How did you and the other lords decide on whom to behead?" the emperor asked.

The Terror hesitated.

"By discovering the guilty party, my lord."

"I am not a mandolin. Do not attempt to play me like one."

A giggle came from the other end of the room. The prince cut a glance at the wriggling tortoise seated on a raised cushion by the desk. The tortoise stared back at him in hair-raising defiance. "He was picked at random," the Terror admitted.

"In what fashion?"

"We assigned the attendants who had visited your apartment in the last few days a number. One of the generals turned over a cup of dice." As the emperor chuckled darkly at this explanation the prince looked at his father in an imperceptible squint. "You knew, then. That the man was innocent."

The emperor walked across the salon to the empty birdcage. He fiddled with the latch of the cage, swinging the hatch shut and opening it again, and as the Terror watched his father, who seemed somehow much older than He was only a few months ago, it seemed entirely possible that there was no theft—that this old man had simply forgotten to lock the cage last night, and His bird escaped on its own, unaided, through the balcony window. *That the sole reason I was killed in court was as sacrifice to His pride.*

"It matters not in the end," the emperor said, shutting the cage door for good. "Now. Tell me of my country."

They took tea together. The Terror prepared it. He brought the water to a boil over the cook-flame as his father remained sullen and withdrawn, the deep wells under His eyes speaking to how little sleep He was getting. Hoping to lift his mood, the prince told Him that the checkpoints on the Road Above were in good order. That bandit attacks were at the lowest incidence rate since the time of his grandfather. He did not mention that the opposite was true for the Road Below; that more people than ever fell prey to thieves and murderers on that long, unattended road. *A man stopped me on my way to my sister's village. He said he needed help moving his wagon, which was just over there, behind the trees. Yes. I was a fool. I had only three copans to my name. I don't know what he was expecting. But he gutted me for it anyway.* Yes, the Terror said, the land was thriving. "The fleet on the eastern coast finished construction not a few weeks ago, every boat manned by the finest nauters the land has to offer." He did not mention that the fleet cost three times as much as was first estimated and that the Throne was now well in debt to the Five Families from whom the raw materials were purchased. He told his father that everything was prepared for tomorrow, and the people fall over each other to see His caravan pass their way. He did not tell him that those people were hungry, that because of the Endless Summer, their bodies littered the road-sides, throat-parched and sunburnt. *That our children drank from the rice paddies and bloated with sickness.* He told his father every-thing He needed to hear. But the honeyed words did little to stir the emperor from His mood, which of late had grown intense in its inwardness.

The emperor put His tea down. He rubbed His sunken eyes. He did not care about checkpoints or bandits or people.

He spoke of the one thing He did care about of late.

"I had another dream last night. A dream more vivid than all the others." He shut his eyes to recall it, as His son made a show of interest. "A tiger with a cherry bough in its jaws emerged from the brush of my private garden. I followed him through brush and meadow and even across the sea. It walked upon the waves as if they were solid ground." The emperor spoke of the tiger with a hushed reverence. It was known that the tiger and the cherry bough was a symbol of a long and prosperous life. Your lola had sewn the bough onto her father's clothes, which was the only explanation you and your brothers had as to how the man drooling in his rock-ing chair was still alive—that there must have been some truth to what they say about tigers and cherry boughs, since your great-grandfather, your granjo as you called him, for reasons of which you are still unsure, refused to die, despite the barrage of ailment and injury that comes with old age.

Death spurned, a life stretched beyond its means. These were the recent dreams, intense and all-consuming, that had of late been haunting the emperor with their otherworldly promises, inspiring His coming Holy Pilgrimage. Imagery and portent that compelled Him to journey to the new lands across the sea to find the key to a door that had up till then remained locked, for all men; even those born of a god.

The secret to eternal life.

He was not journeying to meet the people of His land. The pilgrimage was a means of collecting enough materials for the long journey across the sea, and beyond—wherever it might lead.

"Do you think I will find it?" He asked His son quietly. "Across that channel, that Great and Unending Sea?"

It worried the First Terror, to hear his father sound so uncertain now, the day before the journey. After all, once his father was gone, it was he who would rule in His stead, and he had many plans for the layout of this royal salon. "You will find what you seek across the waters," he assured the shrinking man. "In the new lands you will find the secret to eternal life. That is what your visions say, and so it will happen, because you are the sun under which all doubtful shadows flee. Is that not so?" He held his father's hand. "Well, Father? Is it not so?"

"It is so," his father said, swallowing some burble of emotion. "You are right, it is so."

"I am glad to hear it," the prince said. "Have you said your goodbyes to Mother? There will be no time for that in the morrow."

For the briefest moment, a mysterious expression came over the emperor, one His son could not quite read. Then it was gone. And the man was shaking His head. "Later tonight, after my final address, I will visit her."

"Good. And when you do, if you could let my son know that I am here, and greatly anticipate our reunion tomorrow—"

"Yes, yes," the Smiling Sun muttered, "your words will be relayed, if I remember."

"How has he been?" the prince asked. "The last time you went down there, was he hale?"

"Why would I know that? His health is of no concern to me."

"Did you speak with him? He is an adept conversationalist. Perhaps tomorrow you two might—"

"You test my patience, child."

The Peacock bowed.

"Deepest apologies, My Smiling Sun."

The emperor sank into His chair. He nudged His teacup away. "You have a knack for worsening my mood." He sighed. "Come," He said. "Tell me what tomorrow will bring. Tell me of my journey. Erase any surprise, any unknowns."

The prince did so eagerly, not wishing to get on His bad side, not this close to the end. "I will tell you of all that will come to pass tomorrow, and the days to come. I will tell you the tale of your pilgrimage."

"Then speak on, child." The last ruler of the Moon Throne shut His eyes once more, His sleepless body now warm and weighted by the tea. "And make your words as honeyed as our drink."

"This is the tale of tomorrow, and the week to come."

Tomorrow, Father, you begin the most important journey of your life. On the sweet breath of early morning you will depart by caravan, eastward, to the shore where the voyager fleet awaits your arrival, to bring you to the land of your fabled dreams.

You are so close to godhood.

It will be a journey of five days to reach the coast. Down the scenic Road Above, you will pass through the most spectacular of vistas and enjoy the fruits of the five provinces as the people, who yet believe this to be a mere spiritual pilgrimage, rise to greet you with their finest offerings.

On the First Day they will offer you their richest harvests. You will indulge in a feast of the most aromatic teas and the softest beds of rice, in a celebration hosted by Lord Yinn and Lady Panjet in the grand courtyard of Monkey Gate.

From there, after your night of revelry, you will head east, for the Bowl of Heaven. On those crystal waters you will spend the

Second Day, enjoying the freshest catch from the Thousand Rivers while taking in the lush comforts of my brother's pleasure boat. I have many opinions on the way Luubu conducts himself, as you well know, but what has never wavered is my high regard for his abilities to host an honored guest, and I am certain he will hold for you a party so grand that even you might reconsider leaving this country.

The Third Day will have you remain in the Bowl, where you will tour the textile fleets of Lord Induun, beholding the most extravagant of tapestries and the softest and most supple of carpets, all of which have been woven for that very day. Their patterns telling the story of your enduring rule. These carpets will travel with you on your long journey. They will remind you of home.

On the Fourth Day, your road will meet with the quarries of Lord Waag. Through the cleave of earth, you will be shown the night-black ore that makes our finest weapons. You will visit the forges, and they will present you with a blade sharper than any that has ever been crafted. May this blade protect you during your travels through the mystic and wild lands unknown.

And finally, the Fifth Day, the Last Day. That is when you will reach the Divine City at the end of the world. That inspiring cliff-side view of the Great and Unending Sea. There, a performance for the ages awaits you in the grand plaza, and you will enjoy the people's finest dancing before the last dregs of day. Whether you choose to visit Joyrock is up to you. No one will begrudge you, if you do not.

The sun at its last fall, you and your party will board the voyager fleet, loaded with the fruits of the land, supplied for years to come, and upon the unfurling of the sails, you will set off on your great adventure.

To a new land.

You will turn, Father, as the ship disembarks, and you will see all of us standing on the cliff's edge, bidding you farewell as you vanish into that limitless sunset. Fireworks exploding in the dark-red evening sky. And you will know in your heart that though you might be gone, you will never be forgotten—come the day that you return, having conquered death, the land will embrace you as it ever has: with warmth, and love, and the deepest of pride.

There is nothing to fear, My Smiling Sun. The hosts of good fortune remain your steadfast allies. I will remain in this palace, keeping stewardship over your land, and not a single day will pass that I do not lead the people in fervent prayer for your safe travels, your hearth kept stoked by me, for when you come back to claim it.

A giggle broke from the dark.

"You have a most loving son indeed, My Smiling Sun."

Both father and son looked across the salon at the tortoise resting on the blankets in the corner. The prince looked away in revulsion, while behind the veils of sheer Induun fabric, the massive creature let loose its mad giggles, which filled the room like gas escaping from a cracked pipe.

"Strange creatures, the tortoises."

Your lola was holding a phone to her ear, and in the other room, the radio was on; both objects good comparisons, she said. "They were tuned to a certain channel. They had access to a world we cannot see. They could smell moods, taste motive. And they could communicate with one another over great distances." On the radio, an announcer detailed the most recent victory; cannons detonating a coastline; planes shot out of the air like ducks; the enemy battalion obliterated. "A great power, those creatures had," she said. "And a kind of madness, because of it." She sighed as the phone rang on. "Is it any wonder, then, that the Throne had such use for them?"

The emperor nodded at His pet tortoise.

"Why do you interrupt us?" He asked the creature.

The giggling died away. "The Commander of Tiger Gate would like to confirm that your son will be joining her for tea tomorrow, My Smiling Sun."

The emperor turned to the prince. "I thought you were joining my caravan tomorrow."

The prince paused, in careful deliberation of his response. "I thought it prudent to first ride with the collections caravan on the Road Below, to ensure they get off to a good start. A small sacrifice, I think, to be without my company for a day while I make sure the materials for your long journey are being properly transported."

The emperor was not pleased, but as ever, He had a difficult time refuting His son's points. "And what's this about tea?"

The prince lifted a shoulder. "A drink with a friend, nothing more."

A deep sniff came from the tortoise, and it fell once more into a bout of giggles as it smelled from the prince's aura the ticklish spice of desire. "A friend and nothing more," it whispered to itself, deeply amused. "A friend and nothing more."

"Confirm the invitation, tortoise," the emperor said, not nearly as amused as His pet.

"Yes, My Smiling Sun."

The creature suddenly lifted its head. Its neck long and tensed.

The call went out.

You think of your lola, on the phone, hunched and anxious for the operator to pick up.

Briiiiiiiiiing-briiiiiiiiiiiiing.

"Briiiiiiiiiiiing," she would sometimes sing along.

She was always calling home—not your home, but the home across the sea, the one your family came from—to tell them everyone was safe, that you all barely even noticed the war. As the phone rang, she would wipe the drool from granjo's lips. She would shoo the cats out of the room. She would hum and move things around in the kitchen or yell at the housekeepers for some minor transgression. She would wait.

One of your older brothers, who was interested in such things, tried to explain to you how it all worked. How there was a woman somewhere, at a switchboard, connecting sockets with wires.

"Like this," he said, throwing his arms around in the air in a way that made you laugh. And so it was with the tortoises: one made a call, the line was connected, and the call went through. Simple business. Though sometimes, a more thoughtful guard or messenger might gaze at the creatures and wonder who was operating the switchboard.

Click.

Southeast—at the top of the watchtower, above the din of traffic moving through the dusty courtyard, the tortoise of Tiger Gate Checkpoint lifted its head, its neck long and tensed like its brother in the Palace, as it received its message. It nodded. And to the sentry who waited upon the creature, it said: "This one is told to confirm the invitation to tea, tomorrow, with the Commander."

With Araya the Drunk.

Titles were hard to shake in those days. They branded a person as sure as a hot iron on a flank. Some titles were cultivated. They offered a kind of protection, social or otherwise, to those who wore them, whether that be as a warning or a feint. So it was for the commander of Tiger Gate Checkpoint, Uhi Araya, who was known in most circles of the military hierarchy as Araya the Drunk. *The Lady of the Flask. The Blushing Fiend. Our Stumbling Maiden.* A jovial woman of short, round stature, a creature of her comforts who achieved her successes despite, or in some cases because of, her reliance on the drink, becoming in short order the overseer of the first checkpoint that lay on the infamous Road Below. A powerful position that yielded many benefits for her. *We always wondered how she got to where she was—what connections she had.* Her reputation preceding her as someone quick to laugh, and quicker to offer a swig of something debilitatingly joyful even while she took bribes on the side and bumped up the taxes of those passing through her checkpoint on larks and whims. *She said she didn't like the look of me. And then she turned us back. She didn't even return our papers.* This was Araya. Or, it was the side of her she presented to the world. Burping and cockeyed. A flirt and sometimes a hard-ass.

But there was another Araya that few people knew of. An Araya who had been working since the beginning to achieve something that was all but impossible. This was the Araya who unraveled the pouch of poison in her office, after it was confirmed the Terror was coming the next day. She leaned forward and sniffed the powdered mixture in the stone bowl, her nose tingling from the smell like sweet lightning. "Oh," she said, blowing her nose, her eyes watering. She did not know how she was going to get this into the First Terror's tea without him noticing.

She looked through her shelves, something to mask the taste.

"Shit," she said as she knocked a bottle of ink from the counter.

It all came down to her.

So said her contact, the tongueless savant of the gray rivers, some weeks ago, as he signed the plan months in the making onto her quavering palm. *With my shapes drawn onto her damp skin I told her the time had come: that finally we knew the schedule and route of the Pilgrimage.*

It was time to devour the royal family.

There was a knock on the door. "Commander," said a muffled voice, "a message by tortoise has come in for you: Lady Sova of the Panjet Estates would like to discuss your availability for her daughter's coming-of-age—"

"Later, Raami," she grunted as she wiped the ink off the floor, making it worse with each circle. "I'm a bit—I'm a bit busy at the moment."

"Yes, Commander."

His footsteps receded. With a sigh she slapped the dripping cloth into the bin and wiped the residue on her fingers on some inner fold of her robe, then returned to the mortar and the small pouch beside it.

Brittle leaves poked out of the pouch like knives.

Ordinary poison would not fell a royal. The long history of assassination attempts over the centuries of the Moon Throne's reign had told us that their bodies, born as they were from a god, were hardier than our own more mortal flesh. We did well to remember the story of the poor fool who tried to slip a pinch of the Judge's Kiss in the Third Emperor's tilted ear, to no effect—how the emperor woke up with only a small headache before he had his would-be assassin punished; the skin of the man's children stitched to his back, to wear for the remainder of his days as he was made to walk the roads of the country loudly extolling his ruler's virtues.

Araya remembered. That was why her hands continued to shake as she attended to the mixture on the table, grinding away till the powder was as fine as silk.

"This will not end well," she said with an empty smile.

With a pair of tongs, she added more leaves.

Idlit, it was called. It was a plant, snipped from the mossy earth of the deep forests by the old tribes who yet harvested there. *With our gloved hands and our opal knives we cut the weeping stems with blades as sharp as Soma's wit.* The small animals that made the mistake of chewing on this oily leaf convulsed on the misted forest floor, and the ones who did not die on the spot lay paralytic on the moss bed as the larger creatures of the basin emerged from the brush, sniffing their acrid helplessness in the air. *Poisons of the head and of the heart had no effect on princes or emperors. But poisons of the bone and of the flesh still had their purchase.*

On her palm, I told the commander that on the day of the First Terror's visit to Tiger Gate, when she served him tea as decorum dictated, she would spice his drink with this lovely mixture. I pressed the small pouch into her hand and with a warm touch I told her to take care. Too many idlit leaves, and the Terror would no doubt smell the addition of the unusual ingredient with his heightened sense, and he would kill every guard at this Gate before any of the paralytic had entered his bloodstream. Too few, and the man would feel nothing but a slight tingling in his extremities. *A turgid erection perhaps, but not the outcome we were hoping to inspire, especially in a man known for his virility.*

The effect of idlit was immediate in small animals, but in humans, when ingested with boiled tea, paralysis was delayed for the length of an afternoon meal. I told Araya she would need to make sure the Terror was on his way through the gate shortly after ingestion. In no uncertain terms the paralytic needed to come into effect when he was well east of the checkpoint—far enough from the border town so no help could come to him or his men.

I told her that the more Peacocks took part in the tea the better but that if only one person drank the tea, it must needs be HIM— the tea of the finest quality, to ensure he would drink it all. The ambush awaiting the caravan would be massacred in short order otherwise.

As she pulverized the leaves, she whispered to herself, "He's alive," a common prayer she recited when she was feeling anxious; *some of us under her command tried to guess who this He was— copans tossed in the pot—my bet on an old lover—mine an abandoned child—*the He of her prayers in her thoughts as vivid as a waking dream as she finished this fateful recipe. She took a swig from her flask to still her nerves. She brewed a practice pot of tea and served her imaginary guest. She imagined his gaze on her, like a falcon on a scurrying rodent, scrutinizing the movements of her wrists as she poured. She thought up questions she would ask, compliments she would give. He was handsome, and liked to be reminded of that. She would smile, demure, and tell him his sons were his spitting image.

"Yes," she said to the empty room as she poured a cup to the brim, smiling graciously at the wall. "I think you are right. This will be a wonderful week for our Smiling Sun. Yes. I too hope that He remembers us fondly."

Tea spilled over the brim.

She cursed.

Before she left our clandestine meeting place, I grabbed her hand and I reminded her of the price of failure. That the prisoner of Joyrock she worked so hard to free would remain chained in that infernal labyrinth, and her own life would, too, be finished. That we would make no effort to save her; likely to live out the remainder of her days as a skinless ornament decorating the emperor's apartments. Araya breathed in deep. *And as she walked out of the temple, to her destiny, I prayed for her: May this child dance the steps of the Rhythm. May her performance be deemed satisfactory to the spirits and sages of the Sleeping Sea. May this child live to see our country returned to the hands of its people.* A prayer that danced around in Araya's mind as she held her face in her hands until a hurried knock on her office door startled her back to the surface. She said to hold on a moment as she put away the mortar and pestle, almost scooping up the remaining dried leaves with her bare hands before thinking better of it, and with a spare cloth herded the poisonous ingredients back into their pouch. She opened the door.

"What is it?" she said to her second.

"Apologies for the interruption, Commander," young Raami said with a short bow.

"You interrupt nothing—come, why do you call on me?"

"The Sugo siblings," he said. "They've laid siege to the cripple again."

Araya sighed—how quickly the thought of tomorrow's assassination disappeared from view. Raami told her that if she wished, he would take care of the situation outside, *for when I looked at her, the woman I would die for, she seemed tired, defeated—and I felt as though I had failed her.* But she said no, no, she would go.

"It's my job, after all," she said bitterly.

As the commander rushed out of her office, into the harsh midday sun, to deal with the gathering crowd of sentries congesting the line of travelers trying to make it through before the fall of night, this body wishes now to explain to you the nature of the checkpoint that Araya the Drunk ruled over.

Gates, they were called.

And they were everywhere. On main roads. In gullies. On cliffsides. On lonesome stretches between nothing. Everywhere where the land pinched on itself, impassable but for the narrow road that funneled through it, one would find a massive gate of ironwood timber and flexioned rope pulleys to collect the toll and inspect your papers; these fortresses overseen by watchtower tortoises, the eyes of the emperor, who in the paranoia of his later years commanded more and more of these edifices to be constructed throughout the country.

These checkpoints were similar to the ones of your time. You remember well the stopped breath in your lungs when you and your family traveled by train to the northern province to visit your distant relatives and your train was stopped at the border station for a random search. The soldiers yanking bags from the overhead carriage like unruly children from tree branches. You wince to remember the sound of ripped fabric and popped latches. Belongings searched with sticks and cold expressions. The man in the sharp blue uniform with puffed cheeks, reddish, as if he had just taken wine, is printed in your memory. How he coaxed the papers out of your lola's grip. Her chest rising and falling in deep breaths. You thought something was wrong with her, that she was sick, but you were yet young—you had never seen her nervous before.

In the car ahead of yours someone cried out; a helpless sort of cry that faded as they were led off the train. You never saw this person, not even as you and your brothers pressed your faces to the window, but for years after that day, you would imagine them, always with a different face, for in truth they could have been anyone.

"Thank you," the man in the blue uniform said, dropping the papers in your lola's lap as he went to the next seat. She bent over to pick up what had fallen. You and your brothers watched the man go down the aisle until she snapped at you, telling you not to stare. You thought she was teaching you not to be rude, as was lola's job. But not this time. This time, she was teaching you how to survive.

Such was also the case for the people of the time before trains and radios. Those who traveled the unpaved Road Below did so with the awareness that this trip might be their last. *We traveled with twice the water we thought we needed. We never traveled alone. And we never traveled by night.* There were the desperate few who tried to travel alone on the Road Below. Most of the sun-baked corpses hidden in the brush and the paddy fields belonged to these men and women, their bodies stripped of valuables, even their teeth, which sold well depending on the shine, and if you knew to whom to sell them. If the bandits didn't open your throat, then the animals of the forest did, and if not the animals, it was the distempered sun and the long stretches between here and nowhere, the last canteen emptied and the mouth left to wither, *telling myself I'd rest for just a moment underneath that rock, in the cool shade of it, just for a moment, and only then did I learn that a moment could last a lifetime.* And if somehow you made it through all these hazards, then perhaps your end would come near the finish line, as you dragged your tired horse through the gates of some checkpoint where you were attended by a sentry, no older than fifteen, who was foul of mood and who greeted your exhaustion as a sign of disrespect. *The day was fucking endless and these faces kept coming, and none of them seemed thankful at all that you were doing your duty, that you were keeping the country safe! And the fucking heat. It was hard not to take it out on some of them. Just to watch them squirm.* A torn-up document, in tatters in your hand, as they shoved you into a wagon headed straight for Joyrock.

Tiger Gate Checkpoint, Araya's checkpoint, sat on a cliffside road like a dead roach. It had two gates of heavy timber, each of such size that they required the strength of five men to lift by turning-wheel, and between which a long courtyard stretched where the people filed through, timidly, and with averted eyes. *Just let us through, we prayed, just let us through.* It is here, in the dusty courtyard of that forsaken fortress, where Araya met the brawlers who were making a mockery of her command.

You notice a change in the light.

Your eye is drawn by the angle of the firelight and the formation of the many dancers onstage. You focus on the body all the lines seem to converge on. You focus on this moonlit body. One hand is tucked behind this body's back. You think this a strange affectation until you see that it is not merely a move but an intrinsic part of the character this body plays—a life, shaped by its missing left arm.

Your lola pressed her finger into your shoulder.

You remember her tracing the ball joint where your arm met your torso. She was not gentle. "It was the left they would cut off," she told you. "Like so." Her hand making a chopping motion against your shoulder. "The left arm represents your pride. Your warrior's heart. If you dishonored your position—if you abandoned your post or fled from battle—cutting off this arm would tell everyone you met, at a mere glance, that you were a coward."

You asked her what if someone lost their arm in battle? Or from sickness? How could anyone tell the difference?

"The cut was specific," she told you. "High up, the wound treated in a way that made the scar twisted in a particular fashion." She shrugged. "They had a different view of missing limbs in that time. Not a kind one. If they didn't think you were a coward they thought you were a leper, or an unskilled fighter—bad luck, whatever the case. A Man or Woman of Poor Fortune. Bad luck spreads as sure as disease. You did not want them believing any of these things about you."

You thought on this.

You asked her how they did it.

She smiled, which was rare for her to do, an exception made that day as she was amused by your bloodthirsty curiosity and was more than happy to entertain it, seeing as it concerned the Old Country.

"If they liked you, they'd have their best swordsman do it. The best of them were able to remove the arm in one cut. Straight down. They would give you as clean a wound as you could ask for. Yes, if they liked you, it was almost a mercy."

Her smile colder as she added, "But they rarely liked you."

And no one liked the young man from the north.

"Break it up, you dogs!" Raami shouted, pushing his way through the crowd. "Commander's here! Break it up! Back to your posts!"

Araya shook her head as the young, bored workers of Tiger Gate returned to their stations without enthusiasm, beckoning the next anxious traveler down the line. At forty, she was more than twice the age of those under her command, and she felt that difference keenly as she stepped into the settling dust cloud and looked down at the bloodied kids kneeling at the center of it.

The Sugos looked up at her, unrepentant; Mae and Vogo, brother and sister hellhounds; children of some distant relation to the Throne, cousins of cousins, enough royal blood in them to shield them from most of Araya's threats of discipline. They didn't even wait for leave to speak before they launched into their side of the tale. *We told the drunk that the one-armed psychopath over there had walked up to us and attacked us, unprovoked. He even broke my dear sister's thumb.* The dagger-faced Sugo sister presented Araya the skewed digit in question, and her brother, spitting out a tooth loosened from the brawl, said, "Fair recompense must be made," which were words they heard their father say whenever he was greatly displeased, which was often.

"Duly noted," Araya said, looking past them both, her eyes on the third member of this disruption. "And you?" she asked.

"What is your part in this, Keema of the Daware Tribe?"

See him as he was: kneeling in the dirt, beaten but not broken, his body like that of a young panther's, slight but powerful, with eyes that bounced light like polished knives. His gaze flicked only once to Araya's before he in deference looked back at the dirt, his right nostril bleeding freely and unattended. Araya asked him again what was his part in the fight. But he only wiped his face with the back of his one hand.

"Answer your commander!" Raami snapped, his hand on the sheath of his blade.

Araya silenced him with a look. Raami backed down.

"His silence betrays his guilt," Mae said. "Can we get off our knees now?"

Irked by the sister's satisfied smile, Araya gave the young man one more chance. She asked him why he struck out at his fellow sentries, but again he refused to answer, for he knew more than anyone that when it came down to his word against theirs, there was no influencing the weights of the scales of judgment, preordained as they were by blood and influence.

"Punishments are in order, I suppose," Araya said. Keema's eyes widened in surprise when her imperious gaze swept over not only him but the siblings as well. "All three of you will go without evening meal for the traffic you've made in my courtyard. Sugos, you're on stables duty tonight. Horses and orooks cleaned and fed, and all their waste shoveled and carried off to the cliffs. The stables will shine as bright as His Smiling Sun's ass when you are finished." Araya's minor blasphemy making all of them flinch, even loyal Raami.

"Commander," Mae said, seething, "my brother and I have our freed hours tonight. A wagon waits to bring us to the tea estates."

"I'm aware," Araya said brightly. "The wagon will be notified to go on ahead without you. Now, off you go. You have a busy day ahead of you—we think some of yesterday's feed was spoiled; the horses have been making a mess in the hay. Raami, make sure they get to the stables in time, please." Her second saluted her and shoved the Sugos on their way, the two of them unnervingly silent as they were herded off. When they were gone, Araya turned to the young man and she said, "As for you, Keema of the Daware Tribe— Boy Who Is in the Habit of Starting Fights His Commander Must Finish—I'm sorry to say I have to punish you too. But I can spare you the worst of it, if you tell me the reason for all of this trouble."

But all he did was bow his head. He just wanted this to be done with.

"I accept whatever punishment you have for me."

She stared at the back of his head; the short black hair, cut close to the grain; the faint scarring on his neck. And she said, "Fine. You're on clearing duty for the rest of the afternoon."

He grimaced.

"Go," she said.

He uncoiled from his bow, and without protest he walked off to his unseemly duty.

Keema of the Daware Tribe.

That was how he introduced himself to Araya three months ago, when he came to her, half-starved, begging her for a job. Keema of the Daware Tribe. He said his title plain and direct, as though it were a matter of course that not only would one know of the

Daware Tribe but that it should be obvious why he was proud to be of its people. And Araya, who had never heard of this tribe from the north, not amongst the long list of them that had been cut through by the emperor's men during the Marches, quite liked the title that this kid had bestowed upon himself, liking its rhythm and the fire with which he said it, which is why she said his name in full any chance she had. Saying it even then, under her breath, with a fond half smile, and some regret, as she watched him go.

To the place no one else wished to go.

The latrines of Tiger Gate—the long hut that hugged the southern wall of the fortress, and the place where the sentries loosened their bowels. Inside the hut, wooden benches were propped over a trench. Holes were carved out of the seats of the benches, *the lot of us sitting knee to knee more often than not, relieving ourselves. Toe-curled and sweating and pretending we were the only ones in that fucking room.* The natural forces of the world coaxed the waste down this slope into a steepening shaft that terminated in a hole on the side of the cliff; the waste dropping into the chasm between the Spires, much to the displeasure of the animals who lived in the forest basin below the fortress.

Unfortunately for the sentries of Tiger Gate, the shit shaft, as it was called, had an irregular surface, and went very narrow at points, resulting in frequent blockages. One of their number was required to climb into the trench with a pole to break apart these congestions before they got worse. *It was the worst assignment on the rotation schedule.* Bartering was not uncommon to get out of latrine duty. *Coins, favors, things we'd "confiscated" from a traveler—we'd slip these tokens into each other's palms and trade our way out of the shit shaft.* The Sugo siblings were the most notorious of all the officers for their expert trading, having never climbed into that odorous trench despite their having worked at Tiger Gate for years.

But with the arrival of the young man from Daware some months ago, such considerations amongst the sentries quickly evaporated. There was no more bartering, no more gambling on rolled dice. Not for this duty.

We just made him do it.

He was down there often.

Below the latrines, with both feet braced against rock, and his back bowed low to accommodate the low ceiling, Keema worked a pole into the calcified blockages that populated the shaft. The powdered bandanna tied around his mouth did little to protect him from the fumes that choked that dark and humid artery, but he worked through the stench, taking as few breaks as his body could stand, not wishing to drag the assignment out for longer than was necessary.

"They're going to kill you."

The voice came from above. When he poked his head out of the trench he saw many small, soot-stained feet facing him. The orphans who worked the bellows and cleaned the halls were on break from their chores, and it seemed they had business with him. The loudest of them, a boy with a cleft lip, said, "You like rolling around in the shit, piggy?" He was new, trying to earn his place amongst the other children the only way he knew how, but the coarseness of the sentence, lilted by that childish rasp, and the lisp of the cleft, was of such a surprising combination that Keema was less insulted than amused; he even laughed.

"I do," he replied. "Oink-oink."

The children burst out laughing too.

"Have your laugh," the boy with the cleft lip said, trying to fight off a smile. "Keep on rolling. You pass out down there, we won't come and save you. They'll ask us to, they'll ask us to reach into that hole with our little arms, but we'll say no and you'll die down there. Piggy."

A girl behind him echoed "piggy" with a shy smile.

Keema made a face as if he were thinking very hard about this proposition. "I'll try not to pass out then," he said finally. And then, looking at the others, "One of you said someone is going to kill me?"

"The Sugos," a boy in the back of the group said—the one with the bruised eye. "We heard them in the stables."

"You'll be gutted in your sleep," the boy with the cleft lip said.

"You shouldn't've stopped them," the bruised boy said, almost angrily. "They hit us all the time. Now they're going to kill you."

"Shouldn't've stopped 'em," the shy girl echoed.

Keema took this in.

"Thank you all for telling me," he said, bowing his head in gratitude to the orphans, which was an act of grace the children were not used to receiving, nor expecting. When he lifted the bandanna over his mouth and dropped back down into the trench, the orphans were unsure what to say or do, so they hung around the entrance to the latrines for a while, keeping watch for any would-be assailants until they were shooed off by an overseer and shouted back to their duties, polishing the braziers and preparing the tables for evening meal.

Underground, the narrow tunnel swelled with Keema's grunting. Sweat clung to his eyelashes. Shit flumed down the chute and off the cliff. He had hoped that he might avoid retaliation from the Sugos if he remained silent and told Araya nothing about them beating one of the children earlier, but it seemed fortune was yet again not in his favor. For the rest of his time below the earth he thought about how he would protect himself that night; where would be safest for him to sleep; and in this way he was kindred spirits with Araya that day, for death was on both of their minds.

Raami saw the mood writ large on her face.

The somber cast to her eyes, and the reluctance of her step, as if she were trying to drag out the remaining hours of the day as they toured the checkpoint together to ensure all was in good working order for the First Terror's arrival on the morrow. It was not only her expressions, or the minor moment of blasphemy from earlier— *I still could not believe she had so crassly referenced the emper-*

or's . . . bottom—that clued him in to her secret self but also how she drank openly and without shame from her flask that afternoon, without even making a modest attempt to hide her vices. Her jokes were dirtier, too, her smile wider as she made him blush. *But she could not hide from me her distress. There was much I did not know of her in the end. Of her past. But I knew enough to love her.*

On the southern wall, after they had conferenced with the head archer, Raami stopped her. He squinted against the harsh glare of the sun to look her in the eye. "If there's anything I can do, Commander," he said, "anything not strictly on the list of my responsibilities, please let me know."

She smiled at him blankly.

"Anything at all," he said, "that I can do to ease whatever burden you might carry."

Her smile, which was practiced over the years, its mettle tested in a variety of difficult situations that would have meant the end of her life had she not been able to beam through them, collapsed a little. Some unattended infrastructure of the heart, a hairline fracture in the supports, threatening to buckle under the weight of her second's sudden moment of generosity. A brief hesitation that rent Raami's heart.

And then she looked at me like the hopeless child I was.

"You can help the inspectors with the last of the line," she said before she walked away from him.

Life in the gate carried on as day tripped into dusk.

While Keema unclogged the viscera of his colleagues, the sun was beginning its descent behind the Spires—the massive eruptions of earth looking much like the outstretched fingers of a dying giant in those late hours—yet despite the darkening sky, the heat did not abate; the influence of His Endless Summer yet strong; the air still a heavy and suffocating cloak that draped about the shoulders and kept frustrations high.

A braying mule of a checkpoint guard laughed in a woman's face as he told her the seal on her manifest was outdated, that they used a new seal now, and that she would have to come back with the proper ornamentation. A fight almost broke out between two men standing in line, ostensibly over a shove, but it could've been anything—the trading of blows prevented only when a third traveler stood between them and talked them down. *We all wanted to get through. No need to make it harder for one another.* A chorus of babies howled into the humid air, sucking dryly on the breasts of mothers who had little left to give. Water rations were shared between those who had enough to spare and those whose canteens ran empty as the sentries flipped through documents in an unhurried manner. *No need to be proud; we were all thirsty in this heat.* The tortoise, perched in the watchtower like some monstrous eagle, kept a watchful eye on them all, sniffing the air for the sour scent of treason while sunlight fell below the high walls and the fortress was submerged in blessedly cool shadow.

It was but an hour from the closing of the gates when a great screech halted all movement in the fortress.

"Gather!" the tortoise cried. "It is time for His Evening Address!"

All work was ceased. Keema gasped for breath from the latrine trench. Araya, who had been staring at her right hand, which had gone numb as she was signing the receipt of a rice shipment, left her office in something of a fugue state, joining the others in the courtyard, everyone at a breathless standstill, as the tortoise's high-pitched warble let loose its master's words.

"Evening falls over our glorious country!"

From His balcony high above the world, the emperor kept an eye on the sunset as He gave His final evening address to the tortoise behind him; his tired and morose voice translated into a jubilant cry by His network of giggling creatures. "The exit of the sun brings us a most celebrated night. I foresee a lake of stars and quiet dreaming. We could not ask for a more beautiful entrance to this most holy week."

He paused, glancing at His son, who lounged on the pillows as if this place were already his.

His son gave Him a nod of confidence.

The emperor frowned: "I wait in great anticipation to hold in my palms the grain of your harvest. To listen to your stories of troublesome trout and snapped lines. To lose myself in the endless patterns of the carpets you weave and to wield in my hands the sharpest of your forgings. Already in my mind's eye I can see the performances you have been practicing now for many months and the fleet steps of your spirited bodies—all of the beauty that this country has produced, and will continue to produce, even while I am gone, every day under the gaze of this Smiling Sun. In the week to come, may we honor one another with our presentations."

As we listened throughout the country to the cry of the tortoises—listened to the yearning warmth of his words—we forgot for a moment the state of our lives, and we believed Him.

We believed He did this for us.

"But first, we must endure one last sleep. First we must dream of the perfect days to come, in this last night before our grand adventure. Fret not as the sun falls behind the hills. The light will return come the morrow. But we must allow the tapestry to scroll its focus. To bring us the sweet sorrow of the fall of day."

From His mountaintop, He gazed at the dot of light in the horizon.

That single wavering candle.

"The pleasures of this truest night."

The candle blew out.

With a wave of this body's hand all the braziers are snuffed out in this Inverted Theater. The movement is sudden, as is the disappearance of the light, the darkness you are submerged in so complete you can feel it as a presence that surrounds you, blocking sight of even your own hand. It is not so much an absence as it is an overwhelming smog. You can feel it in your chest. The tightness of your breath. The darkness is closing in on you.

Such was the quality of night in the Old Country, or what they then knew as the true dark, which, when the sun fell from its daily perch, was total and unyielding.

What else could they have hoped for, with no moon in the sky?

Your lola put a cigarette out on the wall.

When she pulled the cigarette away, there was left on the cream-colored surface a small black scorch mark.

"They called it the Burn," she said.

The hole in the tapestry of the sky that the Moon once called home, or so went one of your lola's less likely tales; how, after one of the First Men unstitched the Moon from the sky with the tip of his spear, freeing Her from Her determined place in the heavens, She offered him one wish, and that wish was a kingdom.

A hole in the sky like a cigarette scar, the Burn was why the checkpoints shut their gates after nightfall, why the animals burrowed deep into their nests, why so few people braved the roads at dark, for there were far greater dangers than brigands that stalked the fields of a land stripped of its moonlight.

Listen to the world close its gates.

It is the sound of a thousand locks turned at once, for upon the fall of the sun no time was wasted in slamming shut their doors, in all the villages and the cities. The checkpoint gates groaned into the dirt. The travelers who did not make it through the courtyard inspections were herded back, no room to spare for the night, the lot of them forced to run back to the border towns, knocking on the doors of inns whose owners now charged double for entry. And like mice upon the sudden flick of the light switch, the roads were cleared, not even the bandits risking the lightless world and its many teeth; those who had no choice but to spend the night outdoors rubbing themselves frantically in masking scents, of concoctions of dungs and oils that blended their humanity in with the trees and the brush. Such was the case of the ambush team, east of Tiger Gate, the twenty ferocious men and women who, in the woods above the cliffside road, became as still as deer as they waited out the night and listened to the howls that lanced the misted hills. These assassins watched the world from their dark purchase, the daggers of light that pricked up throughout the land, of braziers and candles and torches—these small seeds of fire doing little to shrug off the thick, suffocating blanket of night, but it was something, it was safety, and the people huddled around these holy sources, praying that they would live till morning.

"For tomorrow," the First Terror said, toasting his father.

And then he put down his cup and he made to leave the royal apartment, but the emperor stopped him at the door with a look.

"You leave so quickly," He said.

"Come, Father—I have been here the entire afternoon," His son gently reminded Him.

If the emperor heard the chiding tone of His son's voice, He made no show of it. "There is a room upstairs readied for you. You will sleep here tonight."

"With gratitude, Father, I must decline." He gave a bow that his father did not believe. "I will be staying with my own sons. There is much to discuss with them, concerning plans for the week."

The emperor turned to the balcony. "So be it."

"I will return at dawn. You will not even know I was—"

"Send someone in on your way out."

His son stood there, deliberating whether it was best to press the point or not. The tortoise smelled from the prince the aura of hesitation. It giggled softly into its blankets.

"Good night, Father," he said.

When the salon door slid shut behind Him, the emperor looked around His empty apartment.

He glanced at the empty birdcage and shivered.

This damned country.

He went outside and rested His two aged hands on the balcony railing, His long fingernail, used to scoop his snuff, now clicking on the lacquered wood, restless. His sunken eyes took in the dark landscape peppered with tiny lights, His mind at work, wondering how many people out there wanted His head—a creaking noise above made him flinch, until he reassured Himself that it was but the wood settling against the high winds of the mountains. He breathed out, His shoulders tense as He looked out over the country He ruled, never clearer than it was to Him now, when he was alone, with Himself, how desperate He was to be rid of all of it.

"There is no love in this place," He whispered tiredly as He sat down on the balcony chair, in dire need of an outlet.

The timing could not be more fortuitous—the door slid open and the socked feet of a royal attendant stepped inside. When the young man in a rabbit's mask arrived and asked the emperor what it was he could do for His Smiling Sun, the emperor did not even bother to respond. Without turning in His chair, He merely held up a finger, and the attendant went stiff, *as if my spine had turned to stone, I could not blink my eyes, hot tears rolling down frozen cheeks,* the emperor's fingers making shapes in the air, the attendant's body contorting in accordance with these shapes, *my scream breathless and silent as my arm twisted out of its joint and my leg snapped back, my heel pressed between my shoulder blades, His fingers weaving the invisible threads in the air as my body folded inward and inward,* until all that remained of the man was a box of twisted flesh that somehow still rattled with breath, *my breath on my toes, and my eyes, bulged from their sockets, peering through this cage of limbs at My Smiling Sun,* who looked down on His creation with a satisfied air, remembering once more His immense power. *And when later I was discovered, like the discarded toy I was, a guard sympathetic to my state brought me to my lover, who with trembling hands held me to their breast before I then breathed my last, and returned to the Sleeping Sea, wingless, and free.*

The satiated emperor sat back down in His chair while the flesh box gurgled behind Him. He sunk into the cushions like a lion might just after feeding. He did not remember falling asleep. Sleep came upon Him suddenly, like a spring wind down an alley; brief but deeply felt, and lasting just long enough to dream.

And what a dream it was.

He was floating high above His land. Clouds bowed out of His way as He looked upon the provinces below and saw the produce of the people bubble out of it like so much froth—rivers of tea swirling around fat stalks of rice grain, all of which was curtained by luxuriant folds of carpets and tapestries. At His side, the seven emperors who had come before Him bowed to Him and told Him that He was carrying on their great work—even His father, the Seventh Emperor, whom He had killed, told Him that he was proud of Him. All the heavens were celebrating His triumphs. All that awaited was for Him to make the journey across the Great and Unending Sea to find His reward.

"I will!" He swore to His ancestry. "I will find my due reward!" And on a ship borne on a wave so tall that even the stars moved out of the way did He make His approach of the new land, following the constellation of the tiger and the cherry bough, which leapt ahead of Him in a silver streak, charting the path ahead, the starlight of such brightness that not even the shadow of Death dared approach this vessel.

'Tis a long journey, the tiger said to Him. One best not made alone.

And when the emperor looked to His side, His eyes widened,

for He saw the person who was meant to join Him on His divine journey, and He wondered how it had never occurred to Him earlier, this inspired plan.

He woke from this dream with a gasp.

He knew what He had to do.

The emperor's footsteps echoed down a dark stone staircase.

Below the palace this staircase went, cleaving a steep path into the heart of the mountain. Long ago, many emperors past, this stair had been constructed, each step steep and dizzy with spiraling ornamentation. It was a dream of the Third Emperor, born with the gift of heightened perception, who ordered the creation of this haven free from earthly distraction. *None of us lived beyond the end of this great project. Those of us who did not die in the construction and the tunneling were killed to protect what was down there. Our bones became a part of the edifice of this mighty prison. Our skin dispersed into the air. Our blood in the water that poured down each step.* Torch flame licked moist stone; it whimpered and twirled against a bellows of wind that drafted up the narrow passage. The soldiers who walked with their emperor tried to stay brave the farther down they went; they tried to convince themselves that these halls were not haunted by the unquiet dead. It was a relief to them all when the stairs finally opened up, into a magnificent dome so wide it could fit an entire manse in its berth. *This dome, our masterwork.* The ceiling was punctured by clear flowing waterfalls, and the walls were covered in rich mosaics, composed of blue and black shell tiles, which depicted in swirling, painterly impressions the old tales from the Time Before: The fall of the Moon, Her salvation at the hands of the one who would then become the first of the emperors, the rise of the Throne, and many more. *We were only allowed to depict the approved tales, the tales that showed the Throne as a mighty tree of humble origins that had not, and would never, stop growing.* It was on the other end of the dome, where all the carved lines on the wall converged, where the most important element of the room lay.

The Wolf Door.

One hundred wolves of solid gold snarled and bit at the small knob in the center of the door, each wolf lifelike in its movement, its hunger, as if they were real and had simply been frozen into statues at the instant of the hunt's climax.

A single guard stood before the Wolf Door. Near him was the simple cot and stove that was his life's sustenance for the past six months. His face was obscured by the mask he wore—that of a peacock. He bowed deeply upon the arrival of the emperor and His retinue, while piked warriors formed a deadly avenue between them. "My Smiling Sun," the prince's son said, his voice echoing in this water-swollen dome. "Is it already time for my relief?"

The emperor walked past him and withdrew the key from His robe without comment. It was a jagged spike of a key, with a handle of silver, its teeth a heart attack of needles. The eyes of one hundred golden wolves glinted back at Him, the slit begging to be filled. He inserted the key and turned it—the wolves unclenched their jaws, and the red doors groaned inward, a rush of air flowing into its dark entrance. The emperor smoothed out His robe. He was nervous.

Before He entered, He looked at the person at his side who was supposedly His grandchild. The young man's face was obscured by the peacock mask, so if there was a resemblance between the two of them, the emperor could not see it, but what He could see was the toll that the past six months down here had taken on him. A nervous energy radiated from the young man's shoulders, his hands kept flexing, as if to work out a tightness in the joints that would not leave, and he seemed to turn his head slightly at sounds that only he could hear. *Voices in his head—voices of the dead. We whispered and we snapped and we would never leave him.* The boy was not the first to fall prey to the madness of solitude, especially not in this cavern, not in this silence, but the emperor was nonetheless disappointed that someone of His blood had proven to be so weak. It was just as well that He had forgotten this creature's name. "Your father sends his regards," He said. The Peacock's shoulders ceased their trembling. "If you like, upon my return, we can go up and see him together, while my guards protect the Door in your absence."

"A most generous proposition, My Smiling Sun." The boy gave Him an awkward bow, halting and quick. "But if it please you either way, I would remain here and see out the completion of my duty."

"So be it," the emperor said, not caring.

As He walked through the Wolf Door, He glanced at the captain of the royal guard and in that glance confirmed to the captain His order.

Kill the boy.

And when the doors groaned shut behind Him, the dozen men of the royal guard slowly fanned out across the room, blocking the exit. *We, the most loyal of all the emperor's men, would do as He bid, even when we did not understand the reason for the order.* If the boy noticed their formation, he made no note of it; he simply walked over to his little campsite at the side of the room, where he crouched below the mural of the shattered Moon, joining the men in their tense silence.

The captain, who wore a mask of a red-cheeked and laughing demon, stepped forward. One of his hands rested on the hilt of his sheathed blade. "You are Jun Ossa, are you not?"

The boy in the peacock mask did not reply for a moment. "Yes," he said quietly, without pride. "I am."

The men shared glances with one another, for of all of the prince's many sons who rode under the banner of the Red Peacock, it was Jun who inspired in their hearts the most fear.

"This must have been a rather dull assignment, compared to what you are accustomed," the captain said, shaking his head. "I cannot imagine a whole year down here."

"It is a great honor," the boy named Jun said without affect.

"Why don't you come over, my lord, and tell us about it then," the captain said with a smile in his voice. "Tell us how you fared these past few months, in this place. Tell us if the rumors are true that the murals come alive at night." The captain had begun a slow walk in the boy's direction, his easy hand a little tighter on his hilt. His men continued to push out to the edges of the room. "Tell us anything you like."

Jun looked at all of them.

"You cannot kill me," he said. "She will not let you."

"We are just coming to talk," the captain said.

"It is too late for talk."

There was a great sorrow in his voice that gave the captain pause. But the infamous warrior said no more on the matter—he sprinted to the end of the room, where he dove into the shallow pool of water, gone, upon a small detonation. The men looked at one another, confused, for the pool the Peacock had leapt into had no exit. One of them even chuckled.

"He really has lost his mind down here, hasn't he?"

Behind the Wolf Door,

the emperor walked into a room no larger than a prized servant's quarters. In the center of the room was a small island of stone, surrounded by a moat of crystal-blue water that illuminated the dark. This was the island where She sat. Even the emperor, the most powerful man in the country, averted His gaze in Her presence, His eyes remaining on the floor as He spoke to Her, like a child come in for a scolding.

"I know it has been some time since I have last visited, Mother. I know that we did not part on the best of terms. I hope that your stay in this room has given you time to think about the necessity of my actions—why I did what I did to keep you here. But that is not why I have come. I have come because I have been having dreams,

Mother. The most spectacular dreams. I have seen the tiger and the cherry bough. I have seen the immortal berry. The Many Heavens want me to go on a journey. They want to make me a god. And they want you to come with me." His voice was heavy with emotion. When She did not reply to Him, He continued. "A new land awaits us, Mother, and I think you will agree that it would do both of us some good, to be away from this country for a time. I have accomplished my great works here, and you, yours. Our internment is over. Across the sea we must go, to the new land where . . . we'll find . . ."

His words trailed off when He noticed the small rock by His feet. He noticed more rocks; some were in the moat of water, more yet were spilled over the ground, a trail of them, small and jagged and chalky, all leading up to a broken mesh net. The net once hung from the ceiling, suspended over the water, but someone had severed the rope with a knife.

The mystic trap that had restrained Her for so many years was broken.

She was free.

Oh, the Eighth Emperor thought.

"Mother," He said. He swallowed nothing. His voice as close to pleading as it had ever sounded in His life. "Mother, wait."

She did not wait.

The red doors swelled like a belly full of air—the jeweled eyes of the wolves popping off like buttons—before they exploded outward with such force that the soldiers in the cavern could only blink before their blood was painted onto the muraled walls over the pool of water in which the prince's son still dwelt, the emperor's high and panicked whimper the last noise He made in this earthly realm before He became a cloud of blood and bone, embedded into the walls of this ancient mountain, *where He joined us, the ones who had built this place, in our restless eternity.*

High above this explosion was felt—the plates in the royal dining hall trembling off the table and the finely polished porcelain vases shattering into many little shards from the unearthly vibrations. And in his pagoda, amongst the quartet of girls who served him, the prince fell to his knees, clutching the needling pain behind his right eye. His Peacocks fell upon him and asked him what was wrong, but his voice was empty and his throat too clenched to speak—he vomited onto the carpeted floor ropes of fresh green seawater.

The country shivered.

It was as though a finger had been run down the spine of the land of the moonless night. From the western mountains this shiver ran, all the way to the eastern shore. *Not one of us escaped its chill*. It was a collective feeling, come over by all, from the farmers of the Yinn terrace lands to the dock workers in the Divine City. *When it reached us, we woke up with a startle, thinking that the world was ending; that our bodies had finished their time on this Earth, and this shiver was the release of our spirit into the Sleeping Sea*. The cry of woken babies scored this night of change. The gambling games in the pleasure barges put on pause as the old men and women playing dice now rubbed their arms, warming the small hairs that pricked up from some unknown fright. The fishermen of the Thousand Rivers peered out their boarded windows to perhaps catch sight of the culprit of this bodily premonition, a nightmare spirit perhaps, come to visit them from the water and sated only by the fresh salt tears of the young. *But we saw nothing and no one. We had no explanation for the trembling of our body, which lasted for but one soul-freezing moment.*

Even the prophets of the city night markets, who read the fortunes of passing folk by drinking deep the water from their cupped palms, for but a small fee, an affordable price they assure you, had no explanation for the divine symptom they now experienced, which felt like nothing less than the salted breeze of the Sleeping Sea blowing through their bellies.

The world had changed. The apes sojourning through the dark forests beyond the torchlight of man held one another as the shiver came and went; their eyes shining in the dark as they understood this portent; the days of great upheaval that lay ahead of them.

On the balcony of his private ship, the head of the country's textile production stood, staring into the unforgiving night.

"Something's changed," he said to the imposing woman behind him.

How right they were—for the emperor's death had redirected the currents. Where once all roads led across the water, now, that night, they led somewhere else altogether—unbeknownst to any of them, that was straight to the unlikely doors of Tiger Gate Checkpoint, where the course of the week to come would be determined, by fire, and blood.

There would be no sleep for the sentries of the gate that night.

They lay in their barracks, the heat so intense they went without clothes or blankets, the hard-packed floor carpeted by their naked bodies that breathed in and out, in rhythm with the hearts that pumped full and rich with blood. *The shiver had passed, but we still felt strange. We felt changed. We did not know what it was, but there would be no going back.* Some of the guards lay awake, not sleeping—some just listened to the night, as if hearing it for the first time, amazed that it could be so loud and so alive. *It was like we could hear the world again.* Others turned and twisted in their restlessness and coiled into themselves like fists. *Like every part of our bodies was activated.*

Keema was in the far corner, away from the others. He had just drifted off when the shiver had awoken him, his body upright against the clay wall, where secretly he touched the small knife strapped to his thigh, assuring himself that it was still there, an eye kept on the barracks door for any Sugo who might disturb him. But when the shiver struck him, a strange mood came over him: a heightening of the senses. He began listening to the fat beetle on the ceiling beam as it clicked its wings. The hipbone that cracked as a sleeper's leg stretched out. A man who sighed out from somewhere amidst the twisting bodies. The rustle of a hand reaching across the ground to touch another hand. *We felt like we were on fire.* Summer was all the guards knew, yet on this new night there seemed to be an undiscovered heat. Keema's hand massaging the dent of his bare chest as he breathed raggedly, then rubbing the sweat from his palm onto the thin straw mat beneath him, his eyes half-open when from the corner of the room he heard the telltale moans of those who would forgo sleep. *We fell into each other in those barracks; we felt like we had no choice but to do so.* He staggered to his feet, stepping over the other restless bodies, and wandered out into the courtyard half-dressed, a finger grazing his bare ankle before he left.

Out in front of the barracks he stood, paralyzed for a moment, itching for something without having a clue what that something was or where to start looking for it. It was like the shiver had cleared out his body, emptied it. Like now he needed something to fill it.

Through the courtyard he walked, slipping back into his sleeveless shirt as he passed the night shift at work. Soldiers unracking weapons and polishing the blades and spear tips smooth with oiled cloth, bouncing moonlight off the curved metal. *It was like we were working out an itch. We just needed to do something.* From the corner of his eye he saw dice gambled stealthily by torchlight, shaken in wooden cups behind backs and rolled out into depressions in the dirt. Two reds. A promise to pay up after the shift. *We lost our money and it felt good.* Discreet jokes were muttered in passing. New arrows were whittled from spare wood, nocked and tested on the pincushion dummy that stood by the north-facing wall. A bored guard drew the curves of a woman's hips in the dirt with his big toe, while behind him arrowheads made their home in the target dummy's face, letting loose arterial sprays of straw and stuffing. *We had never been so awake.* In this evening restlessness

Keema circled into the main thoroughfare of this tiny fortress, and he joined the gathering crowd of men and women who stood around a makeshift arena, where pairs dueled each other into submission.

"They used to dance."

"Dances of such strange magicks," your lola said. "It was the people's magick. But as the reach of the Throne grew, and the ownership of power was decided, dancing slowly lost its favor, relegated to the stale corners of tradition. It was dueling that became the way to express oneself." She smiled as she watched a group of youths your age walk down the street—you hid your face from them until they were gone, which she found very amusing. "Even in courtship," she said, putting out her cigarette, "dueling ruled."

A bow, an invitation.

The boundaries of the arena were established by the standing bamboo torches, the center of which was a cloud of dust as the two guards within the square sparred. *We needed to work out this itch.* The children who were still awake watched with half-lidded curiosity from their blankets by the roaring brazier fires. Keema watched as the powerful woman lifted her opponent into the air as easily as one might an empty barrel, and he thought for a brief moment that it was beautiful the way the man was held like a bow beneath the night sky, before he was slammed into the ground. She helped him up, the both of them bruised and smiling as they bowed to each other. *We stomped and howled and cheered at the edges of the arena.* And when they cleared the battlefield, they did so arm in arm, and Keema felt in the pit of himself a small aching seed of envy.

Raami, whose jaguar-like face was cleaved by his cocky smile, strode out into the arena alone with hands held out in challenge. No one was accepting the invitation for a beating. *He was the best fighter of all of us. No one wanted to get their nose broken in.* His taunting finger circling the air around him. He even promised to take on the next chore rotation of their choice, but still no one accepted. Keema stood to the side, watching everyone whom Raami challenged laugh and decline the beating. "Is there any amongst your number who isn't a coward?" the second asked playfully, and Keema, in a moment of bravery, stepped forward.

He bowed deeply.

"I would fight you," he said.

Raami turned, and his face fell. *We watched in uncomfortable silence as Raami stared at the crippled man for what felt like hours. You could see it in the second's eyes. His calculation—asking himself just how much respect he would lose in our estimation if he entertained this unexpected request. He even looked up at the western wall, where Commander Araya stood, as if she would tell him what to do.*

He made his choice in the end. He turned and walked out of the arena. He said he was in need of some water, and he left the poor bastard there, bowing to no one.

Even we felt sorry for him.

Keema stared at the ground. His face hot. He didn't want to look up. As honed as his body may have been, as practiced and articulate his joints and his flex, there was still that whimpering child within him who did not know how to handle such embarrassment. *We all drifted away after that, to other parts of the checkpoint, to pass the time of this restless night. We laughed amongst ourselves, made loud conversation. As if through force of will we could forget that any of that had ever happened.* A luxury not afforded to Keema, who did his best to still his beating heart.

He breathed in; he stood up straight. He set to work putting away the standing torches. *From our patrols on the tops of the walls and from our secret dice games we watched him.* Those glancing eyes, scrutinizing and pitying, burning the back of his head, forcing him to hide his hurt, to calcify, for he had learned over the years of living in this country that one's pride is inextricably bound to the odds of one's survival. And as he brought the last of the standing torches to the secondary storage house in the northern end of the compound, each step brought him further from that moment of rejection, until with enough distance he, too, could mock his self of mere moments passed. How ridiculous it was that he had even tried to duel Raami. *Such a fool that boy was!* he thought with a shake of his head, a wry smile. He promised himself that he would not make the same mistake twice, told himself that such risks were not worth the reward. And gradually the humiliation, once so vivid, peeled off of him in layers as he walked more upright and past the orphans, who did not meet his gaze— the boy with the cleft lip observing him for a time, as if in consideration of some deep commonality between the two of them, before he found more interest in an ant crawling up his chest—the young man from Daware unaware as he packed away the last of the standing torches that he was not as alone as he first thought.

A fat knife came unbuckled.

Vogo's friends stared at Mae with some wariness. *There was a thirst for blood in her eyes that we did not share.* It was a look that she met with some hurt. "We're not killing the bastard," she said. "We're only . . . giving him a reminder of his place. Right, brother?"

The ox of a man nodded. He reminded the others that the fresh scar they were going to give the boy was but fair recompense for his transgression against royal blood; a small price to pay for what was, in essence, blasphemy. Mae added, "He's a proficient fighter, one arm or not, so don't let him get a word in—just pin him down quick and I'll do the—"

She silenced herself and hid her knife; someone was coming. They watched from the dark as Commander Araya met Keema outside the storage house and spoke with him in private. Too far to hear their low voices, the Sugos and their cronies could only make out Keema's expressions lit by a nearby torch: his surprise, and his hesitant acceptance of her invitation. "What now?" one of the men asked as their quarry was led away.

Mae sheathed her blade.

"We'll have him later," she said. "Come. We have other business yet."

They ran off.

Keema hesitated at the threshold of Araya's office.

She looked at him.

"My invitations are not given lightly," she said.

He entered and slid the door shut behind him. Hanging pots of jerin powder kept the room cool. The walls and floor were lush with drapery woven by the textile fleet, the rug beneath his sandaled feet patterned with a complex network of curling vines and jewels. *In the tilting ships that housed his looms, we wove these masterworks for our Lord Induun. The fabric stained with our salted sweat and the blood from our broken fingernails.* Shelving units were populated with rolled-up scrolls, bound reams of parchment, bottles of ink, brushes, and tied-up bundles of spare quills— and a tea set, immaculate in both craft and upkeep, which the commander now lifted by the tray handles as she invited him to take a seat.

Over a small fire she prepared for them both a cup of bitterroot tea, plucked from one of Lady Panjet's private reserves. *Six days a week we spent, bowed like supplicants over the rows of shrubs, picking only the best of the leaves; the backs of our necks burned by the unblinking sun.* Keema bowed, honored when Araya used her own water rations to feed the pot, and he thanked her.

"You're welcome, Keema of the Daware Tribe," she said, chuckling.

They waited for the brew to steep.

"I hope it doesn't bother you," she said, "that I've been taking such pleasure in speaking your name."

"It does not bother me, Commander."

"Please, just Araya. This is a casual drink. You can speak your mind here."

Keema shifted uncomfortably in his seat, quiet and shy, until his commander took pity on him and changed the subject.

"You must be wondering why I invited you to tea. Would you mind if I guessed what you're thinking?"

"No, Commander. I would not mind."

"You think I feel sorry for you after Raami rejected your offer to duel." She looked at him. "You think I've always felt sorry for you; even the first day we met, when you came here begging me for a job. You think I've invited you here for tea the way a master would invite their dog to rest their head on their lap." She tipped the teapot; a long unbroken stream of red liquid splashed into porcelain cups. *At Lord Waag's kilns we baked the ceramics, working with gloves frayed and worn until even the details of our fingers burned away.* "Do not misunderstand me. I do feel sorry for you. My pity for your situation is deep. But it is not why we share tea this evening." She put the teapot down and looked at him. "I have something to ask of you," she said.

She picked up her cup with both hands, blowing gently; he picked up his cup with his one hand, his etiquette yet unpracticed, as he took a sip too quickly and burned his lips. She smiled as he watched and copied her and blew on the surface as she did. Steam peeled off gentle ripples. Floral notes danced under his nose. The apple in his throat bobbed deeply.

"When we first met," she said, "you made a 'Dawaran vow' to serve me. I had never heard the like before, and the phrasing has stuck with me ever since."

"All warriors of Daware swear their unbreaking fealty," he said. "Our word is stone. No promise is taken lightly. No vow unfinished." He spoke as if reciting scripture; with reverence; with pride.

"What is the consequence of breaking such a vow?"

"We do not break vows," he said.

"Perhaps not intentionally," she suggested. "But nothing in this world is for certain. We are but dancers to the Rhythm. What if you were tasked with protecting someone, or something, and you failed? What then?"

"I would sooner end my own life than live with such shame."

"So there is nothing more important to you than seeing through such a task?"

"Not in all the world."

She smiled, as if she were hoping he would say that. Outside, a horn signaled the midnight hour. "Time runs so quick these days," she murmured. When she turned to him there was a resolve in her eyes. "The favor I would ask of you is a simple one. There is something that I would like delivered to the outskirts of the Divine City. A parcel that is very precious to me, as well as to the person whom it would be delivered to. An antique, passed down many generations. Why do you furrow your brow so?"

He touched his forehead, his betrayer. "I am only wondering why you would trust me with the delivery of something so valuable." He looked at her. "We are strangers."

"I thought I had more time," she said simply. The words, said aloud, seemed to cause her pain, as she suddenly touched her chest. "My options are limited. Tomorrow will be—it is—my time is limited, and of all the sentries who work in this fortress, it is you I trust the most, to at least try to complete the delivery . . . aside from Raami, but I need Raami here. I know that you have a history of successful mercenary work. In a tight spot, you, Keema of the Daware Tribe, are my best option." She lifted a shoulder. "You will be paid, of course. Fifty copans in advance."

Some tea dribbled from his lips. "Fifty?"

"Fifty," she said, amused. "A deal on my end, considering the distance you would be traveling. Have you ever been to the eastern shore?"

"No," he admitted. "There was no reason. Someone like me would never be let inside the Divine City." Most people weren't—unless they were being taken to Joyrock, in chains.

"A fortunate thing for both of us then," she said, "that the person accepting the delivery will not be inside the city proper."

"Who is it I would be delivering the parcel to?"

"Know for now she is someone of considerable importance to me. Her details, I'll share should you make your vow." She steepled her fingers. "That is the favor. A long trek, a simple delivery."

His brow furrowed again. "Will I still have a job here if I return?"

"No," she said. And then, after some consideration, added, "In fact I would suggest that you did not return west at all."

Keema's eyes widened. "Why not?"

"For your own good," she said, refusing to elaborate any further. "I do not expect an answer tonight. Think on it. Tomorrow morning, before the prince's arrival, come to me with your response. For now," she said, "let's enjoy this tea."

Though there would be no chance of him settling into the tea now that the room was charged with such mystery, he nodded, and they said little to each other as they finished the last of their drink in that jerin blue room. When the tea was finished, she thanked him for his company and he said his good night; at the door, she stopped him.

"I never understood why you wanted to work here," she said. "I never understood why you begged for a position. You must have known that the others would not take kindly to you. That the work would be difficult, demeaning. At the time I assumed you just needed the room and board. The paltry pay. But in knowing you these past few months, I've come to suspect you could have no shortage of good-paying mercenary work, despite your condition. Which means you had another motive to work here all along." She tilted her head. "Am I right to think so?"

He was quiet. His eyes on the door. In almost a whisper, he said, "A water reader once drank the sweat from my hand and told me my fortune. She told me that I would find what I was looking for at Tiger Gate."

Araya, surprised that this young man would put any value in such readings, asked, "And what is it you are looking for?"

But on this point he would not speak further. He only smiled, unreadable but for the embarrassed brightness of it, which prompted an ache in Araya's chest, as she wished there had been more opportunity these past few months for such beautiful expressions. "I've always spoken true, you know. I do like your name. It is old-fashioned in its way. Few people are 'of' something these days. We are commander 'this' now, or sentry 'that.'" *We are Farmer and Fisherman.* "Quarryman Keema, maybe, or Dueler Keema. Soldier Keema." *Too many of us were soldiers.* "But Keema of the Daware Tribe, I've always liked."

"Most people do not," he said. The words came out of him from deep within, like an unexpected bubbling.

She lifted her eyebrows.

"Fools, the lot of them, then."

She said this casually, as if it were a matter of course, and he felt the need to hide his smile, which he imagined looked very foolish. He walked out of her office with the eyes of the fortress on him once more. *All of us wondered what they had spoken of in there.* But this time Keema didn't much care. Raami had resumed his position outside Araya's door; whatever awkwardness had passed between them at the rejection of the duel now seemed distant to Keema as he passed the man. But Raami, who yet stirred with guilt, offered him a brief nod of acknowledgment.

"Go on, Daware man," he said gently. "Go get some rest."

Time was running to its close.

It is an agitating sensation, almost pleasurable—the feeling of coming up to a steep and impenetrable deadline. It puts you in mind of the egg timer, which was your lola's favorite toy. She used that cranked ovoid contraption when she steeped her tea. She used it when she baked with the clay oven. She used it to startle you awake from a nap. When you think of the egg timer, you think of old hands, white-knuckled, winding the spring. You think of tension wire, held at a gasp between two opposing poles. You think of its insides ticking, ticking away; a sound that has never left you, just as she has never left you; you hear it now, in this very theater, distant but unmistakable; the clicking of its aluminum tongue; the tapping of this moonlit body's foot; we wait.

Horses reared in the night.

A wagon raced through the city between mountains. The driver spurred the horses down crooked alleys while, high above, whistles cried out from the road to the palace. The driver waited tensely for the guards at the city gates to check his documents. They commented that it was rather late to be traveling. They asked him if he knew what the commotion was up on the mountaintop. The driver said he did not. He was in a hurry, he said. When the guards saw the royal seal on his papers they told him to stick to the main road; they wished him good luck. And he nodded in thanks before he snapped his reins through the stone gates that rolled shut behind him.

Through the dark of the moonless night, the wagon hurried through the valley known as the Emperor's Cradle, where howls echoed over the rolling hills of the Panjet tea plantation—the towering mountain of the royal capital behind him, when the driver came upon a fork in the main road.

Left, or right.

After a brief pause, he directed his horses down the road to Tiger Gate.

"It's almost ready," your lola whispered as she stared into the heart of the boiling pot of water.

Tick-tick-tick-tick-tick-tick.

The egg timer twists on itself as the Sugo siblings snuck into the shadows of the eastern gate. Vogo and his friends distracted the guards on duty with a bag of dopha powder, sharing the huff, while Mae prowled into the pulley system and, as casually as one might wait for a carriage or a phone call, took the knife that she used to slice open contraband to saw at the old rope that wound the great wheel. *We knew the prince was coming 'round to visit the next day, and we thought it a good joke, and justice done, if when the Peacock came the eastern gate wouldn't open for him. Araya the Drunk would have a new title that day, and if the prince did not strike her down on the spot, she would be laughed out of the country.*

Yes—we thought this was a brilliant idea, at the time.

The rope was as thick as a man's torso. Mae was unable to saw through even half of the hemp before another rotation of sentries came marching through. She and Vogo and the other workers, drugged out on their powder, fled into the far corner of the fortress, the job only half-done. *We hoped half-done was enough.* And in the shadow of the latrine hut, they celebrated anyway, breathing deep the dopha, dazzling their senses. Vogo laughed with a breathless hysteria as his sister crab-walked for his amusement. Teary-eyed and mentally gone, he wiped at the green powder at his nose while one of their cronies, who fancied himself an amateur scholar, took it upon himself to teach them the origins of dopha, explaining the process of shaving the jaxite stone that was mined from the heart of the eastern quarries, until Vogo drawled, "Shut your mouth," sitting on the dirt, too dizzy to stand. "Just fucking shut it." His sister, his best friend, slumped down beside him. She was tiny next to him.

"We'll cut the cripple up tomorrow," Mae said, dozing off.

Vogo sighed.

"My head is the sun," he said.

Time ticking away beneath the struts of the tortoise's watchtower.

Keema leaned against one of the watchtower struts, watching the orphans play a game of sticks. The game was a surprisingly complicated affair, with rules that yet eluded him, but he stayed anyway, to distract himself from all that had occurred that day.

"It's simple," the boy with the cleft lip said, holding up one of the sticks like an instructor's wand. But the more the boy explained the game, the less Keema understood. He was happy to listen away, and watched many rounds of it, which were quick and frantic and populated with giggling. The children liked having an audience.

"Was that a good move?" Keema asked.

The boy snorted. He explained why it was not a good move. Keema listened in earnest. He stayed for much longer than any of the orphans had expected him to stay. He even tried a round of the game himself, but he lost before his stick even touched the dirt. Though he was a proud young man, he did not mind losing to the children that night. He did not mind that the boy with the cleft lip talked to him as if he, too, were a child, slowly articulating points of good strategy. He did not mind the company on that strange and lonesome night.

A night that seemed so long; so brief.

Araya stilled the shaking of her hand with a tip of her ever-reliable flask as she waited out the hours to morning in her quarters, but the burn in her throat and the fire in her belly brought her little solace, her nerves still singing from the shiver from earlier—a shiver she could not help but interpret as divine warning for the trespass she was about to make against the royal family. The prince. A man who had once told her how at ease he felt in her company whenever they shared tea and whom she, despite herself and all that she had been working toward for so many years, did like in turn.

A pinch of idlit; that's all it would take.

She turned to the wall, where on a mantel hung an object of her ancestry. It was ever to family to whom she turned for comfort, and that night was no exception. She bowed to the spear, old and nicked, with a blade that gleamed like a silver leaf, and she prayed that she would be brave enough when the moment came—for whatever came after, whether that be her life, or her spirit's gentle delivery to the Sleeping Sea's embrace. And as she prayed, you look at the totem in your hands.

That old weapon.

The spear is almost the length of your entire body, though even you have to admit you have never been very tall. You touch the tassel; it is surprisingly soft to the touch, like fine red hair. The other dreamers watch you in wonder as you hold the spear up, the blade glinting in the light of the braziers that now line the aisles of this amphitheater, the weapon handed down from parent to child in your family for many generations, going back even before the crossing of the Great and Unending Sea. Your lola used to bow to the spear every morning before breakfast, as Araya did then, and your lola would bid you bow, too, and you thought of how unfair it was that it was only you she called on to perform these old gestures of tradition and not any of your nine brothers. But once an object of annoyance and shame, the spear now takes on a different weight in your hands as you ask yourself if it and Araya's is one and the same. It is. But as for the why, and the how—

Hush.

Do you hear that?
   This moonlit body stands at the front of the stage.
   Its ear raised to the sky.

He's come.

The people of the border town west of the fortress were the first to hear the approach through the cracked open windows, *but we knew better than to investigate that crazed driver roaring down the road.* The sighters on the wall of the western gate spotted the vehicle next as it clattered down the Road Below. It was a transport wagon from the palace, the stitched insignia of the Throne fading in and out of pools of roadside torchlight. Four large wheels creaked under the weight of the wagon's body as it churned through the dirt, slowing to a stop just before the imposing wooden gate that blocked all westward traffic. The driver stood on the seat of the carriage and held above his head a document. He shouted that he had come on royal business. He held his document higher. Through a spyglass, the sighter on the wall spotted the unmistakable red seal that clinched the parchment. They had no choice but to let him in.

Three short horn blasts from the watchtower woke the sentries. "Open the gate! Royal business! Open the gate!" *We stumbled out of the barracks and the mess hall—from our sleep, from our games.* A quartet of men gathered at the gate's wheel and with a heavy groan the wooden gate began to rise—barely off the ground when the wagon spurred on, the canvas roof ripping itself on the wooden teeth of the gate as it squeezed into the courtyard proper.

Araya ran out of her quarters still holding the spear. She glared up at the watchtower as she ran, shouting up at the tortoise, "Why did you not inform us of a royal visit?"

But the tortoise only sputtered. "No news! No news!" it cried. "Do not blame this child, the palace is quiet! This child has no news . . ."

The two horses stomped and snorted as they dragged their charge into the fortress. Sentries flooded into the courtyard to show their respect to this unexpected royal caravan while the orphans were scooted away, along with Keema—*we did not want the sight of him offending our royal visitors*—he and the children forced to watch all that then followed from the distant shadows, unseen. The western gate slammed shut with a thudding finality. The children receded farther into the shadows, sensing some dangerous quality to the night, while Keema, compelled by the scene before him, took a step forward, his eyes stuck on the midnight driver who stepped off the carriage.

The driver was wearing a palace mask carved in the likeness of a laughing demon, with bright-red cheeks and a mouth full of sharp teeth. He held a scroll in his hand, holding it up in the air as if to show everyone, the archers with nocked bows included, that he was otherwise unarmed.

Araya snatched the parchment from his fist and read the note by the torchlight Raami brought to her, her lips moving as she read.

Too far away to hear what they said, Keema relied on Araya's expressively dubious face and the driver's beseeching gestures to gather the scene in his mind, but it was only after Araya herself had gone into the wagon and then emerged minutes later, visibly shaken, then retreated to her office to speak with the driver in private, that he heard the talk from the others as to what in the abyss was going on.

A visiting dignitary had died.

So they said. Some important woman from the south, who had dropped to the floor upon the mysteriously stopped beating of her heart. *That's what I heard from Yeera, who heard from Doga.* The woman was being carted back home. *Her home was far away.* The driver was told to make the journey as quickly as possible, so that the dignitary's family could perform the Rites of the Body before the energies of her spirit had fled this earthly layer. *That's why they were at our checkpoint at that ungodly hour.*

But this did not explain the dread feeling that seemed to emanate from the wagon. It did not explain why when Keema looked upon the wagon he thought it might open its jaws and swallow him whole. All eyes in Tiger Gate were on that vehicle. Raami stood before the snorting horses, a bead of sweat rolling down his brow as he looked to Araya's quarters—her door shut—and then back at the wagon, which he was ordered by her to inspect. The wagon's manifest was in his hands. It listed all of the corpse's belongings. He had gone through similar checklists before, countless times, but now, *that night there was nothing I would rather have done than shrink away from that thing. I even tried to take a step toward it but was unable to complete the movement. Like I was stopped by some invisible leash on the heart. I cannot explain it.*

I looked for anyone else I could order to do my task. A faithful man might think it some alignment, that it was the Daware man I locked eyes with first. But the truth was it was a matter of practicality; that I lost no favor in my subordinates by shoving forward our lowest member.

And though Keema's heart pounded no less quickly than those of his fellows, he took the manifest from Raami's outstretched hand without complaint, *and our esteem of him rose, if but a little, at his bravery.* Past the horses he went, and around the car to the rear, where the entrance flap waited for him, the canvas pinned back, making a triangle of impressive darkness. He breathed in and climbed inside, wondering if that damned water reader was happy, having cheated him out of what little coin he had, telling him that foolish and false prophecy of what he might find at this checkpoint; this was not what he was looking for at all.

Inside her office, Araya smiled.

Her hands shook, not from the lack of drink, but because the driver had just shared with her a secret so vast in its implications that her body struggled to contain it. She shook, and she smiled, and she said, "It is not possible, that this is how things have turned."

The driver, whose face he had revealed to her from behind his demonic mask—a face that shocked her, his identity one of the last people she expected to see here, tonight of all nights—nodded in understanding. "Nevertheless, that is the way of things. She has entrusted you with the knowledge of Her presence. If you understand that, then you also understand why you need to let me through, Commander, sooner rather than later."

"That shiver I felt . . . was it—"

"Yes," the driver said. "It was."

She held herself.

"Gods."

"Commander," he said.

"I need a moment." She leaned forward in her seat. She thought she was going to throw up. "He's dead. He's really dead." Her mind, once blank, slowly filled with possibility. When she somehow found her breath again, she looked up at him. "Where are you taking Her?"

"Far from here. Somewhere to rest, and where She can make Her plans."

Upon hearing this, Araya decided to adapt.

"I have an alternative route for you," she said.

In the wagon, Keema winced.

The unmistakable smell of death permeated the hold; that stale musk that made the air cloying and heavy. He worked quickly. He unscrolled the manifest and checked the list against the items in the hold. He checked the large, heavy pots, the ponderous sacks of grain, and the large cloth bags filled with what he assumed were the dignitary's dresses and nightwear. He touched and poked at the belongings of the dead. He kicked at a bag of clothing. He lifted the heavy lid of one of the pots, a perfume scent wafting out its mouth and up his nose. He put the lid down and stuck his hand in, his fingers sinking into a satisfying mound of royal flower rice. And he continued on to the black curtain that divided the wagon in half, where he was surprised by the rapid pace of his heartbeat as he yanked the curtain aside.

There She was.

The aged body was, in the Old Country, an incomprehensible thing. The oldest person Keema had ever known was one of the matrons of the pleasure barge, where he worked for some time as a guard. She had laid claim to fifty years when she passed—a remarkable age, and one she might have lived beyond, had it not been for the stress of her many debts. Up till that night, her memory was his benchmark: the most age a human could have.

The corpse of the woman before him now was so old he could barely comprehend it. Her skin was the color of a rotted prune; pinched to the bone yet still somehow deeply wrinkled. She was bald, Her eyes sunk deep into Her skull like two dark craters. Her little body was draped in a loose, ornately patterned robe, and She was sitting in a cross-legged position, with skeletal hands resting on Her bone-drum knees, as if She were in some deep meditation.

This person was dead, of that he was certain, but what he couldn't believe was that She had died only that day—She looked as though She had died before the world was born.

In morbid awe, he approached Her, his right foot crossing the curtain divide. But this was his first mistake that night, for suddenly there was pain—pain as profound as a needle shoved through his eye and out the back of his head, and he dropped to the floor of the wagon.

Sometime later, he woke.

The glazed world snapped into focus. Araya was crouching over him. He blinked several times, his vision clearing along with the pain that had been so blinding and was now all but gone. He was lying on the courtyard dirt. "Why am I out here?" he asked.

"You fainted," Araya said. "The driver dragged you out."

"There's someone in there." He pointed limply at the caravan.

The commander nodded. There was a light in her eyes from the torches that made her look touched by a revelation. "I saw Her too," she said to him. "Hers is a sight not easily forgotten." He tried to get up, but she put a finger on his chest and pushed him back down too easily. "Stay. I would not have you faint again just yet."

"Please, Commander," the masked driver said, standing behind her. "Time is limited."

Keema touched his temple. "I think I'm—"

But his *I'm fine* was snapped in half when beneath his back he felt the ground begin to tremble.

We heard them before we saw them.

The distant rumbling of hooves, echoing through the valley. The pebbles dancing on the ground. The people of the border town beyond the gates knew who was coming. *We knew those horses. We knew that war cry.* And as the blurs of red poured in from the darkness, pounding up the dirt road that led to Tiger Gate, the people pressed their backs against their doors and covered their mouths with their hands, holding their children close, *for at the sound of their thunder we knew naught else to do but cower.*

They all wanted to cower, even the sentries in the fortress who just that morning felt good and powerful as they shepherded travelers through their strict and mercurial inspections, for there was not one person in the land of the moonless night who did not recognize the trembling of the earth and the violence that it foreshadowed. The mysterious driver staggered backward, breathing quickly, as if on the brink of a panic attack.

"Please," he begged, "you must not let him in. He will kill us all."

"What have you brought to my door?" Araya asked him.

"Banners," the sighter on the western wall shouted, her voice tight. "I see them all. The Brigade of the Red Peacock!"

The fortress took in a sharp inhalation. Some of the sentries disappeared into doorways. *My body took me into one of the storage shacks, where I barricaded myself inside and prayed for morning.* Others stayed rooted to the spot, all initiative gone, their bodies in a reflexive state of paralysis. Vogo Sugo, still high off the dopha powder, was stroking the hair of one of the horses, while his sister, Mae, was shuddering in terror on the steps along the wall. Four of the sentries who still had the wherewithal to act sprinted across the courtyard to open the western gate, but when they reached the turning wheel, Araya's voice boomed, "STOP! THE GATE STAYS SHUT!"

Not a person spoke after that; the only sound was that of the rising stampede of the hoofbeats, like a boil bubbling up to the rim of a pot. *We all looked at her as if she had lost her mind—to not open a gate for a prince was blasphemy.* "We know what happened to Fox Gate Checkpoint, when they were visited by the brigade at night," she said to them all. "The pyre of their bodies could be smelled across the entirety of the Thousand, only for it to later be discovered they were innocent of their charges. We find out what they are here for first. This is lawful. This is . . . this is right."

And so no one acted. They just waited as the band of warriors came up the cliffside road, led by the prince himself; *the sword of the western valley; the emperor's claw.*

The First Terror.

"May I speak to your commander?"

The surprisingly gentle voice lilted over the high walls and into the ears of all in attendance in the courtyard. The guards under Araya's command turned to face her, their eyes wide and their shoulders shaking, and she saw them again for the children that they were. "What would you have us do?" Raami asked, but she put a finger to her lips, and she mouthed to him, *He can hear you.* And then she began to hum as if there were nothing extraordinary or frightening about this moment, and she went up the steps of the wall, having learned a long time ago that being a good leader was simply a matter of not expressing how you truly feel. *It worked. We believed that she would save us with that calm smile.* She rested her hands on the edge of the wall and blandly counted in her head the number of hollow-eyed warriors below whose red armor made the western road a river of blood. Her gaze followed the line of warriors down to the termination point just below her, where before the massive wooden gate the First Terror stood, on his sandaled feet, beside his snuffling horse.

He smiled.

"Hello, Commander Araya. Nice to see you again."

There stood Saam Ossa, the first of the emperor's triplet sons, the First Terror, and Scourge of the Valley. He was, as ever, clean-shaven, handsome in a vague way, where there was nothing notably striking about the face but nothing off-putting either, his hair short, with a slight wave to it. Unlike his warrior sons, he did not wear armor but a stark red robe and black breeches that were tied off at the shin with string.

"My lord," she said, bowing just so. "It is an honor."

"Thank you for saying so, even if you don't mean it." It put her on edge, how charming his smile was. "The hour is late. I know. My presence disturbs the peace, and for that I am truly sorry."

"Nonsense. We serve at the pleasure of the Throne."

"Again, thank you for saying so, though I must say—and please understand I am not accusing you of anything, I simply state this as a curious observation—it *is* notable that you have yet to open your gates for us, even though it must be very clear by now who we are."

"It has been a strange night," she replied. The archers at her side were by then no longer at her side, having now backed up enough so that they were out of sight of the brigade—one of them, a boy who was no older than fifteen, looked at his commander *and I realized that I was standing beside the bravest person I would ever know in this life and I craved to be held by her.* "News from the palace remains uncertain, and tensions are high. I made it a blanket policy for anyone approaching at this late hour to be questioned first, before allowing them through."

"Safety is the best policy," the First Terror replied with humor after listening attentively to her. His smile never wavered. He pointed at her. "It is good to see you, Commander Araya. Very good. The last few weeks have thrown into relief how special you are, as I visited many other checkpoints my father had built and spoke with their commanders. At the last checkpoint I visited, the commander was too scared to come out and speak to me. He sent his lieutenant instead. A scared little man whose hands shook, like this, while he read aloud his commander's official greeting from a roll of parchment. He pissed himself as he bowed to me. It was a sorry sight." He held up his hands, what-can-you-do. "I missed your bravery. You were never afraid to face me yourself. It was always refreshing to spend time with someone who saw you for what you were; just a man, who has collected one too many titles during his time on this earthly band."

His smile faded just a bit, just enough for her to notice.

"Unlike my brothers," he continued, "I've never enjoyed being called a Terror, though I cannot deny that the title is accurate, especially on a night like tonight, where time is short and my mission is urgent.

"A wagon has passed through this way just recently. I know that you have seen it through your gates, the signs abound, the tracks below my feet match its description. I'm sure you've figured out by now that we're looking for it. As for why, well, the driver stole something precious from the capital and killed one of my sons in their escape." *In that abattoir below the mountain we found Jun Ossa's peacock mask, shreds of his clothing, and, most damning of all, the bone necklace that was his most prized possession. His father wept as he held the necklace in his grip.* "For that reason, amongst others, I will hunt this wagon down to the ends of the earth. And I will do so while doing my title of Terror justice." There was no smile on his face anymore. "If you did your diligent inspection of his wagon, which I am sure you did, and if you employed the quick deductive and reasoning skills that I know you possess, then you'll know that the precious something that I am looking for is the body of an old woman in the cab of his carriage. An extraordinarily old woman whom I am very fond of, and whom I would like to return home as soon as possible. This is why I am here tonight, Commander. And I will go forth stridently, with or without your aid."

"Monkey Gate Checkpoint is some miles north of here," Araya said, after swallowing nothing. "I think that is the best chance you have of catching up to them."

"Again," he said kindly, "a good, worthwhile effort."

He then dropped his gaze and looked straight through the gate.

His voice cold and quiet and heard by all.

"Mother," he said.

I know you're there.
  I can smell you.
  Can you smell me?
  The blood of my father on my clothes?
  My son?

Anyway.
I've come to bring you home.
And Commander.
Thank you for your good service.
And your company.

He raised his hand to the gate.

But I'm coming in now.

And then the egg timer snapped.

Brztztztztztztztztztztztztztztztztztztztzt—
"Oh!" your lola gasped, startled.
Water boiled over the rim of the pot.
"It's time!"

Something large hit the western gate.

The once-unyielding timber construction buckled, as if sucker-punched, and all the fortress flinched from the impact. The children scurried into small burrows, and the crowd of sentries in the courtyard looked up at their fellows who stood atop the wall. *We shouted up at them, asking them what they saw, what was hitting our gate, but they did not respond—they did not even hear us.*

And then the second impact came.

A crack ran down the face of the western gate. The light of the brigade's torches could be seen through the opening. *How could we tell the others what we saw? How could we explain to them the power of the First Terror?*

"Mercy!" Someone ran up the steps to the parapets, shouting this word. It was the Sugo sister. Araya stared at her dumbly as Mae shouted down at the brigade, "I have royal blood! My brother and I—we are one of you! Please, we will open this gate! Simply spare us! Vogo!" But when she turned, her brother was nowhere to be seen. *It always fell to me to save us, ever since we were kids.* Snarling, she enlisted the aid of her cronies, "You all, with me if you want to live!" and she and the men headed for the gate's turning wheel.

"No, Mae!" Araya shouted, coming out of her stunned interior, and as she ran to stop them she shouted at Raami, "Get the eastern gate open! Children first! Go!" Raami nodded and gathered men of his own for the task while Mae and her friends began to push against the wheel for the Terror. It had yet to complete a single revolution when Araya nudged the tip of her spear against Mae's back. "I said leave it. We cannot open this gate."

"You stupid fool!" Mae screamed. With dilated pupils she pivoted on her heel, swiping the spear to the side with the back of her hand before she stuck her knife into Araya's side.

From the other end of the courtyard, Raami saw Araya stumble backward. *Through the crowds of my fellows who ran in terror, I saw my commander, wounded, and as I saw her touch the hilt in her side, I felt the wound as if it were my own.* Mae was already back on the wheel, shuddering as she pressed with all her weight, unable to budge it forward, for her cronies had abandoned her. "Spare—us—" she grunted, before she winced, and her breath stopped, her body slumping to the ground.

Grimacing, Araya yanked the spear out of Mae's back.

A third hit.

The crack widened into a fissure. Keema had joined the others at the eastern wheel, the gate that led into the terrace lands slowly groaning to life, the wooden teeth lifting from out of their deep furrows. Eight sentries in all worked the wheel, double the requirement, and yet the resistance seemed to them so much greater. *The wheel had an impossible weight to it, fighting us in a way it never had before.* The sabotaged rope within the pulley-works now trembling from the tension, hemp hairs splitting away as the orphans were sent under the gate's slowly widening gap—the boy with the cleft lip sprinting down the dark cliff road with the other children, not knowing where else to run but forward. Some of the men tried to squeeze through the narrow gap as well; two of them made it through before the rope in the pulley-works snapped like a tendon; the wooden slab slammed into the dirt. *And we stared at the broken gate, knowing in our hearts that we would never see it opened again.*

A fourth hit.

Half of the western gate had begun to slump forward. By then, a calmness had come over Araya, even as she bled profusely from her side, her courage fed by the panic of those around her. *We did not understand why she was not frightened at all; why she smiled.* The guards under her command, stunned by her serenity, followed without question, their jangled nerves calmed by her surety as they armed themselves and prepared for the coming breach. Raami stood by her, alongside an outfit of trusted warriors. *We were moths to her light. It was the only light we could see.* And Araya looked at them, not understanding why they joined her side, what reason there was for their loyalty, or their bravery. She wanted to

tell them that she was sorry. That their deaths were on her con-
science. That she wanted nothing more than to sit and drink. But
instead, she told them where to set up the barrels, and where to tip
the tables, and where to hide if they did not wish to fight. She sent
a man up the watchtower to sever the tortoise's head, so that it
would not be used by their enemy after they breached the fortress.
And as she gave out her instructions, Keema pulled a sword from
the rack, and he joined Araya's line of warriors before the fractur-
ing western gate. "Where would you have me?" he asked. But when
she smiled at him, he knew that he was to be rejected from a fight
for the second time that night.

Fifth hit.

A cloud of splinters flew out across the courtyard. A diamond
shape had been punched out of the gate, through which they could
see the manes of the snarling horses and the glint of the Peacocks'
blades.

"Keema of the Daware Tribe. There you are." Araya sounded as
if he had walked in on her dice game and was pleasantly surprised
by his visit. She told him to drop the sword in his hand. And then
she handed him her spear. "I would have you go to the outskirts of
the Divine City. In five days there will be an army encampment, out
in the fields of soma. A soldier named Shan will be there. I would
have you offer her this spear."

Keema hesitated—this order did not strike him as sane. With
the spear he pointed at the western gate, soon to cave in.

"I'll fight," he said helplessly.

Sixth hit.

"The emperor is dead, Keema," she said. The words were so improbable they bounced off his ears with no registry. So she drove the words in. "He's dead. Believe this truth. There is not enough time for you not to. The Smiling Sun is no more. He is as dead as anyone has ever been, and this world will soon fall gloriously apart. And that wagon over there is the hook that will ensure its unraveling." She looked at him. "Ride that wagon east. Bring this spear home." She smiled as blood dripped from her grip on her side. "And maybe whatever it is you once asked of that water reader, perhaps you will find it there."

Behind her, Raami shouted for men to line up along the wall.

"Is this what you would have me do?" he asked. "Leave?"

"Yes," she said. "On your oath as a Daware man, swear to me you will leave."

He looked into her eyes.

"I swear it."

"Swear that you will bring this spear with you to the coast. Swear you will bring it to a soldier named Shan."

"I swear it," he said. "What would you have me tell this Shan?"

There were tears in Araya's eyes.

"I do not know, Keema of the Daware Tribe. What would you tell someone whose forgiveness you sought? Think on that, and when you get there, tell her something kind."

She smiled.

"Go then," she said. "Your ride is leaving."

He turned—the wagon was being drawn away by the rein-snapped horses.

And he ran.

Seventh hit.

The fissure was wide enough to fit an arm through. One more hit and the gate would crack open. Whoever did not pick up a weapon ran into the barracks and the officers' building and barricaded themselves within. *I was not a coward! I was not going to die for that fool of a commander!* Others tried to escape through the latrine trenches, only to slide off the edge and plummet into the misted abyss. *My last prayer spent in hope that I would find dignity after death.* A wall of sentries crossed the span of the fortress, with Araya at their center, her legs bent and her back hunched as she draped a long blade across her shoulders—her anxiety made manifest only in the tremble of her bottom lip, which she bit, till it bled, and stopped. Raami stood beside her. *I did what I could for her wound, but there was too little time to treat it properly.* And as she bled, Keema ran up to the departing wagon and threw his spear into the hold, then himself, wincing as he joined the old woman's cross-legged corpse amongst the other et ceteras of the deceased.

The wagon charged forward at the closed eastern gate. The First Terror, standing before the western gate, focused his last strike. The sentries who watched the wagon wondered how the driver intended to leave. But then it happened, as if in syncopation— as if this strange new night had accounted for this moment and had made art of it by creating in it this timed rhythm—for when the First Terror slammed his hands forward and punched open the western gate with his fist of wind, wide enough to allow his soldiers passage, the eastern gate, at that very instant, upon the twitch of the dead old woman's finger, blew open.

Like a powder keg—

the sound cracking the eardrums of every warrior in Tiger Gate Checkpoint, a tinnitus howl in Keema's ears as through the canvas flap he watched the gate that had stood tall for years soundlessly kicked in by what seemed like nothing, and with such ease, as if it were a handful of twigs blown away by the breath of a red-faced child. The wagon careening through this freshly made cataract while in a world of silence and raining splinters a broad-chested man with a red tattoo on his face staggered into the courtyard, touching his helmet at the place of his ear, so stunned by the explosion from the east that he forgot for a moment where he was or why he had wanted to get into this courtyard so desperately, the warrior-drug in his stomach reversing the order of his adrenaline, pulling him into a heady high as he knocked at his ear and heard nothing, not even when he tried speaking out loud—"Father," he said, the only word that came to mind—and it terrified him that he could not hear it; his terror cut mercifully short by Araya's approach from the smoke and the whispering fall of her long blade as it cleaved his neck. His head bounced against the dirt. Blood geysered into the starless night. Araya was a soaked demon that hummed a tuneless note as she slashed left and slashed right. She took down an arm, a leg, another leg, three bodies piling up behind her until she turned just in time to see the swing of the club as the horseman's weapon clipped her shoulder and sent her tumbling to the ground, silencing her—her mouth filled with dirt as the other horses stampeded into the courtyard and crunched her head beneath their hooves, the dam broken and the brigade streaming like red water into the shattered checkpoint. The guards of Tiger Gate were trampled and skewered at the bright ends of thrusted pikes. *We were cut to pieces. Those of us barricaded in the mess hall and barracks were burned alive.* Raami tried to stop the flinging of the torches, but he was soon overwhelmed. They threw him into the pyre with the kindling, the

Peacocks laughing as he writhed in the flames that billowed its black smoke into the moonless sky.

Keema could see the smokestacks from the wagon.

He stood inside the berth of the wagon, looking out through the rear canvas opening, from where he watched Tiger Gate go up in flames. He could feel the wheels juddering over uneven road, and the tight turns the vehicle made around cliffside corners, bringing him far away from the destruction, but he did not feel safe, or good. He swallowed dryly as he listened to the distant shrieks, and the give of collapsing timber.

"They're all dead," Vogo muttered.

Keema turned. By the rattling pots of rice deep inside the wagon, the Sugo brother was crouched, half-hidden, his face buried in his knees. He was rocking back and forth. There was a limit to the things Keema could be surprised by that night. He walked over to Vogo, to say or do what he did not know; in the end he did nothing; he just stood there as Vogo reached out and hugged his leg and wept. As the man found comfort in his leg, which probably could have been anyone's leg, Keema looked to the rear of the wagon again, to see if any riders were following, and his eyes widened when he saw the orphans running down the road, after them. The boy with the cleft lip was ahead of all of them. He was reaching out for Keema.

Keema shrugged off Vogo's grasp and ran to the end of the wagon. He held his hand out.

The boy, with heaving breath, reached for him.

A scream—the children were scattering to the sides of the road to make way for the coming Peacock, who galloped at a pace reserved for demons. The boy with the cleft lip was lagging in his speed; he could not match the wagon's horses. Keema shouted at him to get to the side of the road, and the boy obeyed, hugging himself to the cliff wall, narrowly avoiding being trampled by the warrior's snorting stallion.

With the purple-bruised sky behind him, the warrior seemed to Keema of almost mythic proportion, a portrait commissioned by some free-band to memorialize the best of their killers, and he thought it appropriate, and even good, that this man would be his death, this moment of grim appreciation cut short when the behemoth warrior leapt from his horse like a frog from a lily pad and fell through the rear of the wagon, colliding with Keema, who let out a breathless *oh*—the dropped weight of the two of them so great, and so sudden, that it cracked the rear axle of the wagon in half.

The back of the wagon slammed onto the dirt road.

The Sugo brother yelped.

The horses whinnied as they pulled this slow and dragging object down the unkempt road. Wheels popped over ruts in the dirt. More Peacocks were coming around the bend. *We cheered on our brother to kill the bastards. We chanted his name as we sped onward to meet them.* The world of the wagon now tilted as the warrior slid down this newly made ramp, along with all the objects in the hold; the pots tipping over the rear lip of the wagon and bouncing onto the road before shattering into great clouds of perfumed rice while the canvas bags of clothes ripped open against the friction and sent the old woman's robes and scarves off the cliffside like so many cotton and lace birds. The old woman herself began to slide, her cushion creeping down the ramp, until the driver, in a moment of sheer instinct, reached back and grabbed her collar while with the other hand he kept tight observance of the horses' reins.

The warrior with the peacock tattoo was at the bottom of the ramp, looking for purchase. He grabbed the Sugo brother's leg. The brother simply grunted as he was dragged down. Keema watched from his tenuous hold on a knot of canvas as the two men below him fought. But though Sugo was strong, the Peacock was stronger.

"I—Help—I!" the brother shouted as the Peacock covered the crying man's face with his massive hand. Keema slid down a bit and kicked at the behemoth warrior. The warrior was not bothered by these attacks. With a bleeding nose and a bloodlust smile, he pressed the Sugo brother's face into the floorboards of the wagon, Vogo's arms spasming out to the sides from the pressure as Keema continued to kick the snarling warrior in the face. Blood shot out of the Peacock's nose. A tooth jerked from its socket. But he did not release the brother. "I—I—I—" the Sugo brother cried as the warrior squeezed his face with his gauntlet until, with a bloodcurdling pop, he deflated.

Death was instant.

Bone slid into brain and in that bright firework behind his jellied eyes Vogo was propelled out of his body, as if two hands had shoved him off the edge of the last precipice of this world, his spirit crashing through the heavenly bands, the banners of color and sound that lay like sediment between these choruses, until he dropped into the churning waters of the Sleeping Sea, where upon the cold detonation of its surface he scattered, like pieces of a dropped porcelain plate, into the hours that bind our days, *and I thought about my mother who jumped from a cliff when I was little, and I wondered if this was what she saw when she ended things, as I ended things,* what remained of Vogo gone far away, and yet not far at all, as the crisscrossing waves closed over these pieces of him like linens folded by a pair of loving hands.

The Peacock warrior grunted.

There was a squelch as he threw the dead boy overboard, the corpse twisting over the speeding dirt like a doll. Keema's stomach seized, vomit building up in his throat, but he was afforded no release, for the Peacock then grabbed his leg and dragged him down next.

They were eye to eye now. Keema was overwhelmed by the man's sour and angry breath. He fought against the powerful hand that held his throat. Red-eyed he watched the man's other hand rise up, a fist backlit by the bruised-purple sky, the knuckles curled and ready to punch his head through the wagon's floor. But then, as Keema wheezed, he saw the warrior's eyes dilate so suddenly it was as if the pupils had dropped through a surprise chute.

The man bolted upright. He grabbed at his own face. He screamed as if overwhelmed by a pain in his head from an unknown source like an invisible needle through the eye. Whatever had come over him, the warrior was in such pain he did not even notice Keema kick out at him, not until he was already falling backward, crunching onto the road, where momentum rolled him off the cliffside, until, noiselessly, he dropped off the cliff.

More were coming.

The road behind them was congested with riders just as they reached the first bridge. The wheels of the wagon beginning to judder over the rough-hewn boards of the Berum Chasm Span.

"I'm losing grip!" the driver shouted.

The collar of the old woman's robes was sliding through the angry curl of his fingertips. When She slipped free, Keema pinned Her to the tilted floor with his body. The corpse was so insubstantial that holding Her down was like holding a bed of loose old parchment. The smell of Her like an unearthed thing from beneath ancient bedrock. As he held Her, he could hear the brigade not far behind them, their hunting screams as they spurred their horses forth. There were dozens of them. They would drag Keema out of the wagon and rip him to shreds; he knew this. He squeezed his eyes shut as he held on to Her.

He did not want to die.

They were near the end of the bridge when Keema heard the prince's voice in his head—that calm, avuncular, and awful voice that said,

"Just let go."

And he did. He let go of his bodied grip on the corpse that was not a corpse as Her eyes drew open, and he let Her rise, just so, until She was sitting upright and looking out at the bridge between cliffs and the chasm below it. Three Peacocks had begun galloping across the bridge. *We would make our father proud that night. We would bring his mother home.* And although Keema would only be told Her true identity later that new day, even then, as he watched Her raise Her arm, with Her hand curled upward as if holding an ecstatic fruit, a deep part of him understood that She was not of the mortal world.

The sky rose from its purple tint into a dark-orange blush as She held Her aged hand high and slowly curled in Her fingers, forcing the wooden boards of the bridge to crack and splinter, a great trembling running through the supports. And Keema flinched when She squeezed Her hand into a fist and the bridge blew apart.

Three warriors dropped into the depths between the ancient hills. *We fell with our father's name on our tongues.* The Peacocks in their freefall disappearing with the remnants of the bridge into the forest canopy far below—the First Terror rearing his horse at the cliff's edge, running in a fury to the chasm's lip as he shouted his children's names.

In the tattered wagon, Keema pressed his back to the wall.

He looked up at the old woman, who wore a cruel smile.

"Avert your eyes, mortal," She said. "You forget yourself, before your empress."

It is only now that you realize you've heard this tale before.

At least, a version of it. You don't know what tripped this memory. It comes on you suddenly as the dancers and this moonlit body clear the stage: the day your father told you the tale of the stolen Moon, and Her journey to reclaim Her country. You do not remember why he told you this tale, after all, he seemed perpetually annoyed by your lola's efforts to share with you everything she knew of the Old Country, but what you do remember is the great pains he took to describe the battles and the swordplay, and how he kept interrupting his own tale to assure you that this wasn't a love story. That it was about camaraderie; that it was about a revolution; the important things. And to you, it seemed strange of him to bring any of this up. You never thought it was a love story, for in his story there was no love. There was only a long road of bodies.

The end of his tale is lost to your remembrance. You know only that it takes place in the span of five days, and that there is much blood yet to spill before the end.

But outside of the tale, you remember your lola shaking her head and tsking from the other room, and once your father had left to go on his afternoon constitutional, she came over to you, and said, "Do not heed his words to the letter." She told you that that was but one version of the telling; that your father had learned this way from your granjo, who had his own feelings about life and what was worth his attention. And then she sat on her favorite chair in the kitchen and rolled out a cigarette, even though by then she was very weak and could barely hold a breath. You wanted to go out and play, but she told you to wait and listen. She told you this was important.

"The old men would have you believe it shook out one way.

That the road was but pain and glory. Sometimes, perhaps, life whittles itself down to these essences. Sometimes there is nothing we can do but sit in it." She took a long drag and blew gray smoke up into the ceiling, where it lived like an opaque and swirling cloud of shape and texture. "But listen well when I tell you that your father, and your granjo, are wrong."

What were they wrong about? you asked.

She shrugged.

"This is a love story to its blade-dented bone."

THE FIRST DAY

—

in which we offer our finest harvest

Light breaks—

From behind the stage's white-parchment backdrop, a light rises, diffuse yet bright, and you know this to be the sun. As this stage-sun lifts, the dancers are revealed from the dark, the light casting them and this moonlit body in striking silhouette, these bodies postured tall and strong. You see these legs rooted to the floor, veins of rock dug into the earth, and these arms, curled around the chest like vines tough and unyielding. These chins lifted high, basking in the languid sunrise. When you see these bodies, you no longer see the stage but towering rock and wind-blown trees. You see the natural wall that separated the emperor's cradle from the rest of the country to the east.

You see the Spires at dawn.

You know this place. You had seen it yourself, not in person, but as an oil painting, done in the style of Old Meridian, where the lushness of the natural world was the focus. Even in your youthful disinterest at the time you remember the intense beauty of the image: the light that fell in great shafts through dramatic cloud breaks, draping over the mighty thrusts of land. Trees erupting from stone in thick, verdant brushstrokes, and mists that rolled down these hills like curls of gray hair down an ancient shoulder, making mystery and danger of the dirt roads that curved around these towers of rock like thin knots of twine around a dead god's fingers.

This painting, however pleasing to the eye, is forever linked in your mind with discomfort and tedium, for you saw it on one of the days you were tasked with walking your lola through the dockside markets. It was a chore you dreaded, not only because the wheelchairs of your time were made of wood and wicker, tending to snag on every irregular surface, but also due to her temperament on those walks, when she was at her meanest, taking out on you her frustrations with her decaying body. "Why are we sitting in the middle of the street?" she would snap—"Hurry it up, you lazy ass." The woman bonking you with her cane like you were an untrained donkey in between her fits of coughing. She was only in that wheelchair for a short time before she passed away; those were the last days you had to spend with her, but you did not know this at the time. All you knew was that fortune smiled on you that day, when she discovered the quiet, tarp-shaded artisans' corner and bid you to stop.

There, in a triangle of light at the end of the alley, she gripped your wrist and pointed at the framed image hanging on the clay wall.

"Home," she said.

Your lola sat transfixed by this painting for much of the afternoon. She even tried to buy it before the shopkeeper's price wilted her excitement and she settled for simply beholding it with her loving gaze, pointing out to you the subtle patches of green in the rock of the hills as she told you of the foolhardy fortune-seekers who would scale these cliffs with naught but a frayed rope and a rusty chisel to mine the precious jaxite inside. She spoke excitedly, forgetting that she was bound to the chair that you captained. You remember the chill you felt when she turned to you and gave you the warning all children of the Old Country were given: that to fall from the Spires is certain death. It was a piece of wisdom shared by everyone of the Old Country, regardless of station, even the First of the Terrors, who, as the last of the Berum Chasm Span crumbled from its obliterated supports and pebbled down the side of the cliff, knelt at the cliff's edge and grieved for the sons who had fallen in. He keened. He wailed. And with tears in his eyes, he glared across the chasm at the near-destroyed wagon that made its flight around the turn of the far hill, and he made this promise to his remaining sons: "They will not get far."

Your lola sighed. She looked very small as she sat before that grand painting of a place she had never been, before she then turned to you.

"I'm done," she said wearily.

This moonlit body breaks from its life as a mighty rock.

And it becomes before your eyes a creature at the brink of its life. A being reduced to snarls and whinnies. Hooves punching into the dirt as it drags an impossible weight up a steepening rise, red-eyed and exhausted and choked on its own mangled reins; a stray arrow stuck in the nape of its neck.

The light behind the parchment wall halts its rise.

The day begins here: at the moment of this creature's passing.

DAWN

The horse fell.

It tipped over without ceremony at the last rise in the cliff road. A thick cloud of dirt and dust plumed over its capsized body, clinging to the hot, still air as the masked driver, coughing, climbed out of the carriage. He looked down upon the fallen creature, its twitching legs a false sign of life, and he bowed his head.

"Forgive me," he said.

And then, as if in sympathy with its fallen brethren, the second horse lay down as well, and the driver knew what was to happen when he saw the foam sizzling from its snout and its teeth chattering as if suffering the onset of winter; his suspicion confirmed when it collapsed onto its side. *I told him he should not have chosen these creatures. I told him that they were too weak for our purposes. I told him he should have listened to me.* The masked driver shrugged off Her Whisper like a gnat off his shoulder. They had left the palace in a hurried state thanks to Her, and the only means of transport he could find was this two-horse canvas wagon not meant for the speed or distance they intended to travel. But try as he might to direct the blame at Her, he could not—everything in the end came back to him.

"I pushed them too hard," he said.

He crouched beside the creature and placed his hand on its distended belly, feeling through the hot skin the untethered stomp of its heart. It did not have long. He buried his hand in its thick black mane as the horse wheezed and trembled. He could feel it all: all of the terror in the creature's last moments, and was almost glad when it finally went limp, its last movement a strange, reflexive kick of its back leg into the air as if to strike the sky before resting on the ground for the last time. The masked driver prayed for the two horses that lay before him. He prayed for their safe passage into the

Sleeping Sea. He was not the praying sort until rather recently. Now it seemed that prayer, prayer to the world, the spirits the world cradled, and to the Sleeping Sea that dwelt beneath it all, was all he had to stop himself from losing his mind. But his prayers for the horses were interrupted when She called to him, with urgency, *for I demanded that he attend to me,* and upon the command of Her Whisper the masked driver had no choice but to get up. He rose from his kneel with reluctance. He told Her he was coming. The hand ax twined to his belt bouncing against his thigh as he approached the wagon.

Perhaps it was this sound that provoked what happened next; the sound of a weapon, tapping against his thigh with a casual, accidental menace, that tensed the mood enough to snap. Had the masked driver approached the wagon with more care, he maybe would have avoided what was to come, but in his emotional state, with the First Terror's cruel whisper still clinging to his eardrums, he had forgotten that he and the empress were not alone—that, in the madness of the attack on Tiger Gate, they had picked up an extra passenger.

And so, when the canvas fold of the wagon parted and a young man leapt out, he flinched, his old instincts flaring, and he punched this stranger in the face. The young man stumbled backward against the wagon, where he touched his chin and frowned at the blood on his fingers.

Hear the drums fill the theater—the brazier flames spitting and roaring as the young man looked at his attacker, who had already put his hands up in apology, and charged at him with a scream.

"It's preemptive," your father said.

"In a time of peril, it's act first, or be acted on," he said, which were words you had never heard him say before; the merchant who sold luxury carpets and textiles now, somehow, a military strategist. "If we don't invade K_____, the enemy will." These supposed words of wisdom sourced from his new friends from the pub, where he went to grieve your lola after her sudden passing, and then, eventually, simply where he went. He would host impromptu salons with these other men in your home, their drinking and their bluster carrying on through the night, and you would see how desperate your father was to fit in with them; this man who had so few people in his life he could call compatriots; how strangely people behaved when they were lost.

And so the two lost warriors fought in the dirt.

Their grunts and their punches echoed throughout the valley of rock spires while up in the trees that overlooked the road, hanging amongst the tangle of branches, an old ape watched them with a look of disappointment while pulling out from a cloth satchel a joint. Another ape reached out and lit it for him, and as he sucked in the smoke, the rest of his caste, a family of green-snouts thirteen strong, joined him in watching the humans dance. *Humans fought and we gave our eyes eagerly to their come-together.* Some of the younger apes hollered encouragement at the warriors—Keema made the mistake of looking up at them before the driver's fist swiveled his head—but the fight for the most part continued on as though the apes were not there, the young men elbowing the air out of one another's stomachs, kicking at shins, scratching, anything to hurt the other no matter how tricksome. They did not break focus even as the apes spat fruit stones into the air in exaltation of their ruthless performance.

The old ape with the joint did not celebrate the warriors. He sat without energy on a thick branch that only just supported his weight as he gazed down at the brawl with something close to pity, as he puffed and streamed smoke from his wide, scarred nostrils. *In that Endless Summer I gave my eyes to too much hurt. My son and daughter, dead by hunters, their teeth stolen from their mouths, I see them always. I saw them then, in the two warriors fighting in the road. No good. Hurt in my chest. Moving on was the great desire in this body, no wish to be witness to more pain, but I gave my eyes to the battle anyway. I smoked, and I gave my eyes in hope, hope that this come-together would not end in stopped breath.*

The two humans rolled over each other, each attempting to pin the other to the ground, to get the other one to stop moving, to dominate him, the dirt getting in their eyes as they rolled, and in their mouths, until they were forced to part to clear their faces. One of them blinked to get the grit out, while the other, afforded some protection by the mask he wore, took advantage of the moment and flew at his stunned opponent with a knee to the gut. But the one-armed human, blinded as he was, sensed an approaching blow and he braced himself, much to the excitement of the younger apes, who hooted, *glad to give our eyes to these humans of high skill,* as he absorbed the knee-blow, then wrapped his arm around the masked driver and tossed him to the ground. He fell on him. Grunts echoed down the cliffside corridors. The aged ape let out a long breath, smoke dissipating in the humid air. *Nothing would come of this.*

But as you watch this brawl in the theater, translated into performance by this moonlit body and its partner dancer, you have the sense that these two bodies do not want to stop, even if they could. You watch the jerked and halting movements of the two creatures circling each other and striking—this moonlit body kicking and spinning and then pressing its partner into the floor—and you understand that the dance could stop at any time, that both participants know that nothing will come of the fight, and yet it goes on. It goes on, even as greater concerns loom in the distance. Even as the First Terror makes his way northward to the next gate, on the hunt for them. Time ticking away on an egg timer in another era.

Keema screamed as he drove the masked young man into the ground. The driver, winded, kicked him in the thigh. They fought for nothing, which is why you see yourself in them. You remember the time you and your friend Jadi fought. He had bumped into your shoulder, hard enough to knock you back into a stranger's arms. You were embarrassed. He was sorry. And you knew he had meant nothing by it, that it was an accident; that Jadi was joyfully clumsy. You knew he cared about you. But something in you needed to claw his heart out anyway.

Your lola had died. Your lola, whom some days you hated, capricious as her mood was, leaving you always trying to guess if today she would be kind or not, if she would slap your hands or not. Your lola was dead, outlived by her own father. And you were on fire.

And it felt so good to let it burn.

The masked driver wrestled his arm free and gripped Keema's throat, searching for the pinch that would make him faint, and Keema, red-faced, breath-choked, pressed his hand to the driver's wooden mask, his fingers scrambling over the old etchings and demonic curves until they found the eyeholes, fore and middle finger digging in, ready to blind him, the aged ape looking away as the two warriors were caught in this unending knot of pain, with Keema so lost in the moment he was even beginning to smile, and the driver forgetting all that had led him to this fight, all that he had left behind in the past six months as he focused on this one goal, his fingers pressing into Keema's flesh, his nails digging into the skin of his throat, ready to draw blood, ready to tear the whole thing out, when their fight was interrupted. *I had had enough of these children.*

The wagon exploded.

Upon the drumbeat, a plume of wood and cloth and dirt shot off the cliffside. The explosion was swift and loud. Shrapnel peppered the canopy of the forest basin far below, causing the birds to quit their purchase on trembling branches. The green-snouted apes shrunk back into the trees, their eyes glowing in the dark brush in wary watchfulness, *for we saw Her, and we wanted no part of Her schemes.*

The two warriors parted from each other, hacking and coughing in the thick cloud of dirt the explosion had created. Pieces of canvas fluttered down from the sky. Keema rose to his feet, his mind catching up to what his eyes beheld. The two horses were gone. The wagon was gone. A wooden piece of axle fell from the sky, striking the dirt not two paces from him. He wiped a film of dust off his face, noticing in his periphery that the masked driver was still on his knees, bent in prostration in the direction of the obliterated wagon.

"Forgive me!" the driver shouted, "I lost myself!" And for a moment, Keema smirked as he looked down at his cowering antagonist, but this feeling of superiority did not last long; when the last blot of dust and dirt was blown away by a hot breeze, clearing the choked air that surrounded where the wagon once lay, a dead chill settled in the pit of his stomach as he looked upon the old woman sitting cross-legged amongst the rubble—her eyes shut but still somehow staring at him.

Keema slid down to his knees as the driver had done and he bowed his head, while up in the branches the old ape nodded in approval, glad that the young warrior was capable of at least this much wisdom. *My father told me of Her strength. He told me that one day She would pass through this land, and woe to any creature that did not bow to Her presence. But though my caste begged that we leave should we become captured in Her wrath, I bid them wait. I wished to give these eyes to this moment. I felt something of great importance occurring before me.*

Keema's heart paced quicker the longer he stayed prostrate, the heat of the rising dawn sun burning the back of his neck and arm. He side-eyed the driver, who was still pressing his mask to the ground.

"Yes," the driver said, to seemingly no one. "Yes, I understand."

"I agree, Your Highness," he said.

"If that be your will," he said.

Keema watched the mad driver stand up and walk toward the debris. He pulled a seat cushion down from a tangle of branches and dropped it on the ground, and, after he placed Her body upon the cushion, he lifted Her up over his head as if She weighed nothing at all, and carried Her the way royal children were once carried by their servants during the parades, back when the people still had parades, out to the edge of the road,

where he treated with the apes.

"The empress recognizes the Green Hill Tribe," he shouted up into the trees. "Long has it been since She has treated with your caste, but it is with great fondness that she recalls the elder Five Scar, who sang up to Her in praise when She yet ruled the night. He was beautiful and brave, and few days go by when she does not think of his whistle-song—even now, as She makes Her way east, to undo the Moon Throne's hold over Her land—a mission with which She would be most grateful for aid."

The smoking ape looked down at them from his branch. "Have the two boys finished their warring on our territory?" he asked. The younger apes behind him snickered.

The driver was silent for a moment. "I offer my sincerest apologies for that display."

The ape shrugged with his hand. "No matter. Young warriors fight and the sun rises on another day. We of the Green Hill give our respects to the lovely Moon." With an appraising look, he added, "If the wind speaks the truth, we also give our thanks to Her for ridding us of that emperor, as well as our sorrow for the loss. We held no love for the man, but we recognize that such action is no easy measure."

"She accepts this thanks," the driver said after a moment.

"And we remember with sorrow old Five Scar," the ape said. "The empress has been gone for much time, so perhaps She does not yet know that he was hunted down for his teeth by the same men She called family."

The driver said nothing to this.

The ape pointed to the tower of smoke in the distance. "You come in the wake of great destruction."

The driver nodded. "It will grieve no ears to hear that Tiger Gate Checkpoint has fallen—a casualty of the empress's escape from the palace. The man you know as the First Terror gave chase, and in his fury burned all that lay in his path. The commander of the checkpoint helped us through. It was she who told us of a team of warriors who lay in wait amongst these trees. A plan to ensnare the First Terror, which now will not come to pass. Have you encountered these assassins? We have need to speak with them."

The ape nodded. "We have. Humans of cruel eyes and unknown intention are not welcome sights. We spelled them to sleep with our dance." He took a final puff of his joint and then ate it. "We enjoyed their wares."

Behind him, the other apes wore various assortments of human gear. Helmets and pauldrons. A bandanna on one; another brandishing a curved sword like a fishing rod.

"I see."

"I would not continue your search for them. They will not wake for many days."

"That is unfortunate." The driver took whispered conference with the empress. He looked up at the apes. "She would then know if your caste will help us more directly. We make for the eastern coast. We have been told that people gather there, and soon—in a matter of days—they will rise up against the Throne. We would join them. But it is a long journey, and we are in need of protection, and transport."

The ape chuckled.

"No," he said.

A subtle, unnatural wind picked up, fluttering the dry leaves that clung to the branches. The green-snouts in the background began to hoot. "This is a surprising answer," the driver said. He sounded nervous to Keema, as if even he was afraid of what might happen should the apes refuse Her request. "I would beg you to reconsider."

"We will not," the ape said, paying no mind to the quaking leaves and the swirling wind. "If it is Her intention to strike us down for this blasphemy, She may. But this ape can smell the limits of Her human flesh. She is . . . old. She does not have long." He said this as the irrefutable fact that it was. "She will not make it to Her destination if She destroys every creature in Her path."

The quaking leaves began to settle; the dust winds dying.

The driver breathed out, relieved.

"She asks this then," he said. "Why is the Green Hill Tribe abandoning Her in Her time of need?"

"'Abandoning' . . . A daring accusation, coming from Her." The ape made a dismissive gesture. "But this one does not wish to argue who abandoned whom, and when, however many hundreds of years ago. The only relevant truth in this moment is that we will not help you because our caste is small." A great sadness came over his sunken eyes. "We cannot afford to offer you our protection on this journey during which you all will perish, because to do so will mean the end of our tribe."

"She says that some might consider this a worthwhile trade," he said, "for the payment of a Throne's end. What better sign of hope is there than the emperor's death?"

"One man. One man is dead." Agitated, the ape settled back on his branch, blinking in an unhurried way as one of his caste tossed him a fruit. "He was not the first bad man to build his checkpoints, and he will not be the last. Your come-together with that one over there this morning proves only how little his death means. More fighting will come. Another emperor will soon be standing in his place, by another name. Do not tempt me with death. Such things are useless to me."

The driver was silent for a long time.

"She understands what you say," he said. "She asks no more of you."

The ape covered his face with his large hand and then peeled it away, as if unmasking himself. "In peaceful parting, we offer you and Her this: down the road, where the cliff once more meets the ground, and the Spires end and your rice farms come into view, there is a wagon. It is abandoned on the side of the road. If no one has yet claimed it, you will find it there, not far from the first of the farmers' compounds."

"Abandoned?"

The ape shook his head. "We do not know for certain. We dared not approach, for the wagon smelled of death."

"This is a generous offering," the driver said, ready to start moving. "You have our thanks."

The ape bowed his head. "Then this one gives you his eyes in witness to your passing. This humble caste prays to the Sleeping Sea and the Inverted Lands for your good fortune, and in recognition of Her, we offer you these seeds to eat on your long march east." From the branches rained small nuts and seeds. Some of the seeds pinged off his mask. But the driver thanked the apes anyway and grabbed what food he could, keeping balance of the empress on his head as he did so, leaving the rest that he could not carry on the road behind him.

Keema watched them walk off.

"It would not be wise to follow them," the ape said. "Their path leads only to bloodshed." The creature of the forest then looked down at Keema in a furrowed way, as if confused by his presence. "The other two reek of royal blood," he said, sniffing the air, "but you, you have no such smell." Keema, who had never spoken to an animal before, aside from the tortoises, did not know what to say, so he bowed, which had always been his last resort when proper etiquette was beyond him. This amused the ape greatly. "What is your name, little one?" Nervously, he told the creature his title, in full, for the first time feeling silly as he did so; but like Araya, the ape treated his name with seriousness, and significance, and with his face resting thoughtfully on leathery hands, his old eyes took him in, before he asked him the question whose answer Keema had for so long been searching for.

"And what is your part in this, Keema of the Daware Tribe?"

The driver was near the second bridge of the Spires, where the cliff road began its gradual declination into the terrace valley, when he heard the catch-up of footsteps behind him. He humphed in light surprise when he saw the one-armed sentry following them at a distance.

"What would you have me do?" the driver muttered to his empress.

I told my glorified donkey to watch this stranger, and nothing more. We could ill afford to be further delayed by his antics.

"As you will it," he said dutifully.

And so, for a time, the three of them walked the road in silence.

Eastward the sun rose, crowning the Spires around which the road spun, the heat such that even the rocks were sweating. With audible relief they stepped into the deep shade cast by the neighboring towers of rock, and when they came upon a boulder sitting in the middle of the road, knocked loose by the explosions from earlier, they sidled through the narrow passage between the rock and the edge of the road, the driver's stomach tightening as he imagined those Peacocks falling into the abyss—all of whom he still cared for, in the part of him that would never die. *It was us or them, I told him.* But the driver would never again be able to take solace in the death of another, and he said nothing to Her in response.

The Burn in the sky smoldered like a black moon above their heads. As he walked, the driver could feel a change in the empress's mood—Her hot aura of impatience now a blue yearning, pointed upward, and when he glanced up from under the cushion he carried he knew that what Her attentions were focused upon was the cosmic rip in the sky She had once called Her home. But he knew from bitter experience what would come of broaching a subject She had no wish to speak on, so he left Her to Herself, and instead focused on his other present issue. When the last bridge came into view, and beyond it the road that bowed in greeting to the expanse of Yinn terrace lands, the driver turned on his heel.

"You fight well," he said, his voice echoing off cliffsides.

His compliment caught their follower at a disadvantage—the young man seemed unsure whether he should thank him or ready his spear. "So do you," he replied, almost begrudgingly.

"But you should not follow us."

"I follow no one," he said. "My path happens to lie east, with yours."

This, the driver did not believe. "You walk behind us like a lost pup. You fight well, and the spear you carry is formidable, but serving us will afford you no protection under Her Strength. You would find more safety in the arms of a bandit."

Their follower stood up straight and proud, and when he spoke his teeth were bared. "My name is Keema of the Daware Tribe and I do not seek safety in your company. I made an oath to the commander of Tiger Gate to walk this road, and a warrior of Daware always keeps his oath. This spear," he said, holding forth the weapon of his former commander, "will be delivered by me to a soldier named Shan on the eastern shore outside the Divine City."

The driver stopped again. His demon mask tilted at the spear.

"Did you know that your commander was a traitor to the Throne?"

"No," Keema admitted after a moment.

"She was in league with powerful forces, plotting to assassinate the royal family. She blasphemed against the natural order. As far as the laws of the divine are concerned, you are freed from your oath."

"It changes nothing," Keema said.

"It changes everything." The driver carried on down the sloping road. "She is cursed and dead and you are free. Only a fool would believe themselves beholden to such a person."

"Then I am a fool." Keema chased after him. "But I will be a fool who holds his oaths."

"If your Daware people were as stubborn, then it is no wonder they are gone."

"Do not insult me."

The accusation rang out amongst the Fingers. The look in Keema's eyes, the seething anger, was enough to make the driver bow his head.

"I'm sorry," he said. "I take back what I said."

Keema, unused to apologies, and unsure what to say in response, only nodded. "Speak again about my people that way and I will finish what we started back at that wagon."

The driver did not bother turning this time. "You would lose," he said. Keema made to challenge him, right then and there, but the driver held up his hand. "She will not let us fight again. She would sooner crush your head like a berry than allow me to waste any more time."

Keema, his pride bruised, kept pace with the driver's hurried step, more determined than before to dog them. "What is your rush anyway?" he asked. "The bridge is out. The brigade cannot catch up to you now. The chase is over before it has even begun."

"This is not a chase," the driver replied testily. "To call it a chase would imply we had a chance to begin with. No," he said, "they will find us. He will find us. It is only a matter of when."

He was quiet.

"Not even the trees stand in his way."

What creature in its right mind
would stand before a grieving father?

Gods help the tea planters and free-band riders who crossed paths with the brigade that morning, for nothing would stop their stampede. With a flick of the prince's wrist the stray rivers of the valley that lay in their path parted. *We the rivers had no choice but to* part. The trees bent out of their way. *We the trees opened the way to this royalty.* But the homes of the workers who farmed the tea plantations, unfortunate enough to be built in these outward places amongst the trees or on these slight hills, could not move out of the way. *I looked out my window just when they came—my mind not registering what my eye beheld. No matter. It all came falling on top of me anyway.* Upon the crown prince's snarl the houses shattered before him, and he and his sons rode through the debris of timber and hay and cups and tables while the children left in their wake screamed. *I heard it—the pop of his bones as my father was trampled underneath their wretched hooves.* These people less than bugs to the First Terror, who had been raised properly on his diet of royal sycophants; the sort of man whose depressed mood was helped by the eradication of these small wooden blights on the land. The trees shattering in their wake. The river waters breaking upward like frightened cats, the furious horses galloping underneath these watery arches as they, by the Terror's hand, cheated their way through the sun-fried land, the sons following the father on his mission of blood.

MORNING

They arrived at the Yinn terrace lands, hungry and tired.

Neither boy wanted much to be in the company of the other, but already they were bound by mutual need, for only fools walked the Road Below alone. The only other soul they encountered was the corpse of a traveler stuffed into the brush, their throat opened and their pockets thieved. Much to Keema's surprise, the driver stopped and bowed his head in respect of this stranger's passing; his hurry put on pause for this brief moment of prayer. *For eight days I had rotted under the sun, after the man who promised me safe passage robbed me of my coin and my life. For eight days, no one offered*

me respect or prayer, until the masked demon crossed my path.
"Travel well," he whispered.

It was not until they were well past the Spires that they began to see more signs of life—when, like a curtain slowly parting from a bright window, Lord Yinn's verdant terrace lands announced themselves from around the next hillside bend, the compound that the apes had spoken of not far in the distance, the terra-cotta buildings and stepped rice terraces hugging the side of a mighty foothill draped in banners of sunlight. It was there that the driver recognized an opportunity to rid himself of the one-armed man at his side.

He told Keema that they would not make it far without supplies. "I have visited this compound before. It is the Alvo Estate, overseen by Lord Yinn's nephew Sui Yinn Alvo, who has always been a reckless fool in the matters of safety and security. The compound's storehouse is rarely guarded, the lock easily undone—just there, at the height of the terraces, where the last of the buildings meets that tree line near the top. Do you see it?" Keema squinted against the sun over the hill, and he nodded. "If you follow this side path, it will bring you right to the storehouse's porch." The driver then explained how the lock on the storehouse could be broken into. On Keema's brow there was an almost imperceptible twitch.

"Should not the man with two arms go foraging for supplies?" he asked.

"I'll be occupied with searching for the wagon the apes had spoken of," the driver replied. "Once I have . . . requisitioned it, and you have gotten our supplies for the road ahead, we'll meet just over there, beyond the last of the allotments."

But Keema was unconvinced. "If you know the layout of this compound, shouldn't you sneak in while I go wagon hunting?"

"No," the driver said.

"Why not?"

Because the driver planned to ride off without him. But as this was not something he wished to say aloud, he gave Keema another, equally honest, answer. "The truth is I do not trust you yet. I am going to take the wagon because I do not want it leaving without me."

"I can say the same."

"You can," the driver conceded. "But the all-powerful god riding on my head gives me leverage, for She does not trust you either." Keema averted his gaze from the old woman. The driver smiled behind his mask. "Get us supplies for the road and perhaps we will save a seat for you."

"Do not speak to me like a child," Keema said as he left on his task.

I told him that he was a fool. The empress's words pierced the driver's mind like a sharp rock as he willingly parted company with the Daware man. *I reminded him that we could not hope to make it east by ourselves.* The driver grunted at her as he climbed the hill opposite the compound for a better view. "It had to be done, Your Eminence," he said, navigating the steepening slope that cut through the foothills. "He needs not be dragged into our battle. And the farmers here are good people. They will catch him, and, with some luck, take care of him."

Our mess was everyone's mess; the Daware man's life was fair trade for the success of our mission.

He sighed. "If that is how you expect me to think, then you have been teaching me the wrong lessons these past six months."

They spoke no more of the matter. At the top of the hill, he looked over the compound from behind a cluster of rocks. It was then that whatever feeling of pride and justice he had been flush with evaporated, for he soon found the wagon the apes spoke of and discovered that it was not abandoned like they had claimed but was, in fact, tended to by several hungover soldiers of the Throne.

Five armed members of the royal guard lazed under the compound awnings, awaiting food and drink from the put-upon farmers. One of the soldiers danced around with his blade drawn, laughing, his pants nowhere to be seen. *I told him once again that he was a fool—how was he going to take care of this alone?* He ignored Her, his expression tightening when he noticed the insignia

of the Moon Throne embroidered on the wagon's canvas awning as
well as the soldier who every now and then emerged from the compound to check on it. The young man winced as he lowered Her
and Her cushion down on the ground. "It is nothing we cannot
manage, Your Highness," he said, his voice suddenly hoarse.

Then take care of it, I said.

He breathed out small breaths in quick succession, like he was
about to jump into cold water, before he scurried toward the
wagon—cursing those trickster apes under his breath, and himself.

In one of the allotments, a girl sighed.

With that defeated sigh she upturned the cup she had found floating in the ankle-deep water and let the paddy murk drizzle out of
it. She sloshed farther into her allotment, where she found more
floating debris amongst her crop: a sandal, a small wooden comb.
A ratty piece of a grown man's underclothing. She collected these
scattered objects while in the other terraced allotments her fellow,
much luckier, farmers began their day's work, making one last pass
through their fields before it was time to load up the wagons with
their rice pots and head to the village for the fete. She tutted and
cooed over her rice sprouts, many of which had been stomped on,
and tossed the miscellaneous garbage into a cloth sack as quickly
as she could, not wishing to be left behind when the caravan left the
compound. One of the other farmers, a boy not much older than
her, was kind enough to give her a hand in the cleanup. *I suppose I
was fond of him. Sometimes we would sleep on the same mat. He
was so afraid of touching me he would sleep with his arms to his
sides, like this, as if he were inside a narrow tube, which I thought
was funny, and which I liked.* Together they picked out from the
water the unfinished rice cakes and cups until the boy nudged her
and said in a whisper, "They're coming," and retreated to his own
allotment.

"Farmer-girl!" called the hungover soldier.

Her back stiffened. It was the same man who had hounded her and her fellow farmers the night before. She turned with the most gracious smile she could muster as the Blade of the Throne approached her. He cut a pathetic figure in the unforgiving daylight; his eyes, swollen from the drink, wandering about her body before he presented her his bare, mud-caked foot. "I seem to be missing a friend," he said. "You haven't seen it out here, have you?"

She opened her sack and handed him the sandal she had found. The Blade mumbled a thanks as he sat on the bank's edge and slipped it on. "I found more of your things out in the water," she said. "This comb. This bag of jerin."

He laughed. "What better way to start off Holy Week, eh?"

"Many of my sprouts were crushed by your men."

Her annoyance was tamped down by the look he gave her, the joviality in the man's voice lessened just enough to chill her. "Now, now," he said. "A whole night of sound rest, under our protection—not everyone is so lucky. No bandits come to slit your throats in the night, no wolves to tear away your babies." When she would not meet his eye, he dug into his pocket, pulled out enough copans to buy a few sweets at market, and pressed them into her palm. She forced herself to bow in thanks. He nodded, pleased. "Now that we're friends again, my men and I are hungry. We also have need of sustenance for the road ahead. Ah! Would I be pleased if you showed us the way to the storehouse."

I could have pushed him over the edge of the paddy. The fall wouldn't have killed him, but it would've broken something, and I would've liked that.

"This way," she said.

Together they headed in the direction of the storehouse. The girl made sure to keep a good distance from the soldier, for she had heard the stories from the other women. It was then that a flash of movement out in the road caught her eye: a tighter squint revealed the masked young man darting from behind various rocks and furrows. He was headed for the soldier's caravan, parked on the side of the Road Below.

She smirked at the appearance of this thief.

"What is it?" the soldier said.

"Beautiful day," she said as she led the man farther up the terrace steps. *I did my best to keep his eyes on me and away from the road. I did not know what the masked stranger was up to, but I knew it would not be good for our visitors.* "It must have been quite the night you and your men had."

"Lot of energy needed releasing," he said, grunting up the hill after her. "I think we released it capably."

"Indeed," she said, while below, the masked stranger leapt into the caravan.

He would have looked first.

As the driver neared the wagon he realized the apes were correct in one regard: it did indeed smell of death. But whatever warning signals were going off in his head were overridden when he thought he heard the approach of a soldier's footsteps. So he went in, in one heedless jump, and it was within that dark space that he experienced an odor not unlike that of a corpse that had shit itself before passing. His whole face wrinkled behind his mask, the smell tangible, the film of it coating his throat with each breath he took. With a nauseous heave, he opened up the canvas flap and leaned out of the wagon, lifting his mask just enough to gulp untainted air while light lanced its way through the gap, revealing the source of the stench.

"This one does not recognize you," the tortoise said from the dark.

It was smaller than its brethren of the court, just shy of massive, the breadth of it swallowing the majority of the wagon's interior. But there was something wrong with the creature. Its shell was cracked and pus-drooling, and its legs, those malformed stumps, lay useless at its sides; all it could do was knock its stumps on the floor as it lolled its head in thought and sniffed the air again, reading his scent. "You have the blood in you," it giggled. "A prince's blood." It sniffed some more; and while the creature was preoccupied with rooting around his aura, the driver unhooked his hatchet from his waistbelt; he envisioned in his mind two hacks, maybe three, to end its life. "But your purposes . . ." the tortoise said, lost in its own world. "You are at a cross with the Throne. A prince's son at cross-purposes . . ." Its freewheeling eye fixed itself on the hatchet raised into the air. The creature lowered its head in submission to him. "Let this one live," it giggled. "Please. Let this one live. A bargain! A bargain can be struck!"

"Forgive me," the driver whispered.

He swallowed, his grip on the hilt trembling.

But the hatchet, once raised, never came down, *for we were there too,* and the young man who was once the pride of the Red Peacocks, who once carved his father's name into the flesh of a weeping man's back for the crime of a disrespectful expression, now gazed at his trembling hand as the fingers opened one by one until the hilt slipped from his grasp and the weapon clattered to the floor. *And we made him look at this hand, this hand he once covered in our blood, and we made him remember*—his eyes welling with tears as the voices in his head, from another life lived heedlessly not long ago, came surging forth from the dark cracks of his mind, as they had done for the past six months, with the empress's help. *We made him smell the burnt flesh. We made him feel the slickness of our blood.* "Forgive me . . ." he cried, "please forgive me . . ." *BUT WHAT WOULD FORGIVENESS DO FOR US, FOR ME, WHEN HE SLIT MY FUCKING THROAT?*

The theater is cacophonous with the shrieks of the dead. You hold your ears tight, but it does little to block out the screaming. The tortoise's head shrinking back as it watched this broken man collapse in on himself, *and we, the people, the ones this bastard had struck down and burned and shot, we swirled around that pretty little skull of his and we clawed at the walls and we wailed and we said do you remember us, you demon, do you remember spilling our blood at your taloned feet and now here you are DOING IT AGAIN,* and he groaned as he clutched at his head, his throbbing eye, and begged them to cease the pain, begged them for their release. "I—I'm s-sorry . . ." The hatchet at his feet now long forgotten, the young man now a boy shuddering on the floor.

The tortoise extended its head. It observed this young one's weeping with its mad eye.

It deliberated on this fresh opportunity.

On the other end of the compound, a storehouse was raided.

The lock, undone, lay in the warm grass, the opened double doors revealing shelves of clay jars of rice grain, ropes of dried-out meats, pouches of spices, and a variety of preserved things in jars that tasted sour on Keema's finger. He passed by tools and materials for rebuilding broken equipment and buildings. He grabbed a fistful of rice and strips of jerky. A piece of meat dangled from his lips as he jogged down the narrow corridor of the storehouse with the empty sack he had swiped from a hook, the sack growing fuller and fuller as he went. He came upon a knot of canteens, but none of them had water. He took them anyway. All of this went into the sack, and when it was time to go, he knelt down and, with his teeth and his hand, he knotted the bag to the end of his spear like a bindle. With the excitement of having finished half his task, he charged out of the storehouse—nearly colliding with two people on his way out.

"Oh," the farmer girl said.

The soldier, startled, put a hand on the hilt of his saber.

Keema stepped back. They looked at one another for a moment, each of them trying to figure out the situation before the others. It was the girl who finished her calculation first—she stepped forward and stood between the two men.

"There you are, Serro," she said, smiling at Keema; she turned to the soldier. "Serro thought it would be a good idea, in the spirit of His Holy Pilgrimage, to stock the larders of you and your men for your journey to Rabbit Gate."

The soldier did not remove his hand from his hilt. "Did he now?"

"Yes! Many little snacks and foodstuffs for you to enjoy. Serro, did you find all of the goods?"

She beseeched him with her eyes.

"Yes," Keema said. "All of it is here. I put in some extra jerky too."

"Good. Why don't you go along and bring it down to their wagon?"

Keema nodded and went off to do just that.

"Wait," the soldier said, approaching Keema, circling him. "I don't remember you from last night. And I'd remember if there was a man of poor fortune in our company." The soldier jerked open the mouth of the sack and looked inside; he let out a pleased grunt. "The beef looks good."

"There's more inside the storehouse," the girl said. "Come, sir, I'll show you."

But her insistence only stoked the light of suspicion in the soldier's eyes. He could feel something was off in the girl's obsequiousness, her panicked smile, and in the young man's stiff posture; the scuffs and tears in his clothing; his cut lip; the deep bruise on his neck. He frowned. "Why don't you stay with us, Serro," he said. "I'll walk you to the wagon when we're done. I need to check on the creature anyway."

"If it is all the same," the girl said quickly, "Serro has other tasks to get to in preparation for the caravan. Would it be all right if he goes on ahead of you?"

"No, it would not be all right," the soldier said with a smile. He patted her shoulder and pushed her on ahead toward the storehouse. "Now, you were showing me my breakfast."

The driver groaned.

He was huddled in the corner of the wagon's hold, gripping his head as the voices came and went. *We circled his thoughts and made him twitch. We made him suffer as he made us suffer.* He was only half listening to the tortoise as it spoke to him—the rest of him was trying not to vomit.

"This one smells your guilt," the tortoise said in its halting voice. "The salt stink of it comes off you stronger than this one's own stench. Many deaths stain your hands. Their blood runs deep in your soil, prince's child. But now you are here, trying to clean those hands in whatever water you can find. This one would offer you water of a sort. Stay your hand. Make peace with this one. And this one will remain quiet to its brothers."

"A bluff," the driver croaked, his nose pointed toward the canvas flap, toward air. "You've told them about me already."

"Trust," the tortoise said. "Either you trust this one and let this one live, or you strike this body and seal your fate." The tortoise lowered its beak onto the floorboards and looked up with its swiveling eye. "This one will scream its last. The soldiers will come. Perhaps you may outmatch them, but," it said, eyeing his sorry state and letting out an instinctual mad giggle, "perhaps not." The hatchet lay on the floor not far from the driver's hand, but he had no desire to look at it, much less lift it; an overwhelming nausea—more powerful than the nausea the tortoise's odor inspired—washed over him whenever he looked down at that glinting blade. *How many of our heads had he split open with that hatchet under his father's proud command?* The driver felt a bubble rise in his throat. He turned away from the hatchet and swallowed deeply. He wished for death. "And why have you not called the soldiers yet?" he asked.

"This one is no friend to the soldiers," the tortoise said. "They take this one to Rabbit Gate, where it will be hoisted up into a watchtower to live for the rest of its days. A great honor, which this one wants no part of." It lifted one of its malformed stumps. "Ever since its wretched birth in the palace heat beds, this one has been known as Defect. Born wrong. Its connection to the motherweb imperfect—frayed, like old thread. But even though this one misses many messages, this one knows that something has happened in the palace. This one can read the shiver on the eastward wind. This one knows the emperor is dead."

It looked at the driver as if daring him to deny this fact.

"What is it you want?" the boy asked.

"To live," it replied. "It would go east. It would lie on the shore and feel the cool water of the Great and Unending Sea on these . . . things . . ." it said, lifting its stumps with great bitterness. "This one does not want to rot with the birds in a lonely watchtower. This one wants to be free. It wants to go east, with you." It nodded to its own dream. "In return this one will help you. Many tortoises lie between you and your destination. This one can read the air. Defective this one might be, but it can still read the signals. This one can help you choose your roads."

"And all you want in return is freedom."

"Not all," it said.

"This is everything."

The girl gestured at the food in the storehouse and the soldier grinned as if he were meeting old friends whose company he had missed. As they walked down the corridor—he was too tall and had to duck under the intermittent beams—she offered him this and that, his arms brimming full with the ingredients for a hearty breakfast; but his attention never strayed far from Keema, who played the obedient servant near the back of the storehouse, still weak from the night before and uncertain if he could take on a man so large and imposing.

"That should be good," the soldier said, to the girl's relief, for there were almost no more eggs to give him. *Once we had left the storehouse, he told me to bring the food to the kitchens and have something special prepared for his men. With my arms straining to hold all the food he had chosen, I watched him and the one-armed stranger walk off together to the wagon by the road.*

As the girl wondered if she had doomed the whole compound to the pyre with the lie she had told, Keema was led through the compound proper, the soldier at his back. The farmers, delayed by the cleanup and the field-check, rushed to load their caravans with their rice offerings, while under a purple cloth awning by one of the main houses five soldiers lay on mats, surrounded by emptied jugs of wine, chuckling at the busy people moving around them, calling for refills or for company. *We had to do what the drunk bastards said, but we also could not be late for the fete.* A woman feigned flattery at one of the soldiers' slurred advances. *I was holding a pot of rice grain heavier than my own child, but he didn't seem to notice the strain, or care.* In one of the houses lay a man the soldiers had beaten half to death the night prior, though none of the soldiers, drunk as they were, could remember why this had come to pass. *They had asked me for a joke—in front of everyone, as they danced around drunk on our wine, they asked me for a joke. They did not find the joke I told them funny.*

They were young, and on the edge.

They were not so different from the soldiers stationed in your dockside town—the same ones your lola went quiet and still around, the way deer might when a pack of wolves prowl in the distance—the same ones your father came to admire the more he listened to the radio. They were soldiers, far from home, and shadowed by the presence of death; the deaths of others; of their own. They were youths, proud and strong, some of them cruel, many of them scared—of course they drank themselves under the table; of course they broke windows and smashed bottles and seemed always ready to beat someone into the ground. They were bottomless, drinking all the wine in the compound, grabbing at any body that might come near, farmer or not, their hunger rare and frightening.

On your way home one night, a grunt sitting on the low wall outside the pub watched you pass. A pint cradled between his thighs. His left eye was missing—shot, you supposed, right out of his skull. He seemed unashamed of any of it.

"It looks better up close," he said, smiling.

And it did.

"Come on, Serro," the soldier said, prodding Keema forward.

On the last lonely stretch of path before the main road, when they were clear of the compound proper, clear of the farmers and the other soldiers, the man's demeanor changed. He seemed to relax, his hand leaving the hilt of his sword; he was even looking gently at Keema as he cooled himself with a paper fan he'd slipped from his sleeve.

"My uncle was like you," he said, as if he had been waiting to say it for a while. "He, too, was a man of poor fortune. He ran out on a debt from one of Luubu's table games, and when he was caught, he paid the price with his left arm. Doomed to be unlucky for the rest of his life." He shook his head. The wagon was in view now. "Everywhere he went he was shunned. Even my mother, his own sister, wouldn't let him in the house, should he 'taint our thresholds.' Poor bastard died alone; hanged himself from his own rafters." Keema, unsure where this was going, only listened, not that the man needed any encouragement to continue. "All that to say, *Serro,* I can't help but notice those cuts on your arm. Those bruises on your neck. The way that girl bossed you around. Like you were a stranger. Makes me wonder if those farmers are mistreating you."

The man was looking at him earnestly. This, Keema did not expect.

"No, sir," he said. "They have welcomed me kindly and with open arms."

"Have they now?" The man sounded amused, the way a parent might be amused by a child who was a terrible liar. He snapped his fan shut and stopped walking. "I've always felt poorly about how I treated my uncle. I was only a child, but even children are capable of kindness, and I gave him none. I even made fun of him with my friends." He breathed out his demons. "So, in memory of my uncle, I will show you a kindness: if these downfield slackjaws are laying unwanted hands on you, give me a sign, and perhaps my men and I will stay an extra night. Perhaps some lessons will be learned over a roaring fire."

It was strange—though Keema knew the farmers were innocent of these transgressions, a part of him was pleased to hear this offer.

A small part.

"These farmers have done nothing to me," he said.

The man held his gaze, in study of his honesty, before he shrugged and gave up. "Thought I'd ask," he said, continuing on.

They came to the main road. Keema saw that the wagon was still there, and not stolen, and he wondered what had become of the others—if the driver had decided the wagon wasn't worth the trouble and had walked off with the empress and without him—but all his wonderings were cut short by the smell; a stench that emanated from the wagon's direction, its intensity growing as they approached the road. Keema grunted.

"I know," the man said wearily. "Now imagine traveling with the damn thing." He stopped at the compound's entrance. "You can go ahead. I'll . . . stay here. Just put the supplies in the back."

As Keema crossed the road, he asked himself what he was going to do, now that he had lost his party. Traveling the Road Below alone was, for him, a last resort; he supposed he could go looking for the driver and the empress, but who knew how far from the road they had strayed. He could ask the farmers for a ride to the next village—that girl seemed friendly enough—and from there find someone to take him to the Bowl, if anyone was going that far east, but he did not have any money to pay his way across the country. The weight of the spear was heavy against his shoulder. It would be no small task delivering it. Suddenly, he thought of the brawl from earlier that morning. He wanted to fight the driver again. In his mind, there had not been a victor. His pride as a warrior was at stake. He supposed this was why he felt such relief when he tore the canvas flap of the wagon open and saw the boy in the demon mask staring back at him from within.

The boy was not alone. A tortoise sat behind him, gazing at Keema with its unblinking eye, its mouth open as if to scream at him, silenced only by the driver's raised hand.

"Everything all right?" the soldier asked from the side of the road.

"Yes," Keema said. He untied the sack from his spear and lifted it over the wooden lip, handing it to the driver, and then, looking at him but speaking loud enough for the soldier, he said, "These should be enough supplies for the long journey."

"Good," the soldier said. "Just make sure it's out of the creature's reach. The damn thing doesn't stop eating."

Once the bag was secure in the hold, the driver looked down at Keema, his eyes behind the dark slits of his mask in new appraisal of him. And it was then that a kind of messaging passed between them; in their locked and silent gaze a tightening of the first knot of trust; a contract, signed by a nod of the driver's head, before Keema closed the flap, and returned to the soldier's side.

The driver breathed again.

He opened the sack. He touched the rice; he smelled the jerky. He opened the canteens—empty. Aside from the lack of water, the Daware man had spoken true: there were enough foodstuffs to last a journey twice as long as the one they were taking. He peeked out the canvas flap. The two men were halfway back to the compound. He wondered how Keema had negotiated himself into such a position and how he intended to negotiate himself out of it.

"Who was that person?" the tortoise asked.

"He's with us," the driver said.

Once he was sure the way was clear of soldiers, he ran back to the rock cluster at the top of the hill, where the empress waited for him. *He expected me to be none too pleased that he had taken a tortoise on board with us, but I made no comment on the matter. I had old debts to the tortoise castes. The boy could do what he liked with the creature, even if it was, unequivocally, a burden.* The driver gingerly lifted Her cushion and brought Her back to the caravan, where She was none too pleased to be sat next to the tortoise's stench, though the Defect, for its part, was no gladder for the company.

"Our most honored Moon," it said scornfully.

The driver had no time to explore this moment between them, for he needed to get the wagon moving. He crept up to the front of the carriage, staying on the side opposite the compound's entrance, and greeted the beasts of burden. The soft-tempered orooks cast their kindly gaze on the masked boy on his approach. He was glad to discover that the animals were not of strict allegiance, eager as they were for a scratch between their eyes, where the first of their hard quills began. Snuffling, snorting, the orooks' thick hooves stomped into the dirt, and they followed the driver, who coaxed them out onto the road by their reins, the transition of the wheels from soft dirt to the hardpacked pebbled road not a quiet one; the whole vehicle groaning and clacking as it shifted its weight onto the new terrain. With his head low, the driver climbed onto the front of the carriage, glancing back at the compound, looking for movement, but no one seemed to have noticed that their ride was leaving.

The soldier at Keema's side had his mind on other matters.

The flap of his paper fan and the choral buzz of the cicadas in the dry grass overwhelmed any other sound he might've heard from the road, and his interest in Keema had yet to wane. "I think we have something in common," he said.

Keema, thinking frantically of a way to return to the driver, had his interest piqued by the man's observation.

"I think we are both wondering how in the abyss we got here." The soldier chuckled after he said this. His fan flapping slowed. "I admire you. You're trying to rebuild your life here, even if it isn't the easiest road." He smiled; a subtle one. "The same goes for me, for I've taken a job, a very special job; the kind you are offered only once in your life, if that, and once I finish this job, I won't have to wear this damned uniform anymore. I'll have enough money to buy my own compound. No more kissing the feet of Lord Yinn's men. No more shepherding tortoises to their . . . fucking . . ." His voice trailed off, for two soldiers were now running toward them, one of them waving and yelling. "What in the heavenly band . . ."

The soldiers were pointing at the road. The man turned around.

Their wagon was rolling away, driven by a masked thief.

The shouting reached the heart of the compound.

From the kitchen window the farmer girl watched the remaining soldiers scramble to their feet. A jug of wine was kicked, scattering red liquid over the dirt as the soldiers ran toward the shouts of their leader. The girl and the others in the kitchen looked at one another and then went outside to see what was going on. From the surrounding allotments the farmers put down their tools and watched as the hungover soldiers sprinted down the road after the runaway wagon, shouting for the driver to halt. *I sat down on the bank and watched the fools run like I was at a traveling show. Even the hardest-working of us took a break to see what happened—though I think it safe to say none of us expected what happened next.*

To the untrained eye, it was as though the middle of the road had been punched in by a giant, invisible fist. The men fell into the hole so suddenly that only one of them had the wherewithal to yelp in surprise; the rest simply tumbled in and over one another in a breathless silence, a ball of men at the bottom of a shallow pit, one of the unsheathed swords slicing open the leg of his colleague, who let his feelings be known through his bloodcurdling scream. *When we heard the screaming, we went down to see what had come of them.* The farmer girl moved through the gathering crowd, her gaze set not on the hole but on the road ahead, watching the one-armed stranger catch up to the fleeing wagon. He tossed his spear into the hold, and then himself. And then she turned away. *I pretended I saw nothing, relieved that "Serro" had gotten away. I joined the others at the strange pit's rim. The soldier I had showed to the storehouse lay at the top of that writhing mass of bodies, groaning for assistance. That was the moment we all looked at one another, the same thought in our heads: that it was time to decide what to do with these boys.*

The farmers crouched over the hole with all of their tools.

It was Her doing.

Keema learned this after he had caught up to the wagon and had explained to the driver—between gulps of breath—what had happened to the chasing soldiers, and the driver sighed and shouted into the hold at the old woman: "Your Highness, you must be careful with expending too much energy! You will not be much use to the others if I deliver you spent and dead!" When She did not respond, he shook his head and focused instead on the long stretch of the Road Below that spun out in front of the trotting orooks. Keema settled into his seat beside him. Their speed was about half that of a horse's gallop, but it was faster than a walk, and enough to toss a breeze against their hot skin.

"There is a tortoise in this wagon," Keema said.

The driver said nothing for a time. And then he said, "It won't be a problem."

The road curved around one of the many low hills of this valley of rice and harvest, when the driver said, "I did not know the compound was visited by soldiers of the Throne when I sent you in."

Keema did not know if he believed him, but he let it go all the same. "We are alive and we have transport."

The driver nodded.

Keema touched the wooden frame of the carriage, patted it. "I'm going to see what supplies this thing has."

"It's Jun, by the way."

Keema paused at the flap and turned.

"My name," the driver said. "It's Jun."

The smell was bracing inside the wagon.

Keema hugged the wall as he squeezed around the tortoise's large, cracked shell, thinking in his mind *Jun, Jun, Jun* as he undid some of the knots in the canvas to let in some air. A cross-breeze flitted through the new opening in the canvas. As the Defect's stench left the wagon, Keema heard the creature sniffing at his back, trying to read his intentions. "If you wish to learn about me, I suggest you ask," he said as he unfastened the last knot. The Defect stopped sniffing.

"This one apologizes," it said on the tail end of a light giggle. "It simply desires to know its traveling companion."

"Traveling companion, eh?" Keema smirked. "I am Keema of the Daware Tribe," he said. "For now, that's all you need to know."

"You smell of fear. And sadness."

Keema cut him a glare and the creature bowed its head and giggled, he presumed apologetically. The strange creature watched him look around the wagon, taking inventory. Aside from the food he had stolen from the farmer's compound, there wasn't much of use. A narrow chest filled with a soldier's spare clothing. Some pouches of deodorizing powders hanging from the roof of the wagon like holiday decorations. Words were etched into one of the support beams: *Nalan fucked Jovva here.* Behind him, Keema heard the tortoise giggle again. He asked it what was the matter. "This one is amused by you, Daware man," it said. "You do not seem to care at all that you are in the presence of a god."

He had taken care not to look in the direction of the old woman sitting beside the tortoise, cross-legged and motionless as a corpse, for he was terrified of Her, unable to forget that cruel smile she wore after she had destroyed the bridge.

"I do care," he said to the Defect.

Once he was done looking around, he sat down against the rear lip of the wagon, heavily, the night and the morning catching up to him suddenly. He tilted his head back a bit so he could see the slate-blue sky through the fluttering flaps. Faint screams played out in the fringes of his memory. A pillar of smoke rising in the sky. *Tell her something kind.* He shut his eyes.

A few moments' rest couldn't hurt.

But there was one last interruption.

The rattling of a loose board in the floor of the wagon. Keema's brow furrowed; he opened his eyes. He looked at the dancing board. "This one knows nothing," the Defect said almost defensively. "This one only saw them put the creature in. It knows nothing more."

Keema sat up. It was easy enough for him to pry the board up with the tips of his fingers; it released itself from a crooked nail with a satisfying give. He put the board down and looked into the dark hole, and it was then that he had the briefest flashback of the soldier telling him of a very special mission he had undertaken. Keema had assumed the man spoke of contraband; drugs, illicit materials such as historical scrolls or palace documents. But no contraband was discovered in that small hidden compartment; only the Defect's strange claim.

A bird.

The bird was no larger than the size of his hand, its plumage vibrant, almost unnaturally so, its purple sheen glowing in the dark of that small hole, twitching, its twig legs kicking against some sort of restraint. A knot of string kept its beak shut, and a series of bindings over its wings and around its legs ensured that it could not move. With care Keema lifted the bird out of the hole, its eyes, as black as burnt coals, regarding him with fury, as if it dared him to crush it in his hand.

"Give this one the bird," the Defect said with a sickly light in its eyes. "This one is hungry."

Keema ignored the Defect, and the creature grumbled as the bird wriggled on the Daware man's palm, out of its reach. "It must have been stolen from somewhere," Keema theorized. "The palace maybe?" He put the bird on the floor. The bindings were made of a black cloth of such material he did not recognize, and on these bindings was small, delicate writing, in a script he could not read. He thought he would ask the tortoise to read it, but he did not trust the creature to withhold its appetite. Nor did he consult Jun on what to do with the bird; no, he did not give it a second thought; it seemed a matter of course to him to free that which had been imprisoned. He took the knife strapped to his thigh and cut the bird free—the bindings of such delicate composition that, upon the first snip, they disintegrated into ash.

"Strange," he said.

And then the bird, realizing it was free, flew at his face. It attacked him in a flurry of wing-flap and talon-scratch before it zipped out of the canvas flap like an arrowshot.

"Is there trouble?" Jun called out from the front.

"I don't know," Keema said, stunned, pulling a purple feather, streaked in blood, from his hair.

The bird was free.

Up into the sky it flew, with only a single, maddened song in its angry beak. The creature letting loose a bloodcurdling whistle as it eclipsed the sun.

Free. Free.

Its song like a needle in the ear.

Free.

MIDDAY

High above the land the bird flew.

Higher than any bird would, or could. *Free.* Its feathers unaffected by the lancing of the fiery sun, its small black eyes beholding the country that staggered beneath it. To the west, the bird gazed upon where it had been stolen from: the black horizon of mountains that were the royal aerie. To the east, it looked upon its possible destinations: the Thousand Rivers, the rising lip of the Bowl of Heaven, and beyond.

But for reasons even the bird was attempting to decode for itself, it did not flee from the immediate territory. Instead, it looked down at the tiny wagon far below. It thought of the young man who had freed it; the warmth of his eyes as he cradled the creature out of that dark hold. Unusual. Kind. Repayment of service must be made. Curiosity must be followed. By these two tenets the bird did not evacuate the midwestern expanse of terraces and hill land, but rather remained and decided to engage in some brief reconnaissance.

The purple arrow soared west. It passed the ruined remains of Tiger Gate. It circled around the long stretch of the Spires that ran vertical up the country like the bones of a spine. And then, not far from Monkey Gate to the north, it saw something curious; someone it did not expect to see ever again.

The First Terror and his brigade, storming through the land.

Upon his snarling horse the Terror looked up at the sky behind him with a frown, sensing something that was not quite right—the fleet shadow of the bird gone as quickly as it had come, leaving little evidence of anything to be suspicious of but for the deathly smell that graced the Terror's sensitive nostrils.

"Is something wrong, Father?" his eldest son asked.

"It is nothing," the Terror said with rare uncertainty.

Soon they reached the Road Above, which would take them through Monkey Gate Checkpoint, and from there to the terrace lands into which their quarry fled. It was there that they slowed their horses, for Lord Yinn's wagon train was up ahead, the wagons ornately painted and the men heavily armed, and there were grave consequences to not offering a lord his due respect—especially for a prince who aspired to be emperor. And so the First Terror bottled his rage and his grief and made to give the caravan his brief greeting. Like a body reacting to the threat of a punch, the whole caravan flinched at their approach. Horses whinnied and the Family Men who rode alongside the wagons tensed up but did not dare to raise their weapons at the prince, their gazes averted as the Peacocks trotted up the line. *None of us wanted any trouble from the bastards, all of whom looked ready to cut the heads off the first person who crossed them.* The brigade headed for the most lavish of all the carriages; the little brass bells that lined the eaves of the lord's carriage giving off a melodic tremble when the door was opened. From within the plush womb of the carriage, Lord Yinn smiled like an old cat. Gout prevented the man from rising to meet the Terror, so he had the child who fanned him with a broad-rimmed paddle bow in his stead.

"My prince," the lord said. "Fortune's bounty showers like gold from parted fingers as we are granted this chance meeting on the long and lonely Road Above." As was the style of the time, his house color, the white of the rice grain his tenants harvested, was painted as a streak across his eyes, the white cutting across his blemished skin like a scar. "It pleases me to see we are headed in the same direction. Please, join me in my carriage! Join me and tell me how you fare this fine day of His Smiling Sun's summer."

"I fear I cannot today, Lord Yinn." The Terror eased his eager horse. "We are limited for time. A fugitive of the Throne flees and we give chase."

The man, given to overwrought emotion, put his small hands on his cheeks, both horrified and touched. "That you, in the midst of your chase, stopped to speak to me . . . I am breathless with honor, my prince."

"I'm glad this is so. But you are right, my time is short. So if you will excuse me—"

"Oh, but you mustn't go yet! You must tell me everything about your prey. Is it anything to do with the commotion from the palace?"

The Terror gazed upon Lord Yinn's oblivious expression. "Yes," he said carefully. "They are related. I am curious what you've heard though. I didn't know you were in the city."

"Not the city. I was taking tea at my cousin's estate up north— within earshot of a tortoise, of course, to hear His Smiling Sun's address—when we felt the quake in the earth and the, uh"—like most people, Lord Yinn could not find the words to describe the shiver—"and what followed. Was it serious?"

"News will be shared of the matter shortly, my lord. But have no fear—the Throne remains strong."

"With you taking care of us, it is impossible to fear anything," Lord Yinn said reverently. "You are always so calm."

"Thank you, Lord Yinn."

"I am always telling my fool nephews to be calm like you. Our rock in a troubled river. If there's anything me or my caravan can do to be of use . . . We are headed for the Bowl to attend your brother's celebration. I will tell my men to keep an ear and eye out for anything suspicious as we go!"

Great, thought the Terror. The land is saved. "A gracious offer," he said. His horse stamped in the dirt. "Now, if you will forgive me."

"Are you sure you do not wish to sit in the shade of my carriage for a bit?" Lord Yinn called after him. "There's tea!"

"Another time!" the Terror called back before snapping his reins and galloping away, muttering, "Fucking idiot." He looked upon the road ahead, congested with many finely woven canvas wagons and guards. "Get out of my way," he said. And upon his cold whisper, all the men and women who stood in his path parted from the road's center like a cresting wave.

"There's little he cannot do," Jun said.

"Of his brothers, he has the most control over his powers. With but a thought and a gesture he can shift water and redirect wind. He can carry his Whisper across valleys. He can make water leap from a bowl. And with enough focus, he can even blow down a checkpoint gate." Jun was silent for a moment. The orooks made their unhurried pace down the winding road. "We may have gained some time destroying that bridge, and if it were anyone else who chased us, we might have lost them for good. But distance is almost meaningless to him. The land cannot stop him. Other than sudden elevation and sheer rock, he just . . . goes through it."

"Goes through it?" Keema asked.

"Like a bull through lace curtains." Jun's demon mask turned to him in a chill-inducing gaze. "I thank you for the supplies. You did a good turn to the empress and me, even though we did little to deserve it from you. But you need to understand the danger you are in, should you stay with us—how unlikely survival is." He looked at the road ahead. "We will be coming up to the Village of Five Sisters soon. It is as good a place as any to disappear. I won't try to convince you further to go your own way, for you've proved your use, but if you value your own life, you'll part ways with us at the village. You'll make your own way east. That is my recommendation."

Keema knew Jun spoke true. He knew that if he were wise, he would get away from this strange party as fast as possible. That the only oath he had made was to deliver Araya's spear, and that he owed the people he rode with nothing; but still, he was reluctant to part ways with them.

The reason was simple.

"You will find what you seek at Tiger Gate."

Never would he forget the water reader's grip on his wrist as the grayed man drank deep the cold water cupped in his palm—the grip at once trembling and firm, as if his wrist were the only tether that held the reader above the swirling tempest of his own prophetic madness. And never would he forget the clarity he then saw in the reader's eyes as he relayed to him his vision, tasted from the rivulets of water: that Keema's search, lifelong and unending, would find its completion at Tiger Gate Checkpoint. "You search for purpose," the reader said. "You will find it there."

"In most unexpected company."

Keema looked into the eye slits of Jun's laughing demon mask, certain that this was what the reader had spoken of, for what more unexpected company could he find himself in than this driver, a broken tortoise, and the Mother of Emperors? None of this, however, was he willing to share just yet—he was afraid Jun would think him a gullible idiot should he reveal himself to take so much stock in a water reader's word—so he made a show of deliberation and told Jun that he would come to his decision when they arrived at the village, which seemed to satisfy Jun enough to not push the point. "Do you have a plan?" Keema then asked. "If the Terror is as unstoppable as you claim, how do you hope to outrun him?"

"If we stay on land," Jun said, "there is no hope. He will catch up to us, and he will kill us. The only way forward I can see is to make it to the river just beyond Rabbit Gate and lose him in the sprawl of the Thousand, where not even he can predict the changing turns of the river bends."

"I thought you said he can control water."

"Only so much of it. And his Peacocks are landmen through and through. They rely on their horses as much as they do their swords. Put them on a boat and they lose much of their strength. Even we might stand a chance against them, should they overtake us."

Keema looked at the orooks, who could pull great weight at the expense of great speed. "At this pace, you won't make it to Rabbit Gate until evening."

"It will be close," Jun conceded.

"You will also need a boat."

"We'll find one."

The two boys went quiet as they considered this doomed expedition.

Steadily the road became more congested.

It was a reliable quality of the Road Below that where one wagon went, so went many. Loath as anyone was to venture forth on the road alone, even with armed guards, the people often waited till they saw another traveler happening by before they themselves set out. Groups accumulated naturally, an unspoken agreement between them that they would keep one another safe till their destination. Civilians on their own wagons, on caravan trains, families on foot, all of them coming from the surrounding farmlands and communes, pouring in from the various side roads that fed into the Below. *We carried with us all of our finest grains, our sacks of rice and our pots, to offer up to the emperor's men, who waited to collect this harvest at the Village of Five Sisters.* There were enough people on the road that some of them had no choice but to walk or ride near the royal wagon that carried the defective tortoise, though they made their displeasure evident by their sour expressions and their pinched noses.

"Trinkets! Trinkets!"

And of all the travelers who came out that day, beware the man in finery who smiles to you on the Road Below. Beware his promises.

"Trinkets! Trinkets! Excuse me, sirs of the Moon Throne, would you be interested in purchasing a trinket?"

Yes—of the many carts and drays and buckboards trafficked down the Tiger–Rabbit Stretch there were but a few that stood out in their extravagances—only a few whose designs had been labored over, not content to be painted in the colors of their lords' houses, the off-white streak of Lord Yinn's banner, but rather were bursts of color and intricacy of construction that drew the eye to their shelves and wares—a dangerous strategy indeed for any traveler in those days. Enter the trinket seller, from the right, catching Keema off guard as he came up as if from behind a passing cloud. "Trinkets!" he called out. His wagon was painted a sunset orange, his driver a sleepy rumple of a man who kept to his own business while the seller did his work catching people's attention. He tapped the side of his wagon with his stick and it opened on the side like a love-worker's folding screen. *It is all a performance, this business. People trusted you if you first blinded them with color.* Behind this false wall were shelves of the strangest objects. The trinket seller used his fancy stick to point at various items, walking alongside the moving train while his driver spurred the horses. He pointed at an ornate rug. "Woven by one of Luubu's consorts herself!" A glowing lantern with a frame of jaxite-colored rock. "Guaranteed to stay lit through an Emperor's Night." A small black box with a single hole poked through the top of it. "One lost soul, trapped inside this gaani square. Put your ear to the hole and listen. It will whisper to you the coming weather. It is right half the time." He pointed at objects from the old world. Coins long out of print embossed with the faces of emperors long dead. Scrolls of secret histories and outdated laws. An edict, signed by the Third Emperor, that forbade the practice of water reading. And he pointed at a box filled with beige, nondescript tubes. "Fireworks, for the celebrations of the week to come. Colors the like of which you have never seen with your young eyes!"

"That," Jun said, pointing at the mask of the smiling fox. "How much?"

"This delight, carved by the artisans of the northern estates?"

"Yes, that delight," Jun said, "made cheap by a poor child's hands. I'll buy it off you for two copans."

"Come, certainly we can discuss a price for—"

Jun held up the two coins.

The seller's face flattened; he made the exchange in the end. Jun took his new mask, and started moving the orooks a little faster to get away from this man.

Keema, on the other hand, could not stop looking at these mystical wares. His history with shopkeepers was a list of depressing consistency—most of them shooing him away, in fear that he would scare off their other customers. This seller seemed to have no such compunction. Pretending to be a transporter for the Throne had its benefits, Keema thought. But there was a problem. "I have no money to spend."

His savings were still at Tiger Gate, hidden behind some loose timber.

"Oh, is that so?" the seller said.

While the seller did his best to hold their attention, inside the wagon, the Defect heard giggling. It picked up its head. Looked toward the rear. *We were close. We gestured for the trinket man to keep them busy.*

Jun had redirected their orooks to the other side of the road when the trinket seller followed, sweating. "Wait, wait! No money, you say? I completely understand. No matter who you are, rock worker or royal attendant, the times are challenging, purse strings tight. So, my lords, in recognition of this fact, and of your mighty efforts to serve our glorious country, I would like to offer you a peek at a certain . . . collector's item—free of charge, of course!" Even Jun's ears perked up at the word "free." The trinket seller bowed deeply, making a valiant effort to keep up with the wagon, gesturing for his put-upon driver to keep pace. "Think nothing of it. It is but a cursory and small gesture that I'd like to make this auspicious Holy Week. So please," he said, unveiling the so-called discount shelf, "look, but do not touch."

Keema, chewing on a strip of jerky, almost spat out a cloud of meat when he saw what was being presented.

Arrayed across the shelf were small tablets with pornographic etchings. "This one is a personal favorite," the seller said with a wink as he pointed at the crude stencil of a woman being taken by a lusty wolf. There were many varieties of smut on display, of seemingly every possible combination. "Do the classics grab your fancy?" He presented a man and woman, horizontal and moaning. "Or do you prefer the less conventional pairings?" He showed them such surprising couplings, with legs pointed in every direction, that both of them were unaware of the commotion in the back of the wagon. *We lit the canvas. Blew on it. And once we had gotten the fire going, we ran, and we didn't look back.*

If it were not for the Defect's overpowering odor, Keema and Jun might have smelled the angry musk of the flame; instead, they were unaware of the fire that crept up the rear canvas flap, until the tortoise itself shouted, "Blaze! Blaze!" They broke into a run, each of them going down one side of the wagon, meeting at the rear. They tore the flap off and beat it into the ground, stomping the flames out with their sandaled feet until it was naught but blackened ash.

Sweating, they looked around for the culprit. People traffic flowed around them, indistinguishable.

The trinket seller was also gone.

"What in the abyss was that?" Jun asked.

He flinched when a woman on a horse spat at the dirt at his feet before speeding away, *my heart pounding, never having done something like that before, I couldn't wait to tell Momo what I'd done to these dogs of the Throne.* From the looks in the eyes of everyone else who passed, it was clear that she was not the only one who wished to show them how much they cared.

"We should keep moving," Keema suggested.

In agreement, Jun sat at the head of the wagon, taking charge of the orooks' reins while Keema walked behind the wagon, spear in hand, protecting the rear; a precaution that in the end was unnecessary, for no one else dared to come near them, *our point having been made.* And though for the time being the trinket seller had evaded retribution for his part in the canvas burning, this gave Keema little grief—after all, he had already gotten his revenge.

With the spear tucked under his arm, Keema pulled the stolen object out from a small pocket stitched to the inner lining of his jerkin.

He studied the pornographic tablet.

The tablet was thin, like a biscuit, light and fragile-seeming, and made of a ceramic so red it brought to Keema's mind the color of a freshly pricked finger. The drawing that defaced the tablet was done with black ink and fine brush, the lines careful and studied and unhesitating. There was a cleanness to the depiction of the embrace that at once allured Keema and clashed with his own experience of physical closeness, which was either the blood-stroke of battle or the secondhand descriptions of drunk men who were less than artful in their retellings of brothel exploits.

The drawing was without dimension, as was the style of the time—depth only beginning to be experimented with in the formal arts, as seen in the emperor's most recent tapestries and commissions—the limbs of the participants of this particular dance existing on the same plane, no detail left to the imagination, as if both bodies were pressed up against the surface of the image, straining to break through. What was uncommon, but not entirely rare, was that both of the lovers were male.

A furtive glance to the side told him that he was alone, that it was safe to look closer. Whether he had chosen this particular tablet on purpose or whether it was the one easiest to swipe, this was not a distinction Keema was quite ready to articulate, though less from shame than uncertainty and inexperience. Unlike your time, where masculine pride is propagandized to advance the war effort and certain arrangements of the family are idealized over others to encourage the repopulation of the ranks—your grandfather, for the limited time that you knew him, was preoccupied with making sure that you and your brothers had what he deemed appropriate appetites—the joining of these like bodies was not disparaged in the era of the Eighth Emperor, who was known to have had an expansive and welcoming taste when it came to the lovers he took to bed, and broadcasted such sentiments out through his tortoise network in the days when he hoped to bring to his threshold the most attractive lovers in the land.

The black ink lines depicted the bodies of two broad-chested men, without clothes. *We were hired to pose for the artist, who was well known for these tablets. It was the first day we had met one another.* The larger man was lying back on a pillow, his hands behind his head, in a state of utter relaxation, while the slighter man lay over him, fondling his partner's large member with one hand and tipping his chin upward, to the sky, with the other. *Both of us had heard tales of such jobs taking ill turns, but this one was easy. The artist was not pleased that we kept laughing as we held each other's cocks, but he did not tell us to stop. He only asked that we stay still for a few more minutes. He paid us well.* The joy in the act captured in the expressions of the men drawn on clay. The beginnings of a smile, even a laugh, *in the midst of a single moment of intensity, as we were told to look into each other's eyes and hold this gaze.* And in the midst of his own stirred feelings—a looseness to his walk as he accommodated a growing hardness—Keema was in wonder of the certainty of the men's expressions as they looked at each other. As if there were no fear at all in what the other might be thinking. As if both of them were there, and nowhere else. *It was a job in the end.*

But it was not without its pleasures.

By the end of the day Keema would lose the tablet. He would assume he lost it in the village they were soon to arrive at, amid the crowded bustle of the square, the tablet bumped loose from its purchase by a divot in the road and pressed into the earth by the oblivious feet of passersby. He would be disappointed that it was gone. But the image of the embrace would remain. It would become a thing he could return to in his mind when he pleased, elaborating on the details, giving life to the still image, and in this way it would become his, for this was the fate of all fantasy.

You know this well.

After your father removed the family radio from the living room and brought it into his bedroom, where he could listen to it for as long and as uninterrupted as he liked, you and your brothers, deprived of your serials, had no choice but to rely on memory to keep yourselves entertained through the summer months. At first you simply recalled the stories of Captain Domingo and his misfit crew as they journeyed into the heart of the empire. You took turns being narrator, doing your best to recite word-for-word certain favorite episodes. *All of the inquisitor's men aimed their rifles at the church windows. For the crimes against the viceroy, Domingo must die. But in their sights they did not see an unsuspecting target but a man who never went into battle without a plan—a man who, with a wink, revealed the detonator in his gloved hand.* But the more you all reenacted these events, the more you allowed yourselves to deviate from the script, until you were telling one another stories completely made up, starring you, your brothers, your friends. It was these stories that were the most fun to tell, and the sorriest you were to finish when the key jangled in the front lock and your father came home from work, tired and angry.

"He's here!" shouted a man on the wall. "The prince is here!"

It is familiar, then, what the sentries of Monkey Gate Checkpoint felt when the First Terror's presence was announced—the urge to flee while decorum and the rules of respect demanded that you stay put and welcome in a man who might cut your head off on a whim. *We lined up as quick as we could down the courtyard. Our commander rushed out of his office just as the horses entered the first gate.* A distinctly childlike fear kept their eyes on the floor as the Terror leapt off his horse. He walked briskly past the bowing commander and climbed up the tortoise's watchtower with little effort, surprising the creature with his sudden appearance. Traffic in the checkpoint stopped, every sentry quiet, the Peacocks dead-eyed and still, as the prince and the tortoise communed with each other above them all. Both panicked and relieved, the tortoise asked its lord what news he had from the palace, for none of its brethren were answering its call, but the Terror only held up his hand and silenced the creature. "I have need of your eyes," he said. "Last night a wagon came through Tiger Gate Checkpoint. Your sibling in the Tiger Gate watchtower must have seen the wagon, and who was driving it, before it was killed by the traitorous commander. I would know who is driving the wagon and who rides in it. And I would know where it now is."

The tortoise nodded as it giggled in mourning for its lost sibling. "It saw, it saw." The tortoise shut its eyes as it recalled its sibling's final transmission. "Yes, it saw, in the driver's carriage . . . a young man. Who, these ones cannot say, for he wore the mask of a laughing demon." The Terror furrowed his brow and with patience asked if there was anyone else. "None that these eyes can see, before the light of the falling blade." The creature shuddered.

"And on the Road Below? Have any of your brethren seen it?"

The tortoise whimpered, overwhelmed by the memory of its sibling's death, and the smell of the Terror's urgency and rage. It stretched up its head to the sky and called out to its siblings along that southern road, far away—over the foothills and dense forests of the terrace lands, to the long and unkempt road congested with pilgrims traveling east; a road that wound through the hills to the Village of Five Sisters, where its sibling nearest to Tiger Gate was stationed, and where, it learned, the people were getting restless.

The reaping had yet to begin.

Hundreds of farmers from the nearby sectors of Lord Yinn's terrace lands were congregated in this moderately sized town, cupped between the five distinct hills that gave the village its name, the people stuffed into alleyways and balconies, far too many for the village to accommodate, *but we had no choice but to come—you either showed up or they forfeited your lease to the next family,* the people confused and angry as they sweated under the midday sun amongst all their produce, for the emperor's collections caravan, due some time ago, had yet to arrive.

The mood grew more tense, more alive by the hour. The tortoise up in the village watchtower near the central square cringed from the red stink of agitation that wafted up from the crowd as yet more farmers came in through the gates with pots of rice and roped livestock and sheafs of buckwheat. *Few of us had any sleep last night. We were wakened in the middle of the night by a strange and intense shiver, which left us restless and feeling . . . different.* There were murmurings of trouble from the west; of an inexplicable stack of smoke that stained the sky above the western Spires, and the sound of a mighty explosion that some chanced to hear in their sleepless pacing during the night, but because no one had any explanation for such events—no news from the tortoise, which was normally so forthcoming with such information—this talk only added to the air of frustration that had been building up in their hearts since early morning. The few royal guards who happened to be in attendance fielded questions as best they could, which is to say they told the people that all that happened was ever according to His Smiling Sun's plan. *We knew there was a chance that things would become violent. We decided to tell the local Older-man to start the performances and the games.* And so, upon the sound of the horn blast and a brief speech, the youths in the drumline picked up their sticks and the dancing arena was opened. And amongst the shouts of the feet-stompers and the cheering of the crowd, the tortoise in the watchtower looked amongst the faces until it saw, entering from the western gate, a wagon of the Throne, driven by a young man wearing the mask of a smiling fox.

Within the wagon, the Defect's head was swiveling in near every direction. "There are . . . many . . . smells here. This one is . . . having difficulty focusing . . . on a thought."

The imperious village tortoise followed the newly arrived wagon with its beak.

"It has seen this one," the Defect told Keema. "It is confused why this one will not let it into its thoughts. We should not stay long."

Keema relayed this to Jun in the front.

"I hear you," he said. "We just need to stop for water."

The crowd parted for them swiftly, knowing better than to get in the way of a royal wagon. One of the hapless guards ran up to them, asking if they had any news to share from the palace as to the collection caravan's estimated time of arrival. Jun apologized to him and said he didn't know any more than anyone else, and the guard, dejected, slumped back into the crowd as they pulled up to the water pumps. They were unaware that across the town square a woman watched them from the shadows. Their attentions were on the long line of thirsty people who waited their turn for water rations, the line wrapping around some of the homes and down a terra-cotta alley. Jun looked at Keema. "If this village is where we part ways, I ask only that you leave after I return. I'd rather the wagon is not unprotected while I'm gone."

"I'll keep watch," Keema assured.

Jun's new fox mask gazed at him for a long beat. Behind him, the dancers bowed, all in a line, at the end of the first performance.

"Okay," he finally said.

With the knot of canteens in hand, he leapt off the wagon and headed toward the line, declaring loudly that he was here on business of the Throne and needed to get through quickly. Grumbling, the people made room for him at the head of the line, where he thrust the canteens into the hands of the broad-shouldered Provider, for though much had changed about Jun in the past six months, he still knew how to act like a prince's son. He waited with crossed arms while the angry Provider worked the pump. *I would've kicked the little bastard into the dirt, had he not just come from a wagon of the Throne.* Meanwhile, up above, the tortoise relayed the scene to its sibling to the north, characters and all.

The Terror drummed his fingers.

"It is possible our quarry changed masks," he quietly told his sons, whom he gathered around him at the base of the watchtower. His Peacocks, hungry, waited with eager breath for their father's command. "Regardless, whether or not it is them, we can still act against them."

A man locked his arms around another's chest.

Keema winced as the man then drove his opponent into the ground. At the edge of the arena a child holding a skewer of sweet rolls laughed loudly from his perch on his mother's shoulders. *We watched the fighters, and we roared, and we let loose our belly fires. The bad spirits quit our bodies and floated up into the sky.* The drumming settled into a rhythmic, earthen pulse, and new pairs sprung from the crowd, dressed in ceremonial skirts, ready to spar in honor of this blessed day. Keema stood up on the seat of the cab to get a better view of the arena. His heart bounced, for even in times of trouble there would always be something alluring about the fight, but whatever joy he felt was briefly lived, for when he looked at the arena, all he saw was Raami, pointing to the crowd in challenge, and Araya, standing on the wall, watching over them all with her drunk smile, and even Vogo, clinging desperately to his leg, whispering, *they're all dead,* which swiftly blew out the candle of his excitement while the crowd cheered, and he looked away, unable to watch.

"Excuse me, sir."

Keema looked down. Standing by their wagon was a wiry woman of secretive expression, her hair cut short, unevenly, as if by her own hand, without the aid of a mirror—an anxious energy radiating from her as she looked around to see if they were being watched. "Are you the ones transporting the new tortoise to Rabbit Gate Checkpoint?" she asked.

"Yes," he said warily, his grip on the spear reassuring itself.

"Good, good. I'm the liaison," she said, as if that meant anything to him.

"Okay," he said.

"So," she said. "Are you ready to hand it over?"

"I don't know what you're talking about," he said.

Her relieved smile faded. "The . . . delivery. You do have it, don't you?"

Keema, now believing this person to be unhinged, said curtly, "I don't know what you're talking about." He waved his spear. "Move along."

"Do not fuck with me, cripple," she whisper-snapped, startling him. "The bird. Do you have the bird?"

In a rush he remembered the vibrant purple devil he had freed, but not before it scratched at his face, and the soldier he had met at the compound who told him he was tasked with a secret mission, one that promised to pay enough to risk even treason. The woman's hand was outstretched, trembling, waiting for that which only he could give, and Keema felt a funny kind of embarrassment, a pang of guilt, for allowing the bird she so desperately wanted to get away. He did not know what to tell her, other than that he was sorry. Fortunately, he did not have to suffer her snarling for much longer, as Jun climbed into the cab with the full canteens and said that it was time to leave.

"Are you coming with us?" Jun asked him.

"Just go," Keema said. And as the orooks were spurred on and the wagon wheels creaked to life, he held up his spear-hand to the woman and said to her, "My apologies, stranger. I hope you find what it is you are looking for."

Veins of rage popped in the woman's forehead as they pulled away. "I hope for your sakes that this is nothing but a laugh you are having at my expense. You do not realize the wrath that will— YOU DO NOT REALIZE THE WRATH THAT WILL FALL UPON YOUR HEADS IF THAT BIRD DOESN'T—" But it wasn't long before she was swallowed by the noise of the crowd. When she was out of view, Jun regarded Keema with a tilt of his mask, but Keema, who had no answer, simply shrugged; it was on their way through the eastern gate of the village that he explained it had something to do with that bird he'd freed.

"I see," Jun said.

"What is it?"

Jun humphed. "I have the feeling that much is happening, just out of our sight."

How right he was.

Ten minutes prior, by the watchtower of Monkey Gate, the Terror had told his sons what he planned to do. "I will let them go." He held up his hand in anticipation of his Peacocks' protests, silencing them before they even spoke out; patient as ever, he was not one to miss out on a teachable moment for his children, even when pressed for time. "No, there is no use in informing the village guards. I would not trust the local regiment to apprehend them; nothing would come of that but disaster. Besides, I would not be deprived of my hunt. Our hunt. We must catch them ourselves, which means cutting off their means of escape. They make their way east, likely to the Thousand Rivers. And we know that the only way out of the terrace lands on the Road Below is Rabbit Gate Checkpoint."

"But Rabbit Gate is yet without a tortoise," his eldest said. "We cannot command them to shut their gates from here."

"Not directly," the Terror conceded.

And so, to the tortoise of the watchtower, he said this: "Relay this message to the soldiers of the Village of Five Sisters: The Crown Prince would have them send a messenger to Rabbit Gate Checkpoint, with haste, on horseback. The messenger will carry this note."

A royal order to close its gates, to any and all travelers, regardless of identity, until the Brigade of Red Peacocks arrives.

Beyond the last of the awnings, into the land unprotected from the sun, the empress's wagon rode, its passengers oblivious to the conspiring of the First Terror. They went opposite of most traffic, the people yet streaming into the village expecting to offload their harvest cargo for a caravan that would never show up. Keema and Jun drank deep from their canteens, the water almost hurting as it went down their parched throats; it took rare discipline to not finish their rations in one angry gulp. "It's easy to forget how thirsty you are," Jun said absently, turning away as he lifted his mask and drank. Keema agreed with a pleased hum, and after he wiped his moistened lips, he went in the back and gave some water to the Defect, pouring it into a shallow wooden bowl he had found in the clothing chest. He glanced at the old woman and asked Jun if She drank. He was told that She did not. *Such mortal concerns were beyond me.* Not so for Keema, who announced that he needed to relieve himself.

"We aren't stopping," Jun said as Keema climbed out.

Keema chuckled. "I'll catch up."

He leapt from the wagon into a bush on the side of the road. He felt his whole body relax as he went, as if every muscle for the last twenty-four hours had been held in complete tension until that moment. The dirt was so hot it hissed. He let out a reflexive sigh. In a languorous gaze he looked down the road from which they had come, tensing for a moment when he saw a horse galloping toward him at great speed, and relaxing when the rider passed him and the wagon, uninterested, and was soon far off in the distance. Keema did not give the rider another thought until he had returned and the Defect shouted, "This one smelled a messenger! He rides for Rabbit Gate! Stop him!"

He and Jun squinted at the vanishing rider on the horizon. Heat waves blurred him into the backdrop. "We'll never catch up to him," Keema said. "We'll never catch up."

"What message does he carry?" Jun asked.

"This one does not know!" the tortoise said. "This one can only smell his urgency."

From behind, Her Royal Whisper slapped Jun on the back of the head. She was yet too strained, too weak, to stop the rider, but She had enough in Her to deliver Her commandment.

I demanded they act quickly!

A strange fortune then arrived, as if waiting for its cue: a small object swooping down from the sky like a comet, striking the man on the horse, cleaving him from his saddle soundlessly. At first Keema thought it was the work of bandits, that someone from the surrounding brush had twirled a rock from a sling, but then the "rock" flapped back up into the sky, disappearing into the light, while the rider's horse, startled, ran down the road, then stopped by some roadside brush. Rising from their seats, Keema and Jun stared at the figure in the distance. He rolled on the ground. He was alive. There was still time for him to catch up to his horse. Keema and Jun looked at each other.

"No," Jun said, his voice dried and weak. "We can't kill him." *What is a murderer if he doesn't murder? He was nothing more than his father's son. No matter what, he would always be that monster's spawn.* "I won't," he whispered tightly, holding his head.

Keema looked at Jun as if he were mad.

"It's him or us," Keema said.

He picked up his spear and ran.

Someone was coming.

The messenger had hit his head. *I was so dizzy. Didn't know what had just happened, I couldn't . . . piece it together right away.* He had somehow found himself sprawled on the ground when a minute before he had been flying on the fastest horse the regiment had. *Proudest moment of my life was being handed the royal order. I thought, Yes, this is it. I was finally moving up.* Blood dripped out of his nose. He touched it and shivered. He fell back and rested for a moment before he tried to get up again. He wondered where the travelers were. Where was the help? *My nose was broken. Cassa would never let me hear the end of it.* He looked around for help. He saw a person in the distance running toward him. *I remember putting up my hand. Calling to them—nasally, stuffed-up, holding the blood up my nose. I laughed. Help was coming. I was going to be okay. My nose wouldn't stop bleeding.* So focused was he on the promise of help that his eye did not register when the person stopped and threw something into the air. The arc of the spear glinted at its apex before it fell out of the sun and pinned him into the earth.

I screamed.

The young man had now caught up to him, was staring down at

him. *I screamed*. The young man had only one arm, but that one arm was strong, and when he gripped the pole of the spear, he pulled it out with ease. A spout of blood painted a line across the dirt. *I screamed*. And then he shoved the point into the messenger's heart. *I—I don't know what happened after that. I don't know*. The man, empty-eyed, sunken, as Keema felt the last throb of his pulse run down the spine of Araya's spear and into the palm of his hand.

Jun looked away as Keema pulled the weapon out with a sickening squelch. He grabbed at the man's ankle, which was so thin all of his fingers wrapped easily around it, and he dragged the body off the road into the surrounding brush, where he searched the messenger's robes and skirts till he found the royal order to close Rabbit Gate Checkpoint. He was relieved to find this order, for this death to be justified in his eyes, and he nodded to the stiffening body in some acknowledgment of what he had done, of tough luck and well wishes, and he walked back out on the road as if nothing had happened. People were coming in both directions. Some of them had seen what had happened to the rider. But no one stopped Keema as he made his way back to the wagon, flicking blood from his spear. They looked away, and they kept quiet.

We moved on.

AFTERNOON

A body lies on the stage.

The dancer had come out from the wings only to fall as soon as they had emerged. And there, to the side of it all, the body remains, unmoving and unattended, as the tale continues. The corpse ever in view on the stage boards.

"She just stopped," the one-eyed soldier said.

Remember that sacred night. It was just the two of you in that dark room, and he seemed much smaller there than he did outside the pub, less certain of himself, as he sat on the edge of the bed and recalled for you his nightmare. "You see a lot of bodies, when you're over there. So many, most of them stop being bodies. They're just . . . things. It goes on and on. You can never predict which ones will be easy. Which ones will stick."

He sniffed.

"She just stopped," he said. "And I looked at her, and I wondered what the point of it was." He leaned away from you, but when you reached for him, he did not shrug you off. He let you feel his breath through his back; the ribs, expanding underneath damp skin. "Why did we do any of it?"

"For the greater good."

Your father said this without hesitation, as if it were printed in ink from the telegraph of his mind, delivered by some cold and distant signal. He and one of your older brothers were arguing again. Dinner was getting cold. "For the greater good" was your father's answer to all of your brother's moral queries about the war that would not end. "Do you think any of this was given to us for free?" he asked, gesturing at his house, at the table, covered in fine lace, and rich food, cooked by your housekeepers. "People died so that we could live. Others suffered so that we may prosper. This is the way of the world. To believe otherwise is to never grow up."

This did not convince your brother. When he was finally drafted, he ran away, unwilling to give his life for a cause he did not believe in, and you never saw him again. You can still feel his kiss on your forehead. It felt like goodbye. Your father never forgave him for that.

"What son?" he would say to any who would ask.

"My son is dead."

So the First Terror believed as he led his Peacocks southeast through the Yinn terrace lands, following his mother's scent in the wind. He told himself Jun was dead, even though the tortoise's description of the young man in the laughing demon mask gave him pause, for he knew that the emperor's First Guard had owned a mask of that same description, and the First Guard was dead, painted into the walls of that bloodied cavern far below the earth. They found Jun's peacock mask down there, too, and his prized bone necklace, and so much viscera it was impossible to tell where one body ended and another began.

"What if it is him?" his sons asked him as they cut through the foothills. *Our father would not see what we did. Could not. We loved him for that, and we were frustrated by him because of it.* He silenced them with but a look. Stop this silliness, that look said. Never would he birth a son who might betray him—he could not conceive of this possibility, his love for them all was so great.

He shooed away his doubt. He cleared his mind and left it but a temple for his vengeance.

His son was dead.

Objects were all that were left in the end.

In the slow-drawn and lopsided wagon, Jun touched his bare neck. It was a thing he did so often in search of comfort, once. He would touch the necklace, woven out of tiger-lace and ornamented with the bones of his fallen brothers, and he would feel their presence, and their presence would give him courage. But he had left that necklace behind. And now he felt only a deep absence as he withdrew his hand and looked at the old woman with a frown.

"I am sorry you have found me so lacking, Your Highness," he said.

Her whisper was a cold finger in his head, scaring off all the other voices that had since taken up residence there, while she explained to him his lack. She spared no detail. *I told him that ever since we had left the Palace he had made one wrong decision after another. His choice of heart-sick horses. His insistence on abandoning the Daware man at the time of our greatest need for useful bodies. His baffling recruitment of the defective tortoise, who was a near-literal deadweight. And his inability to do what needed to be done, when it came to it—our journey nearly premature in its ending, had the Daware man not been there to take care of the messenger on horseback.*

To say that I found him lacking would be an understatement. Worse than useless, he was an active hindrance, and I told him that if he wished to find any absolution for his wretched life, then he had best change course in his behavior soon, else we were all doomed.

The once-favored son of the Crown Prince, so feared for his merciless butchery, bowed before the corpselike old woman, trembling and close to tears. "I will do better, Your Highness, I will."

Good, I told him.

"But I swore I would never kill again," he said. "In your honor I swore it."

A tiresome oath, I thought at the time, but I knew the boy needed it. He needed to believe he could change. So I told him fine, if he insisted on staying his blade, if he truly would not take another life again, then we best bring with us someone who would.

"You want the Daware man."

Yes.

"What is the difference, Your Highness, between killing someone with my own hands and hiring someone else to do it?"

I told him to tell himself whatever he liked, I cared not, so long as he did what I bid. If he was not capable of that much, then perhaps I would simply replace him.

"We know so little about the sentry. We do not know what he wants."

Then get to know him, I said. We were in a situation of limited options, and there was plenty of time yet, before we arrived at Rabbit Gate, to learn the worth of his character.

"Yes, Your Highness."

Should he find the Daware man to be satisfactory, he was to bring him to me, so that I might bind him to our cause.

Jun stood up. "By your will," he said quietly.

Do not disappoint me again, child, I said.

I would not be so forgiving the next time.

Keema was in the driver's carriage, limply holding the reins to the orooks as he remembered the blood that sprang from the messenger's chest; how it was like pulling a cork from a wine cask. A thirsty revulsion building in his throat as he played the moment in his head again and again. It was not the first life he had taken, and he doubted it would be the last, but still, this made it no easier to move beyond. He would not forget the scratch of the man's heel into the dirt as he writhed under the weight of the spear, nor the final shudderings of his body.

They were well east of the Village of Five Sisters by then. The foothills leveled out into long, flat stretches of rice paddy allotments and bunches of yet-unclaimed forest. It was, despite the heat, a beautiful day. The sun, wheeling off its midday perch, bounced its light off the paddy waters, transforming the horizon into a field of shimmering gold. A hot breeze carried on its current the smell of a sweet porridge, wafted from a roadside cauldron and ladled out to hungry travelers, a half-copan a bowl, by a young woman who was flanked by three large farmers wielding sharp scythes. *She insisted on feeding the Road Below, and we insisted on protecting her.* When Keema saw them up ahead, on instinct he averted his eyes, keeping them on the reins and the orooks, but when he drove the wagon past these people, they did not glare at him or shout anything un-kind. The young woman and her guardians glanced once at the insignia of the Throne, painted on the side of the wagon, and they bowed deeply to him.

"Good day, young lord," the woman said.

"Good day," he replied, his voice cracking.

He turned back to the road, a light feeling in his chest. He knew that it was not him that they bowed to but the Throne, and that it was not out of love that they did so but fear. Still, as it was before, with the soldier in the compound, he could not help but feel some kind of satisfaction in being respected, however indirectly. It was almost enough to forget that not long ago he had just killed a man.

Jun emerged from the hold. He fell into the empty seat and stared out at the passing landscape while picking at the paint-chipped edges of his demon mask, which he had put on again much to Keema's disappointment, as he thought the fox was much cuter. It was clear from Jun's restless energy that he wished to say some-thing but did not know where to start. "Thank you," he said. "For taking care of what I could not."

Keema grunted.

After some time, watching a beetle crawl across the lip of the carriage, Jun nodded at the spear that sat between them. "Will you really bring that thing across the country?"

"Yes." Keema's answer brooked no argument.

"Your commander must have meant a great deal to you."

"She—" Keema began, but he stopped himself, for it occurred to him only then to ask himself what she did mean to him. In truth he knew almost nothing about Commander Araya. He did not know she was a traitor. All he knew was she liked to drink. That she was very close to Raami. He knew the rumors about her and the First Terror's casual relationship. But other than that, he could recall little more of the life she hid behind her smile. "I had not known her for very long, but she gave me work, and shelter. And she spoke to me as few others do." He was surprised by the emotion he felt—this sudden warmth, and loss. "She . . . respected me."

Jun leaned back. "I've met her a few times, briefly."

"You have?" Keema said, surprised.

"Yes. My duties brought me through Tiger Gate on occasion, likely before you arrived. Every time I came, there were more orphans living in that fortress than before. It seemed like she never said no to a lost child. I always wondered why."

"I'm not a lost child."

"I didn't mean to suggest that."

"I'm taller than you."

This made Jun laugh, and not unpleasantly to Keema's ears.

"So you are," he conceded.

"Who are they?" Keema then asked. When the boy in the mask merely stared at him, he clarified his question. "The people Araya told you of. The ones she would have you meet."

"The Five Families." He said this with little emotion, as if it were of little interest that the five heads of this country's industries were plotting a coup. "Apparently they've been planning for this week ever since the emperor first announced his pilgrimage. Even as we ride, their private armies prepare to gather at the gates of the Divine City for an assault on the Fifth Day, when the emperor is meant to arrive." He chuckled grimly. "We made their job considerably easier in that respect."

"Oh," Keema said, sounding disappointed.

Jun looked at him. "What?"

"I'd assumed you were meeting with people not as . . . wealthy."

"Of course we are," Jun said. "We want to win."

They passed the Syta compound.

An argument was being had outside its gates. One man was shouting at a few others, who listened to him with crossed arms. *The caravan had left for the village reaping without my harvest. I told them I just needed another hour, and the bastards left anyway, and now my life was ruined. I was going to lose my allotment. I was going to be investigated for blasphemy. Joyrock was all but certain. Oh, the others gave me their excuses, but I knew they wanted me to fail. They wanted my paddies for themselves.* The shouting escalated to the tipping edge of a fight, a man grabbing another by the front-robes, before they saw the insignia of the Throne on Keema and Jun's wagon, and immediately dropped their heads in a bow.

"Good day, my lords," they said.

"Good day," Keema replied while Jun lifted a finger in acknowledgment.

Keema did not feel the same lightness in his chest as he did before with the porridge server. When they were some distance away, he craned his head and looked back. The men were still bowing. They would not get up until they were out of view. He slumped in his seat, feeling something in his stomach, close to queasiness. He noticed, from the corner of his eye, that Jun was in study of him.

"Who were you before you were a sentry of Tiger Gate?"

Keema looked at him with a cocked brow. "Why?"

"Because I'd like to know," Jun said. "We can sit in silence, if you prefer."

"I was a mercenary," he said. "I rode with a free-band company when I was younger. That was before I lost my arm. And then I took whatever work I could get after that. There wasn't much. Longest job I had was working as a guard in the Bowl. A pleasure barge. I threw out the drunks who bothered the love workers. That was where I was at, before Araya took me on."

"How did you lose your arm?"

Keema did not like revisiting that memory, which was why he now had a stock answer, should the question ever come up.

"I lost it the way everyone loses an arm," he said.

"How is that?"

"Bad luck."

Jun chuckled. He did not push the matter.

"And you?" Keema asked, starting to enjoy the conversation. "What's your tale?"

The masked driver thought about his answer for a time before he gave it, carefully. "I was a high-ranked warrior, in service to the royal family. I reported directly to the First Terror." Keema, who had already suspected as much, nodded for him to go on. "The last six months I was given the order to guard the Wolf Door. Do you know of it?" Keema shook his head. "It is a door, deep below the palace. It is the most treasured area of the capital. And it is where She was kept." He nodded to the back of the wagon, as if the She of his tale needed any clarification. "Every six months a new guard is ordered to stand before the door, and for six months, that guard is the only person who stands between the world and the heart of the Throne." He shrugged. "It's more a symbol than anything. A rite of passage. It was my turn to be that guard before all this started. It was the proudest moment of my life when I was selected for the duty."

"What happened then?" Keema asked.

Another shrug, this one more defeated. "She changed my mind."

"And then you killed the emperor?"

He nodded at the back. "She did."

"With a blade?"

"With Her mind," he said. "She blew him up. Like a sneeze. Painted Him against the walls of the cavern."

"That is incredible," Keema said, shaking his head.

He then furrowed his brow.

"I thought the emperor was all-powerful."

Jun nodded.

"So did He," he said.

The wagon slowed as they came upon a congested road.

They were behind a stopped passenger caravan. The people sitting on the benches inside the caravan avoided their gaze, except for a child, who openly stared at them from behind his mother's arm. Keema wondered what was going on; Jun stood up on the seat to see how long the wagon jam was. He could see as far as ten canvas roofs—there seemed to be a blockage on the road up ahead, the vehicles directed onto a makeshift side path. He said as much to Keema.

"Is there space to go around the others?" Keema asked.

"I don't think so—else we'd just sink into the paddy water."

"I wouldn't try anything fancy, my lords," a man in the passenger caravan said. He did not meet their gaze. "There's a Daido up ahead."

Jun sighed into his seat. "Shit."

Keema echoed this sentiment with a grim nod.

"I guess we're waiting."

Your father had carved one, once.

He was always so disdainful of your lola's stories, so it was a surprise to you all when, shortly after her passing, he tried to sculpt this magical trinket. If there was ever a time when he was good with his hands, it was well before you came into the world, but when the need arose for a blessed object to be placed on your lola's altar—her little Daido statuette gone missing along with her sepia-toned daguerreotype, stolen, your uncle was certain, by one of the pallbearers—your father took the task upon himself to sculpt a replacement.

You and your brothers knew that your father had never sculpted anything in his life, but, as affected as he was by her passing in the week after the funeral, you all decided, without speaking once about such a decision, to let him try his hand at the task, and to hold your tongue as he muttered and cursed in the backyard over the small cube of rock he had purchased from a quarryman. Whenever he was not at the textiles house, he was out in the courtyard working at the block—or, inevitably, the new block he had purchased, with the old one lying discarded somewhere in the yard for you or your brothers to trip over during one of your chasing games. Your uncle, at first proud of his brother for making these beginner's attempts, was soon rolling his eyes as the housecleaners dragged the stone out of the house and drove the rock down to the local artisans to salvage the mess.

Your father was, if nothing else, persistent. At night, swaying in your hammock, listening to your brothers' snoring and the music of your neighbor's radio through the open window, you heard him chipping away at the rock.

You heard his night song:

"Fucking hell!"

He finished eventually; a month's time, and much poorer than he began, the quarrymen in town counting their coin with pleasure. You found him kneeling before your lola's altar in one of the side rooms of the house, the Daido held limply in his bandaged fingers. He wore a pensive expression, one that you recognized meant that he did not want to be bothered, but when he noticed you walking by he asked you to come in. "Look," he said, like he was your child, showing you what he had made; he handed the little statuette to you.

The Daido, traditionally, was the effigy of an old man, in crosslegged posture, with one hand held up as if to stop someone from passing him and the other hand held out, palm up, as if asking for coin. The many replications you have seen in the artisans' corner ably captured the old man's calm yet distant expression, and his gaunt, near-starved frame. Your father's Daido looked more like an angry baby: the texture rough, more stone than person.

You told him it looked great.

He asked you to sit with him. "She must have told you about these things," he said as you handed it back to him.

Your lola did, in fact, tell you of the Daido, many times over. You told your father that no one was sure who the old man was, his true name forgotten, only his title remembered: the First Beggar. Your father turned the statuette in his hand; the granite caught the light from the window in a glittering spray and it seemed, for a moment, magical—as if your father, almost on accident, had imbued it with some sort of spiritual essence. You told him that if ever there was danger, of spirits or beast or otherwise, this Daido would appear, on the road or on the field, or even sometimes on the surface of a river, and the statue's presence would warn the people not to continue on their path. To turn back or go around. No one would question the Daido. And no one, ever, walked past it.

That afternoon was so strange to you; a one-off, never to repeat itself. The next morning, your father would go on to become subsumed in the news of the war. But you would never forget the day you felt you'd really seen him.

The brief opening, now closed.

The Daido sat in the middle of the Road Below. The farmers, hushed and reverent, changed the course of their wagons, going down the precarious turns of the rutted paths that cut between the paddy allotments, barely wide enough for one direction of traffic. Proper respect was shown to the Daido; even the wagons seemed to creak quieter as the line inched forward. *My father said that if you talk too loud near a Daido, then whatever's behind it will snatch you up in its mighty claws.* They were frightened into silence, all of them, even Keema and Jun, who did not so much as breathe as they approached the turn in the road. Keema had seen only one other Daido in his life—their appearances more common back in the reign of the previous emperors, when there were yet more forests, and springs—and so when they finally met the Daido, he was surprised, because it was smaller than he expected it to be.

He watched quietly and with some disquiet as everyone who

passed the Daido left behind a coin, some of them placing it with care in a pile in the statuette's hands, others not daring to get close, flicking the coin from their horse or wagon, the ground around the statuette glittering with iron and bronze chips. Jun handed Keema a coin and let him toss it over to the Daido. It clinked into the growing pile at the Daido's feet. Satisfied with the luck they had purchased, Jun, who had taken the reins again, made to spur the orooks before he heard Her voice.

I told him to stop.

Just for a moment.

"What's wrong?" Keema asked.

"It's Her," Jun said.

It had been a long time. A very long time, since I had last seen him. I knew it was not him. That this was but a statuette, carved clumsily from old rock.

But still, it was . . . lovely.

Keema heard sniffing. He looked over at Jun and saw that he was crying; wetness beading on his chin. Keema looked away, uncomfortable.

"These are not my tears," Jun said. And then, to the back: "Are you done yet, Your Highness?"

I told him I was done.

There was no more to remember.

Jun snapped the reins and the orooks groaned as they pulled the wagon forth, down the diverted road. He did not explain what he meant when he said that those tears were not his; he left the moment where it was and continued on as if it had never happened.

"It is not easy, to be bound to her."

He said this sometime later, apropos of nothing, the two of them riding along in a thoughtful silence. There was grim humor in Jun's voice as he wiped the tears off his chin. The way he spoke reminded Keema of the high-borns in the teahouses. A practiced curve to his words. Indirect, but always hitting its target from around a corner. A game of words. "It is not easy," he said again, "but I do it for what I believe are just reasons. I have not lived well. I have much to make up for. So I follow Her, in the hope that I might find some measure of redemption. This is what I live for now. This road will likely end in my death, but there is no other road for me."

He turned to Keema.

"She would like to speak with you," he said plainly. "She would like to show you what it is She fights for. And then she will likely bind you to our cause, if that is truly what you want." He was quiet for a time. "From one stranger to another, Keema, I would advise you to think well about what you want before you treat with Her."

He then nodded.

"Go on. She's waiting."

As Keema climbed into the wagon's hold, he was unaware that the pornographic tablet slipped out of his cloth folds and landed on the seat of the driver's carriage. As the canvas fold closed behind him, Jun picked up the tablet. And he made a "huh" noise as he tilted it against the light.

Keema shivered.

The mood inside the wagon was noticeably different from before. The dark hold, lit up by the shafts of light that fell through the canvas tatters, had the solemnity of a temple service. Little details that had always been there only now became apparent. Two small wooden charms, tied to one of the knots that held the canvas in place; cat-shaped trinkets jangling on small hooks. There was a dampness to the light, as if another layer of canvas had been draped over the roof, blotting the sun enough so that it was only just noticeable. Keema felt himself pulled toward the back of the wagon, where She waited; the pull inexorable, like a hand wrapping itself around his own as it drew him farther in, to a place where few were permitted.

As was proper when addressing his elders, Keema knelt before the old woman, who as ever remained cross-legged and eye-shut and in all ways dead to the world. He sat on his feet and paid Her his respects, bowing his head just so. *Once the young man had come, I prepared to tell him everything—but before I could speak, the damned creature interrupted me.* "Be careful with this one," the Defect muttered to Keema, pawing at him with its stump. "Think twice . . . before you let Her in."

He smiled at the tortoise's concern, even as he was unnerved by how similar the words of warning were to Jun's. "I will be careful," he said, and no sooner had he spoken those words could he then feel it, from the dark—a coaxing-open of his mind.

"Hold on to yourself then," the Defect said, "for she will not be gentle."

When Keema turned back to the old woman, he flinched. Her eyes wide open—great furious orbs, with small dagger-point irises, gazing at him as if to swallow him whole. The sight horrified him, regret bubbling up his throat, a need to shout that he had changed his mind—to flee—but before he could change the course of his life for what was known and safe, he felt a bright pain, like a finger flicked against his forehead, and he fell backward into the waking dream.

The Moon falling into his mind.

He saw Her suspended in a black parchment sky. *He saw how beautiful I once was.* In the dark and vast plain within his mind, he stared up at the perfect circle of Her. *Back when I was still called Shadow Star, the Sibling of the Sun, the Night Warden and Day Ender; the Eye of the Sleeping Sea.* He understood why they called Her empress. *But this was before the time of the Throne, when my province was yet the sky; when I illuminated the stars and I danced with the tide and under me the Water swelled and receded, our dance ongoing and eternal.* He saw the world of night as it once was. The cool bath of soft light that gilded the leaves. *The flowers that slept curled under my cold and loving touch.* He saw the world when it was quiet. *Long ago, before the counting of days. When there was only the rise of the sun and the fall.* The Moon cracked in half like an egg and She, as he knew Her, emerged from the broken shell: that old woman, that strip of cracked leather. *Cracked, and dying. I had kept myself alive through unnatural means. I had slowed my own heart so that I might continue on in this body. I have done this while the worst of them had kept me imprisoned beneath his royal apartment for decades.*

Keema saw the room She was kept in. He saw the cavern, and the Wolf Door, and the many guards who had over the years stood before it. And She showed him the room behind the door; the small, dark space She called home, where She sat surrounded by a moat of water, and, suspended above the water, a pentagram of nets, filled with old stones. *I could not flee on my own*—blinded, muted as she was—*and so I convinced someone to help me.* Keema saw a flash of a guard in a peacock mask, standing outside the Wolf Door. He saw the withered emperor tossing and turning in bed, haunted by dreams of immortality. *I poured such vivid dreams into my wretched son. False promises of things He craved. I needed Him distracted. I needed Him weak, before I struck!* Keema flinched when the emperor transformed into a cloudburst of blood. *And now that He was gone only three sons remained. Three Terrors that continued their reign over this despoiled country.* Keema shivered as he was presented the silhouettes of the men who haunted so many whispers in those days—one that prowled, one that slinked, and one that was little more than vapor—the three demons of the Throne looking at Keema as if he were a small animal in the brush. *I told the Daware man to not be fooled by their presence, they were not all-powerful, for they were born with a weakness—the triplets given only a fraction of what they were due, but a third of the power that one emperor might share. It was because of this that they craved the power withheld from them since birth; why they would have it by any means necessary—do you understand, Keema—do you understand, Keema—do you understand*—Her

Royal Whisper interrupted by a sudden vision—*of teeth gnashing on a bloody bone as three little boys ate their mother's body—they would eat me, and take into themselves my power*—"And like that," Keema trance-whispered, pale and shaking, "they would rule for another bloody age"—the Defect watching with concern as the young man and the empress stared at each other with synchronous blinks, the young man speaking Her words—"Soon I will die," *but before I pass from this world and return to the sky,* "I will end my sons," *my greatest loves,* "who love me so much they would devour me whole." *I will go east and meet the people,* "the ones that Commander Araya had spoken of," *and if necessary I will give them my flesh so that they may eat and inherit enough of my power,* "to end the Moon Throne once and for all." Keema, shaking, as this prophecy left his mind, and his eyes once again opened, and the old woman was back into Her old position, seated and quiet, Her eyes shut, but Her lips, chapped and aged, ticked into what, in the right light, seemed like an expression of command and confidence. *This was my plan.*

"You are bound to Her now."

The Defect sighed, its disappointment tempered with some sense of inevitability, as if it were aware of Her power, Her draw, and could only begrudge Keema so much for giving in. "But what this one said before . . . it remains true. . . . Hold on to yourself. Whatever influence of Hers may come. Hold on to yourself."

The words reverberated in Keema's head as he returned to the driver's carriage, unable to cease his shivering.

"Do you have clarity now?" Jun asked, breaking the silence.

Keema did not answer. He was gazing at the road that danced over low hills. It all seemed at once both profound and irrelevant. Some frivolous grandeur. An unknown way to be alive. He didn't know what to say.

"Yeah," Jun said, to the silence. "Me neither."

They rode past the last of the rice terraces.

Dusk bruised the sky, the sun cracking over the jagged horizon. On the last of the Yinn-owned farmlands, the oxen dragged forks through dirt while old men blew protection powder around the coops and onto the paths that led into the howling forests. Guards patrolling the acreage eyed the passing of their wagon with a casual suspicion until they were out of view.

The road was long and empty at this late hour. The last people Keema and Jun saw that day on the road were the Sky Beggars; a line of half-starved outcasts, at least thirty souls long, from child to grown woman, walking in a rhythmic shuffle down the side of the road. Barefoot. Some of them were missing limbs, eyes, or ears. They held above their heads empty wooden bowls as they recited the old prayers for the summoning of broken clouds, and rain—praying for the end of this Endless Summer. One of the beggars glanced at them with eyes as empty as the bowl over his head, *and I looked at the young man wearing the mask of a laughing demon and I smiled, for no mask can hide the truth of a man,* and Jun whipped his rein and the orooks went forth a little quicker than before, until, over the next hill, the beggars disappeared from view.

He looked over at Keema, who was still in a silent, distracted mood, and he was suddenly glad that he was not alone in this—that now there was someone like him, bound together to Her.

"Do you regret staying?" he asked.

"I am of the Daware Tribe," Keema said, dully. "And when a man of Daware makes an oath, he holds to it, no matter the cost." He sat up straighter. "I would sooner cut off my own arm than break my word."

"Where is Daware anyway?"

"South," Keema said, after a pause. "Past the last of the Thousand, where the end of the river bleeds into fields of stickle-wheat and valleys of poisonous flowers. Upon the deadly petals of the bora rose, the warriors of Daware made their oaths. To us, to break an oath is to break the promise you made with your own life."

As Araya had done before, Jun asked him what the consequences were, of breaking an oath of Daware.

"My life must be ended."

Keema said this without fear or hesitation. He showed Jun the small knife he kept strapped to his thigh by cord and sheath. He told Jun that the knife was of his father's making. It was a knife of deep-blue stone, with a hilt made of black leather and threads of colorful string. A beautiful object, made and given to him, he told Jun, by his parents with the knowledge that one day it may end their son's life by his own hand. It was his mother who showed him how to disembowel himself correctly. How to do it with certainty, from right to left, with hand on the hilt, all the way through. How to let the blood enrich the soil and cleanse what you left tainted by your ineptitude and your fouled promises. How this was the only appropriate act of forgiveness.

None of this was true; Keema had only heard about the practice of self-disembowelment a few months ago.

But it was what he said.

Jun considered Keema's words—of what would become of him should he fail his task—and, after a period of thoughtful silence, during which he considered the falling cry of day, and the dark and lightless Burn in the sky, he said, with what sounded like a smile, "Since failure is all but certain, I will say it now: It was nice knowing you, Keema of the Daware Tribe."

NIGHT

They were on the precipice of it.

The black curtain of true night was draping itself over the last of the fields and hills. The orooks were tired but they kept pace with the snap of Jun's reins while Keema played the Eye, keeping vigil over the road behind them. The empress told them she sensed him on the southward wind. *I could feel the approach of my son. I could feel the distant echo of hard hoofbeats in the dirt.* "You won't see them coming," Jun said. "Not until they're already here."

"They're thirty strong," Keema replied, gazing over the canvas roof. "Of course I'll see them."

Jun did the thing that annoyed Keema, where somehow, even with the mask on, he let it be known that he was smirking. But as the land around them began to rise, and then steeply fall, funneling toward some grim point of termination, that masked smirk fell away, replaced by a somber voice that chilled Keema to hear it: "I have something to tell you."

"What is it?"

"The one who is chasing us, the First Terror . . ." Jun's voice fell away. "I don't think we will outrun him." The wheels bumped over the rough grooves in the road. Keema waited for him to work out what he wanted to say. "The Terror has good reason to want to kill me."

"Because you killed his son," Keema said, remembering what that man's voice had said last night over the gate.

Jun was silent. Two fields away, the shadows of true night flooded the land. "The Terror will do whatever he can to end my life," he said.

"We can make it to the river before that happens."

"I won't make it to the river." Jun laughed as if startled by his own thought; by the truth of it.

Keema sat down. "What are you saying?"

"If I die," the boy in the laughing demon mask said, "you're the only one who can bring Her east. And I hope that if and when that time comes, you remain a man of your word. Your word as a man of Daware."

The torch signs of Rabbit Gate came into view in the dusk-driven horizon like many little orange teeth. The fortress sat at the mouth of a small canyon pass, beset by clumps of thick forest between which Keema could see nothing but blackness. He felt as though they were driving the orooks into the maw of a giant demon. He stood back up on the carriage seat. The road behind them was empty; there was only the encroaching dark.

"One more thing," Jun said, like a man at the noose thinking of one last request. "The tortoise is coming with us."

"We need to pass through Rabbit Gate," Keema reminded him, "and Rabbit Gate is expecting a tortoise delivery from us. For us to pass through and not deliver a tortoise . . . It is not possible."

"You are right. It isn't possible," Jun said, his hands white-knuckling the reins. "And it isn't relevant at all to our journey, our mission. But still. I cannot let the creature die." Before Keema could make any protestations, he said, "In those six months I spent in that fucking hole, the empress unveiled my eyes, and She broke me, and I learned the price of taking a life. Let the messenger on the road be the last who needs to fall on our journey east. Let him be the last nail driven into the wall. I will not have another creature die by my hand. Swear that you will help me bring the tortoise to safety. Swear it!"

Keema's head hurt. "Moments ago you told me that no matter what comes to pass my one goal was to bring the old woman east. Now you speak as if the tortoise is your greatest priority. Which is it? Who do you want me to shepherd east?"

"Both of them." Jun's mask turned toward him in all of its laughing insanity. "Swear it."

Keema breathed out.

"You're mad," he said.

"Swear it!" Jun shouted. "Swear you'll save the damned creature's life! Even should I die! Swear it!"

"I—"

"Swear it or you're a fucking coward!"

In a cold rush the curtain of night swallowed the road.

". . . I swear it."

The night-blind orooks stumbled in their gallop before switching over to scent, following the trails of warm human musk to the fortress gates.

Before they arrived, Keema checked in on the Defect. He asked the creature how it was doing as he squeezed water out of one of the canteens and massaged it onto the hot shell with a scrap of cloth, as the sentries had done in Tiger Gate to their tortoise. "This one has been worse," the tortoise replied with a grateful sigh.

"We're almost there," Keema said. "Rabbit Gate nears."

The creature looked at him with its small, pained eyes. "This one heard what you and the masked one spoke of, in regards to this one. What is your plan then?" it asked, its tone both doubtful that Keema had a plan and hopeful that he did.

"A warrior of the Daware Tribe never shares his schemes," Keema said. "This is so the only one who can foil his plans is himself."

"Keen words improvised on the spot." The Defect shook its head. "In simple words: bullshit."

Keema laughed. "A wise tortoise, aren't you?"

"Not that wise. . . . after all . . . this one is here, trusting you." After a moment of looking at him, with the old woman silent and prostrate, it said quietly, "This one dreams of eastern waters."

Keema squeezed the last bit of water out, to the creature's audible pleasure.

"You won't see the top of that tower," he said.

"Daware man!" Jun called out.

Keema climbed back out onto the carriage. Reins were shoved into his hand as Jun went inside. Keema asked him where he was going.

"To move the empress out of sight," he said. "I doubt she'd be happy if I let you do it." While Keema drove the orooks forward, trusting them to find their way through the lightless road, he heard the careful movement of someone navigating precious cargo around a crowded room. He wondered where Jun was planning to put the old woman's body. He imagined the Mother of Emperors being covered in one of the old canvas sheets in one of the hold's compartments, and he found it within himself to smile at the thought. And then he was hit with another image, out of nowhere, almost as if someone shot it right into his brain from across a field: *I showed him what must happen. I showed him how he would tell the guards at Rabbit Gate that their tortoise had arrived. I showed how he would watch impassively as the tortoise was dragged out of the wagon, its mouth held shut by my powers, the thing wide-eyed in terror and fury and unable to speak, not until we were already well on our way through the opposite gate, with no obstacle between us and the river docks. I told him that this was what must happen.*

Keema gripped the reins.

They'd arrived.

Against the dark, the torchlight of Rabbit Gate Checkpoint was like a minor sun as they approached. Two sentries met them at the well-lit western gate; women both, young in age, not more than thirty years between them, yet owning that stone-cut gaze earned through a lifetime of difficult trials. "Long travels," the first said with a welcoming gesture, her smile fading when she saw Keema's missing left arm and Jun's strange mask. Curtly, she said, "You've arrived just in time. We're about to close the gates for the night."

"Let's get on with it then," Jun said, putting on a performance of a tired worker of the Throne. "We don't want to keep you all longer than necessary."

"Kind of you," the sentry said, nodding to her partner. "We're going to look in the back if that's all right."

Jun nodded.

But just before the other sentry began her way to the wagon's hold, Keema had an idea. "Just a minute," he said. The sentries stopped, brows cocked with impatience. What he was about to try was risky, and required the aid of a person he did not know how to communicate with, and who might not humor him even if he could somehow tell Her his slapdash plan. Yet he had to try. "The thing's been making strange noises the whole trip from the palace," he said. "Sickness, I think. Best keep your distance. Never know what might pass between a tortoise and a human, cough-wise."

"A sick tortoise," the sentry repeated, dubious. "Never heard of the like."

"Just our luck to be carrying one. Isn't that right?" he said, nudging Jun.

The laughing demon mask gave the subtlest of nods.

"I'd warn your commander too," Keema said. "In case you might have need of some physicker or whomever."

The two sentries glanced at each other, but orders were orders their shrugs seemed to say. *I went into the back of the wagon to see if these strange men spoke the truth, and when I pulled back the canvas flap I almost retched.* She gave her partner a nod, *the thing looked as sick as any creature I'd seen,* and the partner said to the young men in the carriage seat, "Go on then. Just over there. We'll let the commander know you've come."

They rolled through the first of the gates.

"What are you doing?" Jun whispered.

But Keema didn't have time to explain. He just asked this: "How do I speak to Her?"

"With your mouth."

"She can hear me?"

"If she chooses to."

In the wagon he crouched beside the bundle of cloths and blankets and bags of rice that he supposed she was hidden under, and said, quietly, urgently, "You are a being of great power. I've witnessed this, not only by your mighty acts the past day and night, but in the images you've shared with me. Things both great and small. The destruction of a bridge, or the slowing of your own heart. With humility, I would ask you this: Slow this Defect's heart; make him appear otherwise dead." The tortoise shook its beak, not liking this idea. But the wagon was beginning to slow down, and they were running out of time—he heard voices, Jun's, saying to someone to hold just a moment—and he heard the rattling of the pulley chains. The tortoise heard it too. It let out a pitiful mewl that shook the baseboards. "Please, Mother of Emperors, our Unstitched Moon," Keema whispered into the blankets. "I beg—"

Fine.

The word was not spoken or whispered but imprinted somehow onto his mind. Delivered to him in the sudden image of a young girl's hand opening. A thing flying out between Her fingers. Keema heard the troubled breath of the tortoise slow, its rasp and rumble fading out until it had no breath at all. He held his ear close to the creature's head, which was resting on the floor of the wagon with eyes half-lidded and tongue lolling out of its beak. He heard and felt nothing.

A shout from outside.

"Is the creature ready, Keema?"

"The thing's dead!" he shouted back.

Silence followed. Then a disturbed murmuring. Keema climbed out of the wagon and met with Jun, who was standing before a gang of sentries, each of whom were large and muscular, chosen for their strength to lever the creature onto its new home. They seemed confused by his claim, staring at him as he explained again that the tortoise that they had brought from the palace had, at some point, he was not sure when, died.

"They can die?" one of the men said.

Jun's impenetrable mask stared at Keema. Keema stared back at him. "It's dead," he said once more. "Please go fetch your commander."

Wouldn't normally take orders from a cripple, but these were special circumstances. The commander of Rabbit Gate arrived in a harried walk, his hair an unkempt wave, as if someone had only just startled him from a nap. "It cannot be so," the now sweating man said. He asked for a reiteration of this most unbelievable news. "I had no idea they could die."

"They do," Keema said, "and this one did."

"I'd like to see it for myself." The commander had a lot riding on this creature being installed, for Rabbit Gate suffered from not being connected to the Throne's network. With grim determination he opened the wagon's singed flap and recoiled from the odor that escaped.

"It smelled like that before it died," Keema told him.

"What awful creatures," the commander muttered, holding the back of his hand to his mouth, faint. He sent one of his men in his stead—the sentry scrambling back out a moment later, green-faced, confirming to his superior the news.

The commander crossed his arms; he did his best impersonation of a leader. "I assume," he said, "there is protocol for this unfortunate event."

Jun clasped his hands behind his back, curious as to what Keema would say next.

"It's a body like any other," he said. "The thing was defective, it seemed, and prone to sickness. We'll dump it on our way east to the Bowl. Somewhere where no one will have to smell it again."

It took some time for the commander to agree, but in the end, seeing no other option, he did.

The orooks grumbled against the late-night hour and Jun's urging reins. Neither of the young men spoke as they rattled across the courtyard, their shoulders tense as they passed lines of guards who wrinkled their noses at them, and yet looked on with grim curiosity, and some disappointment, that they did not get to see the tortoise's corpse. But for all of the sniffing and squinting, none of the guards dared approach. Nearly as quick as Keema and Jun had arrived at Rabbit Gate had they left, tipping down the final slope of the rocky pass, toward the welcome sound of rushing water.

Spheres of torchlight lit the way down to the river shore. The dock was attended by but a single sentry, who asked to see their permission form if they wished to take out one of the boats before he was knocked out by the butt end of Keema's spear and stuffed inside an empty barrel. As Keema began moving supplies out onto the nearest skiff, Jun unmoored the other ships along the dock, kicking them out into the water, while She pushed the boats down a current of Her own making, far enough that no one could make use of them. They worked quickly, while back at Rabbit Gate, the guards began lowering the gates. The commander, apprehensive since learning of the unfortunate demise of his promised tortoise, paced around the courtyard, agitated, as the last of the braziers were lit. *My brother cursed me before he died, as punishment for sleeping with his wife. Before his last breath he slipped uncooked rice into my pocket, and he told me that I would never be settled in this life. It was impossible to not believe him.* He rubbed his arms, covered in goosepimples, and he flinched when his second approached him.

"Ready to close for the night," the boy said.

He nodded, distracted. "Good, good."

He could not escape the feeling that something was wrong.

At the dock, Keema and Jun were determining a way to move the giant tortoise from the wagon onto the boat they were illegally requisitioning when they felt the wind shift direction—wide ripples flowing out into the black river water, cutting against the natural current. The old woman's eyebrow twitched. *He was here. I told them there was no time.*

"We need a ramp," Jun said helplessly. "We can slide it onto the boat."

In the end there was no need for a ramp. Both of the young men stepped back as the limp tortoise began to levitate out of the wagon, held aloft by the empress.

Never let it be said that I was without mercy.

The great wheel turned under the strained effort of four men, but the gate's lowering stopped halfway, the process halted without ceremony upon a large, booming sound that made the commander begin to perspire. His sentries murmured in confusion over the jammed wheel. They shouted that they had need of a mechanic to take a look inside the pulley system.

"Abyss take it all," the commander muttered as he crossed the courtyard to meet them.

That was when he heard the whisper on the wind, like a whip on the ear.

Out of the way, please.

From the dark burst the Brigade of Red Peacocks. Their arrival so sudden that there was no scream or yowl from any of the guards on duty that night; just the instinctual recoiling as they either dove out of the way or were trampled under hoof.

It was then that the tortoise began to stir, believing for a weightless moment that it had died back in the checkpoint—that it had left its mortal form and joined the warm and dark waters of the One Mind, floating on its soft, rippling currents of thought and memory—until it heard the shouting, and the broil of hoofbeats, and it realized it was not dead but very much alive, a fearful burp caught in its throat as it saw that it was hovering over the rotted planks of the boardwalk, heading toward the berth of a wide skiff, suspended over all by Her ancient and steady power. It mewled, its voice delirious and sloppy, while the brigade poured down the hill like a spill of red wine. Jun went ahead of the tortoise, moving netting on the boat out of the way as the flailing creature was lowered onto the boards. The wood groaned under its weight, one of the benches cracking under it. The boat bobbed deeply, the displaced river water splashing against the dock struts.

"*Stay there.*"

The voice shot into Keema's ear like a bee, with a powerful gust of wind. He took up the ax on the ground and chopped at the restraining ropes. The boat began to sigh away from the dock. He scrambled aboard as Jun lifted one of the poles and pushed them out into the water, just as the brigade reached the last slope of the hill. Keema picked up the second pole, and together he and Jun worked the boat out into dark water. The Defect, dazed, asked again and again what was going on as Keema and Jun poled frantically into the heart of the river, Keema, sweating deeply, glancing back at the shore, where he, in a heart-stopping moment, witnessed the eerie sight of the brigade, torchlit and quiet, gathered at shore's edge.

It was like he was watching a play, some experimental entertainment on some pleasure barge, where the crowd parted until there was just one actor, one man, climbing off his horse and standing in the center of this clearing. Unsheathing a wicked blade that seemed kissed by starlight. The First Terror held up his free hand, and their boat stopped. And as the man's hand drew inward, so did the water, the surface of the river trembling as the current began to reverse toward the shore. Keema and Jun fought against the inverted water, but to no avail, their poles dragging backward along the riverbed. And then they stopped, the boat twirling in place, stuck in the middle of the water, coming no closer, going no farther, as a single bead of sweat ran down the empress's temple, *as I did all I could to counter him.*

The Terror boomed with laughter at this unexpected development. Then, impossibly, he stepped out onto the water as if it were solid and sure, and he sprinted across gentle waves. Each step was light, provoking on the water's surface only the slightest of ripples. A rock skipping across a royal pond. An avenue of tiny detonations. And he leapt as if pushed up into the air by some swell of water and wind, and fell toward a startled Keema.

His blade, drawn.

But it was dark, and the blade was long. It sank into the thick, calcified, and unyielding materials of the Defect's carapace, Keema's face not so much as a few inches below the blade's hungry edge, the First Terror's arm dislocated from the sword's impact with the shell, his shoulder popping. He laughed with a crazed delight before he withdrew a smaller blade, not much longer than a dagger, with his other arm and stabbed it at Keema's face. Keema ducked out of the way, and the blade pinged against the shell. He scrambled to the other side of the boat while the Terror gave chase, searching blindly for the spear or the hatchet, but before he could reach the weapons, a sharp wind knocked him off his feet. He twirled in the air and slammed onto the floor of the boat, the vessel bucking under him, the First Terror's hand gripping the air, using the wind to drag Keema toward him as if on a leash—until Jun tackled the older man.

The Terror let out an airless humph. In his and Jun's deep-grunted wrestling the water around the boat behaved erratically. Spouts of water shot up into the sky in violent geysers. The boat spun down the river as the brigade, unable to do much more than helplessly watch their father engage in battle, followed the boat on their horses at a light trot down the river's bend. The First Terror punted his knee into Jun's belly, eliciting a gasp so painful even the tortoise winced, and with a pitiless backhand, reflexive, almost as if he were disciplining a spoiled child, he slapped Jun across the head—the wooden mask snapping off, thudding against the floor of the boat.

Jun slowly stood up, lowering his hand from his face. The First Terror's eyes widened as he looked down on the young man with the tattoo of a red peacock's wing on his face. The tip of the wing ending just at the far corner of his left eye.

"My son," he said. His voice choked. "My son."

His words cut off, when Keema, from the side, swung his ax.

The flower was cut from the stem.

Its red petals strewn.

The Terror's head rolled between Jun's feet, blinking at him. Keema, with labored breath, dropped the hatchet. It clattered onto the wood, next to the body, which was slumped against one of the benches, its severed neck spurting red.

Keema looked at the now-maskless Jun, and after some mysterious calculation behind his eyes, the former Peacock picked up his father's head and he held it up into the air so that all of the brigade might see it. And along the coast, the horsemen slowed to a dead stop as they bore witness to their lost brother, who now held their father's decapitated head in his hands. *We did not believe it. We could not believe it.* The sons watching in a broken silence as the boat sailed down the river, propelled by the empress's blessing.

"I lost," the First Terror's head whispered, the man dumbfounded by the first lost battle in his life. He would have time yet to ruminate on such a failure, in private, once Jun opened the lid of an empty rice jar and placed the stunned head inside, covering it up with the lid, unable to stomach the sight of him. As for the body, together they lifted up the arms and the legs and let the corpse drop into the water to feed the many hungry fish that lived amongst the twisting weeds.

"There's blood on my beak," the tortoise muttered.

They could no longer see the brigade. There was now only the network of rivers ahead of them that was named, appropriately, the Thousand. Jun fitted his mask back on before he could face Keema again. And there the day did end, with the two warriors staring at each other with a wary and distrustful gaze once more while somewhere, in the dark space between this world and the Sleeping Sea, She wept, in both grief and joy, for the end of Her son, the First of the Terrors.

THE SECOND DAY

—

in which we offer our finest catch

The father leaves the stage.

It was sudden, such things always are, though you knew it was coming—ever since your lola passed, he was not the same. He rarely smiled. He spent most of his days not at work but at home, listening to the radio. Listening to the advertisements for the war effort and who can help and how. At dinner he rarely talked about the merchant's game. Instead he would talk about the front. He would talk about glory. He would talk about being a part of something bigger than himself.

And then, like that, he became a part of something bigger than himself. He joined the war. He left at night, without telling anyone; a coward's exit that you witnessed only by chance, awake as you were by the window, watching one of the neighborhood cats leap up the balconies—that was when you saw your father, walking away from the house, with a bag packed for his one-way trip. He stopped in the middle of the road and turned to look at your house, in remembrance, in farewell, and the two of you made eye contact. He made no expression, none that you could see at least, but he did open his mouth, to say what, perhaps even he did not know, for he merely closed it again without saying a word. And then he was gone, swallowed by the shadows of the alley, the sound of his heavy footstep on cobbled road the last of him that you remember. It seemed then, and even now, as but a dream. Your father was gone in one willful movement, and you heard a small snip, somewhere inside of yourself, which was the sound of your life untethered from this earth.

Fathers leave in all sorts of ways. Some of them leave in the dark. Some leave only in their heads, while their bodies remain, staring at the world around them forever distantly. Others fade out over time, like an old photo rubbed raw.

Many, gone in an instant.

If there is anything you understand about the Red Peacocks, truly understand, it is the quality of their silence in the moments that followed their father's beheading. You understand what it means for one moment to pass into another and for the world in that quick transition to take on a new blue color and weightlessness.

Yes, you know this quiet.

The sons of the First Terror stood at the edge of the water, unable to comprehend the image of their brother holding up their father's head. Dumbly they watched the body tossed overboard, sinking like a rock into the dark water. There went the man to whom their lives were in total devoted, the disturbed waters flattening out, the world now a large and nauseating place. One of the Peacocks doubled over and threw up. Others began to shake. The eldest of them began to strip, readying to dive into the water to retrieve the body. *I would not allow him to be pecked at by fish*. But none of them said anything, just as you had said nothing when your own father had left, for there are moments in this life that speak clearly for themselves.

On the boat, which slipped into the untrackable maze that was the Thousand Rivers, the empress, witness to the sundering of the second of Her children in so many days, said nothing either, Her tempests kept private in some distant inner realm.

The First Terror, who to Her would always be the babe named Saam, was in many ways a stranger to Her. After She had birthed him and his brothers, with the promise from the emperor that She would be freed once She had done so, she knew her sons only as vague presences of heat and life on the other side of the Wolf Door. Once, when he was little, of six years of age, Saam snuck out of his room at night, and ventured down into the cavern to see Her. Even then he was powerful enough to dispatch the guard charged with protecting Her door, skewering him with a spear of water before he walked up to the door and placed his hand on the snout of one of the many golden wolves, and She winced, from the depth of Her feeling, as he asked Her if She was there, and if She loved him. He fell asleep curled against the door, and the next day he was discovered by his father, and was brought away to be punished—a punishment severe enough that he never tried to come back down again.

That was what the empress thought of, as passing river birds bowed their heads, and fish parted from their prow.

As for Keema and Jun, the revelations that night were still as raw as freshly skinned lemons.

Words would not do justice to the moment.

So they fought.

The old woman made no effort to stop them this time. *They remained little boys to the end. Their foolish battling was rocking the boat, but they would not listen to me, and I had not enough in me to stop them with any grand eruption, still recovering was I from moving that blasted tortoise and destroying those boats. So I let them have their moment.* In the impenetrable dark, the near-blind

Keema and Jun fought in a desperate way, more vicious than they had the morning before. Blows came from nowhere as they tussled blindly around the tortoise's girth. It seemed not to notice, or care, when Keema kicked Jun into its hard shell; nor did it pay them any mind as Jun rebounded and tackled Keema between the boat's wooden benches, his mask slipping free again, his face dug into the crook of Keema's neck, his breath hot on Keema's skin as he punched the Daware man's side as if working out a dent in his partner's body, while Keema grabbed at the rolled-up fishing net behind his head and shook the webbing loose, then wrapped the net around Jun's head, ensnaring his face, only for Jun to bite right through it.

If one were to stop these young men and ask them why they sparred with such violence, they would struggle for an answer. Perhaps, after coming up with nothing, Jun would say that it was his familial duty to protect his father's honor; that etiquette demanded he combat the young man who felled him. Or Keema, struggling to reply, might finally say that upon discovering Jun's true identity as a Red Peacock, as a dangerous agent, he had no choice but to make a token effort in taking him down. But the truth of the matter was they fought because Jun was grieving and Keema was terrified and Jun was exhilarated and Keema was joyful and Jun was exhausted and Keema was repulsed.

They fought because it was the easiest language they spoke.

But even young bulls have limits to their earthly energies, and soon their breaths ran ragged, and they found themselves standing in the middle of the boat with heads resting on each other's shoulders, taking unenthusiastic swipes at each other's bellies while the boat continued on its gentle journey down the river current. As they caught their breath, the sounds of night gradually came alive around them. A family of toads ribbited from tall grass, while a marshland bird craned its neck and sang out a mournful warble. And then, without notice, Jun put his palm against Keema's chest. The Peacock's hand remained there for a moment longer than Keema expected it to, on the hot and sweat-damp skin, trapping under its palm the rapid beat of Keema's heart, before that hand shoved him away without ceremony. Keema, wide-eyed, tripped backward over one of the benches. He fell on his ass. In the mess of netting, he began to laugh.

I asked the children if they were done.

Her words shook the last bits of fighting mood from their hearts. Jun put out a hand, Keema got up on his own, and together they lit the lantern at the bow of the boat, cracking the candle afire with some spark stones they found in a small satchel beneath one of the bench boards. The lantern lit the dark riverway and the avenue of tall weeds, allowing them to take stock of their supplies: other than the food and water from the wagon, there was a mud jar filled with dead bait, a rolled-up net, and a replacement hook for the pole lashed to the side of the boat. Jun checked the health of the boat, testing the ties on the pontoons with his foot, bouncing a few times. When the leftmost pontoon bumped up against a sudden turn in the river, he grabbed for the pole, about to push the boat away from the land, but he was beaten to the task by the empress, who, with but a thought, pushed the boat back on its course. *I told them that I would steer for the night. Jun attempted to protest, but I allowed no argument. They were in no state to get me to the eastern shore alive. I needed them rested and not stupid from exhaustion.* Jun had no choice but to relent; he lashed the pole back to the outer lip of the boat before he sat down opposite Keema on the benches.

The boat's lantern, whose incense warded off the more irritating of the bugs that swarmed about, was the brightest object in the Thousand that night. To the predator birds that passed high above, they looked like an orange dagger, cleaving through a black sheet of sheer Induun fabric.

The light was just enough to see each other.

By the delicate glow, Keema saw Jun's face in full for the first time since the start of their journey. It was an unexpected face. Not because of the peacock tattoo; Keema had already suspected his identity, if not outright then ambiently, like an itch without a name or location, until suddenly there it was. The unexpected quality was more from the delicacy of his features. The small, slightly upturned nose. The tapered chin. The eyes that reminded him of broken porcelain. This delicacy of his offset by certain scars, like the one that split the rightmost part of his bottom lip, and the hook scar on his left eyebrow. A fainter scar that ran down his neck. A chunk of his right ear, the lobe, missing. A body that had seen battle. Keema had difficulty looking away. His mouth was dry. These sensations were strange to him. He was then aware that the blood of this person's father was still drying on his hand. He stuck his hand into the river's black water and washed his face, then splashed water on the back of his neck. When he was done, he was disappointed to see that Jun had put his mask back on.

"Why do you wear it?" he asked.

Jun's muffled voice replied, "A peacock amongst its ostentation is mighty, but a peacock alone will be torn apart by those he once hunted." He was quoting someone, and though he did not tell Keema who, Keema could guess those were his father's words. "Our journey would be much harder if everyone we encountered knew that I was once a part of their nightmares." Keema thought this was a fair point. Jun added, somewhat quieter, "And that aside, I no longer wear this tattoo with pride." He paused. "I would rather it never be seen again."

"You will wear this mask for the rest of your life then?"

Jun looked away.

"If I must," he said.

They readied for bed. Keema nestled between the benches of the boat, rolling up the fishnet into a makeshift pillow. He listened to the night. The breeze breaking through the tall grass avenue. The lapping of the water on old, near-rotted wood as the boat was pulled down the river by Her invisible hand. The small detonations of toads leaping off lily pads. And he found that he was not ready to sleep. Not yet.

He rolled over and looked through the bench gaps at Jun, who lay at the end of the boat. "When did you get it?" he asked. "That tattoo?"

He doubted he would get an answer. Not that night, anyway. But then he heard Jun shift.

"I was nine."

Back at shore, the Red Peacocks congregated by the dark river's edge, on their knees, in supplication. The warriors were silent, penitent, as the eldest amongst them dove into the brackish depths of the river and searched for their father's body.

"You get your first feather after your first kill. That's how it was for all of my . . . brothers, and so it was for me. The first feather earned you your horse, and your sword."

Some of the Peacocks still hoped it was a trick of the eyes. That their father was whole. That the play was only a play and the actor was backstage. That he was waiting for them at the bottom of the water with a game smile, a ready quip.

"He does it himself, the tattoo. It is only you and him in the room, and he looks at you like you are the strongest warrior he had ever known, and you believe him. You feel safe before he sticks you with the needle. He makes the pain . . . good."

Thirty-three sons standing by their horses beneath the torchlight of the docks remembered; little boys unsure what to do with themselves as they watched the bubbles break the surface of the placid river while their eldest brother's hands combed the riverbed, the rocks and the silt, searching; his fingers slipping between slick watergrass while fat bubbles of air quit his nostrils and the crooks of his open eyes, until, inside the thickest patch of watergrass, his hand wrapped around a cold ankle.

"The tattoo was the proudest day of my life. I liked that when people saw it, they knew not to fuck with me. They knew who my father was."

The river surface burst. The waterlogged body was brought up like some old treasure of the sea. The thirty-three sons fell on their knees before their father's corpse.

"They knew I would do everything in my power to serve his word."

It was then that, from far off in the dark, Keema and Jun heard the Peacocks' collective wail. Jun raised his head at the sound, then thought better of it and lowered his head again. "How foolish I was," he said, "for believing any of it."

Through the gaps in the bottom of the benches Keema could see the small of Jun's back.

"Who was your first kill?" he asked.

This, he did not expect an answer to, and was not put off when Jun, after a moment of quiet, said:

"Another time, maybe."

"Why not now?" the voice said.

Keema was for a moment not sure if he had not fallen asleep by accident—that he had not somehow dreamt the muffled voice that came from the rice jar at the tortoise's side—until he heard Jun say, in a rigid, near-fearful voice, "Do not respond to him."

"It was a boy, not much older than he," the voice in the jar went on. "A thief who had pocketed the ring of some minor lord. Do you remember, Jun, how I gave you my favorite knife? How I showed you where on the boy's body to slip the blade for the quickest death? Do you remember how the child fell to his knees and begged you for mercy? He called you 'my lord.' 'Please, my lord,' he said, like a prayer. The fool had no idea what mercy was. He wriggled, didn't he? He even fought back a little, he got a few good hits too. But I stopped anyone from interfering. I wanted you to earn it. And you did. You pinned him to the ground and you stuck him with a knife, many times, until he—"

Enough, I said.

Her Royal Whisper cut short his grim tale, and the head in the jar, still obedient to his mother's word, said not another word about Jun's kill, for even in this state, even defeated, he could not help but listen to Her. He had only one thing left to say, and he said it quickly, and quietly, as if to slip a note through a closing door.

"I do not know what you think you are doing here, Jun, or what you are trying to prove, or to whom. But what I do know is that you earned every single one of those feathers on your face. You are a Peacock to the end."

After that, he said nothing more, and Keema, hoping that the night was over, rested himself once more on the rolled-up fishing net in a bid to catch some rest before morning—his mind at the edge of sleep, when he heard amongst the choir of night bugs and birdcall the sniffling from the other end of the boat, and a whisper, Jun's voice like a croaked prayer, as he said, to the night, to no one, "I am sorry . . . forgive me . . . I am sorry."

DAWN

The Prince of the Honeyed Word breathed out.

Long and low was the sigh of Luubu Ossa, the Second Terror, and full rich with pleasure, for he had learned that his father was dead, and the news, even a day later, had yet to lose its flavor.

"The guests will be arriving in two turns of the glass, my lord," his attendant said. "How would you like to spend your time till then?"

He leaned on the ship's railing.

"I think I'd like to paint," he said softly.

It was early enough that many of the servants aboard the *Cav-Meer* were only beginning to wake, the cleaning girls yawning as they carried buckets of water into the guest rooms and the kitchen staff preparing breakfast in quiet diligence, pots bubbling as their knives chopped through stalks and roots with the easy precision of those who had dedicated their lives to the craft. *We were the best that the country had to offer. No expense was spared for this momentous day.*

In one of the guest rooms, which was recently redone to the Second Terror's beguiling specifications, the windows were striped with iron bars, and a series of small holes had been carved out, through which the briny air of the Bowl whistled. One of the cleaning girls, new to the ship, shook her head as she dusted the corners of the room. *Made no sense, that room—you could hear everything that was happening outside. I thought: what noble would want to stay in a place like that?* Indeed the room was loud with the shouts of ferrymen, the ringing of the bells of changing guard rotations, the slap of the water against the hull of the ship. She asked the older girl what the point of the holes was, only to be shushed, kindly but firmly.

"No questions," the older girl whispered, pointing at the pipes along the wall that carried all manner of sound. "Just work."

The easel and paints were brought out and propped in his favorite place on deck, underneath a wide sun umbrella. Luubu picked up the horsehair brush and got to work; his subject nothing less than the light and shadow of the Bowl of Heaven. He was a good painter, trained by royal tutors, and was amongst the vanguard exploring realistic depictions of depth in their work. His brushstroke captured the way the dawn light necklaced the rim of the great crater and dripped in long sheets down the crater's walls. He made sense of the colorful shatter of light that was reflected off the stained-glass windows of the royal pleasure cruises. He understood the geometries that composed the hulking forms of the apartment barges. The bold, multicolored strikes of the Induun family junk ships. The dark smear of the imperial prison fleet. The silver banners of the royal veraschafts. The smoke that rose in long curls from the snuffed-out night-watch braziers. The morning patrol boats that rowed their scheduled routes in small gangs, like flocks of waterfowl, gliding between their behemoth brothers, poling the dark water for contraband.

His brush suddenly stopped, mid-sweep. He squinted at the horizon. He gestured for his attendant and muttered into his ear.

"Understood, my lord."

The attendant walked down to the lower deck, to the tortoise's perch, from where he sent a message across the waters of the Bowl to the captain of the seventh apartment barge of the northwest arc. And then, without question, the captain piloted the barge a few degrees starboard side, until, from the deck of the *Cav-Meer*, Luubu nodded, satisfied with its angle, and how it blended in with the other ships.

He resumed painting. It was a consuming task. He paid only small mind to the breakfast of fruits and honey and sweet rice cakes laid out beside him on standing trays. Not even the fattened flies that drank the syrup bothered him as he focused on the horsehair brush and the canvas. It was not until his attendant informed him that the Families were arriving that he even considered stopping—he looked over the railing and watched with an imperious expression the procession of boats that had come to dock alongside his own.

They were all there, disembarking from their finely hewn vessels, with extended family and their porters; the lords of the Five Houses, the Yinns and the Maadas and the Panjet-Waags, and, before them all, the most powerful, and his least favorite, if the way he squeezed his brush in his fist was any evidence.

Induun.

The name gives you a familiar pang. It is a name you've heard sporadically throughout your life, the first memory coming ready to mind the cold trail of months that followed your father's sudden departure. Those were the months you became aware of money, and scarcity, when your uncle convinced one of your older brothers to give him access to the family coffers—to help, always to help— and disappeared not long after with all your coin. Not long after that, the hired help disappeared, the dust accumulated on the shelves, and your little brother sneezed, as it fell to you to dress him in the early morning. Your older brother, ashamed for falling for your uncle's tricks, took charge of the house's accounts. He sold off his precious motorbike, along with old family heirlooms, so that you all might have something to eat that week.

"Proper Induun weave," you recall him saying in the foyer as he tried to convince the prospective buyer to raise his price—using much the same language as your father once did at the height of his negotiations. "Made from a true loom of the Sisters' House. Come, feel it in your hands. Tell me that is not worth the extra coin."

"This is as much Induun as the cheap foot rugs down in Hawker's Alley," the buyer said. You could practically hear him shaking his head. "I won't pay more than seven fifty for it."

"Then you won't pay anything at all for it," your brother told him fiercely. "You will leave this house without this priceless carpet, and you will be all the poorer for it."

A risky gambit, one that you were sure was not going to pay off, but the buyer finally relented, for even hundreds of years later, the name of Induun still held its weight as that of quality craftsmanship, and your brother knew it.

Let this clarify Luubu's irritation as he watched the Induun family board his ship. He was the Second Terror, the ruler of the Bowl, every ship at his ready command, and yet—and yet—he was forced to recognize the fact that he shared that power. He shared it with the Five Families, but most of all with Induun, who owned and operated the massive textile fleets of the Bowl and the trawlers that dredged the crater's watery depths for the gelatinous worms that produced the high-quality thread the weavers of the fleet used to create their masterpieces. Even the workers were aware of the balances of power. *It was to the Second Terror that we put out our hands in worship, but it was to Induun that we put out our hands in service.* Luubu's brush tapped against the railing as he watched the Families board the *Cav-Meer*. He wondered if he could get away with it—poisoning them all today, in one fell swoop, during breakfast. He sighed and reminded himself to have patience; he had come this far. Once things were settled, maybe; once everyone knew how close he was to holding their leash.

Later.

For now, the performance.

On the *Cav-Meer*'s spacious deck, Luubu informed the nobility and the Families that the emperor and the First Terror were delayed, and that they would be enjoying a private celebration later on. "The Smiling Sun, in His infinite generosity, would have us instead enjoy the good company and wonderful performance that was meant for Him." His voice somber, reverential; a well-practiced mask; though even he would not be able to hide his glee, if he knew that his brother was at that moment a headless chicken.

The breakfast was laid out in bowls and mats before the many personages in attendance, along with fresh-caught trout and carp, steamed and with bellies slit open, bursting with moist white flesh. Serving boys and girls holding carafes of rice wine and fresh water circulated through the many cousins and siblings, pretending to be unseeing and unhearing founts of food and drink as they filled the cups and wandered through the many strained conversations held that day. *We were all playing the game now, attempting to discern who knew what—if anyone had any news of why the palace tortoises yet remained silent.* The nobility of the Old Country were scared, but they maintained their facades of decorum and jollity, hiding behind their feigned blushes and laughing not too loudly at rude jokes, while Luubu, who of late did not have much of an appetite, sat quietly on his throne of pillows, where he was served a simple tajeline; his porcelain spoon swirling around the creamy innards in an uninterested way while the important members of the various families approached him, one by one, and made their expected overtures.

"Lord Djove Induun, of the Textile Fleet,"
the attendant announced.

The de facto head of the Families approached first, as was dictated by court etiquette. The short, unassuming man was dressed in plain garb that day, almost in defiance of the fact that his workers created the most beautiful fabrics in the country. Luubu did not like him for this false display of modesty, and he did not like his expression, which was one of ever having overcome some grave disappointment, and he did not like his wife, whom he considered ugly, with too many teeth—the same for his ward, that tall, ungainly girl who acted as his bodyguard.

"Welcome aboard the *Cav-Meer,* my lord," Luubu said with a forced smile. "How fares the textile trade these days?"

"What?" Lord Induun said gruffly, cupping his ear.

The man was hard of hearing since childhood, a result of almost drowning in the Sereven River—*no one liked to speak of it, but I know that it was his sister who tried to kill him, I saw it happen as I took in their laundry, I saw his sister push the little boy deep into the river water*—the sounds of the world, ever since, coming through to him as if through a thick sheet. A tragic tale with a silver lining, for the injury rendered him impervious to Luubu's Word—and Luubu, who relied so much on bending others to his will through simple inflection, had to rely on more traditional tactics to get his way with him.

"I said, 'How fares the textile trade?'"

"Adequate, my prince," came the annoyed reply. "A break was in order, my thanks for the invitation to this little get-together you've thrown here."

The word "little" struck its target. The attendant holding the tajeline grimaced.

"Think nothing of it," Luubu said, after a moment.

But Induun was uninterested in the prince's hurt feelings. "I was hoping to speak to your father," he said. "He has been well delayed in signing off on the newest lease agreements between my House and the Throne. A pity He could not make it."

"His Smiling Sun lives by a demanding schedule."

"One would hazard that guess, by proof of His lack of attendance to the events you hold." The man offered one of his rare smiles. "A demanding schedule indeed."

"Come, my lord, there is no need to fire across the bow. Not today of all days. We are here to celebrate His Smiling Sun, are we not?"

"A strange sort of celebration, when the guest of honor is not in attendance."

"As I said, He was delayed. I know you will see Him before the week is out."

"You have always prided yourself on knowing. But this time I can't help but wonder if you know as much as you believe."

His smile, mysterious, and not forthcoming, unnerved Luubu, and in a moment of weakness, he flexed his Word.

"Go fuck your brother to death."

The fan that cooled Luubu's throne stopped, and the attendants within earshot stared in horror as Lord Induun's eyes widened. His hand, trembling, coming up to his face, while Luubu sat forward, a hungry smile on his face as he wondered if he had actually done it, if he had broken through—only for Induun's hand to cup his ear once more.

"I'm sorry, I didn't catch that."

Luubu sat back against his pillows. He waved his hand as if batting a fly. "I said show in the next one."

"Lord Erso Maada, of the Fisheries."

Convinced now that the lord of textiles was up to something, Luubu decided to find out what he could from the other lords; he began with Lord Maada of the Fisheries, ox of a man, famous for his short temper and his penchant for slamming doors off their hinges, for though he was strong of body, he was not strong of mind. He slipped under the sway of Luubu's Word with little effort, and upon asking him "Is Lord Induun plotting against me?" the man, famous for withstanding a thousand blows at the Battle of Jongo Bridge, crumpled as he said, "Your suspicions are correct. Lord Induun is plotting against you." But when Luubu asked him in what manner this plotting would take place, the large man frowned, as if fighting with himself, and he shook his head. "I do not know. We agreed that it would be best if only he knew the details of the treason."

"We?"

"He . . . approached me to join his cause. I have not yet committed. But even if I had, he would have told me nothing."

"Because he is resistant to my influence, and you are not."

"Yes, my prince."

Luubu took this in. "He aims to kill me."

"Yes, my prince."

"And I take it all the heads of the Families are together on this. You and Yinn and the Panjet-Waags."

Sweat poured down the ox's face.

"We are, my prince."

He took this news in, in grim silence, and told Lord Maada to forget this conversation—which Maada did, the words he and the prince had shared curling up and dying off the vine of his mind before he had even reached his seat cushion, forgetting he had just betrayed the confidence of his fellows.

"Lord Albra Yinn, of the Terrace Lands."

Luubu confirmed what he had learned with the jelly-spined Lord Yinn, who would not have even needed the provocation of his Word to give up all his secrets—though he had few that were of any use to him. For his own entertainment he told Yinn, **"Rub your nipple,"** which the lord of rice did with abandon as he spoke. "Induun spoke to all of us after it became known that the emperor was planning to leave the country. He told us that he would take care of everything. That if we followed his word, then by the end of His Holy Pilgrimage it would be the Families who wielded control of this country."

"What do you know of the commotion in the palace?"

"But rumor," the lord answered as his finger attacked his nipple beneath his robe. "A skirmish. Deep within the palace. Frightful bloody business, they say."

"Do any of you know that the emperor is dead?"

Lord Yinn nodded, with a groan. "We all do."

*"Lady Suso Panjet, of the Tea Estates,
and Lord Kasma Waag, of the Quarries."*

Lord Waag, already drunk off the rice wine, had little to offer Luubu other than the fact that Induun had been plotting his coup for many months; but his wife, Lady Panjet, had something of more substance to add. She chuckled from behind her sleeve as if she were a blushing maiden many years her junior and said, demurely, that her world was small, decidedly so, for she was concerned with only the growth of her precious leaves. "I have no time for such politicking. It seemed only best to leave those matters to Lord Induun."

Luubu sighed. "So you know nothing of Induun's plan to assassinate me."

Her voice lost a step. "That is not quite true."

He finally deigned to look at her. "What do you know?"

"I know that it will happen today."

He almost coughed on his drink.

"Today?"

"A supposition on my part," she said. "Induun has not told me the truth of the matter, wisely, for now I cannot tell you the truth of the matter, can I? No matter how you pressed me for information." She seemed reluctant to add that last part.

"Then what leads you to believe that my assassination will happen today?"

"The release of the schedule of His Holy Pilgrimage," she answered. "I knew for some time that on the Second Day we would be gathered on the *Cav-Meer* for the day's celebrations. All of us lords and ladies. And you. It seemed the ripest time to strike."

Something was off about this description—an illogic. "But until recently," Luubu said, his brow knit, "you would have assumed the emperor would be in attendance. Were you planning on striking Him down, too, at the same time? Striking me alone I can almost fathom, but striking my father at the same time . . . You would've been slaughtered."

This mere thought made Lady Panjet sweat. "Again," she said, "I know not of Induun's plans. But it was clear to me—and I suspect to Induun—from the start that the emperor would not be here."

Luubu narrowed his eyes. "How was this clear to you?"

She looked at him innocently. "Because His Smiling Sun never comes to your parties."

A bell chimed.

It was time. The nobility took their seats beneath the line of sun umbrellas while on the other side of the deck the dancers prepared behind the folding screen. *We held one another's hands and felt each other's fear. We pretended it was a game, just like we used to do under the kolba tree, with Haas and Djina—a performance like any other.* Two women and one man, dressed alike in fine, silk-shimmer robes, emerged one by one from behind the screen while Luubu simmered on his pillows, still bruised from Lady Panjet's casual blow—even telling her to shit herself had provided little comfort, no matter how humorous he found her waddle as she left his company. Scowling, he at first gave only cursory attention to the performers, but they were of such high skill he could not help but be pulled into their dance.

The prince was smiling—we were doing well! Each move connected into the next with grace, bringing to mind the image of a carp leaping out from one body of water to the next. Who was the carp and who was the water changed throughout the dance. Sometimes it was the man who was skipping through water, sometimes he was the water, sometimes the women were the sun and sometimes they were the currents pushing against the carp's struggle. *Our fears dropping away the further in we went, for this was what we loved most.* The dance terminating in a violent and triumphant burst that brought the gentry to their feet, with Luubu clapping along, which made the performers beam with pleasure. He got up and met them on this impromptu stage while an attendant followed him with a paper umbrella.

"A worthy dance for the Fisher's Day this Holy Week," he said. "The three of you should be quite proud of yourselves."

We bowed and we told him that we were very proud.

"Yes," he said. "I am sure that the emperor will be eager to see it for Himself one day, when I tell Him of it."

He had heard they had to pull his father's teeth from out of the wall of the cavern of the Wolf Door. He remembered this now, to cheer himself up.

"Triplet dancers," he said, looking at the three beautiful young people before him. "Quite the thing. Looking at you now, I cannot help but think that your parents must be god and goddess indeed. Please, go ahead, you may speak."

One of the women bowed. "In our humble opinion, my lord, they were, but we thank you for saying so nonetheless. It is an unbounded generosity."

He wasn't listening. "Though surely you did not come out all at the same time. One of you is the oldest, one's the youngest. One is the . . . middle."

It was a strange observation, and it made them and the crowd laugh nervously to hear it, though it was not intended as a joke. They told him that yes, she was born first, she second, and he third, he being the "youngest" of the three of them. "But only by brief moments. We do not recognize such divisions." They glanced at one another with reflexive fondness. "We are one in cause."

"Except when deciding who will do laundry," ventured the man.

The gentry laughed appropriately.

"I wonder," Luubu said, his voice trailing off into the clapping waters. A bird squawked from high above, its shadow flashing across the deck. "I'm envious, I suppose. I have always had some difficulty negotiating a relationship with my own brothers. Even my parents." The audience shifted in their seats, the dancers averting their gaze to the polished deck floor. It was as if he had disrobed in front of them. No one was sure what to do with this sudden admission from a royal prince. "Being in the middle," he continued, unbothered by the change in mood, "it is easy to be looked over, is it not? Forgotten. It is never intentional, I understand that. It is just the way the eye and mind work. We look at the beginning"—he gestured at the eldest of the triplets—"and the end"—the youngest of them—"but never the middle," he finished, with his eyes settling on hers, *and I had to stop myself from taking a step back, from recoiling from that silver gaze.*

"Could you dance for me again?" he asked.

The triplets glanced at one another, *wondering what we had done wrong, for we were certain that we had not made one mistake in our performance.*

"It would be our pleasure," the eldest said.

"But just her," he said, looking at the middle child. "Today we give the stage to the unseen and the passed-over. Today we celebrate the shadow."

He gestured for the music to start up again and for the dancer to take her place, and when he returned to his pillows he did not recline; he did not touch his bowl of fruit; he sat up in full attention as the "middle child" emerged from behind the folding screen, this time alone. If there was any doubt as to her talents based on what time she was born in comparison to her siblings, those doubts were soon erased, for she somehow took up all three parts in herself, switching ably between them so that there was never any confusion in the narrative, none of the grace lost in the translation from three to one. *We were so proud of her that day.* If there were any mistakes, any trips or slips, they were inevitable; snags that anyone would encounter performing solo such a complicated move set, the mistakes thus easily forgiven in the face of all of her immense skill. The applause was full-throated. Even her siblings were caught up in the display, and clapped with the rest of the crowd, no one clapping harder than Luubu himself, who was at the brink of tears. "Brilliant! Brilliant!" The woman breathed deep, flush and pleased by the reception. "Again!" Luubu shouted joyfully. "Do it again!"

This instilled some pause in the dancer, who was wiping sweat with a towel handed by one of the attendants. She looked to her siblings, but they could do nothing for her. The gentry, too, were not pleased to have to watch the same performance again, but all Luubu had to do was stand before them, and say, **"This is exactly what you want,"** and they all found themselves nodding until they believed the notion was their own. Djove Induun, who did not nod, sat in calm observance, occasionally leaning over to whisper something in his wife's ear, or to give an order to his ward, his attentions never entirely leaving the Second Terror, who returned to his pillows once more and gestured for the music to reset. The middle child returned to the folding screen. The fisher's dance was performed a third time. If anything, it was even better than the last, now that the dancer had an idea of what it meant to perform alone. She pressed herself into the floor at the end, her skin glistening with sweat as the morning sun marched ever upward and brought with it the heat of the day. "Phenomenal!" Luubu cried, leaping to his feet. "Again! Again!" He gestured to the gentry, and he said, **"You all want to see it again! Let her know how much!"**

The words seemed to transform them.

"Please! Again!" a distant nephew of Lord Yinn cried. "I must see it again!" The gentry were on their knees begging for the dancer to dance. *His words had infected us. We would've done anything he told us to do. We would've barked like dogs.* They begged and they demanded, and so, with quavering voice, she said, "If it pleases you all," and she went back to the folding screen, a slight trembling to her legs. *Behind the screen we held our sister, we asked her what we could do, but she shook her head. She said she could do it.*

The fourth time, it was clear she was getting tired; the dance was a long and difficult one. Some of the arcs she made with her hands, and the waves with her back, were less refined, choked by a growing exhaustion, her mouth parched from the hot sun, which now flooded the Bowl of Heaven with its searing light. *I could scarcely breathe.* Her siblings, standing to the side, were petrified for her. "Again." After the fifth dance, "Again," and the sixth, "Again," the eldest approached the throne of pillows with her head lowered in respect, and suggested that maybe her sister was getting a bit tired, and if it pleased her lord, she could return in a few days, tomorrow even, and dance for him in private then. "But tomorrow isn't today," he said, as if she were a lovely idiot, "and today I am in the mood to see her dance. I am a flawed creature, you know. My moods are capricious, my desires even more so. I have a hard time knowing what it is I want from moment to moment!" It was something he had been told by an old friend, before they had tried to kill him. He chuckled, and she mirrored his chuckling without confidence. "So I would much prefer to hold on to this moment while I can."

"It is only—the body can only withstand so much."

"I'm sure she's practiced the routine more times in one day than she has for me here. But I hear your worries. This is quite a different situation than a shaded practice room. It might be she just needs a boost in her confidence. From you, perhaps." He looked at her fully in the eyes, her wideness soon matching his, as he said, "**You think that she can dance for a longer while yet.**"

Her face changed upon hearing the words. Relaxed. Filled with utter belief. *It was like hearing wisdom for the first time in my life. A cool water on the mind.* "Yes. I think . . . yes, I am sure she can dance for a longer while yet."

"You will tell her that as the eldest, it is your duty to encourage her to keep dancing."

"What else is an older sister for, my lord?"

"Go on then. Let her know how you feel."

The crowd gathered on the deck that day watched as the older sister met with the younger and made her inspirational speech. Confused, hurt, the younger sister returned to the folding screen to prepare once more, while behind her, her beloved sibling smiled as wide as a lantern.

Dances eight, nine, and ten were expert, but there was a sense that the movements were descending into flails and spastic motions. The Terror said that it was just a matter of a lull. She would find herself in time. There were no breaks between the routines. No water. The attendant bowed to his ear-level and whispered, "My lord, I wonder if she is a bit tired now."

My feet were bleeding.

"My lord, perhaps a break is in order?"

I was painting the floor in red streaks.

"I think not," Luubu said to the insistent attendant. "And no more suggestions, or I will make you eat your own cock. I'll make you enjoy it too."

The attendant shrunk away.

The performance lasted another hour—enough time that even Luubu was beginning to get bored, though he could not admit it to the others, as this was all his idea. He was thankful when it ended rather abruptly, after a poorly timed fall snapped the dancer's shin bone. *I heard the loud pop before I felt it—and then I was on the floor, screaming.* She vomited from the pain and the heat, some of the nobles looking away or recoiling, a few even laughing, as she was dragged away, weeping, by her distraught siblings.

"Is that the best your fishermen have to offer, Lord Maada?" Luubu called out from his throne. The deck shook with raucous laughter, and the ox of a man, his face flush, stood up, walked across the bloody footprints on the floor, and bowed to the Second Terror. "I apologize on the dancer's behalf for that shameful display."

"Do you now?" Luubu stared at him from his pillows. With his Word, he commanded Maada, **"Say what you want to say."**

Maada's thick neck strained, like he was choking on his words.
"Let it out," Luubu said with a light smile. **"Don't hold back."**

"I—I think you are—a—d-d-demon."

The words caught the breath of every person in attendance.
Maada's wife, Zuza, stoic even when her child died of the Cough in
her arms, now bit her lip and put a hand to her chest, certain that
this was her husband's end.

"I am not a demon," Luubu corrected, feigning hurt. "I am a
god. Which makes your words blasphemous. You do know what
the punishment for blasphemy is?"

We knew. We knew where the flayed men writhed.

We knew of Joyrock.

"Please, my lord!" Zuza shouted. "He is a stupid man, not
worth your eye. Have mercy!"

Without looking at her, Luubu smirked. "A stupid man, she
says. Such a stirring defense from your banshee." He enjoyed looking down at the groveling Maada, and indulged in this feeling for a
little while longer before he then lifted his hand. "Oh, get up. Like
I care what you actually think. Go. Back to your seat. You and your
skin."

The large man grunted to his feet while Luubu congratulated
himself for this display of restraint, rewarding himself with more
tajeline cream, his hunger sudden and ravenous. He was so busy
with his fruit that he did not notice when the red-eyed, humiliated
Maada had given Djove Induun a quick glance on his way back to
his cushion. It was a glance that spoke volumes to those it involved,
for it was, in part, a giving-in. A concession.

An agreement.

Lord Induun lifted his chin in acknowledgment of this glance,
and Maada lowered himself beside his wife. She handed him a cup
of tea and did nothing more, for she knew from bitter experience
not to touch her husband when his pride had just been wounded.
There were days when I could not love him at all.

The mood soured after that. The people drank their tea and for
the most part kept silent as the river singers were brought out to
present the village storm songs, all of which were written for the

emperor, whose absence became more apparent the longer the morning wore on. It was to everyone's relief when the river singers were led away and Luubu suggested a break, having organized a visit to one of the nearby pleasure barges. Upon a tortoise communication, the *Cav-Meer* and the vast *Sudak Koyo* pleasure barge intercepted each other, and a bridge was formed so that the Families could cross back and forth at their leisure. "Will you not be joining us?" Lord Induun asked Luubu at the gangway, noticing that the prince was staying behind.

"Apologies, my lord," the Second Terror said. "Royal business calls."

"Off to the prison fleet again to see her?"

The words, as intended, flicked at Luubu's nerve. He frowned. He did not deign to answer. "Enjoy the barge," he said, walking away. "Enjoy the games up to the last of your coin."

"I will," Djove said.

He was a man of his word. He went in and he played the dice, and he smiled graciously when his numbers came up short. He enjoyed it all—but not before he nodded at his ward and the tall girl, unobserved, flipped a red teacup on a table by a certain window, and left it there, on its head.

Luubu's private ferry departed from the *Cav-Meer*'s hold shortly after all the nobility had boarded the barge, oblivious to the chain of signals the inverted red teacup had precipitated.

His ferryman knew where to take him without needing to be told, and the prince's private boat pushed off, threading between the wide berths of the *Cav-Meer* and the *Sudak Koyo* before it headed toward the northeastern quarter of the crater, where the low shapes of the prison fleet waited like crocodiles.

Luubu gazed up at the sun that rose above the rim of the Bowl—a breath escaping his lips at the beauty of the heavenly gilding. His finger twitched, yearning for a brush. He sighed.

If only he could capture this too.

From far off, a spyglass glinted.

The glass flashed in the dawnlight from the fifth deck of a distant apartment barge—impossible to distinguish from any other reflective surface that bright morning. The young girl holding the spyglass watched Luubu's private ferry disappear and reappear from behind various masts and passing hulls. *We were waiting for the convergence. The movements of the Bowl were such that every thirty minutes there were alignments. Clear sights down an avenue of vessels. Luubu's vessel was soon to pass through such a convergence.* "No deviation," the girl said.

The man beside her nocked his arrow. *When I was five I shot a man in the eye from across two fields—only reasonable that I had taken Induun's notice.* His arrow, the head of which was carved from moonrock and jaxite, strained against the V of the string, eager to fly. *The arrow was worth more than my parents' earnings; I did not intend to waste it.* The weapon was trained on the ballista boat that sailed across the emerald waters, on the prince who stood at its railing in observance of the dawn. *I had been working for this moment my entire life, and there it was.*

Redemption.

"No ships are crossing," the girl said. She studied the sails. "The wind is easterly, but only just so."

The man smiled as a bead of sweat rolled down his cheek.

There was no stopping now.

The string, tensed to its limit, begged for mercy.

The girl with the spyglass was holding her breath. "Wind is east-northeast," she said. "Whenever you're ready."

I was ready.

His fingers released the string.

The arrow lanced across the water.

As Djove Induun and the other lords and ladies played dice and watched theater aboard the *Sudak Koyo,* the private ferryman heard a sound. A peculiar noise, like a humph, followed by a wet snort. *There was but one rule to follow, and that was don't look at him unless he told you to look.* But the ferryman broke protocol. He looked back. He had to. His reward a vision of horror.

He looked upon the sight of the Second Terror, heaving at the floor; an arrow stuck in his throat.

"H-Help m-me," he said, through sucked breath.

MORNING

Change was coming.

It came upon a ripple from the north that danced across the fingertips of the waterweeds. If Keema and Jun had been awake, they perhaps would have felt the disturbance in the wind, that subtle flex and shift that, like it had the first night upon the death of the emperor, exclaimed some great change in the country. If the empress were not deep within Herself, living off the sustenance of old memories as She had learned to do in Her isolation behind the Wolf Door, perhaps She would have taken notice of it as well—perhaps would even have been able to taste Her child's blood in the air. But She was absent. Not even the head in the jar was keen to the ripple, trapped as he was in the replaying of last night's battle; the shame of the loss; the sharp bite of the ax on the back of his neck; his wondering of why his favorite son had betrayed him.

So it was that, in the deep morning of the Second Day, only our tortoise was present to the moment—the Defect of Heat Bed Three, perched on the boat like a rock on a child's hand, blinking as the world around it shivered. Prone to all manner of aches and pains and psychic false-positives, the creature lifted its head skeptically, more annoyed than curious as it looked north, in the direction of this "flick." Unable to see past the tall grass, or through the glare of the midmorning sun—its eyes still unadjusted to such pure, unfiltered light—it paid no further mind to the strange sensation, supposing the flick was another symptom of its deficiencies, or perhaps some errant signal from the Burn. With a slight grumble, it lowered its head and resumed its numbering of the many delights this avenue of water had to offer, for there were few things that tortoises liked more than counting. Eight bulbous toads, twenty-three scurrying fish, six spiderwebs glinting in the dew light, and—the Defect snapped at the air and swallowed—one fat-bellied fly.

It purred, deeply enjoying the sensuous world of the Thousand Rivers that enveloped the boat. Thirty-three cicadas trembled on thick stalks. The dark river water skipped with nine leaping frogs. Two minutes of gentle breeze kissed the tortoise's open wounds, the cracks in its chitinous shell, the ooze, and provided it a relief like none other. It snapped the air again; swallowed a second fly.

Yes. For the first time in its brief life, there was hope.

I watched the Defect from my half-wake.

The empress, only just reemerged from Her submersion, observed the awkward, heaving movements of the Defect; listened to its labored breath with annoyance, and pity. *How far the tortoises had fallen. In a reflective mood, I asked the creature if it knew who I was.*

The tortoise lifted its head at Her Whisper, though it had not the flexibility to look over its own shell to see Her.

"Yes," it giggled softly. "This one knows."

Who was I then?

"You are the Moon that fell on our mother's back."

You laugh.

The fall was always the funniest part of the tale. To this day you aren't sure if your lola made that part up to make you laugh or if it happened like she said it did, in that absurd way that life and myth often work out; an absurdity that made the tale so easy to recite to your little brother, long after she was gone, and you two were waiting in the ration line—he stopped crying once you got to the good part.

You told him how once the Moon came unstitched from the sky and all the people watched in horror as it hurtled toward land. Your fist mimed the moonfall's trajectory, your mouth playing out the rumble of its atmospheric entry, the other poor bastards in line glancing at you, annoyed by the sounds you were making, but you didn't care, you were desperate to entertain this kid. Your little brother's big eyes watched your fist fall toward the open palm of your other hand. You told him that for two days the people watched the Moon grow bigger and bigger, so hopeless they had even stopped begging to the gods and spirits of the world for mercy. Some made their peace with one another; others fought, not knowing what else to do. The sky burned red. The clouds broke apart like ripped fabric. It was all going to soon end.

Those were not your words but hers, and you were surprised by how little you had forgotten of your lola's telling. Your little brother sniffed and wiped his eyes and asked what happened next.

Of all the possible saviors, you told him, it was the most unlikely that deflected the apocalypse: a tortoise. Your little brother made a face, which made you only insist that it all was true—that the creature was as big as a house, with a shell as hard as iron, and that day, when everyone else had given up, it was the tortoise alone who made the slow march across the field that lay in the moonfall's path. Hundreds of years old and slower than a tugboat, but it made it.

The ration line came to you, the tale on pause as you pulled the frayed tickets out of your pocket and handed them to the woman behind the counter, who recognized you, your family. She asked you about the brother who ran away from the draft. She said she was still waiting for him to take her to dinner. Walking back to the house with more parcels of food than you were expecting, weaving through the gangs of soldiers clustered around town, your little brother asked you how a tortoise saved the world.

You remembered asking your lola the same question, with the same level of disbelief. You told him, as confidently as you could manage—trying not to laugh because you could see that he was more invested than you thought he'd be—that the tortoise's shell, famous amongst its clan for its impenetrability, absorbed the brunt of the moonfall's impact. But it didn't save everything. There was an explosion that forever marked the world, resulting in a bowl in the earth, and many rivers that ran fractal from it, the country scattered with moonrock.

The limits of your storytelling ability were proven that day when your little brother asked what became of the tortoise after the impact, and all you could remember was the smell of your lola's tobacco smoke. Stuttering for a conclusion, you told him that the tortoise was hailed a hero of the land and lived the rest of its days being fed grapes on a lavish pillow, which did well enough to satisfy him; happy endings often do in a pinch. But he wanted more detail, asked more questions, until mercy was finally granted when the other kids called him to play with them in the alley and he left your side without any further inquiry—though you knew as well as anyone that was not the true end to the tale.

I asked the Defect if it knew the rest.

The creature lifted its head high into the air—an exaltation—and answered the empress in the affirmative. "When our mother caught you on her shell," it said, "you asked her what boon she would have of you, and she told you that she missed her children, and would like to be able to speak to them whenever she pleased, and for her children, in turn, to be able to speak to one another. And so you granted her wish. . . . So yes, this one knows you very well," the tortoise said, "for you are the Moon who cursed us with this gift."

The body of the empress, that frail old form at the head of the boat, remained shut to the world, the eyes still closed, the legs still locked in their meditative cross. To look at the body offered no hint as to the regret that the old woman felt at that moment. *But I needed the creature to understand that I gave that gift out of gratitude. That it was not a curse but a blessing.*

"This one does not need reminding on that account," it said with acid to the old woman. "This one does not need to be told how to see the world."

I may have had regrets, but I still had my pride, and I would not be spoken to by some whelp in such an obstinate manner, so I told the creature that it would do well to remember its place. I told it that this brief freedom it had found on this boat would not last; that it would be unhappy again in short order once the novelty of that freedom had faded.

"You are a bitter old thing," the Defect said. And then it entertained Her not a moment further, choosing instead to ruminate some more on the nature of beauty and the joy of counting the blades of grass, and fish. But the empress was successful in reminding the creature that this was all fleeting.

It did its best impression of a sigh.

When the Defect was first born from the inverted womb in the Shrike Room beside the heat beds, it received, all at once, like a waterfall, the memories of all the tortoises that had come before it, and all that now yet lived. The first few weeks of life were akin to the storms of the abyss as it learned to parse the assault of imagery and sound and sense, to understand the context it had been given and its place in the world. But with enough time it was able to attain an awareness of what it meant to be a tortoise, for all the memories it had been given were those of pain and humiliation, of themselves and of others—and yet there were precious few memories of joy.

The cicadas rattled.

The frogs skipped.

"This is a beautiful morning," it said.

The creature pocketed the memory. The quiet river and the rolling clouds and the tall yellow grass. It pocketed the sweet smell and the light snoring of the small humans who flanked its shell. It pocketed the fiery sun and the green-gray water and the sound of directionless birdsong. Turned it into a memory worth keeping. And it promised itself that one day, when it was safe to, it would share with its brethren this memory of a beautiful morning; without chains, or hungry heart.

I told the creature that it was correct in this respect.

It was, indeed, a beautiful morning.

The Defect sniffed, satisfied.

A turn came in the lazy river.

There were objects up ahead that the tortoise did not recognize, for there were few tortoises that lay claim to the rivers or its people, and there was much they did not know about Lord Maada's domain and the nature of fishing. It did not understand the function of the objects that hung off the ends of the long bamboo poles like dewdrops off grass tips; why the mesh nets the bamboo held aloft were filled with graveled moonrock.

It did not know they were traps.

You suspended the bag of tea over your little brother's cup, just as your lola had once done. You slowly lowered the bag till it was enveloped by the steam of the liquid, and you let the bag dangle just above the water. You told him how the Moon and the Water were once lovers; how the Water grieved when the Moon quit Her heavenly perch and fell to the earth, no longer able to capture Her radiance in its reflective embrace. You told him that after the moonfall, the fishermen of the Old Country discovered that water would react when it got near moonrock. When held suspended just above the surface, just out of reach of the water, the water would shriek.

"How?" asked the perpetually curious boy, as he lowered his head to better see the hair's distance between the teabag and the water.

You told him that everything can shriek, or laugh, or weep—that there was more to this world than what human eyes could see, and ears could hear. It just so happened that when the water shrieked, a strange effect occurred in the world. The threads along which the Rhythm pulsed would become knotted. The spirits in the trees and the grass would flee. And the animals caught in the troubled waters would be stunned. Such as the fish.

You dropped the bag into the cup. He giggled as it splashed. The trap stopped working once it was no longer suspended over water. The trick was finding the right weight, the right distance. The fishermen were good at that.

"What does the water's shriek sound like?" he asked.

The theater is quiet.

This moonlit body touches its ear, telling you to listen, and now all of you are listening for it—there, the water calling for Her.

Like a boy trapped in a high tower.

The empress winced.

The traps stretched on for the entirety of this river, a nuisance in the tortoise's ear, like a swarm of gnats, but to Her, it was all unfathomably painful. *I could not bear it, not again—that knife, twisting, twisting.* Like a chest slamming shut She collapsed into Herself, just like She did those many years ago, when Her son trapped Her behind the Wolf Door, Her power disrupted, and the boat, untethered from Her control, drifting sideways, spinning gently until it bumped against the side of the curling river, the bump jolting enough to startle the two young men awake.

Keema leapt to his feet.

The first thing he did whenever he was startled awake was to grab the nearest weapon at hand, which is why he held Araya's spear in a tight-knuckled grip, awake in an instant, his eyes darting around, taking in the riverway. He asked the Defect what the trouble was, but the tortoise, who had no context for where they were, did little to assuage him: "This one is worried. This one does not know why we stopped."

Jun got up a bit slower, his mask half-off as he rubbed his tired eyes. When he saw what had happened he told the tortoise that it was fine; Keema lowered his spear as Jun pushed the boat from the river's edge with a pole. "They're traps for the fish," he said. "Like the bowls people use when they camp, or the nets you'd see outside the richer villages along the Road Above. Do you hear the sound of it?"

"This one does," the Defect confirmed. "Like a howling from far away."

"Humans can't," Jun said. "But animals can, and the spirits, Wherever They Dwell." He gestured to the other end of the boat, where the empress sat. "Unfortunately these netted traps have the funny side effect of making Her all . . ." He made a flittery finger gesture near his head, lacking the words. "She'll be gone till we get off this stretch of river, away from this noise. Come, Daware man, help me push."

Keema retrieved the other pole and the two of them worked the boat down the stretch of river, weaving between the rock-net pendulums that hung in their way.

"It's strange," Jun said. "All these nets are out, but no one attends them."

"Where do you think the fishermen are?" Keema asked.

Gone, we were gone.

Jun shook his head. "I don't know."

It came from nowhere.

They poled down the river for a while longer, Keema's muscles sore, begging him for rest. He pushed through the pain, not wishing to be outdone by his partner. He looked ahead of the prow. The river seemed endless with the traps, the poles evenly dispersed along the water's curling length, a new one every few meters, all of them as unattended as the last. "How did you sleep?" Keema asked, straining a bit as he pushed against the riverbed.

"Well enough, considering," Jun said, grunting. "You?"

"Dreamt I was at the beach."

"Sounds nice."

"I've never been to the beach," he said. "Never seen the ocean. Just heard of it. But there it was in my dream. Like I'd always known what it was like to be there. And in the sky I saw—"

Jun stopped rowing. "Do you smell that?"

"Yeah," Keema said. His nose crinkled. He lowered the pole and held the spear aloft again. "I smell it."

It smelled like iron.

We never saw it coming.

In the distance, where the river straightened out, they saw the dark edges of a dock sticking out from shore. *We were supposed to be protected. We were owned by Maada Fisheries. They were supposed to protect us.* Boats were lashed to the dock, but all the boats were empty. Some of them, unmoored, drifted out with the current.

"It's not right," Keema whispered. *It wasn't right, what happened wasn't right. Maada failed us.* The closer they rowed to the dock, the more potent the smell of iron became, until it was like a sick film on their tongue. Jun retched from behind his mask. Keema took the smell in stride, though he tried not to breathe through his nose, reminded of a few unpleasant memories he preferred to keep back of mind, of corpses he had known. The empress could not help them here. *The sound disordered the world; I could no longer direct; I was gone in a hole in myself.* The closer they got, the stranger the scene became, the dock slick and wet, dripping, but what it dripped with was not water.

"This one is not at peace," the tortoise muttered, and Keema saw why.

It was blood. Everything was painted in blood. *It killed us all.* As if someone had taken great big bucketfuls of blood and doused the dock boards with it, and the boats, and the walls of the homes that made up this small and now silent village. *It came through the windows. It broke through the doors.* An arm hung off the side of the dock. When their rightmost pontoon bumped into the dock strut by accident, the arm slipped off the edge and gulped into the water.

Jun opened his mask and vomited overboard. He sprawled over the edge of the boat, spitting into the water, dry-heaving. His body no longer able to handle the smell of blood he once thrived on.

Keema, trying to keep himself steady, asked Jun if he could rise. Without answering, Jun struggled to his feet, using the pole as leverage. "I need to—I need to get out of here," he croaked.

"I wasn't looking to stay much longer anyway," Keema said.

Together they poled the boat past the docks, with Keema putting in most of the effort, as Jun had difficulty breathing, much less boating. Keema kicked the villagers' boats that floated dead in the water out of the way, and when one of their pontoons got snagged in a trawling net, he had to reach in the water and work the pontoon free with his hand and his teeth, doing his best to ignore the chewed-off foot snagged in the net and the snake of intestines that drifted past his shoulder. Red liquid drizzled off of him as he rolled back onto his feet and picked up his pole again. Shallow-breathed, Jun watched the Daware man work with a quiet admiration, as he alone carried them down the river until the smell of iron dissipated, along with the taste of bile. The water they rowed through soon clearing up, becoming translucent silver and gold, and no longer that swirling wine-dark murk.

Keema glanced back once or twice more at the fishers' village as they rounded the river bend, and he wondered what had happened back there. He worried that they had not yet escaped whatever it was that did it.

That monster. It held my child in its teeth as it smiled.

"Oh gods," Jun croaked. "It's—I can still feel it on me. My tongue."

"We're almost out," Keema said. "Keep poling."

"Right," Jun said, as if he had forgotten. "Keep poling."

They were now a half length's way down the new river. Above them, fat white clouds sat on a blue-carpet sky. Glass-winged cicadas flitted between the branches of low-hanging trees. The day was hot, and it was calm. Aside from the nervous and persistent giggle of the tortoise, the world offered no suggestion that a massacre had only recently taken place. Keema focused on his poling, to steady his own frantic heart, and at a certain distance he began to believe that they were out of immediate danger. He told Jun as much, and they allowed themselves to pole a bit slower, though Jun did not stop muttering this new mantra of his.

"Keep poling. Keep poling."

Slowly their nerves came back down.

What had happened back there?

They shared their theories. Marauders, drugged-out and out of control. Family Men, sent by Lord Maada, or Silver Monkeys, sent by Luubu, as a show of force, for blasphemy. Maybe the villagers killed one another. Keema suggested that one, though he admitted it was unlikely. Deeper into the Thousand they went, wondering aloud—for they were afraid of silence—about what was capable of such carnage. Some demon, from deep within this nest of rivers. A thing that did not understand the destruction it wrought. A thing that lived only to eat.

Maybe, Jun had said.

Maybe.

They had entered a new section of river, the edges of which were crowded with overhanging trees and thick tangles of roots. Keema offered to row alone for a time, as he noted the slow, exhausted pace of Jun's pole. Jun was grateful for the reprieve. He sat down with a heavy breath as Keema pushed them through the shadowed water, the sunlight breaking in small pinpricks through the thick canopy of leaves above. In time he noticed Jun whittling something in his lap, a small carving knife applied to a hard white object in his hand with an almost aggravated energy.

"That's a bone," Keema said, realizing this as he said it.

Jun hesitated before he acknowledged this with a nod. "It is a bone. Yes."

"Animal bone?" Keema asked.

Jun snorted.

"It is the bone of my brother," he said with a hint of pride. "It's a piece of his shoulder blade. I used to keep it on a necklace, but now I just carry it." Keema did not know what to say to that, so he remained quiet. "He died taking an arrow for me," Jun said. "After we performed the Rite of the Body on him, my father gave me this bone, and he taught me the ways of scrimshaw." He glanced at the rice jar under the bench, as if expecting the head to pipe up. He did not. "It's how we give thanks to the dead after they're gone."

"What do you write on it?"

"Nothing new. There's not enough room. See?" Jun held up the triangular bone, the size of his palm. It was covered in words and runic script, deeply etched, like the sun-starved ramblings on a prison wall. "I just go over the old words and make them deeper when I'm . . ."

He trailed off. Shrugged.

"I get it," Keema said.

"What do you do to distract your mind?" Jun asked.

"Nothing," Keema smiled, almost confessing to the dancing. "I should find something though."

"It helps," Jun said. He scratched deep into the bone. "It doesn't fix anything, but it helps."

For a time, the sounds of the river were overwritten by his scratching, and Keema was surprised, and somewhat unsettled, by the comfort he felt, listening to it.

Birdsong broke from the branches—

a free-form twittering that caught both of their attentions. Keema was then greeted by an acquaintance he did not think he would see again: the bird with purple feathers, alighting upon the Defect's shell, chirping happily at him. He let out a humored huh, which prompted Jun to ask what was the matter. "That's the bird," Keema explained. "The one I found in the wagon. The same one that knocked the rider off his horse."

"How do you . . ." Jun paused to spit some leftover bile from his mouth into the river. "Apologies. How could you know that it's the same bird?"

Keema lifted his shoulder as he stared at the purple little thing, which stared back at him unblinkingly. "I just know."

"Strange that it keeps returning to you."

"Maybe it's thankful for how I freed it."

"A thankful bird. Perhaps it is a spirit of the aerie." Jun chuckled. "Perhaps you are blessed with the protection of some minor god. A lucky thing, for a man of poor fortune."

"Perhaps," Keema said. "Why have you come back anyway? We

did not part on the best of terms on our first meeting." He pointed at the still-healing scratch on his cheek, which the bird tilted its head at, as if not understanding why a simple scratch might bother him. "We have little food to spare," he told it. "And nothing that I think you might find suitable to eat." A little quieter, he added, "Right now's not the best time to visit. These are dangerous waters."

But the bird did not seem to mind any danger. It pecked at the Defect's shell and flew in circles around them as they passed the next few moonrock nets, though for all the bird's playfulness, Keema noticed that it did not go near the empress's body. For the most part it seemed to prefer Keema's company alone. It sat on top of his head as he worked the water, and he played a game of seeing how long he could keep it there before it flew away. Jun got up, finished resting, and picked up his pole.

At the end of the river, without warning, that bird kicked up off Keema's head, scratching him for a second time as it jumped into the air and darted ahead of their boat, squawking, demanding their attention.

That was when they came upon the fork in the river.

The path on the left was a narrow channel that disappeared out of view behind thicker, darker foliage.

The right path was wider and clearer—this was the path the bird was fluttering around, beseeching them to follow. And it would have been the obvious path to take, were it not for the Daido that blocked it, the statuette floating above the water as if dangling by fishing wire.

"Now, this is a choice," Keema muttered.

"I think the answer is obvious," Jun said. He pointed to the shaded left path. "We take the route without the Daido. We avoid spirit business. We stay alive."

There was logic in his words, but Keema could not help but feel pulled toward the other option. "The bird wants us to go past the Daido."

Jun scoffed. "Let us agree that the bird has no say in the matter." The purple creature squawked at that. "The left path seems to favor the north. North is the Bowl. The closer we get to the Bowl, the more likely we'll find main thoroughfares, and more directions. The path on the right," he said, now pointing at the Daido route, "is but a small distance away from the violent massacre we just passed back there. It would not surprise me at all if what lay behind this spirit wall is the creature that tore those poor bastards to shreds."

Some small part of Keema thought it best to trust the bird, but he couldn't make a good argument out of it. "You tell me to ignore the bird, but if it is indeed a spirit of protection like you yourself suggested, then maybe nature itself is giving us a sign of where to direct ourselves."

"Nature would see me drawn and quartered." Jun's voice had taken on a flatter tone as he said this. Neutral. Matter-of-fact. Certain. "Nature would have me gutted. Nothing in this world will ever meet me and not want to slit my throat, because I wear the mark of death on my face. Because I had served death proudly." He looked at Keema. "I envy anyone who can still trust nature. But I am beyond nature's grace. That bird knows what I am. It can no doubt smell the blood that stains my body. I believe it would lure us into certain death. I cannot find it within myself to trust it." And then there was a moment when he did not talk. He just thought. "But you have more than earned my trust by now, Keema of the Daware Tribe. If you truly believe that going right would be best, I will listen."

With a dry throat, Keema returned the mask's gaze.

"Okay," he said finally.

"We go left."

The bird went wild as they poled the opposite direction of its frantic call, but soon they could no longer hear the creature, it having likely abandoned them as lost causes. As they poled down this shaded and narrow slice of river, Keema repeated Jun's words from before. " 'I am beyond nature's grace.' " He snickered. "Didn't realize you were a poet."

Jun's ears burned red. "I said what I had to, to stop you from making a dumb fucking decision."

"Sure, sure." He batted a low-hanging branch out of the way. Smiling now, eager to tease because teasing was more fun than being afraid, "Nature's grace is a lovely thing to behold, isn't it, my princeling? Oh! How I yearn for nature's grace to save me from the shadows of my soul!"

The river trees grew thicker above them; the sunlight darker.

"Fuck you," Jun said, though even his mask could not hide the swell of his cheek as he smiled. "Fuck you and your one arm."

"Grace! My Grace!"

And darker.

"I'm done with you." Jun focused on his poling. "I'm done with your foolishness."

"That's fine then," Keema said, laughing.

We watched them. And we waited.

"This one is confused as to why it was not consulted about which direction would be wisest to go," the Defect said.

"Consult you?" Jun said. "I forgot you were even there."

"This one highly doubts that."

And we waited.

"I can't believe there are still moonrock nets way out here," Keema observed as they passed yet more of the traps. "That village's territory must stretch on for a while."

"It's a river, there are fish, of course they'd pole here."

Until . . .

"How long is this river, do you think?" Keema asked.

. . . the right moment. His question met by two sheets of rope netting that snapped up on either side of the boat like walls, ending their journey.

One net blocked the way forward, the other the way back.

Easy catch.

"Back up!" Keema shouted. "Back!"

Jun raised his pole hook and tried to bring the net down, but it was as taut as bowstring. "We need to cut through the—" An arrow pinged off the bow of the boat. Jun crawled backward into Keema's side, and Keema held his spear out, looking into the dark of the riverside woods for movement. Shadows grew from the brush, at first only a few, but those few turned into many, until two dozen strong men and women faced them on both banks. Bows drawn. Spears held out. Eyes cold and dead.

"This one would have voted to go right," the tortoise said.

MIDDAY

Through shade and beams of light, the leader emerged.

A woman with cords of gray-and-black hair, her skin deeply sun-wrinkled. She was garbed in functional attire, three pieces of billowy fabric, her arms bare, revealing that combination of tight muscles and lax skin that comes with the territory of living through your work; of years spent in the rivers summoning nets from the water and heaving large things off boats. Laugh lines were etched deep around her mouth, but there was no merriment in her face that day.

"Who are you?" she asked.

It was a question whose answer Jun knew would determine whether they survived the next few moments. He noticed the tattoos on these warriors' arms; circular signs and symbols that were the unique tongue of the fishermen of the Thousand. "We are travelers," he said. "Pilgrimaging to the Divine City to see the end of His Holy Pilgrimage."

"Pilgrimaging?" The woman laughed. "Then you are the first pilgrims I've seen who carry with them a vat-grown tortoise." She tilted her head at the creature. "One that seems born broken, if these eyes tell the truth."

The tortoise hissed at her.

The woman smiled, as if she had not reckoned to be so entertained by their catch. She walked up to the very edge of the riverbank while the lean men and women behind her held taut their bowstrings and twirled sharp rocks in leather slings; the slings whistled angrily. "I'd know more of this cast before I believe the story they perform. You," she said, pointing at Keema, "how did you come by this tortoise?"

Keema glanced at Jun, who shrugged.

"We stole it," Keema answered.

Her smile only grew wider. "Do explain."

"Back in the terraces of Lord Yinn," Jun added, "we found ourselves in need of transportation, so we . . . requisitioned a royal wagon. The creature came with it. It travels with us now." He stared at them hard. "Which means it is also under our protection."

"Let's hope no one needs to challenge that. And who's she?" Her finger pointed at the old woman, who sat cross-legged by the tortoise.

"My grandmother," Jun said.

"I'm sure she is." Her eyes back on Jun now. "Your mask. Remove it."

"I would rather not. I'm sensitive to the light."

The air tensed with the sound of tightening bowstrings.

"If you don't want to become a pincushion, I would remove it now. For everyone's peace of mind."

Keema raised his spear as Jun's hand went up to his mask. Their eyes meeting once, as if to say, *Get ready, this will not end well,* before he pulled back the band and removed it.

An agitated hush descended on the dozens in their company, for not one person missed the tattoo of the Red Peacock on his face. The woman's good humor gone as her eyes darkened and the men and women behind her muttered amongst themselves. *We wanted her to let us loose. We wanted her to let us rip the bastard apart.* For here before them was a Terror's foot soldier, a person they could funnel all of their frustration and fear into as they skinned him alive, *my fingers itching to release the string, for Sayla, for Mardo, for all of them—how I begged to make a hole in his throat, make him sing.*

The woman tsked at Jun.

"You dirty little peacock." She shut her eyes. "Son of the First Terror, we cannot suffer you to draw another breath. For all the citizens of this country you have put to the torch in the sick name of your father, I would see you peppered with every arrow at our mere disposal." She raised her hand. Jun flinched. The tortoise let out a terrified honk. Keema readied to throw his spear into her throat. But before a single quill could be loosed, a voice rang out.

"Tak-Lina, lower that hand!"

And the woman, Tak-Lina, did lower her hand, and the archers behind her and across the river lowered theirs, too, at her wide-eyed command, though one bow was fired by accident. *It was my second time holding a bow outside of practice.* The loosed arrow thunked into the wooden boards at Jun's feet, but he did not flinch, staring unblinkingly at the river woman. She stepped forward, her face one of awe as she asked, in a quiet, tempered voice, "What did you call me?"

When Jun replied, there was a different aspect to him that Keema could not identify—a hundred small variations of expression and posture and inflection that suggested it was not Jun who spoke but someone else through him, his spine straightening, his chin lifting to meet this Tak-Lina's gaze, the young man no longer a bow-backed, scurrying cat but a creature imperious and even haughty as he stood on one of the benches and addressed his ambushers. "I called you Tak-Lina, and I would have you cease your prattle. Enough threatening the lives of the ones who now serve me. Speak to me as you once had all those years ago. As the one you once worshipped."

Yes, it was the empress who inhabited Jun's body, *for we had passed the last of the moonrock traps and I had returned to the world of the living, only to find my servants in danger of being killed by an old friend. It was clear to me that it was necessary to intervene.*

The face of the woman named Tak-Lina went through many transformations. The awestruck reverence melted into a deep nostalgia that then warped into a face hot with fury—that fury tempering itself into something cool and distant, as if this were the state she needed to remain in if she wanted to protect herself.

"What's he on about?" one of the men asked another. "Who's Tak-Lina?"

"An old name," she said quietly. "One I have not gone by in a very long time." To Jun-who-was-not-Jun, she said, "I thought that old woman there looked familiar, but what were the odds, thought I, that She of all people would drift down my river, of all the rivers of the Thousand."

Not-Jun smiled. "You know as well as I that there are no odds in this world. There is only the Rhythm, and the Dance. That we are but the dancers."

Tak-Lina nodded, as if it had been too long since she had last heard such words. "I admit," she said, "it is a neat trick, this speaking through a surrogate. Little more impressive though, than the emperor and His tortoises. Any reason why you cannot spill speech from your own mouth?"

Not-Jun sighed. "I am old, Tak-Lina, and I have only a handful of breaths, and not many more heartbeats left to spend in this form"—they said, gesturing to Her body—"I use them sparingly."

"Interesting time to leave your palace."

"Leave. An amusing choice of word, isn't it?" Keema flinched when Not-Jun looked at him with a wry grin, unnerved, and glad when the empress's surrogate returned their gaze back at their quarry. "I did not *leave*. I escaped. After many years of effort."

Tak-Lina folded her arms. "And now that you've escaped, here you are, in the sticks. Going where? Doing what?"

"Going east. To undo what I have started." Not-Jun stood at

the edge of the boat, their hand sweeping over Keema, the Defect, themselves. "These are my servants. They shepherd me to the eastern coast, where people hungry for change await my arrival. People who would take the land back and make it their own. I will offer my body up to them, in a great Consumption, and bestow upon them what god gifts I have left to offer, so that they might cleave through walls that till now have remained impenetrable."

"They ate people?"

Your little brother blinked, his eyes wet, and all of you glared at your second oldest brother, who was never good about reading a room, having thoughtlessly made a comment about the royals of old eating the flesh of humans. All of you were in the dining room, the meager ration meal finished, your bellies rumbling. It was meant as a joke: that if times became desperate enough, if it came down to it, you all could do what the royals once did in the Old Country and eat your brethren. Some conversation followed about who would be eaten first. Some laughter. But your little brother was still stuck on that note of worried fascination.

"Did they really eat people?" he asked. His fear worried the rest of you, because when your little brother did not sleep, no one slept.

"No, they didn't eat people," another assured him. "Right?" he asked, turning to you.

They all turned to you. This was not surprising—you were the one, after all, whom lola poured all her tales into. And so you told them that it was not what they were imagining. Again, parroting your lola, you even sounded a bit defensive as you told them that there was a ritual behind the consumption of human flesh, the Rite of the Body. That they only ever ate the dead, and when they did, it was out of a sense of duty and love, not hunger. You said that it was usually only someone in power, like a local governor or lord, or emperor. That the practice dated back to a time of eld, when a new god would replace an old one in the pantheon, devouring their flesh, and in doing so, taking in themselves the old god's memories, and their power.

With a smile you told your brothers it would do little good to eat each other just yet. You cast a bitter look to your father's portrait above the mantel. Between you all, you said, there was very little worth inheriting.

Not so with the corpse of the Moon God.

"I seek nothing less than to undo the grand tapestry of the Throne," Not-Jun said as they looked head-on at Tak-Lina, whose expression was dark and unreadable. "My time is done. I cannot wield my power as I once did. I can count on one hand the number of times I can intervene before I have spent my last." Not-Jun smiled weakly. "I am running out of time. For the first time in our very long lives, I beg of your assistance. The apes have already refused us, and I suspect that will be the case for most of those who still dwell in the forests and the water . . . so it is with prayer that I turn to you for help. Let us pass. And if you are able, help us travel through the Thousand. Help us go east, to meet with the rebellion that now gathers on its shore."

"The shiver," Tak-Lina said, after a moment's pause. "Was that your doing?"

"Yes. When I killed the emperor."

The breath of the warriors who accompanied the river woman was stolen from their lungs at this bold statement. The empress saw this spark and took the opportunity to stoke the flame.

"By my hand I blew apart my own child as if he were no more than kindling. And this warrior of the Daware Tribe," she said, gesturing to Keema, who still held his spear as if to skewer any who might come at them, "this warrior has slain the First Terror."

"Impossible," a man shouted.

"The rumors are true then?" someone cried.

"Oh gods, oh gods."

"Then, this is it. The water readers spoke true! This is our time!"

"Quiet!" Tak-Lina shouted. *On her command we fell quiet, for she was our Kaara, and we trusted none more than her.* The troubled waters of her expression hardened into something steeled and furious, the corner of her mouth twitching into a broken grin. "You are an unbelievable creature, My Gracious Moon. You act as if it is charity for you to bestow upon the people your so-called gifts. But this . . . need of yours to bestow that which should not be given freely has corrupted this land beyond recognition." She breathed out, clutching the large-beaded necklace that hung low on her chest. "By your gift I have watched your sons wipe whole tribes away upon their backhand. I have seen them bleed rivers dry. I have seen the sky, for years now, refuse to yield a drop of water." She cast a withering gaze upon the tortoise. "By your gifts those damned creatures see all and report all, and strengthen the hold of the Five Families. Friends have been thrown into the pit of Joyrock, never to be heard from again. I am glad that the Throne no longer has you under their yoke, truly, if only so that they can claim less power for themselves . . . but you have much yet to answer for, for all the *gifts* you have bestowed." She looked at the old woman's body sitting at the head of the boat. "You call me Tak-Lina, but Tak-Lina is a creature of the past. Like you, *Empress*, I have changed. Our old skin is shed. I am Kaara of the Jogon River now. I work the rivers, and I break bread with my people. When the emperor saw it as his right to close his teeth on our waters with his stone sluice gates, we saw it as our right to take it back. We, of the Thousand, will take back the Bowl of Heaven from the Second Terror." Her people, on her command, drew back their bows once more. "And you will take it with us."

I told the Daware man to lower his spear.

Keema, with reluctance, obeyed Her Royal Whisper. Araya's spear came to a rest at his side as this scouting party robbed them of their weaponry. *The Daware man wondered why we did not fight back, or flee. Never mind that my strength was almost depleted, the reason I stayed our hands was because of a debt.*

A debt I owed to Tak-Lina.

We would meet with her people. The least we could do was find out how we might be of use before we escaped their chains. Keema accepted this. He looked at Jun, relieved that his body had returned to normal, his eyes downcast as he allowed his hatchet to be taken, along with the long blade that had been dropped by his father on the floor of the boat. He saw one of the fishermen spit in Jun's face, and he was overcome with the urge to deal the bastard a blow to the head, but he did not move, Jun giving him a subtle shake of the head to stay his hand; his legs hiding the rice jar that sat beneath one of the wooden benches.

"Do we need to bind your wrists together?" Kaara/Tak-Lina asked. "Or will you be good?"

"You have nothing to worry from us," Jun said sharply.

Keema held up his one arm. "You can try."

Kaara/Tak-Lina raised an eyebrow.

"Humor," she said. "Interesting."

Shortly after, they journeyed north, to the Gathering.

The group moved as one.

They traveled slow, and with great deliberation, through the many rivers. *We of the Thousand learned when we were young that one cannot row a river with a distracted mind—the world was waiting to swallow those who did not step sure across its surface. Rivers* had a habit of changing their minds, the myth waking from its slumber to shift position, and a boat, certain it had come this way before, might circle on its own path and make a trip not planned for, into territory dark and deadly. *The unprepared travelers decorated the trees and the grass with their bones. We acknowledged them; their cold hands still gripped tight to their oars, as if it were not yet too late to flee.* Keema had traveled by boat a few times in his life, but it was only now that he appreciated how easily one could get lost in this place as he rowed with the fishermen and observed their vigilance. Come the forks in the river, they relied on the sun's coordinates as well as dowsing rods cut with finger blood to show the way, and when they were not dowsing the currents, they were rowing in tight formation around the captured boat, watchful as hawks for any strange movements the two warriors or the tall grass might make. Some of the fishermen murmured to one another, wondering if it was true that the emperor and the First Terror were dead. Others had less lofty thoughts on their mind, a man grinning at them as he tapped on the curved knife in his belt, as if to say *just you wait.*

Keema glanced at Jun, and it surprised him how much comfort he found in the other's gaze, despite the red tattoo that sparked in the others so much ire. Between the two of them was a silent agreement, that once the empress was satisfied, they would depart from this company of rebels as soon as the opportunity presented itself—but that would be only if they found a way to navigate out of the Thousand on their own.

Vines draped over the Yan-Tsi River like unkempt braids of hair. The trees along the border of the river fell away and tall grass took its place, the river becoming a curling avenue not unlike the narrow and crooked squeezes of your dockside town. Sometimes, Keema noticed, the tall grass moved—rustled, as if brushed aside by the passing body of some large creature. *We all knew to never go into the grass. Even if your boat was on fire and the water was filled with biting fish, you never go into the grass.* "I've an uncle who stuck his hand in there once," one of the more even-tempered fishermen said, when he noticed Keema staring into the thicket. "Did it as a joke, he did. Said he could feel a water-fae's tits. But when he pulled his hand back out, all the flesh was gone. There was just bone."

Keema, unsure if he was in a position safe enough to speak back, remained silent, not even nodding, but he soon found that the fishermen of the Old Country were a talkative sort, even a group such as this, who presented themselves as bloodthirsty rebels, for the work, made up of long stretches of nothing, demanded a kind of fellow-feeling and camaraderie to survive it; when one man started up, the others could not help but start up, too, even in the company of the despised.

"No one's ever going to believe that story," a woman rowing behind him said. "Except you, when your fool uncle told it. But that's all your family is, I suppose. A tree of fools."

The man shrugged. "More fun to believe it than not. 'Sides. No one can ever truly know the Thousand."

The woman rolled her eyes.

The man told Keema the story of this river they now traveled, the Yan-Tsi. How the Yan-Tsi took its name from the snake demon that fell in love with the three beautiful brothers of Twin Fan Village—the same village whose carnage Keema and Jun had been witness to earlier. The snake demon did everything it could to capture the young brothers' affections. "Gold, gifts, whatever he could think of, but it was to no avail, for he was the demon who had swallowed whole their ancestry, and who could love a demon with that much blood on his hands?" Keema could feel Jun listening; it was obvious to them both that this tale was not told by accident. "It was only after many years of trying to win their hearts that Yan-Tsi realized that this would be the first battle he had ever lost. When one morning he heard the three brothers complain about their fellow villagers, and how nice it would be if they had a river of their own to tend to, the demon knew what he must do. And so he used the last of his grim magick to transform himself into this coiling river we now travel." It was but one of the many thoroughfares that spun across the Thousand Rivers, each one of those thousand rivers claiming its own piece of myth and history. "And if you're alone out here, you can hear it all the better—the rattling end of his long tail, for a love that would never be his."

More tales followed, none of the others wishing to be outdone. Tales that sprung from the territory of the Thousand like weeds. The backwards songs one might hear from the trees, that predict the migratory patterns of jeweled carp. The shimmer in the air that, if looked at from the right angle, would resolve into the peculiar vision of a black moon and a blue sun, which people said was the true sky of this world. And yes, they spoke more of the tall grass that would eat the flesh off your finger if you were careless. But however much the fishermen spoke, the boundaries of their courtesy were clear, for they did not once address Jun, or even look at him, aside from the few glares they threw at his back like darts; such small gestures would do to satisfy them until a more fitting punishment was delivered at the Gathering.

Jun, for his part, did nothing to attract their ire. He kept his eyes forward and his expression neutral, his poling sure and unhurried—though his mind was alight and agitated as he made sure not to look at the rice jar hidden beneath the bench.

The midday bugs swarmed the water's surface. Fidges and qweeks with little needles for mouths and wings that vibrated like little motors as they drank deep the blood from an unattended arm. Attracted as they were to large carcasses, most of them buzzed about the Defect, rapturous black clouds that sucked up his odor and ooze. But the ever-hungry creature made no move to snap at them. Keema asked it what was the matter. The Defect let out a giggle that turned in on itself, inspiring in Keema's mind the image of a boy tripping over his own sandals. "This one feels . . . strange," it said. When a particularly fat fidge slammed into Keema's cheek, he went to relight the incense lantern, suggesting to the creature that whatever it was feeling might clear away with the bugs. "Perhaps," it said, giving a doubtful giggle. It did not tell Keema that there was a sound in its head that belonged to neither fidge nor qweek nor empress—a whisper, distant, and ebbing, in and out of its mind, like some vulnerable and staticked channel.

As Keema struck the flint and lit the lantern's wick, he noticed

Kaara/Tak-Lina, rowing her one-person skiff alongside him. *I told him not to trust Tak-Lina.* He shivered to hear Her Royal Whisper. *I told him that she was not human, but a river spirit near as old as I, and as mercurial as one would expect a river spirit to be. But he didn't think it wise to be rude to their captor, so he offered the river woman a curt nod.*

Kaara/Tak-Lina was standing on her craft as she rowed. Her strokes were much smaller than those of her compatriots; where theirs were grand and powerful, like a horse's gallop, hers were brief, caressing, the difference between a whisper and an exclamation; and yet she covered just as much distance, if not more so, with such simple movements. She noticed him noticing, and smiled. "I am curious how a cripple finds himself in the stuff of gods and rebellion," she said.

He bristled at the word but did not correct her. "I swore an oath, and I intend to keep it."

"Oaths do not spring suddenly from the earth as like weeds. Where were you before you swore this oath?"

"In the earth," he said, with an odd pang of tenderness, "shoveling shit down a small tunnel."

Kaara/Tak-Lina chuckled. "And this Daware Tribe the Gracious Moon spoke of. Tell me of it. I have not heard of them."

He rowed with a thoughtful look. After a pause, he said, "It was a tribe of warriors. The greatest warriors this land had ever known."

She did not mock him for this statement. "Where did they make their home?"

Keema glanced at Jun, who seemed lost in his thoughts on the other end of the boat. "In the storm-riddled western plains," he said, "burned away by the emperor's men some time ago. They forged their oaths under the clap of lightning, as unyielding as the metals they used to forge their blades." He looked at her. "I am the last of them."

"You have my condolences for this loss, warrior." She bowed her head. "I hope that their end was mighty."

"I've yet to witness an end that was," he said. The words were spoken without thought, and Keema was not sure if even he believed it, but Kaara/Tak-Lina seemed affected by them.

"I have lived a long time," she said. "And the longer I live, the more it surprises me, and saddens me, how wise the young must become to live in this world."

Without another word she rowed ahead of them, in one unbroken glide, to the head of the group, where she began to converse with one of the fishermen, leaving Keema a little stunned by her warm words before he remembered that they were her prisoners, and began once more to paddle.

Their journey was almost at an end. The last landmark they passed was one of the Maada sluice gates. They spied it from across the wide stretch of the Yurna River, but they did not approach the black-rock gate that welded shut the mouth of the Lesser Yurna, for on either side of the gate were small compounds flying both the banner of the Throne and the banner of the Silver Monkey, the symbol of the Second Terror's personal army.

"On the other side of that gate is a dead place," Kaara/Tak-Lina said to the empress, to everyone. "A riverbed dried out, the fish choking on hot rock. This gate has been closed for two years now, ever since they found the contraband fabrics in the basement of a village along the Lesser Yurna. Three rolls of mid-priced Induun fabrics that the fishermen found from an abandoned basket floating out in the main straits, unclaimed. For that reason alone, they killed this river. And Lord Maada let it happen without a fight, because the village was a small place, a piece in a game given up for the sake of larger riches to come." And then she moved on, ending the moment before it had time to settle in the stomach, the black gate lingering in the back of Keema's senses for a while yet as they rowed on.

"Yes?" the Defect said suddenly. It swung its head into the air and spoke to someone neither Keema nor Jun could see.

"What is it?" Keema whispered. "What's wrong?"

The tortoise's beak mouthed words it did not speak.

Then, "This one thought it heard its mother's voice."

"Your mother?"

"Their god," Jun clarified. "The one who binds their minds together. It is not surprising, I suppose, that you can hear her now. She isn't far."

"Where is she?" Keema asked, curious, for this information was not common knowledge to the populace.

"The Bowl of Heaven," Kaara/Tak-Lina answered. "Held as an 'honored' guest aboard one of Luubu's prison ships. We have been working to free her for some time. Plans are coming together." She nodded at the Defect. "What do you hear your mother say, creature?"

"This one cannot understand her. This one is not sure it is even her at all."

"If you hear anything that can be of use, let us know," she said. "Any aid you provide will go some way toward what leniency the Gathering will show you all."

"How much farther, then, till our execution?" Jun asked.

Kaara/Tak-Lina hummed.

"Not far now."

Indeed it was not—the entrance, easily glanced over by someone not looking for it, was two bends of the river away. Three of the fishermen rowed ahead of the group and pressed their boats up against the wall of tall grass; the grass moving aside with ease, like a false wall, revealing behind it a small riverway. The tortoise boat was ushered through this opening first, Keema beginning to sweat as he rowed with Jun down the last length of the riverway, and they came upon the Gathering of the River Clans.

AFTERNOON

A town on the water.

That's how you described the Gathering to your little brother, who was not so little anymore. He was taller than you by an entire head; his growth spurt was sudden, as was his desire to go abroad to study, despite the dangers of overseas travel in those days. He knew you were the saddest to see him go, of all your brothers, and so he humored you with his company in the weeks leading up to his departure, the two of you making many walks together, sometimes toward chores, mostly toward nowhere. And you felt very old, even though you were not old at all, when he put on his patient listening face while you remembered aloud yet another one of your lola's stories.

"You shouldn't be embarrassed," he often said. "I think it's neat that you remember so many of them."

Yes, you thought, rolling a cigarette. Neat.

Anyway—the Gathering. The name explained itself. The two of you walked along the docks of your town, your hat threatening to fly off into the sea as you gestured at the boats—the skiffs as slim as blades of grass, the fat tugboats, the puzzling catamarans, even the warships—and you described to him how the fishermen of the Old Country would congregate to form this collective and discuss amongst themselves the trials of the day. How they would lash their boats together, with ropes, with planks, boats of all different sizes, and create, in effect, a temporary town on the water, stepping across this complex web of pathways and ladders and platforms. The location of the Gathering always changed, for those in power were made nervous by these meetings, and sometimes tried to infiltrate them with paid accomplices.

It was said that a fisherman was never lost, for he had two homes—his village, and his Gathering—and he was never far from either.

No matter how far he rowed, you said, he was never lost.

Your brother turned to you with tears in his eyes, and you thought you would crumble. "I won't be gone forever," he said. "I'll come home when I can." You tried to tell him you were just telling him a story, but your voice couldn't even manage that, so you hugged him, and you told him that you would miss him.

"I'll miss you too," he said.

And then he picked you up, too easily, and he threw you in the bay—his laugh high and flutelike as you detonated the water.

It was as fine a farewell as you could've hoped.

Not everyone gets to say goodbye.

You couldn't point a finger into the crowd of the Old Country without finding someone who had experienced some great, unsettled loss. All of the people in attendance at the Gathering had been pushed, in some way or another, into trying to take back what they felt was rightfully theirs. *I lost my mother; I lost my child; I lost the only man I would ever love.* You could see it in the way they behaved that day as they prepared for an attack long in the making—an attack they knew they would likely lose. *I lost my river; my dignity.* An attack that would likely end in their violent deaths.

They laughed. Loud and joyfully. They traded stories with the fervor anyone might have on their Last Day. They made silly faces as they painted one another's cheeks with protective runes, and they sang full-throated as they sharpened their knives and whittled their arrows. *We didn't see the point in being grave about it all. If you know what's coming, then what's the value in being miserable about it?* From far away, the laughter was a crackle of noise, like some distant fireworks lit in honor of a hero's passing—and up close, it was almost overwhelming, a bright and wincing joy that would make one realize there is no correct way to shake hands with pain. One of the weavers repairing the nets, and strengthening the thick, arrow-catching cloth armor, laughed particularly loud that day. She was but one of many, and were you to cast your gaze about the crowd she would be likely lost amongst the shuffle of notable people—her life up till then a modest one in comparison with those who had been fighting since the beginning. *My name was Mira of the Narada River. I was once a member of Induun's textile fleet, and I brought all I knew of the weave to my new people.* A woman of thirty years, a respected age in those days, and for many, the mark that you had reached the last quarter of your life, for there were all too many ways to fall afoul of Death, and she knew that as well as anyone. *My name was Mira, and I was the last living member of my family.*

She was a patient teacher as she guided the younger ones through the finer points of the weave, and was quick to laugh at herself whenever she pricked her own fingers on the needle. "No matter how long you do something," she said, "you can always fuck it up." Her attitude was a great balm to those around her. She would not be party to the coming infiltration, she would not be slitting throats in the dark, but she was here, and she was helping.

It was only when word came around that Kaara's people had returned that her laughter died, and a wound that had never truly healed began to bleed again, *for I had heard who was traveling with her.*

And I knew what must be done.

The scouting party approached the Gathering.

Keema gave out his own startled laugh of delight when he saw the dozens of boats congregated in the center of this hidden reservoir. He had only heard whispers of such a place, and had never thought he would actually see it—it was grander than he could've hoped. Large cargo ships and tiny two-man skiffs abutted one another, amongst likely hundreds of other crafts of varied size, all of them connected by an impossible sequence of wooden planks and rope bindings, creating surprising walkways between the vessels. The whole enterprise bobbed and shifted, making it seem like a living creature, contracting and expanding with each breath. "Our own miniature Bowl," Kaara/Tak-Lina said with pride before she remembered why she had brought them here in the first place. "Come."

They were shown to a long platform along which many other smaller boats were lashed, and where a group of formidable-looking men and women waited—nearly all of them staring at the Peacock in their midst. Jun let out a little breath.

"All right," he said quietly, with acceptance.

When their rope was knotted, Keema was told to stay with the tortoise, under the watch of a mountain-sized dockmaster, while the others were taken away to meet with the admiralty. There was no time for words when he and Jun were parted. He watched in silence as Jun lifted the old woman above his head and stepped off the boat without threat of losing his balance, as if he had made this step many times before. Kaara/Tak-Lina led him away; he and Keema spared one last glance at each other, the look in his partner's eyes burning like the afterimage of the sun in Keema's mind. Most of the party then left, except for a leftover contingent of guards who were tasked with ensuring that the man from Daware did nothing suspicious. Keema ignored their hostile gazes, and he sat down on one of the wooden benches of the boat, overcome with a feeling of impatience, of uselessness. He wished he had said something. But what?

Goodbye?

Not knowing what else to do, he turned to the tortoise. "And how are you faring in all of this?" he asked.

The Defect looked at him with its little eye and its big eye. "This one is eager to see what happens next."

"You sound almost excited."

The Defect did not deny this. "This one appreciates their cause. They wish to free themselves. This one understands such desire." It sniffed the air deeply. "This place smells of red certainty. They do not know if they will succeed in freeing the Bowl, but they are certain they will try."

"You said your mother is held in the Bowl?"

It nodded.

"Have you ever met her?"

It seemed confused. "The mother? No. This one has not met the mother. Not in the way you humans mean. You do not meet the land you walk on, and this one does not meet its mother. But this one feels its mother, underneath its thoughts. Its mother is the land its mind walks on. Its mother is what binds it to its siblings. It is because of its mother that it is never alone." It nodded like it was agreeing with itself before it turned to Keema. "This one would know of *your* mother."

"Didn't have one," Keema said. Some of the guards were talking with one another, but he couldn't hear what they spoke of.

"Were you also grown in a palace vat?"

He smirked. "No. I was born like a human, as far as I know. But she was gone before I'd ever had a chance to meet her. Same with my father. I was raised by . . ." He furrowed his brow. "Can you not read my thoughts? Do you not already know this?"

"The smell of your aura, and your blood, does not tell this one the secrets in your head," the tortoise said. A sad giggle. "All this one knows is that you smell of worry. It comes off of you in a most vivid color."

"Am I now?" Keema said, amused. "What color is my worry?"

"The color of a gray and broken sky." The tortoise looked toward the gathering of boats. "This one is also worried."

"You do not think this will end well?" Keema asked.

"No," whispered the voice in the jar, "I do not."

A chill came over Keema. He looked at the dockmaster and the guards to see if they had heard the third voice on the boat, but a glance told him this was not so; it seemed Kaara had told them he was not much of a threat, for they were now casting only a casual eye in his direction.

The jar was by the bench before him. Keema continued to speak with the tortoise, hoping to make it clear to the voice in the jar that his input was unwanted, but forcing small conversation was never one of Keema's strong suits, and he found himself awkwardly expounding on a growing bruise he discovered on his lower back, until the First Terror mercifully made his interruption. "Boy," he whispered sharply. "Boy, I know you can hear me. Open this jar."

"No," Keema said, keeping his voice quiet, his eyes staring ahead.

"Open this jar. Open it before I make myself known. It is not as though I have much left to lose." He could almost hear the head smile. "And I can be quite loud, as I'm sure you'll remember."

Keema's hand was a fist.

"This one thinks it best to humor him," the Defect said.

With a breath, Keema lifted the lid of the jar, just enough to reveal a crescent moon of darkness, a slice of light illuminating the First Terror's narrowed eye.

"Does that satisfy you?" he asked.

"Yes," the Terror said.

"What do you want?"

"To look upon the face of my killer."

"It doesn't seem like I've earned that title just yet."

A laugh.

"My attacker, then."

"You did not leave us with many alternatives."

"Please do not get me wrong, boy." He seemed to take great pleasure in calling him *boy*. "I am not angry." And he did not sound angry. His whisper was light, friendly even. "In forty-five years I have not once lost a battle. Forty-five years. Only once had Death ever come close to inspiring my last breath. A nobleman tried to have me killed after I had relations with his mistress. He shot me in the back with an arrow like a coward." He chuckled as if he were at a dinner party and Keema were some diplomat from an overseas land he was trying to entertain. "Young fool that I was, I didn't see it coming. I told myself I would not make the same mistake twice. That no one would have a clear shot at me from behind again." He looked up at Keema with an unreadable eye. "Turns out I am still that young fool."

Keema was watching a gigi bird leap from rope to rope before it struck the water; it flew away with something silver and flapping in its tiny beak.

"Where is my son?" the Terror asked.

"Not here."

"You cannot turn him against me." The head said this with a quick confidence. "He may be confused for the time being, but he will always be loyal."

There was an instinct in Keema to correct the matter, to tell the Terror that he had no intention of turning Jun against anyone or anything, until he realized he did not care one whit what the Terror might think. "The matters between you and your son are none of my concern."

"Of course they're not, you peasant," the Terror snapped.

The dockmaster perked up from his parchment, briefly. He stared at Keema for a beat before returning to his work.

The head found his composure.

"But that is beside the point," he said, quieter. "In time Jun will remember where he is from. He will remember the true nature of his heart."

"He will return to me."

Jun's lips were dry. His heart was in his mouth. There was an uncertainty to his step as he followed the fishermen into the heart of the Gathering, as if his legs would give out at any moment. Such symptoms of cowardice shamed him, and he told himself that he was simply water-sick; that the bob of the platforms they walked across was playing a trick on his stomach. He told himself that he was not scared, even as his body wished to wilt under the wrathful gaze of the many men and women lined up to see him. The voices in his head were volcanic. *We laughed as we told him that even if he denied it to himself, we knew the truth—we saw his FEAR. He was right to be afraid. We screamed at him that he was right to piss himself, because they knew, they ALL knew what he had done. And justice would be served.*

He told himself he was not afraid, that whatever may come, he deserved it and would greet his end with solemnity. He held on to this last vestige of pride as he stepped onto the central platform, where the admiralty waited.

Twenty-two men and women sat in a half-moon, facing him and the empress, whom he knelt beside.

Kaara/Tak-Lina was the first to address the impromptu court. She told the men and women of the admiralty the story of their encounter, and Jun found that, to her credit, she presented each detail in a fair way, without pressing for evidence to be interpreted one way or another—though he noticed she did leave out the detail that she knew the empress from a time long before that of Man—or perhaps, he thought, the admiralty already knew. When she was finished, she joined the other twenty-two, taking her seat at the right end of the half-moon.

A man seated in the center spoke. *My name was Tajeem of the Cicada River.* He looked as though he could snap Jun's neck with only a squint. "We would speak to the empress first," he said. "She may elect to use Her own body, or speak through her surrogate, it matters not to us. All we ask is that She do so with haste."

Even as Jun nodded, he could already feel Her taking control. Like a cold worm wriggling up his spine and into his brain. He tried to relax into it.

She wrested control of him with a fist.

"I am here, men and women of the Gathering," Not-Jun said to the hushed appraisal of the admiralty. And though She was coming dangerously close to expiring the last of Her energy, *I knew that if I did not inspire these people with my presence, we were doomed,* and so She made the eyes shimmer a pale, unearthly blue, and a white aura emanate from the shoulders in spirit-laced tentacles, *but even without the glowing eyes, and the light, the transformation was obvious; all of us felt Her royal aura, ebbing off Her surrogate's shoulders. It was a power beyond compare, and it overwhelmed us.* "After so long, I have escaped the clutches of my children. I have removed the emperor from this world, and the First Terror, and I will not stop until the others can no longer torment this country." A wind buffeted the water and the robes and the hair. It made music of the wooden charms that dangled from the bow. She was an old rope tether, straining to hold a great weight, but She was caught up now in Her own performance; the entire platform lifting into the air, just enough to make the stomachs gulp, and for the world to seem impossible and great. And then She gently lowered it, and She brought back in the wind and the light, the only remnant of Her show of force the light in Her eyes. "Forgive me, for being away for so long. But I am here now. And I wish to help."

Even the unsympathetic Kaara/Tak-Lina seemed stripped of words.

"Then it is true," Tajeem said, wiping the sweat from his brow. "The Gracious Moon has finally returned to us."

"Blessed Moon!" came a cry from on high.

"Our Lovely Light!"

It was an exaltation given from deep within; one that the people could not deny. One by one, the admiralty bowed their heads, and by decorum's standard, Kaara/Tak-Lina, too, followed suit, her face expressionless, as if she were not surprised by the direction of this meeting, even if it were not the direction that she'd hoped. And as the elected heads of the Gathering bowed to them, *our hearts Hers entirely,* Jun felt the empress's swell of love in his own breast, as Her subjects looked upon Her with awe, with adoration, and he heard Her thoughts as She wondered how long it had been since She had last been worshipped in this way.

How long, and how lovely.

Keema had felt it even from where he sat.

As soon as the wind had begun to stir, he knew who it was who stirred it, and like the dockmaster and the guards, he could not help but feel the spark of awe when the heart of the Gathering began to shimmer in a heavenly light. Word was quick to spread about the empress's show, and the once fatalistic mood shifted into something more hopeful, for the balance of strength was beginning to tilt in their favor. It wasn't long till only one guard remained on watch, while the others ran to find out more of what was happening. The Terror seemed amused. "And like that, She has won Herself a new following." Keema found himself nodding in agreement. "Anyway," the head said, "while we wait for our laurels and palanquins, I'd ask of you this: did my eyes deceive me last night, or do you carry with you Araya's spear?"

The name, spoken from his lips, was enough to shake Keema from his distracted gaze. "What of it?" he asked, wary.

"Did she give it to you?"

"Of course she did."

A sigh left the jar, like a ghost escaping through a crack in a gravestone. "I did like her," he said. "She would have produced a fine child for me, if she were able." Keema at once wanted to shut the lid and to hear more; he said nothing and did nothing; this, giving tacit approval for the head to continue, which he seemed to very much want to. "The nights I spent with her, there was a meaninglessness to them that I hope we both enjoyed. But there were times when I would look up at the spear that hung on her wall and ask her of its story, and she would smile, and deny me its history. 'Don't ruin this' she would say. I could have found out more on my own, but it never felt right to go skulking in places she did not wish me to skulk. The desires of others never prevented me from doing what I wished before, but for some reason, hers did." The jar was quiet. And then, he said, "She was still alive when I returned to Tiger Gate."

Keema's breath tightened. *Go on,* he wanted to say. *Shut your mouth,* he wanted to say.

"Our horses had trampled her into the ground. Not one bit of her was left unbroken. She could not even lift her head as I knelt at her side and stroked the hair from her eyes. 'Uhi,' I said, 'Oh Uhi, why have you done this?' She denied me even that." He made a strange sort of sound, a sad laugh. "All she asked me was if you had gotten away, and when I told her that you had, she passed on to the Sleeping Sea. I went to her office, to retrieve the spear and let it lie with her, but it was gone. Till now, I wondered what had become of it."

There was an excitement of conversation farther down the dock. But Keema did not see it, not really.

"I'm glad it is not lost," the Terror said. "Whoever you were to one another, I am glad she trusted someone enough to hand it off, before the end."

That was enough.

Keema put the lid back over the jar. The First Terror sighed once more, but he did not complain—but as the circle of wood slid back over the hole, the left eye disappearing in the dark, he heard the Terror say, tensely, "Wait."

"Something's changed."

A new wind shook the grass that circled this reservoir, and before Keema could so much as say *What?* the Defect's head shot up into the air, as if pulled up by some invisible and urgent hand, and it let out a honk, loud and abrasive, like sand punched into the ear. The dockmaster yelled, "Shut your fucking pet!" but the creature would not be controlled. It let loose another honk. *We heard it on the other side of the Gathering—and we, on instinct, thought the emperor was giving an address from beyond the grave.* A third honk, like the blast of a war horn, one that seemed to come from the creature's very depths. *The horrid cry a sound we knew too well, heard it at some point in our passing through the checkpoints, when something was terribly wrong.* The whole of the Gathering on edge—Jun, the old woman, and the admiralty all turning their heads toward the dock, where Keema cupped his right ear and pressed the other into his shoulder as the defective tortoise, at a volume almost unnatural in its shrieking heights, proclaimed, "HE'S DEAD! LUUBU IS DEAD! THE BOWL OF HEAVEN HAS BEEN DROPPED FROM HIS FINGERS!"

"THE SECOND TERROR IS DEAD!"

The Defect cried this news like a young herald on a notice-boat, fully and without guile. It would not stop until it was heeded, and even then, more was needed to accommodate this breathless creature. It was an unusual situation, of the sort that none of the admiralty had dealt with before, including Kaara/Tak-Lina, who had been around for much longer than any of them, and so new protocol was established on the fly. Connection planks were removed and boats were cleared out of the way so that the Defect's vessel could be brought closer to the center of the ring, where it could explain itself in full. But even extracting clear information from the creature was difficult in the beginning, *for the creature seemed to be on the verge of hysteria, between every statement loosening a joy honk or a terror honk or a don't-interrupt-me honk, none of us were sure*—no one present in the Gathering having the tools to decipher its more abstract noises, its desperate flailing. It took time, but eventually the tortoise settled down long enough that they were able to determine the following, later confirmed by their own scouts, who had their ear to the city's chest.

Mere hours ago, Luubu, the Second Terror, and de-facto ruler of the Bowl of Heaven, was shot through the neck with a stone-tipped arrow, from the fifth deck of a noble apartment barge. As Luubu's driver tried to get away, a second arrow slammed deep into the Terror's back. The pincushioned prince was brought to the nearest medical deck, where word spread that he was dead on arrival. *When we learned of this, I reached for my husband's hand. I held it.* The Bowl of Heaven was yet quiet, for news of Luubu's death was, much like the emperor's, kept secret. But while the public at large had yet to learn of the assassination, rumor, even in those past few hours, had been working through the prison-fleet ranks, guard to guard, up the hierarchy, to those at the top, the captains, the wardens, and the generals, all of whom found themselves with no one to answer to, or to ask for help. Neither did the textile company heads nor the heads of the weavers' guilds know what to do, their fabrics now with no one to receive them for to-morrow's Holy Week events—Lord Induun unable to help with co-ordination, for he had already departed for the Divine City. No one could stop the word spreading from vessel to vessel, the fiery news destabilizing the structures through which it burned. And so it was that a window of opportunity had presented itself to the admiralty of the Gathering, the Bowl vulnerable as it adjusted to the sudden loss of its head.

With a reverence in its voice that Keema did not know the crea-ture was capable of, the Defect said, "For the first time in this one's wretched life it has heard the voice of its mother! And her voice is glory! The mother is glad that this one is free!" A wild pride in the swing of its head. "The mother sees all! She has confided in this one of the events of the Bowl of Heaven so that it may bring help. So that it may bring reinforcements to come and save it and all tor-toises throughout this burning country!"

It honked triumphant in the air—but if it intended to receive applause, none arrived.

Admiral Tajeem stood up from his bench in the center of the gathering. He looked to the empress's surrogate. "Do you trust this creature, Gracious Moon?"

I did not yet know. "My senses have dulled over the years," Not-Jun said. "My ties to the world are limited to what is around me. What is and isn't is . . . cloudy. But I have felt a loss, of something, a presence—like a thread, cut before its time. But what that loss, that presence, is, I cannot say."

A murmur rippled through the arena. "Whether this is true or not matters not in the slightest." Kaara/Tak-Lina shook the mood with her absoluteness. "Before we intercepted the Lady Moon, the plan was to strike the Bowl tonight. Everything is in its place. We have the timings of the vessel alignments and the ballista boat rota-tions. We have the people on board the barges, waiting for our sig-nal. Canalway Twelve will be unprotected. If anything, I believe this is a sign—we must carry out our strike."

"She is right," Shala of the Worthy River said. "With the hierarchy in chaos, we could also strike the prison fleet—perhaps even release the tortoise god from its prison."

Another woman countered, "We would be throwing their lives away! The prison fleet is alive with tortoised patrol boats. With no set routine! Not a man could make it through, not at our strength."

"We would be fools not to take advantage of this situation."

"We already are, by attacking at all!"

Voice countered voice, argument swelling.

Kaara/Tak-Lina's eyes widened as Not-Jun stood up with his glowing eyes.

"I would be the one who rips the wall off the tortoise mother's cell," they said, to Keema's immense surprise, and also Jun's, though he was not in a position to express it. "I will help you dismantle my child's Bowl of Heaven."

The Defect held its head high in praise of Her.

I told him that I was not changing my mind.

In a small houseboat at the edge of the Gathering, which belonged to one of Admiral Tajeem's mistresses, and loaned out against her wishes for the use of the empress and Her party, She and Jun argued. The houseboat bobbed on the water as he paced in frustrated circles, explaining why they could not go off on this side mission— telling Her that these people were not equipped to survive an assault on the Bowl, and that going with them was all but certain death. Outside, Keema leaned against the wall, guarding the door, just as he used to do when he worked the pleasure barges. He made no expression, while inside, Jun shook his hands at Her. "We had a plan—a decent plan. Treat with Araya's people. The Five Families have resources. They are organized. They have—they have an army. These fishermen . . . have boats, and nets."

This was no "side mission," I told him. I had a responsibility to save the tortoise god who had caught my first fall. If I could save her, this would go a long way to unraveling the hold of the Throne. And this was the truth.

But I did not tell him the deeper truth. I did not tell him that I liked being worshipped by these people.

That I craved it.

"We are heading into a bloodbath," he said, staring daggers at the corpse-quiet old woman. "We have only just escaped the palace, Your Highness. We need to find a safe place, where we can think wisely about our next course of action."

I told him, once more, that I was not changing my mind.

"Abyss take it all, Your Highness, this is not wisdom! We cannot embark with the Gathering simply because you miss being loved. They do not love you, they just—"

Keema never heard the rest of the sentence; it was interrupted by a loud crash, like a body slammed into the floor.

Jun's face was pressed into the carpet, while his hands were pulled back and twisted into a painful helix. His feet were in the air. Blood welling in his head. His right hand twisting up and up, the veins popping red, the pain so great he started to piss himself.

I told him that he forgot himself.

"I—I—I—" he said.

I told him that I am a god.

"I—"

That a god needs no mortal's permission.

No false emperor.

No human.

She twisted him harder.

And no little whelp coward like him.

"I—I'm s-s-s-sorry!" he cried. "Please, God, I-I'm sorry!"

Good.

Jun dropped to the ground just as Keema slammed open the door. The boy was curled into himself, shaking like a wet dog. The old woman had not moved an inch, Her eyes still shut, no sign on Her of the violence She had just enacted on Her grandchild, Her servant. *I told him not to forget his station again. That he was but a stain of his father's bloodied seed.*

That by my grace alone was he deemed worthy of breath.

The boy wept. It was a loud, keening weep that started in the stomach, like some great, ulcerous pain. Keema hesitated before he entered. The malice in the room was pungent. When he did finally find the resolve to come inside, it was like penetrating a sheet of ice, his entire body shivering as he helped the weeping boy to his wobbling feet, and together they staggered out of that shadowed house. The empress, left behind on Her little cushion, alone.

In the quiet hum of that empty room, Her ancient hand, once balled into a fist, now relaxed.

I had overreacted.

They were well away from the houseboat when Jun pushed Keema away. It was a shrug that then became a hard shove, definitive, and strong enough to knock the Daware man on his back foot. He recovered swiftly enough, physically, he did not fall on his rear, but he stared wide-eyed at Jun, who seethed, and spat, humiliated in a way he had never been before—the feeling like a new egg in the old Peacock's stomach. His skin prickling, hot, his leg wet with his own piss and beginning to itch. When he took a step, he stumbled over, still weak from the attack, but when Keema reached out to help him, he warned him back, letting loose an incomprehensible snarl before he stormed off, alone, disappearing into the heart of the Gathering.

He went across planks and over railings. Tried to slip into the throngs of people who walked these connected decks, tried to lose himself there, but he was as noticeable as a torch in the dark. The people recoiled from him. They looked down at him from high-up railings, from nets, from behind mastheads. *There went the prince's butcher. There went the demon.* He winced at the memory of Her twisting him like a wet towel; the way Keema looked at him afterward, like he was a thing to be pitied. *You are a monster. You are not deserving of pity.* He needed to move, but he did not know where to. He couldn't leave. He couldn't stay.

His father felt the pain radiating from his son. He looked up at the crescent of light that lined the top of the jar.

"Jun," he whispered. "Do not wander in this place."

But his son was lost in the Gathering now, in no state to realize that he was, for the past few minutes, being followed.

By a woman, with a knife.

While the others celebrated the news of the death of the emperor and His progeny, Mira watched the Red Peacock, waiting for her opportunity. From her friend's boat she lay in wait for the bastard to emerge from the houseboat. Through the network of the Gathering she kept pace with his stumbling flight, the knife solid and sharp in her hand. *I wondered if this is how he felt, when he hunted my sister's family—this power. This ease, in stalking one's prey.* In an alley between steep vessels, where the sun was blocked by the masts and the world was but shadow and water, he stopped to gather himself, and she took in a breath. *I had never killed anyone in my life.* Pearlescent barnacles, latched to the hull, warped her reflection as she approached him—his back tightening as he sensed someone behind him. *But if I was ever to kill someone, then why not him?* The boy did not even turn around. It was like he knew. *Just do it, Mira!* She gripped the knife tight and stepped forward.

If she was capable of such an act, she would not yet discover it, for Kaara then appeared, as if she had come in from the water itself.

"He is a guest," Kaara said. "He is under Her protection."

And that was all that needed to be said for Mira to lower her knife hand.

The boy had turned around by then. They looked at one another. To her, he seemed somehow smaller than before, the demon of her memory now smudged, looking more like the young men she had known in her youth than a Terror's child. And to him, she was as a stranger. A woman in a fisher's robe. Her dark-brown hair tied up in a loose bun. And apart from the knife she held in her trembling grip, she reminded him of a friendly aunt; of the people his brigade passed so often on the road, unremarkable and easily forgotten. The both of them very tired that day.

"I know you," she said.

Jun did not doubt this. "I killed someone you loved," he said. It was a guess.

She nodded.

Correct.

"Three years ago, in Jerval's Field. We had run away from the textile fleet, with many others, after the revolt in the *Gorga*. The debts our families owed to Induun yet unpaid. Your brigade gave chase. It did not take you long to find us." She swallowed. "Jerval's Field. It was early morning. My sister and her husband were beheaded by your brothers. I was hiding under a body. And I saw you. Covered in blood. A hatchet in your hand. My nephew was ten years of age when you struck him down. His name was Sarva. He had caught his first trout not two days before his death. It was the largest anyone of his age had ever pulled from the water."

"I remember," Jun said.

"So you admit it," she said. "You admit to his murder."

He looked at her. His eyes red. The empress's words echoed in his head.

You are your father's stain.

"I do."

Mira covered her eyes. *I would not have him see me cry.* Kaara put an arm around the woman's shoulders and led her away. "That will have to do for now. Come, let's get you back to the others." Kaara spared a glance for Jun. "And you. I would suggest you return to your boat. Mira is not the only one who wants to put a knife in your back."

"Wait," Jun said.

Kaara paused. Mira turned her head, enough that he could see her profile.

"I will come back," he said. "After I am finished serving Her will . . . if I am still alive after all of this . . . I will come to you."

She narrowed her eyes at him.

"I swear it on my father's head," he said. "I swear it on the empress's will. On the ground I walk and the air I breathe. When this is over, I will return. On my knees I will come, and with any blade or weapon of your choosing you may take my life, however you might wish." He bowed, his lip trembling. "You may have my neck."

"Your word means nothing to me," Mira said. She turned away. "But should that day ever come, I will be ready for you, Peacock. For you, and your neck."

When he looked up, the two women were gone.

It wasn't long after that, that Keema found him.

"I found you these."

A new pair of breeches. *I had been washing my clothes and turned to fetch something, and when I came back, someone had stolen one of my pants, right off the rack.* They were black and loose, so he kept them rolled up at the shin, the cord in the hemline tied tight. He washed his soiled garments in the water, hanging them to dry on the side of the tortoise's boat. He thanked Keema for the clothes.

"Are you all right?" Keema asked.

Jun didn't bother to answer.

Keema watched in silence as Jun put the mask back on, his hands shaking while he did so, like an addict lighting a bowl of duri leaves. He didn't ask where he had gone, or what had happened to him in the heart of the Gathering; nor did he ask why he put the mask back on when everyone already knew who he was. He simply stood by his side and waited.

There were some hours yet to pass before the Gathering had finished its preparations for the attack. With permission from the admiralty, who wished to keep the peace between the fishermen and the empress's party, Keema took their pontoon boat and brought Jun to the shore at the edge of the reservoir, a small outcropping of rock and wet sand, bordered by an imposing wall of tall grass that they were warned not to approach. Jun sat down on the sand. Keema leaned against a boulder. Neither spoke; Jun far away and Keema wondering where he was but not knowing how to ask, for there had been so few opportunities in his life to practice such kindness.

Keema remembered the love worker who briefly took him under her wing, back when he was still a guard on the pleasure barge—how she would sit with him during his moods, and then, bored of his stoicism, would stand up and offer him her hand to dance. He was always resistant at first, a part of him fearing what might happen should he actually enjoy it . . . but she always got her way in the end. "Come, kitten," she'd say, pulling him to his feet, "there's nothing in this room to fear—this is nothing more than the old magick." Together they would move as one, telling stories with their bodies, of the greedy monkey and the forlorn husband, and the bending of ancient bamboo. He enjoyed it so much that he continued the practice even after she was gone from his life, and he had no one else to bring him out of himself. In his empty rented rooms and makeshift campsites, he would stand up, and move, and he would remember that at least he was here, breathing this air.

He wanted to show Jun this side of him. He wanted to stand up and reach out and offer Jun his hand and ask him if he would like to dance. But he was afraid, and in fear he could find no words to pull out of his parched throat.

And so he tackled him.

Offshore some fisher boats glided by. *We watched the weird young men fight for a time in the sand. We wondered if we should tell someone. We didn't.* They rolled over each other. Keema managed to roll on top of Jun and pincer his arms to his sides with nothing but the tension of his thighs.

"Do you submit?" he asked.

Jun's disbelief of the situation faded; wherever he had gone, he had returned.

"No," he said.

He kneed Keema in the crotch. Keema's eyes popped and he fell on his side, pressing his forehead in the sand, thrown of breath as his hand cradled his pain-throbbed genitals. Slowly, they rose to their feet, in unison; with one finger, Jun moved his mask back into place, the move subtle and cool; Keema snorted, and attacked. *We took bets. I was the only one who had a woodcut coin on the cripple.* And for the third time, they dueled. Keema dodged Jun's punch and grabbed his wrist, tossing him over his shoulder. Jun fell onto his back with a breathless humph, but didn't waste any time in tripping Keema's ankle, knocking him to the ground, where he then pounced, Keema struggling underneath him, wriggling his arm free before he knocked Jun's head aside with his elbow—a hollow thunk reverberating as his elbow collided with the edge of the mask—the boy withdrawing his arm in a vibrant, vibrating pain. He was drooling. They rolled down the shore, the sand in their hair, the both of them red-eyed and wild of voice. Both of them kind of spent. Rolling, one atop the other, and back again. "You— submit—do you submit . . ." Keema breathed out, only for Jun to shake his head before pressing his hand against Keema's cheek, smushing it into the sky. *We didn't stay long to watch. It soon became obvious this was a fight with no victor. We had other business anyway.* A few fishermen remained to watch as the two warriors fought like back-alley thieves, until finally they rolled off each other and lay sprawled in the sand without another breath to spare.

A draw.

"Probably . . . stupid of us . . . to do that. . . . before tonight . . ." Jun said.

This made Keema laugh, which in turn started Jun up laughing too.

No winner at all.

In time they got up again.

In time.

"How long has it been since you slept?"

Jun looked at him.

"I slept in the boat," he said.

"I mean really slept. Slept long enough to fall into the Sleeping Sea."

Jun turned away.

"Two days," he admitted.

Keema frowned. "You should have a rest."

"Not in this place," he said quietly. "It's not safe in this place." He laughed quietly too.

"I'll keep watch," Keema said.

"You'll keep watch," Jun repeated, laughing as if he didn't believe him. But Keema nodded and said it again.

"I will keep watch."

And there, in Jun's eyes, was a dared temptation to believe him.

"An oath, then," Keema said. He was sitting upright now, his head bowed in Jun's direction. "I swear to watch over you, Jun of No Tribe, for the next few hours while you sleep. I swear to protect you from any spirit or animal or living or dead thing that may mean you harm or mischief. I swear you will wake up again, and I swear that you will be rested."

"One of your famous oaths," Jun said lightly, but Keema could tell that he was moved by it, by the way he wouldn't look at him. As if defeated, Jun fell onto his back and shut his eyes. "Fine. At least I know that if you fuck this up you have to disembowel yourself."

"I hope that brings you much comfort as you sleep."

"Oh. It does."

They were both grinning.

For all of his paranoia, it did not take long for Jun to fall asleep, curled up in the sand. His breath evened out; he rolled onto his other side; and Keema, sitting on the boulder above him, did his duty. He kept watch over the sleeping Peacock while nursing what was probably a new bruise on his rear, and he watched the tall grass for movement, and he watched the water for anyone who might approach. Every now and then a boat passed by, some of them stopping for long enough for Keema to stand up, *and we would drift just beyond the shore, wondering if we could do it—if we could take them*—but the boats would always leave in the end.

Keema glanced at Jun on occasion, to make sure he was still there, he told himself; to make sure that what Jun feared most had not in fact happened. That nature hadn't taken its revenge. That the sand hadn't eaten him whole. That a wolf hadn't dragged him into the grass. His occasional glance became more frequent over the next few hours. The demon mask slipping off his face in his restless sleep, revealing to the light his dark eyelashes, his full and parted lips. He wondered what it would be like to run his finger along those lips, and then, ashamed that his mind had been so distracted, he returned to his task. He watched the grass, the sand, the water, as he listened to the light and dreaming breath. His oath upheld throughout the remaining hours before the return of the reconnaissance party, for no one, and nothing, had disturbed his sleeping charge.

She reached out, once, an hour before the horn blew.

I wanted to know if he was healthy. If he was still able to fight that night.

"Yes," Keema whispered, looking at him now. "He's fine."

Good, I said to him.

I left it at that.

And the small hairs on the back of Keema's neck prickled a bit at the passing of Her unearthly presence.

DUSK

Upon the fall of the sun, the signal was given.

The admiralty led all of the clans in prayer while a group of children played a row of small golden bells, calling out to the spirits of fortune. *May the river carry us safe on our passage. May the things in the dark recoil from our bow.* On the hull of Tajeem's ship, the final blessings were painted. And Kaara/Tak-Lina swiped her bloodied palm on the prows of the boats that would lead the charge. *May we be doubtless in our search for freedom.* The unfurling of the Gathering occurred without collision or bump; their movements practiced as they unlatched the boats from one another and directed their oars toward the exit rivers, the entire construction dismantled in less than half an hour, ship following ship, silently in one another's wake as dusk burned above them.

With their weapons returned to them, Keema and Jun had returned to their boat, with the empress and the tortoise, and they were about to take up oars when Kaara/Tak-Lina glided up to their side and said, "Don't bother," and with a wink carried them forward on a summoned wave; the wind tousling their hair as they joined the departing line.

And they were off.

Night, falling like a dead man.

The lantern blown out; the world cast back into that total and unforgiving dark; the sky as black as the Burn itself. Throughout the Thousand, the rivers were emptied of boats, the trawling lines pulled and the traps left out in the waters—the people of the river villages shutting their doors as they put their children to bed in their hammocks and made their rounds to the windows, ensuring the latches were bolted and that no nighttime creatures would be finding their way inside, while northward, the Gathering flew.

They were sleek as carp, cutting silk through the water, the reflection of the sky shuddering in their wake; the stars shaking like children in the cold. All around them was a lightless world. They turned onto a thoroughfare, the tall grass now well behind them. In the far distance, small lights burned like beads from a broken necklace. Tree lines and mountaintops were visible only by the stars they blocked.

"I feel you there," the voice in the jar said softly.

"Jun," the voice said.

"Speak to me, Jun."

Jun did not speak.

A black shape towered on the horizon—the crater that was the Bowl of Heaven.

The quiet fleet entered one of the main straits, empty of civilian vessels. They were an arrow, aimed for the twelfth canalway. The massive wall of the crater continued to lift into the sky, and Keema wondered if the walls were higher than even the palace mountains. He noticed that unlike the other rivers to his left and his right, which were peopled with torches and lit-up wooden towers, theirs was almost completely dark. He would on occasion hear something odd on the wind, but whatever it was, was too far up for him to pick up anything other than an echo of a scream. Their boat passed at least three dark, unattended watchtowers. They bumped into something in the water, but Kaara/Tak-Lina's wave had already pushed them on before Keema could see what it was that was floating in the water. *I was singing a song that my friend hated. Neither of us were looking out at the water like we were supposed to. I was too busy laughing, driving him mad. And then I went silent. "Finally you shut up," he said, smiling, and when he turned around, it was just in time to see my throat being opened by a knife from the dark.*

Canalway Twelve approached like a hungry snake. The tunnel entrance was abandoned, the guard station demolished, the ballista boats shattered, *a fight we'd finished not a few moments before the first of the ships arrived*, the bodies strewn across the water.

The dark tunnel swallowed them, their ears popping from the change in pressure.

"Do you get nervous before a battle?" Jun asked in that black passage.

"Yes," Keema said. "I get nervous."

Jun chuckled.

"Why is that funny?" Keema asked, a little insulted.

"Fear is not something my brothers would ever admit to. I've never met any warrior who would admit to such weakness."

"It's not a weakness," Keema said.

"Oh?"

"Fear keeps you alive."

"Not always." Jun tilted his head. "Not when fear kills your good ideas. Not when it makes you run and your enemy shoots you in the back with his arrow."

"My fear has never guided me wrong," Keema said.

Jun shrugged. "Either way, it was not an insult. Not intended, at least." He made a strange and unreadable gesture in the dark. "It's interesting that you are so proud of your fear."

"Are you not afraid before a fight?"

Jun took off his mask and looked at him. His face appearing and disappearing along the tunnel wall of torchlight.

He was smiling.

They were out of the tunnel.

They spilled out into the apartment district. The twenty-third. The southwest passage. Massive apartment barges towered over their paltry ship like great ocean beasts surrounding minnow. *We were awake in our berths. The overseers believed we were asleep. They did not know we were waiting for the lighting of a torch.* Shouts rang out ahead—panicked, terrified. Something large crashed into the water and sounded to Keema like an entire building had lost its balance and fallen in. *They did not know that we were mighty.*

And then it was quiet again. It was time for Keema and Jun to part from the main line. Kaara/Tak-Lina nodded at them as they headed their own way down the dark waterways between the looming barges. Without her wave, they were forced to row with the oars they had been given—*A loan, I told the Peacock, when I handed him the oar, so make sure you return it after this is done.* They pushed through the water in silence, passing beneath dank woodwork and rickety catwalks and stone arches; between the lesser barges, where the lights were never on and where if one looked with enough care one would see the movement of hungry eyes shining against distant torchlight. *Not all of us were part of the plan. Some of us watched, and wondered. We whispered, "What if?" What if it was all about to end?* While fires bloomed in the direction from which they had come, they made their way to the northeastern quarter of the Bowl, cutting across the wide central expanse to the prison fleet, where, once they were close, Jun turned to the Defect, and said, "Your turn." The creature raised its head and listened to the vibrations of the threads in the night and led them through the ink-black spots between torchlight, its whispering giggle directing them, "Yes, this way," and "More to the right," for Keema and Jun were, for all intents and purposes, working blind as they wended their way into the spiderweb of the prison fleet.

"Stop," the Defect snapped.

A torchlit patrol boat came around the hull of a massive junk ship. A man at a swiveling ballista stared into the dark as his oarsmen pushed the boat onward. One of them lifting his nose into the air. *Thought I smelled something foul—but what didn't, in those waters?*

The boat moved on, and the party sighed. On they went, and the closer they got to the center of the fleet, the louder and more frantic the tortoise became, its head whipping around as if trying to see over its own shell. Jun tried to quiet it down as it loudly murmured, "I have arrived, my God, I have arrived . . ." They passed under a banner, stretched between two giant ships, celebrating the Holy Week. Keema sensed something amiss. A feeling that raised the fine hairs on his arm as he looked out into the dark and quiet avenues of royal ships. There were no more boats. No perches from which the Terror's Silver Monkeys might strike. It seemed all the forces of the Bowl were already heading toward the Gathering's strike points.

"Tread with care," he whispered.

The royal prison barge lay ahead of them, the second largest ship in the prison fleet. Keema felt a sense of vertigo as they approached it, as if they were but ants crawling up to a fallen tree. The Defect's head, like a dowsing rod, pointed toward the heart of the vessel and said, "Right there. Please, my Gracious Moon, free my mother! They are right there!" Jun snapped at it to be quiet.

They drifted up to the sheer rise of the hull, just under the area the tortoise was pointing eagerly toward. They all looked to the empress. *I did not tell them how tired I was; how spent, from all of my behavior back at the Gathering. Pride, I suppose. I had brought them here. If I did not do my part, what manner of god was I? So I pulled what little energy I could out of my increasingly empty bag, and I made them an opening.* The starboard wall of the barge was shorn off like old skin, with the popping of hundreds of nails pried out of their sockets, Keema staring in silent awe at this display of magick, as the wooden wall shattered into the water in many small detonations, their boat careening over the disturbed waves. She had revealed a cross-section of the interior of the boat; a dark honeycomb of rooms and cells on display like the naval exhibits you once liked to visit. None of the lights inside the boat were on. There was no one inside. Keema noted this to the others, unnecessarily.

"Perhaps they have abandoned their posts," he suggested.

"I don't know," Jun said again.

"There it is," the Defect said. "There!"

On the lowest level of the barge, in the widest and tallest of the unlit rooms, as large as a warehouse, there was the shape of something large and round. Tortoise-shaped, perhaps, but in this thick night, and from their distance, it was impossible for them to be sure. "Gracious Moon! I beg you, save this one's mother!" the Defect cried. *But I, too, was troubled. Something was off about the tortoise god's presence. I had so little left to spare—we needed to be sure what it was we had come to save.* Jun nodded, and he and Keema rowed closer up to the side of the barge, next to the mildewed and barnacled siding. It was Keema who volunteered to go up and check it out.

"No, I will," Jun said. "This is my duty."

Keema shook his head. "Of everyone on this boat, my death would be the least inconvenient."

Jun scowled, started with a "But—" and then *I threw up my proverbial hands and said for SOMEONE to go,* and before Jun could protest, Keema leapt off the boat. He had chucked the spear before him, landing its point just below the entrance to the prison, and was now scaling the wall of the barge, the cracks in the hull providing him with just enough footing that he could launch himself up, by his one arm and his two feet, like a panther—throwing himself, in a heavy pant, onto the floor of the hold. He scratched his thigh on a broken wooden board as he wriggled inside, blood seeping from the wound. Wincing, he signaled to the others below that he was fine with a wave of his hand, and Jun moved the boat farther out so they could get a better view of him and the interior.

It smelled awful—as if there were thirty Defects in the room with him, oozing pus. Breathing through his mouth, Keema twisted the spear out of its wedge in the wood and made his way in. He didn't get very far before a voice from the dark said,

"Stop."

Upon the man's Word, he had no choice but to obey.

Every muscle in his body went rigid, only his eyes remaining mobile—two terrified orbs, darting in every direction that could be conceived, while the rest of the body remained as still as stone. A breathless grunt escaped his unmoving lips. His frozen chest. It was a fear that Keema had never known before. Not even his small finger accepted his command. Someone could walk right up to him and lick the side of his face and steal his spear and he would not even be able to flinch. His pupils tunneled into pinpricks as a bright flame was ignited on the other end of the prison holding.

There, by the torchlight, and the shadow of some behemoth creature, stood a man slight and small. He was dressed in a very fine black robe patterned with intricate red designs, a thick scarf wrapped around his neck, its colors red and black. The man seemed the type to have never sat on anything harder than a pillow; delicate, his posture that of someone who had just woken up. Bored, tired. Someone who was waiting for his dance partner to return. "You made it," he said, his voice fine and rich in the way older voices often were—though his had a hard rasp to it, as if sore from some recent injury. He was perhaps in his mid-forties. The same age as—

"My brother," the man continued. "You are the one who beheaded him. The boy of the Daware tribe."

A strangled noise quit his mouth.

"Oh, right," the man said. "**You can speak.**"

"You are Luubu," Keema said, dry-mouthed.

The Second Terror smiled. He walked past a teeth-clenched Keema and toward the massive cataract in the wall, stopping himself at the broken edge.

"She's down there, too, isn't She?" he said.

"She'll rip . . . your face off," Keema struggled to say, his frantic lungs still swelled against his rictus muscles.

Luubu made a show of thinking about this.

"Good point," he said, nodding to someone in the far back.

The nod was the signal.

From the rails of the prison barge deck large mesh sacks were tossed. The heavy sacks sailed through the air, trailing behind them long umbilicals of rope that, at the termination of their length, went taut as bowstring, thrumming, as the sacks swayed above the brackish surface of the crater's waters.

I felt it immediately.

Beneath the moonrock traps, the water began to tremble.

It began to shriek.

He had captured me.

The old woman, silenced, was powerless as Luubu looked down at Her from the ship's cataract. His own ears, closed to the world with plugs of wax, were deaf to the sound of the tremoring water, his Word still powerful as he waved down at Her and shouted, "Hello, Mother!" And "Hello, nephew!" And ". . . hello, brother." Behind him, Keema, red-faced, grunting, tried to take a step forward, in vain. His hand, tight around Araya's spear, would not budge. He wanted to vomit. He looked around the room for anything that might help him. And it was then that he took true notice of the large shape half-hidden from torchlight. His eyes widening as the dark resolved, and he saw what it was.

What had become of it.

"My god! I am here! Where are you!" the Defect cried.

Keema felt the bile rise in his throat as he looked upon the gargantuan shell of the tortoise god, cleaved in two. Half of the creature's face yet uneaten, its mouth opened as if in mid-scream, the flesh all but gone. The god had been hollowed out like a tajeline. And its corpse smelled like nothing Keema had ever smelled before, the underside of death, his eyes watering, the salty tracks running down his frozen cheeks.

Luubu smiled down at the little boat in the water. His voice entered their heads, though his lips made no movement. *I told them that I was sorry, but I had eaten the god they were searching for. That it took a long time. There was so much . . . flesh. The womb had already been taken to the palace many years ago, to feed the heat beds, but what remained on the body was nothing short of a feast. It was a project that lasted over the course of many months, and only now, standing here, looking down at them, had I reached the end of it. I told the defective tortoise that if it was any consolation, its god was a resilient creature.*

It was alive for most of it.

"No . . ." the Defect murmured.

Yes, I told the tortoise. And with each awful bite I gained more access to the One Mind, until the whole network was mine. I saw through the eyes of its brethren and I heard through their ears—and, just that day, I had opened my way into the Defect, tricking the creature into believing its Mother was reaching out to it.

Luubu sighed with pride.

What a joy it was, to discover not only my beloved mother in your company, but my brother's head too. What a—

"LIES!" the tortoise cried. It honked pitifully into the air. "MY GOD! ANSWER ME! MY GOD! YOUR CHILD HAS COME FOR YOU!"

"It is bad form to interrupt someone when he's speaking," Luubu said to the creature with some distaste. He gestured at his men. And Keema heard from somewhere above him the creak of wood: the large, turreted ballistas, loaded with thick iron-head bolts, spun in the direction of the boat in the water. *The night thrummed with loosened bowstrings.* He saw the brief glimpse of bolts as they shot past the hole in the wall of the barge, their serrated metal tips catching the light of the torches in one instant before they sank deep into the Defect's shell, five of them peppering its body, and one, aimed by the truest shot the Silver Monkeys had, pinning the sobbing head to the floor of the boat.

It was dead, its god's name lost on its withering tongue.

Black bile oozed from its ear hole.

Jun shrank back, begging the old woman to do something, in his panic kicking the rice jar, the First Terror's head rolling out into the spreading pool of tortoise bile, but the empress did nothing, for she was a breathing body and nothing more, no longer able to fight back against the scream of the water—the energies of the natural world stopped along these frozen threads—all of her efforts focused on holding her consciousness together.

Keema clenched his teeth, his furious gaze trained on Luubu, his spear hand trembling against the restraints of the prince's Word.

"You . . . are . . . a coward," he said.

The Second Terror looked at him as if he had forgotten he was there. He looked at one of his guards. "Why does this boy still live?"

And when Keema turned his head, he saw a man from the dark, with silver paint on his face, lunging at him with a needle-thin dagger aimed right for his heart, and he knew there was no avoiding its plunge, that he would die right there, and he thought of how sorry and pathetic an end that would be for him, the stupidity that had brought them to this discursive point, when a spout of water shot through the hole in the barge and punched him out the other side like a rag doll, his limp body tossed into the water by the river spirit Kaara/Tak-Lina, upon one last desperate throw before the shrieking water dissolved her and he fell into the dark water of the Bowl, bruised, and broken, and lost of consciousness.

And at the end of this Day, there is silence.

The audience is quiet as the players leave the stage, leaving only this moonlit body under the light of the brazier. You hear the change in the atmosphere. The utter quietude of it. The voices of the ancient and of the dead receding, too, for but a brief time, to make space for the one who would tell their own story.

At the end of that Second Day, as I felt my senses robbed from me for the last time, I knew that if I did not act, and did not act swiftly, then all would be lost. We stand before the Third Day of the Holy Pilgrimage, this most fateful Day, and we perform a dancer's swap. *I had gone quiet for too long—I had let my body rot in its disuse.* And for a day, we trade one voice for another. A move that is only appropriate, considering the events that are soon to follow. In this Inverted Theater, out of time, and out of place, this moonlit body allows Her Royal Whisper to enter in full, to tell the tale as she would tell it. *How on the Third Day I made a choice I never thought I would make.* The tale of a wrathful child's revenge, and the breaking of the Bowl of Heaven. *So hear me, audience of the theater—listen to the Moon on High, the Empress of the Eight Sons of the Moon Throne, for I have a tale to tell.*

THE THIRD DAY

—

in which we offer our finest weaves

It began and ended here.

The Bowl of Heaven, they called it, for from its depths sprung an eternal font of water that fed the land. Throughout my time on this Earth, the Bowl had been a mark of pride for the people—proof that humanity had been chosen by the gods to rule this country. Yet for me this crater was not a gift of the five heavens but an embarrassment, a shame, deep in my bones. When I looked upon this crater, what I saw was a deep scarring of the earth. I saw the rivers of fault and blame, spreading out from my hands.

I saw my body, falling.

The crater was where they found me after I had quit my place in the heavens. At the bottom of the burnt-out basin, atop the cracked shell of the wounded tortoise god who absorbed the brunt of my impact, my new, fragile, human form draped unconscious over the bleeding creature. I do not know for how long I slept, but when I woke, the tortoise god had carried me to the nearby village, where I was surrounded by supplicants, on their knees, their heads bowed low, and their hands out, begging me to touch them. I was finally here; no longer were these people distant abstractions to be witnessed from high up and far away; they were now up close, and so loving, it was an intensity beyond measure. I rose up to meet them, but when I slid off the mighty shell of the tortoise, my legs, new and never used, swiftly gave out beneath me and I collapsed into the dirt. I rolled onto my back as the people murmured and cooed over me, and through their ministrations I looked up at the sky, at the dark Burn high above, until the crowd parted for the warrior who had cut me free from the stars. He touched his forehead to the dirt and he told me he was glad that I had made it down safely, before he reminded me, softly, that in exchange for what he had done, I had promised him his heart's desire.

"And what is it that you want?" I asked, with barely a breath to ask it.

"Sons," he said. "I would like sons."

It is not hard to remember the old days.

My time as the Moon is never far from mind. The days of cold milk forests and silver rivers are a sacred hideaway in the isles of my memory. I dream of rare midnight flowers curling open to the night sky, drinking up my radiance, and of lovers in the woods, dewy and flush, breathing in my moonlight through their skin. I was once a great beauty.

I was the second creation of the Weaver. His Pale Eye. I watched Him stitch together the carpet of stars, and I bore witness to His eight consorts, who breathed life into the barren land like bellows stoking a fire, the canopies of trees billowing up from the canyons like smoke. I was there from the beginning, watching the first seeds take root, and the rivers pulse and overflow. I was there when the first of men came crawling from the Water, like babes bare-fleshed and weak, squinting against the light. I was there when they picked up that rock, and struck down their brother in the woods. I was there at the first spilling of blood.

There is much of my experience in those days that I cannot translate into human speech. Beauty and terror unutterable to your muscled tongue. Believe me only when I say that the world back then was like that of the ripest berry, swollen and bursting in the teeth. Those were the days before gates and brigades; before the Red Palace and the Northern Estates and the Divine City. Those were the days when the animal castes still populated the fields and forests, strong in number, their homes not yet cut down for their timber, their burrows not burned out for their metals. When the bears and the wolves still commanded the mountains and the rivers still bucked with shimmering fish. But of all the wonders that were on display below my pale eye, there was nothing I loved more than to watch the dancing.

The people were fewer in number in those days. They had to fight for their place alongside the other castes. To compensate for their lack of fang and claw, the Water taught them the magick of the dance. The people danced for the earth, and the earth giggled and swelled and made the harvests ever richer. *We called it The Palm Beats the Dirt.* They danced for the rivers and the fish, and the fish leapt into open nets. *The Spring Fills Our Basket.* They danced for the sky to bring rain for the grass and thunder when fire was in need. *The Arrow Pierces the Cloud.* They danced for the people. They imbued the builders with the gift of strength and the artists the light of creativity. And when my sibling Sun would retire, and it was my turn to take position in the sky in our eternal vigil with the Great Dark, the people would perform for me, and me alone. I drenched their land with my light, in pools and valleys, I made their paths safe to travel, and they gave to me their wonderful dances that told tales of lost loves and great battles.

When I cast my reflection into the heart of the ocean, and visited my love in its Inverted World, it would ask me what I thought of the newest dances it had taught the people. And we embraced, as I told the Water that each dance was finer than the last.

"It is all for you," they whispered in my cold and luminous ear.

If only there were a way to prolong the inevitable. If only there were a way to hold a moment in your hands and keep it alive forever.

But nothing, and no one, lives forever.

Not even gods. We are mighty, but we are not invulnerable. Death simply must work harder to catch us—another few hundred years, a few thousand perhaps, until from our fallen corpse a new god is born, like a molting, and whatever we once were disappears. Our likes and our loves gone, as a new order rises in our stead. Up until the days of humans and their dances, I had lived for a very long time. The surface of myself had become pocked and cracked and cratered, and I knew that if I let myself remain in that form any longer, I would disappear; a new Moon would take my throne, and it would no longer be my light that the animals and the forests bathed in. It would no longer be to me whom the dancers presented their finest arts, but some other lesser creature who would not be able to appreciate and love the same things I did; and such a thought I could not bear.

I would rather there were no Moon at all.

To the strongest of the humans, I asked of him this: free me from this Tapestry, and I will answer your heart's desire. The man, who hungered for more than life would ever offer him, accepted my task, and he built a blade longer than any blade had been built before, which he used to cut the stitching around my body. And as I came tumbling from the throne that the blessed Weaver had given me and fell toward the earth, I believed I had done it. I had tricked them all. I had tricked even Death itself. For I knew that if I remained missing from the sky, no new Moon could be birthed from my corpse, and there would be nothing left on heaven's throne but an infertile Burn, a scar that would remain as proof of my eternal rule, and no one else's.

When I woke in my new form, earthbound, and mortal, I entered some of the happiest years of my life, as I enjoyed the dances up close, and even learned some of them myself—the feeling so much more tactile, and present, than the strange, upside-down workings of my dear Water's Inverted Theater. I even came to enjoy the warrior who freed me, who was himself a most skilled dancer, and lover, and I did not mind when he requested of me that I take on the form of a woman, to better fit with his desire. But always, beneath all of my moments in their company, I was aware of the world I had left, and the one I was yet expected to create.

"I want sons," he said.

Sons, he said, and the lands of his brothers, for nothing tastes so sweet to the human tongue than the squeeze of stolen fruit. So I gave him sons, and I gave those sons the power to not only survive in this world, but to take it for themselves. And in this dynasty, I lost myself. I forgot about the Weaver and the Stars and even the Water—the Burn above my head all but a small reminder of how far I had come. All that mattered was my family and throne.

The tortoise god once wondered aloud if they had done the right thing, catching me the day of my fall. The first sluice gate had by then been constructed, the Gora River choked of water.

"What did I save that day?" the god asked.

I could not say.

Many generations later, I looked up for an answer.

And my son looked back down on me.

From the dark cataract of the ship, very little of Luubu's expression was visible to me, but I knew that he was happy. His trap had ensnared us, and the wretched Defect had been slain by the ballista bolts, and the Daware man was nowhere to be seen, but my son, who had orchestrated all of this misery, seemed to think of nothing but of how glad he was that I was there, to see him triumph. But his joy, I think, would have been tempered slightly, had he known that his success was only partial, for I had been trapped once before by the moonrock pentagram, by his father—trapped, for a very long time—and I by then had a sense for when one might strike; which is why, the closer we came to the prison fleet, I in my well-founded suspicions took a precaution, and before we arrived at the boat in which we believed the tortoise god to dwell, I had done something reckless and unwise.

DAWN

I split myself.

Inadvisable. That is what Jun would have said if I had shared my plans with him before I took matters into my own hands. Over the brief time that I had known him, he had been becoming more and more impertinent, but in this instance he would have been right to chastise me. I had only so much of myself left to spend, and to divide myself between two bodies took effort and strength I had barely the reservoir for. But the choice proved wise, and from two separate points of awareness I watched the events of that night unfold: from my body, and from the eyes of a small gorion bird, perched atop the railing of a nearby prison vessel.

The bird was distant enough that it was only mildly affected by the trap's dampening power. Through its beady eyes I saw the moonrock sacks sail over the railing, and I saw the swivel of the ballistas, and the flash of metal before the bolts found their target in the tortoise's body. I saw Jun crouch over the tortoise's head, stroking its bloodied beak, as the patrol boats came out from Luubu's ship to seize us. And as my body drowned under the weight of the screaming water, my small wings beat furiously, and I flew high above the Bowl, and below the morning-dark skies.

I took stock of the city.

The crater echoed with the sound of battle. Luubu may have tricked his family into his trap, but there was little he could do to the growing rebellion but engage it in the many little skirmishes that were occurring, at once, throughout the Bowl.

My little bird observed from the railings and rafters the fighting. Many of those revolting were the workers who lived in the dirtier apartment barges, who worked the trawling ships and the textile fleets. Kaara/Tak-Lina and her admiralty's tactics were that of confusion. The night had begun with the spark of small fires throughout the Bowl, with missing patrol boats and strange commands from superiors, delivered through the flash of coded messages across ship prows. Half a crate of explosive powders, stolen from Lord Waag's foundry, was used to sink the largest of the barracks-boats, while the other half was used to hold hostage the *Shrik-Soso* pleasure barge, which was wide enough to provide cover from ballista fire for the other insurgents.

Now, in this early morning, the heads of the captaincy of the most important ships were being severed. Men and women young and old took up arms and charged through the deck halls and even climbed up into the netting of the sails like spiders up tilted webs as they overthrew the masters and backbreakers, while patrolling ballista boats sprung bolts into their chests, spearing them overboard into the water. I saw three men pinned to the hull of a ship by a single discharge, like a stack of parchment stuck to a needle. I saw a fire lit in the berth of an apartment barge, the flames rising from the lowest and the poorest of the decks to the highest, the people flinging themselves into the water to save themselves, where they were cut down by the blades of Luubu's brigade, the Silver Monkeys. As for where Kaara/Tak-Lina was in all this, I did not know.

At the time I assumed she had been as affected by the trap as I had been, and was, I supposed, dispersed into the cold waters of the Bowl in many droplets, trying to re-collect herself.

The sounds of the fighting were everywhere; one could not escape them. However, there were parts around the Bowl where it was noticeably quieter; where the smokestacks from the flames were but thin black lines on the horizon of these protected neighborhoods, and the boats had time to draw the water collected overnight from their bilges. It was in such an area, in one of the wealthier pleasure bays within the crater, where I discovered the Daware man's body, floating in the water. My bird landed on him and was relieved to find that he was not dead, just unconscious, his pulse a slow and distant drumbeat below my talons. But no matter how many times I pecked at his chest, he did not stir, and in time I was forced to abandon him when a sudden torchlight illuminated his body and shadowed men in a slim collector's skiff dragged him aboard. *Troubled times, like that day in the Bowl, that was when we went out hunting—no one notices a trotter here or there gone missing.* I followed them at a distance as far as I could, but the skiff soon disappeared into the interior of a massive pleasure barge. I studied the markings emblazoned on the side of the barge so that I could remember it and told myself that I would soon return after I had finished my reconnaissance of the crater at large.

And while this was all occurring, I was still aware of, but not yet focused on, the senses of my body—not until we had stopped and I was parted from my son, and Jun, somewhat violently.

We were brought onto Luubu's pleasure ship.

A man I did not know carried me. His hands were large and rough, and the sense of myself that was royal was offended that he touched my person. I fixated on this affront as I was brought to a small, private room, where I was kept under lock and key. The man with rough hands placed me on a sitting pillow like an old, used-up toy.

I thought that perhaps with enough effort I could use the last of myself to pop open this blasphemous man's head, but the thought was fleeting, and with time I was able to remember myself as well, as the rules were yet the same: do not spend all my coin on one game. This body had enough for only one more physical act, and I intended to make it count.

The room was as florid as one might expect from one of Luubu's royal cruises. There was a bed wide enough for five humans, with sheer curtains that parted the mattress from the rest of the room, and on the other side of the room, a long and plush lounge sofa and tea table carved from a single piece of red gannet wood. This was the room for visiting dignitaries, for people the Second Terror wished to impress his wealth and status upon. For a room of such pedigree, I was surprised that the screech of the moonrock trap seemed unusually loud in here; with some surveyance—I could yet project myself some distance from my body—I discovered a series of holes in the wall, too small to crawl through but large enough to let in all the sounds from outside. There were also two openmouthed pipes that erupted from the corner of the room. I projected my mind upwards and I followed these pipes. One went up to the bridge of this ship, which was, curiously, empty, and the other went from this room to the outside, as if designed to more clearly pick up the noise of the Bowl, and in this way it seemed that this room had been built just for me.

I could go a bit further. Luubu's trap was spread out, diffuse, not as acute in its disruption as the Wolf Door's; I could not move so much as a book or a teacup, but I could at least spy into the adjoining rooms and see where the others were being kept. My son was in the room across the hall from me. His head was placed on a dinner plate, which sat atop a stool in the middle of an empty room, cleared of all furniture. Someone had taken the effort of decorating the plate with some sliced fruits and finely cut greens. *It was Deegan who did it, the crack-up. He was the one who plated the royal pig. Luubu approved of the scene. The head on the plate, less so.* He seemed aware of my presence in the room.

"A fine day this is turning out to be, isn't it, Mother?" he said.

I moved on until I found Jun. He was down the steps, in the lower deck. They had thrown him into a small closet that was once used for storing various tools and materials for fixing the ship's odds and ends, but the shelves had been cleared out. His mask had also been taken from him. He was kicking at the door, trying to break it open, when it suddenly did, the lock splintering outward. He was briefly jubilant before three men appeared and beat him into submission. Enough so that when he was deposited back into the closet, it was all he could do to crawl into the corner of the room and cover with his bloody hands the tattoo on his face.

"Having fun looking around?"

The brass voice came from one of the pipes in my room. I pulled myself back into my body.

"Strange," the voice from the pipe said, "that this is only our second time meeting each other. That the only other time was when I was born. For what it is worth, I would like you to know that it is a pleasure to have you aboard my finest craft. It's okay, you don't have to speak, I understand why you prefer silence. I would, too, at your age. I just wanted to check in before everything gets started. To let you know that you are in my care now, and that I intend to keep you as close to myself as possible." There was a smile in his voice that would have made a human nauseous. He went on to talk some more, but I was uninterested in what he had to say, so I focused my efforts elsewhere for the time being. My little bird was circling the inner wall of the crater when it spied something curious.

Two long boats, filled with masked men.

They glided silently through one of the canal gates, no one there to witness their entrance, for the gates were destroyed in the uprising, and the guard posts were on fire, draped with bodies, or simply abandoned. The twin crafts cut across the water at a deliberate and watchful pace. The way their many little oars dipped in and out of the water reminded me of the small legs of a centipede, running across a bedroom floor. By the make of their dress, cloaked and hooded, I could tell they were neither rebel nor Silver Monkey, but a third party whose identity I could not yet determine. But I was too preoccupied with thinking of a plan of escape for my body to be further concerned with these new arrivals.

The main issue I was confronting was that being a small bird was somewhat useless. This was not the bird's fault. If I could have inhabited a person, I would have, but the unwilling mind of a human takes great effort to wrangle; I did not have the strength to wrangle, only coax, and the bird happened to be the only creature in reach who was open to my whispering.

With my options limited in what I could do on my own, I had to resort to allies, and the sole ally I had who was not in Luubu's capture was the Daware man. I was worried that communication would be difficult between us, since I was a bird, and he was not, but he had proven himself capable on this journey. I flew back toward the pleasure barge into which he was taken, trusting that, once I freed him, we would find some method of alliance.

As I flew, I checked in on my body. Luubu was no longer speaking to me through the brass flower, and there was no one coming to interfere with my body, which meant I still had time to act before my son did something regrettable. What exactly his plans were, for me, for Saam and Jun, I did not know.

I did not care to find out.

MORNING

Had they all been so violent?

Even the Third Emperor, the softest of my boys, turned cruel in his later years. In those days I was a more active parent; I even delighted in teaching my sons the way of the world. The Third and I spent much time in the Bowl, where I showed him the secrets within its waters. The worms that emerged from the spout of the Sleeping Sea; worms that spun silk in their bellies. And together we wove fine carpets and tapestries the likes of which I think are yet to be matched in quality.

He was, perhaps, too soft. Those who craved his power beheaded him. I took our revenge, and afterward I sewed my son's head back onto his body, but I saw that ever since then he was not the same. He shied away from the things he used to like to do. He let the people weave the carpets and he shrunk away from the light. Fear weighed on his shoulders every day. Once, on the banister of the pleasure boat, a small bird landed gently, and my son flinched, and I watched him as he, without a word, used the power I had given him to break the bird's neck.

The creature dropped into the water like a rock.

"There is nothing left to fear, Mother," he said softly.

Blame is an endless circle.

And I seemed to be standing in the center of it.

As I returned to the barge that had swallowed the Daware man, a few stray arrows almost clipped my wings. I had flown too low and had glided straight through some battle below that I was not taking notice of. *The boat was almost under our control before Overseer Sengyyna lit the signal that called for help and before we knew it we were firing arrows at a patrol ship that was coming up on us. Olan didn't make it. Right through the eye the arrow went. I had failed countless oaths that day, but that was the one that hurt the most.*

The barge was quite a distance beyond the battle. It sat heavily amongst other pleasure ships of its kind, like a family of walruses on some little-visited shore. I circled its massive form, searching for a way in, but for all of my searching I could find only one entrance:

a docking bay that opened up in the rear of the ship, where visitors landed their skiffs.

I landed upon a railing within the docking bay, taking care not to be seen and shooed away, and I listened to the people coming and going, hoping to pick up a piece of information, a clue, that would tell me where they had taken him. This did not prove difficult, for he was the only one-armed person that had come through that day. I learned that such a person of his description was taken into the deck two floors up. There was a conspiratorial hush to the way they traded this information that worried me as to his fate, so I flew quick through the ship, only once being spotted by a young cleaner who tried to bat me off with his broom. He chased me, but I quickly lost him in the crowd of people walking toward the main staircases; everyone else didn't seem to mind that I had come, though some covered their heads with their hands as I flew over them.

When I found where the Daware man was being kept, I saw that I was right to be concerned. With some expert and well-timed flutters from ceiling beam to ceiling beam I was able to get deep enough into the third deck to discover what the people here called the Toy Room. *We were the toys of the pleasure chest. And we never got out.* In the shadowed recesses of the pleasure barges both fine and suspect one is bound to find such places, where a person may be taken and through long-term means be rendered into only a breathing body for the pleasure of those who might find use for it. The mind scrubbed out through cruelty. *I was broken, I was. They took these sticks, hard and pointed, and they, they, they—*

These Toy Rooms were not against the law, but they were frowned upon when it came to terms of good taste, even though it was well known that Luubu partook in such company. *He whispered in my ear that I never loved anyone but him, and his Whisper curled around my thoughts and I believed it, I believed he was the only one I had ever loved and when he left I scratched at the walls to get to him until my fingernails snapped off in the cracks in the wood.* It was here where I found the Daware man, his arm and right leg chained to the boards of the cell in which he was kept. He had by then regained consciousness but still seemed dazed and disbelieving of his situation. He had been beaten. His left eye was swollen, his bottom lip broken. And his spear was gone, presumably lost in the waters of the Bowl.

A woman almost as tall as the deck itself was walking up and down the cells with a pleased smile. Her torch-thrown shadow passed over the cages, making the inhabitants shrink back into the wall. *We dared not look at her. We knew what horrible sounds she would bring out of us, should our gazes meet.* When she was far enough that I felt safe to venture out, I swooped down through the bars of the Daware man's cell and found myself wondering how to speak to him, for he just looked at me with a blank expression and said, in a whisper, "You are not the bird from before." He wore a weak, bruised smile. "Are you that bird's friend? I would keep my distance if I were you." He made a pained expression, staring at his empty hand, and though he said nothing, I knew his thoughts were of defeat. "I am an oath breaker," he said, close to tears. "I am a man of poor fortune."

I cared about none of this. I tweeted at him and I flapped my wings, but this aroused no useful response in him; he merely smiled at me, as if he was humoring me. He made no effort to interpret or understand, his mind too tired to engage in such decoding; all he wanted was to enjoy this little bird that had chosen to visit him. It was an immensely frustrating experience. "If you see a guy in a palace mask," he said tiredly, "tell him I'm looking for him." I needed use of the Daware man's body, but I could not leave the bird and enter his mind. I was worried that the slightest bit of resistance from him would dissolve this shadowed self of mine. I had to choose my next action with care.

The fearsome woman was coming back around from the end of the corridor. With no recourse, I decided to leave the Daware man for the time being. He seemed not to mind as I took flight once more; he gave me but a slight nod of farewell before I slipped through the bars.

I regrouped outside of the Toy Room. After a brief moment of helplessness up in the rafters, where I fluttered my wings in frustration, it was clear to me that nothing would get done unless I got it done. With more ship yet to explore, I decided to see if there was anything I could put to use; a key maybe, or a tool the Daware man could use to free himself. Through more eavesdropping I discovered that the keys to the cages were held by the warden, and the warden only, and he, at that moment, was entertaining himself up on the Zoological Deck.

I had never heard of or been to such a deck before, and when I flew up the main staircase and entered the large, vaulted space, I was dismayed by the many animals I saw, caged and suspended from the ceiling like ornaments. There were bug-eyed bats and colorful parrots and, bathing in a tub of water, a family of gannets. A small, gray-haired monkey pressed its snout against the bars, reaching out to me as I flew past. Cats roamed the hall, lazing on the edges of tables until they got in the way of the games and were shoved off. When I looked down, I saw that this deck was not only a prison for animals, but also a gambling hall, with many low square tables on which people played cups and dice, and other longer tables on which many white stone tiles were placed in dizzying patterns to overcome their opponents through some opaque means of divide and conquer. As I searched for the warden in these back halls, I discovered something else of infinitely more promise—or rather, I heard it: the large, bellowing roar of a bear, coming from the other side of the hall.

A drunken crowd cheered around a cordoned-off area, where the black bear, leashed to the floor with mighty chains, was seated on a pillow too small for it, while a man with fine cheekbones dusted his face with vibrant blue makeup, as was custom those days for performers. He and the bear were performing a stage play. The man was the aggrieved spouse who wanted attention from their lover, and the bear was the lover tired of his spouse's henpecking. The crowd fell into raucous waves of laughter whenever the man said something along the lines of "You used to call me beautiful! You used to say I was the water to your parched throat! And what do you say to me now?" to which the trained bear would roar, and swipe the air as if dismissing these complaints.

The bear's strength was immediately appealing to me. I had a vision of ripping free the shackles from the Daware man with its teeth. The creature would do. But as I made my way to the performance arena, I was forced to perch on an unoccupied bench and pause, for I realized that, back at my body, back in the royal cruise, there was someone standing in the room with me.

It was the man from before.

The one with the large hands who had carried me in that way I did not like. He picked me up and carried me out of the room, not nearly as gently as Jun used to. When I saw that we were headed up the main staircase, I knew where he was taking me. It was, after all, only a matter of time.

The servants bowed their heads as we passed.

I was brought into a vast room, minimal in its presentation. The floor was made of a black wood that shined, and the walls were long red panels, on the faces of which were the brushstroke paintings of his banner creature, the silver monkey, in various positions of yearning and fury. The room funneled toward a simple blackwood table, at which Luubu was seated on the farthest side, and where I was then seated opposite him. Fine plates arrayed with delicate slices of silver-eye white fish were placed on mats of Induun silk, each slice of fish interrupted by a vegetable of surprising and vivid color, red and purple and silver.

Luubu dismissed the man who carried me, and then we were alone, apart from the attendants who stood in the shadows of the room, waiting to be beckoned. "I wonder if you had ever known how desperately I wanted this," he said. "To share a meal with you."

I said nothing.

"My brothers had much the same desire. To spend time with our mother. **Listen to me.**"

The power of his words overwhelmed my weakened state. I had no choice but to open myself to him.

"It is a strange thing," he said, "to know where you've been our entire lives, but to not be able to go to you. The First tried to sneak out to you once. This was when we were little. I never learned what our father did to him as punishment, and he never spoke of it." He pushed the food around on his plate like a discontented child; I could still smell the flesh of the tortoise god on his breath. "Strange thing. So close, yet so far. We felt you in our dreams. For nights on end we would dream of the Moon so bright in the sky that it was blinding. We would sometimes share those dreams with each other. But as brothers do, we grew apart, and we kept our dreams to ourselves." This thought seemed to cause him great anguish, or that was what he wanted me to believe, for he turned away from me dramatically. "I think we all have been holding out hope for the day one of us became emperor. The day we would be given the key to your room and we could finally spend some time with you." He breathed in, and turned back to the table. He poured tea from a heavy stone pot and I could not help but enjoy the sweet perfume of its steam. "I don't even know what tea you prefer," he said. "I hope this one is all right. It was grown not far from here, in a reserve that I own. Never let it be said that only Lady Panjet grows delicious leaves." He smiled. "On another day, another situation, I would've brought you there. That reserve. The flowers turn gold at sunset." His smile became more muted. "Ah. Well." He sighed and ran a hand through his black hair, which was thinning. "The plans I made to get you here . . . it would exhaust even you to hear of it. All I will say is that it is a lucky thing that Jun took the tortoise with him. It made eating the god all the more worth it, because I'll tell you, that was hard work. The weeks of eating its chewy, tasteless meat." He let out a high and fluttering laugh. "I kept it drugged so that its meat wasn't tense when I ate it, and it slurred like a drunk as it begged me to stop. But how could I stop? Every bite brought me closer to a kind of . . . becoming." He shut his eyes. "I hear them all now. The tortoises' messages. Their memories. I can even smell what they smell. The silver fear that lifts from the people's shoulders. Their red fury. Father really fucked up, didn't He?" He put down his cup. "Oh, Mother!" he exclaimed, falling on his back, a pillow there to catch him. "If only He hadn't kept you down there, things would be different! I was lonely! Father only had eyes for the eldest, but you, you would've seen me. If you were there, you would've listened. You would have told me what I needed to hear." He crawled over to my body. He put his head in my lap and took my limp hand and placed it on his cheek. "If I had a bad dream you would've stroked my hair and told me it was all right to go back to bed. And when I woke, you would've given me the courage to go on with my day. It was so hard, growing up without you, Mother." He was whispering now. "All the things we could've done if you had been there."

He used my hand like a comb. He sighed against my touch.

"I have a busy schedule today," he said, in a distant, thoughtful voice. "I'm going to torture my brother. He's just a head, but he can feel pain yet, and certainly humiliation. And if you're wondering why I am compelled to meet him with pain, just know that you have missed much during your time behind that Door. I will probably have his son killed in front of him. Skinned alive. I could have my Silver Monkeys take him against his will, right in front of his father." This thought seemed to amuse him greatly. "I haven't decided. But there's time yet to mull over those matters. Right now, the two of us have business with each other." He nodded in my lap. "Yes. A most urgent business, Mother. Because now that I've had the taste of one god, I find myself hungering for something a bit more substantial."

He looked up at me with wide eyes.

"I think I'm going to eat you."

And as he said this, the midday chants rang out through the Bowl, for the day was by then half-done; his hand resuming its grip on mine as he combed my fingers through his hair for a little while longer; and I felt acutely aware that we were all running out of time.

I once asked him why sons.

The man who unstitched me was very honest about what he wanted. There was no false modesty in his answer, and when he answered a question, it was clear and direct. There was no game with him. I liked him for that. But when I asked him why he wanted sons to inherit his legacy, he never gave me a satisfying answer. He would go on about tradition, about rights of succession, about strong bodies versus weak, but if I were to press him on matters of tradition, or strength—if I reminded him that I was a god, and that with my power I could help him change tradition, and give him a child who was strong regardless of how they presented to the world, he would become testy, and ask why I needled him with such pointless questions. I told him I asked him this because my time as a human woman had been a pleasurable one, and the other women I met and spent time with seemed as capable as any man their equal. But this had little impact on him; always the man would find a way to remove himself from the conversation without engaging with me. At the time I told myself this was fine, that I had an oath to answer, and it didn't matter what my opinions on that oath were; I would fulfill it regardless.

I always wondered though. Across the many long and bloody campaigns of my offspring, I'd ask myself if things would have been different, had one gotten through; if there had been an empress to answer for all the emperors. If the earth would drown in so much blood had she been there to stop the swinging of the blades. I had many tempting fantasies of such description. But I think now I know that, even though she would have been a welcome respite and perhaps even a soothing balm to the burned hand of the people, it would not have been enough. I had seen what happened to all of those sons I gave birth to. How they were molded by the world they had been given, for even the man who had started it all did not know why he made the choices he did. It is all a spiral that feeds into itself with the gathering weight at the center we call Power.

That was what occurred to me as I was trapped with my sick child on his fancy boat. It was an old lesson that everyone in the old village knew: You can fault the dancer, but more often than not, it is the dance itself that has to change.

Luubu gazed at me with a love so infinite it presented as a mad and indecipherable pattern. It was overwhelming and violent in its hunger. And even now it remains hard for me to determine how I feel about the men who had sprung from me—what to do with my deep hatred, and my bottomless love, for them.

MIDDAY

The day was slipping away from me, and I had to act.

I swooped into the performance arena without heed, and, I admit, a bit panicked, for Luubu had rattled me. I thought little of the bird's safety as I flapped over the cheering crowd and arced toward the bear. The spear-armed guards that haloed the arena did not notice me, nor did the male performer who was at that moment trying to "woo" the uninterested bear by pulling up the hem of his silk robe to reveal his naked legs. The bear, tired from the long day, stretched its mighty jaws and yawned.

I dropped the bird into its mouth.

And then, I was the bear, and I was choking on the little bird flapping in my throat. With a heavy roll I fell onto all fours and hacked up the creature. The bird slapped onto the floor, drooling with my saliva, twitching a little before it wicked the fluid off its wings with a few resolute beats. The performer flinched.

"What is this?" he asked.

I looked at this man, and as the bear, I was overwhelmed with fury, for this bastard had been my tormentor for many years, the awful plays he made me perform, and the many nights he made me go hungry as punishment for his bad reviews. There was no argument: I back-swiped him into the crowd. He let out an airless oomph and flew into the benches as a cannonball would into fortress timber. As the man groaned amid a pile of cracked rubble, the people laughed, believing this to be a part of the act; they even laughed as I pulled with all my weight against the unyielding chain that bound me to the floor; it only went quiet when the guards, who knew my actions were not part of the script, leapt over the cordon and began to circle me with their submission spears. One of them jabbed me in the thigh. *We shouted for him to calm down. We shouted his name. We tried to frighten him with our spears. Remind him what happened last time he tried to escape. But nothing worked. The creature was berserk.* Frustrated, I clamped down on the chain with my jaws and I ripped the entirety of the chain hook out of the floor. The wood splintered, metal bolts flew, and the chain hung loose from my neck like an untethered leash. I looked around. The guards stepped back. The people clutched their chests. There was a hush on the Zoological Deck as it dawned on everyone in the audience that I was free.

And then I charged forward.

Only one guard was foolish enough to stand his ground. *I couldn't move—I couldn't move.* I leapt on him hard enough to send his body through the floor, into the lower deck. As I ran, I roared to make the throngs of people clear the way. This unfortunately had the opposite effect, for in their panic they tripped and stumbled over the dice tables, tossing chairs, and stepping over one another, going in every direction but the safe one. I kept my head down as I ran, butting out of the way anyone who couldn't see themselves out of my charging line. I burst through the gambling tables. I destroyed the cages that kept the bats, and the bats screeched and skittered through the air. I took some satisfaction from this destruction, but I did not pause to indulge in it, and leapt down the main stairs and headed for the Toy Room.

I like to imagine what the Daware man must've experienced in that moment. What he must've thought when he heard the crashing and roaring and stampeding from the floor above. I imagine him trying to stand up, to rise and meet the chaos on the upper decks. I imagine the sound inspiring him to try to get free but straining in vain against the chains that bound him. How he must've frozen in place when he heard the sound of a large creature barreling through the paneled walls. The sound of screams, of pleas for mercy, of doors crashing out of their frame. And what terrified blood must've pumped through his temples as the last door fell forward and a breathing, snorting, bloodied bear came trundling down to his very cell, past all the other cells, as if he alone had all the bad luck in the world—a man of poor fortune indeed.

He pressed himself up against the wall. He was holding his breath. Perhaps if there was time, I would have indulged in the fear he seemed to take of my presence as I towered over his cell door, for humans have such a funny way of scrambling. But there was no time.

"You're fucked, cripple," a gaunt man cackled from an adjacent cell.

The Daware man shrank as far into the corner of the room as his chains allowed, which was not very far at all. I ripped the cell door off its hinges and entered, my body too large to fit my entire self, my snout taking in the rank smell, and my black eyes in scrutiny of his injuries, as he looked at me with unrestrained terror. From outside this squalid prison I heard the march of armed guards coming down the main steps. Poor of time, and believing that I would have time to properly communicate with him later, I decided to free the Daware man before attempting to convince him who I was. I broke the hooks that bound his chains with my feral bear strength. The manacles, still locked to his wrist and his right ankle, came free from the wall with loud pops. I was about to scratch his name into the wood, to prove my identity, but as soon as I had displayed my claw the Daware man, deathly still up till that moment, broke into a run, squeezing through the narrow gap between my girth and the doorframe. He tripped into the corridor, falling on his face, then scrambled to his feet like a frightened child. I cursed myself for not writing the name down before I freed him, but this curse came out as an angry roar that only made him run faster.

There was nothing to do but to chase him. He ran straight down the corridor, in such a panic that he ran into the chest of an approaching guard. The two men spun around each other like a dancing pair. As I came barreling down the corridor I saw that they were fighting over the guard's weapon, the Daware man at last winning as he yanked the spear hard from the other's grasp and sprinted off. The unarmed guard gulped at me before I batted him out of the way.

The Daware man was going up the stairs, fighting against the terrified flow of people coming down, all of whom were headed to the barge's docking bay. A squadron of soldiers rounded the corner and pointed at me with spear tips brandished in the glow-light of the wide corridor. I snorted and followed the Daware man to the upper decks. I heaved with tired breath as the endless staircase zigzagged all the way to the top of the ship.

I could smell the clear, salty air, and I knew we were close to the top deck. At the head of the last flight, the Daware man glanced behind to see if I was still chasing him, and he cursed with loud disbelief when I turned the corner and gained on him. He rushed out the doors.

A gray-bright afternoon sky greeted us both, the rest areas and the tea tables of the sky deck all but abandoned but for a few old men who were so entrenched in their routine that they could not be bothered to end their ginseng gossip because of a loose wild bear. As the Daware man, in a rather pathetic bid for time, tipped tables and pots over to slow my charge, I tried to think up a way to communicate with him. I tried to speak, but those only came out as roars. I tried to stop chasing him, but he continued to run all the same. My bear brain could only think to keep going—my path interrupted by the whistling of a ballista bolt and its musical thrum into the railing on my other side, the shot so close the small hairs around my snout had swayed as the bolt soared past me. Another bolt wedged itself into the wooden board beside my paw. When I stopped, I saw, with a rather hopeless feeling, that all along the perimeter of the top deck there were manned ballistas on swiveling platforms, all of them aimed at me.

Up ahead the Daware man had cornered himself against the end of the vessel. More bolts flew over my head as I ran at him, desperate now not to die. When he saw me coming, he looked over the railing, judging the distance from the sky deck to the water. Unfortunately for him, we were on one of the tallest pleasure barges in the Bowl. The fall was a swan dive off a high cliff. The landing would not be kind. But all it took for him to find his motivation was another glance at me, and the angry bolts that peppered the deck, before he made up his mind between the lesser of two evils, and leapt.

A bolt ripped through my ear—I roared at the sky as I leapt after him.

We fell into the water.

It is only by the grace of the Water's love for me that our fall was cushioned. I could feel the surface dimple below us, and though the collision was not soft on our bodies, I knew that it could have been much worse. For a moment I floated suspended in the green waters of the Bowl of Heaven and I remembered what it was like, to move with the Water; I remembered floating high above, directing the tides. I remembered making the Water laugh into waves. Air bubbles came out of my snout as I, for once that day, indulged in a moment and stopped. Even as the bolts humphed into the water around me, I was unhurried. I swam up. Swam toward day. And once I broke the surface, I paddled myself toward the Daware man, who had fallen unconscious from the drop. This marked the third time he had blacked out on our journey, and as I carried him in my open jaws, I hoped that he would not wake up mind-bent and useless to me. The guards continued to fire at me from the top deck, but they missed all of their shots, for this was likely the first and only time they had ever had cause to operate the ballistas on the pleasure barge.

It was a long swim to the crater-side docks, but it was an uninterrupted one, for everyone else in the Bowl was busy with the matters of the rebellion. I could smell above the murky tang of the crater waters the scent of smoke and fire. Somewhere in my periphery a boat was burning but I could not be bothered to stop and look. I did not stop swimming until we reached the stone steps of the dock, which were slick with bay water, and I, drooling water from every bit of my fur, climbed up and deposited the sleeping Daware man onto the floor. He would wake soon, so I set to work. In time, he coughed water from his mouth, and he held his sides as if to stop his lungs from falling out, his coughing fit ending when he blinked and looked up, and saw, cleaved deep into the crater wall by my throbbing claw,

I AM THE BEAR.

He turned to look at me. He was shaking from the water. His dark hair plastered to his forehead. "You're . . . Her?"

I nodded.

He let out a small laugh.

"Why? How?"

I blinked at him, and he chuckled, because of course I could not answer him, his chuckling serving only to make him wince. He lifted his tunic and scowled at the reddened skin that had slapped against the water. "I guess I should keep the questions for later then," he said. "But I should thank you first, for—"

His words were interrupted—or I could no longer hear him—for at that moment something changed. I heard something. The sound of a crunch. It was happening right at that moment, and the pain of this nameless loss was more profound than any I had felt before. Even my fall from the heavens was a kindness compared to this pain. It was a pain so vivid it prompted me to roar. I roared in the Daware man's face, the breath so hot and forceful he was startled off his feet. On the ground, he asked me what was wrong, but there was no way for me to tell him what happened.

That Luubu was eating my finger.

His head was still in my lap. He had slipped my pointer finger into his mouth, fitting it between his molars, before he bit into it. It was a hard and decisive bite, as if biting into a carrot. He looked up at me as he gnawed on it. The white of the bone stuck out between his suckling lips. His eyes were unblinking, like a fixated baby, as his tongue worked the flesh from the bone. Whether he took any pleasure in the action I could not tell, for he ate without much expression, only an animal urgency, as he chewed and swallowed.

I could not think.

I was, for the first time in my earthly existence, scared.

Far in the distance, I heard the echo of someone shout. Shouting for my attention as Luubu's eyes fixated on me with great love and daring. The shout of the Daware man, who had spied the approach of a ballista boat.

"Watch out!"

He was pulling at my fur. He was telling me to move. As the ballista rope twanged and let loose its charge I started running, trying my best not to listen to the crunch of bone between eager teeth. I felt the bolt as it missed my rear. Together we ran down the long dock that outlined the crater's edge, trapped between the water and the massive and impenetrable wall that made up the crater's southeastern curve. But I could not run as fast as before, distracted as I was from the delirious pain. I staggered, and the Daware man saw me staggering.

"What do you need?" he asked. "Tell me what you need!" I roared at him in mounting frustration. A second bolt parted us, our ears ringing as the metal tip collided with the stone wall. We heard a third bolt being loaded. I tried to move, but Luubu was humming now as he chewed, and blood was pooling from my hand, and we both looked at the ballista boat expecting a swift and sudden end to the day, when some strange magick occurred.

A small shadow fell out of the sun.

It was the blur of a purple bird, descending on the man at the ballista, clawing and flapping at him with a ferocity unusual to creatures of its kind. The man screamed.

The bird was pecking out his eyes.

The driver of the boat tried to help his partner, but in his panic he swung at the bird with his short blade, and the bird, without much effort, moved out of the way, the blade wedging itself into wood while his partner screamed about his eyes, his eyes.

There was something familiar about that bird—a feeling, small and warm. I had the suspicion that we had met once before, this bird and I, but in my weakened state, there was only so much attention I could pay to the creature. The Daware man seemed to have met the bird, too, from the way he stared at the scene. Perhaps if I had known what I know now. If I could've gone back . . .

. . . well.

What's done is done.

It was thanks to the bird's intervention that we were able to get to safety. Beneath a stone archway, shaded from both the sun and any passing patrol boats, I made it clear to the Daware man that I needed a moment to rest, for something else was happening back on the royal cruise that required my undivided attention. He seemed exasperated as I sat down and did not budge, forced as he was to stand guard over me with no weapon but his fist, his new spear as lost in the water as his old one. But he was irrelevant in that moment.

Someone was sneaking onto Luubu's ship.

I felt them arrive as Luubu napped, tired from the meal, his head still in my lap—the twin long crafts from before now sliding up to the side of his cruise without a sound but the gentle lapping of the water. From the crafts, a few dozen masked men disembarked. These men were swift and they were quiet and they moved as one organism, the ones in the front acting as eyes for those holding bows in the back. Sudden corners were crept upon. Footsteps listened for. Blades slid out of polished sheaths. Luubu's Silver Monkey guards were dispatched with little effort. The blood from their split necks painted the walls while the masked men in the rear held between them, with care, a wrapped corpse, carrying this body up the decks of this royal junk ship.

No one was spared in their silent assault. *I had just finished clearing out the kitchen when a blade snuck its way into my back. I felt myself tremble as the knife went in many times.* A trail of bodies left behind them as they made their way up the many waxed blackwood steps. They crept past Jun's storage closet. Jun heard the strange noises but did not know what to make of them, thinking that maybe it was the Daware man come to help him, a tentative smile breaking on his face before he heard that it was not one but many footsteps that crawled up the length of the boat—up into the apartment deck, where the two Silver Monkeys guarding the First Terror's door were beheaded in two blurred strikes. Fountains of blood sprouted from rent necks, presenting their arrival as they unlocked and opened the prince's door.

Their father's head was silent as one by one his sons entered, carrying with them his body. The pride he felt upon seeing them was of such magnitude that even I could feel the echo of it in myself, tears falling freely down his cheeks, the saltwater dropping onto the sliced fruits on his plate as he beheld them all and whispered, "My sons, my sons," while they unwrapped his body and took out the needle and the thread of fine silver.

It was not a perfect repair; none of them had ever had to return a missing head to a body before, there were bound to be flaws in the design, but the strength of the blood that he had received from me in his birth took the healing the rest of the way. The silver thread was a little loose in some of the seams, stretching but not snapping as he rose up in a body he had believed gone for good, but the stitching held, and he was whole again. Each one of his sons, he kissed on the cheek, and they beamed at the touch of his lips, proud that they had for once saved him.

"Where is our uncle?" the eldest son asked.

Saam pointed up at the ceiling.

On the floor above them, Luubu slept in my lap.

It would have been a perfect time to strike, but Luubu was not their next destination, a fact which surprised both me and his sons, as the Terror led the way down the steps instead of up, all the way back to the locked closet that Jun was held behind.

"Open it."

Upon his father's command, the eldest broke open the door with a decisive kick. Jun leapt to his feet, on guard, his shoulders relaxing a bit when he saw his brothers, and his father, though he went tense again when his father stepped into the closet with him. Behind the First Terror, a deep and simmering ambivalence seethed off of the Red Peacocks' shoulders. *Never would we forget how our brother once held our father's head in the air—never would we forgive him for that trespass.* I could sense their resentment, as could Jun, who backed away slowly at his father's approach. But his father did not share his sons' sentiments. It seemed that being without a body for a time reminded him of how brief and trivial our many earthly arguments often were.

"I will offer this to you only once," his father said.

And he held out his hand.

"You could have thrown my head away at any point on your

journey," he said. "You could've tossed it into the tall grass or into some secret river, never to be seen again. But you did not. You kept me close. You kept me safe." His gaze on Jun was soft, even after all that had happened, and if there was ever any doubt that he loved his children, let this moment dispel that doubt completely. "I do not know what you and my mother spoke of in that cavern. I do not know what she said to you. What . . . memories she made you relive. In many ways it feels like you went down there as one person, and came back as someone else entirely. You are almost unrecognizable to me. A strange thing to admit about one's own son, but there it is. I do not understand you, or the choices you've made these past few days. And yet, you did not throw my head away. Which tells me something vital: that you were never really gone. Changed, but not gone." His hand reached out even farther, waiting. "Jun. You can come home."

Jun stared at that hand.

"All of it, I forgive," his father said. "All of it, I will let go. Just come home."

Jun shut his eyes, welled with tears. Every part of him wanted to take that hand in his own. It was a pull stronger than the Weaver's heavenly knots. But his father was correct. Jun had come far. And he stepped away from that hand, until his back hit the shelving.

There was no hiding the heartbreak on his father's face. He seemed not to know what to do with himself. He looked away. "That's fine," he said, leaving the closet. "That's . . . that's fine." He glanced back only once, with his reddened eyes.

He smiled.

"I'm going to save you all the same."

He closed the door, and barricaded it shut with a chair. Jun slipped down to the floor, weeping.

The Red Peacocks ran up the stairs without him.

Luubu was awake by then.

I had not noticed this until he rose from my lap as if from the dead, the chewed bone of my finger in his hand as he gestured for his attendants to leave the room. As they padded through the side doors, he stood at the head of the tea table, facing the entrance of his court. Whatever hope I had that the finger he had eaten had yet to work its way into his system was quashed by the confidence and awareness with which his slim body moved, how even the air itself seemed to part from his step, and I knew then that the First Terror did not know what arena he was stepping into.

"Why have you stopped? We need to keep moving!"

The Daware man was pushing against my body. I roared back at him. He threw his hand up at me and left, shouting back that he was going to look around for something useful. I let him go. I needed to focus.

The Brigade of the Red Peacocks filed into the room.

Like in a wordless dance they entered, in two lines, the honed bodies of these lifelong warriors stepping into Luubu's court without fear, their ears plugged with makeshift wax stoppers. They were followed by their father, who briskly walked in the violent stitching on his neck, and a long sword drawn and thirsty. Thirty-three red-tattooed warriors and their beloved leader faced the ruler of the Bowl of Heaven, whose hands were clasped behind his back, politely waiting for them to make a move. Before the First Terror addressed his brother, he looked at me for a long moment, and I saw that Luubu was right; he was not the only son who craved to see me and to spend time with me—perhaps, even, to devour me. "It is quite the game you've been playing," Saam said, still looking at me but speaking to Luubu; or perhaps both of us. "The music you've been piping into my room is atrocious."

"I thought you liked those songs," Luubu said.

"Always playing the innocent, even now." He walked farther into the room, until he and Luubu were separated only by the table. "You've lost, brother. My sons have protected themselves from your Word, and you know as well as I that your influence has no purchase on me. Whatever blade you might keep under your robe will be deflected. Whatever warrior you send to die on your behalf will die on your behalf. But know that I am gracious enough to offer even the likes of you an honorable death." He held up his sword. "Kneel."

"Kneel and you'll make it quick?" Luubu laughed. It was a forced laughter, the braying of a goat. "I'm impressed you were able to return to your body. You look great."

"Kneel," Saam said as he began his walk around the table, his blade at the ready.

"I see that losing your head hasn't shaken free any of your stubbornness." He sighed and got on his knees. He even closed his eyes, though he smiled like he was a child waiting to be given a sweet.

"Whenever you're ready, brother," he said lightly.

Saam paused halfway down the table. His mouth tricked into a smile. "What is your game here?"

"The game is simple," Luubu said. "I'm waiting for you to cut off my head. Here I am, brother. Certain victory lies before you, as it always had."

"If the past week has taught me anything, it is to be anything but certain." The First Terror shrugged. He approached no farther. With a raise of his left hand, he signaled to his Red Peacocks in the back, who drew their arrows.

But Luubu said, "Stop. All of you." And the ten archers froze in their drawn position, the arrows stopped inside the bows' quivering tension, their fingers unable to release the string. His Word had gone straight through the wax. A light breath escaped the First Terror's lips, as he realized something about Luubu was different—his eyes widening when he saw the pool of blood in my lap, realizing what it was his brother had done. He broke into a run, toward Luubu, his sword gusting toward its target, but Luubu pointed at him and said, "**You stop too.**" And the First gasped as his legs locked into position and he staggered to a halt, caught, for the first time, under the influence of his little brother. Luubu was grinning wide now. He wasted no time in flexing his potential. He pointed at one of the archers. "You. Kill the brother standing to the left of you."

Without hesitation, the archer turned and shot the man in the back of the head. The arrow pierced the skull and the man dropped to the floor. The First Terror made to scream, but Luubu put a finger to his lips, and said, "**Quiet.**"

A torrent of grief swirled in his older brother's stopped throat.

Luubu started walking around the room now filled with these pliable humans. "Amazing. Just one finger, and I can do all of this." He stood next to another Peacock. "**Show the room your ass.**" The man bent over and pulled up his skirts. "**Shit yourself.**" As the waste crawled down his leg, Luubu continued down the line, chuckling to himself, muttering, "Even Djove won't be able to resist me now." But speaking that lord's name aloud gave him pause. He looked around the room, at all these dolls under his command, at his disposal, and he sighed. "It's somewhat amusing," he said to the First, whose eyes were red and wet. "I'd dreamed of such a scenario for so long. To see you stripped of all your unearned glory. But I am so much bigger now. My aims higher than your station. And now I just want to hurt you as fast as possible." He told the Peacocks to spread out and stand around the room until they were evenly dispersed. They did as he commanded. And then he turned on his heel and swiveled toward his brother. "Look at your sons. Look at them look at you." He gave a short nod. "**Now kill them.**"

The First Terror tried to fight it, his teeth gritted to the point that it would not have surprised anyone if they had shattered; his arm moving of its own accord, like a snake from a basket, as it pointed the sword at the son closest to him. His eldest. The veins in the arms like thick worms as he tried to redirect the swings. *My father was coming toward me. I had never seen him panicked before. I had never seen him scared. That's what terrified me the most; not that he was going to kill me, but that even he could be broken.*

There was nothing I could do; the scream of the moonrock trap was still omnipresent. I cursed the Red Peacocks for not taking care of those devices. I cursed the First Terror for not taking care of those devices. I cursed Luubu for using them. The closer the First Terror got to his son, struggling the entire way, trying to slow himself as much as possible, to buy time, to hope for some kind of blessed intervention, the more my son grew distressed, and frightened, and rageful, and I in such close proximity to him felt all of those emotions too. And I as a bear roared as he raised his sword in tears and hacked off his eldest's head. The arterial spray almost beautiful in its utter force as the head rolled away, and the First Terror, half-drenched, turned to his next of kin. *And when he looked at me I pissed myself and everything that had made me feel safe in this world was now gone and then he brought the sword down on me, but I didn't die and so he brought it down on me again and I screamed until I couldn't scream and my father continued on with his task in silence,* and in this manner the Brigade of the Red Peacock was ended, the blackwood floor turned red.

I roared.

The sun was in mid-set behind the westward crater wall, and I roared for my son who could not roar. I roared not for the end of the brigade that had through its actions earned this bloody farewell, but for my grandsons who were, in the end, little boys cut down by a large sword. *I begged him to stop, but he couldn't and then he swung, my father swung,* and I felt them cry as I did the ache in my own body. *I cried out to him, but he did not cry back.* In that room, they were of me, because we all shared the heat of that mental sympathy; of a father who could not help himself. *He said nothing. He said nothing.* He tried to make the deaths quick, but however quick they may have been, that did not make them pleasant. *We bloomed into the ceiling.* The death of a human had never repulsed me. And yet that day I roared.

I roared until the Daware man returned to me. He asked me what was wrong but I could not answer him; even if I could speak I would not have the words, for the agitation was deeper than words. I let loose a low keening and as I did so he told me that there were people down the docks, a fight, between rebels and the Silver Monkeys, and before he could explain the situation further I charged forth. This is the central problem with leaping into the body of an animal—you are swept up in the animal's being. Anger was not just anger, it was a ball of fire in my head. Indignity could not be shrugged off; it needed to be won back. Agitation needed to be acted upon. There was no wait and see. There was only now. I needed a fight; the Daware man showed me to one.

The skirmish was significant in number: ten Silver Monkeys hounding twenty civilian fighters, hacking at them with quick swipes of their short swords. From the positioning of the boats that were jammed up against the dock, the story seemed to be that the Silver Monkeys had pursued this rebel contingent all the way from one of the lower apartment barges. One of the fighters was on his back, cowering from an attack. *I held up my arms to protect my face and the Silver Monkey hacked through them, as if they were nothing but branches.* The smell of blood only stoked my bear rage. I cared not who fell under my claws, I leapt at the first human I came across. It happened to be one of Luubu's men; as I wrung him out like a doll, the rest of the skirmishers were scattering, shouting at the sudden appearance of this hungry bear. I clenched my jaws and the body between my teeth let loose a final death-twitch. I tossed him into the crater wall. I found another one, abandoned by her partner, who had taken away the boat for himself in a panic. She put her hands together in prayer before I clawed her apart. I snorted and growled inside her opened belly, but the boats were now leaving, and there was no one left to maim. And as my agitation died down just a little bit, the First Terror dropped his blade, having finished off the last of his sons. Luubu bid him to sit at the table with him and me, and he did, with hollow-eyed obedience. Not one part of him was dry.

"**Serve us,**" Luubu said, pushing the teapot toward him.

Again, he complied.

The Daware man ran up to me, slipping a bit on the pool of blood spreading out from the Silver Monkey's discarded corpse.

"It is very difficult to not know what you want to do!" he shouted.

I lowered my head to the ground.

"I don't know what's going on," he said, exhausted. He put his hand on his knee and breathed out. He looked out at the boats and the smoke. "Is Jun . . . does he still live?"

My bear ears pricked up.

As if in sympathy with the Daware man's thoughts, Luubu lowered his cup of tea, and he looked over at his brother serenely. "Oh yes. I completely forgot. There's one more."

The closet door then swung open.

But when Jun emerged, he saw no one behind it—just the chair that had been propped against it now tipped over on the ground. He stepped into the empty corridor. A voice came from a brass flower in the ceiling.

"**Come upstairs,**" Luubu's voice commanded.

And like all of the Second Terror's victims that day, the last of the Red Peacocks had no choice but to obey.

DUSK

I think of Jun.

It was an easy matter to break him. I did so, I admit, with relish. I had spent many decades in attempt to breach the moonrock trap behind the Wolf Door, and more years yet in pursuit of someone whose will I could bend in accordance with my own. When I finally found him, I did not hold back. I unleashed on him the frustration and impotence and fury that clung to me during my long imprisonment.

Many guards came and went upon whom my efforts to seduce were wasted. I would spend time studying them as they stood in that cavern, probing at their thoughts as they pretended that nothing was wrong, looking for memories or motivations to exploit. But when I tried to manipulate one, one of two things would occur: either they were completely unaffected, well trained to withstand such assaults of the mind, or they broke like cheap wood, and were then dragged out in some gibbering heap by their comrades, utterly useless to me. I needed the person who stood between these two states; someone who would break, but not so much that they could not serve me. What luck it was when he was assigned to me, for I was nearing the end of my life and I had limited time to accomplish what I desired.

It will always remain interesting to me that the first and only guard I finally broke was a Red Peacock, and not just any Peacock, but one of the most favored. Jun was an experienced killer by then, having gutted all sorts for the sake of his father's proud smile. He had galloped into rebel encampments, into flocks of free-band warriors, into the homes of both murderers and innocents, his blade, his hatchet, smiling in his hand; his mind peaked and valleyed by confusion, by regret, which he hid behind an almost perfect mask of loyalty. I suppose it was my luck, then, a favor of fortune, that he had recently burned down a rice farmer's house and was, to say the least, affected by the memory.

I smelled the stink on him as soon as he entered the cavern. It wafted from his sunken shoulders. The sweat of a young man who stands on the edge of himself. From there the rest was easy—all I did was pull on a thread, then let the whole thing unravel. He remembered the smell of burning peaches from the farmer's open window. He remembered the charred hand that reached out from the flames. He remembered the child who ran into the house for his parents. The burning beam of wood that collapsed on him. The dull impact that killed the child instantly. I made him live the moment as the mother who burned alive. I made him live as the father who tried to save her. I made him live as the child who knew only terror before the wooden beam crushed him into the Sleeping Sea.

I made him relive these memories and more in the dark of that cavern. I snuck the smoke into his dreams, with some variations on the theme. Sometimes it was his own brothers whose throats he opened. Sometimes it was his father he pushed off the cliff. And then I brought in the other wounds. The intense, needling regret of unrequited love. I made love smell like spilt blood. And he would shiver and weep in his sleep as in his dream he leapt onto himself and stabbed himself in the back with that bloody knife, given from his father.

He was an ugly thing when he cried. In the heights of his overwrought tears I wondered how he could be in any way related to those first people who danced under my moonlight—how this back-bent dog of battle was worthy of his own breath.

When he was ready to take it, I started the whispering. The insinuations. The blame. I crept around his brain palace until there were no secrets left for him to hide. I made light of his perversions and threw into relief his dark dreams and his moments of shame, of which he owned many. He tried to fight back. He defended himself, he made his excuses. Predictable. I was the more practiced hand in the realm of the mind, and it was a rather easy thing to tear down his defenses, wall by wall—which is not to say I had not learned my lessons from the other men I had ruined. I did not destroy him. But I opened the box that made him go a little mad, so that he would hear the whispers in his head, the hauntings of those he killed, for the rest of his life.

In a few months' time, it was he who was begging me to know how he could earn some ounce of salvation for the soiled ley lines of his spirit.

Not all of our conversations were so contentious. There were nights that he and I spoke of smaller matters, for there was much time to waste before we could finally act. Once I spoke to him about the dances, projecting these memories into his mind, and he saw them just as I had, when I was whole and radiant, and he agreed that the people were very beautiful. And in his dreams, the dreams I did not touch, a lover's hand would caress his cheek and gently peel off the red tattoo, like it was nothing but a wet piece of cloth, and he would wake up weeping until I pulled him back under and gave him softer dreams to sleep by.

I mention this all because it is important to the moment in the tale that now follows, when Luubu called him upstairs. That there was something I did not anticipate happening during those six months that I warped him in that cavern. An attachment of some kind, the coordinates of which even I cannot pin down with my finger, but which made itself known by the worried pang in my breast as Luubu lured the boy toward certain death. I did not care for Jun. Not because he had a loathsome past; in truth I did not care about that, I had known people much, much worse, and loved them still. No, I did not care for Jun because I saw so much of myself in him. To look at him frustrated me. The pathetic sound of his cries frustrated me. He was weak and he was stubborn and his heart was vice. But in that cavern he told me he would never kill again, and he did so in a way that gave me something I had not had since I could not remember when. It gave me hope. Hope that things could be different.

And so as he walked up the stairs to Luubu's deck, I reared my bear's head and I roared to the sky that hope would not die that day.

The Daware man shouted as I flung him onto my back.

He was shouting for explanation, for some hint of what I was planning, but I had grown weary of his strange expectation that I should finally answer him coherently from my bear mouth, so I roared once to shut him up and I started my trot down the dock with him clutching the scruff of my neck. As he whispered a fevered prayer that he would not be thrown off, I searched the docks for a way to cross the Bowl and reach Luubu's cruise.

The Daware man did not get a semblance of my plan until I had climbed up to the second tier of the docks to get more height, and stood at the edge of the outstretched pier, eyeing the distance between us and the nearest ship, which was fast approaching. He grasped a thick tuft of my fur, and I took this for acceptance. I backed up from the edge to give myself a distance to run down, and then I broke into a charge. The Daware man cursing as we neared the edge of the stone and I leapt, clearing a great distance of water before we crashed onto the top deck of a passing junk ship. He was thrown off my back from the force of the landing. The sailors around us were scattering but for the brave ones who approached us with drawn sabers. All it took was a roar for them to think twice about coming any closer.

Once the Daware man had gotten himself up on my back again I ran toward the bow of the ship. The ship was headed in the opposite direction of the royal district, but they were nearing the end of a long chain of ships that, to hop across, one after the other, would take us directly there. The Daware man gripped tighter this time as I ran and dug my claws into the wood and leapt—this time onto the broadside catwalk of an apartment barge. A man smoking out his window stared at us with little expression as we crashed into the wall. The Daware man climbed out of the apartment he had been thrown into, tattered paper and cloth falling out of his hair as he beckoned me inside. "There's a way through here!" he shouted. We ran past three lovers who had been enjoying themselves in bed, the Daware man pausing briefly to look at them be-fore I snouted him into the main corridor, where guards on the other end of the hall came running down. In a quick scramble, the Daware man was on my back again.

"Welcome, Jun."

My grandchild had reached the top of the stairs. His eyes wide as he surveyed the room that was almost entirely red now. Red panels, and floors slick with red. In the center of all the bodies sat Luubu, his father, and me.

The table had been moved to the side of the room. Luubu said it was getting in the way of the dramatic presentation of the scene. Ever the showman, he had arranged everything just so. My back was to Jun. Sitting to my left was his father, whose bloody face Jun could see only in profile, and to my right was Luubu, who was smil-ing at Jun as if an honored guest had finally arrived for tea.

"**Come over,**" he said. "No need to be bashful amongst family."

Jun did as commanded and walked through the abattoir. He stepped over the headless bodies and splayed limbs of those he had fought alongside his whole life, those he had slaughtered with.

He tasted their blood in the air.

As he stepped toward us, I was leaping from boat to boat through ballista bolt fire. Wood splintered and I was crashing through walls with the Daware man, crossing the sectors of the Bowl as fast as we dared. I roared and I leapt as Jun padded softly across the bloody floor and took his seat on the empty pillow that faced his father. "Do not worry about all this mess, nephew," Luubu said, waving at the dripping room. "It is all part of the weave. What they call . . . divine punishment. **Say this is so, brother.**"

"It is divine punishment," the First Terror repeated.

"You see?" Luubu said brightly.

He then took my hand and bit off another finger.

I staggered.

I crashed into the mast pole. I felt as though I had been cut in half. The Daware man had taken another soldier's spear and was fending off those who would end me while I tried to recover. I grunted and etched the floorboards with my claws as I endeavored to rise. *Follow, Daware man!* I roared, and I think he was beginning to understand me, for he leapt on my back quickly and we were off to startle the passengers of the next boat. We were almost there.

I heard lips smack.

"I could've had children too," Luubu said as he wiped the blood from his mouth. "I could've whored myself across the land like my brother here, and grown my own sons and daughters like bushels of wheat. But it seems I was the one child who remembered the responsibilities of his position—the requirements of grace, and control, that are asked of a prince. Only a woman worthy of my attentions will carry my seed in her basket. And that child will one day inherit all that I have to offer. He will not have to vie for my love or my attention. He will never have to feel jealousy, or wonder if my estimation of him is greater or lesser than mine of his brothers, for he will have no brothers. There will only be him, and he will be happy."

Luubu washed my blood down with a cup of tea. His pupils were wide, as if drugged.

"I see so much now," he said. "As the tortoises had seen the colors of the invisible world, I see the frayed threads that bind you all together. I see the poison that seeps from father into son, and the rot that builds in the son who has been led astray. I see your hatred, Jun. Your renouncement of all your father's ideals. Because of Her, you have turned your back on the path of the blade, and you insist that you will never kill again." Luubu shook his head. "A pitiable outcome. Your son is lost, brother. He is wayward, because your attention strayed. You have failed him as a father. **Say it.**"

"I have failed you," the First intoned, looking through Jun.

"Tell him he is a disappointment."

"You are a disappointment."

Jun withered.

"You offered me an honorable death," Luubu said, to the First Terror. "And now, I would offer you a similar kindness. I will bring your son back from his wayward path. He will be a Red Peacock once more." He leaned over and picked a long, gleaming object up off the floor. "Here, Jun. **Hold this sword.** You know it well, do you not? It is your father's famous blade. I found it amongst your effects when we captured you."

Jun took the grotesquely long sword in his hands, his arms buckling a little from the surprising weight of it. Blood still stained the metal, but in the reflective sheen of its surface he could see his own bewildered eyes.

"You already know what I will ask you to do with that sword."

"Please," Jun begged. "Don't do it."

If ever there was a day Luubu could be swayed by another man's word, that day was long past. "The man in front of you is responsible for making you who you are today," he said. "He is the reason that tattoo on your face will remain till the end of your days, the reason you will be marked outcast long after this is all over. You hate him, don't you?"

"Yes," Jun said weakly. "I do. But I do not want to kill him."

"You do. I smell it on you. It comes off of you like a stench. From the truest part of you."

"I won't do it." His voice was wet. "I'm different now."

"Different, no." Luubu frowned with sympathy. "No one really changes. Our parents make us who we are, and that's all there is. You speak as if we can will ourselves into being who we are not. But every movement we make, Jun, we make under the influence of others. **Wield the sword and ready it.**"

In an expert motion Jun hefted the handle as he once dreamed of doing with this sword in old childhood fantasies of himself as his father's successor. But now his bottom lip trembled.

I roared as we ran across the long deck of the final ship.

"Bring the point to your father's chest. To the heart."

The metal nudged aside the wet clothing and revealed the naked chest. The apple of the First's throat bobbed deeply as he looked into his son's eyes. Saam blinked, his eyes wet.

"There is nothing to forgive," his father said.

"Jun," Luubu said. **"Do it."**

The sword pulled back and readied its dive as I leapt off the final deck and landed with all my weight against the *Cav-Meer*'s hull, my jaw clasping over the rope that suspended the largest of the moonrock traps, my weight bringing the sack down into the water in a geyser, the barrier disrupted,

and I was free.

And all of my spirit returned to my body and before Jun could thrust I grabbed his wrist with my three-fingered hand, and I opened my eyes, and I looked at him; the boy stunned, the tears streaking down his cheeks, as I shook my head, and told him, "You can let go now."

His hands opened. The sword dropped to the bloody floor. Luubu shot to his feet and staggered backward.

"Mother," he cried, **"be silent!"**

"You will have to eat more than two fingers for that to work, my son," I said.

I said.

I said!

What I felt, speaking with my own mouth, after so long, it was at once exhilarating and tiring. My lungs punched for breath, those old cloth bags, but the breath tasted so good on my tongue. I knew that I did not have long; that I should use my words sparingly.

"My son," I said, "I free you from his Word."

And the First Terror doubled forward onto his hands, gasping for air. He released the scream he had been forced to hold in that entire afternoon. He screamed loud enough that the blood on the floor trembled. The red panels broke outward. His face snapping in Luubu's direction.

"**Be still!**" Luubu cried. "**Be silent!**"

But I had freed Saam, and I had disrupted the trap, which meant he had little issue not being still, not being silent; he rose to his feet and told Luubu that he was going to kill him now, and before Luubu could have any say in the matter his older brother ran toward him, the blood leaping from his sandals with each step. With a flick of his wrist he twisted the blood of his sons upward into funneling spikes that arced toward Luubu's face.

But Luubu had eaten two of my fingers. It was enough for him to deflect the blood bolts. He smiled with the awareness that he now edged Saam out in strength, that he could still win the day.

The two of them collided in the center of the room and the ceiling was blown away by the force of their impact, the top of the cruise sheared off its hinges, the wooden beams and the finery and the paneling all flying up into the air of the Bowl, letting in the burnt evening sky. In the midst of this explosion of energy my two sons were reaching for each other with hands gripping the air in eager desire to strangle the other; the closer each of them got the more powerful the surges released. The boat cracked down the middle like a man breaking open a tajeline.

Jun had slid back into Luubu's throne of pillows while I held my ground. Large waves of water rolled out from the boat and throughout the Bowl. Apartment barges rose higher than they were constructed to handle. The prison fleet smeared against the wall of the crater. A poorly made textile ship splintered apart and released into the heaving wind thousands of streams of vividly colored fabrics, along with the people who helped make them. A small girl flew briefly into the sky, her neck snapped, her eyes dead.

I knew that my sons had to be stopped before the entire Bowl and everyone in it was destroyed. I staggered toward them, hesitating only a moment, out of nostalgia I think, and out of remnant love for them, until Saam looked back at me and said, "It's fine!" Brusquely, a dog bark. "It's fine! I'm ready! Do it!"

And so, as Luubu snarled and finally wrapped his hands around Saam's throat, I brought my own hands together and with those hands compressed the air around my sons. Folding it and folding it, like sheer Induun fabric, until they fell into each other's arms, their last sound that of Luubu's small and terrified gasp before I brought my hands together one last time, and smashed them together into a single small coin of flesh. A royal copan. And no sooner had the coin dropped to the floor than I picked it up and swallowed it.

The waves settled. The debris that had been swirling above the city now crashed back into the water. The crater filled with the sound of a thousand brief detonations as I crumpled to the floor, my grandson running to me.

EVENING

He carried me out of that sinking ship.

In my falling awareness of things I felt him hold me in his arms. They were strong arms, with the grip of a human who carried with him precious cargo. This, I approved of, even though my own sense of decorum wished to still be carried on that pillow above his head. I was still a god, after all, even if I were now a dying one.

I heard him call the Daware man's name. The Daware man was on a skiff he had cut free from Luubu's disintegrating ship. The Daware man called his name back.

If one listened, one could hear it in their voices.

One can tell a lot, even in such a state, by the way someone speaks another's name.

We were on a boat leaving the Bowl.

I was laid on my back, staring at the orange-and-purple evening sky. I remember having the thought that soon night would fall. In my delirium I remembered how the night used to be mine. How I used to be the night. My finger pointing upward.

I used to be right there.

That Burn.

"It's okay," Jun said, lowering my hand. "Rest."

"We're almost out," the Daware man said as he poled us forward.

The world turned black as we glided through the tunnel and out the sluice.

I remember going down a river.

I could see the wall of the crater shrinking in the distance. I remember Jun looking down at me with a tenderness that surprised me. I remember looking at his face and thinking that it was beautiful. He was beautiful. That the world was lucky to have such a beautiful person in it. And I wondered at myself, and why I had ever thought to hurt this beautiful person, or the world he lived in. Looking at him, I wondered at the things that I had done.

The Daware man told us that there was a blockade ahead. A broken river checkpoint, destroyed in the rebellion. It was effectively a dam.

He told us we would have to disembark.

And then I was lying beside a fire.

It was a small fire, but it seemed impossibly bright against the moonless night. A camp in the wilderness. The two of them were seated on either side of the fire. In that moment did they remind me of the old guardians of the city beneath the Sleeping Sea, who protected the black pyre on which flowers bloom and are uplifted on the draft of the eternal flame. I could see them that night, soaring into the air above that little campground. I could see them lighting the stars on fire.

"You'll make it to the eastern shore," Jun said. "You just have to return to your sleeping state."

"I will not make it to the Divine City," I told him. I could tell that they were unused to hearing my voice, my true voice, aloud. It must have sounded so odd to their mortal ears. What is the sound of the voice of the oldest tree? What is the song of the Moon? "I will die here," I said.

They said nothing to this, for they knew this to be the truth, and there was little reason for me to lie.

"You have not failed me," I told Jun.

He did not answer me.

"But I do have one last request. Of the both of you."

And the both of them nodded.

"I will not make it east," I said once more, "which is why I would have you consume this body." My hand on my chest. Their eyes widening. "Consume this body, and take what little power I have left to offer. Return this body, and end the life of my last child. The Third of the Three Terrors, who yet rules the eastern shore of this despoiled country. Consume this body, and end him, and once you have done this, offer my bones to the sea, so that the Water may give me back to the sky, a new Moon born to the night."

"A simple request then," Jun joked, his voice strained. The Daware man smiled grimly, and I let loose a rattled chuckle.

"Far from it," I said. "But I would make it all the same. Swear you will do this."

They both swore, without hesitation, and this made me glad.

I looked up at the sky once more.

The constellations burned.

I was falling asleep.

I asked them if they knew a lullaby. I missed the old songs. But my protectors had lived their lives as warriors in this bloody land, and they confessed to me that they knew no lullabies. The Daware man and Jun, all they knew were war songs. They knew the battle chants. The victory cries. The bloody verse of mercenaries over strong drinks, a lover on their lap. I told them that was fine. A war song would do. Just sing.

And my last thought that night, in that world, in all of my many years, was of how strange my ending was. These two young men singing me to sleep with untested voices, singing of all the dead that had passed their blade, and of all the dead that were to come. The flames leaping, throwing their laughing shadows onto the surfaces of the ancient boulders that surrounded us as they sang of conquest. How strange, their chants of battles won and lost. How amusing, how one boy would teach the other one the words. A rare excitement in their eyes as they stomped the beat into the earth. The two of them raising my spirit into the bloodborne night on their hoarse, ugly, beautiful singing. I thought how strange it was that I ever feared the end. That I had ever tried to escape it. And like that, it was done. My hand releasing from its fist. The battle fought. The life slipped from this old tether.

THE FOURTH DAY

—

in which we offer our finest weapon

Her tale is told.

When Her voice leaves the theater, all that is left behind is silence; a silence with such weight, you can feel it on your shoulders, pressing you into your seat. Onstage, this moonlit body, and its fellow dancers, having performed Her tale as She willed it, now lower to these knees, heads bowed to the floor, a finality to their movement that only confirms that Her voice is gone, and will likely never return. You are not sure what to think when the curtains draw shut for the first time since this performance had begun, a panic in your breast when this moonlit body disappears behind the swift meeting of the drapes, and the theater comes alive with light.

The brass bowls, relit by the spectral attendants and their sparking sticks, roar once more with fire, the tapestries that hang off the walls and eaves bright in all of their gloriously splintered patterns. You blink, as if waking from a long dream, feeling full, if not yet satisfied, your arms stretching to work out the cramps of sitting still for too long, until you realize that the other shades have begun to rise and exit the theater. Out they go, in single file up the aisles, with all that occurred on the Third Day going with them present in the way they carry themselves—an exhaustion to their step, a stupor, and in some, a bounce, the story a part of their body now. And as you watch them leave, you clutch your family's spear close to your chest, giving space for the shades to move past you and join the line headed for the exits. You ask the tall shade beside you why everyone is leaving, thinking that the story could not possibly be over yet—hoping this wasn't the case, for all the loose threads that yet remained—and with some kindness, and some condescension, the shade leans over and tells you what is happening.

"Intermission."

With nowhere else to go, you follow the line out of the theater and into the ornate lobby, which is decorated with yet more banners, floating lanterns, and trees that erupt from the floor and press up through the high ceiling, a fluttering sprinkle of flat-brimmed leaves falling all around you as you press up against the far wall and play observer, as you tended to in these sorts of situations. Toadmen wander the crowds of shades with trays, serving drinks. One of them ribbits when he passes you and you politely tell him you are not thirsty, but he presses a cup into your hands anyway. The cup is smoothly hewn of a dark wood, a dull gold liquid sloshing inside. It tastes how you imagine light tastes to a shy flower. You wonder how well this drink would sell at the pub where you work.

You smile faintly. You had been so caught up in the tale, you had forgotten your own. All that awaits you on the other side of this dream.

You are not looking forward to picking up that mop again.

With this cup of light in your hand, you walk around and pick up some of the conversation between the other shades. The talk is casual. No one speaks of the tale. They instead share tales of themselves; of where, and when, they were before the dreaming tide brought their spirits here. *I'm lying amongst forty others, in a room with a ceiling so low you have to walk on your knees when you need to go to the bathroom. We spoon our bolt-action rifles like old lovers.* Another says, *I am asleep within my blade. It is the third night, and we are soon to pierce the veil of the fourth heaven—on our way to a battle over the sun itself.* It is nonsense to your ears, but the more you listen, the clearer it is that not only are you all from different places but also different times, different eras, and it strikes you as notable, special even, that you are all gathered here in this place outside of time. You wonder if there is a reason you all share this space today, if there is any greater link between you all than mere happenstance. *In the canopy of a great tree, I made my camp. There are no more people in the land where I dwell. From the Red Plains to the Dead River, I am alone. I was young when the weapon fell from the sky. I was young when my country was ended, on the whim of a bastard.*

Not all the tales were grave.

He is stroking my hair as I sleep.

I feel safe.

A woman is hailing you.

She is hard to miss, for she is one of the few here who is not a shade. She is solid, with skin and hair and cheeks, a familiar look about her that you cannot place. Her details resolve as you approach; she is tanned, like the fishermen who work the docks of your town, and like them she is very thin and wiry, and the way she moves has a slink to it, as if she had never known a straight line in her life. Her eyes are gray and cutting, their attention on you—or rather, on the spear you carry—so intensely that you recoil.

"Who are you?" she asks.

A funny question to begin with, considering she was the one who beckoned you, but your dedication to politeness compels you to answer. You tell her that you are a merchant's child, but as soon as you start to speak, you notice she seems less interested in you than the spear you hold. She asks you if this is the selfsame spear from the tale—the same spear that Keema had sworn to bring across the country in Araya's name. In a moment of pride, and characteristic sheepishness, you say you suppose it might be. You say you come from a time that was many, many years after the time of the tale—in the time of trains and radios—and that this spear had been handed down the successive generations of your family. You say that the line of inheritance was long and not very well known. Your father, and your lola, could only trace the spear's history back to your great-grandfather's passage across the Great and Unending Sea. Who owned it before then was anyone's guess.

You say you were surprised to learn that Commander Araya had the same spear. You wonder if the two of you are related by some distant means.

Great, great, great, great, great, great, grand—

She asks you if she may study it. You hand her the spear after a moment's hesitation, some bone-deep part of you reluctant to let it go. Her sleeves are pulled back; her hands reach out; the grooves and etches are explored. There is something intimate about the way she explores it, as if her fingers spoke the tongue of the spear and they were now in deep conversation, no inch of its length left untouched. Her expression is melancholic. You feel like you are watching a reunion of sorts, friends from long ago, meeting again after all this time, the intensity such that you even feel a little embarrassed for staring. She observes aloud that the details of the spear are different from the tale's description, pointing to the markings that cover the shaft: a series of bumps and grooves, almost like musical notation. You nod, and tell her that you are not sure what the markings signify; not even your lola had a tale to explain them. But the woman shrugs, and says she knows well what they are.

"They are dance steps," she says. "This is an old form of notation. One from even before the time of this tale."

The fine hairs of your attention prick up. You ask her what kind of dance it is.

She seems to have forgotten you are there. "The people would etch these notations on their weapons, on the inside of their armor, so that the steps were never forgotten." A low breath leaves her lips as she takes stock of the spear once more, before handing it back to you. "But I've never been one to read such markings. I do not know what dance this spear foretells."

She turns and walks away. You make to follow her but a bell chimes from up in the canopy and the sound rings in your ears loud enough that you shut your eyes, and when you open them again, you are in the theater, back in your seat, the tall shade nodding at you before they turn toward the stage. You look for the woman, but she is nowhere to be seen, your task made impossible as the brazier lights dim out and the drums command your attention with their steady, pounding beat. The curtains part once more, for the final stretch of this tale, but you find that your attention is split. You are listening to the drums, and you are also listening to the spear, your thumb running over the grooves and etchings on the shaft, trying to imagine who had carved these notations, and what movements they describe. You still do not understand how you are now holding this object, the math not adding up, for if the spear was lost on the Third Day, gone in the waters of the Bowl of Heaven, then how did this weapon come to hang on your family's mantel centuries later? And why is it here now?

The tall shade nudges you and you look up. The stage is open, and you see the bodies of two dancers, sprawled on the floorboards.

You feel a chill, as you think for a moment that they are dead— followed by relief, when you see the subtle rise of their chests and you understand they are only sleeping. You see one of the dancers kick and tremble. You hear them groan. And you understand that whatever sleep the man was having, it was a bottomless one, many leagues beneath the surface of the Sleeping Sea—trapped in a dream as restless as wolves.

A dream as real as day.

The last that Keema of the Daware tribe remembered of the world was standing with Jun at the edge of the river, helping him scrub clean Her bones in the water. Whatever flesh of Hers that they hadn't eaten, and hadn't been boiled off in the pot, would go on to feed the fish and the waterweeds. They did not speak as they worked—what, Keema thought, was there to say, as he held Her femur in his hand. No comment seemed appropriate. She tasted like old jerky, unsalted, dank. Her texture was rough and sinewed; there was no softness at all to Her. The meal seemed to have lasted for hours, though in truth it was not so very long, there was not much of Her to eat at all, small and aged as she was. He had never eaten human flesh before. He thought he was going to have to fight to keep Her down, but the sad truth was that he had eaten very little these past few days, and this was, in many ways, the first proper meal he'd had in a while, though he tried not to think of it that way; he tried to remind himself that what they had done was but a duty, done by Her request. He glanced at Jun, whose hands worked the bones in the water with a fevered focus, and thought better of asking him how he was doing. They would speak in the morning. That was what Keema thought, when they finally finished, and brought the bag of Her bones back to camp. And so he lay down that night by the dying fire with little thought as to the inner workings of his body—the chemistry of bequeathment and inheritance that began as the acids of his stomach met the gnarled and potent flesh of a god.

Let this then explain his dream. Why upon the shutting of his eyes, he fell immediately through the heavenly bands, as a rock might through endless sheets of colorful parchment, a silent scream on his yawning mouth until suddenly he stopped, and he found himself standing at the edge of the Last Road of this existence.

You know this road.

You remember it from her stories. It is the road that marks the border between this world and the next. A road on a high cliff that overlooks the endless roil of the Sleeping Sea. The Red-Cloaked

Fisherman once sat upon the edge of this road, with his stool and his rod stringed with the unbreakable strand of hair plucked from the head of his true love. The same road that the solemn warriors of the fifth heavenly band would walk, cutting down any coward soul who yet clung to the cliff's edge, not ready to fall. It was the road for wanderers—for those who had never known a home, not even in themselves.

This was the road where Keema met
Uhi Araya for the final time.

The dream was such that he did not feel surprise when he saw her, only relief, as she approached him while riding astride a tortoise. She rode without reins, like a god on some mystic steed, and her dress was that of a person who had been on the road for a very long time. None of her clothing matched, neither color nor cut, the fabric old and weathered from near constant exposure to the elements. She looked as though she had seen and been through much. But she smiled anyway when she saw him, and after she had taken a healthy swig from a jug tied to her waist—alcohol, he could smell it, even from where he stood—she spoke to him. "It's been some time since I've crossed paths with another wanderer."

Keema lowered himself on his knees, his forehead kissing the ground in supplication. "Commander Araya," he said, his voice choked.

She chuckled.

"I do not know this Commander Araya, though I'd like to know what she's done, to deserve such humility from you, stranger."

When he looked up at her, he saw that there was not a glint of recognition in her eyes. Whatever life she had once lived was far behind her now, in this outward place. "She saved my life," he said.

"A thing worth saving," Not-Araya said seriously.

He looked up at her.

"Do you truly not know me?"

She shook her head. "No. I do not. Your face stirs nothing. But do not look so crestfallen, child; all I've known on this walk is this landscape, these clothes, this creature." She patted the tortoise's shell as she looked out over the cliff's edge. She looked at Keema, and smiled warmly. "But you seem nice enough. If you like, you can walk with us for a time."

"Where are you going?"

"This is the Last Road," she said, as if he were a cute fool. "There is no going. We are already here."

They walked alongside each other down the road, while the tortoise ambled slowly behind them.

He asked her how long she had been here.

"Too long to say," she said lightly, staring up at the swirling clouds. "I remember my first moment of awareness. I was gripping the side of this cliff, doing all I could not to fall, while someone, some strangely dressed warrior, was standing above me, telling me to let go, or else he would cut free my fingers. He told me to embrace my end." She shrugged. "Clearly, I was ready to do no such thing, so I traded places with him, and have been walking this road ever since." She was silent for a moment. Keema could hear the distant crash of wave against wave far below. "There are no days here," she said, "or nights. There's only the churning of the Sleeping Sea, and the wind that kicks up the cliffside. Some days it is beautiful; others I wonder why I keep walking. Why I do not . . . let go, as that warrior once suggested I do. But I cannot help but feel that something here has been left unfinished. So here I am. Araya the Wanderer, Who Walks the Last Road in Search of Her Destiny." Then, with some concern, she asked, "Why does your face fall so?"

"I fear you walk this road because of me," he said.

"Do I now?" she said, with one cocked brow.

"I broke the oath I made to you," he told her, falling back down to her in supplication. "In life you asked me to bring a treasured family spear to the eastern shore of our land, to return it to those who would care for it. But in my travels the spear was lost to me, gone forever in the waters of the Bowl of Heaven. I failed you. By my honor I should have ended mine own life. I—I should have done what must be done, but I hold on to my life like a coward. And now by your unfinished business are you here, doomed to walk this road along the edge of heaven for eternity. I do not deserve your forgiveness."

The words came out in a heavy rush, mannered, stilted; the way he always seemed to speak when he was truly nervous. He expected her to turn on him. To punish him in some way for this failure.

He did not expect her to laugh.

"You young men," she said in tears. "So serious." When she was done laughing, she reached down and grabbed his arm. "Come on, boy, stand up, I can't stand groveling. Here, have some of this, it never fails to cheer me up." She tipped the jug of alcohol into his parted lips. He coughed until he was on all fours once more and she was laughing all over again. She crouched beside him. "Maybe you're right," she said. "If what you say is true, maybe I should be furious. Maybe I should haunt you for the rest of your living days until you are dragged here with me. But though I remember nothing of my life before this road, I do have a feeling when I look at you, and that feeling isn't fury." She shrugged. "So let's have that be the end of it."

He wiped his mouth. He was aware this was a dream. Or close to a dream. Yet his throat burned and already he felt the spirits hit his head in a buzzy way. "I will do everything in my power to find that spear again. I swear I will try till the last of my days."

"Will it make you feel better if I pretend to care?"

"Yes," he said earnestly.

She took another swig. "Then your humility has been acknowledged." She looked at him as she drank. "Though I must say, there is a strange aura about you. Don't you think so too?" She looked down at the tortoise, who sniffed Keema, and shut its eyes in agreement. "I know not how to explain it," she said; then, with some suspicion, "How did you come here?"

"I don't know," he said. He tried to remember where he was before this. The muddle of his mind made it difficult to keep the events of his life in order. But somewhere in there, there was a spark. "I ate a god," he said.

Araya's eyes widened.

"We have only just met," she said, "so forgive me for saying that that does not sound like a very wise decision." He conceded that she was right with a shrug of his shoulder, and said nothing as Araya walked up to the edge of the cliff, looking out into the Sleeping abyss. She went quiet. Her eyes were eastward, staring into the black-and-blue horizon as a sudden wind kicked up, tousling their hair. "Whatever your situation may be," she said, "it seems you have a more pressing concern to deal with." Her hair flowed in the wind like black waterweeds. Like ink spilled from its well. "The Wall approaches. It will arrive in a day's time, if the taste of this dread wind is any sign."

The words carried with them a foreboding that sat heavy in Keema's stomach, though he knew not what they meant. He asked Araya what this Wall was, but she did not tell him; she had other interests to speak of. "This spear I tasked you with delivering. Whom did I want you to bring it to?"

"Shan," he said. "A soldier named Shan."

"Shan," she repeated, looking out into the abyss.

"That was all you told me. Just a name. You said you wanted me to tell them something kind."

"Oh."

She turned away so he could not see her face, but he saw the way her shoulders sunk; her hands touching her belly.

"Well," she said.

"Are you all right?" He approached her.

"It is a pretty name, don't you think? Shan." Araya the Wanderer breathed out, her hands falling to her sides. "If you happen to find her," she said, "I hope you do tell her something kind. That would be enough, I think."

She climbed back onto her mount, her jug firm at her side. "It seems we both have business to attend to," she said. "Best we get on with things while we still have the time. The road waits for no lady." She nudged the tortoise with her heel and the creature began its slow march down the unending road of this reality's keen edge.

And then she stopped it, turned to Keema, and asked, "What is your name, anyway?"

He let out a breath that was almost a laugh.

"Keema," he said, "of the Daware Tribe."

She tilted her head, as if the name rang familiar, from a place she yet did not recognize. "I like that name."

"I know," he said.

She smiled again, and nodded. "Farewell, then, Keema of the Daware Tribe. I wish you luck in the day to come."

"I will find your spear," he said. "And I will bring word of your passing to your family. Your spirit will rest easy."

She laughed—her laugh seeming to come from far away. As in a dream, things clipped forward; somehow, she and the tortoise were already small in the distance. "Worry not for me, Man of Daware!" she shouted. "It is you the Wall is coming for! You who must wake up!"

What Wall? he wanted to ask. But he had no chance to reply.

The ground gave way beneath his feet.

He fell.

His body dropped through the blood-red sky, the cliff face rushing past him like an endlessly running scroll, his clothing buffeted in the freefall. He did not scream as he plummeted into the abyss—it all happened so quickly he did not have time to scream. His body puncturing the black like an arrow. Reality betraying its unusual shape to him as he fell through an open window of a farmland kitchen into the mouth of a crying child and out the side of a mountain from whose great heights he saw the edges of this old country—the Wall that Araya had spoken of, as tall as the sky itself, in full view now—dark and impenetrable. A bubble in the pit of his stomach as the curtains of this towering Wall parted, and a giant eye, desperate and hungry, was revealed—the thick lid of this eye snapping open, and in whose fat pupil he saw his end. But all falls, no matter how visionary, must come to an end; all nights melt off from the fires of day; his journey to the edge of heaven, and the words he had shared with Araya, doomed to be forgotten upon waking. But what might seem a pointless loop along the long line of this journey would, come the opening of his eyes, remain in the unspoken text of him, for he had taken part in the consumption of a god, and no mortal in this earthly domain can resist such almighty transformations.

Come the first needlings of light over the horizon of trees, he would know how far he and Jun had come.

DAWN

You hear a plucked string in the Theater.

It comes from behind the wings. You think of a woman's finger curling over a taut, freshly tuned string of silk and gut, her thumb pressing gently into this string, letting the casual weight of her digit bend it until, like a lover rolling out of bed, the thumb falls away, and the string releases its built-up tension. And upon the springing of this magicked note, the two bodies onstage rise as one, as if waking from a deep slumber. *I woke up different.* You jump a little. The others in the audience, too, are caught off guard, for all of you realize this is your first time hearing Keema's voice, whispering through this theater. You do not know how you know it is him, but you do. His voice is harsher than you expected it to be, his tilted tone like a shadow coming out from between your legs, reminding you of the young men of your town, who hung out on street corners or balconies with cigarettes in their lips, their squints so performatively cynical it circled back around to sweetly earnest, though you still hurried past them on your way home. *The world smelled different. I smelled different.* The dancers move around the stage as if confused by its construction, overwhelmed by the floor, the curtains, the proscenium. They move without looking at one another, without being aware of one another, a strange synchronicity to their bodies that tricks your eye, making you think that you are seeing a mirrored image of the same man. The dancers touch and sniff and study the stage. They do not yet realize their connection. They are still becoming aware of the world, of themselves. Of a change they cannot name. One of the dancers touches the air in wonder. The other touches his own cheek. *I knew I was different now. I could feel it.* The dancers hold themselves. *I was so hungry I could've eaten a whole fish. An entire orook. I could've eaten the quills.* A stomach rumbles. The world, it seems, is coming at them from every direction, so vividly it is almost unbearable. A second note is plucked from that far-off guitar.

The sun rose to a sound as sweet and sharp as a sugared lemon.

Light streaked across the valleys east of the Bowl in thick strokes of gold paint. The sea green and hay-yellow grass was flooded with heat. A barrage of butterflies shattered the light off their wings as they peppered themselves over a thatch of wildflowers. Keema could smell the perfume powder of their wings, the musky sweet nectar they drank from ecstatically colored pores, but he didn't know that was what he smelled—that his nose had become so sensitive to such a small detail of the world. All he was aware of was that something in the air smelled vaguely sweet, and made his mouth water, as he lifted himself up from a dream he could no longer remember.

"Hale morning, Keema." The voice, no louder than a tired croak, filled his ear like cold water, and it inspired in his body a delighted shiver. When he turned to the person who spoke to him, he saw cold gray clouds driven with black iron nails—he saw a stormcast sea swirling around two dark whirlpools—and he felt a profound vertigo, as if he were looking into the heart of an endless chasm, and it was like he was falling, his breath caught in his throat, until he put his hand on the ground to steady himself, and he realized that all he was looking at was nothing more, and nothing less, than the gaze of Jun's eyes. *I could not look at him, not that morning, not yet.* He did the orator's trick, and looked at the bridge of Jun's nose—the scattering of sun-freckles, the near-invisible sheen of oil—as he asked him what they should do for breakfast. *We would eat well that day, for it turned out that the skiff I had taken from the* Cav-Meer *belonged to the Red Peacocks, and they had stocked their ship well.* They decided they would eat simply, some porridge, maybe some jerky. But when Keema opened the bag and reached in for the food, he paused, holding a strip of dried meat in his hand.

Dark red and cragged.

His thumb ran along the cracked surface of the meat. The minute fissures and small hairs once invisible to the eye. He pressed it up to his nostrils, the flesh savory and acrid, a tinge of iron from a pat of dried blood, the leftover spoils of the dead. The cow was dead, he could smell its story, its haunches rotting in a field beyond a small farm ruled by a tyrant who no longer cared that his livestock were sick. Illness had stained this meat. The white fear of a creeping death. He was crying. It was all too much.

"Keema."

Jun's hand was out. Keema wiped his eyes and tossed the stick to him and started chewing a strip of his own—the muscles in his jaw at work like arms kneading dough, saliva-glistened beef melting slowly on his shivering tongue. He fetched the hand pot—warm and hard like the arm of a lover in the woods who needed something, *anything but this,* the lip of the pot cragged and uneven, forged by a man who had thousands more pots to make that day, *just let him rest.* Keema brought the pot to the newly started fire and began making the porridge. So invested was he in his own sensory experience of the world, he did not notice Jun across the camp, feeling the fabric of his pants between his thumb and forefinger, as if in the stitching there was hidden the answer to a riddle long lost, in the friction between skin and thread.

"Do you feel different?"

Keema hummed as he poured water from a canteen into the pot. His hum trembled the top of his skull in a pleasing way. From the other side of the camp, Jun listened to him hum, and watched him pour the water. *As he poured the water into the pot I was poured with it, and as I filled up the container I wondered how much we had left for the journey ahead.* "Five full canisters," Keema said. "Don't worry, we should be fine." *And when he said this, I smiled, for now I wasn't worried.*

I trusted this person with my life.

Keema blushed as Jun got up and went somewhere private.

Behind the boulder, he relieved himself.

The sigh bubbled up from the bottom of his lungs, releasing into the air his humid and spit-dried breath as he splattered urine against the rock and the dirt. The crackling sound brought with it old memories of campout days, when he and his brothers hunted together, and cooked together, and pissed in brushes together. *We were not as close as our father wished we were. But there were days when it was only us. Us, and everyone else.* Jun shut his eyes. When he was done, he didn't return, not immediately. He instead leaned forward and pressed his forehead against the coolness of the rock, and he stood there, remembering the smell of blood in the room where all of his brothers had died, along with his father. It was strange, it happened only yesterday but already it felt so distant, like it was but a story that someone else had told him in passing. There were some memories inside of him that were like picking up a sharp rock, but not this one. This one was like a note scribbled on a piece of ripped parchment, worn from its time in the pocket, the message dire, but the writing soft and faded. He looked down at the soles of his bare feet. He had washed them the night before in the river, but there was still a slight darkness to them, some mixture of dirt and dried blood that would not go away for a while yet. He tried to rub some of it off with his thumb, but it did little to clean the foot and just made his thumb dirty too. *He had been gone a while by then. I wanted to tell him the food was ready, but I could sense that he needed some time by himself.*

Jun flinched, and glanced behind him. A bug scattered from the grass.

"Keema?" he called out.

From the other side of the boulder: "Food's done!"

He slipped his sandals back on, glancing once more behind him, certain that he had heard something—a whisper on the breeze. But the moment came and went, and he found that relieving himself did a great deal to make him feel better. He walked back to the fire with a lighter step, and when he saw Keema crouched over the pot, bouncing a little on the balls of his feet as he stirred the porridge, Jun was filled with warmth. He sat down by the flame, and as the stew popped and boiled, he listened to the gurgling pot—and the trill of birdsong high above, like a sharp green color twisting around a fingernail—and he asked himself when was the last time he had a calm morning like this, when there was no rush. No schedule to keep. No danger. Even the voices in his head were unusually calm. *We were there. But it was different in there. Some change— some clearing. We could not muster the energy yet to hound him.* Not as he smelled the thick and floral aroma of the porridge. When was the last time someone made him breakfast? *When was the last time I was served breakfast?*

Never.

Keema smiled. The pleasure of waking up to someone, whether friend or lover, preparing food for you was a pleasure denied him for most of his life. He had seen others do it. When he was a guard on that pleasure barge, his feet sore from the long nights spent standing in place, he would watch tired lovers leave their rented rooms at dawn, hair disheveled and eyes dreamy as they went to fetch breakfast for their partners who waited for them in bed. He would feign disinterest. He would nurse a colorful envy. This is why he took such a rare pleasure in being the one to cook someone else food for once. They may not have been lovers, but when Jun returned from relieving himself and made a comment about the delicious smell, it pleased Keema in a fluttery way that Jun was pleased, and he set to ladling the food out into small bowls for them both.

Their stomachs were empty carts waiting to be filled. This did not strike either of them as strange, despite their meal the night prior. *We tried not to think of Her—we tried not to think of how She tasted.* They tucked into the food and ate in silence. Keema caught Jun looking at him from over the rim of his bowl. He could feel his gaze like a hot breath on his forehead.

He smiled.

Jun could not help but look at him. *I thought he had died in the Bowl when that spout of water took him. When I saw him again, bringing us an escape boat from that sinking ship, I was almost knocked out from relief. I had the urge to hold him. I could not stop staring at him. It felt as though I were in a dream, to be sharing breakfast with him now.*

Keema looked up from his bowl, startled by this admission. It gladdened him. "It is like a dream, isn't it?" he said. "To still be alive, after everything that happened yesterday."

"Did I—?" Jun began to ask, but he believed the question to be mad. He threw it away. "Yes," he said, echoing Keema, "it is like a dream . . ."

"I had a dream last night. But I cannot remember it. There was water in it. I think." Keema spoke with his mouth full. Wet, masticated rice fell onto the dirt, and Jun's lip curled.

His father, if nothing else, had taught him manners.

Disgusting, I thought.

Keema felt the word like a knife in the side. "I—I apologize," he said, wiping his mouth, finishing his chew. "The dream I had," he continued, "it is like the shadow remains, but I cannot make out the shape that is casting it." He frowned. "But I know the tortoise was there."

Jun's expression darkened as he remembered the creature's death, and to Keema, it was like the clouds had blotted out the sun, both of them drawn into the pit of themselves as they remembered it like it was happening right at that moment, the bolts flashing through the dark, piercing flesh and wood, vibrating like tuners, tongue lolling out of a slack beak, eyes snuffed of their vital fire, a black bile spilling out of its—

Jun heaved.

The ground splattered with digested porridge and dark flecks of meat. It was the most rancid smell Keema had ever taken in, somehow more potent and unbearable than the latrines at Tiger Gate. Jun, shaken, wiped his mouth with the back of his hand, and after he kicked some dirt over the vomit, he collected himself.

I wondered if he was all right.

I was fine.

"I'm fine."

I wanted to change the subject.

He changed the subject to one that always gave him comfort to discuss. Future plans. "It is because of Her that we now have the means to finish off the last of the Terrors," Jun said, his hands trembling slightly. "The Third lives in the Divine City on the eastern coast, within a palatial walled-off fortress."

"Of all the Terrors, he is the one I know the least about." Keema winced from the smell of the vomit. *How in the abyss did it smell that bad?*

Jun laughed, unsure what to say to that. He went on, "It would surprise me if you did know anything about the Third Terror. Much effort on the emperor's part has gone into keeping him out of the eye of the citizenry. Even I have never met the man."

"Truth?"

Jun nodded. "Truth. My father—"

His voice caught.

Father.

The word was like a stick in my throat. Keema swallowed dryly. He waited, unhurried, for Jun to continue, and after Jun inhaled, resisting his tears—*I would not cry, I was strong, I was strong*— flattened into Luubu like a coin, bones crunching from the impact, dead—he touched his throat, steadied himself, and said, with a cracked voice, "My father, he rarely spoke of his youngest brother. Few people of the Throne ever mentioned him, much less within hearing of the emperor. I do not even know what god gift he had inherited from the empress, though I know that he was born strange."

"Strange?"

I had been called strange before.

Was strange good?

"Monstrous," Jun clarified. "A demon. The Wrong One of that batch of triplets." Jun looked off to the side, morose again. "Though I guess they were all the Wrong One in the end." *I hated myself for feeling bad that he was gone.*

I hated myself for missing him.

I was beyond redemption.

"It is not strange to miss your father," Keema said.

"What?"

Startled, Keema said "What?" back at him.

Jun's eyes were sharpened knives.

"You keep doing that."

Doing what? I wondered.

"That—talking like I just said something."

What joke was this guy trying to tell?

"There is no joke here," Jun said. "I assure you of that much. Now, stop. It's making my skin crawl."

"I didn't say you were joking."

"Have you marked me for a fool? I know what I heard."

"What did you hear?" Keema asked, annoyed, on edge.

Jun laughed harshly. *He was playing with me. The Daware man was playing a game. I did not understand it, but I did not like it.*

"There's no game," Keema spat.

Jun's eyes widened. "How did you—?"

"I—"

Keema put down his bowl. His hand was shaking. He was scared. Why was he scared? The accusation. He felt it too. But there was something else that he was beginning to attain a dim awareness of, and he felt like an utter fool for not seeing it before.

The way he looked down at his feet. I could see that he was as confused as I. I—I could feel it. I started to feel less sure that he was doing any of this on purpose.

"I'm not doing anything on purpose," Keema said.

He did it again.

"And so are you."

Jun's shoulders tensed.

"We're both doing it."

He was right.

"Our thoughts," Keema said.

"We can hear each other," Jun said.

Almost.

The stories are everywhere, you cannot avoid them. Every day you tell a story to yourself; the details of your day become a part of your myth. It is reordered. It is made sense of. Your lola told stories about the country she had come from; your father told you the stories of himself, his destiny for greatness. They are private stories told on stages behind thick curtains, seen only by the teller, and no one else. But what was happening in that moment, on that Fourth Day, was the pulling back of the curtain. It occurred to both Keema and Jun, as they looked at each other from across the ashen fire pit, that a door had been opened, and a threshold crossed. They could hear each other's story. That inner narration. The same narration that you can hear in this very theater. The realization made Keema's skin prick up. He felt like his blood was not his own. He looked at his arm, his hand. *And I asked myself: Where had my bruises gone?*

"Healed, most like," Jun said. "Resilience was one of her . . . gifts. It was how my father lived past his beheading." *The father whose head you chopped off.*

The thought, careless, accidental, slapped Keema across the cheek. "He was trying to kill us," Keema reminded him.

"I know." *I told him to fuck himself.* "I know." *I told him to fuck himself.*

"You fuck off!"

Jun held up his hands. "Stop reading what I'm thinking!"

"Stop throwing your thinking in my face!"

And then we returned.

"Who is that?" Keema asked.

The clearing gone, the peace gone, and he was agitated once more—and we had our opening. "Who the fuck was that?" Keema asked, looking around.

Jun put his hand to his forehead as if overcome by a great head-ache. *Killer, Murderer! we cried. We burned alive and we fell at your arrows and what do you have to say to us now? Why do you get to keep on living, YOU BASTARD?* "Just," Jun breathed, "just give me a second." He fell on his hands, his breath labored. *If we could've stopped his lungs we would've. We would've made him choke on his own thoughts, because he didn't deserve any of it, not this morning, not this breakfast, not the man across the fire that he fancied, this pervert murderer whore we HATED him we SCRATCHED and we BIT and we SCREAMED,* "just a second," Jun cried, Keema crying with him, "I just need a second," *UNTIL HE brought out a cold cloth and threw it on the fire of himself . . . and we . . . stopped . . . for now.* He sniffed and he wiped his eyes. "I'm sorry," he said, doing his best to even out his voice—to regain control.

"I'm sorry."

The two young gods slowly raised their heads, their eyes widening as they saw the state of the camp. The boulders that surrounded them had been pushed outward, with deep furrows in the earth trenching their path, as if the boulders had been dragged away. One of the supply bags had ruptured, grains of rice fanning out from it. Every object scattered from them as if they were the epicenter of some great and forceful wind. "They just started moving," Keema said, dazed. "They just . . . started moving."

Jun rose to his feet. "*We* should get moving. There's little point in remaining, and I . . . I could do with the walk."

"As could I," Keema said.

They started packing quickly. They saved what rice they could. Keema threw more dirt onto the fire pit to make sure it was dead. *I glanced at Jun to make sure he was all right,* and Jun growled, "I'm fine," *though it was obvious he was not.* "Fuck you, not obvious," Jun muttered. There was no question as to who would carry the bag of bones. Jun snatched it up before Keema could even think of approaching it. Keema made do with carrying this spear that was a poor replacement for the one he had lost, and a few other of the sacks slung over his shoulder.

In silence, they set off east.

MORNING

You think of thought.

There were times in your life when you wished your mind could be read, or tuned to like some frequency on a radio. Times when you did not want to do the work of speaking your piece. Like when you and Jadi fought that day shortly after your lola died, scrappy, bruising, and afterward you knew it was your fault, the fight, but you didn't know how to tell your friend that you were sorry. How easy it would've been, if you could've just opened a door and let him walk inside and see the mess for himself.

But you know as well as any guilty party that no one thought stands alone. That there is a city within you, populated by both high- and lowborn beliefs, interjections, prayers, rantings. You once thought of pressing your finger into Jadi's eye until it popped. It was not a thought born of malice, it was one of curiosity, of strange play, gone as quickly as it had come; harmless but for the fact that you held no dominion over such thoughts; that it called into question your own control over yourself. And sometimes you wonder, even now, if maybe your mind has a mind of its own.

What would Jadi think if he saw, paired with your apology, the image of you blinding him?

With how much charity would he greet such thoughts?

It was not long into their journey that Keema and Jun had to contend with such a problem.

In the morning light, there were no shadows to hide in.

They crossed the plains that lay beyond the Bowl in plain sight, over the wide tracts of grasslands interrupted by veins of water hidden amongst the weeds, which meant there were many opportunities to snag an ankle, if one did not step with care. It gave Jun and Keema an excuse not to speak to each other, focusing instead on their steps, both of them hoping that silence would stop the leakage of their minds. *But I could not help but think of the blood in Luubu's court. A sea of my brothers' blood. The iron and pungent smell of it trapped in my nostrils.* And as Jun thought of the violence he had witnessed yesterday, Keema could taste it, the iron, the sweat, the gelatinous marrow on his tongue. He looked at Jun. *I wondered if he could hear what I was thinking? I could hear what he was thinking. I could hear him thinking what I was thinking. I could hear him thinking what I was thinking what he was thinking.* The thoughts were sparks from a roaring and unbounded fire. The fire was spreading up the trees of their inner forests. Keema tried to control it. He made a game with his feet. *I was a snake winding between grass, my feet went one in front of the other, over the water and between the rocks*—but Jun was annoyed by the interruption of his own thoughts—*I was alone, my family was dead, I was alone*—which made Keema sneer. *You're alone? I've been alone my whole fucking life.* Sometimes they were direct images, arrow-shot straight from the mind. *The corpse of an ox pulsing with maggots; my hand kneading the maggots like rice. A man pulling on his shirt to show his hard nipple—pinching it till it bled. An old woman laughing with a pipe in her mouth.* Sometimes it was just noise; the loud, angry, unshaped noise that plays beneath the mind and is rarely if ever shown as it is. *Never.*

Never never never never never never . . .

One leap took them over a thin stream. Low clouds rolled over slight hills up ahead. Keema remembered what he had overheard back at the campfire, where the voices in Jun's head had said *the man you fancied.* He didn't mean to remember it; he wasn't trying to embarrass Jun, it just came to him unbidden as he leapt over the stream, *and I wondered what that was about. I thought I knew but I couldn't be sure, couldn't be sure I heard it right, because everything about that moment was so strange.* And when he turned, he saw that Jun had yet to cross the stream with him.

"It didn't," Jun said, "it didn't mean anything."

I was lying.

"You're lying?"

Yes. "Fuck." That was all Jun said as he hopped over the stream and walked away from Keema. Keema was a bit amused. His heart was also beating fast. *He said he was lying.*

Jun paused in his step before he hurried on, not looking back.

Separating.

Physical distance lessened the volume. Private thoughts, meant for no one but the person thinking them, became harder to hear. They were quite far from each other, a field's worth at least, when Jun thought the words *He was a cripple*—why, he did not know. It was a random murmur that nonetheless presented itself to Keema in a poisoned whisper. And Keema, not helping matters, remembered on a lark the vibration that ran up the bone of his arm as he swung the ax into the First Terror's neck. Jun knew that Keema was not remembering the details of his father's death out of malice. But still. Farther and farther from each other they went. The god-tether that bound them growing lax as hill and rock and river came between them. And the next time Keema looked for Jun, he was a speck on the other end of the field, almost silent but for the faraway crinkle of the sound of a house on fire—the wooden timber in his memory breaking in half, in a sudden, heart-stopping crack, the child looking up at the falling ceiling with big eyes, as Jun passed through a low, rolling cloud of mist that then turned him into shadow.

Both of them, finally, were alone.

You know what it is to be alone; to walk the halls of an empty house, with no sound but that of your own breath, and the traffic from outside. These days you are the sole attendant of the house that was once your father's. Your brothers are either gone, or dead, and you do not make enough money from your job at the pub to pay for help to sweep the steps and beat the rugs. The big clock in the hall remains unwound, the stopped hands always tricking you into thinking it is either later, or earlier, than it is. Amazingly, your granjo is still alive, slumped in his wheelchair in the living room, gazing emptily out the bay window. You feed him, and bathe him, all on your own, and only sometimes does he move to slap your hands away.

The war yet goes on, but the radio remains off.

It is still in your father's study.

Sometimes on your way to work you think you see the one-eyed soldier from years past. You do a double take, your shoulders sinking when you realize the person sitting on the low wall outside the pub is someone else. The rest of your day spent below a cloud as you remember what it was like to be touched.

Your little brother calls regularly from abroad.

"What are you up to?" he asks. And, "When are you coming?"

You've made up so many stories for him by now, it is easy to make up more—you spin tales of all your friends and brightly lit nights, and he is gracious enough to believe them. And though your granjo no longer moves, sometimes, when you are feeding him, you think you see the light of judgment in his eyes, along with the question you've been asking yourself every morning for a very long time now.

What are you still doing here?

But on you go. Your movements automatic as you live through each day and sleep through each night. You know what it is to be alone.

You've been too scared to be anything else.

It's why Jun walked alone.

There was a slight wetness to his scalp as he exited the cloud. He shook the dampness out like a dog, and when the sun revealed itself, he squinted, following the path of light down into the valley. Giant rocks erupted from the earth, and on the tip of one of them he saw a family of black foxes sleeping under the heat. Two of the younger ones were fighting over a bone that seemed human-shaped. His stomach rumbled with the memory of cleaning Her bones in the river, so he moved on. *He was alone, like he was always meant to be—like we always knew he would be.* "It's fine," he said as he slid down a slight ramp of dirt. "You can talk now. I just didn't want him to hear it."

We showed him the charred hand reaching out of the burning window and he only sighed. We told him what we thought of him, but he knew the words already and even repeated them alongside us until we grew weary of his games and searched for another line of attack. We found one.

We told him that the Daware man would never trust him.

Not with that tattoo on his face.

He winced. *And we knew we found a ripe target.* "I never thought he would," he said. "I wouldn't trust me either. I'm talking to myself now, aren't I?" *Yes, he was. He was going mad. The Gracious Moon had seen to that. She had started the unraveling, and all that would be left of him was a pile of string.* "So long as I finish what we started," he said, climbing over a rock, "I'm fine with that." *We knew he was only playing the part of martyr. We knew he wanted to survive.* "Of course I do." *We knew all the things that even he did not know about himself. The things he had no time to consider during this journey but which nonetheless existed in the secret spaces below his heart. He will never love. We told him so.* A tear falling from his left eye, which he wiped away as he reckoned with that. "I have not come this far expecting love."

We were running out of ways to turn him against himself. We

*raged. We pulled at the curtains. We told him that the Daware man
did not trust him and did not like him.* This made Jun chuckle. "I
think he does. At least a little."

And we knew we had lost.

Then, it was quiet. It came unbidden, but welcome, the quiet,
and Jun had the opportunity to sigh at the beauty of the valley; at
the way the sun bounced off the grass, and how the clusters of trees
chuckled against the unfurling breeze from the north. He looked in
the direction he had come, at the rise in the earth that now separated him from Keema; no signal shared between them now, not at
this distance.

The voices were at least right about one thing.

He was indeed alone.

As was Keema.

The young man of Daware was small amongst the vast stretch of
field that surrounded him. With Jun lost to his sight, his mind
slipped into a place he tried not to let it slip. He thought about
death. There were mercs in some of the less reputable teahouses
who between drinks would talk about how they wanted to go—
what the most honorable way to be offed was—and even he sometimes entertained such notions, especially when he drank, thinking
that it would be all right if the awkward road that had been his life
ended at the skewering end of a thousand spears. A death to sing a
song by. But that was rarely how things went. The mercs who
prophesied their own mighty ends were often the ones who died in
dark alleys, gutted, their hands holding in their insides. Keema had
seen people die screaming while on fire. He had seen them starved
on the side of the road. Quartered in public for treason. The body
ejecting all it held. The smell of piss and shit and vomit. He had
made those things happen to other people.

He remembered the messenger he had speared.

I screamed.

There was no other way.

I screamed.

He had to die.

Keema tripped into one of the hidden streams in the grass and banged his chin against the ground, splitting it—and in the distance, unbeknownst to him, Jun winced in pain, though he did not know why the bottom of his chin throbbed so. Keema cursed and picked himself up. He touched the blood on his face. He put the bags down and washed his face in the stream and it did not take very long for the blood to stop, a few minutes perhaps, and when next he touched his chin he could no longer feel pain. The healing of his body quickened, making him feel both powerful and freakish. Shaking his head, he picked the bags back up again and hefted his spear. He continued walking.

The plains stretched out all around him. He was taken back to the time before all of this, when he traveled alone between the far places of this country.

A boy scaling a mountain.

Sitting in a cave, listening to the rain.

Humming as he followed the curling path of a forest brook.

Being alone, in and of itself, never bothered him. He liked that he could keep to his own schedule. That he was self-reliant. It was only when he crossed paths with families or groups of friendly travelers that he remembered there was no one at his side to watch over him at night.

The dark nights.

Sometimes there was a wildness about it, like he could feel the heartbeat of the trees, and in those moments he craved to run his tongue up a man's back and make him howl. Twisting wordlessly in on himself until he was able to postpone the feeling that he was missing something vital about the world. As he maneuvered through the field of rocks that had appeared from out of the plain, he thought it strange, the thoughts a man has when he is alone, even when he heads toward battle. Or was it the other way around? Was it the prospect of the coming battle that made his blood ignite? His own coming death? He looked in the direction Jun had gone. The blue sky interrupted by thrusts of earth. It was a tickly feeling, to know that there was someone close by who liked him. But by then he knew better than to expect the best of such situations. He was too burned by the past to make the first move. And he knew that Jun was too preoccupied with all he had lost to even begin to think about desire. It was best to just let things lie and see how they may or may not play out down the road.

That was what he thought, anyway.

But he still enjoyed the knowledge of it. And he desired nothing more than to leap on Jun and start sparring. He wanted to fight him. He wanted to get kicked into the dirt and then trip the other guy onto his back. He wanted to wrestle. He wanted to climb on top. To look down and tell the guy exactly what he was going to give him. He shut his eyes tight, as if to make them explode from the pressure, embarrassed by himself, not realizing that as he did so, behind him, he had made a rock shoot up into the air, gone into the cloudless sky.

He felt like an idiot.

His self-berating was interrupted when he heard some surprisingly unpleasant birdsong, and the purple bird that had been following him since the beginning now made itself known from a nearby tree branch. And with his heightened senses, Keema could smell the bird, even from its distance, and he was surprised by the pungent odor that emanated from the creature's little body.

Across the way, Jun was listening to the world.

In the strange conversations he and the empress shared in those six months by the Wolf Door, when they had firmly established their antagonistic relationship, She had told him about the Rhythm.

You remember your lola's finger, tapping a beat on the side of the kitchen table.

"Everything moves in time," she said.

The Rhythm dictated that time.

You hear it now.

The drum, pounding the beat.

The dancers, holding the beat on their toes.

Long ago, people had an easier time hearing the Rhythm than they did now. Their bodies tuned to the earth. The empress said that Jun would probably never be able to hear the Rhythm. That he was only human. She said it with a sneer.

There are no words exact enough to describe a piece of music and there are no words to describe what he heard as he walked barefoot on the earth. The soles of his bloodstained feet crunching over dried crumbs and hot, yielding pillows of grass. Through the ground he felt the boulders to the south, their beat faint, but it was there, coming in clearer with focus, his body still unaccustomed to its frequencies. Centuries of erosion and chipped faces. A thousand years of waiting; but a slice of a beat that would not make itself known for many decades yet.

Jun was small.

He was standing on the edge of the world.

He walked into the shadow of a tajeline tree.

High up amongst the threaded palms were the hard shells filled with creamy nectar. His mouth salivated, but he had neither the tools nor the inclination to climb this narrow, branchless tree. He supposed he could use Her power, to practice here—knock a fruit off its perch. The skin on his arms prickling, a voice seeming to come from both his inner ear and the bag of bones he cradled in his arm, as it whispered, *Here are the steps.*

"Okay," he said.

He put down his bags, his sandals, and he stood before the tree. As he bowed to it, he tried to remember the woven patterns She had once showed him in the dark, and he was surprised by how readily the memory of it bubbled up, as if it were responding to his request. He did his best to follow the instructions. Facing the tree, he spread his legs so that he stood in a wide squat; his hands rested on his thighs. He clapped twice. He leapt, and landed with his right foot forward, his left foot back; his right hand coaxing the air. The transitions were clumsy, the movements rigid. But he persisted, and as he rolled his shoulders back and leapt and changed the position of his legs, he began to feel some gradual change in the world. He could hear, distantly, faintly, the pulse as his feet connected with the ground. Left hand out, coaxing. Right foot back, back, tapping. He could begin to feel the tree respond. He felt the fine little tendrils that wound up its trunk tingle and swell. He felt the tree bend, as if pulled by the gravity of his dance. And when he landed once more in the return position, his feet slapping into the ground in that wide squat stance, with both palms face-up, a tajeline fruit landed in his hands and he yelped.

Keema wondered at the tingling on his palms.

Like something hard and smooth had just slapped them. He worked the feeling out with a few flexes and continued walking while his friend the purple bird flew overhead. And as he walked he could feel in the earth the faint pulse of Jun's rhythm. As if he were feeling the footsteps of someone on the floor below him. He could tell by the beat that Jun was dancing.

Don't be shy, kitten, whispered the voice of the consort from his past.

"I don't dance," Keema said, to her, to no one.

But kitten. These are no ordinary dances.

This is the old magick.

As he walked, his walk began to keep the time. He did not do it consciously. He was a piece of driftwood on a rippling wave.

He leapt over another hidden muddy brook.

Jun felt Keema land on his feet.

He cracked the tajeline over a rock and drank from the halved shard. The fruit was not yet ripe, its insides more liquid than cream. The fluid was overwhelming in its sweetness, but also cool and refreshing. He licked his lips and wiped them on the back of his arm. The hard-shell halves falling away as his steps went in sync with the beat of his friend through the earth.

Soon Jun stopped—he listened—smiled.

He heard the sound of running water.

The Comosa River ran cursive through the plains, its banks staggered by low-hanging tajeline trees. The tajeline fruit sticky all over his hands and face, he decided to go for a quick wash. He slipped down a sudden furrow in the land and slid onto the silt shore of the river. He put down his bags and crept up to the water. He knelt beside its cool, flowing touch and dipped his hands. A small fish swam between his fingers and skirted away from him and he giggled. He cupped his hands and brought the water to his face and rubbed it in, with gradual intensity, as if to rub the tattoo right off the skin. But alas, only the juice released itself from his body.

He smelled himself. He looked around; he could not see Keema, though he knew he wasn't far off, the beat of him faint but still present. Alone by this river, Jun decided to bathe the rest of himself. He pulled off his jerkin and the bandages around his abdomen and he slipped out of the trousers Keema had gotten for him from the Gathering, and his underclothes. He stepped into the water.

A shiver ran up Keema's legs.

The purple bird looked at him curiously as he slowed his walk, confused as to these sensations in his body.

He felt cold, but pleasurably so, as if he were taking a long-overdue bath. He wasn't frightened of what he felt, for some intuitive part of him knew that Jun was the cause of it. As he walked he found himself focusing on these incoming sensations that were alien to his current experience of walking across the hardpacked dirt and grass of the plains under a hot, unblinking sun. It was a shiver that ran the length of his body, all the way up to his neck, and then back down again, till the coolness seemed to even out at his waist. And he laughed as Jun washed his armpits. Some trick in the transmission; Keema more ticklish than the person bathing. And then there was the very odd sensation as Jun rubbed down his arms, and Keema looked at his phantom left as it went damp and cold and was soothed by the other man's touch. He used to miss his arm, but that was a long time ago; what he felt now was not nostalgia, just a distant and unnerved curiosity. More pleasurable sensations followed. As he walked he sighed as his scalp was worked. He gasped a little when a finger flicked across a nipple as the arm dropped to the side. He felt himself growing hard.

Jun's eyes widened.

He knew he was not alone. Not quite. He knew Keema was aware of him, for he was aware of Keema. The door between them was both an exit and an entrance. As Keema experienced the physical reactions of Jun bathing, so, too, did Jun experience Keema's; the quickened pulse, the blood flow, the stiffening. And it was a feedback loop of another sort. The act of bathing, for Jun, turning from a practical matter into something else entirely.

And I thought: this was not a bad thing.

He remembered back when he was still a Peacock, he and a few of his brothers had been given special seats to the presentation of a singing recital by one of the local lord's daughters. They were there in representation of their father, who could not make it that night. It was one of the first shows Jun had ever been to. He remembered not thinking much of her singing. His brothers had better voices.

But the joy she took in performing for an audience was infectious. And there was a give-and-take between her and her listeners that night, their mood changing her inflection, the way she approached the melody, which in turn heightened their mood and provoked it. One was dependent on the other. There was no beginning, and no end. A completely average voice and yet he never forgot it. And he found himself making this comparison as he stood in the shallows of this cold river; how he was her, in a way, in this moment. This bath had become a performance, with an audience of one.

It was an audience he was glad to perform for.

His hands lowered beneath the surface of the water, and he swore he could hear the sound of Keema's breath in his ear. The memories of the week obliterated from his mind as his hands touched the bone of his own pelvis. Tracing the contours of the muscles, the faint map of veins, the lines of sinew that arced downward.

By then Keema had stopped walking. He was leaning against a tree, staring at nothing, feeling those hands, those fingers running past the edge of his pubic hair, pulling a tuft, twirling it. Keema smiled in an almost manic way. He felt the hands go everywhere but where he wanted them to go. Between the legs, in the crook between the thigh and the crotch. A finger running along the base of himself in a way that made his legs turn to jelly and he slipped to the ground in an almost chortled moan.

Jun smiled, pleased with himself until Keema retaliated, the moment becoming much like their duels as his hand slipped underneath his shirt, and he ran circles around his own nipple. The dizzying delight of it interrupted by a sudden hard pinch. Keema grinning mischievously while somewhere, far out of earshot, Jun shouted into the river, "You piece of SHIT!" His shock giving way to laughter. The nipple recovering from the attack. Not quite sore, but close. Sensitive and alive to his touch now. His other hand slipping back, to his firm bottom, Keema's eyes very wide now, rubbing himself through his skirts as Jun's index finger traced the curve of himself—but before it went any further *we showed him ourselves as he last saw us* Jun withdrew his hand as his mind was clipped with the images he tried hard to keep away from himself, the charred hand reaching out of the flame and the child in the fields stuck with arrows and the river bloated with corpses that he tossed yet another into and the boy lying limp under him with a back full of knife holes. *We made him live it*. He could smell the bodies covered in their own stink. He could smell the rot baked under the sun. He retched; Keema went soft, for though he could not see what Jun saw, he could feel his sudden distress, and he could even smell in the air the faint whiff of burnt timber.

They grabbed their belongings. Keema stood up. Jun crossed the river with his bags held over his head. *And we were louder in his head than we had ever been as we told him that this was the fate he deserved. We were his guilt, and we would rob him of every intimacy.* He dressed in great agitation, slinging his bags over his shoulder, and picked up the bag of Her bones, a little embarrassed that he had done what he had done in such close proximity to Her. A river boat passing behind him, the fishers giving him a slight wave as he pulled on his brother's Peacock mask and gave a polite nod back, his face once more hidden. The women on board conversed with one another, laughing, deep into swapping the local gossip about a drunk, his niece, and their three dogs. *This was his life as it would ever be.* And with sunken shoulders, a head full of noise, and the remnant grace of a tingle on the tips of his fingers, he walked on, as did Keema, who had by then lost sight of the purple bird, neither of them far now from the road that led to the Divine City.

To Swan Road.

Keema heard the road before he saw it; the rolling of wheels and settling of wagon wood. The bray of the beasts of burden. The people shouting over one another in the midst of conversation energized by anticipation, by circumstance. It was the penultimate day before the end of the Pilgrimage, and everyone was making their way east for the final celebrations. Hundreds of wagons were dragged by horse and ox, hundreds of groups on foot streamed down this wide dirt channel. There were even stalls set up on the sides of the road, manned by shopkeepers who had smelled an opportunity for foot traffic. *I asked him if he'd heard the rumor that the emperor was castrated by His mistress during the Fisher's Day, but he said he'd heard that it was the First Terror who was castrated and it was the emperor who did it.* He smelled it, the sweat of the people—*I couldn't find my mother*—and the horse waste and the aromas of the stick foods sold from the roadside stands *It was fucking hot and I was selling pan-pan sticks for overmarked prices; yes, it was the best day of my life.* The closer he approached, the louder it got. And he knew that it was not only Jun's inner voice that he could hear. *I remember we groaned when we saw the cripple coming toward the road from the fields. We tried to move out of the way. It was bad luck to be so close to his kind.*

I pushed my children toward the other side; I didn't want them to smell him.

He looked . . . weathered. We felt bad for him. I thought we should give him some coin.

But we didn't want to risk it.

It was everyone's.

As he joined the people traffic he felt all of the voices pour into him as one. *We had been traveling for TWO DAYS and she wouldn't stop TALKING. I wanted to drink poison and die in front of her, but I knew even that wouldn't shut her up.* He thought his head was going to crack open. *My daughter had died the day before but I was loyal so I was not going to miss the emperor's celebrations but I couldn't stop thinking about her bloated lips because they found her in the river, they found her in the river and they don't know who put her there.* He tried to press forward; he was following Jun's pulse, Jun was somewhere ahead. *And then I saw this creature slink past me and my whole body shivered because he had only one arm and I feared that he had just made me sick and of all the things I needed—I SAID HEY, WATCH IT—I can't find my mother—stick it in her stick it in her all the way make her moan—feet all stubbed and bloody from practicing all last night and I pulled off the nail of my big toe like a scab—He coughed in my face and I wanted to vomit—Smell, smell everywhere It's crawling up inside me—I will never be satisfied again I will die like this, hot under the sun surrounded by these fucking people—COME ON COME ON COME ON COME ON—there, a cripple boy, I had one like him in the Toy Room back on the Induun pleasure barge, I made him love me—What is it like to have only one arm, he's kind of cute—But we should remember to keep our distance—Keep distance—Stay away—HEY! TOO CLOSE!*

A hand shoved his back and he went staggering forward, dizzy from the heat and the noise, and he tipped and began to fall, the gravity of the drop lifting his stomach, the sweat curling up over his forehead, and once he fell, he would be kicked dead by this overwhelming world and he was okay with that because this was how it was always going to end for someone like him, trampled underfoot by people who didn't give a shit, *and I thought, Maybe if I just land on my face and break my nose through my skull I could finally get some goddamn rest.*

But then someone caught him.

Two hands lifted him up and he thought he might dissolve with relief when he saw the masked boy staring back at him. By the tight grip on his shoulders, he could tell that Jun was also having a rough time of the noise—*Two weirdos blocking everyone's way, yeah, of course we told them to get a move on—Our bodies still rotting in the bastard's mind, worm-thing pushing out of eye socket*—but something happened that neither of them expected. As they stood in the middle of that crowded road and stared into each other, the voices started to dim. *Lost lease and now itchy asshole couldn't leave it . . . couldn't get by it.* And in that tangle of theirs, which they had found themselves in after Jun had caught him, their hands on or near each other's chests, they could feel the beat of the other's heart. The rhythm of it. *He left a flower in one of my sandals with a note and I burned the note without reading it and then I ate the flower because I would never forgive him.* And Jun, with immense sweat beading on his chin, said, "She told me about this. The Rhythm. It's everywhere." Keema nodded in quiet awe. His palm now pressed into Jun's chest, and Jun's into his. *Told the two perverts to get a room. They didn't hear me.* And their bodies syncopated in their rhythms. The feedback loop went lax. It became loose. The sound continued to dim further, until it was only the low roar of a far-off shore. Only a few voices got through. *I wanted to go home, I wanted to go home.* And Keema realized it was not sweat that poured down Jun's chin but tears, for finally, in the calm of this syncopation, *we were quieted, the river cleaned of bodies, the knife taken out of the child's back, and a cold rain falling on the burning house, until the hand in the window slipped away and all that remained was smolder.*

MIDDAY

Swan Gate.

There were few beautiful gates in the Old Country. These were structures not meant for beauty. But Swan Gate, and its sibling checkpoint on the Road Above, Trine Gate, were the rare exceptions.

Both gates were the last stand between the rest of the country and the noble houses of the eastern coast. Jealous of the mountain cradle His Smiling Sun claimed dominion over in the west, the Five Families and their compatriots strove to finance and construct their own ornate signs of power. Trine and Swan Gates were but a small percentage of the many mighty constructions that peppered the eastern edge of the land, all—at least in some part—made possible by one of the Five Families. It was Lord Waag who had led the efforts to build the opalescent and wing-tipped structures that composed Swan Gate, the materials that now shimmered in the noonlight in the distance mined from his most precious quarries.

The effect on the people was immediate and powerful. *I reared the horses and told the others to come out to look.* When Swan Gate came into view, one had to pause, if for a moment, to appreciate its overwhelming presentation. *I held my child over my head so that they may see over the people. Look, I told him. Look at what our lords had made possible!* The smooth white rock wings coming up over the gate itself, which was a hinged slab of solid green jaxite. *My father died helping build that eyesore. His superior did not believe him when he said the scaffolding was weak. It would take too long, his superior said, to rebuild it. Keep going, he said. Twenty men and women died that day as the bamboo shifted and the wooden poles beneath them snapped. My father was crushed beneath them all.*

This brief tale was caught by Keema's new senses, though he could not see from whom, as he and Jun walked with the people toward the grand gate. Behind its behemoth walls lay the Fissures, where the land, cracked from Her Impact, erupted into a maze of canyon and tunnel and alien formation. This was the dividing line, where Soma's Fields met those hallowed canyons.

Past those canyons were the estates.

Amongst those estates, His Summer Palace.

They were close.

A wind was rising.

It was in the sway of the surrounding trees, the play of the leaves. The gathering of the people's hair. The steady flapping of the wagon's canvas flap. In the dilated state of their new senses none of these details were lost on Keema and Jun, who saw the wind now almost as a physical object; as a brush that curled through the air and swept along its horsehairs all the moveable elements of the world. It was the wind of portent, dragging itself eastward, to the estates, to the shore. Pulling the people toward a gate that was, mysteriously, shut.

The heavy jaxite jaws of Swan Gate were dug in the dirt. No one was able to pass. A crowd that was hundreds strong had already begun to accumulate in front of this gate, shouting to be let through.

This was exceptional.

They had closed it on us with no warning, no explanation, and the damned archers on the wall wouldn't tell us when they would be opening it again. We were stuck outside, in the heat, with no idea whether it was best to turn back or wait. Keema and Jun wove through the mass of people—*I thought, Of course this was happening to me, first Jela leaves me and now, well*—slipping between the backed-up wagons and the wheeled platforms that had, tied to their surface, statues carved in the emperor's likeness—*for months I had labored over this, so that I might receive His blessing*—and carts filled with contraptions and pieces of art to be presented at the divine celebrations, the two of them trying to get closer, so that they might learn why everything had been stopped.

In the heart of the crowd they listened, and though not everything they heard was useful they were able to sift through the noise to get the story of the gate that day. *Wonder if it's true. Stupid reason to keep it shut if it is. They don't need a tortoise to inspect us. No concern of ours if it doesn't want to work for them anymore.* Keema and Jun shared a glance. "The tortoise isn't working?" Keema asked, to which Jun nodded, and said, "We can find out more."

But there was scant information to be gleaned from the growing irritation of the people forced to wait; just that the gate had been closed for a while now, probably because of the malfunctioning co-operation of the tortoise within, but maybe not, and the sentries up on the wall holding those bows refused to speak.

It was a bit farther up when they heard, coming from somewhere to the right, someone think: *Five fucking hours I had been waiting in front of Swan Gate. I had come all the way from the*

Palace City for this. Dragging this wagon full of fucking useless trinkets to the ass end of the country to make a profit that I could've doubled if I'd remained with my old partners. I blamed my driver. I blamed my ex-wife. I wondered if maybe I lit those fireworks something would happen—if that would get the dumb bastards behind the gate to open up. With a shiver, Jun and Keema both experienced the same icy recognition of that puffed-up voice.

The trinket seller.

The man who had distracted them earlier that week while someone else tried to burn their wagon down. It did not take long at all to pick him out from the dust-choked crowd. He was still the same plush gentleman as before, looking in Keema's eyes not unlike a preening bird. The day had not been kind to the seller. He was scuffed, scratched, and he even had a bruise going up his neck to his cheek, which was easily explained by the man himself. *They could have just said no deal. They didn't have to accuse me of grift. They didn't have to push me off the goddamn platform.*

"This man," Keema muttered.

"Don't kill him," Jun said. "Let's talk to him first."

"You Red Peacocks are much too merciful."

Jun chuckled.

When the trinket seller saw the two young men approach, his eyes glanced over them before he avoided eye contact, *for I believed they were beggars come to ask me for pocket change, and charity makes fools of us all,* but when they coughed for his attention, he reevaluated them, seeing better the confident way they carried themselves, and he wondered if maybe he was faced with prospective customers. *I prided myself in my discernment of whom I allowed in my good graces. I was an excellent judge of character.* He was about to launch into his sales pitch for why this piece of rock, tied to the end of a rope, was in fact of divine origins, when the faces clicked, his memory as bright as a cloud break as he said, "Oh shit."

"Good day, fellow traveler," Jun said.

They were going to kill me. This was how I was going to die. For going along with a stupid kid's plan! "Look, gentlemen, it wasn't my idea. It was—it was"—he seemed to be looking around for someone to blame—"it was a jape! Just a jape! No real damage was done, I trust? It's all a matter of, they didn't know you were one of the good ones, okay? They saw the royal wagon and they smelled the tortoise, and the people, they're so temperamental, they wanted to let off some steam so they asked me to play a part in their little scheme but that's all it was, just a, just a scheme in the end really."

"What say you?" Keema asked Jun.

"I say horseshit," Jun said. "What did you mean they didn't know we were one of the good ones?"

The trinket seller looked up from his obsequious posture and very quietly said, "You are rebels, are you not? Of the Gathering?" He clarified: "I passed through Rabbit Gate not long after you did. I heard the story of the wagon driven by two young men of your description and a renegade tortoise, chased by the First Terror himself. You both made quite the topic of conversation on the traders' routes."

"Is that so," Jun said.

I prayed that they believed me. It was almost the truth! Though what they actually said was that the wagon was driven by a cripple and a masked freak—but they need not know about that. "It is so, it is so, young master."

"Maybe I'll believe you if you spin some useful story for us."

Oh thank the gods, thought I. "O-Of course, anything you like! Please just ask, I'm here to serve."

"Why is this gate closed?"

The trinket seller made a small, dismissive gesture. "Internal politics, so I've heard. A misbehaving tortoise that won't sniff a soul." He then looked between the two of them. "And what became of your renegade tortoise? Has it found a new home yet?"

Keema tensed.

Black bile, pooling at the feet.

"It is no longer traveling with us."

"I'm sorry to hear that, Mr. . . . I apologize, I haven't caught either of your names. You are?" he asked Keema.

Keema straightened up. "Death."

"Ah."

Jun shook his head and pressed the topic at hand. "So no one's said anything more than that? Was hoping you'd have more of an ear to the ground, being so congenial and all."

The man began to sweat. "Very kind of you to notice, young master, but truly the gate guards have been their usual antagonistic selves. Questions are met with warnings, which are then met with shouting, which in turn is met with more warnings." The trinket seller then looked on at the crowds with a surprising sobriety. "They won't stand for it much longer, I don't think." He shrugged, his mustache fluttering in the rising wind. "And so I've decided to wait." *For a revolution or a massacre, I didn't care.* "The gate will open in time—though I have heard that the commander of Swan Gate is particularly hard-nosed about conceding ground."

Within the checkpoint,

the commander was at that very moment trying to hold on to what ground he could. As he stood before the stubborn tortoise, trying to convince it to work again, he could hear the crowd outside the gate; the shouting was only getting louder by the moment. His personal aide was doing his best not to look bothered, but unable to do much about his trembling lip—*my father told me this job was a bad idea*—his sentries beginning to lose nerve in the face of all those raging people on the other side of the wall. He knew that his soldiers were scared, but he was a man of the Throne, *I was the goddamn commander*, and he would not let one civilian through without going through proper inspection procedure, *for once pro-*

cedure was lost, all was lost. A country either had total security or none at all.

"So help me, tortoise," he said, holding a perfumed handkerchief to his nose, "that crowd of thousands out there, in the heat of this day, thirsty and tired, they wait on your obedience. Hear me, I am trying to protect you from them. They will look for anyone and everyone to blame for their inconvenience. They will look to you."

The tortoise didn't bother to lift its head. "This one will not comply. This one is finished with this task."

"You cannot be finished. You are never finished. One's duty to one's country is never finished!"

"This is not this one's country," it said.

"Blasphemy!"

"There can be no blasphemy when the god being blasphemed is dead."

And it did not speak only to the rumor that the emperor had been assassinated, for what the commander did not know was that the tortoise, every tortoise, had felt its own god's passing. Now that Luubu was dead and the web that bound them had crumpled, the creatures had become distant lighthouses to one another in the dark, able to send and receive only the most basic of information and images; and it was in such a dark place that they received, from somewhere, from one of their number who no longer was, the image of a morning spent drifting down a calm and sun-touched river. A morning spent alone, in the company of oneself, unattended by sentries or diplomats or generals. No sniffing the people they did not want to sniff. No reading of thoughts or emotions, no picking out treasons theoretical and real. There was only the river. The sky. And itself. And this alone was enough to make the creatures reconsider the chains that bound them to their wretched watchtowers.

The people had begun to fling things over the wall at the archers. A bag of jerky pelted someone in the back of the head. The commander frowned. He told the tortoise that it tried his patience. It was unmoved.

"This one is done," it said.

More food sailed over the walls. We shouted down for the people to stop before things escalated. This was not what the people wanted to hear. *"Escalate?" I shouted back at the man, "I'll escalate this rock up your ass if you don't open this gate!"* "Oh dear," the trinket seller said as the crowd throbbed with agitation. They stopped throwing food and started throwing harder objects. The archers cursed. *I got hit with a fucking ladle!* The archers promised the crowd that soon they would start throwing much sharper, more pointed things back if they did not stop. The commander heard this, but he didn't care; he just wanted the tortoise to be under his control again. But Keema and Jun could see the bloody outcome of this feud. They could see the gate soon to be littered with bodies. "This wouldn't have happened last year," the seller said. "The whole world has been turned on its head this past week it seems."

"We should do something," Jun said to Keema. "Before it gets worse."

"What? You want to try opening the gate?"

He nodded. "It wouldn't hurt."

Keema thought on this.

I was curious to see if we could even do it.

This, Jun agreed with.

The trinket seller heard the words "try opening the gate," but he did not understand what they meant. *That gate was ten full-grown warriors tall, and ten times heavier than that. When the masked freak and the cripple said they meant to open it, they sounded as though they had lost their minds. If this was so, then I feared for my life.* "As well you should, if you keep calling me cripple," Keema said to him before he and Jun walked away, leaving the trinket seller by his wagon, stunned.

The two of them went unnoticed as they took up their positions in the back of the growing crowd; there were enough people present that the archers took no notice of them, lost as they were amongst the visual noise of the riot.

They shut their eyes. They silenced their minds. They listened to the Rhythm. They could feel the strength of the wood that composed the towering gate. The rope bindings and the mighty cogs that turned with the wheel. They could feel the hours and days and weeks that went into this gate's construction. They could feel the pulse and ache of the trees that were cut down from the forest to the north. The ageless sunlight once imprinted on their branches. They could feel the years, and the life, of this object, which to them in their mode of focus breathed just as deep as the humans that stood on top of it. The wood had flex, and tension. It bled energy.

It was in this deep study, which they undertook with one arm each held out toward it, that they felt the resistance give. They took the sounds of shouting, the crackling disappointment of the crowd, and they used that force against the beams of wood. *We were thirsty and we were tired and they wouldn't tell us anything. But we knew what had happened in the Bowl. We knew that it was possible to break through.* They let the two energies speak to each other. *And from my wagon of useless trinkets I saw them do it.*

I saw it happen.

The gate began to lift.

When the commander heard the sound of the wooden teeth of his gate being dragged upward—a sound he only liked to hear twice in the day, early morning, and late evening before true dark—he cursed and climbed down from the tortoise's watchtower. "Who's doing that!" he shouted. "Who is at the wheel!" His sentries approached him, baffled. *We told the commander that no one was. The wheel was unmanned.* "Then explain to me how that gate is rising!"

He stormed over to the wall but saw for himself that the wheel turned on its own and, in that moment, felt himself surrounded by worldly quantities that he did not understand. As a man who left the mysteries of the world to the emperor and the scholars of the Inverted World, he greeted this unexplainable moment with fear, and anger, and an irrepressible urge to snuff it out. "Stop the wheel! You three, grab those handles!" But the sentries' hearts were not in it, for they believed that to do so would be an interference with the divine. *We believed it would be blasphemy.* And besides, the turn of the wheel was too sure and strong, too inevitable, for them to fight against it. *So we pushed with it.* A group of sentries gathering at the wheel, aiding the divine power in its obvious will to have this gate be opened to the people, despite the status of the tortoise, and much to the commander's fury. The gate had risen enough that the first of the people were able to squeeze through, despite the archers shouting for them to not enter. The commander called for the archers and the more loyal of his infantry to follow him, and together they formed a line across the courtyard, where the crowd of confused civilians emerging from the still-opening gate met them.

None of the civilians knew why the gate was opened now all of a sudden, and they were even more confused that they were being stopped again by the commander and his archers. A scrawny man who had not planned to pilgrimage to the Divine City but ended up doing so out of parental guilt—*my mother warned me that if I did not go cheer for our emperor, my firstborn would be cursed*—and wanted little to do with any of this somehow found himself at the front of the pack, and, after a long standoff between the two groups, a hand shoved him forward, and he, unwilling spokesperson for the people, said in his ineffectual voice to the imposing commander, "Please let us through."

"Turn around," the commander growled. "All of you. This gate is closed until further notice."

The scrawny man looked back at the crowd for help. An older woman shook her head at him. "No?" he said. "No. Let us through. Please."

"Archers, draw your bows."

They did so, and the crowd recoiled.

"All of you trespass on holy ground. If you value your lives, you will turn around, and return at a later time when we are fully operational."

"Fuck you," a voice from the crowd said; a kid, on his father's shoulders.

And then the eastern gate began to open as well. But this time it was not Keema or Jun who was pushing it up but the sentries themselves. The commander turned and shouted, "Stop! Stop before I have you executed for insubordination!" They did not stop. *We had to follow the will of the world. The world wanted these gates opened.* "Archers! Fire!" Some of the archers lowered their bows, but three loyalists released their arrows at their fellow sentries. A quill punctured a man's spine. He crumpled over the handlebar of the wheel. *Murderer! we shouted.* And a rock pinged off the archer's head, breaking his nose, and then it was done, the momentum was too great to stop, the people charged forward and the commander was relieved of his position, *beaten by five of us till he stopped fighting back and pulled into a building for tie-up,* while the archers and soldiers surrendered, and the wheel was turned, the final road to the Divine City revealed to them from behind the steady and inevitable rise of the jaxite door.

Swan Gate was once again open for passage.

"Forgive me, forgive me!"

The trinket seller bowed until his head kissed the road. "I did not know you were gods! Please, forgive this humble purveyor of small delights!" The people traffic moved around them, the crowds funneling into the gate. Some passersby gave the three of them a side-eye. *I told her it was probably an older man who liked being shamed by younger gents. I wanted nothing to do with it, that's for sure, the jinxed perverts.*

"Hey!" Keema said, catching the comment. Then, to the seller, "All right, stand up, will you? We're not gods."

"No, no, quite right, you two aren't gods," the trinket seller said before he gave them an ostentatious wink. "Well, then, young-masters-who-are-not-in-any-way-responsible-for-the-gate-opening-on-its-own, I see you carry with you many bags, and though I have no doubt now as to the un-limits of your strength, everyone can do with a bit of comfort now and then, which is to say it would be an extreme honor if you did me the courtesy of riding in my wagon on our way to the Divine City."

Keema looked at Jun. *How about it? I asked him. Shall we accept his offer?*

Jun looked back at him. *I said that we should. I was done walking.*

"All right, Trinket Man," Keema said. "We'll ride with you."

"Blessings!"

He ran back to his wagon and shouted at his sleeping driver to get the horses moving. "Right this way, young masters!" They threw their bags into the hold, the seller wincing as his wares were crushed underneath their stuff. Jun eased Her bones onto a pillow in the back. As there was not much room inside, the two of them sat on the back steps of the wagon, while the seller and his driver sat in the cab. Keema smiled as the wheels started rolling. They passed under the frame of the last gate. *I asked Keema why he was laughing.* "Feels like we're back where we started," he said, "riding this wagon."

Jun nodded. *I told him I was surprised he remembered that, considering it was a thousand years ago.*

Swan Gate receded from view.

I told Keema that we were near the end now.

It was almost over.

Keema leaned against the lip of the wagon. He watched the road unwind beneath them as they rolled into the mouth of the fractured canyon.

Almost.

AFTERNOON

They rode through rock.

The procession of pilgrims, hundreds strong, shuffled down the road that cleaved through this steadily blooming canyon. *We prayed that there would be no dust storm to delay our passage.* Striped rock that had been smoothed out by millennia of salted winds towered above them, cutting off the hot glare of the sun for many blessed steps. The people kept to the main road, which was beaten into the rock by the soles of the many brave travelers who had come before them—the road sometimes branching off in tempting directions, with signposts that told the direction of nearby quarries, *and though there were those of us who had family or friends who worked Lord Waag's mines, and his northern forges, we did not sway from our path. Many of us wished to see the emperor off on His journey. Others wished to see whom He would pardon from the prison of Joyrock. And there were those of us who had nothing else to do but go forward.*

In these static hours, where little of note came to pass but for a gecko scurrying up dusty rock, or the odd family of bats crashing out of a hollow in the canyon walls, Keema observed the people who marched behind the trinket seller's wagon. The quiet families. The merchants and their guards. The caravans that made up half of an entire village. If he reached out, he could feel their exhaustion. Their confusion from the frightening silence of the tortoises all over the country. Their unearned hope that once they reached the outskirts of the Divine City, all would become as it was once again—a hope for a return to normalcy, even if that normalcy was fear and distrust and hunger, for at least the fear, the distrust, the hunger were familiar. During the ride, Keema would look at Jun. *There was nothing I wanted to say to him in particular. My eye traveled to his masked face of its own accord.* And sometimes Jun looked back, and Keema would feel a little kick in his stomach that he would nurse with some tired pleasure.

"Once this is over," Keema said, "what are you going to do?"

"If we live, you mean."

Keema smiled. "If we live."

Jun thought of Mira of the Gathering, and the promise he had made to her, of his life. It was a thought he did not want to sour the moment with, so he guarded it from Keema, who saw only a blur of a woman's face in Jun's memory. "Do you have someone who waits for you?" Keema asked hesitantly.

Jun chuckled. "No. No, I do not." He breathed out. "To speak honestly, I don't think I have a good answer for you. I have not thought too far ahead of our task." *It was hard for me to imagine there would be an "after."* "What about you?" Jun asked. "What will you do?"

Keema swallowed, and tilted his head, pretending to give it a good long think. "I don't have any plans either."

"Is that so?"

"Yes. It is so."

"Then after this is done," Jun said, looking off to the side, at nothing, "maybe we can help each other. It would be a good thing to have a travel companion for a bit, while we get things sorted."

Keema shrugged nonchalantly.

"That's not a bad idea."

It was a rocky ride. Their shoulders bounced together. And in their heightened state such contact was like the meeting of two exposed wires.

Keema gripped the rim of the wagon's entrance. He was embarrassed by how happy he was, to be sitting next to someone. He tried to hide it, his delight, but it was too expansive. *I was unused to such touch.* It flowed over the lip of his soul and onto the floor. Jun, not being as deprived as Keema when it came to the nourishment of physical contact, took notice of the pleasure radiating from his friend. He pressed gently into Keema's side; Keema pressed back. They sat together with elbows touching, with lightning on their skin. They watched two children fight over a snack. A man on another wagon tapped two sticks together to make a beat, a woman wondering aloud to her friend how long they had been walking for, and how it could be that a body could get so tired and still keep moving. On occasion the trinket seller would leave the driver's carriage and walk alongside the two of them, making frivolous conversation, pointing out things they passed that readily explained themselves.

"Down that way is Corcova Quarry," he said, pointing south. "Most of the land's moonrock comes from there."

Then:

"Ah! A shiver-gecko. Have you heard of the princess of old who poisoned her sisters with the blood of these geckos? Would you like me to recount it for you?"

Keema or Jun would tell him not to bother, but he would launch into the tale anyway. *I was going to get in good with these strange gods if it was the last thing I did. Every ounce of luck they had to spare would be mine.*

But whatever luck these young gods possessed, they seemed reluctant to part with it, no matter how I entertained them, so for most of the time I left them alone and sat with my fool of a driver in the cab.

As the seller and his beleaguered driver bickered loudly, Keema and Jun sat in silence. To anyone who saw them, they looked like two tired travelers who barely knew each other but had decided to share a seat at the back of someone's wagon out of mere convenience, which would be true in its own right. But as they gazed at the landscapes they passed, the bubbling rock formations that arched over the road like old fingers, they were walking through each other's minds. Past the doors both open and shut. And it was near the end of some long and little-visited corridor where Keema, with trembling lip, showed Jun a memory he had never shared with anyone, for he knew that if he did not share it now, it might stay locked within him forever, and that was a possibility too unbearable to entertain, and this was how Jun learned of the tale of Keema's lost left arm. And when he did, he looked at Keema with reappraising eyes through his mask, and he said nothing, for some memories do not need commenting on.

You may wonder what it was that Jun saw behind that memory-door. What pain, and what bloodshed, that was secreted away for so many years. But this was a tale meant for him and him alone, and matters little in the scheme of the story told on this stage to-night, so this moonlit body will leave it where it lies.

If this does not satisfy you, then imagine this:

Imagine a great battle in the courtyard of a towering fortress. Imagine a sword, whipping out of its sheath, and a leap of blood as Keema, wide-eyed, watches his arm fly across the battlefield.

Imagine whatever lie you like.

"The wind's picking up," Jun said with his hand in the air.

A dust storm soon arrived.

The people's prayer remained unanswered; such was the erratic na-ture of the wind that day, and no one saw it coming. As the dust from the rocks was whipped into the air by the wind in stinging gales, the people searched for shelter, some finding solace under wide umbrella-shaped formations, others in the hollows that speck-led the canyon sides like pores in a well-risen loaf of bread. The trinket seller ran around, and, after apologizing profusely, he told them that they would have to take shelter as well, for the horses refused to fight the grain of the current. "Unless, young masters, you have it in you to stop the storm yourselves?" They told him they did not. Cursing, the trinket seller and his driver brought their wagon into a hollow in the rock while Keema and Jun ran into one of their own down the way. It was empty, yet unclaimed by any of the travelers. As the dust winds shrieked they felt snug in their dark cave, protected from the storm outside. As Keema relaxed against the smoothly curved wall, it occurred to him that they were alone together, and from there the memory of the river was not far at all. He knew Jun knew what he was thinking about, but Jun seemed determined not to bring it up; the masked man put a small rock on the ground between them. "We should practice," he said. "While no one can see."

"What are we going to do with a rock?"

"See who can pull it toward them first. Keep your hand behind your back," he said, "and I'll keep mine behind my back too. See if we even need to gesture at a thing to make it move."

"And see who's stronger?"

"Sure."

"We putting any bets on this?"

Jun grinned. "I wasn't aware you had any money to bet with."

Keema gave him a rude gesture. The dust winds screeched and howled as they took their positions on opposite ends of this dark hollow. Their hands behind their backs. Jun, with a focus in his eyes, brought the rock, which was about the size of a fist, up into the air. Keema felt him do this the way one can feel a flower burst open. The rock levitated in the center of the cave like a dark thought.

"Okay," Jun said with gritted teeth. "Start pulling."

Like before, to Keema, the rock was a thing that was a part of him, as was the cave and the winds outside and even the other body who stood before him. To pull on the rock was to flex a muscle he did not know existed until today. It started drifting toward him. He was calling it home. But unlike before, this time there was resistance. It was like he was pulling the rock through mud. Like it was fighting against some opposite-facing current. And over the brim of the rock he saw the intense knit of Jun's eyes and remembered that they were fighting for dominance over this rock, and so he pressed his bare feet to the ground and pulled harder with his mind, the rock now jerking in both directions, unable to choose its master, the winner of this impromptu competition between boys whom the world had tricked into believing they were men, that old, base spirit of friendly battle coming up as they began to taunt each other. Jun shouting with hoarse voice, "I know you have one arm, you half-boy, but come now! Pull! Do you have only half a spirit?" The rock favored Jun. But then Keema, whose callused heels had begun to feel the burn of being pressed so deep into the cracking ground beneath him, thought back, *The only crippled one will be you after I win and smash this rock into your legs.* The rock jerked back toward Keema. "Brave words to say to the son of the First Terror!" Jun shouted. *He wasn't so terrifying when I cut off his head.* "Way I remember it, he was about to finish you before I distracted him." *Do you often look for excuses when you are about to lose?* "No. Just reasons for my grand . . . comeback!"

The rock shook, torn between two demanding poles, neither of them realizing that in their efforts over this tiny object there were reverberations all around them, slight pulses cascading off their shoulders and trembling the dirt and the dust off the walls of the cave and off the faces of rocks in a fields-wide circumference around their standoff. The people looked up at the ceilings of their caves. *We thought it was an earthquake. A small one, but still, we couldn't help but wonder what we had done to deserve this.* Keema was more desperate than anything for this rock, even though by now he was not sure why, this trivial pursuit of glory, and he thought maybe that was why he wanted it so bad, because it didn't matter at all. And then he pulled so hard he thought his spirit would snap off his spine, but it worked: the rock flung toward him, so fast that it would've gone straight through his head and through the wall behind him if he didn't move out of the way fast enough, the object shattering into many little pieces, the shrapnel flying outward in a sudden cloudburst and catching him in the side of the face. A single slice cut across his right cheek, which he gripped as he staggered backward. Jun ran toward him.

"Are you all right?"

"Yeah," Keema said. He brought away his palm, slick with redness, which looked black in the dark of the cave. *I feared that it had scarred me.*

"It's not that bad," Jun said.

"It doesn't hurt much," Keema insisted.

"I can clean it."

"I said I was all right." *He wasn't looking at me—it must've been bad.*

"You can stop worrying about your face," Jun said, smirking.

"I'm not worrying."

Jun walked away laughing.

He shouldn't have worried.

He still looked nice to me.

The thought snuck out like a mouse in the corner of the room, swift enough that Keema would have missed it if he hadn't been so aware in that moment. He looked at Jun, who was now looking away, walking away, toward the bags. Jun ripped a piece of cloth from the frayed end of a bag and dipped it in canteen water. Keema stood there in dumb fashion while Jun cleaned the wound. The sting was sharp, but he didn't hate it, and he realized that Jun felt it, too, by the knit in his face, the wince of the right eye as he pressed the cloth against Keema's cheek. Their heartbeats now returning to the front of the stage as they stood close to each other in the dark, close enough to feel the current of each other's breath.

The wind howled outside. A beetle on the cave wall scattered. Keema swung his fist at Jun, and Jun, after dodging nimbly backward, broke into a surprised laugh.

"What the fuck was that?" he asked.

"Spar. I want to spar," Keema said, flush, his voice clipped. He dove at Jun. "Come on."

He obliged him. They swung at each other. But they soon found that none of their hits would connect. They could read each other too well. Keema smiled. *I could see exactly what he was going to do.* Jun snorted. *And I saw what his counter would be.* Their fists narrowly avoided. Knuckles skimming across the surface of shoulder blades. Coming back around. They leapt around each other. They did not mind the difficulty in hitting. But they were not aware of something deeper that was happening in the circuitry of their bodies—that the fight was in the process of transformation, as they wove in and out of each other's grasp, the rhythm of it changing as

Keema's fist met Jun's chest and Jun twisted to accommodate its presence. Both of them too caught up in the movement to realize that the fight had instead become a dance as they leapt and grabbed at and pulled under and over. A strange dance, out of time, from another place entirely, pirouettes and side slides, alien to anyone who might've witnessed it, but they were quite alone in that hollow, there was no one to question or to wonder; there was only the two of them, in movement, Jun's hand sneaking out from behind, squirming up Keema's chest like a snake until it stopped just above the heart, and held its beat. Jun's lips behind Keema's neck, breathing; and they stood there like that, against each other. Just breathing.

Keema pressed his back against Jun's chest. Jun's breath hitched. Neither spoke, neither moved. Jun tightened his grip on Keema.

You do not deserve this.

And then he released Keema.

He backed away.

You do not deserve any of this.

"Good spar," Jun said, with no body to his voice. "Let's leave it there for now."

"I—" Keema said.

Jun turned around, and shrugged.

"Let's leave it."

Keema looked at him with wide eyes. *I did something wrong.* He tried to reach into Jun's mind, but he was greeted by a wall with no door. A surface, frictionless and impenetrable. And as Jun receded to the other side of the cave, a coldness came over Keema, and he thought, *Fine, this is fine.* Just as before, with Raami's rejection, the doors of himself slammed shut. He let the emotion drain from his face. And he sat against the cave wall, staring at the storm of dust that shredded past the entrance.

I was fine.

The wind howled.

How long they were sitting there, listening to the dust, they did not know—at some point, Jun had tried to make a joke about the trinket seller's relationship with his driver, which prompted a curt grunt from Keema—but in time, they heard from outside the sound of clopping, *and we thought the storm was over and the trinket seller had returned.* But the dusts raged as heavily as before. The only difference now was that there was a creature's silhouette standing at the cave's mouth. Both boys stood up. *I asked Keema if he saw what I saw. I told Jun that I did.*

It was an elk. For a time it stood there, unbothered by the sandpaper winds, and wordlessly Keema and Jun receded farther into the cave. Another animal appeared, this one a monkey, knuckling its way to the elk's side. *I suggested to Jun that perhaps there was a caravan transporting animals; that some cage had broken open.* But this did not explain how unaffected these animal silhouettes seemed to be by the dust storm—and when the monkey was then followed, of all things, by a strutting peacock, the two young men were certain that they had slipped accidentally into a dream; that during their duel they had somehow knocked each other out and were experiencing the twitching hallucinations a bleeding skull might inspire; this certainty only growing when the animals stepped inside the cave, and they saw their true colors.

The Purple Elk.

The Silver Monkey.

The Red Peacock.

"Creatures of myth."

Your lola sighed, the day before she died.
    "I saw them," she said. "Out that window."
    Who did you see, you asked.
    "The Three Shepherds of the soul," she said, with a shy smile.
"Come to take me to the blessed Sleeping Sea."

EVENING

You call it many things.

It is the place that lies below what is known. Your lola told you it
was called the Sleeping Sea. She told you it is the place we of the
Old Country look to when we are lost, for it is the place from which
we have come, and the place where we, in the end, must return.
Many of her age called it by that name, the Sleeping Sea—preferring
how the title evoked both mystery and an abundance of life. It was
a name that gave them comfort.
    "It is a holy and beautiful place," your lola said to you from her
bed, in a state of mania, her grip on your wrist painful. "I will leave
this body, and as water is taken into the soil so will my spirit be
taken into the land. And in time I will find my way there, that Un-
dersea, and then I will return to this earth, born anew. Do you understand me, child?" Of course you understood, she had told you
this exact sentiment the day before, down to the letter. And like
yesterday, and the day before, you told her yes, you understood—
this time with more bite than you intended, but whether she noticed the fraying of your patience she gave no sign. "I have nothing
to fear, because I am not going anywhere," she said in a hush. You

handed her a kerchief to wipe her tears, but when she ignored the offering, you took it upon yourself to dry her cheeks as she, in a delirious whisper, insisted to you that her route was clear, and that she would not be gone long.

She looked at you with big, wet eyes.

"I am not afraid," she said.

To people like your father, people who were always searching for purpose and who put stock into the notion of the immovable Pattern, they called it the Tapestry's Fray. They saw life, both its past and its future, as an already-completed work. They assuaged their guilty consciences by telling themselves that their actions have been written into the fabric of the world long before they had come into it. Moral responsibility gave way to the needs of destiny. The world and its timelines had been mapped, and the Tapestry's Fray was the border of that great work. The worried edge, and the unyielding hem, that held the image together. When your lola passed away, your father said that there was nothing to be sad about. That her death was expected. That life had a certain design and your lola had fulfilled her role in it. "Her part in the Tapestry is over." As if that explained all of your mortal concerns.

As for you and your brothers, rare was the day when you thought about the place suspended below the known world, for there were daily concerns that pulled you in every direction but inward. But it did come up as your brothers fell, one by one, one dying in the war, another alone in his apartment with a piece of bloody glass in his hand. It came up as you spooned lukewarm soup into your granjo's parched mouth and walked past the dead clock in the main hallway. What is the place we go to when the last seconds of our life have been spent?

Perhaps your eldest brother summed it up best, in the words he etched into the bark of the courtyard tree, before he ran away when you were little.

The End.

That was what the purple elk answered when Keema asked where they were going. From another creature, such words might seem glib, dismissive, an unwillingness to speak plainly to a mortal mind, but from this elk, it was clear to Keema that this was the only true description of the journey they now made.

They were far beneath the earth, where the air was cool and the bones of ancient travelers both man and beast jutted out of the rock like teeth, the five of them traversing the network of bridges that spanned the First Chasm. Without hesitation the elk clopped across the thin stone bridges suspended over the darkest and deepest of pits, and despite the queasy depths that swallowed the stray kicked pebble, Keema felt at ease under this creature's charge, even though he had only just met it. Some base part of him trusted its step and its eye as that base part of him also trusted the silver monkey who led their troupe, casting seeds on the branching bridgework before them to determine what path was real and what path was but a trick of the eye, falling into nothing.

They were more than halfway across the chasm when Jun lowered his mask and sniffed the air.

"I smell flowers," he said.

He had intended this as an innocent observation—the trace element of lilac, daffodil, some curl of perfume, had tickled his nostril and he thought it a pleasant enough way to break the silence. But when the elk tensed beneath him he realized there was more to this detail than he would likely ever know. The silver monkey paused. It asked him from which direction he smelled the flowers, and Jun pointed to the right, and without another word, the monkey led them down the path that favored the left, away from that sweet and foul smell. Keema asked the elk what they were traveling away from, to which the elk replied that there were things that sat along the edge of heaven, born from the darkest fissures within the earth, whose lives were spent in waiting for someone to follow their scent; waiting for someone to walk up and fall into their arms.

The elk told them they would be wise to fear such scents, and that if they wished to survive this journey below, they would heed the words of monkey, elk, and peacock and remain under their watchful protection. This, the two young men had no problem with. And to the sharp, bright, and predatory eyes that glowed from the dark, the red peacock burst open its tail fan, the eyes of the feathers like small coins of fire that warded off any would-be attackers.

The road changed the farther down it they went. Keema and Jun, robbed of words, speaking not to the animals or to each other—neither wishing to speak of the frayed awkwardness of that moment in the cave—observed the changes in their surroundings in a tense and silent awe as it became ever clearer to them that they were journeying into the heart of the realm of the spirits; to a place that no mortal was allowed to enter. What was once a tunnel, digging ever farther into the earth, became a dark jungle path, thick with brush and canopy, the elk's antlers shaking clear the vines that snagged on its teeth. Keema's excitement for what came next taking a purer form than Jun's, who had noticed the red peacock's disdain for the tattoo on his face and could not help but fear that he was being brought to his execution.

Camp was made in a brief clearing. The silver monkey handed each of them seeds that were bright gold in color and had the texture of velvet. The seeds had a cold jelly center that surprised Keema to bite into, but once he was used to the feel of it in his mouth, he discovered this to be one of the most delicious foods he had ever had the pleasure of eating. He thanked the monkey, who made a brief gesture of acknowledgment before it climbed up onto the resting elk's back and picked at its downy fur.

They moved on. The jungle path became a strand of hair. A long black strand as wide as the Road Below, and which curved down into a tapestry of stars; more stars than Keema had ever beheld in his life, and more worlds than he knew existed.

Worlds where energy springs and spoils. This strand of hair winding into the deepest depths of the supposed Tapestry, where the roots of flowers erupt and coil around the dog moons and fire-brands in the sky, and in the stars were etched the pantheon of giant cats and wolves and bears who watched the five of them pass with ravenous eyes, as if waiting for permission to leap from the dark and eat the small interlopers who had gone where no mortal should ever trespass. They walked this strand of hair until they disappeared into the scalp of this long-dead giant whose name is still writ large in the blood of the guilty. And in that nest of hair, the path became a shallow river, walled by the tallest of grass. Here, the world was alive with the sound of rattling bugs, the air textured with the click and the whir of insects flitting between stalks, avoiding the thrown tongues of toads from the dark. The elk's hooves clopped down the avenue of water. The river's surface was so still that their reflection was like that of a mirror, clean and articulate. This area reminded Keema of the Second Day, when they rafted through the Thousand, which now felt like a lifetime ago, and to recall that day gave him a strange and unexpected sense of history. Both he and Jun thought of the tortoise, and the oath they had made to it to see it safely east.

You do not deserve this, the voices in Jun's head refrained.

Keema could feel Jun withdraw into himself. But he did not know what to say to pull him back out. And even if there were a combination of words that would offer his new and only friend some peace, some accord, there would have been no time to speak them, for it was then that the silver monkey paused and the elk nodded, and upon turning to them suggested the two warriors hold fast to its fur. Keema and Jun gripped tight, believing that the creature was about to break into a gallop.

But the animal went nowhere—it merely shuddered.

Shudders.

And nothing observable happens. The creature continues its un-hurried walk, the silver monkey and the peacock keeping pace, and for a moment Keema believes that a trick has just been played on them, for all that he had noticed as unusual was a brief drop in the stomach, as if his body had been startled by something that his mind was yet unaware of, and a ripple flowing outward from them as if from a small impact—but little else.

The tall grass sways. It is only when he turns to Jun to share a questioning look, to commiserate on the oddity of the movement, that he is struck by the thought that his friend seems different. Looks different. Jun hears this thought. *I tell Keema that he looks different too—but in a way that I cannot name, this feeling unsettling me.* But as ever, the answer reveals itself in the many small details. Keema sees it in the hook scar on Jun's lip, which has changed sides. Jun sees it in the reversed part in Keema's hair. The missing arm.

Once left, now right.

Everything is flipped.

Keema looks down at the water and realizes they have entered their own reflection. And with this realization, the silver monkey tells them that they are here, and it parts the wall of grass, revealing from behind it their destination.

It is here that the monkey and the peacock part ways—their roles fulfilled. Keema and Jun bow to them both in thanks as the elk takes them past the border of grass, its hooves stepping onto the surface of the lake beyond it as if it were the keenest glass. The only sound in this still and quiet lake is the light splash of its step as it walks the two warriors down the avenue of lit braziers that float suspended over the dark water and lead up to the mouth of the structure that sits in the middle of this interior place. The center of this ribboning existence.

The Inverted Theater.

The hairs on the back of your neck prick up as a murmur ripples throughout the crowd; a questioning. *It cannot be—they are not—I do not believe it.*

But all of you know it to be true. In this place outside of time, and location.

They are here.

In the lobby they are told to wait.

The attendants disappear behind a sliding door. The elk drinks from one of the fountains as the two warriors walk around the lobby in a reverent silence, a dreading silence. As they look at the tapestries that hang on the walls and the carved spouts that release rivers of water, it is not lost on them, the feeling that they are approaching a moment much larger than they may be equipped to handle. It is in the numbness of their fingertips. The agitated pacing of their step. They are not speaking to each other.

Keema is unable to stand it anymore.

There is no Daware Tribe, he says, out of the blue.

Across the lobby, Jun furrows his eyebrows.

What do you mean?

He shakes his head, more at himself than anyone else. *The Mothers told me my parents died with the name of their tribe on their lips. They thought they heard the name Daware when they asked them where they were from. But it could've been anything. This name that meant . . . nothing.*

It was all I had though. People would ask me where I was from, and I'd tell them Daware. I added to it over time. Picked details from actual tribes to give it weight. But none of it was real.

I just . . . made it up.

Jun looks at him.

And those unbreakable oaths?

Keema looks away.

I made them up—took them from some peoples to the north who used to do that sort of ritual.

Jun does not understand.

Why? Why take that one?

Because it makes him feel special. It makes him feel greater than himself. As though he is a part of a larger network of ideals than his own survival. Because it was the only way to get people to take his word seriously. *Because otherwise I'm just . . . me. Some man of poor fortune.*

No story to my name.

Jun takes this in.

Are you mad at me? Keema asks.

No. I don't really care. I'm more thinking about how we are mortals in the spirit world right now.

That makes sense.

If it helps, Jun says, *the fact that you are of the Daware Tribe is the least interesting thing about you.*

Keema starts laughing.

Jun, glad that his words helped, joins him.

Soon the doors open. The drapes part. Kaara/Tak-Lina stands before them. She does not answer their surprise at her appearance with words, only a stern expression, and a beckoning gesture for them to follow. And then they are led inside, and it is over, this moment between two souls, as fine a way to spend one's last ten minutes of peace as there ever was.

You see them enter through the back.

They look a bit different from what you expect, both a bit shorter, Jun the shorter of the two; they are two aisles away from where you sit, and the shadow and light of the theater are such that it is hard to pick out the finer details of them, but you know Jun by his tattoo, which burns in this sacred place like some demonic sigil, the ink glowing an unearthly red as it reacts to the spirit currents that blow through the theater.

You, the audience, are pin-drop silent as the two young warriors are led up the stage, where this moonlit body awaits them. Kaara/Tak-Lina, her task finished, bows, and steps into the shadows of the back of the stage, leaving Keema and Jun stranded in the middle of the light. Keema, unused to so many eyes on him, to such attention, is overwhelmed, and keeps his gaze on the black polished floorboards. Jun has fallen back on his imperious past, his arms crossed, his chin lifted; it offers him confidence as he asks the only question right now that matters.

Why are we here?

All eyes fall on this body as it approaches them—moonlight shifting around its skin like living tattoos. "You are here because the Rhythm has led you here," this body explains, its voice calm and matter of fact. "You are here because the Pattern has dictated you would be here. You are here because you chose to follow those ancient animals, the elk and the monkey and the peacock, through the impossible heart of the world. You are here because you have always come here, will always come here." This body raises its hand and gestures to the rafters. The lights from the braziers brighten as the depths of the performance hall are revealed to them. "This place, which lies between your world and the next, is the theater where stories like yours are told."

Keema's brow furrowed.

Our story?

"The tales of old. The tales of heroes, Keema, of brave deeds and grim tragedies. The audience you see before you, they've followed you since the First Day of your long journey, and in time, they will see what comes to pass at the end of it."

Jun, with a look of displeasure, for he did not like the idea of being watched, asked, *And what is the end?*

This moonlit body smiles gently. "This body does not know. Time moves around this place in everchanging currents. Right now, at this moment, it knows only that your path has led you here, so that this one can deliver you a warning, and your final instructions."

Whatever doubts and misgivings the two warriors have, their attentions come alive at this last statement.

What warning?

"You know of the fell wind that drapes the land. You have felt it." This moonlit body walks between them. "How the wind shifts east, toward shore, as an inward breath. Keema, you have dreamt of its foretelling. Your Araya has told you of the portent." You see him, confused at first, slowly coming alive as he remembers his dream from the night before. *She was riding a tortoise along the edge of reality.* "But even if she had not warned you, you have both felt for yourself the great inhalation. The strange twisting of the trees. The wind that goes toward the sea, for it is the Water taking in its breath before the great expulsion. The Water knows that its lover is dead. It knows that the Moon has passed on. It can feel Her bones and Her essence, somewhere in the land. In that bag you carry. In those hearts you keep locked away." This moonlit body takes its finger off of Jun's chest. "And it wants Her back."

You see it on the backdrop.

A moving painting of a wave, white-foamed and rolling over the continent. You see the wave, openmouthed like a hungry wolf, swallowing the Old Country. The Great and Unending Sea, rising up into the sky.

Kaara/Tak-Lina—the woman who asked you about your spear—steps into the light.

"You are here," she says, "because you both have broken the

covenant between god and mortal. You have eaten the flesh of the Moon. You have crossed a boundary no human should cross."

"Even now the Water recedes, preparing to rise," this moonlit body says. "In a great wave, a towering Wall—and soon it will approach the shore of your land. It will destroy all in its blind and angry search for Her remains; the same remains you now hold in your arms; the remains you hold in your hearts. The land you journey through, so close to being released from under the heel of the Throne, will be crushed underneath the Water in its final tempestuous throes. Do you understand, Keema? Do you understand, Jun? You are here because it is up to you to stop it."

Fine, the young warriors say, so eager to throw themselves into battle. *We will end the Third Terror, and we will stop the Water from devouring the land.*

But even Kaara/Tak-Lina, so disdainful of these two, has the heart to look away from them, these proud fools, when she says, "It will not be so simple as that."

They misunderstand her. They think she means this statement in its most literal interpretation. One cannot go charging headfirst into battle; heart alone will not win the day; the warrior who does not plan, plans to fail. Trite missives of glory won, and all but useless in this grim scenario. Their warrior's fire sputters out when this moonlit body shakes its head and tells them in no uncertain terms what comes next.

"To stop the Water means your death."

They are quiet.

Now Keema is looking at the floor, his expression dazed, as Jun stands tall and meets the news head-on. The audience is quiet as this moonlit body and Kaara/Tak-Lina explain to them that the Moon is a part of them, wedded to their flesh, and that along with Her bones, their bodies, too, must be sacrificed to the Water's hunger, if they wish to stop its rampage. This body will not let them be under any illusion: if they agree to go through with this final set of instructions, their end is all but inevitable. As powerful as they might be now—as many gates as they might be able to push open with mere thought—they are more human than not, and their human bodies will not survive the Water's crush. They must go in with clear eyes on this matter, or else they will fail. And once they have accomplished their task, and the Water has receded back to its resting state, no one would remember them. Their martyrdom would be rewarded only with the telling of this tale, to an audience who would forget all of it upon their waking. If this was acceptable to them, this body would open for them a passageway, one that would bring them into the Fifth Day as safely as possible.

The rest would be up to them.

"This one is sorry," this body says. "This one is sorry that this is the only choice on offer. And this one is sorry to force you to make this choice in front of all of these people. But this, too, is part of the tale."

It bows.

The reception to its words is mixed.

As Jun listens to this proposal, he smiles—a smile of disbelief, and inevitability. *Of course this is how it goes. Of course.* And when this body bows, and he and Keema are left to think about the consequences of their future actions, his face suddenly clears of all doubt, long before Keema has even begun to digest the idea.

I'll do it.

Keema's head snaps up in shock. Even Kaara/Tak-lina and this moonlit body pause, and ask him if he is sure. He nods. *I started this journey with the expectation that I would not see the end of it.* He does not look at Keema, or anyone else onstage—he is looking at himself. *The empress was always clear on that matter from the beginning. She didn't intend for either of us to make it, and I was fine with that. She told me there would never come a day when I've balanced the scales of my life, that the things I've done to others will remain as scars on this world, forever, and that the same went for Her. Redemption was out of our reach, but we could at least step toward it, and if we died on that long road, then all the better, for everyone. She said we did more harm than good, sharing this earth with those who deserved it. She said it was time to move aside.* The smile Jun now wears is a genuine one as his eyes glisten in the brazier light. *My family is gone. Once this is over, there will be no place for me here. The tattoo on my face will mark me forever as my father's stain. So really, it doesn't matter when I step aside, it's going to happen regardless, with or without my help. I might as well make that moment useful.* He looks to this moonlit body, to Kaara/Tak-Lina, to you, the audience, and says that it would be his honor to give up his life to stop the wave. *My life is yours.* He does not mention the one regret that lingers in his heart. He does not speak it. He says he will stop the wave, and he looks to Keema for accord.

But Keema says no.

He backs away. He tries to pull Jun up from his bow, but Jun shrugs him off apologetically. *No.* Keema's voice carrying throughout this dark arena. *No. No, no, no. NO!* His voice is childish. Childlike. It is angry. Confused. Angrier. *This makes no sense.* The language of another time seeps in, infecting him. *It's FUCKING STUPID. No. I will not sacrifice my—you will not have my body. YOU WILL NOT! Jun, get up—Jun, why do you bow to these people? They are—we were—*and then he stops, as the memory of the Comosa River and the cave pours into his mind, and he remembers life; the static shock of touch up his spine, and the thrilling sensation of two bodies, standing in the dark, listening to each other breathe. He backs away from everyone, his heel on the edge of the stage. You see his back; the knot of flesh that landmarks the arm he lost. His voice cracks. It sounds wet, his voice. You know that tears now flow, but you are too far to see them.

His voice is small when he says, out loud, "I was so close."

He is looking at Jun when he says this. Jun refuses to look at him; he knows that if he does, he will change his mind. Keema is looking at Jun and he is crying.

I was so close.

He looks into the dark.

Why is this my story?

It doesn't have to be.

"Keema," this moonlit body says, venturing a step toward him, and then another. "What tale is told of you, of your exploits, is decided here. We stand in the place where the Rhythm is decided, and from which the Pattern unspools. If you walk away, that will be your choice. And of all things that lie between these heavens this one has seen and understood, it has been witness to and has told the tales of crimes of far greater magnitude than that of a boy who decided to live for himself."

Keema takes one step away from this moonlit body, but no more.

He is not leaving.

He is listening.

"I can make a door that will bring you to His royal palace. Up to His royal apartments. It is the only place high enough to not be destroyed by the wave. If that is the choice you make, the Rhythm will change—a new dance will take its place. In that mountain palace you will spend the rest of your days, as the Water shifts and spoils around you. You can live up there, for years if you like, but the Water will stir, and wait. And there will come a day when you are ready, and you will offer yourself to it. That is all but certain.

"There is another door," this body adds. "To another world.

Another time. You can escape the Old Country altogether, and live a life as rich and as long as any fortunate soul, blessed with the Moon's good luck."

He considered this.

"But my old land will be swallowed," he says.

This body nods. "There is no escaping that point. The wave is coming. And the makings of this life are such that this one can do only so much to aid you in that respect. But come what may, there is a path you can walk that does not lead to your end just yet." This moonlit body touches his shoulder. "You can choose to live. And none of these people here can tell you otherwise."

"Enough," Keema says, exhausted. "Please. Enough." He wipes his eyes.

He does not look at anyone.

You all understand what is being chosen before your eyes, and you wonder if the boy onstage understands that he is deciding between his life and yours—that if the land is swallowed under the tide, the people of the Old Country will be wiped out, the root of your ancestry cut, and you will never have been born. Your life will have been but a dream, a fleeting curl of smoke blown out the lips of some mysterious teller, gone upon the next crossing of the coastal winds. In this place outside of time, in the unknowable and mysterious flex of this Inverted World, this Fray in the Tapestry, any new Pattern might be born, to subsume the old.

No one speaks. From across the stage Jun watches Keema without expression. Kaara/Tak-Lina crosses her arms. The eyes of the audience are on the young man of Daware, and he feels like he is about to throw up.

"Just . . . make this easy for me," he says. He sounds defeated. He sounds like anyone halfway resigned to their fate. "I will do it. I will . . . I will do it . . . just make it easy."

This moonlit body bows to him.

"As you wish."

And then it looks to you.

You.

Upon this moonlit body's gesture, you understand that you are meant to join them onstage, but the old insecurities keep you pinned to your seat—until the tall shade sitting beside you nudges you to your feet.

Go on, they say.

Everyone on the floor and up in the many balconies watches you as you enter the aisle and begin the long walk toward the stage. You hear someone cough behind you. Someone else to your right is murmuring into the ear of their seatmate. Your steps are soft and uncertain. You are a mouse in a cathedral. Even your breath can be heard, from every end of the theater, as you approach the steps. You have a stunned, embarrassed expression as you climb up, and pass Kaara/Tak-Lina, and Jun, and this body. But it is only when you stand before Keema that your embarrassment fades, for when you see his face by the brazier light, you see him as he is, as he was. And you are not thinking about yourself, but of him as you wonder how someone can seem at once so young and so old.

His eyes are in study of you. The spear you hold.

They widen.

"Yes," this moonlit body says. "This is Araya's spear. The same one you lost in the waters of the Bowl of Heaven."

"I do not understand. Why does this shade have it?"

"They are Araya's descendant. One of many. As is everyone in this theater. Everyone here tonight has a root, dug deep, that can be followed into the earth, all the way to where the grave of Araya's family makes its soil. She never told you she had a daughter."

Keema shakes his head, stunned.

"Not once did it come up in the short time I knew her."

"Judge not the parent who keeps silent to their child's cry. There are too many reasons in heaven and earth to disappoint the ones we care for."

This moonlit body steps back.

"But this moment is between the two of you."

It bows.

"Speak your piece."

He looks at you.

Keema of the Daware Tribe. There are bags under his eyes. A weary gray. The day has worn on him, but there is an attention to his gaze that holds you in place. For a time neither of you speak, unsure what it is you are meant to say to each other. He begins by asking you what you know of Araya. You confess you did not know of her existence until tonight. That you did not know you were of her bloodline until this very moment. He asks what you know of your ancestry. Of the people who had come before you. You tell him that you know little. That you know only the name of the boat that brought your lola to the new continent, and nothing before that.

"Then who are you?" he asks, with impatience.

You tell him. You tell him about the dockside town where you grew up. That your father was a textile merchant before he left for the war. That your mother was gone; not dead, just gone. You tell him about your smoking lola, who told you the stories, and your brothers, all nine of them, all of whom you loved. Some more than others. Few of whom you truly knew. Your granjo, who lived in his chair and would not die.

Keema asks you about this war. Who it is between, and what they are fighting for, but all you can remember are the propaganda posters that curl off the adobe walls and waft down the crooked alley streets. You give him half-remembered names, of places, of kings. You stutter to recall how it all began—a gunshot, ringing in a temple—but you speak so vaguely that he squints to understand you. You move on. He asks you if the Old Country is still spoken of in your time, and you hesitate before you tell him that it is, but more in whispers than anything; that like most of the world before a certain time, it has been all but forgotten.

He surprises you when he asks you if you are proud to be of its people. The question seems to come from nowhere, but the way he asks it tells you that this question is no frivolity. He needs an answer. Your instinct is to lie, but the truth comes out before you can stop it.

Sometimes, you say. For most of your life it has been little more than a curiosity, this root that is caught on your heel. You would tell people about it to catch their attention, if they were the kind of person to be interested. You would sometimes hide it—and hide it you could, with your mother's blood—if you wished to be part of the group. Sometimes you made fun of the fact of it. Behind your lola's back you used to mimic the elastic twang of the mother tongue to your friends—no, you would heighten it, make it ridiculous, nonsensical—and you would make them laugh. You didn't think twice about it.

He looks at you, and you cannot read him.

You tell him that most days you do not think of the Old Country at all. That it would be a lie to say that you hold the place close to your heart, that your ancestors speak to you in any profound whisper of the spirit. You tell him that all you have are some stories, and some carpets. A Daido your father carved out of rock that your brother tried to sell, with no luck, to a man who didn't care.

You tell him you live in an empty house now, apart from your granjo. Your lola is passed on, and your parents are no longer in your life. If the radio tells it true, the war will soon come to an end, but it's been coming to an end for decades now, and your brothers are already gone. Some have joined the war effort. Others have moved away to better places, to live better lives.

A few are dead.

You think about them often.

You tell him that you have lived a strange life. Easy in some ways, difficult in others. You are kept awake at night by a rattling shutter you don't know how to fix. Some days you are so alone, you think you will collapse into a hard and dense rock. You tell him that you wish things were different. That you feel as though you have a sack over your shoulder, heavy and dragging, but you have no idea what's inside the sack, or who gave it to you. It's just there. It's just yours. And you regret so many things. You've hurt people, you've embarrassed them, you've embarrassed yourself. You have made so many wrong turns that it's a wonder that you're still walking. It has been a strange life. You say it again, and again.

And then, having listened to you speak your piece, Keema of the Daware Tribe takes in your words, and at the end of it, he asks you a simple question, a question that cuts right to the heart of it: he asks you if you would like to keep on living.

Even if nothing changed; if it all played out the same way.

Would you want this life?

You bow.

You hold out Araya's spear.
Offering it to him.
And you tell him yes.

Behind you, the people fall to their knees.

One by one. A rolling wave. The sea of descendants bowing, with you, to Keema. And when you feel him take the spear from your hands, you glance up at him, and you see that he is yet again overwhelmed. He stands there, at the front of the stage, holding the spear grooved and etched by the magic of the Sleeping Sea, and he nods to Jun, who with swelled chest joins his side. And the narration of their lives rings out in this suspended place.

We will stop the wave.

"Listen well to this body, then. The great wave will arrive on the Fifth Day, come the late afternoon. It will crash over every valley and mountain unless you bring Her to it first and give the Water what it seeks."

We swore an oath to the Lady Moon. To end her royal bloodline. We would finish the Third Terror first.

Kaara/Tak-Lina scoffs. "You play with time the way only mortals do. Recklessly. The Terror can be dealt with later on, but the wave cannot."

We made an oath. We will stop him with Her at our side. This is the oath we made, and we intend to keep it.

"Then the two of you have a very busy day ahead of you," this moonlit body says, and Kaara/Tak-Lina betrays some admiration for them with the quick smile she wears.

"We will give you what aid we can. But know that there will come a point of no return that the wave will cross. When it does, there will be nothing you can do to stop it. It will swallow the world despite your best efforts. As soon as the sun is blotted out of the sky come the late afternoon, you will be too late." This moonlit body smiles. "So do not tarry. Do not delay."

"And do not fuck up," Kaara/Tak-Lina says.

They leave this theater. All of you descendants of Araya remain bowed, silent and reverent, up to the last moment, till they disappear behind the exit curtain. You do not know what else to do to honor them. You hope this is enough. And when they are gone, you stand up, and you return to your seat. The lights go down. This moonlit body and its dancers fill the stage.

And you watch the end.

THE FIFTH DAY

—

in which we offer our finest dance

The drums rise with fury.

And it begins. The air cracks with the clap of bouncing sticks and the thrum of taut animal skin. The dancers leap from the wings, and this moonlit body, at the front of the stage, raises its hands, and the whispering voices of the ancient and the dead flood back into the hall—*our tale coming to its close*—*our long week nearing its end*—the now familiar trappings of this theater something of a comfort to you as you settle into the scene. Four days done, and only one remains. But this time, amongst the whispering dead that chant from the dark, you hear other voices, *our voices,* voices whose tone and timbre are stitched to your memory, no matter how long ago your last meeting may have been—for that, after all, is the nature of family. *We are never far. And we are here, ready to help end this story.* The vision of them comes suddenly—in one moment, you are following the gaze of this moonlit body up to the ceiling, which you realize is not a ceiling at all but the hollow of a great tower, so limitless in its height you feel the emptiness above you pressing you into your seat, your eyes red from the incense sticks the attendants drag down the aisles, tear-streaked and clouded—

and then, you are not in the theater at all, but in the living room of your family home, where a man you know very well, standing by the sunlit window with hands clasped behind his back, turns, and cocks his steely gray eye at you.

"It began here," your great-grandfather says.

No longer is your granjo the glassy-eyed old crumple in the chair. *No longer do you have to care for me.* He is younger in this vision, a salt-and-pepper middle-aged falcon of a man, dressed like a general prepared for battle. He slaps a piece of paper on the long table, a map, and he draws, in clear, confident lines, the positions of the armies, the factions vying for power on the Fifth Day. Here were the nobles. There the loyalists. There the marshaling forces of the Families. He speaks directly and without emotion, so unlike that bitter and mercurial man your lola once described from her childhood, or the drooling thing you were so used to feeding with a spoon, near unrecognizable but for those great chutes of white nose hair, which bristle with excitement as he tells you of the state of things.

"It was precarious," he says to you. "By all accounts the Moon Throne reached its end before even the dawn of the Fifth Day, with the death of nearly all of the royal family." His fingers drum along his forearms. "In this vacuum of power, the land was up for the taking. Many tried. The Wise Men in the palace attempted to seize control shortly after the empress painted the walls with the emperor's blood, but the coup was short-lived, falling under the sword of the loyalists who yet remained." On the table map he tips over the castle token on the western border, his finger sweeping to the center of the country. "In the Bowl of Heaven, the Fishermen's Rebellion was more successful. Many of the ships that still remained afloat after the destruction of the Third Day were brought under the command of the Gathering, to little resistance, for many believed that the cascading waves that emanated from the *Cav-Meer* had been summoned by the fishermen themselves. The only boats they could not wrest control of were Indunn's remaining textile barges, protected as they were by their own private forces, loyal not to Luubu but to the Families." A smile—the old warmonger can't get enough of it. "But where matters would truly be settled was the skirmish on the eastern coast." His finger touches the token that lies on the eastern border of the map; it is shaped like a conch shell and sits along the cliffs that overlook the Great and Unending Sea. "The Divine City. The stronghold of the last of the loyalists, and the residence of the Third Terror."

He taps this area with a stern finger.

"The Divine City began life in the era of the Fourth Emperor as a summer home, a place for the royal family to vacation, and get away from the political troubles of the capital. It was constructed out of the shell of a gigantic sea beast felled by the warrior Handa of the Yabare Tribe, as trade to stop the incursion of the Throne on tribal lands; the shell's top removed, and the city built along its inner walls, the main road spiraling up through the districts, to the highest point, where His Summer Home looked out over all. Protected by the two main gates wrought of nigh-impenetrable jaxite, the nobility cowered in their homes while the honor guard patrolled the alleys, and the last of the Second Terror's Silver Monkeys and the Third Terror's Purple Elks had retreated there as well. They knocked on the door to the Summer Home, hoping to enlist the aid of the Third Terror Himself . . . but no one answered. All they could do in the end was prepare for battle, and make use of home advantage, before the army came. Time was running short." He draws a concentric circle around the token. "Outside the walls, the pilgrims who still believed that the emperor was alive arrived to bid their Smiling Sun farewell, before His passage across the sea. There were thousands of them. They installed their tent and wagon communes around the walls of the Divine City, unaware that they were forming for the nobility a wall of flesh, to stand between them and the armies coming from the west—nor were they aware of the wagon, filled with explosives, that would, when the time was right, be pushed up against the gate of the city and clear a path for Induun's forces." He draws a larger circle around the one previous;

a circle that engulfed them all. "The armies of the Five Families—composed of their own loyal brigades, of soldiers of the Throne swayed from their ranks, and of free-band mercenaries bought with Family coin. Their goal was simple: conquer the coastal city, and claim the land once and for all, under the shared banner of the Houses of Industry. Behind the rise of hills northeast of the city they prepared, the riders and the pikemen and the blade-hands muttering their final prayers before they marched off to what they knew was certain victory." His hands lay flat, bordering this small and necessary section of the map. "This was the state of things, at the dawn of the Fifth Day. The air electric with the prospect of war and the morning prayers sung out by the pilgrims who stood between the proverbial lion and the rock."

From the other room, an old woman's voice calls out.

"But none of them knew the wave was coming," she says.

Your granjo nods to you, and steps aside. The swinging door of the kitchen begs you inside.

You enter the cloud of smoke.

You cough and wave your hands and finally the tobacco clears and you feel, mingled with surprise, a sense of inevitability as your lola smiles at you from across the kitchen table. *No longer do you have to miss me.* She is a little girl, no older in your eyes than a child of ten, her cheeks as smooth as lacquered wood, her once-foggy eyes now glinting with a startling clarity, like an old glass freshly rinsed. Her small hand taps ash into an empty porcelain teacup while the other fondles her prized yellow egg timer, pinching it, feeling it, threatening to wind it up but never committing. You would tell her that it is good to see her again, but there is an aspect to this vision that denies you voice, a reminder that this is still the performance, and that you, for all of your self-possession, are but the audience. But she grins at you anyway, as if she has heard you, *as if I were never truly gone,* and you are caught off guard by how much you missed her sly smile.

"There were signs abounding," she says. She takes a drag and blows a smoke shape into the air. "The banners twisted restlessly in the dread wind, and the air smelled of wet copper, and even their own bodies all but shouted that something was amiss—the small hairs, here, and here, raised like radio antennae." She touches your forearm, the back of your neck. You feel the goosepimples rise. "But the people did not listen to the auguries of the earth. When they looked over the edge of the eastern cliff and saw the ocean's retreat, the silt floor completely exposed, they believed this to be nothing more than yet another peculiarity of a most peculiar week. The dunes, the swells of sand, like a sheet of beige silk laid over a warped floor, on top of which thousands of slick fish gasped and died. No attention was paid to how the Water was marshaling its own forces that day." She sighs, and brushes aside her thick curls. "Tides have gone up and down. Waves large and small have crashed against the rocky cliffs of the eastern coast, but never in the history of all the emperors, nowhere in all of their records, had the waters ever withdrawn completely. One might think it amazing that in the face of such overwhelming evidence, no effort was made to save themselves. But though I cannot help but wish that when the world quirks and shudders, we have the wherewithal to listen, even I cannot deny how difficult it can be, to accept that sometimes, to survive, we must change our course." And then, as if to underline her point, she takes in a long drag until the cigarette in her hand turns to ash.

Another sigh.

"For so long has the Water missed the Moon. Centuries of yearning that manifested itself as a gathering swell beyond the eastern horizon. It would stop at nothing to honor Her bones. Come midday, even the sun would be blotted out by its yawning jaw."

The light outside the window begins to darken.

"The end was coming."

When the both of you hear an agitated shuffle come from the

office down the hall, your lola leans back in her chair, and for but a moment you catch a glimpse of the old woman's spirit behind the child's face, aged and weary, before she nods at you, bidding you to stand.

You know your next destination.

Your father frowns before the tapestry.

He is not even looking at you when you enter his office. He is squinting through a jeweler's loupe, checking the tapestry laid out on his desk for flaws before shipping the piece to its buyer across the sea. *No one gave me any time. It all fell on my shoulders, and no one gave me any goddamn time.* You find it darkly amusing that even in this magicked vision of yours, he is working—that, just like the last time you saw him, walking down that dark alley to war, his back is to you. But eventually he looks at you, and you see that he is but a boy, a teenager with hungry eyes who would always be trying to prove himself to the people he believed were his superiors. *And when I look at you, I feel so many things, so much pride and worry and regret, that it is easier to look away.*

Easier to pretend we are strangers.

"We focus on the particulars," he says, his face pressed close to the tapestry. "We focus on Induun." You sit beside him as he worries over the crenellations, the mirrored faces. The unending fractal. "On the eve of the Fifth Day, Lord Djove Induun observed the lighting of the fires in his army encampment with a satisfaction he rarely allowed himself to feel. For months he had been watching the emperor in fear and madness retreat further and further into His palace, His control over the land weakening because of His refusal to engage with it. Induun, a man of vision, knew that it was only a matter of time before someone else filled the throne their ruler was leaving behind, and it was obvious to him, and to all of his associates, that the man most qualified for the position was he. And now, after so much planning, he was here, about to have all that his heart desired. But because of his old childhood injury, when he turned away from the encampment and headed back to the main tent, he did not hear the song that broke out from fire to fire, the tremulous melody of the men and women who would be fighting in his honor, as they sang of the glorious deaths to come.

"That night, Lord Induun held a banquet for his fellow lords and his generals; a lavish spread of fish and rice and lamb and an unending fount of rice wine and harder spirits, for there was much to celebrate." Your father draws away from the loupe for a moment and gazes out the window. The young man has a yearning look in his eyes. "To have been in that tent, feasting with the five most powerful people in the country, must have been a rare privilege. Merchants all over would have given all their wealth to sit at that table. To have supped with the great men and women who would soon rule the land. Listen." Clearing his throat, he takes out a sheet of paper, a record of all that was said that night in the war tent, and he reads it like a script from a play, reciting to you the speech the lord of the textile fleet made to his compatriots on the eve of the battle.

A toast.

" 'Let tomorrow mark the last day that we must suffer under the yoke of the Throne's tyranny. After tomorrow, no longer will we have to answer to the mercurial wants of a mad leader. No longer will one man rule, but many—all of us, together, deciding the course this country will take, on the rich and prosperous road to come. Yes, my friends. Loyalists still hold the capital, and we have lost the Bowl of Heaven. But these are necessary sacrifices, small pieces in our larger game. They hold the vestiges of the past. Once we have the Divine City, and the grand port, we will hold in our grasp the future. The emperor's timid steps onto the world stage will become, under us, an expanse of trade routes and newly forged alliances. Our tea, our rice, our fish, our blades, and our textiles will spread as the untamed forest does into the fertile valley. Our meager holdings will be as vast as the coffers of the gods.

" 'And so in this spirit, I raise my cup to you all. I thank you all for your participation. I bow to your ferocity, and your loyalty. And

I pray that our continued friendships remain steadfast and strong in the days, the months, the years to come as we build out this empire. Not one man amongst us forgotten.'"

Your father is smiling into the sky until he notices the shadows behind him move. His smile falling, when the shadows speak.

"Someone is always forgotten."

Your brothers are faceless. They are dark clouds that shift and sway. *No longer must you bear witness to us.* Their voices swirling in your ears like smoke in a bottle as they speak as one, and say, "The man named Induun was so focused on that speech, and the feast afterwards, that he spared no thought to the one who stood behind him." Slowly the shades separate from you. They are holes in the air. They bleed nothing but smoke. "You know her. On the Second Day, it was she who passed on the order to take down the Terror of the Bowl of Heaven. Her life spent in service to this man, addressing the powerful. Her life, his shadow."

The brother-shades grimly chuckle.

"She stood in that tent, on the eve of battle, only half listening to the words spoken during that party. She had no interest in the talk; she knew the verse of Induun's rhetorical flourishes so well she herself could have addressed the crowd if such were his desire. And there were other matters on her mind besides speechifying and premature congratulations. A vision of the morrow, and her part in all of it—for Djove himself had promised her a position on the front lines. Her stomach became unsettled as she imagined the carnage she was soon to face. Her hand tightening over the hilt of her blade. She was afraid, but she would not turn back. She had been on this course, set by her mother, for far too long. The shame of stopping now would be too great. It would mean her end." Your brothers sigh. "Not a glance was spared that night for the warrior heading out to her possible doom. Or for the soldiers who would be winning them the day. Or the pilgrims, caught in the midst of all of it."

There was only tea, and laughter.

"It was the eve of victory," your great-grandfather says. "There was no space for introspection or the attendance of your subordinate's emotions. There was only the movement of the tokens across the map. The grim determination of leaders and the unwavering bravery of the man-at-arms. And the pounding of the drums of war."

There was only smoke, and whispers.

"The signs of the wasted world unheeded," your lola says. "No time spent worrying over the lowering tides of the coast or listening to the troubled dancing of the wind. There was only the concern of mortals, who knew only of what was facing them, not of what was coming up from the back. No stopping."

There was only pride, and glory.

"The waiting for incomparable rewards," your father says. "There was no sorrow. No lingering. There was only forward, and the search for the bounty that waited on the other side of the hill, the other end of time."

And there were only ghosts.

"As the two warriors made their way back from the spirit world to stop the wave," your brother-shades say. "The woman who was Induun's shadow, soon to become entwined with Jun and Keema's threads."

Your brothers look at you.

"Her name was Shan. Granddaughter of Djove Induun, and daughter of Commander Uhi Araya. And there was only one thing on her mind. One mission."

The vision is fading—the stage returning.

The light of the brazier-sun stoked to life.

"To rescue her father."

DAWN

She woke before any of them.

Amongst the dozens of campsites, where the hired free-band warriors and Family Men came alive from slumber, no one was surprised to see Shan Araya walking the fields with grim purpose. They bowed their heads as she passed and wished her hale morning, affording her the respect her bloodline demanded, *we gave the Girl of Induun our regard,* but when she was out of earshot, or near enough out of earshot that they could deny having said anything, blame it on the wind, they would mutter some choice names, *though most of us just called her the Child Giant.* It was a name she was well aware of, one that had followed her her whole life, for she had always been taller than most, and broader of shoulder; an oddity for one of her young age.

At fifteen, Shan Induun was not only an anomaly in the prodigious developments of her body but also in ranking. *We would never believe that she earned any of it.* Her life was dedicated to swordplay. She participated every year in the noble games, and every year she came second in the duels, always throwing the last fight in her opponent's favor at her grandfather's behest, as he curried favor with the other Families, and bolstered his alliances. It was only a few months ago that she was named Lord Induun's First Protector, a title that meant little, but still, it rankled her fellow warriors, who did not believe she had justly earned her place at the table—to say nothing of the rumors of her lineage.

Even as she walked the fields that morning, heading toward the main tent, the whispers followed her. *We knew about her mother. The woman who married for love.* It would for her entire life beguile Shan, why her mother, Uhi, had cut short the prosperous union arranged between her and a cousin to the Throne, and instead ran off with a man of poor fortune whose name was written in no ledger of renown. *The scandal was delicious; all of us apart from Lord Induun himself took great relish in spreading the word of this embarrassment.* The elopement, written of in sweaty accounts in diaries and letters, ending swiftly, when the emperor's men discovered the lovers in their northern hideaway and, to answer for the blasphemy, had the man of poor fortune sent to the bowels of Joyrock, where he was to live for the remainder of his tortured days. It was only at the cost of Lord Induun's humbling before the court that Uhi was suffered to live, her life to be dedicated in service to the security of the Throne, where over the years, and with her father's influence, she became the commander of the ramshackle fortress of Tiger Gate—her life lived in wondering if that man of poor fortune yet lived in that abyss below the Divine City. No one could convince her to change her name back to Induun. Forever would she be Uhi Araya, in remembrance of the one she loved, and lost.

Shan grew up apart from her mother. It was agreed by both Uhi and Djove that the girl should not be saddled by the weight of her mother's history; to live with her grandfather, whom she might one day succeed. But there were letters. Letters that even Lord Induun did not know about, hidden in a secret compartment below Shan's childhood bed. *And in those letters I told Shan about her father. I told her of the man named Radle Araya—the craftsman from Lord Waag's forges, who had eyes the color of well-steeped tea, and a smile brighter than the noonday sun. I told her of a man humble and kind. A man who laughed easily and whose love for me I never doubted, not once, in the too-brief days we spent together.*

A man who made for me a spear, out of red korga wood and minerite.

A spear, he told me, that would cut through any boundary that might one day part us.

In the lonely and formative stretches of her young life, Shan would reread these letters with the fervor of a monk poring over scripture. Because Lord Induun never traveled the Road Below, and because he kept Shan occupied with the many duties of her station, she never had the opportunity to visit her mother at Tiger Gate. All they had were the letters they sent to each other in secret, passed from one to the other by trusted servants. The Radle Araya of her mother's letters becoming as mythic in her mind as the giants that once loomed on the southern horizon of that mystic country.

She never told her grandfather about the letters. She never told him of her dreams of the father she had that were as desperate and real as her longing for her mother. She never told him of their plan to one day free Radle Araya from the pit of Joyrock, if even he yet lived—that from the start, their motivations had not been to the Family but to the stubborn fruit of love. That despite his wishes, she intended to ride with the first charge, and to lead a contingent of favored warriors into the Summer Home itself.

She had told him none of this, until today.

Within the main tent, past the quartet of generals who surrounded the map table *as we agreed upon the closing of the routes, and where we might best infiltrate the high houses of the city*, in the back, beyond the last cordon, where few others were allowed to enter, grandfather and granddaughter shared their last conversation on this earth. Djove Induun did not so much as turn around when she addressed him and told him what she planned. His brow did not so much as lift as the attendant finished dressing him. He only breathed out, and waved the attendant off, before his voice went as quiet as a whisper.

"You choose death, Shan," he said. "You do realize this."

"Death is not a certainty."

"For you, today, it will be," he said. "It is vanishingly small, the number of warriors who survive the first charge. These survivors are imbued with either the luck of the gods or of unearthly skill, and I have known you your whole life, *First Protector*. You are skilled at swordplay, more than most, but even you do not have the godly prowess required to defy Death itself." He looked at her as if daring her to retort. She did not. "And you are tall, which means you will be an easy target for the archers. Blame your father for that, but there it is. I see it as clear as day: an arrow, sailing over the wall, and pinning you to the earth before the battle has even begun." He shook his head wearily at this child. "Not the most interesting of ends for the scribes to record as they finish your brief, unsatisfying biography."

"A satisfying biography was never my aim," she said.

The bitterness of her voice brought a sternness to Induun that he reserved for the most heated of negotiation tables. "There are two roads before you, Shan. One road, the road of wisdom, where you stay with the generals in the back line under the defensive umbrellas, leads to life. It leads to a tomorrow where you are on hand to guide the creation of a new order to this country. The other road, the road of pride, takes you through the soldiers not yet tired from battle, and the archers not yet out of ammunition, and the doors not yet beaten-in. It is the road that leads to the harshest conflict. To your likeliest end. The end of your tale." He held up a hand, like a shrug. "You choose death."

Shan did not like argument. She would just as soon lose them quickly than win them after a protracted battle, which is why she said, "Fine then. I choose death. Just so long as we are both clear what is happening today," and then turned heel. But he stopped her.

"Wait. I have one more question, First Protector."

She braced herself to hear it.

"This man. This man you have never met. This man who may be already dead, or, if not dead, then driven mad by the torture. This man who may not even be your father—you risk everything to see him safely from Joyrock."

"I do, Lord Induun."

"At least tell me why."

She closed her eyes.

"What a country we will be," she said, "when we are led by a man who has to ask such a question."

When she was gone, Djove met with his generals.

He gave for them the performance of a man in control of his destiny, as stoic and unyielding as the western mountains, as they went over once more the tactics of the siege. *To this great man we showed the certainty of our coming victory.* He was dressed in simple, durable robing, and his face was painted delicately with his house colors of green and silver, no aspect of him giving away the now-troubled thoughts that stormed within. *He told us that we had all done well; that he wished us good luck on this auspicious day.* Inside, he fumed. The insult his granddaughter had shown him, after he had given her everything she could have needed in this life, was too much; in one spite-filled snap he had told her to go, go do what she wished, her life was her own; and now, as he gazed at the men of war who surrounded him, his anticipation, his excitement, was poisoned by the regret with which he had ended things, for as coldly as he handled his business, there were things in this world he did earnestly love, and she was one of them.

He decided to send for her, to patch things over and perhaps convince her, in a gentler fashion, as he used to when she was very young and just as stubborn, to not throw her life away on this lark. But when his messenger returned, he was told that she refused to treat with him, deciding instead to ride off with her men, for the hills that surrounded the Divine City.

Outside the city, the pilgrims gathered.

Hand-drawn wains formed impromptu markets: wooden boards propped up with hooks and color-dazzled textiles arrayed in sweeping fans for hands to touch and flip through. Inexpensive fabrics and necklaces and rings. Large pots boiled and spat, a gangrenous chicken claw sticking out from the rim of one before a ladle pushed it deeper into the hearty stew; pots that, with the aid of a judicious amount of spices, became floral and savory beacons that diverted the flow of people wandering the tent markets with empty stomachs. As the crowds thickened, pots of jerin powder were put out to cool the air. *We laughed as we opened our robes to the blue embers.* There were shouts from somewhere concerning stolen property. A tent in the western slice had caught fire from a cooking accident. Sandaled feet squelched into human shit. A few children wandered around, lost; not all of them were found again.

The trinket seller and his driver were amongst the thousands in the field that day. He had hitched his wagon amongst the dozens of others that crowded around Gavel Gate, in hopes to be amongst the first to be let into the Divine City, to hawk their wares to the wealthy elite who lived within those high walls. It was of some concern that the gate remained shut, even though the day had begun. The city was occupied, *we could see the small heads of archers up there, looking down at us like we were ants,* and like they had done back at Swan Gate, the merchants tried to shout for these archers' attentions, but not a word was returned from the distant balustrade.

When it was clear that the gates would not be opened for a while yet, the merchants set their sights on the pilgrims of this tent-and-wagon city. The trinket seller rolled his wagon through the narrow paths between canvas halls and planted himself in a patch of field that was getting much foot traffic. "Fireworks!" he cried. "Pearlescent stones from the shores of the Inverse! Tablets of lascivious desire!" He worked the crowds as he did his best to ignore the uncanny sensation on the back of his neck that something was terribly wrong with the world. He tried not to think of the word of the strange low tide along the coast, or the gates that would not open, or the two young gods he had traveled with the day before and who had vanished without a word of thanks for his carriage. He tried not to think about the spreading rumor that the emperor was not coming; the whisper that the emperor was injured; that the Bowl of Heaven was in disorder, for though he harbored little love for the god-king, or the Families, he had no desire to be thrown into Joyrock for blasphemy. *I hadn't gotten this far by stirring the pot. Keep to yourself. Keep clean. Stay alive. This was the way.* He tried to think only of his wagon full of trinkets and the people fool enough to buy them. He ran his throat ragged, shouting his made-up stories of objects stolen from the gods, and he yelled at his put-upon driver to relieve his frustrations, telling him to help or to get out of his sight, until the driver did as he was told and simply got up and left, much to the seller's fury.

"Wh-Where are you going?" he asked helplessly.

The driver wished to see for himself the rumored state of the sea. He followed a group of others heading toward the cliff's edge and saw that it was indeed as described—the ocean was retreating. All that was once invisible under the water was now exposed. Not just the fish and the sharks and the eels and the flattened weed-silk, but also the wall of coral in the far distance, like a line of colorful flowerpots. And on the seabed just below the cliff, the emperor's fallen ships. Eight junk ships—the Smiling Sun's massive wooden beasts, His venture for the new lands yet unconquered, grounded on silt. Seven of them were capsized, *Maada* and *Induun* and other family namesakes on their sides, like toys tipped onto the floor, with only one boat still standing, the *Jorro,* leaning at a tilt, held back only by the last rope restraints tied to the stone hooks that lined the royal quay.

The trinket seller's driver, and others who shared his curiosity, watched the men below try to rescue the tilting boat. *Years of work nearly gone with a low tide. . . . We had never seen the likes of it before. Our only hope was to pull the ships back upright, patch any damage to their hulls before the tide came rushing back in.* A small crowd of onlookers on the clifftop cheered and laughed and shouted pointless instructions as the tiny men far below flung ropes over the starboard railing of the *Jorro* and pulled—thirty men and women pulling now—as they tried to prevent the inevitable slump of the eighth ship.

But like a tired cat, the *Jorro* would not be stopped in its want. The massive boat rolled onto its side and its mast cracked in half like a bone. The men with ropes in their hands staring at the fallen beast in stunned silence.

"Poor fucks," the driver murmured.

As the driver mused on the futility of serving an unforgiving master, the trinket seller was shooed away by yet another unhappy customer. With sunken shoulders he turned to the carriage, wishing to vent to his driver how difficult it was to sell his wares to fools and idiots, and when he saw that the carriage was empty, the seller had a brief moment of self-awareness as he wondered if, perhaps, when in consideration of the many wrong turns his life had taken, some fault might lay with him. *This was not a happy day.* He decided to return to the gate and see if any news had yet come from within. The horses, unused to his presence at the reins, moved only after much effort on his part, yanking left, right, and up, sparing themselves from his onslaught. It was all for naught anyway—when he arrived, the gate was yet unmoved, and the line of wagons had only grown in number. He noticed one of the wagons by the gate, covered fully by thick folds of draped canvas, was unattended by any merchant or driver. *I supposed that, after a week like this one, some of us had simply given up. Went in search of an easier life. Seeing that unattended wagon, even I was tempted to just walk away.* Such was the state of the pilgrims' stretch, when the day then began in earnest.

"What in the five heavens is that?"

The shout echoed out from the middle of the crowd. Upon the woman's shout and her pointed finger, the people looked west, at the horizon of hills, and the light that broke through the gathering clouds.

A black line had formed along the crests of the hills, the distance such that the details of it were smudged and indistinct. It looked to the trinket seller like sediment, hard and compact, the kind that grew beneath his wagon should he neglect its cleaning— but this sediment seemed to be of a graver sort than what he was used to scraping. Hands shaking, he grabbed an old spyglass from his chest of wares and he saw the black line for what it was: an army, hundreds strong, flying the banners of the Five Families and the free-bands who fought for them. *And all I could think was what a waste it was, that I had traveled all this way for nothing.* When a formation on horseback broke from the main line, flying the colors of House Induun, the trinket seller began to sweat, and through his spyglass he saw the woman at the head of this formation raise her hand, flashing a piece of glass against the dawn light. It was a signal. She was sending a message. The seller knew this, but he did not know what this signal meant, who it was for.

"Is it the emperor? Has He finally come?" someone nearby asked.

The trinket seller lowered his spyglass. He was practiced in slipping out of tough situations. He knew when he could get away from a fight, and he knew when it was time to brace for the punch. He turned to the woman, dry-mouthed.

He wanted to tell her that it was time to hide, but he had misjudged the direction from which the danger was coming, because a moment later he was on the ground, and his ears were ringing as bits of wood and rock rained down on him and all the other people who had been knocked flat with him. His ears were bleeding. People were screaming, but he could not hear them. *My husband—he was just standing next to me—had anyone seen him?* It was as if whatever force had pushed him to the ground had also knocked him underwater. And as the world fell apart at the seams, the trinket seller found within himself a reservoir of holy feeling, and as he in a dopey stagger looked around the smoking chaos for his driver, there came, unbidden from nowhere, a prayer at the end of the threading of his frayed mind—for rescue, from any who might be listening.

MORNING

The gates to the Divine City collapsed inward.

From the outskirt hills where the lords observed the carnage, it looked less like an explosion and more like a sudden puff of black smoke, and the unceremonious tipping over of the great stone slab, which they heard only as a series of distant thumps. Djove heard nothing at all. His attention remained on the front-line forces charging on horseback toward the cratered wall—cleaving through the avenue of scattering, screaming pilgrims.

It had begun. Congratulations were served to Lord Waag, who had overseen the development of the explosives, which were made from the materials mined from his quarries, and Lord Waag beamed and told the others he was proud to see his work used for this higher purpose. The lords retired to the war tents behind the hills, while Djove lingered for a moment, watching through the glass as the first of his warriors disappeared into the smoke and rubble of the city wall.

He turned away.

On his way to the main tent, he crossed paths with a breathless young warrior.

"Demons, my lord!" the warrior said. "There are demons who wish to speak with Shan!"

In a dark tent, they waited.

The reserve unit that had captured them stood outside the holding tent, silent, none of them sure how to put into words what they had all just experienced at the crossroads not far from camp. *We were on the patrol, ensuring no secret strategy had been employed by our enemy—no reinforcements aiming to take us from behind, when the Daidos appeared.* One of the Family Men peeked through the tent flap. He did it quick, touching the flap as if it were hot, afraid to look inside for too long. *More Daidos than any of us had seen. Hundreds of them. In a blink, without a sound—they were just there. All of them of different size, some large as a bear, others like little pebbles on the ground. The spirit statues carpeting the entrance of a side road that led to who-knew-where. When we sensed something coming through, we readied our blades, our bows and arrows.*

"What are they doing in there?" one of the men asked.

"Just standing there," another answered. "Just . . . waiting."

We were expecting something with many teeth and evil eyes. We were expecting our sudden death. But what emerged from the Daido gate were but two humans—or so we at first thought. Males, near enough to our age. One had but one arm. The other wore on his face the tattoo of the Red Peacock.

But we soon saw that these were no mere humans. The air seemed to shake off of them as blood does from a wicked sword. With weapons drawn we told them to give up their arms. We demanded to know where they had come from and what they intended to do. And they looked at us, and then at each other, and though they did not speak it was clear they were communicating, for one of them soon gave a small nod, and said that they wished to speak with the soldier named Shan. Give up your arms, we told them once more, but then . . . but then . . .

We heard them. In our minds.

Like a whisper from a rock.

Bring us to Shan.

When none other than Lord Induun and his personal guards arrived, the soldiers bowed with intense relief. "Have care, my lord," the bravest of the reserves said after he explained to Djove the situation in which these two prisoners were discovered. "There is no telling what these demons are capable of." Djove waved the reserve unit away, and his guards filed into the tent. They tried to convince their lord to let them handle the interrogation, that it was too dangerous for him to enter, but Djove Induun would not be swayed from meeting with supposed demons who were in search of his granddaughter.

The armed Family Men divided the tent into two halves; he, well-protected on one end, and the two young demons flanked by spear and sword tip on the other. At first, he wondered why his men were scared at all. These captives were dusty, their clothing tattered from some vicious battle, their faces gaunt and tired in a way that reminded him of the urchins who would come begging through the roads of the Family compounds. He thought he recognized one of them, the shorter of the two, with the tattoo of the Red Peacock chiseled onto his sharp face. As for the other, he was miscellaneous in Djove's eyes, a bone dagger of a boy unearthed from beneath some old and forgotten boulder. He took note of his missing left arm, fearful for a moment that he now shared a tent with a leper, but that fear overcome by the emotions he felt when he saw the spear the boy held. He swallowed dryly.

Once every year he would visit Araya at her checkpoint. They would drink tea together, and have a polite, if tense, discussion about their interim lives. He would make no mention of the poor state of her fortress; of the copious amount of wine she would pour herself. But every visit, he would ask her if she might like to take back the family name, and every visit she would kindly deny him, argument breaking out only when he took note of the damned spear that continued to hang on her bedroom wall.

"Is it not enough that you almost ruined us with your behavior?" he would ask. "Must you also parade your failure before all of your guests? This mockery of love?"

"It is all I have of him," she would say—adding, with a sneer, "and what do you know of love?"

As he looked at the spear in the one-armed creature's hand, he was reminded of all of their petty fights. Of the ways he believed they had failed each other.

The stupid girl.

"Who are you?" he asked quietly.

"My name is Keema of the Daware Tribe," the young man said. "I served under Commander Uhi Araya before the First Terror's brigade attacked, in search of the runaway empress. Araya gave me this spear before she died and bid me to deliver it to a soldier named Shan."

Djove took this in.

I believed them.

"How did my daughter die?"

It was clear by the break in the young man's expression that he did not know Araya was his family. "As anyone might hope to go," he said. "Bravely."

For a long moment Djove did not move. He was a distant and soundless storm. His guards glanced at him; they asked him if he was all right. "I had heard word of the empress's escape," he said finally. "I suppose you are the two guardians who were driving Her caravan."

"We were," the man of Daware said.

"Where is She?" he asked.

"She died," Jun said.

"She died." Djove repeated this with as much credulity as he had to offer. "The Eternal Mother of Emperors, the Moon Incarnate, the Lady of Night, died."

"She spent the last of Herself, killing the First and Second Terrors."

This was news to him. "And Her body?"

"We ate Her, at her request."

The line of guards did a backstep from them. One of the swords was shaking. Djove, whose body did not express things such as fear or distress, felt a slickness in his palms. Keema stepped forward.

I looked at them all and told them, with these thoughts, that it was true. As my voice entered their minds, I presented them with proof that we were in command of Her Gift, while Jun made the tent poles tremble and the straw mats on the ground lift from the earth. It was a show, just as the empress had done with the admiralty. The guards, all men of belief, fell to their knees before them and kissed the dirt. Djove's eyes were wide, but he remained standing. *But we heard this thought, and we did not care who bowed and who stood tall. We told them that the wave was coming and that we were there to stop it, after we had brought down the Third Terror. That if they valued their own breath, they would recall their forces and escape west, for we did not know how far the wave would come before we could cease its march, and we would have as few people as possible be crushed under its mighty weight.* They were words that even Djove could not refuse to hear, for they went right past his damaged ears and into the very temple of his thoughts. For anyone to dare enter this place, his inner self, was a trespass that he could not bear to let pass without punishment. There was even, on the tip of his tongue, the command to have his guards strike these whelps down. *But we heard this thought, and we told him that we did not recommend this course of action.*

Djove Induun bit his own tongue, because he did not trust it to restrain itself. A prominent vein ran down his forehead. It seemed to pulse with his displeasure, his frustration, as he bowed to them.

Neither Keema nor Jun expected this.

"I thank you," Djove said, through gritted teeth, "for your patience. For not slaughtering us, for I imagine it a small feat for you now. Though if what you say is true, if a wave is truly coming to sweep this land away, then I do not think much about your time-management skills."

He stood back up. He walked past the line of guards to their side of the tent. He looked no less furious.

I did not like to lose.

"My lord . . ." one of the guards whispered.

"If Shan yet lives," he said, "then she charges through the city as we speak. She makes her way to the Summer Home at the top of the hill—to Joyrock." *We thanked him. And we told him that if he wished to live, he would retreat now. He glared at us.* "I will meet with the other Families," he said slowly. "But I doubt that even should the horn be blown that Shan will return. She believes her father yet lives in Joyrock, and I fear she would sooner die than fail to free him."

He bowed to them once more.

"Please. Find her." He swallowed. "Send her back to me."

Within the city walls, Shan sighed.

She flicked the blood from her sword as the headless man rolled down the sloping road. "With me!" she shouted, and she and her coterie sprinted up the city's Grand Loop, passing through districts of royals cowering behind slapped-shut doorways, and imperial regiments coming from alleys, from behind, from even the balconies and rooftops. Her men encircled her. "Shields up!" she cried. Wooden shields were raised in turtle formation, catching arrows in the air. Sharp stone heads bit through wood like a swarm of bee stings. *Whatever misgivings we had before we followed the Girl from Induun into battle were shed as she tore through the soldiers like a knife through cheap cloth.* Shan, for her part, was terrified, but she had learned from the best how to hide any emotions that would get in the way of her and what she wanted, and what she wanted was her father.

An arrow sliced across her arm. She gave it a cursory glance before she charged, screaming. Blood sprayed onto the sides of the adobe buildings. It sloshed down the cobbled road.

It ran wet and warm down her cheek.

The demons were gone.

Djove watched them speed off into the fields toward the flash of battle. "My lord," his attendant said, on a tentative approach, "what would you like us to do?"

I would've liked them to give back my certainty.

"Where are the other lords?" he asked.

"In the resting tent, having lunch."

"After I've spoken with them, I would have you sound the retreat." That last word was like bile on his tongue. He closed his eyes. He was about to do the very thing his whole life had been dedicated to fighting: concede. He knew that the heads of the Families would not look at him the same after this moment. He knew that he was, in effect, handing over his power.

What a strange end.

His retinue walked him to the safe area, in the glade protected by a circle of their finest warriors. His step was heavy as he walked toward the mouth of the tent. In many ways he felt like a child being led off to get chastised. *Retreat.* Lord Maada would no doubt come for his position after this. Or the Panjet-Waags. They would tell him today that retreat is the wisest course of action. And then they would come for his proverbial head.

But then, he thought about the spear.

He thought of Araya, trampled into the dirt.

He thought about Shan, cut down by a sword.

What do you know of love?

He stopped, just before he entered the tent. His attendant looked after him, worried. And Djove tensed his jaw, and he breathed in the troubled air, and he stepped inside. The flap shut behind him. And there they were, seated at the long table, all four of them, his rivals, his enemies, his closest friends. Lord Waag was still smiling, though he was considerably more drunk, as he continued to bask in the success of his explosives. Lord Maada and his wife, Zusa, kept to themselves on the other end of the table, for neither of them cared for Waag's bluster or Yinn's theatrics. None of them noticed Djove enter, except for Lady Panjet, who noticed the uncharacteristic slump in his shoulders. "What happened, Lord Induun?" she asked.

But before Induun could answer, it was Lord Yinn, never one to read a moment correctly, who interrupted him with a startled giggle. "It looks like you've brought in a visitor, my lord!"

A small bird had flown into the tent behind him. A bird the unusual color of royal purple. The attendants lining the walls of the tent broke into a panicked chase as they tried to capture the bird and bring it outside. And while the other lords, buoyant on the successes of the day, laughed and kidded about this unexpected guest, Djove stared at this bird, at the striking hue of its plumage, and suddenly, like that, all of the heaviness in himself then lifted. His failures and his victories, and all the loves and hates in his life. They went up, through the ceiling of the tent, and into the sky. For he knew this bird was no simple bird. He knew it before any of them— even before the bird flew into the corner of the tent and came out from behind the folding screen a bird no longer, with a silhouette long-snouted and many-toothed. But Djove Induun needed no obvious hint. As soon as he saw those purple feathers, in the basest pit of himself, where truth makes itself known to instinct and instinct alone, he knew.

"What in the abyss is that?" Lord Yinn cried, scrambling from his seat.

The creature's full-moon eye beheld them all before its jaw unhinged.

Djove smiled in gracious defeat.

And I welcomed my death.

"So began the chase to the center."

Your granjo unfurls a map on the table; a closeup of the outskirt field and the city. "Between the two warriors and the Terror's Summer Home lay a swarming battlefield, an impenetrable wall, and an entire city. More than four hundred warriors fought in the streets, and the field beyond."

"The gate was choked with death," your lola says. "There was no way through the smoke, or the sweeping blades."

Your father stands by the window.

Around him sit the shades of his sons, their hands on his slumped shoulders.

"You can hear it," he says, with his ear to the air.

The screams.

The trinket seller pressed his head into the dirt while around him the fighters raged. He knew the banners, he had sold his pornographic tablets to most of them at some point or another. Rooster's Claw. The Black Dragons. Tempest. The River Snakes. The Hatchet Men. Broken Manse. God Killers. Fortune's Promise. Blood Moon. Summer's End. The Stone Demons. They clashed with the loyalist forces of the Purple Elks and the Silver Monkeys while the people between them screamed and ran. Through the lopped-off limbs and the arcs of blood, the seller dragged himself under the wagon, his breath quick and shallow. *I searched desperately for my driver. I just wanted to see the lazy ass again. I just wanted to make sure he still breathed.*

Half of a man's body slumped into the dirt beside him and he whimpered.

A contingent of loyalist soldiers emerged from the southern gate. These soldiers met the warriors hired by the Families out in the field. The men and women of the River Snakes sang through the torrents of gore they spilled onto the fields. The fight by its own natural momentum closed in on the crowds they surrounded. The crowds surged toward the front gate. People sank beneath the surge, crushed. *I couldn't breathe. Feet were standing on my chest, my neck.* Fists pounded on the portcullis. *We shouted for them to let us in. Shouted until we couldn't shout anymore.* The honor guards that had been stationed outside to create an avenue for an emperor who was never going to arrive formed a line between the free-band and the civilians, trying to keep the peace. *They told us to keep back, but we had no weapons! They thought we were soldiers!* The people were cut down. The honor guard shouted for the free-bands to stop their fighting, to stand down, but their commands, backed by no visible power, fell pathetically to the ground, until a man of Fortune's Promise walked up to them and dropped his hammer on a quaking man's head. Bits of skull exploded. The man of Fortune's Promise was swept off his feet. The honor guard skewered him beneath a gang pile of spear tips. The iron smell of blood mixed with the musk of fur and shit. Fear rose from this quarter like a smog. The trinket seller watched it all from the jail of his fingers, as a child he did not know huddled at his side. His entire body tremored, and all of his stubborn history fell off his shaking shoulders as he became acquainted with the parchment-thin divide between breath and stillness. *It was then, upon the basest moment of my fear, that I saw the two warriors, running toward the fray. And with widened eyes I watched them approach the great wall of the Divine City and witnessed them perform their second miracle.*

Your granjo makes an estimate with his hand.

His hand wavers, and then stops, at the height of his own head.

"About as tall as a checkpoint, a bit taller."

He shrugged.

"Nothing a human could scale."

They leapt.

From beneath his wagon the seller watched it: two bodies, flung into the air as if by catapult. The spear nearly slipping from the man of poor fortune's grasp as he went up, and over. Two archers on the wall staring slack-jawed at the arc of their bodies, like birds burst from a locked cage. They didn't even think to shoot at them. Not even they wanted to ruin this moment. And silently Keema and Jun disappeared over the high wall, the seller whispering a prayer mumbled from the heart before the horn from the northwestern hills let loose its blast.

BRROOOOAAAAAAAAAMMMMMMM—

Over the teeming city the blast rang out, sourced from the hills to the west, where the Family encampment sounded its retreat. The footstep of every Family Man, every free-band rider, halted. *Our leaders were dead, and by Djove's last command we were to bring our warriors back.* The Family Men broke from the skirmish first, for they were the most loyal, and the readiest to follow the command of the lords—the free-banders more reluctant to stop the fighting, their bloodlust at its apex, while the Silver Monkeys danced out of the shadows, cutting off their retreat.

A knife bounced off the sword Shan wielded. She was at the entrance to the second-to-last district. She was almost to the top.

"First Protector!" one of Shan's men said as the baritone howl of the retreat horn cracked the air. "We must fall back!"

But she was too close.

Years, she had waited for this moment.

A lifetime.

"I'm going on," she said to the six bloodied warriors of hers who remained. "Those of you who would come with me, then come with me. Those of you who would turn back, return to camp and tell them that Shan Araya keeps her promises."

The six warriors glanced at one another.

She had, if nothing else that day, earned our respect.

They bowed to her before they ran off, and she had enough energy in her to laugh before she continued on her path to the center of this world.

From the roof of a courthouse, they watched the retreat.

Jun clung to the arm of a statue praying to the sky while Keema straddled the curved awning, his eyes shut, his ears listening to the unheard voices that rose from the stream of bodies below. *I was cold, I was so cold, it was all coming out of me and I was so cold—DAMMIT ALL, I had him, I nearly had him, but I didn't see the knife, it came up out of his robes so quickly, it stuck me right in the side, and I knew this was it, this fucking life—COME AT ME, I screamed, I'M READY, but I wasn't ready—We were trying to retreat, but the arrows kept coming, Therin, he, he, it was in his eye, like a flower, and he smiled at me like we were back in our cot, holding each other, he smiled at me like it was okay—Just come back, just come back—piece of shit motherfucking whore of a man—Yes, I was taking my time, do you even know how good it feels when it slides out of the fucker's belly, like dragging a knife through mud, and he groans under you as all of him just comes out in a flood and I was nearly done right there, just, soiled myself from his flailing—No, nonononono, NO—It was too late—A bird flew over the rooftop and I saw the light and the smoke beaten from its wings and I lowered my blade because what else can you do, when it was all so beautiful?—I was close, one more district, and I was there, I would make my mother proud.* Keema's eyes snapped open. He pointed with his spear at the grand loop's second-to-last revolution. "There!"

She never saw them coming.

Shan was sprinting between the beautiful towers of frozen seaweed and the buildings composed of brain coral as blue as freshly sprinkled jerin, and the hollowed-out crustaceans of ancient size, the things the emperors of old had brought out of the sea to compose their summer palaces, when the two young men slammed into the ground ahead of her.

A spear skittered away. A sack flopped next to their sprawled bodies. She looked to the sky for explanation as the young men groaned.

One of them was a Red Peacock. When she saw the tattoo on his face, she had a sudden and violent image of her mother impaled by the Blood-Red Prince. She charged toward them, her sword drawn. Sensing her, the Peacock leapt to his feet. He held up his hands, unarmed, before he snatched the sack from the ground and cradled it to his chest. The second man came between them, his one arm holding his spear with enough strength to skewer five men through.

"Shan!" he shouted. "Wait!"

The sword almost slipped out of her grip. Her feet skidded across the pebbled floor, her sandals burning from the friction. The young man gazed at her, as if they were old friends too long since met. She reassured her grip on her blade.

"How do you know my name?" she said. "Who are you?"

The young man said nothing, for he knew that words would not do justice to what he could simply show her. He presented her with the weapon that he carried. The spear, carved from korga wood and minerite. Its gleaming tip winking at her. And as he held the spear out to her, all the sounds of the city, the sounds of the dying, the hoarse shouts, the rainfall of retreat all seemed to fade out until there was only her breath, and the whisper of her fingers meeting this object she knew only through the stories of her mother.

"Who are you?" she asked without voice.

"Keema," he said. "Of—"

He stopped.

This part, it was not his story.

"I worked for her," he said. "At Tiger Gate."

She held the spear to her cheek. She did not know why. It just seemed right. The grooved wood was warm, and solid. It was real.

"I'm sorry," Keema said, for by then he knew this girl was Uhi's daughter. "She—it was—" Again, his words, they crumbled in his fingers.

Tell her something kind.

"It's for you."

The Girl of Induun's lips trembled as tears made rivers down her dust-blown cheeks. She breathed in deep.

"A wave is coming," he said. "It threatens to sweep this whole land beneath its crush. We will try to stop it, but this city may be taken. You should go, before it is too late."

Shan wiped her eyes. Her day was not yet done. "Not until I've reached Joyrock."

"Your father," Keema said.

There was wonder in her eyes, of how he could possibly know this. She nodded.

"There may be no coming back from this," Jun said.

"That was clear from the start, Peacock," she said with venom. To Keema, "You have come far to give me this weapon. I thank you for that. Truly. But I have come too far myself to stop here." She looked at the spear with a renewed dedication. "I have to try to free him. Even if he . . . I have to try."

"Okay," Keema said. He would not argue the point. "Then we'll come too. Like you, we also have business at Joyrock."

"What business could you have at that cursed place?" Shan asked as they started moving. "Do you mean to free someone too?"

In a way.

"We mean to kill the Terror."

MIDDAY

At the zenith of the Divine City, all was quiet.

At the top of the sea beast's shell, within the spare bowels of the Summer Home, the head attendant worked, unbothered by the explosions, the screaming. *I have heard much and more in my time under the employ of the Throne. It was all noise to me now.* She continued cleaning the many floors of this grand estate, which sat on the highest point of the city, paying no mind to what she called "The Ruckus," which was any and all business that had nothing to do with her, this building, and the place below it.

Through towering corridors empty of all people or life the small woman scurried. Small she was, and gray of hair, *but I've never minded the grays; they did nothing but make me look more distinguished.* Her way of moving was fastidious, done without hesitation. She knew the whisper of every lantern that lit the dark halls of the Summer Home, the sound of every step. With a practiced ease she cleaned the coral pillars, and the doorframes that were once the jaws of massive territorial sea creatures, and she dusted the lush rugs that yawned for meters down unending corridors—rugs she alone cleaned during the long and unattended days of this grand building. Her steps echoing but never ceasing, the work carrying on as the city outside was torn apart.

Setting down her cleaning supplies, she decided to look out the window, just to see. From the tall windows of the second floor she surveyed the city, her eyes squinting against the harsh light.

A brief chuckle escaped her lips when she saw the three warriors approach.

"Best of luck," she whispered.

The promenade opened up before them.

It was the one place untouched by the battle. An amphitheater of white stone and dizzying coral bushes and trees, and ornate statues carved by the most practiced of sculptors. Eight emperors, as tall as the gates themselves, stood in a circle, presiding over the centuries, each emperor more muscular, more powerful, than the last. *By the Smiling Sun's orders were we made to sculpt His statue as the tallest of them all.* As the three of them passed beneath the gaze of these dead-eyed emperors, Keema had the prickling sensation on the back of his neck that they were being watched. He held fast to the blade Shan had given him in exchange for the spear—a kind gesture, one he appreciated, but nevertheless did he miss that old weapon, feeling strangely exposed now, as if he had given away his clothing. He tried to focus, to not be overwhelmed by the beauty of this promenade, the likes of which he had never seen before; the breathtaking sight of the seaside horizon that cut the space between looming buildings; the bare ocean bed only reminding him of how little time they had left. Gulls squawked overhead. A babbling fountain of water heralded their approach as they walked up the one hundred steps that led to the towering Summer Home. Up above, he saw on the distant second floor a window curtain shift, as if someone had disappeared behind it.

Someone was home.

"Keema! Behind you!"

A spike on a rope flitted through the air.

We, the last of the honor guard of the Purple Elk, the Tines of the Antler, would defend the home of He We Had Sworn to Protect.

Keema let out an oomph, like he had just walked into a piece of furniture. He looked down at his belly. The spike in his abdomen looked back at him. The rope that the spike was tied to came out of him like a misplaced umbilical cord. He touched it with his blade hand. The shock was such that he did not feel much at first. A feeling that something was where it should not be. It almost tickled.

"Jun," he said, as if to show his friend something funny and strange.

And then the man yanked on the rope, and Keema went flying down the steps.

"No!" Jun roared, chasing after him.

Keema bounced to the bottom, where at the foot of the steps he lay, not moving. Purple-armored warriors sighed out from behind thick columns, from dark doorways. Jun leapt down five steps, ten, until he was crouched over Keema's slumped body. "I'm fine," he croaked. He had already pulled out the spike. Blood was seeping through the clutch of his fingers. "Really," he said, his hand shaking, "I'm fine."

The Purple Elks closed in on them like vultures.

The two young warriors looked up the stairs, at where their brief partner stood.

"I'm sorry," Shan whispered, then ran up the stairs without them.

The front doors burst open.

Daylight flooded the dark and curtained hall of the Summer Home. From the shadows the head attendant observed with a dispassionate eye the tall and frantic girl as she slapped sliding doors open, murmuring, "Where is it, where is it?"

"Is it the entrance to Joyrock you are searching for?"

Shan froze—pivoted.

Like a vole, the attendant stepped into the shafted light. Shan's elbow knocked a porcelain vase from its stand; the vase, painted with many purple elks, teetered, but it did not topple.

"This way," the attendant said.

She walked down the side corridor, her shadow long and trailing. Shan walked up to the corridor's entrance. At her feet, an In-duun carpet, the red of deep earth, unfurled the way to hell.

"She followed the woman, of course."

Your lola looks at you with a shrug.

"What else could she do?"

"It's nice to have visitors."

The attendant spoke with the soft reserve of a spouse who had been told that they speak too loudly in good company. "The emperor hasn't visited in a very long time. A pity. So much effort went into the finery here. So many wonderful views. Now enjoyed only by the damned."

Shan could feel the chill of ghosts all around her. *I remember the attendant. When I was dragged into the Summer Home for besmirching His name on the walls of a Shisha temple, it was she who greeted me at the doors. She treated me kindly. She poured me tea in the royal salon that overlooked the verdant sea. She said it was only right that someone enjoy it for once. They called it the Last Kindness; those last few moments of peace, before they throw you in. And a kindness it was, for I cried, to hear the gentle lapping of the waves.*

"Do you not wonder why I am here?" Shan asked as the attendant slid the door open. "Do you not know of all that is happening outside?"

The attendant laughed—dry, like paper slipping onto an attic floor. "I have been here for more than thirty years. I have heard many noises. I no longer wonder about any of them."

"Do you even know that the emperor is dead? That two of His sons are dead?"

The attendant paused. "Which sons?"

"Saam and Luubu."

"Oh." The attendant carried on. She opened the last door down the red hall with her bone-white key. "That's fine then." The lock clicked and the doors pushed open in a loud groan.

Before she even saw what lay beyond the door, Shan doubled over from the stench. Again the attendant tutted, taking the girl's face in her surprisingly strong grip and rubbing with her thumb a powerful smelling-salt paste beneath her nose. "There." She held Shan's face up and gazed into the girl's eyes in an almost loving fashion. Leaning on the attendant's arm, Shan struggled to her feet, her legs jelly, every reactive instinct in her body demanding that she turn away from this room.

Plain and unadorned was the entrance to Joyrock. Four white paper walls met at pleasing blackwood beams. There was no furniture, no finery. The room unfurnished but for the hole in the floor. The hole was a perfect circle, wide enough for a boulder to be dropped through, and it was this hole from where the smell plumed; the smell of viscera; of blood, and shit, stale and ancient. A smell that made shapes in the air that one had to force one's way through, which is what Shan did as she followed the attendant to the edge of the hole. "Most of the blasphemers were dropped in," the attendant said without much emotion. She gestured to the pile of rope ladder hanging on a wall hook. "But for everyone else, for the good ones, there's that."

With the attendant's assistance, Shan unfurled the rope, hooked the end to a bolt in the floor, and let the rungs roll off into the hole. The ladder disappeared into the dark, but it wasn't long till she heard the slap of the end-knot hitting the ground, revealing a drop much shallower than she expected. *It had to be shallow. Nothing important could be broken. The demon needed something to chase, after all.*

"There are two warriors outside," Shan said. "They may already be dead, but if they're not, and they're looking for me, can you tell them where I've gone?"

The attendant looked through her. And though Shan did not

quite believe her when she nodded and said that she would, she thanked the woman anyway, and she held her breath as she looked into the hole.

"I have heard tales," she said, her voice thin and reedy. Her legs shaking as she sat on the lip of the hole and tucked her foot onto the first rung. "Tales that the Third Terror did not kill everyone thrown into the hole. Sometimes he kept them alive. Sometimes for years."

The attendant stared at her with glassy eyes. She did not confirm or deny this point.

Shan looked into the hole one last time. "A man named Radle Araya was thrown into this hole fourteen years ago," she said. "Do you remember him?"

"I remember them all," the attendant said. "He was a kind man, all things considered." She smiled. "He was one of the few I let use the ladder."

Shan could not look at the woman anymore. She was fully on the ladder now. The abyss yawned below her. It seemed to pull at her feet. She shut her eyes and pressed her forehead against the cool stone of the lip.

"Do you think it possible?" she said. "That the man I seek is still alive?"

To which the attendant said, "I have known the one you call the Third Terror for his entire life. I have seen the depths of behavior he is capable of. And even I sometimes struggle to predict his actions."

A small shadow flicked over the bloody promenade,

unnoticed by the combatants dancing between pillars, their weapons sweeping blood across the marble steps. Life was leaking out of the wound in Keema's abdomen. He had to shake his head into focus as yet another Purple Elk came at him from the side with a shanking blade. He heard Jun grunting somewhere across the promenade, his view blocked by coral shrubbery. *I thought to him that we could not fight this many men. And he thought back: I know.* A grimness coming over him, failure seeming in that moment inevitable. His blade thunked into a skull. It was as he tried to wedge it out that something hit him from the side, sending him sprawling onto the ground—pain shooting up from his spike wound. His lungs punched for breath. His vision blurred as he rolled over onto his back. He squinted up at the man in purple robes, face fuzzed, arm up over his head as he brought up a sledgehammer. And Keema, in the strange firings of his brain, imagined what it would feel like when the flat of the hammer hit his face. He thought of Vogo Sugo, of all people. The obliteration of the skull. His essence pushed far into the earth until he came out into the Inverted Country. He thought of falling back onto the stage he had just bravely exited, where he would confess to you, the audience, the magnitude of his failure as he tried to keep his swinging jaw in place. It was a strange and sudden vision of a future that never came to pass, for a large shadow jumped across the frame of his vision, taking with it the man with the sledgehammer like a great wind blown in from the god of good fortune. The hammer dropped, cracking the stone upon which it fell. And as Keema brought himself up on his elbow, and then to his feet, his breath heavy, as if filtered through a rock, he noticed that the sounds of battle were fading. That for every clash of steel there was then a guttural noise—the noise a man might make when falling suddenly into a hole he did not expect—and the quiet spray of liquid, like a snapped fountainhead, and all the water that might break free from the pressure. The noises were a strange comfort to him. It was like a release. A sigh of spring. He blinked as he staggered forward, his foot slipping on the carpet of blood before he met a bewildered Jun in the center of this stone park, painted red.

Jun, wide-eyed, asked Keema if he saw it.

I asked Jun what he had seen.

His friend pointed at the foot of the steps to the Summer Home.

He pointed at the purple-feathered bird who sat there.

Keema's ankles seemed to turn to liquid.

"It's you," he said.

The bird preened. It flapped its wings but it did not take off, as if showing off its plumage. It lifted its right wing, like a salute, before covering its eyes and beak with that wing, like a trained lover would with an unfurled fan. And then, like a fairgrounds trick, the bird withdrew its wing and transformed before their eyes into its true form.

What Keema and Jun saw as they looked into the full-moon eyes of the creature was no less than the history of its creation.

Listen well to this tale.

The Tale of the Demon Prince

"To tell the tale of the boy," your lola says, "one must first know of the birth, which, like all princes of the Throne, occurred deep in the bowels of the western mountain, behind the fabled Wolf Door." Granjo lights her cigarette for her as she continues. "When the Moon was presented with the emperor's bowl of seed, She was bound by the laws of the First Wish to give Him an heir. But She had been imprisoned long enough that She no longer had the desire to follow the law of the First Wish to the letter. And so, for the first time in the long lineage of the rulers of the Moon Throne, She gave Magaam Ossa not one heir but three. It was a small but significant act of rebellion. She drank deep the sour seed and let it take root in Her body, and, when it was time, split the seed into triplets, and in doing so, split amongst them the gifts that, till then, had been given to one. So it was with fury that Emperor Magaam returned to the Wolf Door, only to find three crying babes in the bowl where His seed once dwelt, and then, as He looked upon His sons, a dawning horror as it became apparent what, exactly, the Moon had done."

She chuckles mirthlessly.

"To the firstborn was it given the gift of the power over the elements. Just as the Moon once made Wind and Water dance, during their reign in the Sky, so, too, would Saam Ossa play with and manipulate the natural materials of the world. To the second-born was it given the gift of the power over human thought. Just as the Moon inspired those who basked in Her beams, and earned the praise and worship of the earthbound dwellers who admired Her, so, too, would Luubu Ossa enjoy the reverence and belief that those who listened to his Word would give him. As for the Third. The Last. The most often Forgotten . . . he was given a most unusual gift."

"Unusual indeed," your father grunts. "When the emperor stood over the bowl of crying babes, a new father ready to look upon His sons, He gasped, and drew His prized knife from its sheath, and pressed the blade to the throat of the boy with the wolf's head—and where fur met skin, he drew a bead of rich, royal blood."

Your lola sighs.

"To the third-born was it given the gift of transformation," she says. "Just as the Moon waxed and waned as shifting shadow, so, too, would the Unnamed Ossa enjoy the mutability of form. He would live life as a shapeshifter, as any creature he so desired, though his base form would always be that of a boy with a wolf's head."

"Whatever had stayed the emperor's blade that day," your father says, "whatever fleeting glimmer of love He had for His malformed offspring was never made known to the cursed child. For the entirety of the Third Terror's youth, Magaam showed him nothing but contempt, ashamed as He was that His seed had produced such an ugly and unrefined creature. And as the emperor raged at this feral thing, behind the Wolf Door, in the dark of her prison, the empress smiled."

"The boy was born a beast, and he lived as a beast," your father continues. "Very little about his behavior, his movement, suggested a human lineage. He tore apart his clothes. He refused his table manners, the mats and the dishes. He ate on the floor in the corner. He pissed where he liked. There was no taming such a creature." Your father looks at you, with apology. "The story of the shunned, misbegotten child remains unchanging through the years. It is the same now as it was then. You know the arc, and the characters. The patriarch who despised him. The brothers who pretended he did not exist, in fear that to do so would earn the wrath of the father."

Your brothers crowd around you.

"Sometimes," they say to you, "through the slatted windows of his dark room, the child would look out into the courtyard, and he would watch his brothers spar, with their friends, their trainers. He would watch them sweat and laugh and strike at each other. He would watch them play. And he would pant, and scratch at the wood, and he would howl, desperate to join them."

"A whip kept him in line," your father says.

Your lola nods grimly. "The residents of the palace who had the misfortune of crossing his path were horrified by the sight of him. For but a few years did the emperor withstand the child's presence, the child's smell, the child's many grave disappointments. One day he would be living in a room tucked far away in the royal apartments. Another day, he would be moved to the basement. And then, the locked stables. *Wherever I can no longer smell him,* His Smiling Sun would tell his servants. But it was the day he was found crouched over the ripped-apart remains of a royal retainer—*I had whipped the whelp, not realizing that, small as he was, he could very well fight back*—that His Smiling Sun thought of a way His child might serve the Throne."

Your father lowers his head.

"We need our children to find their place in this world. Without a place, they are lost."

"The labyrinth below the Divine City," your granjo says at the map. "Once a noble playground, fallen into disuse over the decades, no longer where the court held their summer games—no matter. The labyrinth had found a new purpose."

Your lola sighs again, her cigarette finished.

"They dropped him into the hole when he was eight."

Into the warrens beneath the earth.

Through the dark and slick caverns that Shan Araya stalked with torch in hand did the Third Terror live out the majority of his forty-odd years. Her heart beat against her brain. She could feel the Rhythm in every pore of her body. The smelling salts unable to hold back the stench of this abattoir. "Radle!" she shouted into the peerless dark. "Radle Araya!" Her shout met only by the rebounding echo of her own voice, her father's name fleeing away from her as fast as she had spoken it.

She stepped over a broken rib. A pile of gnawed-on bones. Her torchlight revealed rooms with walls in which a moon had been scratched many times over. She discovered the many little gifts that had been piled before a clumsily etched mural of the empress. Things collected from the people who had been dropped in. A bracelet. A ring. A bloody purse-sack. She looked for anything that might signal her father, any effects he might have had with him. But she found nothing.

She did not notice the scratches in the wall below the hole itself—the scratches of desperate escape.

"The maze was a prison for both man and monster."

Your lola breathes out her smoke. "The Third could transform into whatever it was he wished, but his life had been so sheltered, so limited, there were few options that remained to him in the small room of his imagination. He was beaten well for his pale and rabid imitations of his brothers, his father, of any human. And he had seen precious few animals in his time, and not for long enough that he would even consider becoming them."

Your brothers murmur: "For decades he lived in the caverns, doing as he was trained and bid to do. He tortured the blasphemers. He ate them. And sometimes, when he grew weary of this life, he tried to climb out of the hole."

"He would fall," your lola says.

"He would try again," your brothers say.

"Thirty years shredded off his blunted claws."

"His only friend was the silhouette of a woman who stood at the lip of the hole, looking down at him. An attendant who sang to him sometimes at night, as the child howled pitifully below the hole, while throughout his labyrinth, *the blasphemers ran and cried.*"

Shan touched the manacles bolted to the walls.

Nearly every body she encountered was not only lost of life, but desiccated. It had been much time since anyone or anything here had been attended to.

She was deep in the labyrinth now, marking her turns with the arrangement of bones. Torchlight made glimmer the fingernails imbedded in the rock. *We scratched at anything we could.* The hair and teeth on the ground. *It all fell out eventually.* The farther she went, the more she could feel herself unravel. The shouts of her father's name grew more hopeless. Hoarser. There was a ceiling to her breath that her lungs kept hitting. The smelling salts were not enough. The whole world was pouring in through her nostrils, and it smelled like death.

"Radle Araya," she said. "Are you here?"

On she shouted.

"Father!"

Hope all but lost when a voice in the distant dark answered back.

"Is . . . is someone there?"

Your granjo looks at you. "Before they were thrown in, they would be marked. An iron brand on their cheek: a number that told the Third Terror how many years he was to keep the prisoner alive before consuming them. He became good at it. Keeping the body going for longer than it should be able. Though he was still of animal tendency, he learned over the years how to bandage and stop bleeding. For the chained-up prisoners, he would give them water, and he would feed them meat and the stale et ceteras he would be tossed from the mouth of the hole by the attendant. He would release some on occasion. He would unchain them. And then he would chase them. They screamed through the dark."

Your brothers shake their heads. "They did not know he was trying to play."

"He became caretaker and torturer in one," your father says. "A combination that is all too easy to fall prey to."

"Some days," your lola adds, "he would be loving as he chewed up and regurgitated the harder cuts for them. Some days he would sulk and they would not see him at all, and they would go hungry. Some days he raged. Frustrated. Trapped." *He picked up a rock and he slammed it into my head. For five years he had kept me alive and he ended it suddenly and I was grateful.* "And there were days when he just sat below the hole, looking up. He could speak but one word, in a kind of bark."

"That word," your father says, "was 'Mother.'"

"The attendant who sang to him," your lola says, "the attendant who loved him as her own, she knew that it was not for her whom he was calling, but she pretended this was the case all the same. And as she answered his call, and threw treats into the hole, the child continued to howl, yearning for a mother who was not there; a mother far away from that wretched place. He needed Her."

We are called to our parents like sirens.

Shan crouched over the man who was not her father. This man was wrapped in a bundle on the ground. He had no limbs, and his eyes were glazed in cataracts. It was impossible to tell how old this man was. But she knew it was not him. *I had traveled so far in search of the man who had made up the myths of my life. In search of the man who I was told was wonderful and kind and intelligent and who would love me dearly if he ever saw me. I had traveled so far. And for so long. I had come to the lowest place in this land in search of him. And in the end, I had found only a man.*

One, of many.

"How long have you been down here?" she asked softly.

With a gentle touch that he winced to receive, she turned his head. The brand on his cheek burned with the number 20.

His bottom lip trembled. Tears broke from his sunken eyes.

"Your voice is so beautiful," he said, his throat wet. When he opened his mouth, she saw that he had no teeth. "Why has this beautiful winged arkana from the Many Heavens come down here, to this place?"

Shan Araya wiped her eyes.

"I came looking for my father," she said.

He smiled, tear-stained himself. "Many fathers have been through this way."

"His name was Radle Araya." She let out an empty chuckle. "I don't suppose you have seen him around here."

The man looked up; looked past her. "I think I'm the last."

Shan breathed out.

"I am so sorry, my arkana," the bundled man said. "But this place has been so quiet. The child sometimes cannot help himself. Sometimes he does not heed the numbers." His lips touched each other, groping. "Is—is the child near? I have been so hungry."

Shan did not answer at first. She was silent as she sat beside the man who had endured more than any man should.

"You should leave," the toothless man said. "Before he comes back."

She looked around the cell with heavy shoulders.

"I know," she said quietly.

He gasped a little when she picked him up. She walked him down the cavernous corridor, following the bones she had marked as her exit. She held him like a baby. It had been a very long time since the man had been held. His cheek wet her shoulder. "I do not understand," he said. "Why do you save me? I am a sinner. A blasphemer."

He sobbed.

"I am no one."

Such was the identity of all who dwelt in Joyrock.

"And none of them was less of a man than the demon who called those caverns his kingdom," your lola says. "The child was a creature born without a name, who with every passing year was more desperate to escape the hell his father had tossed him into. The drafty halls of the Summer Home filled with his sweet, mournful howl as he dreamed of flight—the attendant listening with heartache to his cry as she lay to rest at night. She was the only one the child had in this world, and she did not take that responsibility lightly. It weighed on her, that he suffered so."

"Soon," your granjo says, "news came to the Summer Home that the emperor was going to leave this country, and that before he did, he planned to close Joyrock. The people of the land rejoiced, believing that he was going to free those he had imprisoned there, but the attendant met the news with grim expression. It was clear to her that the emperor was going to kill his child. And so she felt she had no choice but to finally let him go."

"She dropped the rope ladder for him," your lola says. "And she wept and cheered as he ran out of the house and into the world."

"The first creature he ate was a bird," your granjo says.

"He became purple-feathered and free," your brothers say. "He flew into the midnight sky."

Your father shakes his head.

"And he had no intention of returning."

"The journey to this moment," your lola says, "of him greeting Keema at the steps of the Summer Palace, was a long one. After he escaped from the labyrinth, he became many things in those brief few months when he was free. A bear. A tiger. He enjoyed the crisp fish in the rivers. The dirt and the trees and the open sky that felt as though he would fall into it. But always he would return to his original form, and with his bloody snout he would sniff the air for Her scent. Under scorching sun and blackest night where She once dwelt, he traveled west to find his mother—his truest mission, and his gravest mistake; little did he know that his father had heard of his escape, and was searching for him. It did not take long at all for the trap to be sprung—at a crossroads, not far from the Palace City, where the Third Terror, mid-flight, was caught under the spell of a sleeping poison that sent his small bird form tumbling into the dirt. When next he woke, it was in a cage in his father's apartment, a sigil-spell wrapped around his ankles, trapping him in this form, as the man who despised him most of all smiled at him through the bars.

"The various tortures he endured during that captivity were slight and stupid. Food just out of reach. Water delivered in paltry amounts. Invective and insult drooled over him as his father unleashed His frustrations and His failures on this pathetic creature, both of them trapped in positions that they could not remove themselves from. The child tried to escape, but the cage was unyielding. He saw his brother, the First, and he squawked at him to save him, but his brother looked at him with only a distant curiosity, eyes passing over him, unaware and uninterested in who this bird might be."

"It was coincidence that saved him in the end," your granjo says. "Once he had taken over the tortoise network, Luubu learned all of his father's secrets, including the identity of the bird in the cage in His royal apartments. Craving the power he might earn upon consuming his younger brother, he orchestrated a plot to have the bird stolen and delivered to him. And he would have been successful had it not been for Keema of the Daware Tribe."

"When that lid in the caravan was opened," your lola says, "and that young man picked him up with gentle confidence and unwittingly undid the binding spells around his ankles, the child was greeted with a rare kindness. And he was—though he did not have the vocabulary to describe it himself—smitten."

"We fall in love so easily," your brothers say.

"He was taken with the warrior," your lola says. "His warm touch. His face—the light coming in through the canvas flap made him seem born of a golden river."

"In Joyrock," your brothers say, "very little was beautiful."

"The child had experienced a limited range of wants. Hunger. Thirst. Mother. Father. Brother."

"But desire," your father says. "Desire was new."

Your lola smiles. "After he attacked Keema's face, and gathered himself, he followed the young man who had saved him, and—animal though he might be—he paid back his debts by helping him on his journey east. He took down the messenger who was bringing word of warning to Rabbit Gate Checkpoint. In the Thousand, he surveyed the river before they traveled it. He knew their boat would pass a village that was filled with men and women who, upon one sight of their tortoise cargo and their imperial insignias, would have slaughtered them. So he slaughtered them first."

"Preemptive strike," your father says.

"The child did everything he could to help them on their way. When a fork came in the river, one leading toward the ambush and the other leading past a Daido, straight through an empty river, the Terror flapped its wings and squawked, and was heartbroken when it was unheeded. But still it came back to help, like the lovesick child it was, returning once more during the siege of the Bowl, saving Keema and the empress from the gunner on the swiveling ballista. He tore apart Induun and Yinn and Maada and the Panjet-

Waags after he saw Induun's men capture Keema. And he would've killed Jun, too, but he knew that Keema liked Jun—He knew this, and stewed over it as he watched the two of them duel throughout the week, seething with jealousy."

"It should be me he duels!" your father shouts as the Terror.

"Yes, he knew Keema liked Jun," your brothers say. "For now."

"But now," your lola says, "Keema would only have to look at him as he was, and surely he would appreciate all he had done for him."

"Look."

The Third Terror held forth Djove Induun's head.

Induun's jaw hung slack, his sunken, upturned eyes like that of a priestly martyr. The Terror clenched the head in his jaws as his human arms and legs galloped up to Keema as would a dog, and deposited the head at his feet. A gift. The creature looked up at him, panting.

"He loves you," said the attendant at the top of the steps. She was tearing up at the sight, her hand on her chest. "What a day this is. He returns, and he is in love. My son."

When Keema breathed in and looked down at the wolf-man, when their eyes met, a link was made, and the Terror, through the silent meeting of their minds, shared with him his story. Keema learned of the labyrinth, of the escape, of all this creature had done for him on his journey. He learned of the creature's desire for him, to be with him, duel with him. And perhaps it was some residue of feeling from the empress that he had inherited, but when Keema looked upon the creature's purple feathers on the creature's snout, at his fur and tufted ears, he felt pity. Pity for the body of a full-grown man, hunched and apelike. Knuckles pawing at the floor. Sniffing Keema's feet for acceptance. But that pity curdled when the creature rose to his shaking legs. *Look at me, Keema.* When he stood, taller than any human by many heads. His body muscle and sinew. Thick, blood-pumping veins running across his broad chest, and down his sculpted arms, like his own private Roads Above and Below. Every part of his body seemed to breathe and pulse with power. Even the organ between his legs, which was fully erect, like a stone hammer. *Look at me.*

And Keema stepped back, overwhelmed and repulsed.

"He was denied," your lola said sadly.

"The creature, denied his embrace, shrunk away, embarrassed, ashamed, hiding himself behind the attendant's legs as these new emotions burned like pieces of hot metal in his gut. With despair he watched the Red Peacock wield his hatchet, and Keema, after gathering himself, stand beside his friend, and the Terror did not understand what he had done wrong. He had saved this warrior time and time again. He had delivered him the gift of the head of the most powerful man in the country. He had done anything and everything to earn this warrior's affections. And though he had never thought of himself as princely, in this moment, he believed he had been denied his due."

"And they have the gall to deny you!" the attendant spat.

"You are strong and you are beautiful and it is your turn to deny THEM!" Madly, she shouted, "Go into Joyrock! A woman trespasses in your lair! A woman prized by these fucking fools! Kill the woman and make bitter their victory!"

The wolf-boy trembled with fury. He sprinted up the steps and disappeared into the mansion.

Keema and Jun ran past the snarling attendant, giving chase.

At the entrance of Joyrock, Shan sighed.

The entirety of the rope ladder lay at her feet, for someone had severed it off from the bolt with a knife. The man in her arms was silent as she looked up at the hole. He seemed to be basking in the warmth of her body, the softness of her shoulder skin. She ignored his bizarre nuzzling and wondered to herself how she might get out of here. But she grew worried when she felt the nuzzling stop, the man in her arms trembling like a cold bird.

Wetness dampened her palms.

He was pissing himself.

"He's home," he whispered.

She listened: past the sound of the displaced air at the mouth of the hole, that low and vibrant hum, she heard in the distance the small patter of quick footsteps. Like a sprinter on the other end of a large house. She heard doors slap open. She heard the footsteps become larger. The man in her arms began to cry, murmuring, "I am so hungry," as a true and bone-deep fear took root in Shan. She dropped the torch so that she could hold the spear in one hand and the man in the other, and ran back into the labyrinth. In a panic she went left, and then right, before deciding to go left again, randomly. Straight into the dark.

"He's home . . . he's home," the man whispered. She tried to shush him. She begged him to be quiet.

Someone dropped into the hole.

The sound of the fall echoed throughout the glistening caverns. Shan held her breath and pressed herself into a shallow alcove, clutching the mewling man's face into her shoulder, no doubt suffocating him, but she needed him to be quiet.

Whoever had dropped into the hole began to sniff the air. Large, vibrant sniffs.

She crept away.

The child sniffed the earth.

His fingers gripped wet rock as his snout traced the scent of sweat and skin and dirt. Easy to pick her out of the other scents. She smelled like sweet earth. She smelled like fresh hair. Like wheat. He went faster.

"He's here . . ." a man in the distance moaned, ". . . he's here . . ."

His ears pricked up.

The Terror in a sprint rounded the corner. He saw at the end, slumped against the wall the limbless man, abandoned.

"I'm so hungry . . ." the limbless man whispered.

And indeed so was the Terror. He could have eaten the world in that moment. But for all the times the Terror had been tricked and trapped, perhaps it speaks well of his character, in some small, sick way, that he never learned his lesson. That he remained guileless to the end. For the abandoned man on the ground was not quite abandoned, as he quickly learned, when Shan leapt out of the shadowed alcove and lanced him with her spear. It was but a scratch. A shallow line made down his shoulder, but a palm's length, and bright with blood. A wound any warrior might easily shrug off—Shan herself had dozens like it across her body, just from today. But what neither she nor the Terror knew was that in the forging of this spear, her father had blessed the tip with a fistful of sacred moondust—a magick profound in its effect on both god and demon.

The cut sent him shrieking into the dark, without looking back.

In the heart of Joyrock, he huddled.

Clutching his wound, licking it, the blood sour on his tongue, but no administration would comfort the sizzling hurt that emanated from his shoulder. He sat on the floor beside a broken manacle while blood seeped down his back. As the pain wended its way down into his heart, he felt the darkness of the labyrinth surround him, pressing down on him. He had gone so far, only to end up back here, alone. Slowly, he lay down on his side and shuddered.

He wanted his mother.

He burped.

His hand swelled.

His leg shook, the skin ripping down the bone.

As he transformed, Shan ran.

She turned the slick corners of the labyrinth, not daring to look behind her to see if he was chasing her—a desperate heave to her breath, until she turned the last corner and saw the halo of light in the high ceiling.

The walls began to shake. Bits of rock crumbled down around her. Below her there was some great shrugging of the earth, and she almost lost her step, dropping her spear and catching herself just before she body-slammed the man in her arms. Grimacing, she stood back up, gripping the spear, and she kept going. She headed for the hole. She saw no reason to hope that she might make it out of there alive, but what other choice did she have but to try—even if she had to shatter her fingernails crawling out of this pit, she would try—and she wept, joyfully, when like a prayer answered, the two warriors were there, standing in the light of the entrance, reaching for her.

THE END OF THE DAY

Listen to the inhalation.

On the docks that led out from the cove at the bottom of the Summer Cliffs, the eastward winds howled around the workers as they looked without hope upon all the turtled ships. *We knew there was fighting up above; you could almost make out the sounds above the wind, almost. . . . But fighting didn't matter so much to us. We were dead men already.* Their despondency owing to the fact that they did not know the emperor was no more, and they had assumed that the god-king would be delivering His punishments to each of them personally for their failure to rescue His prized crafts, which were both expensive and time-consuming to create, and were all tipped on their sides, useless. *We were more than dead men.*

They sat around the pier, sharing a strong drink. "Maybe He'll understand," one of the men joked. The others laughed. Their leader, sitting on a barrel facing the shore, slid off his perch and flicked away his joint.

"Do you see that?" he said.

The workers gathered around him, following his finger out to the sea-barren horizon.

Up above, within the walls of the Divine City,

in one of the upper reaches of the nobility apartments, a group of children gathered around the salon window, the girl holding up a spyglass while her brothers tried to wrestle it from her. Their parents were in the midst of being served tea by their servants, doing their best to ignore the noises from outside and the barricade of furniture they had erected in front of their own door, when the mother, with cup trembling in her hand, noticed the children behaving oddly. "I told you not to go near the window," she said, walking over to them. "And what are you looking at anyway?"

Her daughter pressed the spyglass into her hand.

"There's a wall," she said. "Look."

"Of course there's a wall."

"No, behind the wall. There's another wall. Way over there."

The mother, who had, only an hour ago, removed a clump of hair from her head that had come unstuck from stress, breathed in the last of her patience and humored her child. She looked at the wall of the Divine City. And then she looked over it.

"Oh," she said, her lungs empty of air.

Behind her, the servant and the father exchanged a meaningful glance, for they had been having an affair for years now and believed the mother's gasp was simply yet another example of her histrionics.

But underneath his wagon, the trinket seller heard it.

He was clutching his favorite pornographic tablet to his chest, of a woman in a loose robe with legs spread open to the viewer, her eyes welcoming them home, when he slowly lowered his head to the dirt and, with his ear pressed to the ground, heard below all the hoofbeats and bootsteps and collapsing bodies a faraway roar, like an army of lions many hills away.

And he knew that the worst was yet to come.

This is how it began to those who were watching and listening: as a curiosity, too far away to matter, and too big to make sense of. Surely the blue band in the distance was a mere trick of the eye and nothing more, and even if it were not, surely it was not coming out for them. But indisputably, to those who continued to watch, the band rose high and higher, gaining in amplitude to a degree that made the bottom of the stomach drop out, as the body understood the true ratio of their respective proportions.

Spyglasses cracked, as they slipped from the fingers and bounced off the ground.

It wasn't long till the first calls were shouted out from the highest districts of the Divine City to the lowest:

A wave is coming! A wave is coming!

The sun was soon swallowed by its crest. A strange half-light illuminated the land. A colorless twilight that softened all shadows and made the world seem submerged in a basin of ghosts. The people who had given up, the ones waiting along the cliffside that overlooked the shore, they observed the approaching wave with a grim acceptance. There were even vendors handing out food for free, though few had any appetite for meat skewered on sticks. *We couldn't even raise our hands to shoo them away. We just ignored them and they continued on, they as dazed as we were, wandering down the ever-lengthening line of people who had given up and were no longer hungry.*

Some enterprising individuals with tools for this sort of thing measured the distance the wave was from land, and after some quick math done with a finger in the air, determined that they had a little more than an hour left to live. It wasn't much time. Some people spent it alone, others with company. *We fucked right there on the open field. People watched as I put my fingers in his mouth, but it didn't matter. We just wanted to feel good.* And while this subset of the population observed the steady and inexorable source of their demise, the fighting outside the city and within it continued. Honor guards screamed as hatchets rained down on them. Two free-bands had been eradicated entirely, their corpses stepped on and over as the remaining groups warred for supremacy, of what, even they were no longer sure—if ever there was purpose to the battle in the beginning of all this, that purpose had long since evaporated. A furious arrow dug its way into a woman's heel before she could spike another woman's back with her blade. Blood ran down the slanted streets of the Divine City and stained the outskirt fields. A warrior stood atop a dead horse, fending off Silver Monkeys with his broad ax. The wave was rising, and the world was running out of time, and it seemed that no one quite knew how to spend it.

As Keema and Jun and Shan ran out of the Summer Home, Keema glanced at the always-startling view of the coast, and his eyes widened when he saw the blue stretch of wave in the distance, reaching higher than the cliffs, than the walls, than even the highest point of this grand city, and he remembered what this moonlit body had told them: that once it was too late, it was too late. *Finish what you mean to finish before you doom us all.*

What if they were too late?

Jun read this thought. *I told him we couldn't think that. We had to keep going.* And Keema knew he was right.

"What's this?" Shan shouted as the ground began to tremble.

Instinct told them to look behind them.

The Summer Home stood tall and still in the half-light.

"I think—" Jun began.

And then a giant hand burst through the front doors.

The tall blackwood doors ripped apart like paper. The stone-and-coral edifice swelled and exploded. Daggers of refined quarry rock and hard-packed and ancient sea stuff punctured congratulatory banners. All they saw were the tips of the giant fingers coming toward them, like a nightmare, before Jun grabbed Shan—*and I thought to Keema: Push us back!*—and he and Keema propelled each other backward, clear across the now-crackling promenade, narrowly avoiding the massive hand that slapped down onto the front steps to the palace, shattering the foundation.

The head attendant reached up to greet him as he crushed her.

Soon the rest of him emerged. They watched from a nearby rooftop as the hand continued its searching grasp, obliterating the statues of emperors past, before the fingers dug into the ground and pulled the rest of the body out of the disintegrating house.

A man, naked and slick and pulsing as if newly birthed, and as tall as the palace itself. His skin was punctured with large, shimmering purple feathers that flexed out when he breathed. His legs were grotesque in their muscularity, his flaccid penis dripping between them. His eyes were still white and bottomless, that of a panting wolf, but instead of fur, it was purple feathers that decorated his pronounced snout. Somehow, Keema could tell that he was smiling.

"MOTHER," the Terror said, his voice booming as loud as the war horn. There was a hesitation to his movements, as if unused to this new growth. As he stood, the last of the palace fell off his shoulders, and behind him, they saw the backdrop of a blue wave as high as the heavens.

Shan shouted: "We can't fight him here! We need to get him out of the city."

"MOTHER!" the Terror shouted again, grasping at the air ahead of him.

Keema looked around. The shape of the city was a spiral, which they were at the center of; they would be doing the same amount of damage no matter which direction they went. He asked Shan which way they should lure him. She pointed south. "There are few residences that way, so long as you keep him going in a straight path."

"He sees us," Jun said.

The wolf's eye widened. His startlingly human hands reached out as a purple tongue lolled between thick, brilliant fangs. Jun backed into Shan and put her on his back, the nameless man squeezed between them. She did not complain, knowing there was no time for pride in this moment. Keema tucked the bag of bones under his arm and lifted the spear. They tossed each other to the next domed rooftop, landing on their feet this time, while the giant man crashed into the manse they had been standing on. The house bloomed like a summer flower, its petals scattered, a chunk of roof flipping down the curved street before exploding against the delicate eaves of a high-district teahouse. Screams echoed out from within the rubble. "Remember, straight line," Shan said. They leapt two more rooftops away, these ones lower down the incline. Keema nodded and whistled at the wolf-man. He put down the spear and lifted the bag up above his head. "She's over here!"

The beast, half-cast in gray light, swiveled its head. "KEEMA," he said as he took another step forward.

But there was yet an uncertainty to his step, made more difficult because the entire city was a slope, and he was now going down an incline. He misjudged the landing of his right foot. His ankle bent.

He was sent tumbling forward.

Three stomachs dropped. There was no time to leap out of the way. The body, flopping down the hill, hands windmilling as it tried to stop itself, crashed into the courthouse they stood upon. Jun and Shan and the nameless man were separated by the blast. Jun was thrown through the paper shutters of a nearby balcony. Shan and her charge fell into the swirling dust and detritus below. Keema had made it to another rooftop, a coral spire, in brief awe at the destruction: the city looked like a hill a child had rolled down, the buildings crushed and indented into the earth like blades of grass. Clear imprints of the body were left behind on the surface of the high district; giant purple feathers fluttered into alleyways.

The Terror's body was now tangled amid the rubble. He let loose a loud groan as his legs shifted, trying to find purchase to stand, his toes dragging through entire streets. Keema searched for the others, only realizing as he slid down the roof that the spear was gone.

It was stuck in a floorboard.

When Shan Araya fell into the courthouse depths, she thought for sure it was the end. It was an odd sensation, to fall so freely—at once so quick and so slow, enough time to think about her mother. How much time they had wasted being apart. But it was not the end. She had landed on her back, but somehow she was okay. And the man was still, miraculously, in her arms, unconscious, yet breathing.

The wind was knocked out of her; as she recovered her breath, coughing against the smog, she began to realize that what she landed on was soft, with give—it was strangely moist, like skin after a run—and when the thing beneath her swelled with breath, a shiver of revulsion made her stomach bubble when she saw that what she sat on was the Terror's right shoulder blade. She stood up quickly—too quickly—and lost her balance, slipping down the muscular curve of his arm before crashing onto the floor, reflexively protecting the man in her arms as she hit the bottom. Groaning, she looked up. Most of the ceiling was gone, but two-thirds of the walls were still standing. A crow cackled from a drooping beam of wood. She cut her foot on a sharp rock as she stumbled through the still-clearing dust clouds. The long building. And then, squinting, she saw through the dust clouds something large and white illuminate the ruined dark, and she thought for one dazzled moment that it was the Moon, returned to them all.

She gasped and dropped to the ground, on her back, clutching the nameless man close to her.

The wolf's eye had opened. A deep whimper was let loose from its snout as it tried to rise up. The eye was so large, Shan imagined stepping into it and into another world. But then she saw the spear, wedged into the floorboards not far from her, and she had a different dream for it.

She put the man down and crawled forward, pausing, when

the Terror mewled in its rumbling, unsure voice: "W-WHY K-KEEMA . . ."

The moon half-shut, despondent.

She stood up and went for the spear. Her hands gripped the pole as she summoned the weapon from its deep wedge. Her lips twisting. Her palms rough and to the point of bleeding as she pulled, pulled. The moon-eye slowly opened as the wolf's ear perked to the sound of something nearby. She was then silhouetted by this eye, full and piercing and white. Her heart stopped.

The spear zipped out of the floorboard.

"KEEMA?" the beast asked.

Shan said nothing. No wise words. No sentiment.

She just threw the spear at her target.

The moon exploded.

And the Terror howled.

"MOTHER! MOTHER!"

Keema had just found Jun in the apartment he had been thrown into, coming back to consciousness, when the massive body began to thrash. *We felt the world trembling as his fists pounded into the earth. We felt it all coming apart.* The Terror swept his arms left and right, clearing out the space around him before clutching at the bleeding gash in his face. Keema and Jun ran out to the balcony in time to see him rise. There was a sickly countenance to his skin now; a translucency that seemed to sag and stretch and beg to slough off the bone. His remaining eye was a milky white substance without pupil, a furious void. He reached out at the air and grabbed at nothing. He was a child again. He sniffed the air. His snout directed at the two of them, and the sack of bones that Jun carried. "MOTHER? MOTHER!"

When he took another step his knee buckled, and he stumbled forth and fell again, Keema's heart seizing as he watched this man roll toward them; but this time they were ready. With their god gifts they tossed each other out of the way as the ball of limbs bouldered through the city, taking with him building after building. Bright-red coral shrapneled everywhere. "*Fuck!*" Jun shouted, and Keema echoed this sentiment as they flung themselves upward and chased after this writhing form of destruction. They flew through cratered houses and splintered spires and the people who had not yet fled, some of whom were crushed by the body and others who looked around dazed as they stumbled out of the rubble. *We watched the two demons run past us, glad that it was not us that they hunted.*

The Terror had rolled down to the second-to-last district. He was half inside of a wide hall, a magisterial building where forms were filed and trading negotiations were signed off on. Most of the people who had been hiding within that building ran away, though there were some who stayed to fight, impotently sticking the pointy ends of whatever they could grab into the soles of his feet or his hand as he pushed himself back upright. The spears and swords got wedged into the flesh but made it nowhere near anything vital or weak. He bit at a clutch of people. Legs squirmed between clenched jaws. *The last thing I saw was the roof of his mouth before his tongue pressed me into it.* The Terror stood up without noticing the small army that attacked his toes as he clutched at his eye wound and took in another inhalation through his wet nostrils, the breath so strong it made the roofs rattle against the updraft of air. Slowly he turned toward Keema and Jun, who had made it down to a nearby building. *I told Jun that we had to lure him away.*

To which I said to Keema that was a fine plan, if impossible, and did he have any destination in mind.

I pointed toward the cliffside. That was where I thought we could knock him into the ocean.

It was the only plan they had.

"Your mother is here!" Jun shouted; now it was him holding up the bag. The giant raised himself up. Keema and Jun shouted for people to get out of the way—*They did not need to tell us twice*—as they leapt from roof to roof, toward the southern wall, luring the sniffing snout of the beast in their direction. The people scattered through the streets. *To anywhere. It was too much. There were five ends of the world, and to run away from one meant running into another.* They leapt over the wall, and shortly after, the colossus burst through the stonework, the wide jaxite gate coming un-hinged, rolling out of its slot, wheeling through what remained of the pilgrims' tent city like a giant coin, skipping through aban-doned wagons that exploded underneath its weight into clouds of wood shrapnel. The free-bands were no longer fighting, nor the honor guards; they were running away with the people, except for the brave few who helped others out of collapsed rubble, and shouted directions toward the city's exit.

The two warriors bounded through the remains of the tent city, clearing people out of the way with smooth flicks of the hand that carried the crying bystanders aloft through the air—*for one mo-ment, before the end, I flew, and I thought this was it, I was dead—* and landed them not so gently onto the beaten grass beyond the field of battle. At the outskirts, when Keema and Jun turned, they realized the giant was no longer following them. He had stopped just outside the walls of the city, staring with his one good eye at the approaching great wave in the distance.

He was stunned. He was frightened.

The child took a step back. A soldier was crunched beneath his heel. He backed himself toward the hole in the wall that all the ci-vilians were pouring out of, wanting nothing more than to return to the labyrinth, to familiar safety.

"She's over here!" Jun screamed, holding the bag, but the Terror had eyes only for the impending wave.

He took another step back.

And another.

A dark and luminous shadow draped over the river of people streaming into the fields.

The heel coming down on them.

A man held his child to his chest.

If there was one last thing I held in this world, it would be her.

And then a snap of color exploded from beneath the shadow. A frizzle of jerin blue and blood red. Spikes of neon green and serra-tions of royal purple. The colors shot up with increased strength.

White blossoms popped. Constellations of red and orange. The fireworks slung into the air and exploding in a rainbow of furious color while the trinket seller laughed desperately as he lit his wagon on fire, his livelihood. Streamers twirled into the sky. The loud crack in the air caught the wolf's ear. The Terror turned. A dragon's breath of color blew up in his face and he howled, his eye temporarily blinded by the light. He withered from the fireworks, the people, and careened into the now-emptied fields south of the city, following the one thing he had left in the world: the scent of his mother's bones.

He called to her.

"MOTHER!"

And the flow of her scent, like stardust, led him through the resolving dark. Up an ever-steepening hill. But he did not ask where they were going. In his blind groping, his scrabbling, his wolf senses trusted her smell completely, without question.

Up to the cliff that overlooked the sea.

Keema and Jun stood together on the edge of that sharp, dagger-toothed rock that jutted out from the cliff. As they watched the giant clamber toward them, fingers digging into the dirt as it reached up at them, its bellowing and desperate tones for its mother singing through the air, Jun looked over at Keema, and Keema looked over at Jun.

"I would've won," Keema said. "If we had ever had a proper duel. Fully rested. I would've won."

Jun smiled.

"Fuck off," he said, which, to Keema's ears, had the same melody as I love you.

And then the Terror arrived, ready to be delivered into his mother's arms, and the two warriors, with hands pressed into the earth, sent a pulse through the ground and severed the rock from the mainland.

They slipped together into the abyss.

The blue sky was darkening behind the wave as Keema and Jun floated down, carrying each other to the ocean floor. Their feet touched the silt one after the other, sinking into the soft and giving earth. Thousands of fish lay dead around them, but most striking of all were the giant capsized junk ships that surrounded them. The junk ships were towering behemoths. They could've carried hundreds of warriors in their berths. Keema and Jun regarded these vestiges of the Moon Throne. Their sails hanging from their masts like dead skin off broken bones, their hulls cratered, cracked open like tajelines. It was as fitting a backdrop as any, to end the royal line.

"M-MOTHER . . ."

The Third Terror had not fallen as gently as they. He writhed around on the sand, no longer a colossus, but still large, and thrashing. Keema and Jun approached him carefully. *We just had to keep him here till the wave came.* The fall had short-circuited some essential part of him, it seemed, as his body spasmed, his limbs erupting into various large and terrible forms. Wings of black cartilage sprouted from his writhing back before withering off like crumbling charcoal. His right leg shot out into tentacular forms while his left cracked into the backward joints of panthers and lions, toes flexing into paws, a vulture's claw. His arms bristling with purple feathers that shed from him in great plumes, carpeting the silt below him. They could feel the waves of pain coming off his body; pain, and fear, as he looked past the ships, at the leviathan wave that would be here any minute now.

In his spasming, he turned to the cliff's face.

He was going to run.

The writhing creature went tense, like a dog ready to charge, its oddly jointed feet digging into the damp sand, kicking up a spray of it as it ran full-tilt toward the cliff. Keema leapt into its path, his hand held out. An easy swipe sent him flying. He crashed through the soaked hull of the *Jorro.* When Jun leapt and swung the hatchet at the Terror's dangling limb, a tentacle looped around Jun's back and clutched him around the neck, the appendage turning into a white-knuckled hand that brought Jun up to the Terror's wolfish face, all thoughts of escape now gone from the Terror's mind, his remaining eye wide and furious, for he saw in Jun's face the face of his brother, who soaked in all of their father's love, and he saw the face of his rival, who basked in all of Keema's love, and the face of the bastard who snuck away all of his mother's love—in whose body his mother dwelt in that very moment, affording him Her power. And to the rabid child it seemed that all of his problems would go away if he just squeezed hard enough on this tiny body. And so he did, and the veins popped in Jun's neck, his face red, and then purple. His mouth jawing to speak but with no air to speak it.

The force of the squeeze was so great even you feel it now.

The splinters run through the theater, and the stage cracks in half, the audience flinching as the high walls tremble. This moonlit body looks up at the crumbling edifice as a wind blows in and the braziers go out.

Jun is unconscious.

Jun is about to pop.

"Wait! A duel!"

The braziers light up again as the Terror relaxes its grip on the throat of the boy in its grasp; the wolf's head turning to see Keema limping from the destroyed hull of the *Jorro,* holding out his hand, beseeching the child to stop. "A duel." He coughed pathetically. There was blood on his lip, his chin. "I"—blood swallowed— "I challenge you to a duel."

Somewhere, long ago, a young boy clawed at the windows to play with his brothers.

He whimpered to be included.

And now, at the Daware man's unexpected invitation, he could not help but pant with delight.

"Yes," Keema said, strangely moved by the creature's reaction, even now, even with the world at stake. "A duel. Just you and me. If I win, you stop. You just . . . stop. If you win, well . . . you win."

Jun's body slipped out of the child's relaxed grip, and slumped onto the silt. Keema resisted the urge to run to him, keeping his eyes on the child, who was now his own height, if a bit taller—he was on all fours, sitting like a dog waiting to play fetch. His right eye was missing, his fur matted with blood, but he didn't seem to mind.

It was time to play.

The sky darkened.

The people along the cliffside sat with legs dangling as they watched the two small figures down below meet amongst the ruins of His Smiling Sun's grounded ships. *With little else to hold on to, we watched the man of poor fortune face the Demon of Joyrock. We were soon to die, but at least, we thought, we would see one more duel before our untimely end.*

Some of them even began to cheer, as the two combatants prepared to fight.

The water roared behind them.

The boundary was drawn.

Keema drew the circle in the silt with a piece of timber from one of the boats. He did it quickly with Her Gift, the wood moving of its own accord, to his wishes, while Keema stood to the side, clutching at the vicious wound in his side. He smiled without joy.

I thought I was a god.

Why was I still bleeding?

His head was swimming as he asked the child if he was ready, to which the child dug in and jumped around and ran to his end of the circle.

"Right," Keema said, his hand on his wound.

He breathed in.

"Positions!" he shouted, wincing as he drew into his stance. Right foot forward, right hand out. A laugh escaping his lips as he saw the Terror snap into a startlingly professional stance, his naked, muscular body tensed and ready to tear him apart. His snout wet, his many teeth bared.

The two boys, who once wanted nothing more than someone to fight, now faced each other.

"Begin!"

Against the backdrop of the rising wave,
and the dead ships, they rumbled.

It would not go into the scrolls of history as the finest of all fights. It was in fact over almost as soon as it began, for the truth of the matter was that Keema was injured and weak and the Terror was a creature of pure strength whose life had been dedicated to the hunting and killing of prey. To his credit, the Terror obeyed the laws of the duel. He did not bite, and he did not scratch. And Keema put up as good a fight as any in his situation might when faced against a god-child. Four blows, two deflections. A kick rounded into the Terror's jaw, and the Terror taking the blow as a parent might their child's playful slap. The duel ending when the Terror swept Keema off his feet with a kick to the shins, and with his muscled and veiny hand pressed his throat into the ocean floor.

It was over. Keema had no more fight in him.

He patted his hand against the ground in concession.

It was over. It was over.

I'd lost.

The wolf looked down at him. The child's snout was pressed up against his nose, the wolfish breath hot against his face. He was certain that the Terror was now going to eat him alive. He even shut his eyes, to ready himself for the first crunching bite.

But the bite never came. Instead, the child's hand released his neck, and, no longer pinned to the ground, Keema sat up and watched as the child stepped back, and then bowed, as he had watched all the others do after a duel well fought. Beaten, Keema rose to his wobbling feet, and he bowed back. And then the child walked over to the bag of his mother's bones, where he curled up and laid his head, for after all these years, all this time, he was satisfied.

Jun woke up with Keema smiling down at him.

"I had the most wonderful dream," Jun whispered, "that you lost yet another duel."

Keema, with tears in his eyes, laughed. He helped Jun to his feet.

They turned to face the wave. It towered above them at such a height that it was almost impossible to register.

"It's not stopping," Jun said. He sounded exhausted. Replete.

He was right. The wave had not yet sensed them. It was not

shrinking to meet them. Keema doubted it was even aware of their presence. But he was not afraid. He knew what needed to be done.

"We have to make it see us."

He took off his sandals. His toes pressed into the silt. He felt the world on the soles of his feet: the dead flop of the fish, the slowing thump of the Terror's heartbeat. The roiling tremor of the great wave as it tore across the ocean floor in wild grief. *I asked Jun through our link if he felt it. The sounds. The Rhythm that connected us to the wave. And he told me that he did. And I knew that together, we could do it. So I held out my hand.*

And I asked him if he would dance with me.

When Jun took his hand, Keema wanted to laugh, because for his whole life he wished he was brave enough to ask this question, and in the end it was so easy. The meeting of their hands seeming almost inevitable. Jun followed him in the steps that had no name, at least not yet, for the story was still writing itself. One day in the endless loop of history, in the circular currents of its water, where there was no future, and no past, these steps would be inscribed in the shaft of an antique wooden weapon, and would tell the tale of these two warriors.

"I would hold the spear in my hands," your lola says, "and I would wonder what these markings meant. Words and meaning lost to history, but in their grooves my hands would feel a sense of purpose, a sense of warmth."

She smiles, as she sits with your family, and puts out her cigarette.

"I would feel like I was home."

It would only be later, as people recounted what had happened or what they heard had happened, that they would settle on a title for what the two warriors performed on that day. It was a title that, like the other dances of the land, was described in its own movements, in the way two men leapt in synchronicity and landed on solid feet and held each other against the coming end. *And we thought the movements together, and we expressed with our bodies that same thought. We were not ourselves anymore but each other, speaking through our bodies to a wounded and grieving land. And what we said was this:*

The body holds the body.
The arms hold the spear.

And the spear cuts through water.

The water stopped, as if frozen—as if the energies that composed the wave had gone still to listen to the whisper of the sky. And then it split, right down the middle, like a part in the hair, like a crack of the shell of a tajeline.

Like two wings, unfolding.

The people on the cliff watched in stunned awe as the wave unzipped itself. It became two arms of water, reaching out to either side of itself, before turning inward, converging toward the Terror, the empress's bones, and the two young men standing before the end of the world.

The both of them were seized with a sudden fear of the end. A bodily reaction to the walls of water barreling toward them, ready to crush them. Jun ran up to Keema and held him, and Keema cradled the back of Jun's head with his hand, feeling the sharp stubble of his shaved head. Their hearts bird-wing rapid. The two of them slumped against each other, shoulder against chest, like two rocks balanced over some great chasm in an act of trust that seems both impossible and ancient, before they were swept away on that incredible tide. Pulled and pushed in a thousand directions until Keema was sure that his body was going to be torn apart, a fist of water pressed against his ears and his nose and his mouth until he felt it come out—Her, expelled from his body—and he thought he saw the impression of Her in the Water, Her faint smile bubbling into nothing but dark foam as She was returned to her greatest love, and he was glad he had this last measure of peace before the end, before the Water continued to crawl into him and swell up his lungs and his body went into some great ecstatic thrashing, convulsing without breath, and his mind went warm and dull as he wondered if this was what it was like, to be held, and how sorry he was that this was how he found out, and how glad he was that it was over. To the Sleeping Sea he would go, to join the energies of those who had passed before him, and had become once more synonymous with the world. Perhaps he would return as the eyes of a fish, or the pulsing heart of a creature deep below who wakes only rarely, only when time strikes it appropriate to do so, and it stands and brings with it to the surface a mighty pearl the size of the Moon, which it might throw up into the sky to give the people another holy satellite by which to walk on their way to their loving nighttime trysts beyond the village gates. This he might next become, these the last fireworks of thoughts that erupted from his brain as the Water filled him up—or maybe it would be even simpler than that. Maybe he would move up, instead of down. Maybe he would be drawn up into the sky. Higher than even the mountain from which his family might've come. Wherever the warriors of Daware had once laid their claim. Living inside of a dark cloud above the land, as it swelled and thundered before the burst. Maybe he would be the sound of drums itself.

Maybe the rain.

And then, for the first time in a very long time, it did rain. The sky broke open and the grass was fed more than dew and the trees glowed green as they fed from the water that soaked their roots. And the people held out their buckets and their cloth sheets and their open mouths and they tried to catch as much of it as possible. *We tried to fill our bellies. We tried to get our fill.* But there was only so much they could do on such short notice. All they could do was drink deeply from the sudden and surprising gift. Shan, standing in the plains with her warriors, held up her hands to the falling water. The trinket seller picked up the remnants of his blown-up wagon with his reunited driver as he wondered what had become of the young gods he had tried to squeeze for luck.

Over the mountain palace it rained. Over the rubble of Tiger Gate. Over the terraced rice paddies and the mouths of the Thousand Rivers and the fishers' houses. Over the canals and the waterways and the Bowl of Heaven and the canyons beyond. The last of the ape castes gesturing their thanks to the sky. The levels of the rivers rose and overflowed, the veins pumping once more as the land breathed again under sheets of rain, torrents of it. The leaves smacked like drumskins. The people's thirst finally slaked. *We looked up as it poured over our heads with equal fervor. We looked up and opened our mouths and tasted the same taste.* As did the boy with the cleft lip, who sat on a ledge in a small village in the palm of the Spires, where he was taken in by those who cared, along with the other lost children of the land—his tongue held out beneath the cloudburst sky. *And we knew this to be nothing less than the fruit of heaven.*

AFTER

I

The voices are gone.

The theater is once more silent as the footprints of the dead and the ancient, satisfied that their lot has been shared, return to the fabric of the weave. You've become so accustomed to their whispers that the quiet that follows their absence is almost chilling, and you and the tall shade and all the other members of the audience shift in your seats, waiting for this moonlit body to start moving again.

This body rises from its crouch and looks at you all. The finale has come and gone. The story is, for the most part, finished—but no one rises from their seats, for there is yet a loose thread that spills from the end of this tale, caught on the tip of a blood-red spear.

On the backdrop behind this body, the webbed shadows of time and circumstance wheel forth.

This is what happened after.

After the great wave fell.

Once the Third and Last Terror was dead, the world closed the drapes over the end of the Ossan family line, finishing the last days of the Emperor's Summer with two weeks of unending rain. It was under these clouds, gray and cracked and blessed, that Shan Araya rediscovered the family spear, sticking out like a flagpole amidst the rubble of the half-destroyed Divine City.

The days that followed the end were not easy for her. She carried this spear with her, for support, using it sometimes as leverage as she helped clear the wreckage left behind by the Third Terror, freeing the civilians pinned underneath the fallen rock and timber. Time was limited and they had to use any means necessary to get the people out of there before the unending rains filled up those small warrens and drowned them. Sometimes they were too late. A memory that would haunt Shan for the rest of her days was of the mother and son her people found under the collapsed wall of the courthouse, bruised but alive in that small cup of earth. Through a small hole, Shan touched the little boy's hand and told him he and his mother would be freed soon. And they tried. Bloodied hands and snapped fingernails all, they tried. But the stone was too heavy, and it seemed that with each wooden beam they lifted, there was another beneath it. And the water would not stop falling.

It took them both in the end. When their drowned bodies were lifted out of the wreckage, a Family Man behind Shan muttered that it was just as well—that these loyalists had what was coming to them—and she spun around and the Family Man, a kid, no older than thirteen, conscripted from who-knew-what village, flinched as if she were about to strike him, and she saw in that flinch yet another kid, drowning.

She was fifteen years old, but that day she might as well have been forty.

"Go," she said. "Listen for any others."

The spear became her companion during those two weeks of

rain, and her sole source of stability, and comfort, as she catalogued the losses of the day. It kept her on her feet as she grappled with the news of Induun's death, and her own complicated feelings for the man, and it was there, leaning against the corner of the room, as she attended to the nameless man from the labyrinth.

He passed on seven days into the storm, which he watched with great delight from the mat Shan had laid out for him by the open flap of the tent. She had a physiker watch over him day and night. She had the man cleaned and fed. And she felt a great well of emotion when the man asked to be brought under the rain, and he let loose these strange and delighted squeals as she held him under the breaking of the heavens. *Why not,* she would think. *Why not just say he is my father.* Her sadness then inevitable when one day he seized up on the mat, quietly, as if in the throes of a nightmare, and then went limp.

He was dead in less than a minute. The physiker told her that it was a small mercy that the man from the bowels of Joyrock had lived that long. He said it was a shame that they never learned his name.

"Mercy" was a word she heard a lot in those days. The Sky Beggars, holding their sloshing, swollen wooden bowls, sang the word throughout the land, singing that the Emperor's Summer was finished. Gods have mercy, it was finished. But Shan had difficulty seeing such mercy in the world as the dead collected at her feet.

With spear in hand, she looked for the two young men who had saved her from Joyrock, and, if the rumors spoke true, also stopped the deadly wave. She spoke to those who claimed to be there on that day, standing at the edge of the cliff, watching the last battle on that exposed ocean bed. They described in embellished detail the duel between the one-armed warrior and the wolf-man, and because the duel was in truth so brief and did not lend itself well to a tale worth a neighbor's time, the duel became longer and longer in memory, until it became an endless ballet of blows, with even the emperor's ships being used as psychic artillery between the two godlike fighters.

"But that is not even the most surprising part of it," the teller would say to her.

After the Terror was slain—obliterated in all manner of ways, depending on who was telling—the two warriors performed a dance that stayed the wave and cut it in twain. It seemed to be a dance of the old way, from the time when the people were still in communion with the magicks of the world, not just the royals with their poisoned blood. There was some quiet dispute regarding the relationship of the two young men. Some claimed the dance was too intimately performed, too synchronous, too seductive, to have been the product of mere platonic fraternity. One who was amongst the number of witnesses that day swore to seeing the two of them kiss before the water took them, but such gestures were not too uncommon between men in those days in moments of great spirit. "In my eyes they were but brothers-in-arms," a pilgrim told her. "Fellow warriors who fought to the end to protect their beloved land."

She heard many variations of the tale in those two weeks, but it seemed that no one knew anything of use to her.

More, fallen.

She leaned against the spear, tired.

After the rains ceased, and the world continued its stately revolutions, Shan Araya became the new head of the Induun family, and upon the consolidation of forces between the various nobilities not tied to royal blood, for a decade she helped lead her province through a difficult period of transition and instability. In all respects she was a decent leader for her family, and modestly respected, though because she never made a show of her accomplishments, her legacy was rarely spoken of except in the most perfunctory of terms—the more charitable of historians describing the almost impossible situation she had inherited from her predecessor. Pressured by the board of the Induun family, she married the eldest son of Lord Yinn in a consolidation of power; rice was as valuable an export as textiles in the lands overseas, and the two Families were hungry for the promise of profit. The son of Lord Yinn was an aloof man who, in reaction to his father's softness and obsequiousness, entertained no fools, and was generally thought of as an unpleasant and bitter little bug. But he surprised everyone, including

Shan, when over the duration of the first year of their marriage, he fell madly in love with her.

He was as short as she was tall and he looked up at her as if she were his Smiling Sun and his Gracious Moon. There were days when she loved him too. When their union felt right. But because she was forced into this matter—and there was nothing Shan liked less than being forced to do something—she found it difficult to give herself to him completely. Some days were easier than others. Some days he looked at her from across the room so earnestly, she was filled with a desire to give him what he craved, and together they would spend a happy afternoon under covers, much to the blushing of the prudish attendants who were stationed outside their bedroom door.

Some days.

It was a nephew who killed her in the end. A power struggle and an ousting that she long suspected was coming, for the nephew had made his discontent with her leadership known for many years. Poison, in a teacup; that was what did it. Her last thought was a chuckle, thinking that at least her killer had the courtesy of sweetening her drink with honey before he served her her end.

We knot this thread.

So began the spear's long journey. It went into the custody of the nephew who assassinated Shan, but he did not have it for long. Come the end of his life a year after the poisoning—disemboweled, as he was, during the Flower Rebellion, when the farmers of Tran and Syta compound, discontent with the leasing system, and the spiraling debts it put them under, ambushed his richly furnished caravan with the sharpened tools of their trade—the spear shortly after was bequeathed back to one of Shan's many, many children.

The spear traveled through a world of great upheaval. A young woman chronicling the state of the country after the dismantling of the tortoise network carried the spear with her for protection on the long roads Above and Below. The weapon slung across her back, she passed the dehydrated, eviscerated corpses of many tortoises, as she visited the villages that used to house the creatures in their watchtowers, and the gates that were still operational, interviewing the heralds who traveled village to village spreading news the long way around, as well as the guards who had been in direct communication with the creatures prior to the abandonment of their posts. She learned that after the death of their god, the tortoises were no longer connected, and served no purpose to those who once used them. Many of them were killed in retaliation for how they had served the Throne, for all the loved ones they had sent to Joyrock, their heads pulled out and their necks severed, while others were left to die just beyond the village gates or beyond the dismantled checkpoints, starved, or eaten by the animals. In her interviews, she learned that the tortoises had all been heading east, to some unknown destination.

Not all of them died. The young chronicler met one of the escaped tortoises in a hut outside one of the river villages. A kind family had hid the creature there in safety, and at night brought it out to the river to enjoy the sights and sounds of night. The chronicler asked the creature where it and all of its kind were headed, and why, and the creature lowered its head to the ground in mourning, as it told her of the vision of freedom that one of their brethren had delivered to them, of a river, and a bug on its beak, so powerful, so intoxicating, they felt they had no choice but to follow it, and see it for themselves.

"This one will travel the Thousand for the rest of this one's life," the creature said, "and this one will find that river."

It shut its eyes.

"And finally this one will know peace."

With the tortoises gone, news once more traveled the slow way around. The Five Families each had their own heralds that they sent to the outskirt villages, spreading their own version of the state of the country. The people heard enough conflicting reports of who owned what and where power now lay that they were not sure what to believe. A devout sect of penitents even held out hope that the emperor was still alive, for without seeing His body—there was, after all, little of Him left to be seen—it was easy to present alternative theories to truth; easy for the remaining loyalists to believe that He was not dead but somewhere in hiding, marshaling His forces, waiting to attack those they believed to be blasphemers. Violence between the people rose as they fought for the supremacy of their reality.

The young chronicler returned home, and laid the spear to rest with a heavy soul. The future worried her.

Two generations later, the spear went on to live amongst many other family relics in a vault in one of the Induun house-barges in the Bowl. There it lay unattended but for the monthly rotation of servants who dusted the forgotten objects of wealth, as a guard stood at the entrance watching them for theft, while outside the world continued its aching transformations.

Upon the death of the Gracious Moon, the moonrock traps that once stunned the river fish with such reliability now no longer worked, their magick rendered ineffective. The old ways of fishing had to be relearned, the line and the lure, which took time and effort, and caused much friction between those putting in that time and effort, and those who were demanding the same quotas from before to be met, if not in greater quantities.

It was the death of a river child that catalyzed a minor war between Lord Maada's descendants and the exhausted fishermen. After the battle at the Tributary of the Brass Cicadas, won at great cost by the fishermen, Lord Maada's descendants were killed, the dismembered family cast into a lesser river that fed into the heart of the Thousand, and for a brief time, the Gatherings flourished. They even made ties and treaties with the other Families, threatening to become an equal power. But the Induun-Yinn family union, nervous about the precedent set by this successful revolution, as well as the faction's proximity and dealings with the Bowl where the heart of Induun's power lay, determined that the faction was dangerous to their future and must be dismantled. There was another battle. The Battle at the Southern Sluices.

On the eve of the massacre, a descendant of Shan's searched the family vault until he found the spear he had been told such grand stories of. Unbeknownst to his mother and father, who wanted for him a life of quiet safety as a business dealer for their tapestries, he planned to ride with the contingent of soldiers who would attack the fishermen.

"I'm going to be a hero," he told his lover that night. He held out the spear until the blade tip rested against her chin. "Kiss the spear of the hero."

His lover was much older than him, and she was more often than not amused by his youthful rudeness.

On her knees, she smirked, and made him feel like a myth.

During the battle the following day, he hid in terror beneath a capsized boat while the water around him tinted with darker and darker gradations of red. He choked on the bloody water, sputtering it between his lips as he tried to keep his head above the rolling surface. He stayed under there for hours until he dared venture past the dismembered limbs of the soldiers he had supped with mere hours ago, to the shore, where a fisherwoman crouched over one of her own fallen comrades. Seized with opportunity, the young man ran across the sand, the woman turning around just in time to see his panicked face as he thrust the spear into her chest.

Kaara/Tak-lina, done in by a mere child, had enough strength left in her to slip a thin dagger up his chin, and as he scratched frantically at the bleeding puncture, she wandered to the edge of the water and dropped to her knees, smiling as her hand stroked the grooved shaft of the spear, and whispered, "Nice to see you again," before her last breath quit her lips, and she dissolved into a splash of water.

And so it was that the Thousand, too, fell under the rule of Induun-Yinn, the revolts growing in intensity over the years throughout each of the provinces, the Families unwilling to relinquish their power, meeting each of these rebellions with bloodier and bloodier responses. Their attention on the revolts so all-encompassing, so unyielding, they paid little attention to the coming danger from outside their borders.

The spear, after being retrieved from the river shore, continued to lie in wait in the Induun family vault, gathering dust behind studded armors and jeweled chests, until the day came when it was needed once more—many, many years later, when, toward the end of his days, a descendant of Shan's looked around the vault in search of a gift he might offer to the general of an invading army.

We knot this thread.

It was easy for the army from the north to take over the country. Organized and ruthless, they cut through the provinces with little effort. They bled out the Families. The tea estates burned and the quarries were ransacked, and the descendants of Panjet and Waag—the union long ago disassembled—were quartered publicly, as an example to be made to the rest of the populations. Cannons exploded the clay walls and terra-cotta roofing of the manses. The Yinn family, when faced with the armies at the gates of their rice terraces, sent for reinforcements from Induun, but Induun did not answer that call, not willing to risk opening themselves to attack, and so, along with Panjet and Waag, Yinn's descendants, too, were swept away in as few as a handful of days. It was only due to the fact that the invading army was land-based, and inexperienced with the traversing of water, that the Induun family, tucked away in the heart of the Bowl of Heaven, was able to buy enough time to plan for their salvation.

The spear was offered in the spirit of friendship to the army's general, of whom it was known that he had a love for interesting and unique weaponry. With the spear, and the offer of marriage to the sister of the eldest son, the general agreed to let the people of Induun both live and to keep their name, and to continue the manufacture of their fine textiles under the guidelines of their new leadership. And so it was that the spear came under the stewardship of your great-great-great-grandfather.

The brutal man led but the first occupying force—it wasn't long till news spread of the untapped riches the land had to offer. After his army occupied the country for a fruitful number of years, five more countries in search of fertile lands passed their fists over these valleys and mountains over the decades. Upon the invasion of his manses, your ancestor general fled with his family into a faraway town, where he changed his name, and in those difficult and lean years he and his family sustained themselves on the mythic power of the spear, and the colors of their tapestries. When he died of the pale sickness, withered and stenched in a hospice bed, his wife, paralyzed by the sudden freedom to make her own choices after a lifetime of servitude to his wants, opted instead to follow her late husband into the Sleeping Sea, by way of the third-floor window.

We knot this thread.

The spear was thrust into the eldest daughter's shaking hands, and then, in a moment of resolve that would determine her behavior for the rest of her life, those hands gripped the spear tight, as if to choke it. Unsympathetic to her mother's ending of her own life, this daughter, who had up until then considered herself a strange mixture of her parents' sensibilities, of the line between hard and soft, finally pendulum-swung in the disciplined and hard-stepped direction of her father's ascetic lifestyle. With spear in hand she raised her siblings by the ticking second hand of the clock. She entertained no tantrums, and no moments of the soul. She worked as an apprentice to a merchant who traded in textiles across the sea. The merchant worked her to the bone, but she made herself useful to him, with her family's knowledge of the craft, and in time, he helped her start her own business.

Her brothers and sisters both relied on her for financial support. They feared her, for she was not afraid to strike someone who spoke out of turn, or anyone who stood in her way, even if it was her favorite grandnephew. The most tender acts of her life were reserved for the boy who would one day become your granjo. She shared with him the history of her father's conquests and war crimes with pride. And it was to him that she signed away the family business and her beloved spear, before she, too, was claimed by the waves of the Sleeping Sea on the frigid tide of a blood clot.

We knot this thread.

Your granjo was in many ways her duplicate, much to his own parents' disappointment. He even held his chin high like she did, his gaze ever-cast downward even at those who towered over his slight frame. His family tried to have some sway over his life and the business, but he was unmoved by their pleas for him not to bring it overseas to the Unioned Continent, for all too many companies had failed in such reckless expansions. With his wife and daughter and three attending servants whose names he often confused, he set sail for the New World, where he planted his business in that dockside town where you would one day come into this world. It was a struggle to establish himself, for he was not the only merchant king in relocation, but in time he built up your family name and your wealth, while his daughter, who perked up only when he or her mother told her the more fantastical tales of the Old Country, grew up and one day took over. His wife passed at the age of eighty, but he carried on in an almost supernatural way. One day he sat in his chair and he never got up again. At a certain point, it was just assumed your lola had inherited the spear.

We knot this thread.

And there the spear hung, on iron hooks above the mantel, in one of the larger manses of that dockside town, while below it, your lola told you the tales that were one of her sole connections to a world beyond her window. And there it hung while your father in his wild moods stalked the house with feet like iron nails driven into tracks—who then one day vanished in the middle of the night, off to war, with you as the sole witness to his desperate effort to find himself, at the cost of everything. And there it hung as your uncle borrowed what money was left and did not return it, and as your brothers scattered, to join the war, to flee into the wilderness, to die in drunken accidents in alleys that few visited, or, worse, to live wealthy and successful lives against which you compared yourself daily. While you and your granjo live on in that now-abandoned house, you are the undying man's sole keeper. It is a lonely life that you are nevertheless desperate to keep, for who knows what tomorrow will bring.

Or so you tell yourself.

After all, for you, there was no predicting where you are now, sitting in this Inverted Theater. The family spear you had given away now less a spear than a sewing needle, stitching two distant points of time together in one unending embrace. You wondered, as you gave the spear to Keema, why it was you who was chosen to be representative of all the descendants; why you, whose connection to the Old Country was tenuous and variable at best—and, in some essential way, poisoned, considering your heritage. But perhaps now you understand that you are not a representative. That like the spear's journey through time, much of this dance is dictated by chance. You are merely, crucially, no one but yourself, as anyone else is themselves—mere stewards, gifting recursively over the divide of time this spear, that memory, to the people and the place from which they had come—and who, in turn, gift back to you your strange, and sad, and wide-eyed futures.

We knot this thread.

And only one thread remains.

After the great wave was felled,

after the people danced, and the halberds from the north fell upon their necks, and after Induun became the great and only and then the only and forgotten, and the people and their stories were stretched and pulled until they snapped and the seeds went flying, and after one seed took root in a dockside town by an ocean far away from the land from which it came, a merchant's child was pulled into a dream of the Inverted Theater and was told a tale that only few had the privilege to hear, and yet come the end, when but most of the threads of the tale were resolved, they were left unsatisfied.

This moonlit body stands on this broken stage and looks at you.

With all of the dancers, and the audience, it faces you.

You, alone.

Waiting for your answer.

You cough. Nervous. You insist that a part of you *is* satisfied—the part, at least, you share with your granjo, who would have appreciated the bullet-point list of family history that had just been served. But you are one made up of many. And though one yearning was addressed, another stands sprouting from your concrete.

"I thought this was a love story," you say.

Your lola's insistence has remained with you since the beginning, and you say these words in a quiet manner, with a shrug, as if to let these performers know it is fine, it does not matter that much, this thought—that maybe the definition of what a love story is could be stretched to include all that has up till now taken place. You say it like an apology. Like it is a thing to be apologized for. A runaway child, charging through the porcelain shelves: I thought this was a love story. I had hoped this was a love story. You say it with shame, embarrassed at having said it, wishing you could take it back. You say it, worried that you have betrayed some secret part of yourself that does not wish to be exposed—an old gremlin in you, sick and yearning.

You say it with hope. Timid and without conviction. The hope of someone who knows they are about to wake from a dream to a reality they do not understand. The pub awaits, as does your empty bed.

I thought this was a love story.

You regret having said it; as if you know it will lessen the quality of the tale. Rob it, of its smoke and shadow.

But still, you say it.

And this moonlit body smiles. And from the wings the patting of the drums slowly builds, and the curtains behind the dancers rise. Because you are right, this moonlit body tells you; this is indeed a love story. Down to the blade-dented bone. And this body asks its parent the Water if there is a chance—if in the deepness of its waves there remains a mercy to be extracted, and somewhere your lola lights a cigarette in your honor, breathing deep the smoke, lungs like hot-air balloons lifted into an overcast sky, as the drums build, and build,

and sound to you like rain.

It was the fourteenth day of water. Two weeks since the fall of the wave. A fortnight since the people had seen the sky behind the sheet of gray clouds that now hung over them. Water as fresh as the emperor's own supply rat-a-tatted on wooden eaves and the bottoms of buckets. Cupped hands reached out open windows. Dogs drank from dark puddles. For the first time in so many years, no one in the land went thirsty.

There were many homes that were collapsing under the weight of the water, homes whose roofs had not been built to take into account anything that might fall from the sky. Brooms and buckets shooed the flooding out the door. A child laughed and screamed as their wooden figurine went sailing into the village square on a runaway stream, while behind them their parents and their neighbors held up a falling beam that threatened to take down the whole front of the building.

One of the men, while holding the weight of this heavy timber, opened his mouth and drank deep the water from the sky.

It was on the noontide hour of the fourteenth day when Shan heard it. She was sitting in an open-walled salon, observing the curtain of rain as her thumb ran over the grooves and sharp edge of her parents' spear. Generals and Family Men were sitting behind her, speaking of matters of security, of the faction in the Bowl that would need to be dealt with, and of other issues of state. Shan was meant to pay attention, but her mind was far away, present only to the whisper of cloth on wood as she polished the spear and lost herself in the silken texture of the work. The coolness from the rain from the open wall breathed on her cheek in a pleasing fashion. And that was when she felt it: the spear, like a dowsing rod, pointing west.

She stood up.

"First Protector!" one of the men shouted. "Where are you going?" as the door shut behind her.

An attendant hurried after her, popping open an umbrella large enough for the both of them. Shan did not thank the attendant, but neither did she push her away, and the attendant asked no questions about their destination, even though they walked for long enough that the umbrella was all but useless by the time they arrived—the spear taking them into the heart of a copse, where amongst the trees there was a clearing, and in that clearing were the curled-up bodies of the warriors who had saved the country.

"Are they dead?" the attendant asked.

Shan felt Keema's breath on her hand. She sighed, looking at these two bodies, wondering how she would carry them.

"I should have brought more men."

For two weeks, they were gone.

When the wave was cut, and the Water collapsed into them, the conscious forms that were Keema and Jun were taken into the heart of the Water, the way a curl of smoke might be breathed into a nostril. They were taken to a place beyond awareness, or pain. They were, for a time, the Water itself. And then, they were returned. It was during the long rains that the Water, upon this moonlit body's request, gave back to them their bodies. Their flesh made whole again in the quiet and verdant spring of that gathering of trees, where like two creatures of the wood they slept on moss and grass and leaves, unbothered and unaware, and unwaking, until on the last day of the rains, they were found.

They were carried away.

When Keema woke, it was in a room he did not recognize, in a body that felt alien to him, with a girl whose name he did not know sitting by his mattress, crushing herbs into a poultice. When the girl saw that his eyes were open, she stood up without a word and left the room. His throat was too strained to call after her. It was upon sitting up that he noticed it; the change.

He held up his hand and waved his fingers in the air.

The sensations dull and vague.

The god gift was gone. Where before he could feel the minute currents, the throbbing of life from objects once thought inanimate—where each breath was an intoxication of life and flavor, and light was a blinding radiance—and the marks of the other worlds were made visible to the mortal eye, now there was nothing. No vision of the divine. Just the scrape of the wood of the door as it slid open and the daughter of Araya stepped inside. Keema was at once relieved that he was not bombarded by her thoughts, her inner self, and grieved the loss of that once-overwhelming connection.

"I should be dead," he said to her.

"It would seem the world has other plans for you." She shut the door behind her and sat beside him. She told him how long he had been gone, and where she had found him. "I am relieved that you have returned to us. I had never thanked you properly for what you had done—we were parted too soon by the chaos of that day." A flash in Keema's mind—a wolf's head breaking through a wall— gone in his own thoughts for long enough that he was startled when he realized Shan was bowing to him, her head brought low to the floor. "Thank you for saving us, Keema."

Flattered, uncomfortable, he waited for her to rise before he asked her of his friend.

"The Peacock is fine," she said with reservation. "I've already spoken with him."

Relief flowed through his veins like cold water, a heavy breath exhaled; but something in the tone of her voice did not allow him to relax completely. He may have only just come back from the dead, but even he could pick up on the troubled waters beneath the calm surface.

"Where is he?" he asked.

He tried to get up, but her hand suggested he stay put.

"Please, Keema," she said, sounding very tired. "Please, sit back down."

He did. He sat very still, like a small animal on edge, and waited for her to explain herself. Her brow pinched. She was staring at his left arm, or rather the lack of it. The knot of skin that signaled the end of his shoulder. "I had heard report that the two of you were crushed under that wave. But when I found you in that copse of trees, you were whole and hale, and I knew then that you had been . . . saved . . . as if restitched into the fabric of our world by powers beyond my ken." She tilted her head. "Except for that arm. And now I cannot help but wonder why you were not remade whole again."

"I am whole," he said flatly. "Why am I being kept here?"

She bowed her head. "I apologize for the offense. Truly. And you are being kept here because of the necessities of this strange situation. For information. You and the Peacock are in the unique position of being able to fill certain gaps in our knowledge of the happenings of the week of His Holy Pilgrimage. And so I would just ask that you share with me your tale, of how you had come to be in possession of my mother's spear, and everything in between then and this moment. A more complete picture of events would go a long way in helping me deal with the mess left in the week's wake."

"Have you asked this of Jun already?"

She nodded. "He told me a tale that beggars belief, and as I am sure you can understand, because of who he is I cannot take his word at face value. I need your story so that I can hold it against his and sort the truth from the fantasy."

"Is he safe?"

"Yes," she said, the words *for now* left unspoken. She held up a hand, gesturing for him to start. "If you would."

He did.

It took time. He was given food and water. Shan even brewed tea, crushing sweet herbs the way her mother did—a technique described in one of her many letters to her. When he described the attack on Tiger Gate, and Araya's sacrifice, Shan looked into her cup, not speaking, and only sometimes throughout his tale did she ask a few clarifying questions. Yes, her mother was betrayed by one of her own sentries. No, he was not sure if the dream was real—if Araya yet walked the Last Road. There were no windows in that room; by the end, after he had described the enveloping of the wave, he did not know how much time had passed, or when in the day it was, only that he was exhausted. "I assume," he said, "that that is much how Jun described things to you."

Shan stood up and, after telling him that she would be back shortly, she left the room. When he heard a click, he got up and gripped the wooden latch, but as he suspected, the door wouldn't give. He cursed and he kicked it, feeling as though he had just been tricked. All he could think to do was sit back down and wait, to see what direction his life was about to take.

It was about an hour later when Shan finally returned, as promised. When the door opened, he restrained himself from rushing at her in attack.

"Explain yourself quickly, daughter of Araya," he said.

"My second apology, for locking this door," she said, her face drawn. "I only did so at his request."

"Whose?"

"The Peacock named Jun Ossa," she said. "The favored son of the high prince and First Terror, and whose family is guilty of more misdeeds than there is script to record them. It was he who asked me to lock the door. It was only after much cajoling that I was given permission from him to tell you why." Keema, with narrowed eyes, offered her time to elaborate; *but not much,* his dark expression said. She nodded. "You both have done our people a great service. Without you, there would be no people. But the fact of the Peacock's identity remains, and as we move into this new era, freed from the Moon Throne and its influence, he and I agree that it is best that he, in essence, disappear."

More unspoken words: *without you.*

"Where is he?" he asked quietly.

"He is free," she said. "Given a new mask to cover the tattoo on his face, and a bag of supplies to last him a few weeks on the road, to wherever he might choose to go."

Keema's head swam. "I don't understand. Why did he not— why would . . ."

And here, Shan's neutral expression broke into something close to sympathy, for she saw the hurt in this young man's face. She knew this hurt; this rejection. Ever was she too old for her age. "It was a kindness, I think," she suggested. "That was his intention, anyway. He is the last of the Red Peacocks. The enduring symbol of a rule the people, and the land, have come to hate, or will, in time. The road that lies ahead of him is likely a short one. A knife in the dark. A stone thrown from a window. Justice served for some ill he had acted out in the days of his bloodshed. A life that will always be unsettled. On the move. A life he told me that he deserves. When he woke, he knew there was a chance you would want to come with him on this journey, and, in his words, he had inflicted enough pain on the world, and would not add your name to his list."

She looked over at Keema, who was staring at his lap, slumped.

"He is right," she said, after some thought. "If the condition of your arm is any clue, your life has not been an easy one. Perhaps, if I may be bold in saying so, you've earned some reward, and rest."

"Is that why you locked the door? To give him time to leave?"

"Again, at his request, but yes."

He looked then at the door, still half-open, a dark corridor lying behind it. Shan followed his gaze.

"I suppose you have a choice then," she said softly. "You can go looking for him, though he has had quite the head start, and even if, on the off chance you do find him, he may not accept your company. And if he does accept your company, he may not accept your love." His eyes snapped up at her, and she shrugged, as if it were obvious. "And even if he accepts that love, for however long it lasts, the road you would endure would be a difficult one. It would be unsettled, you would always be moving, for he is right, you know—there are many people, and there are many things, that would take their revenge out on this surviving member of the royal family, just as they will the loyalists being dragged out of the Divine City." She sighed. "But if you stay, as he would like you to do, and as I would be honored if you did, then I can promise the wealth of—wait," she said, startled as he stood up and headed for the door, "I haven't even told you—" But she cut herself off, seeing that there was no point in describing the pride and glory that would be showered on him for the deeds he had accomplished. She had not smiled much in those two weeks. It was as relieving to feel on her face as was the coolness of the rain.

"You have made your choice then."

"Thank you for finding us," Keema said, bowing to her, "and for seeing us well again, Shan Araya. But if I would have hope of catching up to my friend, I need to leave now."

"Very well," she said, bowing her head. "Then I suppose there's no point in me not telling you that the last I saw of the Peacock was him leaving the main road, just beyond the gates, in a southwesterly direction." She slapped open the door. The guard in the corridor jumped, startled. "Give me your weapon," she said, and the guard hesitated before he handed Shan his spear—sturdy, but unremarkable—which she then gave to Keema, who was at first at a loss for words.

"Why are you doing this?" he asked.

She looked at him like he was mad.

"You are running out of time, Daware man."

Outside, the clouds broke.

After fourteen days, the skies finally cleared. Night flowed into this world as milk does into a bowl. The people Keema sprinted past were stunned into silence as they looked up and saw that the Burn was healed; a new Moon was stitched in its place in the black canvas sky. Over his shoulder he saw it. The new god of night, like a white, unripe berry hanging off the branch of the heavens, and quickly he paid his respects before continuing on his way, tracking the disturbed grass that he hoped marked the Peacock's path.

When Shan left the Family's temporary headquarters in the ruined Divine City, she stepped carefully into the glowing street, thinking for a moment that she had stumbled into some astral realm, a world elevated above her own, until five children sprinted past her, laughing, their steps slapping dirt into the air, and the guards at her side leaned on their heels as they gasped at the smooth and awesome radiance that hung above them like some perfect ear-ring. The world had weight again, and Shan knew this was real. This bone-white illumination, leaking perhaps from the place her mother and Induun and the nameless man from Joyrock had gone to—on that thread-tripped dream that comes after death. On those fleeting whitecaps. And like so many others that night, she felt as if she could float up from the ground; and her spirit did. It drifted up into the moonlight as Keema ran over hill and field in search of him.

That fool.

In the dark between the trees, upon the snapping of a twig, the masked traveler with the pack slung over his shoulder stopped.

He did not bother to turn around.

"I thought it best that I leave without seeing you again," he said, his voice muffled once more. And then, all he said after that was, "Are you sure?"

"Yes," Keema said. "I am sure."

The young man sniffed. He wiped his eyes beneath his mask before he turned to face Keema. The mask was pale white, and smooth, with dark slits for eyes that were bent in laughter. "Fine then," he said with a wet voice. His shoulders shaking. His voice trying valiantly not to break. "We head west. Is that all right? I have unfinished business, in a village in the Thousand."

He had promised a woman his neck.

"I expect we will make it there in a few days."

He intended to keep that promise.

When I saw the Peacock at my door, kneeling before me with his head offered to me, as I had dreamt he might, my hand did not hesitate—I reached for the knife in the drawer that had been waiting for him.

"I should have enough food for the both of us," Jun said.

"What business do you have there?" Keema asked. "In that village?"

Jun was quiet.

"I would rather not say."

He told me that I could do as I liked, how I liked. I told him I liked to see a Peacock dead. I looked down at my knife. I saw in the blade the oath I had sworn to those I had lost. I saw an end to all of my sleepless nights.

"You avoid my gaze," Keema said. He smiled, heartbroken. "Strange, is it not, that we have come back from the dead and you will not look at me."

Jun turned away from him.

"Why did you follow me?" he asked.

I told the Peacock to make his last prayer. Think of something lovely. And he shut his eyes as I held the knife to his throat and readied to open him. The hilt felt so right in my grip, it was like my hand had been built for just this purpose.

And then, I stopped.

When I saw that bead of blood bright red as berries, drawn from that boy's neck, I stopped the blade. The knife fell from my hands and clattered onto the floor, the moonlight bouncing off its metal. I couldn't do it.

Keema stepped toward his lost friend, and as he did, Jun leaned away, as if to step back, but he did not move. Keema reached up and touched the edge of Jun's mask and lifted it, revealing eyes that brimmed with tears.

Whatever nightmares used to haunt me, this young man kneeling before me was not that nightmare. I didn't know who he was. My hands shook as I turned away, and told him that I had a busy day.

"That's it?" he asked, almost disappointed.

That's it, I said.

I told him I was satisfied.

Keema touched Jun's cheek; the permanent, unfading red ink of his tattoo that the Sleeping Sea had not washed clean. And though Jun flinched from his touch, he did not move from it, and as he wept he asked Keema why they were returned. "I thought I had found it," he cried. "A good death. A death more glorious than I deserved. I do not understand. . . . Why am I still here? Why am I still ugly?" His voice was wracked, almost indecipherable. "What reward is this? What punishment?"

"I do not know if this is a reward," Keema said. "Or if it is a punishment. But maybe it is neither."

He pressed his forehead against Jun's.

The heat immense.

Alive.

"Maybe you are just here."

And here, they found each other.

In the dark forest drenched with rain, away from the torches and the drinking and the dancing of the people along the eastern coast. The agitated mind of the earth and sky now calmed. The voices quiet, out amongst the thickets and ancient trees, where the night bugs were the loudest, and where through the canopy above, sheets of moonlight fell on mossy rock and soft grass; in a slick bright glade, two bodies embraced.

The world was quiet.

They could no longer hear the Rhythm of the ground. The breathing of the trees now subdued to the point of sleep. The pulse of the rocks by their feet all but dead. Neither Keema nor Jun had to say it out loud, for they knew what had come to pass; the Water had taken Her away from them, and now they were themselves again. They would never feel the beat of another life so fully again, and their thoughts would remain their own. Never would one know what the other was thinking.

But where the Eighth Emperor or His sons might greet such a realization in terror, to have lost such control, such dominion, there was no fear, no anger in these warriors' hearts, for as they looked at each other in the full moonshine of that night, they saw that they did not need the power of a god to understand how deeply they were wanted.

Keema stepped toward Jun,

and touched him. His arm, his bony cheek, his lips, and Jun received that touch as he would the water from a waterfall, with eyes closed and face upturned. "You feel like the sun," Jun said. Their hands discovering on each other the scars of war like canyons and mountains, the rough terrain of battle and all the years of blood they had bathed in now slowly washed away in one of the few rains they had ever experienced in their lives. They drank deep this kiss.

"Why are you laughing?" Keema asked, amused by Jun's sudden giggling.

His friend shook his head. "I remembered that there is a theater, somewhere in the lands of the Sleeping Sea, acting out our story." He rested his head on Keema's shoulder; kissed the warm skin there. "Do you think they can see us now? Are they performing this moment onstage?"

"I do not know," Keema said in a distant way, his arm locking around Jun's waist. "Would you stop, if they were?"

"No," Jun said firmly. "They have already seen my life. They have seen my most shameful moments." The pained look in his eyes quickly faded as he gazed into Keema's. "Why would I deny them one of my most beautiful?"

He grabbed Keema's hand and led him deeper into the dark.

They approached it in steps.

The passion was ordered. They did not want to miss an opportunity for delight or surprise. The warmth of a mouth on a finger, a tongue flicking across a toe. Whatever experience Jun had with the act, he was still novitiate, for it was the first time he had ever really felt it before, holding Keema as one would a sacred sight in a disappearing dream. But Keema would not disappear. He was as solid and warm and real as he himself was. And he licked the crook of his arm and the small brown nipple and the hollow of the belly as he felt Keema's foot work him down below and he tasted the salt of Keema and they shared that taste with a kiss and drew blood from someone's lip, whose lip it did not matter, for they both in that moment felt the pain and the pleasure and the fleet taste of iron on the tongue.

There were moments of cold.

When Jun touched the tattoo on his face that would never go away, and which would forever mark him an outsider. Tears beading along the rain on his cheeks as he tried to scrub it off his skin, before Keema gripped his wrist and pulled his hand away, and gently licked the red-roughed skin of his cheeks and his brow.

There was a time of rest.

Keema sat in watchful guard of the night that surrounded them. As Jun slept, Keema sat on his perch, with his spear, and he watched the bending trees and the swaying vines and the sharp eyes that lit up the dark brush. And when he heard a growl, he slowly approached the curtain of vines that separated them from the uncertain night, and to whomever, or whatever, lurked there, he said: "My name is Keema, the guardian of that sleeping warrior. And tonight you will not have him."

A wind rising about his ears—believing for a moment he heard it whisper,

One day, we will.

When he returned to Jun, who was then awake, and wide-eyed, he told him that it was nothing but a small animal with teeth too small to break skin. He lay beside Jun and placed a hand over his chest and felt through the hot skin the frightened pace of his heart.

"I may never sleep again," he said.

To which Keema replied, "Then neither will I."

Jun looked at him.

Into those eyes he did not understand. Keema's eyes as flecked with color and mystery as his thoughts. How long would this person stay with him? How long could he stand the life of a nomad? Would the day come when even Keema would turn him over to those who would hurt him? If there was an answer to these questions, Keema's eyes would not give it up. And as he leaned in to kiss him, Jun wondered if this was why the emperor had everyone wear masks at court. If, for fearful men, it was too much, this life.

And on it went.

A night in the woods, witness to no one but the small monkeys in the trees that hugged their branches and observed with their moonlit eyes the movements of two creatures briefly inhabiting each other. That was what it felt like, becoming someone else, as Jun straddled him, and sat, and Keema entered him with widened eyes, swallowing the rainwater in his mouth and trying not to finish immediately, while for Jun the moment was the edge of pain, it was the grit of teeth and a wince, but pain did not dissuade; pain was a part of it too; it was the offering to the night; to the man he chose to give himself to. Their eyes locked in this ceaseless rhythm as they smiled and dared each other to look away.

They did not.

Every last ounce of energy spent, for they did not stop to rest, even after spending themselves, the moments burned through as quick as your lola's cigarettes. They continued their dance. To rustle into each other. To chase and tackle each other into the brush and start all over again, with renewed fervor, as if to wipe the ink of their bodies from the scroll of history. To evaporate, until the body was ready to join where the spirit already was.

High up.

Above the trees. Where the stars dance and fall like failed incantations.

That is where we end our tale.

With the dancers leaping over the fire.

And this moonlit body, bowing to you in thanks.

You acknowledge the ones who have brought you this far.

You begin with a toast to your pre-pub readers: Erin Jones, Oscar Mancinas, and Doug Koziol. You understand how privileged you are, to enjoy the benefit of their insights, each of them phenomenal writers in their own right, and even better friends. And you would be remiss not to mention that Oscar and Erin have books of their own out right now. You recommend for everyone to look up their work, specifically *To Live and Die in El Valle* and *Tinfoil Crowns*. Both are distinctly terrific.

Next, you thank everyone who supported you on the publishing side of this arrangement. Your agent, Hannah Fergesen, who continues to be best-in-class. Simon Padres for his gorgeous cover artwork, and Chris Panatier, for his stunning dream map of the Old Country (you were indeed spoiled with great artists on this project). Tricia Narwani and David Stevenson and the rest of the team at Del Rey for their countless generosities, along with a special shout-out to your editor, Sarah Peed, who worked with you on this project since pretty much the beginning. Her supernatural patience and sharply observed critiques were bright beacons in a dark time. It is safe to say that without her, there would be no book.

And then, as always, there is your family (and some good friends too). Your arms wrap around them, and you, not wishing to make any of them feel less important than the others, look to them all in alphabetical order: Clarissa, Dad, Emma, Farrah, Ferdinand, Garth, Jason, Kane, Matt, Mom, Nicholas, Quinn, Red, Sara, and Sebastian. And with them in your heart, you remember that, yes, it was all worth it. Every day of it. Today, tomorrow, or the next— your answer is the same.

You would do it all again.

ABOUT THE AUTHOR

—

SIMON JIMENEZ is the author of *The Vanished Birds*. This is his second novel.

ABOUT THE TYPE

———

This book was set in Sabon, a typeface designed by the well-known German typographer Jan Tschichold (1902–74). Sabon's design is based upon the original letter forms of sixteenth-century French type designer Claude Garamond and was created specifically to be used for three sources: foundry type for hand composition, Linotype, and Monotype. Tschichold named his typeface for the famous Frankfurt typefounder Jacques Sabon (c. 1520–80).

CAMPAIGNS
OF THE
CIVIL WAR

CAMPAIGNS
OF THE
CIVIL WAR

WALTER GEER

KONECKY&KONECKY

Konecky & Konecky
72 Ayers Point Rd.
Old Saybrook, CT 06475

ISBN: 1-56852-268-1

Printed and bound in the USA

FOREWORD

IT has been said that Fortune always favors the heaviest battalions, or, as Napoleon put it, that "Providence is always on the side of the last reserve." Military history shows no real exceptions to this axiom, that wars are won by superior strength — by weight of numbers, if the numbers are properly trained and supplied.

The North began the Civil War with all the advantages but two. Her white population outnumbered that of the South by four to one. She had the greater wealth, all the larger industries, the mineral fields, the shipbuilding yards, and all the navy there was. She had all the rank and file of the regular army and two-thirds of the officers.

On the other hand, the South had two advantages which nearly gave her the victory. She was much better fitted for military organization than the North: the great majority of her citizens were country people who could ride and march and shoot; and she had on her side by far the abler generals. The North produced some competent generals in the end — Grant, Sherman, Sheridan, Thomas, not to mention McClellan, Buell, and Rosecrans, who fell by the way. But the South had, in Lee and Stonewall Jackson, generals who have had few superiors in the art of war. If Jackson had been at the side of Lee at Gettysburg, the South would probably have won her independence. And Lee ranks with Alexander, Hannibal, Cæsar, Frederick, and Napoleon, as one of the six greatest captains of all the ages. It detracts nothing from his glory, that he, like Napoleon, finally fell under the accumulated weight of numbers.

Notwithstanding all of her many great advantages, however, the North was confronted by a serious problem. A hundred years before the outbreak of the Civil War, Chatham had said in the British Parliament: "Conquer a free population of three million souls? The thing is impossible!" This phrase has become an axiom in politics. The North faced the task of subduing five and a half million people in deadly earnest, with three and a half million slaves behind them to do the manual labor, while the whole adult white male population took the field. Was victory possible under these circumstances?

It is a popular fallacy that the Great War, which ended nearly a decade ago, superseded, so far as military interest goes, not only Napoleon's campaigns, but our own Civil War. This is not true. Marshal Foch put in practice the main principles that underlay the campaigns of Napoleon; and in the Civil War all the principal strategic and tactical developments of the Great War were foreshadowed: a half a century earlier, America had faced most of its problems and brilliantly solved them. While German staff officers have regarded the Civil War as a mere squabble of amateurs, the British Staff College, for two generations, has made a careful study of the battles of North and South, and the French General Staff has recently (1925) added the history of the American Civil War to the list of subjects studied at the École de Guerre. It is interesting to note, to what an extent technical matters in the earlier contest anticipated the later. In the combats of the Wilderness, the whole technique of trench warfare was foreshadowed; cavalry, for the first time, was used as mounted infantry; many of the modern weapons of war were originated; and the minor tactics on both sides were curiously like those of to-day.

The Civil War will always possess a fascination to the student of history, if for no other reason, because of the two great leaders it produced: Lee on the one side, and Lincoln on the other. To Lee can well be applied the epitaph of Bossuet on Turenne: "He could fight without anger, win without ambition, and triumph without vanity." Lincoln has already passed into legend, and no words can enhance his grandeur: he was one of the two or three greatest men ever born of Anglo-Saxon blood.

The Biblical saying, "Of making many books there is no end," well applies to works relating to the Civil War. There are histories, biographies, and memoirs, too numerous to mention. A list compiled in 1866 gives over six thousand titles, and this has been enormously increased in the sixty years which have elapsed since the close of the war. "Yet," says Major Steele, in his recent book, *American Campaigns,* — "yet, there is no single work that covers the whole war concisely and in a way to satisfy the military student."

It may seem presumptuous on the part of a civilian to undertake this task, but the writer is emboldened by the words of Arnold, in his *Lectures on Modern History,* where he says: "There must be a point up to which an unprofessional judgment on a professional subject may not only be competent, but of high authority.... . The distinction seems to lie originally in the difference between the power of doing a thing and that of perceiving whether it is well done or not.... . As to what is generally called strategy, ... an unprofessional person may, without blame, speak or write on military subjects, and may judge of them sufficiently."

The object of the present book is to give a concise military narrative of the principal campaigns of the Civil War. A discussion of the political differences which brought on the great conflict lies entirely outside the scope of this work.

WALTER GEER

TABLE OF CONTENTS

MAPS

CAMPAIGNS
OF THE
CIVIL WAR

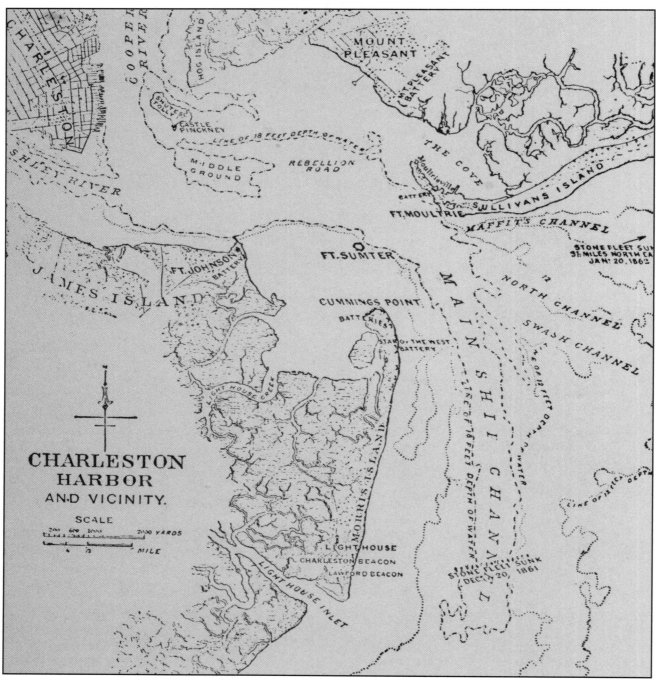

Charleston Harbor

CHAPTER ONE

1861

FORT SUMTER

DURING the first seventy years of the life of this Republic, from the adoption of the Constitution in 1789 to the outbreak of the Civil War in 1861, the control of the Government was almost continuously in the hands of the South. Of the first fifteen Presidents, eight were from that section of the country, and five of these Southern Presidents served for eight years apiece, while not one of the Northern Presidents was reelected. Moreover, throughout nearly all this period, the Southerners, with the help of their Northern allies, controlled one or both Houses of the Federal Congress; and the major part of the Justices of the Supreme Court of the United States were Southerners in every year of its existence. But, in 1860, there was a split in the Democratic party, which had so long dominated the three branches of the Government, and the newly-formed Republican party was victorious at the polls. On the 6 November 1860, Abraham Lincoln was elected President of the United States.

With the exception of some ballots cast for him in the western part of Virginia — now the State of West Virginia — Lincoln received no votes in the slave States. The great majority of the people of the South sincerely felt that they were in danger of persecution and disaster; that the North wished to ruin them. If the Southerners submitted tamely to Lincoln's election, they must expect to see slavery abolished from Delaware to Texas: only independence could save them. It was then that the Southern leaders finally determined to leave the Union.

Since the founding of the government there had been a difference of opinion between the North and the South on the question of the constitutional position of the States within the Union. In the North, it was generally held that the Union was sovereign and the States part of it. In the South, the consensus of public opinion was just the opposite. Every man felt that his first allegiance was to his native State: to her, he owed not merely devotion, but life itself.

From the date of Mr. Lincoln's election, the intention of the people of South Carolina to secede from the Union was clearly shown, and on the 20 December the State formally took this action. The convention which passed the ordinance of secession at once appointed three commissioners, to proceed to Washington to treat with the United States Government for the delivery of the forts, arsenals, and other property of the Government within the limits of South Carolina.

It is impossible to imagine what reception these commissioners would have met at Washington, provided there had been no change in the situation at Charleston prior to their arrival at the capital. But on reaching Washington on the morning of the 27 December, they were confronted by a despatch from Charleston announcing that Major Anderson had transferred his command from Fort Moultrie to Fort Sumter.

Anderson, with two small companies, in all about one hundred officers and men, had been stationed at Fort Moultrie, on the north side of the harbor of Charleston. The two other forts, Castle Pinckney, a small work near the city, and Fort Sumter, erected on a ledge in the middle of the harbor, were not garrisoned. A captain of engineers, Foster, was engaged in putting the latter fort in order for occupancy. Moultrie was commanded by sand hills at a distance of only 160 yards, and was untenable. On the other hand, Sumter was in the middle of the entrance to the harbor, more than a mile from Fort Moultrie on the north, and two-thirds of a mile from Cumming's Point on the south.

Early in December, Major Buell had been sent from Washington to Major Anderson, with verbal instructions, which were afterwards reduced to writing. Anderson was ordered to avoid any act which would tend to provoke aggression, but to hold the forts in the harbor,

The Confederate Flag floating over Fort Sumter on April 16, 1861.

and, if attacked, to defend himself to the last extremity. On account of the smallness of his force, he was authorized to transfer his command, in case of any act of hostility, to the fort most capable of resistance. He was also authorized to take similar steps whenever he had "tangible evidence of a design to proceed to a hostile act."

This "design," Anderson thought that he had discovered, and on the evening of the 26 December, with great skill and address, he transferred his command to Fort Sumter. There can be little question of the fact that he acted entirely within his orders, under the belief that the emergency had arisen which made it his duty to transfer his command to Sumter.

That the authorities of South Carolina had not then any intention of attacking or seizing the forts seems to be proved by the presence in Washington of the commissioners sent to treat with the Government for their surrender. The commissioners were much excited on receipt of this news. After an interview with Mr. Floyd, the Secretary of War, who assured them that Anderson had violated the understanding given to the South Carolina representatives, they made an attack on the President, charging that the faith of the Government had been forfeited by Anderson's conduct. They further insisted that the President should immediately order the evacuation of Charleston Harbor by the United States forces. After a very acrimonious correspondence with the President, the commissioners returned to Charleston at the beginning of January.

As soon as Anderson's removal to Fort Sumter became known, Governor Pickens seized Castle Pinckney and Fort Moultrie. He then proceeded to repair the damage which Anderson had done to Moultrie on evacuating it, and to put it in condition for use against Fort Sumter, should it become necessary. He also took possession of the arsenal in Charleston, and ordered the construction of batteries on Morris Island and Cumming's Point, so as to command the entrance of the harbor, and prevent reinforcements or provisions being sent to Fort Sumter by the Government. These steps were most certainly acts of war, and in fact were so regarded at the time by every one.

When the news of these proceedings reached Washington, President Buchanan decided to reinforce Sumter at once. An unarmed steamer, the Star of the West, was chartered by the Government, and despatched to Charleston. When this vessel arrived at the entrance of the harbor, on the 9 January, it was fired on by the battery on Morris Island, and forced to retire without having reached Fort Sumter. The ship was hit twice, but no one was hurt. Anderson wrote Pickens that, unless this act were promptly disclaimed, he should treat it as an act of war, and the Governor replied the same day, assuming entire responsibility. Pickens stated further that he regarded the retention of Sumter by the United States forces as "an act of positive hostility." In order to clear up the situation, Anderson informed Pickens that he intended to send an officer to Washington for further instructions. No objections were raised, and Lieutenant Talbot left the same evening.

On the 11 January, Pickens sent a formal demand, under a flag of truce, for the surrender of the fort. Anderson refused, but at the same time proposed to send another officer to Washington, accompanied by an envoy to be named by the Governor, to refer the matter to the President. Pickens assented, and appointed Mr. Hayne, the Attorney-General of the

State. Anderson detailed Lieutenant Hall, and these envoys arrived in Washington on the 13 January.

In the meantime, a letter had been received at Washington from Anderson, stating that he had provisions sufficient to last him beyond the 4 March, and could hold the fort against any force which could be brought against him. The administration of Mr. Buchanan therefore allowed matters to drift until the end of its term of office. For this anomalous situation, Anderson himself was in part responsible. His position is stated in a letter written just before the attack on the fort in April: "Had I demanded reinforcements while Mr. Holt was in the War Department, I know that he would have despatched them at all hazards. I did not ask them, because I knew that, the moment it should be known here that additional troops were coming, they would assault me, and thus inaugurate civil war. My policy ... was to keep still, to preserve peace, to give time for the quieting of the excitement, ... in the hope of avoiding bloodshed."

While these events were taking place at Charleston, the other Cotton and Gulf States were not idle. In January, Georgia, Florida, Alabama, Mississippi and Louisiana seceded from the Union, and were followed by Texas on the first day of February. On the 8 February, the seven seceding States organized at Montgomery, Alabama, the Confederate States of America. A month later, they adopted a constitution very similar to that of the United States. Jefferson Davis, of Mississippi, was elected President, and Alexander H. Stephens, of Georgia, Vice-President of the new Confederacy. Both were able men, of large experience in public affairs.

In view of the critical situation of affairs, Mr. Hayne was advised, on reaching Washington, to postpone his demand for the surrender of Fort Sumter until the end of January. Then, after some exchange of letters, the Administration refused the demand, and Hayne left Washington on the 8 February. Before his departure, he telegraphed Governor Pickens the result of his mission, and the same day orders were issued for making the necessary preparations to bombard Fort Sumter. But this action was prevented for the moment by a resolution passed on the 12th by the Confederate Congress, giving the new Government charge of all questions between the several States and the United States Government. Under these circumstances the authorities of South Carolina reluctantly yielded the control of all military operations in Charleston Harbor to the new Confederate Government. Mr. Davis wrote Governor Pickens that he would send an engineer of "military skill" to take charge, and later advised him that General Beauregard had been selected for the position. That officer arrived at Charleston on the 3 March. The next day Abraham Lincoln was inaugurated President of the United States: the opportunity of taking Fort Sumter during Mr. Buchanan's administration had passed away.

The policy of the new President was plainly declared in his Inaugural Address. "To the extent of my ability," he said, "I shall take care ... that the laws of the Union be faithfully executed in all the States." And he closed with the words: "In your hands, my dissatisfied fellow-countrymen, and not in mine, is the momentous issue of civil war. The Government will not assail you. You can have no conflict without being yourselves the aggressors."

Few men in America, if any, have been the equals of Lincoln in political sagacity, and the calm, serious tone of warning which pervades the whole address shows the characteristic political ability of its author.

One of the first questions considered by the Cabinet of President Lincoln was the problem of Fort Sumter. On the 29 March, a decision was finally reached, and Governor Pickens was officially informed, on the 8 April, that "an attempt will be made to supply Fort Sumter with provisions only; and if such attempt be not resisted, no effort to throw in men, arms or ammunition will be made without further notice."

Major Robert Anderson with family

This message again shows the political sagacity of Mr. Lincoln. He unquestionably expected that resistance would be made, and he knew that nothing would more certainly arouse the national feeling of the North than an attack made upon Anderson and his little force.

On the 11 April, General Beauregard sent to Major Anderson a formal demand for the surrender of Fort Sumter, which was at once refused. At half-past four on the morning of the 12 April 1861 the Confederate batteries opened fire, and the bombardment continued without cessation until the next afternoon. An ineffective reply was made by the guns of the fort, until the supply of cartridges gave out. After gallantly defending the post for two days, Anderson accepted the honorable terms of surrender which were offered. On Sunday, the 14th, after saluting his flag with fifty guns, Major Anderson, with his command, was conveyed to the fleet waiting outside the bar, and sailed for New York.

It is remarkable how little we know of the inner thoughts of the great men of the world, and how different their actions often seem to their contemporaries and to historians half a century later. It is very difficult, at this point of time, to understand the mode of reasoning of the Southern leaders in deciding to force the issue of civil war. "A few men more or less at Sumter," writes Professor Channing, "and food for another month or so, would make little difference in the ultimate course of events. But aggressive action on the part of the Confederates would at once bring on the crisis that true policy forbade." The order to open fire on the fort was given, notwithstanding the fact that Anderson had told the Confederate officers who were sent to demand his surrender that he could not hold out for two days if he were not supplied with food. One is amazed today at the lack of political vision shown by the Southern leaders. They little expected the explosion that was to follow!

The President's demand for troops, to enforce the laws, met with a prompt and angry refusal from the Border States. Virginia, Arkansas, Tennessee, and North Carolina promptly passed ordinances of secession, and joined the new Confederacy. Three other States — Maryland, Kentucky, and Missouri — were only kept in the Union by the power of the United States Government, and these States furnished many men to the Confederate armies.

Richmond, the capital of the Confederacy, was situated less than a hundred miles south of Washington; this necessarily made Virginia the seat of the war in the East.

Thus the lines were finally drawn. Twenty-two States remained united; opposed to them stood the eleven States which had seceded, and now constituted the Confederate States of America. After the people of Virginia ratified the ordinance of secession, on the 23 May the seat of the Confederate Government was transferred from Montgomery to Richmond, which continued to be the capital until the end of the war.

On land the theatre of the Civil War was bounded on the north by the Potomac, Ohio, and Missouri rivers; on the east and south, by the coasts of the Atlantic and the Gulf of Mexico; on the west, by the frontiers of Missouri, Arkansas, and Texas. With the exceptions of the battles of Antietam and Gettysburg, which were fought a short distance north of the Potomac, all the principal military operations took place within the limits mentioned.

The terrain thus bounded — approximately one million square miles — was widely diversified in its characteristics. The parallel ranges of the Appalachians, running from northeast to southwest, divided the region between the coast and the Mississippi into two nearly equal parts. Within this area was comprised every variety of country — mountains, prairies, forests, swamps. The armies were forced to cope with every possible physical obstacle.

The frontiers of the Confederacy were far apart. The coast washed by the Gulf of Mexico is 800 miles south of the Potomac; the Rio Grande, the river boundary of Texas, is 1700 miles west of Charleston on the Atlantic. Across this vast expanse of territory then ran but six continuous lines of railway.

1. Richmond, Wilmington, Charleston, Savannah — connecting the Confederate capital with the ports on the Atlantic.
2. Richmond, Lynchburg, Chattanooga, Memphis, New Orleans; and
3. Richmond, Greensboro, Columbia, Atlanta, Pensacola — connecting Richmond with the Mississippi and the Gulf.
4. Louisville, Nashville, Chattanooga, Atlanta, Mobile;
5. Cairo, Corinth, Mobile; and
6. Cairo, Memphis, New Orleans — connecting the Ohio with the Gulf of Mexico.

The railroads of the South were not only few in number, but they were also badly laid out for the strategic demands of the war. The lines were short, and were broken at frequent intervals because of the refusal of important cities to let them pass through. Between Richmond and Savannah, there were half a dozen changes: the most serious break was at Petersburg, where the line from Richmond stopped at the western edge, and the road to Wilmington began at the southern limit. Some of the gaps were filled during the war, but not in time to do much good. As it was impossible to manufacture new rails, those which gave out were replaced by rails taken from less important routes of traffic. It was the same with the rolling stock: in 1864, the Quarter Master General stated that a train could not run more than one hundred miles a day on the main line from Richmond to Georgia, and that a car could not go five hundred miles without breaking down.

On the other hand, the North in 1861 was over-supplied with railroads, and many of them were on the verge of bankruptcy. The owners were glad to place them at the disposal of the Government, and the military engineers rebuilt them as fast as they came under Federal control. The soldiers acquired so much skill in making repairs that by 1864 it was an almost futile operation for the Confederates to break a railroad line. As a striking example of the efficiency with which the Northern lines were handled, we may mention the transfer in three weeks' time of Schofield's Army of the Ohio, thirty thousand strong, from Tennessee to the coast of North Carolina, after the battle of Nashville in December 1864.

The wagon-roads in the Southern States were few and poor — there were no paved highways such as connect the principal places in Europe; but there were numerous navigable streams. Towns were few and far between; food and forage were not easily obtainable; the great rivers were bridged at rare intervals. Except over a comparatively small area, the Union armies met the same obstacles as did the soldiers of Cromwell and Turenne.

The city of Atlanta, the heart of the Confederacy, was sixty days' march from the Potomac, the same distance as Vienna from the Channel, or Moscow from the Niemen. New Orleans was thirty-six days' march from the Ohio, the same distance as Berlin from the Moselle. "Had Napoleon in the campaign against Russia remained for the winter at Smolensk, and firmly established himself in Poland," writes Colonel Henderson, "Moscow might have been captured and held during the ensuing summer. But the occupation of Moscow would not have ended the war. Russia in many respects was not unlike the Confederacy. She had given no hostages to fortune in the shape of rich commercial towns; she possessed no historic fortresses, and so offered but few objectives to the invader. If defeated or retreating, her armies could always find refuge in distant fastnesses. The climate was severe; the internal trade inconsiderable; to bring the burden of war home to the mass of the population was difficult, and to hold the country by force impracticable. Such were the difficulties which the genius of Napoleon was powerless to overcome, and Napoleon invaded Russia with half a million of seasoned soldiers."

The conquest of the eleven seceding States which the Federal Government was about to undertake with an army of 75,000 volunteers, and without the least preparation, was in truth a gigantic undertaking. Without a trained staff and an efficient administration, an army is incapable of movement. It is no small task to keep a marching column supplied with food and forage; and the problem of transport taxes the ability of the most experienced commander. A march of a hundred miles into an enemy's country seems like an easy feat, but unless every detail has been carefully thought out, it may be more disastrous than a lost battle. During the first five weeks of the Russian campaign, between the Niemen and Vilna, a distance of only sixty miles, Napoleon lost one-third of his army from disease. "To handle an army in battle is much less difficult than to bring it on to the field in good condition."

Richmond, the capital of the Confederacy, was situated less than a hundred miles south of Washington: this necessarily made Virginia the seat of the war in the East. The South undoubtedly made a mistake in placing her capital so near the frontier; Chattanooga or Atlanta would have been a better choice. But the Union capital was actually on the boundary, line; batteries on Arlington Heights would render Washington untenable. The capture of either of the capitals might have momentous consequences, and prove decisive of the contest. These facts had a controlling influence on the general strategy of the Civil War. The objects aimed at by the opposing armies in Virginia were:

1. the protection of their own capital;
2. the capture of the enemy's capital; and
3. the defeat of the opposing army.

The approaches to the National capital were blocked only by the Potomac River; and the entrenched line on the south bank, opposite the city, could easily be turned by marching down the Shenandoah Valley. This avenue for the invasion of the North ran from about the centre of Virginia in a northeasterly direction to Harper's Ferry, where the Potomac was easily passable. Throughout all this distance, it was feasible, by guarding the mountain passes, or "gaps," as they were generally called, to prevent interference by the Federal forces. The Valley was fertile, and possessed good turnpikes. From Lexington, at its head, to the Potomac, the Valley was 140 miles long, by about 24 miles wide. Its chief town, and strategic centre, was Winchester, about twenty-six miles southwest of Harper's Ferry. From Winchester, two highways lead westward by Romney and Moorefield; four lead east and southeast, passing the Blue Ridge by Snicker's, Ashby's, Manassas, and Chester gaps. Through Manassas Gap ran the railroad connecting Front Royal in the Valley with Richmond via Manassas Junction. The Baltimore and Ohio Railroad, the main connection between Washington and the West, crossed the Potomac at Harper's Ferry, and followed the course of the river for a distance of 120 miles within the confines of Virginia.

On the other hand, the Shenandoah Valley offered no special advantages as a route for the Federal invader. It led away from Richmond, and the Union forces were liable to be taken in

Fort Sumter on April 16, 1861 with South Carolina troops drilling on the parade after forcing out Anderson.

Map of Virginia

flank, or to have their line of communication cut, by way of the lower gaps. It would there-fore be no easy matter to debouch from the Valley and occupy Gordonsville, the key to the railway system of central Virginia.

The population of the twenty-two States which adhered to the Union was over twenty-two millions; that of the eleven seceding States was but little over nine millions, of whom about three millions and a half were slaves. The slaves, however, instead of being a source of anxiety to the South, as many in the North predicted, proved entirely trustworthy and faith-ful. They raised the crops upon which the whole South subsisted during the war; and they were largely employed in building fortifications.

Regarding the relative numbers of the combatants on the two sides, there are wide differ-ences of opinion. While the Federal statistics are quite complete, official figures are lacking in the case of the Confederacy. Colonel Livermore, who is considered an authority on the question, concludes that there were over a million and a half on the Union side, as against a million among the Confederates. Colonel Wood, a Southern writer, puts the Confederate lev-ies at no more than six hundred thousand. As there could not have been more than a million men of age for military service in the South, the latter estimate is probably nearer correct. There is no doubt, however, that the Union armies were vastly superior, not only in numbers, but even more in resources and equipment. To offset these advantages, the North labored un-der many disadvantages: it was generally acting on the offensive, in a hostile country, where large detachments were necessary, as the armies advanced, to maintain communications, and hold the territory gained.

The self-sustaining power of the South was far greater than has usually been imagined. The area under cultivation was almost equal to that north of the Potomac and the Ohio. The amount of livestock — horses, mules, cattle, and sheep — was actually larger than in the North; and the shortage of the wheat crop was more than balanced by the great harvests of rice and corn.

But in material prosperity, the North was far in advance of the South: in accumulated capital there was no comparison between the two sections. The North was full of manufac-tories of all kinds; the South had very few of any kind. In the North there was also a much larger measure of practical business capacity.

The command of the sea naturally fell at once into the hands of the North. All the navy yards, except those at Norfolk and Pensacola, and the entire personnel of the Navy, with the exception of a few officers, remained under the control of the Government. Moreover, the mercantile marine of the United States, which, in 1861, was second only to that of Great Britain, was almost wholly owned in the North.

The gravity of the coming struggle was realized by neither party. Men of high ability at the North prophesied that the South would be brought back to the Union within ninety days. Only General Scott declared that its conquest might be achieved "in two or three years, by a young able general — a Wolfe, a Desaix, a Hoche — with 300,000 disciplined men, kept up to that number."

Notwithstanding the absolute lack of factories and foundries in the South, and the in-ability to manufacture cannon, powder, and ammunition, the orders first placed in Europe by the Confederate Government were on a trivial scale. Before the war, metals, machinery, rails, rolling-stock, salt, and even medicine, came mainly from the North. The principal staples of the South — cotton and tobacco — brought leather and cloth in exchange from England. There was but one way in which the South could have procured the means of buying abroad the material of every kind of which she stood so greatly in need. Had the Government promptly seized all the cotton in the country, paying for it the market price in Confederate money, sent it to England before the blockade was firmly established, and there stored it, to be sold as occasion required, available funds would have been secured to meet the largest requirements. But this wise course, though suggested, was not adopted. The majority of the Southern politicians thought that England and France, a large portion of whose population depended for their livelihood on the harvests of the South, would not brook interference with their trade, and would never allow the North to enforce the blockade. In the War of Independence, the fleets of France and Spain had come to the assistance of the struggling Americans, and compelled England to let her colonies go; therefore, it was not likely that the North, confronted by the naval strength of England and France, would fail to yield. But, in forecasting the future, the history of the past is not always an infallible guide.

Virginia, the most important State south of Mason and Dixon's line, was not a member of the Confederacy when the Government was established at Montgomery. Her people did not regard the election of a Republican President as a menace, and were not strongly in favor of the secession movement. Many of her leading citizens deprecated the hasty action of South Carolina, and during the earlier months of 1861 there were few signs of unrest. But the crisis was not long postponed. When President Lincoln called upon the State to furnish her quota of troops for the Federal army, Virginia promptly seceded, and, as already stated, her action was followed by Arkansas, Tennessee, and North Carolina.

As soon as the Richmond convention passed the ordinance of secession, on the 17 April 1861, nearly all the officers in the regular army from that State sent in their resignations, and offered their services to the Confederate Government. A few officers only, of whom the most distinguished were Lieutenant-General Scott and Major (afterwards Major-General) George H. Thomas, remained loyal to the Union.

Among the officers who then left the Union service were the two most famous soldiers of the Confederacy — Robert E. Lee and Thomas J. Jackson.

Lee was born in Westmoreland County, Virginia, 19 January 1807. He was the son of General Henry Lee, familiarly known as "Light-Horse Harry," of Revolutionary fame. His mother, Anne Carter, of Shirley, on the James River, was a direct descendant of Robert Carter, who, because of his vast landed possessions and high social position, was called "King Carter."

The Lees were of the oldest, wealthiest, and most patriotic families in Virginia. The original ancestor was Richard Lee, who settled in the Old Dominion as early as 1640. After the Revolution, General Harry Lee served in the Congress of the United States, and was three times governor of Virginia. In his funeral oration on the occasion of the death of

Washington, he pronounced the immortal words, so familiar to every American: "First in war, first in peace, and first in the hearts of his countrymen."

Harry Lee died when his son Robert was only eleven years of age. The family, which seems to have had some financial reverses, had moved to Alexandria, where Robert was placed in school, and worshipped in the same church that Washington had attended. At the age of eighteen he entered West Point on an appointment secured for him by General Andrew Jackson. He graduated second in his class, and for the next five years served in the Engineer Corps.

In June 1831, Robert Lee married Mary Custis, a great-granddaughter of Martha Washington, and the heiress to the beautiful estate of Arlington on the banks of the Potomac.

The Mexican War gave Lee his first opportunity to show his great military talents. General Scott made him chief-of-staff, and for distinguished services he received the brevet rank of colonel. After the war, General Scott declared that Robert E. Lee was the greatest living soldier in America. In 1852 he was appointed superintendent of the Military Academy, where he made a fine record during his three years of service.

In 1861, Lee was colonel of the 5th Cavalry, in Texas, and was generally considered the ablest officer in the Army. He was recalled to Washington, and on the 18 April was offered by President Lincoln the command of the Army of the United States, which he declined. He resigned his commission on the 20 April, and three days later took command at Richmond of the military forces of Virginia.

Though opposed to secession, and deprecating war, Lee felt that he could take no part in the coercion of the Southern States. When the issue was drawn, like so many other men of the South, he considered his allegiance to his native State paramount to his loyalty to the Nation.

In personal appearance and in character, there was a marked contrast between Lee and his great lieutenant, Jackson. Lee was tall, handsome, of distinguished manners and courtly address; he was a patrician, born and bred.

Jackson also was tall, but his form was ungainly, his hands and feet enormous; he was a true son of the soil. He was born on the 21 January 1824 in the little town of Clarksburg, now the county seat of Harrison, but then no more than a village in the Virginia backwoods. His father was a lawyer, clever and popular, who had inherited a comfortable patrimony; generous and incautious, he found it easier to make money than to keep it, and when he died in 1827, every vestige of his property was swept away. The young widow married again, but lived only a year longer, and at the age of seven the boy Thomas found himself a penniless orphan. In 1842, when he was eighteen years of age, a vacancy occurred in the Military Academy at West Point which was to be filled by a youth from the Congressional District in which Clarksburg was included, and young Jackson sought and obtained the appointment.

Owing to his lack of previous training, Jackson's career at West Point was not distinguished, but by application and hard work he finally succeeded in graduating seventeenth in a class of seventy, and his rank gave him a commission in the artillery. During the four years of his stay at West Point, the young Virginian gained in health and strength, and attained his full height of five feet ten. He acquired the erect bearing of the cadets, but never overcame his natural awkwardness, and was always a poor horseman.

There was much in the boyhood of Jackson, as there was much in his later career, that recalls Napoleon to mind. Both were devoted to their families; both were indefatigable students; both were provincial, neither was prepossessing. They both had the same love of method and of order. An inflexibility of purpose, an absolute disregard of popular opinion, and an unswerving belief in their own capacity, were predominant traits in both. Neither sought sympathy, and both felt that they were masters of their own fate.

The soubriquet of "Stonewall," by which Jackson will always be known, was really a misnomer: undoubtedly he could be steadfast on occasions, but he was stronger in offence than in defence. Like the great Corsican, the quality which above all others marked him was mobility — a swiftness in action which puzzled and generally confounded his adversaries, and which usually secured for him success.

Jackson was fortunate from the beginning of his military career. Before the Mexican War, the total strength of the regular army was not more than 8500 men, and nearly all this force was scattered in small detachments along the frontier, to control the Indian tribes. This warfare was monotonous, and there was but little chance to attain military distinction. The 1st Artillery, to which Jackson was attached, was ordered to the Rio Grande, and later was included in Scott's army of invasion. Jackson distinguished himself in several engagements, and came out of the war a major by brevet. None of his West Point comrades had made so great a stride in rank, and his future in his profession was assured.

General Thomas J. "Stonewall" Jackson had few superiors in the art of war.

Many of the generals with whom Jackson was later to be intimately connected, either as friends or enemies, are mentioned in Scott's despatches. Magruder, Ambrose Hill, McDowell, and Hooker, belonged to his own regiment. McClellan and Beauregard served on the staff with Lee. Joseph E. Johnston, twice severely wounded, was conspicuous for his gallantry. Pope was a staff officer; Longstreet was bracketed with Pickett for conspicuous conduct; Porter and Reno did good service with the artillery, and Ewell had two horses killed under him at Churubusco.

After the war, Jackson's battery was sent to Fort Hamilton, on Long Island, seven miles below New York. Two years passed without incident, and then Jackson was transferred to Florida, where his stay was brief. In March 1851 he was appointed Professor of Artillery Tactics and Natural Philosophy at the Virginia Military Institute. This college, founded twelve years previously, on the model of West Point, was located at Lexington, one hundred miles west of Richmond. It was attended by several hundred youths from Virginia and other Southern States, and was the training school of many Confederate officers. In all essential respects the Military Institute was then but little behind West Point: the discipline was as strict, the drill but little less precise.

In the well-stocked library of the Institute, Jackson found every opportunity to increase his professional knowledge. He was an untiring reader, and the campaigns of Napoleon were his constant study. He was an enthusiastic admirer of the genius of the Emperor; the swiftness, the daring, and the energy of his movements appealed to Jackson's every instinct. Ten years passed quickly away, and here we find him at the outbreak of the Civil War.

Marked intellectual capacity is the chief characteristic of the most famous soldiers. Ney and Blucher were probably the best fighting generals of France and Prussia, but neither was capable of conducting a campaign. Caesar, Frederick, and Napoleon were each and all of them more than mere fighting men. No one of their time rivalled them in strength of intellect. It was this, combined with the best qualities of Ney and Blucher, that made them masters of strategy, and lifted them high above those who were tacticians and nothing more; and it was this that Jackson cultivated at Lexington.

Finally, in estimating the relative power of the parties to this conflict, we must take into consideration their respective aptitudes for war. The South undoubtedly possessed a more military population than the North. Not only Virginia, but South Carolina, Louisiana, and other Southern States, possessed excellent military academies. A martial spirit was also cultivated by the conditions of life in the South: riding, hunting, fishing, — unusual physical exertions. The aristocratic regime of the slave-holding States was also conducive to a preference for military, rather than civil, pursuits, and the young men of the better classes eagerly embraced the profession of arms. They made excellent officers, while those below them in the social scale made admirable soldiers. In the North, on the other hand, there was very little of this enthusiasm for a military life. The people there were too busy with schemes for the development of the country, and for the acquisition of private fortunes.

The organization of the Confederate army from the first was superior to that of the Federals. Although a few civilians were appointed to the rank of brigadier-general, all the chief commands were reserved for the graduates of West Point. The Confederate armies were commanded by officers of the full rank of general; the corps, by lieutenant-generals; the divisions, by major-generals, and the brigades, by brigadier-generals. Distinction of rank was uniformly based upon extent of command, as it ought always to be. In the Union army, on the other hand, armies, army-corps, or divisions, indifferently, were commanded by major-generals, to the general detriment of the service. Even General Scott was merely a lieutenant-general by brevet, and it was not until the autumn of 1863 that he was given the full rank of lieutenant-general. The grade of general was not created until 1866. Ignorance of military affairs, and an unworthy jealousy of distinctions of rank, which have always marked our public men, were probably at the bottom of this unwise policy.

The Confederacy was fortunate also, at the start, in having the services of some of the most efficient men in the "Old Army": Adjutant General Cooper, Quarter Master General

Joseph E. Johnston, and Commissary General Northrup; also Colonel Josiah Gorgas, who showed great genius in building up the ordnance service; as well as, in the field, those excellent organizers and disciplinarians, P. G. T. Beauregard and Braxton Bragg. So well did they all do their work that there were remarkably few changes in the personnel of the higher ranks of the Confederate army from the beginning until the close of the war. The only officer to come to the front at a later date was Robert E. Lee, who did not become prominent until the second year of the conflict. As General Cooper never served in the field, his name is not so familiar to the general public; but those who were in "a position to know what he did … will not fail to place him among those who contributed most to whatever was achieved."

CHAPTER TWO

APRIL–JULY 1861

MANASSAS

WHEN the flag was fired on at Fort Sumter, the Nation was powerless to resent the insult. The military establishment was reduced to 13,000 men, scattered in distant garrisons. There was no reserve, no transport, no organization for war. The navy consisted of six screw-frigates, only one of which was in commission; of five steam sloops, some twenty sailing ships, and a few gunboats. Although well armed, the majority of the vessels were out of date; and 9000 officers and men constituted the extent of the personnel.

The news of the firing on Sumter reached Washington on Saturday, the 13 April. The following morning, while Anderson was preparing to evacuate the fort, the President called a special meeting of his Cabinet to discuss the situation. With his own hand, Lincoln immediately drafted a proclamation calling forth the militia of the several States to the number of 75,000 men "to cause the laws to be duly executed"; also convening both Houses of Congress in special session on the fourth day of July.

This proclamation was published throughout the country on Monday morning, 15 April. Its effect in the North was instantaneous and universal. All uncertainty was at an end: the people were ready for war, and the response was simply magnificent. Only the "Old Bay State," however, was prepared. For several months, Governor Andrew had been giving special attention to the equipment and drill of the State militia, and five thousand men were ready, of whom three thousand were fully armed. Within twenty-four hours, the 6th Massachusetts mustered on Boston Common, and started for Washington. The regiment reached Baltimore on the 19 April, a date again to be made memorable by the shedding of the first blood in a great American war. In crossing the city between the two stations, which was necessary at that time, the regiment was attacked by a mob of Southern sympathizers, and several lives were lost on both sides. A few hours later, the regiment reached Washington, and took up its quarters in the Senate chamber at the Capitol. Until then the city had been guarded only by a small force of regulars and a few companies of local volunteers.

The 8th Massachusetts at once followed, under the command of Brigadier-General Benjamin F. Butler, well known in Boston as a lawyer and politician of rather unsavory reputation, who was now to become a national character. As the bridge across the Susquehanna at Havre de Grace had been burned, the regiment made its way by steamer to Annapolis, where it met the full and handsomely equipped 7th Regiment of New York. The arrival of these two regiments at Washington, for the moment, put an end to all apprehension.

Without waiting for the meeting of Congress, on the 3 May the President very wisely called for 42,034 volunteers for three years, for 22,714 men for the regular army, and for 18,000 men for the navy. These men, when enrolled, with the 75,000 previously called out, would raise the available army to 156,861 troops, and the navy to 25,600 men. In his message to Congress, on the 4 July, the President recommended that this number be increased to 400,000 men. In these acts and recommendations Mr. Lincoln showed a comprehension of the magnitude of the task before him which was hardly to be expected from his lack of experience.

The work of organizing and directing these forces was at first entrusted to Lieutenant-General Winfield Scott, a veteran of two wars, but now past his three-score years and ten, and incapacitated by bodily infirmities. Though born in Virginia, he had remained loyal to the Union, and his sound military judgment was of great advantage to the Government at this time. The old general was loath to sheathe his sword, but his health soon forced him to resign from active service.

Out of the twelve hundred graduates of West Point, who, at the beginning of 1861, were still fit for service, a fourth were Southerners, and these, almost without exception, cast their lot with the Confederacy. The defection of Robert E. Lee, in particular, was a sad blow to General Scott, and a great loss to the Union cause.

It was necessary to relieve from active duty many other senior officers in the regular army, who were too old for service in the field, and their places should have been filled by promoting the most capable and promising of the younger officers. Unfortunately, however, the President, in making many of his appointments, was governed too much by political considerations. In the East, Butler and Banks, both men without any kind of military training or experience, were made major-generals of volunteers; while in the West, Fremont was appointed a major general in the regular army, and succeeded in Missouri the brave and capable Lyon, to whose courage and skill the preservation of that State to the Union was largely due.

On the 24 May, after the people of Virginia had ratified the ordinance of secession, the Federal troops crossed the Potomac without opposition and occupied Arlington Heights and Alexandria. A camp was established on the south side of the river, and the line was entrenched from the Chain Bridge to Alexandria. Brevet-Major McDowell, then on duty in the War Department, whose highest rank of command had been lieutenant of artillery, was made a brigadier-general, and placed in command of the forces in Virginia.

Washington now being safe from attack, the Northern newspapers and public began to cry out for a forward movement before the expiration of the term of service of the three-months men. General Scott wanted to wait until the men of the second levy could be made ready for the field. But, in the face of the newspaper clamor, the Government was finally forced to overrule the judgment of the lieutenant-general, and he was ordered to make the necessary arrangements for an advance.

The military situation at this time was as follows: The main army of the Confederacy, 20,000 volunteers under General Beauregard, was stationed at Manassas Junction, thirty miles southwest of Washington. Beauregard, a classmate of McDowell at West Point, had

Before the battle, soldiers who were to fight in Burnside's brigade taking their ease. Their carefree faces are those of young men not yet tested in battle.

been an officer in the Engineers, and the capture of Fort Sumter had added much renown to his already excellent reputation. At Manassas Junction, on the Orange and Alexandria Railroad, a branch line, coming from Front Royal in the Shenandoah Valley, connected with the main line to Richmond.

Near Winchester, in the lower Shenandoah Valley, General Joseph E. Johnston, with about 11,000 men, confronted a Union force of some 18,000, under General Patterson, a veteran of the Mexican War. Although nearly seventy years old, he had recently been appointed a major-general of volunteers from civil life, and given this important command.

At Aquia Creek, thirty miles southeast of Manassas, there was a Confederate force of 3000 men under General Holmes. At Fort Monroe, a small Federal force under General Butler was opposed by Generals Huger and Magruder.

All the Confederate detachments were under the direction of President Davis, at Richmond, who seems to have had General Lee as his military adviser; while General Scott, under President Lincoln, commanded the Union forces at Washington.

There were two main roads running south from the National capital, one from Alexandria to Richmond via Fredericksburg, the other by way of Warrenton. The strategic importance of Manassas was due to the fact that it was located on the Warrenton Turnpike, and on the main line of railway from Washington to the Southern States. Beauregard's position there also guarded the junction of the branch line to the Shenandoah Valley, by which Johnston's army communicated with the Confederate base at Richmond.

Manassas Junction lies on a high, open plateau. The Confederate position was protected by some slight field-works, armed with fifteen heavy guns. To the north and east of Manassas, at a distance of about three miles, flows Bull Run, with wooded heights in most places close to the banks. The stream is winding and sluggish, and fordable in many places, although, here and there, the banks are steep and rocky. The Confederate army guarded the various fords, extending on a line about eight miles long from the Stone Bridge on the Warrenton road to the railway.

In reluctant response to the popular cry for a forward movement, Scott asked McDowell to submit a plan of operations, and he complied on the 24 June. His plan was "to turn the enemy's position and force him out of it by seizing or threatening his communications." He counted upon Patterson and Butler to contain the forces in their respective fronts. Estimating that Beauregard would still receive reinforcements enough to raise his army to about 35,000 men, McDowell thought that he should have a force of 30,000 of all arms, with a reserve of 10,000. At the same time he urged that he might be allowed to put his regiments into brigades: this fact, of itself, shows the very rudimentary state of the Union army.

McDowell's plan was fully discussed, and finally approved, at a council of war held on the 29 June at the Executive Mansion, in which took part the President, his Cabinet, and the principal military officers. McDowell stated emphatically that he could not hope to beat the two Confederate armies if united, and Scott gave him the positive assurance: "If Johnston joins Beauregard, he shall have Patterson at his heels."

It is perhaps unnecessary to state that the operation upon which the Federal authorities had decided was a complicated one, which should never have been undertaken with inexperienced generals and raw troops. It was tempting fortune to subject the issue of arms to the success of a cooperative movement. Instead of relying upon Patterson's ability to detain Johnston in the Shenandoah Valley, the bulk of his army should have been brought to Washington as soon as it was decided to make the forward movement. For this failure, General Scott was largely responsible.

McDowell was ordered to begin his movement on the 8 July; but owing to various delays it was not until a week later that his force was raised to the stipulated strength.

On the 16 July, McDowell issued his orders to march that afternoon. His army was organized as follows.

First Division: TYLER
Brigades: Keyes, Schenck, Sherman, Richardson 9,936
Second Division: HUNTER
Brigades: Porter, Burnside 2,648
Third Division: HEINTZELMAN
Brigades: Franklin, Willcox, Howard 9,777
Fourth Division: RUNYON
No brigade commanders 5,752
Fifth Division: MILES
Brigades: Blenker, Davies 6,207
                                                                                                                                      ———
Total 34,320

There were also seven troops of regular cavalry, and eight companies of infantry under Major Sykes. There were 49 guns, and seven of the batteries were also of the regular army. McDowell's force aggregated 35,000 men, but Runyon's division was held back to guard the line of communications, and took no part in the battle of Manassas. On the field, therefore, McDowell had only 30,000 men.

Through his spies in Washington, Beauregard was kept informed of the Federal plans, and on the 17 July he telegraphed to Richmond that the advance had begun. Davis immediately ordered Johnston and Holmes to Manassas. That same day, Patterson, after advancing within nine miles of Winchester, retired to Charlestown, and telegraphed General Scott that Johnston's force was 35,000 strong, although in fact it was not more than two-thirds the strength of his own.

This left Johnston free to depart, and on the 18th he marched his army by way of Ashby's Gap to Piedmont, where the infantry was placed in railway cars, while the cavalry and artillery proceeded by road. On the afternoon of the 20 July, he had joined Beauregard with the bulk of his forces.

It is hardly worth while to go into the details of the story of Patterson's failure to fulfill the expectations of his chief. As Mr. Ropes says, he "was really more to be pitied than blamed; ... if Scott expected that Patterson would fight Johnston, as he says he did, ... he should have given him orders to that effect, and he cannot be exonerated from blame for not having done so."

McDowell began his advance from Alexandria on the afternoon of the 16 July, and on the morning of the 18th, the greater part of his force of 35,000 men was concentrated at Centreville, twenty-two miles from Washington, and five and a half miles northeast of Manassas. It should have been possible to have attacked the following morning, but the Federal commander was confronted by many obstacles. The maps were poor, and it was impossible to secure local guides. The army was much larger than any ever assembled on the American Continent; the general, his staff, and the troops were alike inexperienced. "To deploy 10,000 or 20,000 men for attack is a difficult operation, even with well-drilled troops and an experienced staff," says Colonel Henderson. "The troops had received no instruction in musketry, and many of the regiments went into action without having once fired their rifles.... Ignorance of war and contempt for the lessons of history were to cost the nation dear."

General Joseph E. Johnston was one of the few who realized that the South's first victory was not "due in any degree to lack of prowess in their assailants."

Stone Church, Centreville, Virginia on the eve of the war's first major conflict. Centreville is on an elevation from which the ground slopes in all directions.

In McDowell's report, he states that it was his intention to attack at once, but he could not get the troops into line earlier than he did. The men were not accustomed to marching, and the supply trains moved with difficulty and in disorder, so that there was a day's delay in getting the provisions forward.

Beauregard's army, then called the Army of the Potomac, consisted of six and a half brigades. It was posted in a line about eight miles long, behind Bull Run, from the Stone Bridge on the Warrenton Pike to Union Mills Ford. The bridge was held by Evans's half-brigade, and the fords to the east by the brigades of Cocke, Bonham, Longstreet, Jones, and

Ewell, with Early in the rear. Holmes, on his arrival, was placed in reserve, as were also the brigades of Jackson, Bee, and Bartow, of Johnston's Army of the Shenandoah, when they came on the field. From these arrangements it is evident that Beauregard expected the Federals to attempt to cross the creek by the fords to the east of the Stone Bridge. This was indeed McDowell's first intention, but he gave it up on account of the difficulty of an attack on that side.

Centreville is on an elevation from which the ground slopes in all directions. The Warrenton Pike runs almost due west, and good dirt roads lead to all the fords. The country toward Bull Run is cut up by small streams; and covered with farms, and thick woods which furnish good cover for troops.

On the morning of the 18th, McDowell ordered Tyler, whose division was in the lead, to make a reconnaissance, but strictly enjoined him not to bring on an engagement.

Tyler advanced along the road to Mitchell's Ford, and opened fire with artillery on the Confederate forces posted on the south side of the stream. He also sent forward two regiments of infantry and a squadron of cavalry into the thick woods along the creek. The troops of Bonham and Longstreet returned the Federal fire at short range, and the Union forces were driven back in disorder. This first affair, small as it was, had a very depressing effect upon McDowell's army, and greatly encouraged the Confederates.

This experience confirmed McDowell's impression that it was impossible with his raw troops to carry the line of Bull Run by a frontal attack. His stay of two days at Centreville, necessitated by the impossibility of concentrating sooner his loosely organized force, had given time for his engineers to examine the position of the enemy, and on their report he decided to turn the Confederate left by making a detour to the northwest with his right wing. Unaware of the fact that Johnston was already on his way to join Beauregard, he also hoped to prevent their junction by destroying the railway to the Valley.

McDowell's orders, issued on Saturday, the 20 July, were as follows: Miles's division, with one brigade of Tyler's division and a strong force of artillery, was to remain in reserve at Centreville, and to threaten Blackburn's Ford. The rest of Tyler's division, with four batteries of regular artillery, was to advance along the turnpike and make a "secondary attack" at daybreak by way of the Stone Bridge. The divisions of Hunter and Heintzelman, about 13,000 men in all, were to make the turning movement. They were to march along the pike to a point two miles west of Centreville, there to take a road through the woods to the right, cross Bull Run at Sudley Springs, and move down upon the flank and rear of the enemy. Five batteries, twenty-four guns in all, were to accompany this column, the whole under the personal command of General McDowell. As soon as this movement had forced the left of Beauregard's army away from the Stone Bridge, Tyler was to cross and join in the main attack. The division of Miles, 6200 strong, was to remain near Centreville to guard the communications of the army.

As anticipated, no resistance was encountered at Sudley Springs, but the turning column was delayed in starting, by Tyler's division getting in the way, and did not reach the ford until nine o'clock Sunday morning, instead of seven, as was calculated.

After fording the creek, and resting perhaps half an hour, the troops resumed their march in a southerly direction. They had proceeded about a mile when the enemy was encountered, posted on some heights near the Matthews house north of the Warrenton road. This was about ten-thirty.

These troops were part of the demi-brigade of General Evans which held the extreme left of the Confederate line. Evans, who was an officer of the Old Army, and a good soldier, had soon divined that the Federal attack on the Stone Bridge was only a feint; and, before long, he suspected that a movement to turn his left flank was in progress. His suspicions were confirmed by a courier from a picket at Sudley Springs, and by a "wig-wag" message from Beauregard's signal officer, Captain E. P. Alexander. Leaving four companies and two guns to defend the bridge, and sending word to Cocke on his right, Evans marched the rest of his command, eleven companies and two guns, to the left, and took up a strong position

Manassas

on high ground about three-quarters of a mile north of the pike, with his left resting on the Sudley road.

On Johnston's arrival the day before, in virtue of his superior rank, he had taken command of the Confederate army, but he wisely left the actual direction of the troops to Beauregard. The latter had formed an ambitious plan of crossing by the lower fords, turning the left of the Federals, and cutting off their line of retreat. In fact, the two generals waited from half-past eight to half-past ten, Sunday morning, on a hill in the rear of Mitchell's Ford for this movement to begin. But the order to Ewell, who was to have been the first to cross, had miscarried, and now, as General Beauregard himself puts it, "the enemy was about to annihilate the left flank" of the Confederate army, "and had to be met and checked there, for otherwise … all would have been lost."

The ruins of Henry House, July 21, 1861. Confederate regiments swarmed from cover and captured the Union position near here.

After despatching orders for the two brigades of Holmes and Early to move up toward the Warrenton Pike, Johnston and Beauregard set off at a rapid gallop to join their troops engaged four miles away. Ewell, Jones and Longstreet, at the same time, were ordered "to make a strong demonstration all along their front on the other side of the Run."

Upon finding Evans drawn up before him, Burnside promptly formed a regiment in line of battle and attacked. Other regiments came forward one after another and were repulsed: there was lack of concert and combined power. The Federal tactics were poor and timid.

Robinson House, Bull Run. It was near this spot that Thomas Jonathan Jackson received the name "Stonewall."

Porter came to the support of Burnside, but Evans maintained his position alone for more than an hour. Then he was reinforced by the brigades of Bee and Bartow; and from the Henry House Hill, Imboden's battery lent its aid.

Meanwhile the leading regiments of Heintzelman's division had come up and prolonged the Federal line to the right. Part of both the hostile lines was in the woods and part in the open fields, and at some points the lines were only a hundred yards apart.

Soon after the arrival of Bee and Bartow, with their four regiments, the right of the Confederate position was taken in flank and rear by the brigades of Sherman and Keyes of Tyler's division. Under the mistaken impression that the Stone Bridge was defended by a heavy abattis, the Federal troops had found fords and crossed Bull Run about halfway between the bridge and Sudley. Thus enveloped on their right, after having maintained their position for over two hours against superior numbers, the Confederates at last gave way and fled in confusion across Young's Branch.

In the angle south of the turnpike there is a commanding ridge called the Henry House Hill, generally level on top, and some two hundred yards across. The inner edge of the ridge afforded some cover both from view and from fire, and formed a good position for a defensive line of battle. Gentle slopes led down from the hill to the valley of Young's Branch; but they were cut up by little ravines, and partly covered with patches of young pines. Upon the northwest brow of the plateau stood the Henry house; and a third of a mile northeast of it, on a projecting spur, was the Robinson house, surrounded by dense trees and shrubbery. Both houses were small frame buildings, and neither had any defensive strength. At the rear of the plateau, along the eastern borders, was a thick fringe of young pines, which merged into a dense oak woods, of considerable extent, lying on both sides of the Sudley-Manassas road.

Jackson, who had marched to the sound of the firing, had formed his brigade in the edge of the pines along the eastern brow of the plateau. He was just in time to support Imboden's battery, which, badly cut to pieces, was withdrawing from the fight. At this moment appeared General Bee: he was covered with dust and sweat, his horse foaming. "General," he said, "they are beating us back!" "Then, sir, we will give them the bayonet," replied Jackson, as his thin lips closed like a vise. Inspired with renewed confidence, Bee galloped back to the ravine where his officers were trying to reform their broken companies. Pointing with his sword to the line on the heights above, he cried: "Look! there is Jackson standing like a stone wall. Rally behind the Virginians!" Bee died that day, but his words will live forever: from that hour, Thomas Jonathan Jackson was universally known as Stonewall Jackson.

Beauregard and Johnston were now on the ground: the former took personal command of the troops, while the latter rode back to the headquarters at the Lewis house to hurry up reinforcements.

It was now about two o'clock. General McDowell, who was present, in direct command of the Union forces, decided to complete the victory by carrying the Confederate position on the

Henry House Hill. He had allowed Burnside to withdraw his brigade, which was exhausted from the morning's work, but he had in hand for the attack the brigades of Porter, Willcox, Sherman, and Franklin, a squadron of regular cavalry, and four batteries of artillery, about 10,000 men. Tyler, with Keyes's brigade of his division, after a feeble demonstration against the Confederate right, had recrossed Young's Branch, and took no further part in the battle. Schenck's brigade and Tyler's artillery were still on the other side of Bull Run. Howard's brigade had not yet come up. The Confederate force on the hill comprised about 6500 infantry, Stuart's squadron of cavalry, and thirteen pieces of artillery.

After the withdrawal of the Confederates from their first position on the Matthews Hill, McDowell placed the two fine regular batteries of Ricketts and Griffin on a hill near the Dogan house, in the angle between the turnpike and the Sudley road. From this position they swept the summit of the Henry Hill with a destructive fire. Knowing the moral support which artillery always gives to infantry, before assaulting the new Confederate position McDowell ordered Major Barry, his chief-of-artillery, to send forward these two batteries to a position beyond and to the south of the Henry house. It was a strange procedure to expose these valuable batteries, without any infantry support, to a close musketry fire, which of course they could not return. Ricketts and Griffin were amazed to receive such an order, but they promptly obeyed, and went into battery near the Henry house, within musketshot of the woods south of it.

Here the batteries were charged by Stuart's cavalry, stationed on the left of the Confederate line, and the Zouave regiment, which had been assigned as a support, at once gave way.

While Colonel Willcox was endeavoring to rally the Zouaves, the 33rd Virginia suddenly appeared from the woods at the south and advanced toward the batteries. At this early date, the uniforms in the two armies were very much alike, and from the direction of the advance Major Barry thought that this was a Federal regiment sent to their support. He therefore ordered Griffin to withhold his fire. A moment later the doubtful regiment proved its identity by a deadly volley, delivered at a range of seventy yards. Every gunner was shot down, several officers fell killed or wounded, and the batteries were rendered useless for the rest of the day. Griffin managed to drag off three of his guns; but Ricketts was badly wounded and captured.

Although somewhat discouraged by this reverse, McDowell had no idea of giving up the fight. The Federals crossed the valley of Young's Branch, mounted the northern slopes of the hill, and gained the plateau beyond the Henry house. Here the fighting became fierce.

The batteries were taken and retaken. The hill at times was covered with the Federal regiments. The enemy more than once was driven back into the woods which bordered the plateau on the south and east, and into which the Federal troops could not venture to follow. For more than an hour, the battle raged backward and forward across the plateau, without any material change in the situation. About three o'clock, Howard came up, but too late to affect the result. Then the Confederates received reinforcements which turned the day in their favor. Early's brigade came up from the lower fords; Kirby Smith's brigade of Johnston's army reached Manassas by rail from the Valley, and marched at once to the field. These fresh troops were placed far out on the Confederate left, thus enveloping the right flank of the

Federals. As Smith led in his troops, he was severely wounded and had to turn over the command to Elzey. Beauregard now ordered an advance all along the line, and the effect was decisive. The Union soldiers, without any show of panic, simply broke ranks, and started home, retiring, for the most part, over the roads by which they had come. The retreat was covered by Sykes's battalion of infantry and Palmer's squadron of cavalry, both of the regular army. "By six o'clock there was not a Union soldier, but the dead, the wounded, and the captives, on the south side of Bull Run."

No effective pursuit was made by the Confederates. "Never did an enemy make a cleaner escape, out of such an exposed position, after such an utter rout," says General Alexander.

Early in the afternoon, President Davis arrived at Manassas by rail from Richmond. Mounting a horse, he rode to the field. To the long procession of stragglers, retiring from the battlefield, he cried; "I am President Davis. Follow me back to the field!" Not far off, Stonewall Jackson was having a wound in his hand dressed by a surgeon. Hearing the words of Davis, he shouted: "We have whipped them! They ran like sheep! Give me five thousand fresh men, and I will be in Washington City tomorrow morning!"

In fact, Jackson seems to have been the only man to grasp the situation and realize the great opportunity before them. The President and his two generals spent the rest of the afternoon in riding over the field. Although it was not sunset until after seven, and there was a, nearly full moon, no serious pursuit was attempted. For this failure to follow up their success, the Confederate generals have presented many excuses. "Our army," says General Johnston, "was more disorganized by victory than that of the United States by defeat."

McDowell intended to make a stand at Centreville, but the men could not be stopped there, and the Federal army retired within the defences of Washington.

The losses at Manassas, which the Federals call the battle of Bull Run, were as follows:

	Federals	Confederates
Killed	460	387
Wounded	1,124	1,582
Missing	1,312	13
Totals	2,896	1,982

Estimated on the basis of the Confederate losses, probably 750 of the Union prisoners were wounded, which would make the total Federal loss in killed and wounded over 2300, or approximately 12 per cent, of the number actually engaged. The Confederate loss was not quite so large — about 11 per cent. These figures show hard fighting.

On the Federal side, Hunter and Heintzelman were wounded, Willcox, wounded and captured. On the Confederate side, Bee and Bartow were killed, Jackson and Kirby Smith, wounded.

In the organization of its first army, the Confederacy displayed more ability than the Government at Washington. Mr. Davis was a graduate of West Point, and had served seven years in the regular army; he had commanded a volunteer regiment in the Mexican War, and had later been Secretary of War. He was acquainted, personally or officially, with most of the higher officers of the Old Army, and his selections for command were generally good. He had the professional soldier's horror of putting troops in charge of men who knew nothing of the business of war. No citizen soldier was given a high command until he had demonstrated his fitness. He did not make the mistake of Mr. Lincoln, with his lack of military experience, and appoint to important commands such men as Banks and Butler.

The Union army of 35,000 men was the largest ever assembled on this Continent, yet it was not organized into higher units than regiments until just before it left Washington.

McDowell's halt of two days at Centreville, necessitated by the "disorganized state" of his army, was fatal. It gave time for the transfer from the Valley of Johnston's Army of the Shenandoah, which decided the battle on Sunday afternoon.

The strategy of the Federal commander has been approved by many writers. For example, General Sherman says: "It is now generally admitted that it was one of the best-planned battles of the war, but one of the worst-fought." Colonel Henderson also writes: "The turning movement by Sudley Springs was a skillful manoeuvre, and completely surprised both Johnston and Beauregard. It was undoubtedly risky, but it was far less dangerous than a direct attack on the strong position along Bull Run."

These opinions seem to be based upon an erroneous impression of the formidable strength of the Confederate position, and it is therefore somewhat difficult to agree entirely with these eminent authorities.

Colonel Henderson writes: "The Confederates were strongly posted…. Even with regular troops a direct attack on a single point of passage would have been difficult."

Mr. Ropes says that Bull Run "presented a formidable obstacle for such raw troops as those which constituted the United States forces."

On the other hand, Captain (afterwards General) Alexander, of the Confederate army, who was present at the battle, says: "Our army was weak and badly posted and could not have withstood a vigorous attack by the force in front of us. Both of our flanks were in the air, and Bull Run could be crossed by infantry in many places. Our centre was a large salient whose lines the enemy could enfilade. The ground on their side was commanding and afforded close approach under excellent cover. On our side it was low and gently rising to the rear, giving no cover whatever, except of the woods."

In McDowell's report he states that he could not make the attack earlier than he did. "I wished to go to Centreville the second day," he writes, "but … I was told that it was impossible for the men to march further. They had only come from Vienna, about six miles, and it was not more than six and a half miles further to Centreville, in all a march of twelve and a half miles; but the men were foot-weary."

Nevertheless, in the face of this experience, of only two days before, McDowell laid his plans for five of his eight brigades to make a night march of nine or ten miles by a circuitous route which would take them dangerously far from his other forces: in other words, he took the risk of having his army split in two by a formidable obstacle. The success of his project depended upon his rolling up the left flank of the enemy, and clearing the path for his own forces to unite by way of the Stone Bridge. It further involved the hazard of forming his line of battle parallel to the Warrenton Pike, his line of retreat; or with his back to the stream; or with his face to the rear.

In fact, McDowell deliberately took the risk of leaving his small rear guard to maintain his line of communications, and cut loose from his base, for the purpose of turning the enemy's left. His main body was further from Centreville than was the Confederate right, and he did not dare to call on his reserves for reinforcements. Unless he won a decisive victory, his position would be untenable, and he would be forced to withdraw across the stream.

But General Sherman is quite right in saying that the battle was not well fought. From every tactical point of view, the attack was badly made. Instead of setting up his headquarters somewhere in the rear, and directing the operations as a whole, McDowell was at the very front, and scarcely exercised any influence on the action. As so often happened in the battles of the Civil War, regiments and brigades went into the battle without any sort of order or concert of action. The assaults were all straight to the front: there was no effort to make a flank attack.

Although the Stone Bridge was open, McDowell did not summon his reserves from Centreville, only four miles away; he did not call Schenck's brigade, and the batteries with it, across the Run; he did not order Burnside back into action; he allowed Keyes to lie idle under cover of Young's Branch throughout the afternoon.

General Johnston says: "If the tactics of the Federals had been equal to their strategy, we should have been beaten." And General Alexander writes: "The Federal tactics were poor and timid: ... there was lack of concert and combined power."

Colonel Henderson, after paying a tribute to the accuracy of the fire, the fine discipline and staunch endurance of the Federal gunners, who were all old soldiers, says: "The infantry, on the other hand, was not well handled. The attack was purely frontal. No attempt was made to turn the Confederate flanks, although the Stone Bridge was now open and Johnston's line might easily have been taken in reverse. Nor does it appear that the cavalry was employed to ascertain where the flanks rested. Moreover, instead of massing the troops for a determined onslaught, driven home by sheer weight of numbers, the attack was made by successive brigades, those in rear waiting till those in front had been defeated; and in the same manner, the brigades attacked by successive regiments. Such tactics were inexcusable."

Mr. Ropes states that the work of Colonel Henderson was not seen by him until his own book was in press, but he met this criticism in advance by the following explanation of McDowell's course: "He did not undertake to coordinate the movements of his divisions and brigades, as he doubtless would have liked to do, because he thought it very doubtful if he could succeed in such an undertaking with raw troops and inexperienced generals, and because moreover it would have taken precious time to make the attempt." Later, Mr. Ropes states: "McDowell could not, with the number of troops at his immediate disposal, turn his adversary's position; he had not a sufficient superiority in force."

As bearing on this point, it may be stated that, at the period of the battle on the Henry Hill, Henderson estimates that the Federals had 16,000 infantry available, while both Ropes and Alexander state that McDowell had under his immediate control not much more than 9000 men, allowing for casualties and stragglers, and taking into account the absence from the firing line of the four brigades of Howard, Burnside, Keyes, and Schenck. All the authorities agree that Beauregard was holding the hill with about 6500 men; but the chances were rather in his favor, as he was standing on the defensive, and the Federal troops, after marching and fighting for twelve hours, were nearly exhausted.

The Federal army should have contained a brigade of cavalry, but it had only seven little troops, and they were mostly split up into small details. The Confederates had 1800 horsemen, but they were split up in the same manner. With the exception of Stuart's charge on the Zouaves, the cavalry played a very insignificant role in the battle.

Beauregard's handling of his troops was equally bad, but fortunately for the Confederacy he had an able associate in Johnston, who hurried up reinforcements at the critical moment, in time to save the day.

Out of McDowell's army of 35,000 men, only 18,500 crossed the Run; and of these the brigades of Burnside and Keyes took little part in the action. Beauregard had about 32,000 men on the field, but he put only 18,000 into the battle. In very few actions of the Civil War were the numbers engaged so nearly equal, but the Confederates had the advantage of acting throughout on the defensive.

Only two officers handled their men well: Sherman on the Union side, and Jackson on the Confederate. It was the latter's wise choice of a position on the further edge of the open plateau, and McDowell's failure to take it in flank, which enabled the Confederates to hold out for four hours against superior numbers, and made their victory possible.

In the opinion of Colonel Henderson, the position chosen by Jackson was the strongest that could be found — a position from which the view is limited, well in the rear of a crest line. The brow of the hill which looks down upon Young's Branch gave an extended view and a wide field of fire upon the advancing Federals, but both flanks would have been exposed. Later, at the battle of Chattanooga, we shall see the dangers of such a position, where the defenders could see the hosts of the enemy preparing for the assault.

The catastrophe of Manassas may be termed one of those unavoidable accidents that so frequently occur in war. But, for a few days, the North seemed dazed: stocks went down, and money went up. Then stern resolve took the place of despair. To the President's call for volunteers, there was a magnificent response: the men enlisted with a spirit that has never been surpassed.

To the South, on the other hand, Manassas was a Pyrrhic victory. It gave their people a very unwarranted opinion of the superior fighting qualities of their troops. To many, the war seemed to be over: volunteering stopped, and even in South Carolina it proved to be impossible to raise sufficient troops to garrison the seacoast defences. The Government indulged in vain hopes of foreign intervention. Few were wise enough, like General Johnston, to realize that the Southern victory was not "due in any degree to lack of prowess in their assailants."

Many of the officers engaged in this first great battle of the war subsequently attained high rank in the two services. On the Union side, Sherman, Burnside, McDowell, Keyes, Heintzelman, Franklin, Porter, and Howard became army or corps commanders; on the Confederate side, Johnston and Beauregard became full generals, and Jackson, Longstreet, Ewell, Early, and Holmes, lieutenant-generals.

CHAPTER THREE

FEBRUARY 1862

HENRY AND DONELSON

DECISIVE as was the victory of Manassas, it is not probable that the Confederates could have captured Washington at that time. Three of the Federal divisions had taken no part in the battle, and were in good condition for the defence of the capital. President Davis discussed the situation fully with Johnston and Beauregard, the night after the battle, and they all agreed that the attempt would be hopeless.

While the loss of the battle was a terrible shock to the North, it caused no wavering in the determination to prosecute the war. On the day after the battle, the House of Representatives voted for the enlistment of 500,000 volunteers. The same day, President Lincoln summoned Major-General McClellan to Washington, and assigned him to the command, under General Scott, of all the troops at the capital. In October, Scott insisted on being allowed to retire from active service, and, on the first day of November, McClellan was appointed commander-in-chief of all the armies of the United States.

Prior to this date, however, on the 4 August, at the request of Mr. Lincoln, McClellan had drawn up a memorandum on the object of the war and his general plan of operations. The main campaign, from which he expected the most decisive results, was to be in the East, but he made a number of judicious suggestions, such as that "a strong movement be made on the Mississippi, and that the rebels be driven out of Missouri."

As the principal military operations of the following winter and spring took place in the West, we shall now turn to the Mississippi Valley.

It will be remembered that when the other Southern States seceded and organized the Confederacy, Kentucky wavered in its loyalty to the Union. The governor was for Secession, but the legislature was for the Union, so the State at first endeavored to compromise by declaring its neutrality (September 1861). Before we take up, however, the narrative of the military operations which this attitude of Kentucky forced upon the Government, it is necessary to trace very briefly the course of events in Missouri. In the summer of 1861, the Confederates made a determined effort to secure control of that State. In August a Confederate force of 10,000 men defeated Lyon, after a hard-fought action in which that promising officer lost his life. Later, a Union army under General Curtis drove the principal Confederate force under Van Dorn out of the State, and in March 1862 totally defeated it in an obstinate engagement at Pea Ridge in Arkansas. This decisive battle settled the fate of Missouri, although the large secessionist population in the State never ceased to give some cause for anxiety.

It was evident to all intelligent observers that the neutrality of Kentucky could not last: its position was too important. On the north the State was bounded by the Ohio River, which separated it from the Union States of Ohio, Indiana, and Illinois; on the south, by the Confederate State of Tennessee; on the east by Virginia, from which it was separated by the Cumberland Mountains, which could be crossed only at certain passes, of which the most important was Cumberland Gap; on the west, by the Mississippi River.

In this territory there were seven principal lines of railway:

1. Louisville and Nashville, running south through Bowling Green 170 miles to Nashville, where connection was made with —
2. Nashville and Chattanooga, joining these two cities, and —
3. Nashville and Decatur, leading into Alabama.
4. Memphis and Ohio, running from Bowling Green via Paris and Humboldt 250 miles to Memphis. From Humboldt, a branch line, 170 miles long, led to Columbus; and two lines, the Mississippi Central and the Mobile and Ohio, ran into Mississippi.
5. Memphis and Charleston, which passed through northern Mississippi and Alabama to Chattanooga, where it connected with —
6. Georgia Central, to Atlanta, and —
7. East Tennessee and Georgia, the main line of communication between Virginia and the Gulf States.

Kentucky and Tennessee

General Albert S. Johnston was one of the ablest of American soldiers. He was stuck by a rifle-ball and bled to death at Shiloh.

There were a few metaled pikes in Kentucky and Tennessee, but the highways were mainly the ordinary dirt roads — good in summer, but nearly impassable in winter and spring.

The neutrality of Kentucky was not long recognized either by the Union or the Confederacy. On the 3 September 1861, General Polk occupied Columbus, and two days later General Grant took possession of Paducah. President Davis then gave the chief command in the West to Albert Sidney Johnston, who was generally regarded as one of the ablest of American soldiers. He was a native of Kentucky, of New England descent. A graduate of West Point, he had served with distinction in the Mexican War. Like Lee, he had been opposed to secession, but when his adopted State, Texas, seceded, he offered his sword to the Confederacy. He was then in his fifty-ninth year, handsome in person and winning in manner, of lofty character, heroic courage, and undoubted ability.

Johnston made his headquarters at Bowling Green, the key to the railway system of Kentucky, where he formed an entrenched camp, with about 22,000 effectives. His line extended from Columbus, on the left, to Cumberland Gap, on the right. In January 1862, Columbus, which was fortified, was held by General Polk, with 18,000 men, and there was another fortified camp at Cumberland Gap.

General Leonidas Polk was one of the picturesque figures of that time. A nephew of President Polk, he had been educated at West Point, but had soon left the army to study theology. At the outbreak of the Civil War he had been for twenty years the Episcopal Bishop of Louisiana; he soon changed his surplice for the uniform of a major-general, and was at once placed in command of the Confederate forces in western Kentucky.

Below Columbus, the Mississippi was guarded by two or three garrisoned forts, and the Tennessee and Cumberland were protected by two forts erected just south of the Kentucky border, where the rivers were about twelve miles apart. Fort Henry stood on the east bank of the Tennessee, and Fort Donelson on the west bank of the Cumberland. Better positions could have been chosen, a few miles further down, at a point where the rivers are separated only by a space of three miles, but the sites were selected at the time that the neutrality of Kentucky was respected, so they were kept within the limits of Tennessee. These two forts were held by General Tilghman with 5000 or 6000 men.

Opposed to Johnston's Confederate forces, General Buell had an army of some 45,000 men, with headquarters at Louisville. General Halleck was in chief command in Missouri, with headquarters at St. Louis, and his territorial department included that part of

Kentucky west of the Cumberland River. The commands of these two generals were absolutely independent. At Cairo there was also a strong Union fleet of ironclad gunboats under Commodore Foote.

On becoming commander-in-chief, McClellan had given this important post in the West to Halleck, whose good fortune was soon to carry him to the supreme position in the army at Washington. Yet he was a worse than mediocre man. He possessed a thorough knowledge of the art of war as it exists in books, and could sit in his study and plan campaigns, but he had had no practical experience of operations in the field, and was later to be responsible for some of the most terrible disasters of the war.

The situation of the Confederates in Kentucky, as Johnston well knew, was extremely precarious. The capture of Fort Henry and Fort Donelson, and the destruction of the railway bridges across the rivers, would break his lines of communication with the garrisons on the Mississippi; would necessitate his retreat from Bowling Green, and would also probably result in the evacuation of Columbus by Polk.

Johnston tried in vain to secure reinforcements: his forces were too small, and the men he had were badly armed. He knew also that the Federal fleet was far superior to anything that the Confederates could assemble in the three rivers.

The plan proposed by Buell for the opening campaign of 1862 in this theatre was for Halleck to ascend the Tennessee and the Cumberland with 20,000 men, supported by the ironclad fleet, while he himself advanced southward along the line of railway to Bowling Green. Halleck did not favor this plan, but wanted the bulk of Buell's forces joined to his own, so that he could move up the Cumberland with an army of 60,000 men, while Buell, with the rest of his command, acted as a containing force in front of Bowling Green. McClellan would not give his approval to either of these plans, but kept urging Buell to advance into East Tennessee, to secure possession of the railroad there, and to support the inhabitants of that region, who were intensely loyal in their sentiments.

In December and January, there were some minor military operations in this territory, the most important of which was the battle of Mill Springs. Here, on the 19 January 1862, General Thomas, with a division of Buell's army, defeated a force of Confederates, and drove it back into the mountains at Cumberland Gap.

George Henry Thomas, whom Professor Fiske terms "one of the most attractive characters in American history since George Washington," was a native of Virginia. He was educated at West

Major-General Don Carlos Buell, Commander of the Army of the Ohio in the Shiloh Campaign.

The Union's western naval base, 1862.

Point, and served with distinction in the Mexican War. Like Lee and both the Johnstons he was confronted with the painful question of allegiance, but, unlike them, his sense of loyalty prevailed over his love for his native State.

It has always been a matter of much debate as to who was entitled to the credit of the plan for the expedition to Forts Henry and Donelson, which struck the first effectual blow at the Confederacy. Halleck claimed the credit, and Sherman seems to accord it to him, but Buell and Grant have also been awarded the honor.

On the 29 January, Halleck received a telegram from McClellan stating that a Confederate deserter had reported that Beauregard was under orders to leave Manassas for Kentucky with fifteen regiments. Three days later, without awaiting further instructions from Washington, or arranging for any cooperation from Buell, Halleck ordered General Grant, with 17,000 men and Foote's ironclads, to ascend the Tennessee and attack Fort Henry, in order to antici- pate the arrival of Beauregard's forces.

Not until the age of thirty-nine did the call come for Ulysses Simpson Grant, who now enters upon the scene of History. Born in 1822, on the banks of the Ohio; educated at West Point, where he achieved no distinction; present in every battle, except one, of the Mexican War, where he gained little reputation, he had been engaged since, without success, in several lines of business. At the outbreak of hostilities in 1861, he was earning a scanty subsistence in the leather trade at Galena, Illinois — a broken, dissipated man, for whom no one would have dreamed of predicting a brilliant future.

When the President's call for troops came in April, Grant raised and drilled a company of volunteers. Presently he passed to the charge of a district, then to the command of the great depot at Cairo. He was soon a brigadier, and in November, at the head of a little force of 3000 men, he fought the battle of Belmont. This was only a small affair, but it made him known to his superiors as a leader cool and adroit in the field, and secured for him the command of the Fort Henry expedition.

The expedition started the 2 February. As there were not enough boats to transport all the troops at once, McClernand's division went first, and landed about nine miles below Fort Henry. General Grant followed with the remainder of the troops, and on the 5th moved his army by boats up to a point four miles below the fort.

Fort Henry was a regular bastioned work, enclosing a space of about ten acres. It was in a bend of the river, so that twelve of its seventeen guns had a perfect sweep of the water, but they were nearly at the water level, which made their fire ineffective against the Union gunboats. The fort was badly located: it was not only surrounded by higher ground, but was perfectly commanded by heights on the opposite bank, where the Confederates had built an- other work, called Fort Heiman.

At this time, General Tilghman had about 2500 men in the two forts on the Tennessee, but on the morning of the 6th he sent all of his troops to Fort Donelson, except about sev- enty men, whom he kept at Fort Henry, under his own command, to hold the fort, and serve the guns, until the infantry was well on its way.

At eleven o'clock on the morning of the 6 February, General Grant moved on the forts, with his land forces, and Foote's fleet consisting of four ironclads and three wooden gun- boats. At a distance of a mile, the fleet opened fire, and two hours later Tilghman lowered his colors and ran up a white flag. The Union troops were so much delayed by the high water in the creeks, and the muddy roads, that the Confederates had time to make good their retreat to Fort Donelson.

Immediately after the fall of Fort Henry, two of the gunboats proceeded up the river and destroyed the bridge of the Memphis and Ohio Railroad. Then they continued on up the river as far as the Muscle Shoals, in Alabama, destroying large quantities of Confederate supplies, and spreading alarm through the whole region.

As soon as General Johnston learned of the fall of Fort Henry, he sent about half of his force under General Floyd to Fort Donelson, and with the remainder of his army, some 14,000 men, retreated to Nashville, where he arrived on the 16 February.

There were two roads leading from Fort Henry across to Fort Donelson, about twelve miles east on the Cumberland. The intervening country was cut up by creeks and marshes, hills and ravines; and was heavily wooded. The water was high in all the creeks, and the roads were in very bad condition. Grant wanted to proceed at once to Fort Donelson, but it continued to rain, and his artillery and wagons could not move. He was also delayed by the time necessary for the fleet to run down the Tennessee and ascend the Cumberland, as he did not "feel justified" in attacking without the coöperation of the fleet. So it was not until the 12 February that his army moved. On that day he started with the divisions of McClernand and C. F. Smith. Another division which had just arrived, under Lew Wal-

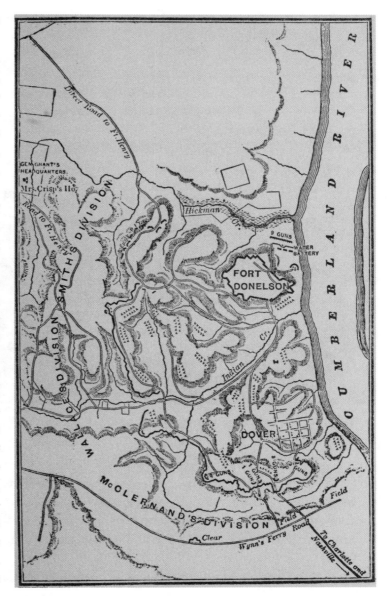

Fort Donelson

lace, and which included a brigade sent by General Buell, went around by water. Before night the neighborhood of the fort was reached by McClernand and Smith, and the troops took up a position surrounding the work. The next day Wallace arrived, the lines were rectified, and some fighting took place.

Fort Donelson was a larger and more elaborate work than Fort Henry. The main fort was an irregular, bastioned parapet, enclosing a space of about 100 acres, nearly 500 yards long in its greatest dimension. It stood 100 feet above the river, at the eastern end of a ridge which narrowed down to a mere neck just west of the fort. Except at this point, the ground sloped

The Cincinnati, the gunboat that fired the first shot in the bombardment of the Fort Henry, Feb. 6 1862, at a range of 1,700 yards.

from the work on all sides. On the north, Hickman Creek, which was unfordable, formed a perfect barrier. On the river side there were two water batteries fifty or sixty feet above water level, commanding the river to the north. About 700 yards west of the main work was another ridge, cut through in two or three places by forks of Indian Creek, and curving from Hickman Creek around to another unfordable stream south of Dover. On the irregular crest of this ridge a line of entrenchments had been constructed, strengthened with abattis. This line, which was two and a half miles long, was what came to be called, later in the war, riflepit — a trench with the earth thrown up on the outer side. Batteries were constructed at nine points in the line, and armed with the guns of eight field batteries. The entire line followed the face of ridges from fifty to eighty feet high, except toward the south where a break was made by the valley of Indian Creek, and faced on valleys or ravines filled with forest and underbrush. The position was a strong one, but possessed the common fault of the Confederate works — it was so large as to need several thousand men to defend it, and a small army in case of an obstinate and protracted siege. "Such conditions," says Mr. Ropes, "made too heavy a draft on the limited resources of the Confederate armies. Thousands of men were shut up in these works who should have been serving in the field with the active armies."

This strong position was held by an army of 19,000 men, commanded by General Pillow, an officer of but little merit. Second in command was General Buckner, an excellent soldier,

whose relations with Pillow were rather strained. On the
13 February, the day after Grant's arrival, a third general, senior in rank to Pillow, came in and took command.
This was John B. Floyd, lately Secretary of War under
President Buchanan. He was a man absolutely unfit for
such an important command, and Johnston made a great
mistake in sending him there.

Upon its arrival, the army of General Grant took
up its position on another ridge about 600 or 700 yards
from the Confederate line, and approximately parallel to
it. McClernand's division was on the right, Smith's on
the left, and Wallace's, after its arrival the next day, held
the centre. Grant now had about 25,000 men on the field,
the divisions were all closed up, and the line was extended around to the right so as to bar the road to Charlotte
and Nashville, the only Confederate line of retreat.

General Grant considered the enemy's works too
strong to be assaulted successfully by the raw troops at
his disposal, and relied upon the fleet to reduce the fort.
On the 14th the fleet arrived, and Commodore Foote at
once took his ships into action. But the gunboats found

*Ulysses S. Grant, a brave, resolute, obstinate
man and a hard fighter.*

no such easy task as the reduction of Fort Henry. The Confederate guns, placed 32 feet above
the river, were served skillfully, and their fire was very effective. Two of the ironclads had
their steering apparatus shot away and helplessly drifted down the river out of the action.
The other two were so badly damaged as to be compelled to withdraw. The whole fleet was
put *hors de combat*, and Foote himself was severely wounded. It would be necessary to send
the disabled vessels back to Cairo for repairs, and further cooperation by the fleet seemed for
the moment out of question.

After he had witnessed the repulse of the fleet, Grant felt that a speedy victory was not
to be expected, and looked forward to a protracted siege. To make the situation even more
discouraging, the weather had turned intensely cold, the temperature dropping to twenty degrees below the freezing-point. The men were without tents, and could not build fires, within
full range of the enemy's guns. Many of them, in their inexperience, had thrown away their
blankets, and were frost-bitten — some even frozen to death. The wagons had not all come
up, and rations were scarce. "The sun went down on the night of the 14 February 1862, leaving the army confronting Fort Donelson anything but comforted over its prospects."

The Confederates also were much discouraged, and Grant's problem was nearer a solution than he imagined. It was feared that the Federal troops would gain the bank of the river
above the fort, establish batteries there to command the stream, and thus prevent supplies
from reaching the defenders. At a council of war held that evening, the three generals decided
to attack the Union right at daybreak, with the object of forcing it off the Charlotte road,
and opening up an avenue of escape. The plan was an excellent one, and it was well executed;

General S.B. Buckner, defender of Fort Donelson.

but it failed in the end because no orders were issued, or arrangements made, for an immediate retreat in case of success.

The next morning, the 15th, the Federal right wing under McClernand was vigorously attacked, and rolled up against Wallace. By one o'clock the Confederates had gained their object, and the road to Nashville was open. Then, in the very moment of victory, Pillow, who had directed the attack, made the fatal blunder of ordering the men back into their works.

At this hour, General Grant arrived on the scene. On account of his wound, Commodore Foote had asked Grant to come aboard his flagship for a conference; it thus happened that the Union commander was absent all the morning. When Grant reached the field, the fighting was all over, and the victorious Confederates were retiring to their works.

Grant sent a despatch to Foote, telling of the events of the morning, and adding, "I must make a charge to save appearances." He asked Foote to make a demonstration with the gunboats and fire a few shells at long range. He said, this "may secure a victory: otherwise all may be defeated."

"It is clear," comments Mr. Ropes, "that he did not expect any important result from the charge; it was, he saw, the proper thing to order, but he relied mainly on the reappearance of the fleet to restore confidence to his troops."

After sending his message to Foote, Grant rode over to find Smith on his left, and gave the order for an immediate assault on the works in his front. The veteran Charles F. Smith, one of the finest officers in the Union service, led the attack in person, and inspired his raw troops with his own dauntless courage. Fortunately for the attacking party, the Confederate troops who had held this part of the line had not yet had time to regain their entrenchments after the morning sortie, and the works were easily carried, although the few troops left in this part of the fort defended themselves with great tenacity. The position thus carried by Smith was found to possess unusual importance: it was an angle inside the fort, which practically commanded the entire work.

In the meantime, under orders from General Grant, Wallace and McClernand had advanced, and reoccupied the positions from which they had been driven in the morning. By nightfall the Union forces again blocked the Confederate line of retreat.

That evening another council of war was held within the fort, and it was decided to surrender the works on the best terms possible. Then ensued a remarkable scene. Floyd, who was at that moment under indictment at Washington for misuse of public funds, said that he would rather die than fall into the hands of the Federals. So he passed the command over to Pillow, who, in turn, transferred it to Buckner, and these two generals escaped up the river on a small steamboat. At the same time, Forrest, with the greater part of his cavalry, succeeded in getting by the Union right, and evading capture.

At daybreak Buckner sent a note to General Grant proposing the appointment of commissioners to agree upon terms of capitulation. Grant wrote back the since famous reply: "No terms except unconditional and immediate surrender" would be accepted, and added that he proposed "to move immediately" upon the enemy's works. Without further parley, Buckner thereupon surrendered his command.

"With plenty of food and ammunition," says Major Steele, "there does not appear to have been any adequate excuse for surrendering at that time."

The Union losses at Fort Donelson were about 2600 killed and wounded, 224 missing. It is impossible to give any reliable statement of the Confederate casualties, but they probably did not exceed 2000 killed and wounded.

There are also no reliable figures regarding the number of the garrison, or the number of prisoners captured. There were probably some 19,000 men in the fort, of whom about a quarter escaped. Badeau states that rations were issued at Cairo to 14,623 prisoners, which seems to be the most trustworthy statement of the number captured. Mr. Ropes says: "About 11,500 men with 40 guns were the fruits of this great victory." Mr. Fiske states: "The surrender delivered up to Grant nearly 15,000 prisoners, with 65 cannon and 17,000 muskets."

The capture of Fort Donelson was the greatest military achievement that the American Continent had yet witnessed, but its moral and strategic results were out of all proportion to its physical dimensions. The two great rivers were laid open for hundreds of miles. There was a panic at Nashville. The State government fled, with the archives and the money in the treasury. Johnston evacuated the city, and fell back to Murfreesboro. Just a week after the surrender, a division of Buell's army occupied the capital of Tennessee. On the Mississippi, the results were equally decisive. Columbus was no longer tenable, and Polk soon retreated as far as Corinth, in Mississippi.

At one bound, General Grant became a national hero, and this he deserved, to be. No criticism can be made of his conduct of the campaign. He had the good sense to rely upon the gunboats to reduce the fort, and, "with a discretion which on similar occasions afterwards he did not always show, he did not waste the strength of his troops by assaulting the unbroken and well-manned fortifications of his antagonists." He well merited the praise which came to him from the public, and the promotion which the Government at once bestowed upon him.

The general strategy of the war in the West may be regarded as a flanking movement on a vast scale, by which, after four years, the left of the Confederacy was at last turned and its overthrow accomplished. At the opening of 1862, of course, no such plan was considered. The Federal objective was to break the Confederate line of defence at its most vulnerable point; and the Donelson campaign was an example of what the text-books call "strategic penetration." The two wings of the Confederate army were at Columbus and Bowling Green, 170 miles apart, or less than one day, in point of time, by rail. The capture of Henry and

Donelson, the destruction of the railway bridge over the Tennessee, and the occupation of Clarksville by the Federal forces, broke the line of communication between the two wings of Johnston's army, and compelled their retirement.

Although this brief campaign was most successful, it had not been free from a certain measure of risk. General Halleck had begun it without any authority from Washington, and without any understanding with Buell either for support or cooperation. Buell was perfectly willing to cause a diversion by advancing in force on Bowling Green, but he was still under orders to invade East Tennessee. He offered Halleck one of his brigades, which arrived in time to take part in the capture of Donelson; and he placed at his disposal eight new regiments then in Ohio and Indiana. He also wrote McClellan, on the 5 February, advocating the postponement of the East Tennessee movement, and finally obtained his approval of the advance on Bowling Green. From that moment, McClellan did all in his power to coordinate the operations of the forces under Halleck and Buell.

To reinforce Grant, Buell had to send troops around by the Ohio River, while Johnston had the short line of the railroad and the highways. This gave Johnston a chance which he failed to improve. He should have left a small force at Bowling Green, to hold back Buell, and himself led the remainder of his army against Grant. Instead of doing this, he sent an incompetent general, Floyd, with 12,000 men to Donelson, while he himself fell back with 14,000 to Nashville.

"In all of the operations of the Civil War," says Major Steele, "it would be hard to find another example of such crass incapacity as was displayed by the Confederate commanders at Fort Donelson.... Not one, but several opportunities offered, ... which, if made use of by a bold and skillful general, might have resulted in a Confederate success."

At the opening of the campaign, Johnston had the advantage of interior lines and could have concentrated his forces more quickly than Halleck and Buell, but after the capture of Henry and Donelson the case was exactly reversed. His line was penetrated; the railway was in the possession of the Federals, and they had on their side all the strategic advantages. Johnston was forced to abandon Bowling Green and fall back to Nashville. He should have left the defence of Donelson to its own little garrison, and kept his forces united; or if he wanted to defend that point, he should have gone there himself. He never would have made the mistake of shutting his army up within the fort to be besieged, and he did not expect Floyd to do so. "He wished Donelson defended if possible, but he did not wish the army to be sacrificed in the attempt." One of his last telegrams to Floyd said: "If you lose the fort bring your troops to Nashville if possible." Any general of average ability would have found it "possible."

All the commanders had cavalry, but with the exception of Forrest's work at Donelson, their role in this campaign was insignificant. The generals had not yet learned how to employ this important arm of the service in the strategic duty of "security and information." Even Forrest, who later became one of the ablest cavalry commanders in the Confederate army, up to this time had done no more than forage and fight. General Grant had cavalry at Donelson, but did not employ it to any extent. It should be stated, however, that his cavalry was made up of volunteers, lately enlisted, and neither officers nor men had had any experience.

This was the first instance in the Civil War in which a river was used as the line of operations, and it furnished nearly the only successful instance in any modern campaign. The ease with which transports can be harassed by the enemy on shore renders the use of rivers as lines of operation very exceptional.

No other Union victory, except Gettysburg, had so disheartening an effect upon the people of the South, and none caused so much exultation in the North, as the capture of Forts Henry and Donelson. "The effect," says Mr. Ropes, "was electrical. It was the first great success won by the Union arms within the limits of the Confederacy." Professor Fiske also chronicles the hopeful feeling throughout the North: "In the gloomy record of the anxious and impatient year which had just passed, this great victory was the one bright spot. The victor became a popular hero."

Halleck, who was personally entitled to so little credit, asked the Government to enlarge his command so as to cover all of the armies west of the Alleghanies, and on the 11 March his request was granted. The territory was divided into three departments, Pope in Missouri commanding the right, Grant on the Tennessee the centre, and Buell at Nashville the left. Grant had already been made major-general of volunteers, and Buell, Pope, Smith, McClernand, and Wallace were raised to the same rank.

CHAPTER FOUR

APRIL 1862

SHILOH

THE first of April 1862 General Grant's command, now called the Army of the Tennessee, was encamped on the west bank of the Tennessee River at Pittsburg Landing, a point about a hundred miles south of Fort Henry, and twenty miles north of Corinth, where Johnston was assembling his army. Grant's headquarters were at Savannah, a small town about nine miles further down on the other (east) bank of the river.

A few weeks prior to this date, Grant had been temporarily suspended, owing to a misunderstanding with Halleck, and the site of the camp was selected by C. F. Smith, who was at first in charge of the expedition. But that excellent officer met early in March with a serious accident, from the effects of which he never recovered.

The ground upon which the camp stood, and upon which the battle of Shiloh was fought, was an irregular triangle, with sides three or four miles long, bounded on the north and west by Snake Creek and its tributary Owl Creek; on the east by the Tennessee; on the south by Lick Creek and its branch, Locust Grove Creek, a small brook in quite a deep ravine. At that time all of these streams were more or less flooded.

The highest ground, about 200 feet above the river, was a ridge lying north of Locust Grove Creek, and from this point the land sloped gradually to the level of the camps, 100 feet below. The ground, uneven and thickly wooded, was mostly impassable for cavalry, although there were several clearings of from 20 to 80 acres. A number of small roads intersected the field, and on one of these, running out toward Corinth, near the west of the position, was a rude meeting-house built of logs and known as Shiloh Church, which gave the name to the battle.

The greater part of the army was arranged across the base, or open front, of the triangle between Owl and Lick creeks, which protected its two flanks. This open front was the only quarter in which the army was exposed to assault. At a later period of the war this line would have been entrenched, and the whole position made impregnable.

The right of the line, near the crossing of Owl Creek by the Purdy road, was held by Sherman, with Prentiss next to him on the left. On Sherman's left, and rear, was McClernand, while Stuart's brigade of Sherman's division held the extreme left, resting upon Lick Creek. From a mile to a mile and a half in the rear, stretching from a point just above the Landing nearly across to Snake Creek, were the divisions of Hurlbut and C. F. Smith — the latter now under the command of William Wallace, owing to Smith's injury. The division of

Lew Wallace was five miles down the river at Crump's Landing, whence a road runs west to Purdy. Another road, parallel with the river, connected Wallace with the Union position by a bridge lately built over Snake Creek.

From Pittsburg Landing two roads led direct to Corinth, only twenty miles away, where it was known that Johnston was assembling an army, estimated at from 50,000 to 80,000 men; but, as above stated, no works of any kind were thrown up on the exposed side of the Federal position; nor was there arranged any line of defence or plan of action in case of attack. Furthermore, there was no possibility of retreat from the position: no bridge could be thrown across the Tennessee, which, at the time, was very high, overflowing its banks. In the rear were deep and muddy creeks, which were practically impassible. The whole arrangement was manifestly faulty, and indicates great carelessness on the part of General Grant. His headquarters were nine miles away, and all the well-known maxims of war, applicable to such a situation, were unheeded by him. Probably there never was an army encamped in the

Shiloh

heart of a hostile country with so little regard to the manifest risks which are inseparable from such a position.

For this state of affairs, Halleck was largely responsible. It was by his permission and approval that Grant, with over 40,000 men, was encamped at Pittsburg Landing, in such an exposed position. But Grant, who was on the ground, cannot escape his share of the responsibility.

Major-General Henry Wagner Halleck. Sherman credits Halleck with having first discovered that Forts Henry and Donelson, where the Tennessee and the Cumberland Rivers so closely approach each other, were the key points to the defensive line of the Confederates in the West.

Halleck had, indeed, ordered Buell to direct his march on Savannah, but in his correspondence he never once intimated to Buell that Grant's army was in peril until it was joined by the troops coming from Nashville. In reality, that danger was imminent.

As we have seen, the army under the command of Johnston had retired from Nashville to Murfreesboro. Thence it marched south over very bad roads to Decatur, in Alabama. Here, about the middle of March, the Tennessee River was crossed, and the march resumed in a westerly direction, the head of the column reaching Corinth, in Mississippi, about the 18th. Johnston had with him some 20,000 men, and he was almost immediately joined by General Bragg, with about 10,000 troops from Pensacola and New Orleans. To this point also Beauregard, his able second in command, directed the forces of Polk, who, since the evacuation of Columbus, had been at Humboldt and Jackson.

On the 29 March, Johnston formally assumed the command of these forces, to which he gave the name of the "Army of the Mississippi." Bragg was made chief-of-staff, and Beauregard was designated as second in command. The army was divided into three corps, under the command of Polk, Bragg, and Hardee. There was also a reserve division of infantry, under Breckinridge, lately the Vice-President of the United States. The army numbered nearly 40,000 men, of whom 35,000 were infantry and the rest cavalry and artillery. There were about 100 guns.

The Confederate forces were ably commanded. Johnston was generally considered to be one of the finest officers in the service. Bragg, who subsequently commanded the army, stood very high as an organizer and disciplinarian, and was a good general, although not a successful strategist. Breckinridge, although a civilian, was a gallant and efficient officer.

Johnston, who was well-informed regarding the position of the Federals, was anxious to strike Grant before Buell could arrive, but it was impossible to complete the organization of his new army before the first of April. Orders for the advance were finally issued on the 3rd. Then, the roads were found so bad, and the weather was so rainy, it was impossible to cover the short distance of twenty miles under three days, so that the army did not get within striking distance until Saturday afternoon, the 5 April. Beauregard felt certain that Buell's army must have joined Grant by this time, and advised that the plan be given up, but to this Johnston would not consent. Accordingly the orders were issued to attack the enemy at daybreak on Sunday, the 6th.

The Federal forces under General Grant comprised six divisions of infantry, and numbered on paper nearly 45,000 men, of whom about 3000 were cavalry. There were over 20 batteries — more than 100 guns. All of the division-generals were men of unquestioned bravery, and perfectly equal to their tasks. Sherman subsequently rose to the command of this army.

In the meantime, the Army of the Ohio, under General Buell, was slowly marching across the country, from Nashville, on the Cumberland, to Savannah on the Tennessee. His force consisted of five divisions, under Thomas, McCook, Nelson, Crittenden, and Wood, and numbered about 37,000 men, with a full complement of artillery, and some cavalry.

The army marched steadily, but without haste, covering about fifteen miles a day. At Duck River, it was found that the bridge had been burned by the enemy, and this caused a delay of nearly two weeks. The movement was not pressed, because Buell had no intimation, from either Halleck or Grant, that the army at Pittsburg Landing was in any danger of attack. In fact, to use Buell's own words, he understood that he was "not to succor General Grant's army, but to form a junction with it for an ulterior offensive campaign."

Nelson, who was in the lead, arrived at Savannah with his division on Saturday, 5 April, about noon, and with one of his brigade commanders, Ammert, saw Grant that same afternoon. Ammen suggested that the division should cross the river at once, and join the army encamped at Pittsburg Landing, but Grant declined the offer — remarking that there would be no battle there, and that they would have to go to Corinth. The same day Grant wrote to Halleck that he had "scarcely the faintest idea" that an attack would be made upon him, but that he should be prepared if it took place. Such blind confidence is hard to explain, when he thought that Johnston had at Corinth, on his own estimate, "not far from 80,000 men."

Sherman, who appears to have been in command when Grant was not at the camp, shared in full the confidence of his chief. On the 5th he wrote Grant: "I do not apprehend anything like an attack on our position." Both Sherman and Prentiss, however, sent out small parties to reconnoitre. Several bodies of the enemy were encountered on Saturday, and on Sunday morning at three o'clock Prentiss

Brigadier-General William H.L. "Lew" Wallace, the author of Ben-Hur, was killed at Shiloh, April 10, 1862.

Confederate soldiers before Shiloh. The Civil War proved that in fighting quality there was little to choose between the soldiers of the North and the South.

despatched an entire brigade to ascertain the extent of the Confederate forces. About six o'clock these troops came in contact with the enemy's first line, under Hardee, and were driven back with loss.

The original Confederate order was to attack at three o'clock on the morning of Saturday, the 5th, but the troops were not in position until late that afternoon. All day Friday they had advanced over muddy roads, hindered by a pelting rain. After midnight a violent storm broke upon them, as they stood under arms in the pitch darkness, with no shelter but the trees. This was followed by clearing weather, and the sun set on Saturday evening in a cloudless sky. Sunday morning broke upon a scene so fair that it left its memory on thousands of hearts. The sky was clear overhead, the air fresh; and when the sun rose in full splendor, the advancing host passed the word from lip to lip that it was the "sun of Austerlitz."

The Confederates advanced to the attack in three parallel lines, under the command of Hardee, Bragg, and Polk. With the reserve of Breckinridge, they numbered 39,630 men, including 4300 cavalry. The first gun was fired at 5:14, as General Johnston was taking coffee with his staff. They at once mounted and galloped to the front.

Two hours later the Confederate artillery opened fire, and Johnston's army advanced with a rush, confident of victory. The Union troops, suddenly alive to the fact that they were attacked in great force, hardly had time to seize their muskets and fall in before the first Confederate line was upon them. Not expecting any attack, and not being in order of battle, for the first few hours they were at the mercy of their antagonists. The resistance they offered was therefore of a fragmentary and disconnected character — each body of troops making the best defence it could, often isolated from the other bodies of troops in its vicinity, and therefore exposed to having its flanks turned by the well-supported lines of the Confederate army. To make matters worse, for several hours there was no commanding general on the field, and each division commander was thrown upon his own resources, with such assistance as he could get from his nearest neighbor.

The first shock fell upon the two divisions of Sherman and Prentiss, which were almost entirely composed of raw troops, and they soon gave way, but for the most part fell back to new positions. This gave time for the divisions of McClernand, Hurlbut, and Wallace, to get under arms and form in order of battle.

Sherman's division naturally retired on that of McClernand, and Hurlbut sent one brigade to their assistance. These troops fought gallantly and stubbornly during the whole day, without the slightest aid from the centre, from which they were separated by a wide gap. Falling back from one position to another, at the close of the day they covered the bridge over Snake Creek by which Lew Wallace was expected to arrive. In his report McClernand states that this was the eighth position he had occupied during the battle.

Prentiss's division, also composed of raw troops, fell back upon the two remaining brigades of Hurlbut, and William Wallace brought up his division to their assistance. About ten o'clock these three bodies of troops, constituting the centre of the army, took up a very strong position, which the Confederates called the "Hornets' Nest." This was located near the centre of the Union line, about halfway between the church and the river. It was a wooded area with dense undergrowth, and was well suited for defence. Here they held out for five or six hours, against the repeated assaults of the enemy, whom they again and again beat back with severe loss. It was in directing one of these assaults, about two-thirty, that General Johnston was killed. He was struck by a rifle-ball which cut an artery in the leg. If a tourniquet had been applied, the wound need not have been fatal; but Johnston, absorbed in his work, paid no attention to it, and suddenly fell dead from loss of blood. His death was a greater misfortune to the South than the loss of the battle.

Finally, after four o'clock, Bragg abandoned these costly frontal attacks, and advanced beyond the Federal position. Hurlbut, finding himself flanked, retired to the Landing. This exposed Prentiss's left, and forced him to change front. Soon afterwards, about five o'clock, the two divisions of Prentiss and Wallace were attacked by the Confederate corps of Polk and Hardee in front and on both flanks. In trying to withdraw his command, Wallace was killed, and between five and half-past five o'clock Prentiss was forced to surrender, with about 2200 men. This ended the resistance of the Federal centre.

The isolated brigade of Stuart, on the extreme left, maintained its position until after three o'clock, and then succeeded in retiring to the Landing, having lost about half its men.

Late in the afternoon there were from 5000 to 15,000 fugitives crowded under the high bluff near the Landing. Efforts were made from time to time to rally them, but they were thoroughly demoralized and would not budge from their shelter.

General Grant was taking an early breakfast at Savannah when he heard the sound of heavy firing at the Landing. He ordered Nelson to march his division up the river to a point opposite the Landing, ready to be ferried over. Then he started up the river himself in a steamer, stopping at Crump's Landing to direct Lew Wallace to be ready to march on receipt of orders. Finding on his arrival that the attack was very serious, he sent a staff-officer to order Wallace to march at once. He then rode to the battlefield, saw Sherman about ten o'clock, and afterwards Prentiss at the Hornets' Nest, which he ordered him to maintain at all hazards. Realizing then how dangerous the situation was, at noon he dispatched an urgent note to Buell, asking him to get his troops on the field at once.

The final Federal position of the day was on a line running from just above the Landing to the bridge across Snake Creek. The left of this position was covered by a ravine partly overflowed with backwater. Here a force of some 4000 men was collected; and a battery of twenty pieces was planted on the bluffs, by Colonel Webster of Grant's staff, just as three Confederate brigades were advancing to the attack. These guns opened upon them, while at the same time two of the Union gunboats enfiladed the Confederate lines. The Confederates, loath to abandon the contest, in which victory seemed almost within their grasp, rushed down into the ravine, and climbed the steep slope on the further side. Here they received the terrible fire of the battery, and the destructive volleys of the Union infantry. Again and again they attempted to reach the crest, but were as often forced to retire. The sun was fast disappearing and little time was left to finish the work of the day. Just as night set in, Beauregard, who was now in supreme command, ordered the troops to withdraw. For this he has been severely criticised, but nothing was to be gained that afternoon by prolonging the action.

In his review of the battle, General Buell, speaking of the final Confederate assault, says: "The attack was poorly organized, but it was not repulsed until Ammen [of Nelson's division] arrived.... Had the attack been made before Nelson could arrive, ... it would have succeeded beyond all question."

As a matter of fact, Ammen's brigade "was ferried across the river just in time to see the end; it had two men killed and one wounded." The arrival of Nelson, therefore, did not affect the result in the smallest degree.

Buell's statement is also directly contradicted by Beauregard's article on the battle. He writes: "After the capture of General Prentiss no serious effort was made to press the victory by the corps commanders. In fact the troops had got out of the hands of the corps, divisional, and brigade commanders; and for the most part, moreover, at the front, were out of ammunition. Several most gallant, uncombined efforts ... were made to reach and carry the Federal battery, but in every instance the effort failed." He adds that, "really the attack had ceased at every point," before he issued orders at six o'clock to suspend hostilities and withdraw the troops from under fire.

Professor Fiske considers General Buell's article as "one of the most masterly pieces of military criticism ... in any language." But Buell was so biased by his jealousy and hatred of General Grant that his statements cannot be accepted without many qualifications.

Mr. Ropes, also, shows his animosity to General Grant in his declaration that the final attack would probably have succeeded but for the arrival of Buell's fresh and well-disciplined troops. He says that, if the Landing had been seized and occupied by the Confederates, they could easily have prevented Nelson's division from crossing, and what was left of Grant's army might have been forced to surrender. "But," says General Beauregard, "in every instance the effort failed."

Nelson's division was delayed in reaching the field through the neglect of Grant to provide steamers to transport the troops from Savannah. They were forced to march up the east side of the river, through a swamp in which the artillery had to be abandoned. The division of Lew Wallace, of Grant's army, took the wrong road in the morning, and did not arrive until after dark. Probably not more than 12,000 men of the Army of the Tennessee were with the colors that night.

"It is evident from all the accounts — Grant's included— that the battle of Sunday was fought by the Union army without any directing head," says Mr. Ropes.

"Fortunate was it for the Union cause that five such gallant and capable division-commanders were on the field. They did all that could be done in the circumstances in which they were placed. But it cannot be supposed that their efforts would not have been better employed and therefore more successful had they found in Grant a general who was capable of assuming the entire control and direction of a great battle. Grant, however, was not a general of this sort. He had neither the ability nor the experience for such a task."

The battle of Sunday was fought by the Confederates with the greatest energy and courage, but it failed of final success because of tactical errors. Their plan was to turn the Union left, so as to cut the Federals off from the Landing, and surround them in the angle of Owl Creek, in which event they hoped to insure a surrender. But in the heat of the conflict this excellent plan was lost sight of, and their strength was wasted for hours in a vain effort to take the Hornets' Nest by a frontal attack. With all his great abilities, it must be admitted that Johnston did not attempt on this day to fill the role of an army commander. He left the general control of the action to Beauregard, and confined himself to directing the assault on the Union centre, where he lost his life.

During the night the remainder of Nelson's division arrived, also that of Crittenden, and early in the morning McCook came up. These three divisions of Buell's army, numbering about 20,000 men, were placed on the left of the Union line. The right was held by the divisions of Hurlbut and McClernand, which still preserved their organization, and the 5000 fresh troops of Lew Wallace. The divisions of Sherman and William Wallace were broken up, but many of the men were in line for the second day's battle.

Grant and Buell determined to assume the offensive as early as possible. Buell took the personal direction of his own troops, and handled them in masterly fashion.

The defeat of the Confederates in the battle of the second day was inevitable. They could put only 20,000 men in line, while the Federals had 25,000 fresh troops, besides at least 10,000 who had taken part in the action of Sunday. As Professor Fiske remarks, the Civil War proved that in fighting quality there was little to choose between the soldiers of the North and the South, so that, under similar conditions, victory always took the side of the heaviest battalions.

The Confederates held practically the same line, to the north of Shiloh Church, which had been occupied the previous day by the Union camp. Bragg was on the extreme left, with Polk and Breckinridge next, and finally Hardee, on the extreme right, next to the river. Beauregard handled his troops bravely and skillfully, and was ably seconded by his corps-commanders. No final or critical stand was made anywhere, and by four o'clock the Confederate army had fallen back beyond Shiloh Church. Here General Grant stopped the Federal advance.

Buell crossing the Big Barren. Buell's army arrived at Shiloh in time to turn a Union reverse into a victory.

Considering the numbers engaged, the losses on both sides had been very heavy:

	Federals	Confederates
Killed	1,754	1,728
Wounded	8,408	8,012
Missing	2,885	959
Totals	13,047	10,699

The Federal casualties amounted to over 24 per cent., and the Confederate to more than 26 per cent. — a larger percentage than in any battle of the Civil War except Chickamauga. In his Memoirs, Grant says: "Shiloh was the severest battle fought at the West during the war.... I saw an open field ... so covered with dead that it would have been possible to walk across the clearing, in any direction, stepping on dead bodies, without a foot touching the ground."

For many years the battle of Shiloh was a subject of bitter controversy in the North. "Probably no single battle of the war," says General Sherman, "gave rise to such wild and damaging reports. It was publicly asserted at the North that our army was taken completely by surprise; that the rebels caught us in our tents; bayoneted the men in their beds; that General Grant was drunk; that Buell's opportune arrival saved the Army of the Tennessee from utter annihilation, etc."

These reports were quite generally believed, and were in a measure sustained by the published articles of Buell, Nelson, and others; even Mr. Ropes, who is generally very fair in his criticisms, has many severe comments to make on the subject of General Grant. But after the lapse of sixty years it may now be possible to take a less prejudiced view of the events and incidents of the battle. The falsity of some of the charges, mentioned by General Sherman, will be apparent from the above narrative, but others may be considered here in somewhat greater detail.

General Sherman says: "We did not fortify our camps against an attack, because we had no orders to do so, and because such a course would have made our raw men timid.... At a later period of the war, we could have rendered this position impregnable in one night, but at this time we did not do it."

General Grant writes: "The criticism has often been made that the Union troops should have been entrenched at Shiloh. Up to that time the pick and spade had been but little resorted to at the West. I had, however, taken this subject under consideration soon after reassuming command in the field, and, as already stated, my only military engineer reported unfavorably. Besides this, the troops with me, officers and men, needed discipline and drill more than they did experience with the pick, shovel, and axe.... Under all these circumstances I concluded that drill and discipline were worth more to our men than fortifications."

On this point it may be remarked that even so good a soldier as Robert E. Lee did not employ field entrenchments at Antietam six months later, in the autumn of this same year. It is therefore hardly fair to condemn Grant and his able division-commanders for not having taken such a precaution at this early period of the Civil War.

Grant has also been criticised for maintaining his headquarters at Savannah, nine miles from the camp. He states that it was his intention to move to Pittsburg, but Buell was expected daily, and would come in at Savannah; he therefore remained at that point a few days longer than he otherwise would have done in order to meet Buell on his arrival. The relations between Grant and Buell had never been very cordial, and for this reason Grant wished to show his rival every consideration. Buell, however, was less courteous: although he reached Savannah on Saturday night, he did not make his presence known to Grant; and they did not meet until one o'clock the following day.

On Friday night, the 4 April, when returning from the front, where firing had been heard, Grant was badly injured by a fall of his horse. In the darkness, with the rain pouring down in torrents, on the way back to the boat, the horse fell with Grant's leg under its body. Only the softness of the ground saved the general from a very severe injury. As it was, his boot had to be cut off, and for several days he was unable to walk except with crutches.

It is well known that Grant, on account of his habits, had been somewhat under a cloud when he left the regular army. On the first day of the battle he was under a terrible physical and mental strain, and it would not be strange if he resorted to stimulants, but there is nothing in any of the reports of the battle to show that he was not in the full possession of his faculties.

In his memoirs General Grant denies emphatically the statement so often made, that his troops were badly beaten on the first day of Shiloh. He says: "There was in fact no hour during the day when I doubted the eventual defeat of the enemy."

This statement is borne out by the account of Whitelaw Reid, who has pictured Grant at the moment of the last Confederate attack. He sat his horse, quiet, thoughtful, almost stolid. "Does not the prospect begin to look gloomy?" some one asked. "Not at all," was the quiet reply. "They cannot force our lines around these batteries tonight. Tomorrow we shall attack them with fresh troops and drive them of course."

It is a principle often illustrated in war that when two armies have fought until their strength is well-nigh spent, the one that can soonest summon its jaded energies to a final assault is almost sure to win. Grant was a very brave, resolute, obstinate man, and a hard fighter. Whatever might be the chances, he was determined to hold out to the last. There is little doubt, therefore, that, even without the arrival of Buell, he would have resumed the battle the next morning with the fresh troops of Lew Wallace, and what was left of his other divisions. He would have had about 17,000 men in line; and the Confederate army was reduced to not more than 20,000 troops, all of whom were in organizations which had been greatly shattered by the casualties of the battle of Sunday, as well as weakened by the loss of many valuable officers. There was at least an even chance of winning. As Grant tersely remarks: "The victory was not to either party until the battle was over."

Grant admits that an immediate pursuit of the enemy after the battle "must have resulted in the capture of a considerable number of prisoners and probably some guns." "I wanted to pursue," he says, "but had not the heart to order the men who had fought desperately for two days, lying in the mud and rain whenever not fighting; and I did not feel disposed positively to order Buell, or any part of his command, to pursue. Although the senior in rank at the time, I had been so only a few weeks... . I did not meet Buell in person until too late to get troops ready and pursue with effect."

Grant was a very shy, modest, unassuming man, and, in view of the somewhat strained relations between Buell and himself, it is easy to understand his attitude. But General Buell, as Grant himself states, was a brave, intelligent officer, with much professional pride and ambition, and Buell himself should, not only have proposed, but even insisted upon, taking up the pursuit with his fresh troops, who had not been engaged in the battle. That he did not do so, was doubtless due to the jealousy of Grant which he showed on this, and on many later occasions. He was far more to blame than Grant for not securing the full fruits of the victory.

On this same subject General Buell writes: "I make no attempt to excuse myself or blame others when I say that General Grant's troops, the lowest individual among them not more than the commander himself, appear to have thought that the object of the battle was sufficiently accomplished when they were reinstated in their camps; and that in some way that idea obstructed the reorganization of my line until a further advance that day became impracticable."

And Professor Fiske says: "I suspect that the true explanation, after all, may be that our peace-loving people had not yet come to realize what a terrible affair war is, when truly effective, and especially when waged against our own kin... . We were satisfied with thwarting the hostile army, and did not appreciate the need for terminating its existence."

More than any battle of modern times Shiloh resembled the conflicts of the Middle Ages, in which knight fought against knight in the general melee. An attempt to recount in detail all the incidents of the day would be both tedious and unprofitable: it was like a gigantic kaleido-scope, in which objects were constantly shifting — but never repeated in symmetrical patterns. For this confusion, there were two reasons, principally:

First, the Confederate attack was made in very unusual tactical formation. Instead of the three corps-commanders — Hardee, Polk, and Bragg — taking charge respectively of the left, centre, and right, as was arranged later in the day, Beauregard ordered that the three corps should advance in line, one behind the other. Hardee's corps, with a brigade from Bragg's, was to constitute the first line, the remainder of Bragg's corps the second line, and Polk's corps, with Breckinridge's division, the third.

Second, the camps in which the Federals were taken by surprise were established to suit the convenience of the several commanders, and without any pretence of system. The army was not in the least prepared to receive an attack — it was not even in order of battle. The resistance, therefore, which it offered to the Confederate attack was necessarily of a fragmen-tary and disconnected character — each body of troops making the best defence it could, often isolated from the other bodies of troops in its vicinity. The course which the battle took was therefore what might have been expected under such conditions.

Of all the battles of the Civil War, that of Shiloh, says Major Steele, is the hardest problem for the military student — the most difficult in which to apportion the credit and the blame.

"It is not an easy task," writes Mr. Ropes, "to follow the movements of General Halleck's mind during the ten days which succeeded the fall of Fort Donelson." It is certain, however, that he did not do what McClellan expected of him, and that was to occupy Nashville at once. He did little except to bombard the Government with applications to be given the chief com-mand in the West. "Give it to me," he wrote on the 19 February, "and I will split secession in twain in one month." Finally, on the 11 March 1862, in anticipation of the forward movement in the East, McClellan was relieved of the general command of the armies, and Halleck's wish was granted. His department comprised all of Kentucky and Tennessee, and the army of Gen-eral Buell was placed under him. Although it was a great advantage to the Union cause to have all the forces in this territory under one general, the appointment of Halleck was a mistake. He had been educated at West Point, but most of his life had been passed out of the army, and he had little natural aptitude for military affairs. He was, moreover, careless, indolent, and inexact to a high degree.

Before being placed in command, Halleck did nothing until about the first of March, when he sent C. F. Smith on a sort of "steamboat raid" up the Tennessee. This led to the selection of Pittsburg Landing as a site for the camp of Grant's army. As soon as Halleck was appointed to the supreme command, he ordered Buell to march on Savannah. This was practically the only act of Halleck's in the campaign which was of value: it brought Buell's army to Shiloh in time to turn a Union reverse into a victory; possibly in time to save Grant's army from capture.

It is impossible to say anything in commendation of the tactics employed at Shiloh on ei-ther side. Neither of the hostile armies on that day was really commanded. The two armies in fact fought without any control, and to this fact nearly all the mistakes can be charged. Neither

Grant nor Johnston established headquarters from which to direct his forces. Grant "visited" his several division-commanders, and issued a few verbal orders, but that was about all. Johnston "was killed doing the work of a brigadier." As army commanders, neither Grant nor Johnston exerted any influence upon the tactics of this great battle.

The Confederate plan to turn the Union left, and hem Grant's army into the pocket of Snake and Owl creeks was never carried out. An attempt was made to turn both flanks, and break the centre, all at once — an effort entirely beyond the strength of Johnston's army.

The Confederate attack, in long lines, instead of deep formation, was also an error. Corps, divisions, and brigades, were soon mixed in hopeless confusion: the action degenerated into a series of isolated combats, which, without any general plan, were ineffective. By eleven o'clock there was not a reserve on the field.

On the Federal side, the tactics were fully as bad. With no prearranged plan, no line or order of battle, it was impossible to have any concert of action. A regiment was rarely overcome in front, but fell back because the regiment on its right or left had done so, and exposed its flank. It continued its backward movement until it was well under shelter, thus exposing the flank of its neighbor, who then was also compelled to withdraw. Once in operation the process repeated itself indefinitely.

In his own story of the battle, Beauregard admits that he knew on Sunday night that at least three of Buell's divisions had arrived. If so, he made a great mistake in staying on the field, instead of retreating at once. The battle of the second day was a useless sacrifice of life. Nothing was to be gained by continuing the struggle against such overwhelming odds.

In later years, both Grant and Sherman were very sensitive to the criticisms of their failure to pursue the enemy, and secure the full fruits of the victory. The explanations given in their memoirs are not at all convincing. Bragg reported the next morning that his troops "were utterly disorganized and demoralized." Breckinridge declared, "My troops are worn out, and I don't think can be relied on after the first volley." Grant and Buell had at least 20,000 fresh men to take up the pursuit, which should have resulted in the capture or the complete dispersal of the Confederate army. In answer to an inquiry from Professor Fiske, regarding the failure to pursue the enemy, Sherman, after the war, made the humorous reply: "I assure you, my dear fellow, we had had quite enough of their society for two whole days, and were only too glad to be rid of them on any terms!"

Grant states that the nature of this battle was such that cavalry could not be used in front; he therefore formed his into line in rear, to stop the numerous stragglers. On the Confederate side, Forrest's men charged a battery, capturing some of the guns, and were of service in compelling the surrender of Prentiss. On Monday, they covered the retreat, forming the last line of the rearguard.

Although much more should have been accomplished, the results of the campaign were on the whole satisfactory to the National Government. Kentucky, and all of Tennessee, except the eastern part, were again under Union control; besides this, the Mississippi was free as far as Vicksburg. To offset these advantages, the Confederate army, which should have been destroyed, was still intact.

CHAPTER FIVE

JULY 1861 — JUNE 1862

THE PENINSULA

ON the 21 July 1861 the streets of Washington were crowded with stragglers from the disastrous field of Manassas, better known as Bull Run. The following day, General George B. McClellan was relieved from command of the Army of the West, and on the 27th, by order of President Lincoln, assumed control of the lately defeated troops in the vicinity of the capital. No appointment at that time could have been more acceptable to the people, the press, and the army.

George Brinton McClellan was born in Philadelphia 3 December 1826. Twenty years later he was graduated at West Point, the second in a class in which Stonewall Jackson was seventeenth. As an engineer with Scott's army in Mexico he won distinction. During the Crimean War he was selected as one of the Government's observers, and his report on the campaign was published by special act of Congress. After serving two years as captain of the 1st Cavalry, he resigned, to accept the appointment of chief engineer of the Illinois Central Railroad, of which he soon became vice-president. At the outbreak of the war he was president of the Ohio and Mississippi, with headquarters at Cincinnati. In all the various positions he had held, he had shown great zeal and capacity.

When the President called for troops after the fall of Sumter, Governor Dennison, of Ohio, appointed McClellan major-general of the "Militia Volunteers" of that State, and he organized, equipped, and put in the field the Army of the Ohio. His operations in West Virginia were "brief and brilliant," and he was the only Union general who had yet scored a complete success. At the time he was called to Washington, McClellan was a man of fine soldierly appearance and engaging manners, thirty-five years of age.

No better picture of the situation at the capital could be presented than is to be found in the general's own statement:

"All was chaos and despondency; the city was filled with intoxicated stragglers, and an attack was expected. The troops numbered less than fifty thousand, many of whom were so demoralized and undisciplined that they could not be relied upon even for defensive purposes. Moreover, the term of service of a large part had already expired, or was on the point of doing so. On the Maryland side of the Potomac no troops were posted on the roads leading into the city, nor were there any entrenchments. On the Virginia side the condition of affairs was better in these respects, but far from satisfactory. Sufficient and fit material of war did not exist. The situation was difficult, and fraught with danger."

Vicinity of Richmond

General McClellan immediately appointed his general staff, and the work of organizing and equipping a large army was forthwith undertaken. Ninety days later, on the 27 October, the general officially reported to the Secretary of War that he had an aggregate strength of 168,318, with 147,695 present for duty. Of this number, some 13,000 were only partially armed, leaving an effective force of about 134,000.

As the new levies of infantry arrived at Washington, they were formed into provisional brigades, and stationed in the suburbs of the city, to be perfected by instruction and discipline. By the opening of the spring of 1862 McClellan had created "as noble a body of men as could have been raised, under similar circumstances, the world over." Exclusive of the detachments

McClellan's headquarters before Yorktown. Appointed commander-in-chief on November 1, 1861, McClellan proposed to strike at Richmond in the East and Nashville in the West.

necessary to guard the defences of Washington, the Potomac, and the lower Shenandoah Valley, which required about 55,000 men, there was a field army 158,000 strong.

On the first of November 1861, General Scott retired, and McClellan was appointed to succeed him as commander-in-chief. But, even before this date, McClellan had prepared, at the request of the President, a memorandum setting forth his views as to the proper method of suppressing the rebellion. War all along the line was his purpose. He proposed to strike at

The Monitor's turret could revolve and hurl two projectiles about every 8 minutes. The Monitor and the Merrimac first clashed on March 9, 1862.

the two centres — Richmond in the East and Nashville in the West — while at the same time expeditionary forces were to assail the principal points on the coast and on the Mississippi. Upon these plans, the subsequent successful campaigns were practically based.

Meantime the Confederate army under Joseph E. Johnston remained in its position at Manassas, and no steps were taken by McClellan to destroy or dislodge it. The Confederates were also allowed to set up batteries on the lower Potomac, which closed the navigation of the river, and the general refused to take any action to capture them. Finally, the last of October, occurred the unfortunate affair of Ball's Bluff, in which Colonel Baker, who had lately resigned his seat in the Senate, was slain, and nearly all his men were killed or captured. The people of the North could not understand this prolonged inaction, and became impatient.

The autumn of 1861 passed, and no move was made. The winter was now at hand, and the roads in Virginia had become almost impassable. To make matters worse, McClellan took typhoid fever and was ill for several weeks, in December and January. The Government debt was piling up, and had reached over half a billion dollars. Dissatisfaction was general, especially at Washington, in Government circles, and in Congress.

Finally, President Lincoln issued the first of his famous "War Orders," in which he directed that the army should advance against Manassas on or before the 22 February — a date chosen doubtless for sentimental reasons. This order was not carried into effect, and two other orders were issued by the President — all for the purpose of allaying the popular impatience.

At length McClellan was forced to divulge his plans, and on the 8 March a forward movement on Richmond by way of Urbana was finally decided upon. The very next day, Johnston withdrew his forces from Centreville and the Potomac, and took up a position south of the Rappahannock, with his right at Fredericksburg and his left at Culpeper Court House. The movement placed the Confederate army as near Richmond as the Union forces would be at Urbana, and compelled the abandonment of that route. It was therefore decided to transfer McClellan's army by water to Fort Monroe, which was held by a Federal garrison, and make that fortress the base for an advance on Richmond by way of the peninsula between the York and James rivers.

On the same day that the Urbana plan was approved, an order was issued forming army corps and assigning the senior general officers to their command. This action was taken without the knowledge of McClellan, and against his judgment that the appointments should have been postponed until the generals had been tried in the field. The organization was as follows:

First Corp: McDowell — Divisions: Franklin, McCall, King
Second Corp: Sumner — Divisions: Richardson, Blenker, Sedgwick
Third Corp: Heintzelman — Divisions: Porter, Hooker, Kearny
Fourth Corp: Keyes — Divisions: Couch, Smith, Casey

Before leaving for the Peninsula, McClellan decided to march his army out to the abandoned Confederate camps at Centreville, in order "to give the troops a little experience on the march and in bivouac, get rid of extra baggage, and test the working of the staff-departments." During this absence, an order was published, without any previous intimation to McClellan, relieving him from the general command of all the armies, and confining his authority to the Department of the Potomac.

Fort Monroe, which McClellan had selected as his base, was a large and very strong work, situated at the southeastern extremity of the Peninsula, about seventy miles from Richmond. His original plan of operations was based entirely upon the cooperation of the navy, which he expected not only to carry his supplies, but also to transport his troops up the York or the

James, so as to turn and compel the evacuation of each and every line of defence which the enemy might take up. When his army had thus manoeuvred the Confederates back to the immediate vicinity of Richmond, he expected to fight his great battle, destroy the enemy's main army, and capture the capital of the Confederate States.

But his expectations regarding the cooperation of the navy, at least for a time, were disappointed. On the 8 March the Merrimac had steamed out of Norfolk, and sunk two Federal frigates in Hampton Roads. The next day the ram had engaged the Monitor, and been forced to return to port in a damaged condition. The vessel was not destroyed, however, and the Federal Navy advised against any attempt to use the James River. At the same time it was discovered that the Confederates had batteries at Yorktown and Gloucester Point on the York which the navy could venture neither to attack nor to pass.

The Peninsula, less than six miles wide at its narrowest point, is a low, level, and marshy region. The highways at that time were all dirt roads. The York River, formed by the junction of the Mattapony and the Pamunkey, was navigable up to the junction joint, where stood West Point, the eastern terminus of the Richmond and York River Railway. Richmond was at the head of navigation, on the north bank of the James.

The only formidable natural obstacle to an advance up the Peninsula was the Chickahominy River and adjacent swamps. This river rises some fifteen miles northwest of Richmond and enters the James about forty miles below that city. Between Meadow Bridge, north of Richmond, and Bottom's Bridge, directly to the east, the river at its ordinary stage is some forty feet wide, fringed with a dense growth of heavy forest trees, and bordered by low marshy lands, varying from half a mile to a mile in width. Within these limits, the firm ground, above highwater mark, seldom approaches the river on either bank, and in no place on both banks. The river was subject to frequent, sudden, and violent floods, and a single severe storm, even of brief duration, would cause an overflow of the bottom-lands, rendering the river impassable for many days, without long and strong bridges.

Of nearly all these facts, General McClellan was fully aware before he went to the Peninsula; but with his "characteristic persistence" he adhered to his original plan even when circumstances had so changed as to make it no longer equally attractive. Accordingly, during the month of March, the Second, Third, and Fourth corps were transported to Fort Monroe.

McClellan already knew that the works at Yorktown, some twenty-five miles up the Peninsula, were held by Magruder with some 15,000 Confederates; also that Johnston's main army would be able to march promptly to this quarter. He therefore "determined to move at once with the force in hand, and endeavor to seize a point — near the Halfway House — between Yorktown and Williamsburg, where the Peninsula is reduced to a narrow neck, and thus cut off the retreat of the Yorktown garrison and prevent the arrival of reinforcements." In reaching this decision he was misled by the erroneous "Cram" map which depicts the Warwick River as coming down to Lee's Mills from the north, instead of stretching across the Peninsula from Yorktown to the James, as proved to be the case.

The forward movement began on the 4 April in two columns, Heintzelman on the road to the right, and Keyes on that to the left. On the following afternoon both columns had been stopped, the right by the works in front of Yorktown, the left at Lee's Mills, where the Warwick was found to be unfordable and strongly entrenched. By means of several dams Magruder had made the river too deep to ford at almost every point; and he had also constructed a strong line of field-works, thirteen miles long, entirely across the Peninsula. "Thus," says General McClellan, "all things were brought to a stand-still, and the intended movement on the Halfway House could not be carried out." In his report McClellan expresses great surprise at this "unexpected" halt, but General Webb says: "Just such a halt ought to have been expected. Nothing less than a continuous front of opposition from the York to the James should have been looked for."

McClellan concluded that the line was too strong to be carried by assault, so he brought up Sumner's corps, and prepared for a regular siege. At this moment he was also on the point of ordering McDowell's corps to move against Gloucester, when he learned that it had been withdrawn from his command and detained near Washington. This reduced the force of 155,000, upon which he had counted at the beginning of the campaign, to about 92,000 men, or some 85,000 present for duty.

To make matters even worse, at this same time the region from the Alleghanies to the sea was parceled out among four independent commanders, and an order was issued from the War Department discontinuing all recruiting for volunteers and closing the recruiting stations. The pernicious policy was also adopted of raising new regiments, instead of maintaining the existing organizations in the field at their full strength. A course more in accordance with well-established military principles would have saved the country millions of treasure and thousands of valuable lives.

Meanwhile the siege operations had been pushed, and the batteries would have been ready to open fire not later than the morning of the 6 May, but during the night of the 3rd the enemy evacuated his positions and retreated up the Peninsula. About the first of May, Magruder had been joined by Johnston's army; and the latter took command of the combined Confederate forces.

The pursuit of the Confederates was at once taken up by all the available Federal cavalry, supported by two divisions of the Third and Fourth corps. About two miles in front of Williamsburg, Magruder had constructed a strong line of defence. Here on the 5 May the Confederates fought a rear-guard action to hold back the Federals until the trains could get well on their way. The battle lasted nearly all day, and that night the Confederates withdrew.

The Union advance was delayed by "dreadful weather and terrible roads," but by the 16 May all the corps were within supporting distance, and a new depot was established at White House. On the 18th, the Fifth and Sixth corps were formed, so that the organization of the Army of the Potomac was then as follows:

Second Corps: Sumner—Divisions: Sedgwick and Richardson
Third Corp: Heintzelman — Divisions: Kearny and Hooker
Fourth Corp: Keyes — Divisions: Couch and Casey
Fifth Corp: Porter — Divisions: Morrell and Sykes
Sixth Corp: Franklin — Divisions: Smith and Slocum

The destruction of the *Merrimac* on the 11 May had opened the James River, and McClellan wished to use that line for his future operations, but his plan was changed by orders from

Topographical engineers compile maps before Yorktown. Erroneous maps played havoc on the execution of war plans.

Washington. On the 18th, a telegram from the Secretary of War informed him that McDowell would advance from Fredericksburg, and directed him to extend the right of the Army of the Potomac to the north of Richmond so as to establish communications with McDowell's corps. The same order directed McClellan to maintain his base at White House. To these orders, McClellan attributes the failure of his campaign, and there is certainly great weight in his contention. Mr. Ropes says: "Petersburg was absolutely undefended, and could be occupied without opposition.... This last line of operations was in truth the one which promised the best results. If Petersburg should be occupied in force by the Federals, it is hard to see how the Confederates could expect long to retain their hold on Richmond."

The Confederate authorities were well aware that McClellan's army, apart from McDowell's corps, outnumbered that of Johnston nearly three to two, the latter being only about 50,000 strong; and the situation seemed so desperate that preparations were made for the removal of the military papers from Richmond. The greatest danger was apprehended from the advance of McDowell's corps, from Fredericksburg, upon the flank of Johnston's army, and it was determined to do everything possible to prevent this movement. General Lee, who was in general charge of the military operations of the Confederacy, accordingly sent Ewell's division to reinforce Jackson in the Shenandoah Valley.

To avoid interrupting the narrative of events in the Peninsula, the story of Jackson's operations in the Shenandoah has not yet been told. Soon after the battle of Bull Run, Jackson was promoted to the rank of major-general; and on the 28 October 1861 he was ordered to Winchester to assume command of the Valley District.

The Shenandoah Valley has already been described in some detail. On its eastern or exposed flank it was covered by the Blue Ridge Mountains, which could only be crossed at certain gaps, through most of which there were good roads. The Valley was connected with Richmond by two lines of railway: the Manassas Gap, mentioned in connection with the Manassas campaign, and the Virginia Central, running from Staunton by way of Rock-fish Gap, Charlottesville, and Gordonsville. A good system of roads connected all of the towns and villages. The main thoroughfare was the Valley Turnpike, stretching from Staunton, near the head of the Valley, to Martinsburg at its lower end, a distance of 120 miles. The main valley, averaging about twenty miles in width, is closed on the western side by the Alleghanies.

The two forks of the Shenandoah River, in the upper part of the Valley, flow parallel to each other, about eight miles apart, for a distance of forty or fifty miles, but separated by an isolated ridge called Massanutten Mountain, as high as the Blue Ridge. At Strasburg this ridge drops suddenly to the level of the Valley, and the North Fork of the Shenandoah sweeps around its base and joins the South Fork at Front Royal. The Shenandoah, thus formed, flows along the very base of the Blue Ridge to Harper's Ferry, where it enters the Potomac. The valley between the Blue Ridge and the South Fork, at the foot of Massanutten Mountain, is known as Luray Valley.

Jackson's command at first consisted only of a weak body of militia; but he was soon reinforced with his old brigade, and later with 6000 poorly disciplined troops under Loring. These, with Ashby's cavalry, raised his forces to about 10,000 men.

The Union troops in this district, about 18,000 strong, were commanded by General Banks, whose headquarters were at Frederick City, in Maryland. General Kelly, with a detachment of 5000 men, garrisoned Romney, a town about thirty-five miles northwest of Winchester by a good road. In January, Jackson marched against this point, hoping to capture the Federal force, but it escaped. This operation, which was attended by great hardships, amounted to nothing in the end.

During the winter, from various causes, Jackson's little army was greatly reduced, so that at the beginning of March he did not have over 5000 men available. Having retired up the Valley, he learned that the enemy had begun to withdraw troops and send them to McClellan. He resolved to check this by a demonstration against Winchester, then occupied by General Shields with a Union force of some 10,000 men. On the 23 March Jackson occupied a ridge at the hamlet of Kernstown, four miles south of Winchester. Here he was attacked by Shields, and finally forced to retreat, after a severe engagement of several hours. The pursuit was not vigorous, and Jackson retired in good order to the vicinity of Swift Run Gap.

Although defeated, Jackson had succeeded in his object of stopping the withdrawal of Federal troops from the Valley, and General Lee was so pleased that he decided to reinforce the Valley army by sending Ewell's division to Jackson, thus giving him an aggregate force of some 15,000 men.

On the first of May, the situation was as follows: Milroy was at McDowell, about forty miles from Staunton, with a Union force of 4000 men, and Schenck's brigade of 2500 was near Franklin, where 20,000 troops of Fremont's army were concentrating. Banks had fortified Strasburg, seventy miles northeast of Staunton on the turnpike, and had pushed forward a force of 20,000 men to Harrisonburg. The total Union forces in the Valley under various commanders aggregated not less than 65,000 men.

Jackson decided first to strike Milroy's detachment, and then to turn against Banks. To mask his movement, he marched over the mountains to a small station a few miles west of Charlottesville, leaving friends and foes to think that he was en route for Richmond. Cars were waiting for his troops, but instead of going east, the trains went west to Staunton. Jackson immediately started his troops on the road from Staunton to McDowell, where on the 8 May he fought a severe and bloody engagement with Milroy and Schenck. The Federals were defeated, and fled toward Franklin to unite with Fremont. Jackson then returned to the Valley, leaving his cavalry under Ashby in front of Fremont to screen the movement.

In the meantime, Banks had fallen back to Strasburg. Shield's division had been sent to General McDowell, and he had only 8000 men, of whom he had placed 1000 under Colonel Kenly at Front Royal, while he himself was entrenched at Strasburg with the remainder.

On the 21 May Jackson started northward with his little army, along the turnpike, but suddenly turned to the right and crossed the Massanutten to Luray. On the morning of the 22nd he took the road down the valley, and the next day fell upon Kenly's detachment at Front Royal. The Federal force was almost entirely wiped out, 154 being killed or wounded, and 600 captured. The Confederate losses were only eleven killed and fifteen wounded.

Banks retreated to Winchester, where he made a useless stand, "to test the strength of the enemy," and then withdrew across the Potomac. After a rest of two days, Jackson advanced to within three miles of Harper's Ferry, to increase the fear at the North, and to give his wagons, with the spoils of Winchester, time to get away on the road to Staunton.

Returning by train to Winchester, ahead of his army, Jackson learned on the 30 May that Shields, commanding McDowell's vanguard, had captured Front Royal; also that Fremont was twenty-five miles west of the Valley Turnpike on the road from Moorefield to Strasburg. Winchester is only eighteen miles from Strasburg, but Jackson's troops were from seven to twenty miles further back on the pike. Banks, in his rear, had 15,000 men; Fremont, also 15,000; and Shields, 10,000, with 10,000 more a few miles behind. Jackson had only 15,000 troops to meet these 50,000 Federals, and he was encumbered with 2000 prisoners, besides a double train of wagons seven miles long. He was in a trap, and nothing but the incompetency of the Union commanders saved him. None of them knew the exact location of the other Federal detachments, and they all stood in awe of Jackson. Fremont was checked by Ashby's cavalry six miles west of Strasburg, and Shields was kept back on the east by a small brigade.

Jackson concentrated his troops at once, and on the 31 May his main body bivouacked at Strasburg. The next morning Ewell's division relieved the cavalry in front of Fremont, and kept him back until the trains and the Stonewall brigade had passed. That night the whole command was at Woodstock, with Ashby's cavalry protecting the rear. The forces of McDowell and Fremont did not get into communication with each other until the 2 June, when both columns took up the pursuit, Shields by the Luray Valley, and Fremont by the turnpike, on opposite sides of the Massanuttens. In anticipation of these movements, Jackson had destroyed the three bridges on the South Fork, to the north of Port Republic, and sent a detachment to hold the bridge at that place for the retreat of his own army. On the 4 June, the Confederates crossed the North Fork, and burnt the bridge. Heavy rains in the Valley, which raised the river, made it difficult for the Federals to throw over a pontoon bridge, and this gave Jackson a lead of twenty-four hours. In a desperate skirmish on the 6th, Ashby was shot through the heart. The death of no other man, save Jackson, could have caused so great a loss to the army. He was the first cavalry leader in this war, or in any war since the time of Napoleon, to use his squadrons right.

The night of the 7 June the hostile forces were thus situated: Shield's command was stretched out over twenty-five miles of road in Luray Valley; Fremont was at Harrisonburg; Ewell's Confederate division was near Cross Keys, and Jackson's main body was near Port Republic. Jackson might now have easily made good his escape, but he had other plans in view. He proposed to hold Fremont back at Cross Keys with Ewell's division, while he crushed Shields with his main body, then to fall upon Fremont with his entire force.

On the 8 June, Fremont attacked Ewell at Cross Keys. Not knowing where Shields was, and supposing that Jackson's entire army was in front of him, the Federal commander made his attack in a timid, half-hearted fashion, only employing five of his twenty-four regiments present on the field. The Federals were repulsed, and the action was not renewed.

At an early hour the following day Jackson set out to attack Shields. About two miles down the river from Port Republic he encountered two Federal brigades under Tyler in a strong position. Here the battle of Port Republic took place. After a fierce action, which lasted for four or five hours, Tyler was driven off the field. In his retreat he met Shields, hurrying with the remainder of his division to the sound of the battle. Shields formed line and stopped the pursuit.

Before midnight Jackson's entire army was in bivouac at Brown's Gap, where it remained until it set out on the 17th upon its swift and secret journey to Richmond. The Valley Campaign was at an end.

During the period of fourteen days, from the morning of the 19 May to the night of the first of June, Jackson's army marched 170 miles, routed forces aggregating 12,500 men, threatened the North with invasion, drew off McDowell from Fredericksburg, and finally, though surrounded on three sides by 50,000 Federals, brought off a huge convoy without losing a single wagon.

Lee had been the first to recognize the weak joint in the enemy's armor: the National anxiety for Washington. Kernstown induced Lincoln to form four independent armies, each acting on a different line. Two months later, when McClellan was in front of Richmond, and it was most important that these armies be combined, Jackson drove Banks across the Potomac, and again the Federal concentration was prevented. Finally, the battles of Cross Keys and Port Republic led Mr. Lincoln to make his worst mistake, and McClellan was left isolated when he most needed help. The brains of two great leaders — Lee and Jackson — had done more for the Confederacy than 200,000 soldiers had done for the Union. From this instance it may be deduced that Providence is sometimes more inclined to side with the big brains than with the big battalions.

A week after Cross Keys and Port Republic, Jackson had vanished from the Valley, and when he appeared on the Chickahominy, Banks, Fremont, and McDowell were still guarding the roads to Washington, and McClellan was waiting for McDowell — 175,000 men absolutely paralyzed by 16,000! Only Napoleon's campaign of 1814 affords a parallel to this extraordinary spectacle. "These brilliant successes," writes Lord Wolseley, "appear to me models of their kind, both in conception and execution. They should be closely studied by all officers who wish to learn the art and science of war."

The use Jackson made of his cavalry was perhaps the most brilliant tactical feature of the Valley Campaign. Such tactics had not been seen since the days of Napoleon. The great cloud of horsemen which veiled the march of the Grand Army had been forgotten. The vast importance ascribed by the Emperor to procuring early information of his enemy and hiding his own movements had been overlooked; and it was left to an American soldier to revive his methods.

To return now to the Peninsula.

On the 17 May, McClellan resumed his advance on Richmond, and encountered but little resistance, as Johnston had withdrawn to the further side of the Chickahominy. The army moved very leisurely, taking three days to cover the twelve miles from White House to the river. By the 25th the corps of Heintzelman and Keyes had crossed at Bottom's Bridge, and taken position on the south side of the stream. The three other corps remained on the north side, extending from the railway to the Mechanicsville Road. This dangerous position, astride the Chickahominy, was taken by McClellan when he was expecting to be rejoined by McDowell, but was not changed even after he was advised that McDowell would not join him. Bridges were built, to facilitate communication between the two wings of the army, but they were liable at any time to be carried away by high water.

In order to secure his line of communications by the York River railway, and to clear his right flank and rear of the enemy, on the 27 May McClellan despatched Porter against

Branch's brigade of Confederates which was at Hanover Court House, fourteen miles north of Richmond. The objects of the expedition were accomplished; and, after destroying the bridges and railroad as far as Ashland, Porter returned to his old camps. This affair has been termed a "useless battle," but General Webb "considers the moral effects of that success to have been of the greatest importance in the subsequent battle of Gaines's Mill."

Johnston's army was now within the entrenchments before Richmond. Having received some reinforcements, it was about 63,000 strong. The army, which had not yet been divided into corps, was organized in four strong divisions, under Longstreet, D. H. Hill, Magruder, and Smith; two small divisions, under A. P. Hill, and Huger; and Stuart's cavalry.

Johnston's first plan was to attack that part of McClellan's army which lay north of the Chickahominy, but when he learned that McDowell had been sent to the Valley, he decided to destroy the two Federal corps which had crossed the river and were encamped within a few miles of Richmond. He accordingly issued orders for his troops to be in position to attack at daybreak on the 31 May.

Major-General James Ewell Brown "Jeb" Stuart, leader of the Virginia Cavalry. In one of his many daring feats, Stuart made a complete circuit of the Union army, marching nearly 150 miles in four days, capturing many prisoners, and losing but one man.

On this day the Federal position was as follows: Casey's division of the Fourth Corps (Keyes) occupied some rifle-pits and a redoubt about three quarters of a mile west of Seven Pines, a tavern on the Williamsburg stage road. The other division, under Couch, was a little to the right and rear. Heintzelman's Third Corps had not advanced much beyond the Chickahominy: the division of Kearny was at Bottom's Bridge, five miles from Casey's advanced line, and Hooker's division was seven miles to the south, guarding White Oak Bridge. Each of these four divisions numbered about 8500 men. It is apparent that General Heintzelman, who was in command of both corps, had not sufficiently concentrated his forces.

To the south of the stage road the ground was swampy, and this gave some protection to the Union left; but to the north, as far as Fair Oaks station on the York River railroad, the country was favorable. It was, of course, to be expected that McClellan would throw his Second Corps, under Sumner, across the river, but the Confederate plans were favored by a violent storm on the afternoon and night of the 30th, which rendered the river unfordable and made the bridges unsafe for the passage of men and guns.

Johnston's plan was simple, and should have been effective. Longstreet was to command the main attack, which was to fall upon the troops at Fair Oaks and Seven Pines. He was to move by the Nine-mile Road, D. H. Hill by the Williamsburg Road, and Huger by the Charles City Road. Smith's division was to remain at the road-fork near Old Tavern, to protect the Confederate left against any movement from the north side of the river. Magruder and A. P. Hill were to remain in position north of the Chickahominy.

The whole plan miscarried through Longstreet's misunderstanding of his orders, which were given him verbally. He got part of his division on the Charles City Road in front of Huger, and part on the stage road in rear of D. H. Hill. Instead of attacking at daybreak, it was one o'clock before the action began, and then D. H. Hill attacked alone. At first the Confederates gained some advantage, but after several hours Kearny came up with his division, and the Union line of battle was reestablished. Later, Hill was reinforced by one, of Longstreet's brigades, and the Federals were driven back to a point a mile and a half east of Seven Pines, where the battle at this part of the line ceased, at about six-thirty.

Huger's division and six of Longstreet's brigades had scarcely fired a shot; but there was a sharp engagement about five o'clock, near Fair Oaks, between Smith's division and part of Sumner's corps, which had marched to Keyes's assistance by way of Grapevine Bridge. The Confederates were repulsed with heavy loss, and the troops of Sumner remained masters of the field.

Before sundown Johnston recognized that his attack was a failure, and he was about to suspend the action, when he received two severe wounds. He was carried from the field, and was incapacitated for service until the middle of November.

G. W. Smith, the next in rank, assumed command of the Confederate army, and he ordered Longstreet to renew the attack "as soon after daybreak as practicable." Longstreet's attack was feebly made, and was repulsed with heavy loss. This ended the battle. General McClellan arrived on the field early in the afternoon, but gave no orders for an attack.

About two o'clock, General Lee appeared at Smith's headquarters, and, by orders from President Davis, assumed command of the Confederate army. That night he withdrew the troops within the defences of Richmond. General Smith, on account of illness, retired temporarily from active duty, and Whiting took command permanently of his division.

In the battle of Seven Pines, or Fair Oaks, as it is variously called, the Confederates lost about 6000 men, and the Federals, 5000. The attack was a complete failure, and left the Confederates in a very disheartened condition. Lee set his men to work strengthening the lines in front of Richmond, and their spirits soon revived, with the sense of security that this gave them.

At the time of his appointment to the command of the Army of Northern Virginia, General Lee was fifty-five years of age, in perfect health, vigorous and robust. As military adviser to the President, a position similar to that of Chief of the General Staff, he had won the full confidence of his chief, but it is a mistake to say that at this time he possessed "the unquestioning and enthusiastic devotion of the army." His only active service had been in West Virginia in the autumn of 1861, and this campaign had generally been considered a failure. His appointment, therefore, "did not at once inspire popular enthusiasm." As he had fought no battles in West Virginia, there was quite a general impression that he would not be an aggressive commander, and this was strengthened when he set his men to work on the fortifications of Richmond. This action, to some of his amateur critics in the public press, seemed a confession of cowardice. Only a few people, who knew him well, then believed that he had the audacity to assume the offensive — to run greater risks and take more desperate chances, than any other general, North or South. These doubts, however, were soon removed, and long before the end of the war, Lee's position was unique — no other commander, on either side, was so universally believed in, so absolutely trusted. "Nor was there ever a commander," says Mr. Ropes, "who better deserved the support of his government, and the affection and confidence of his soldiers."

During the first three weeks of June neither army made any aggressive movement. Lee was engaged in strengthening the defences of Richmond, and McClellan employed his troops in building bridges to connect the wings of his army. These bridges had to be long enough to cross not only the Chickahominy itself, but the marshes on either side, and the task involved no little labor and difficulty. It was, moreover, aggravated by the bad weather which prevailed during the first half of June. McClellan also constructed elaborate field-works on the south side of the river, which completely covered the front from Golding's farm to White Oak Swamp, and rendered this part of the Federal line practically impregnable. Works were also thrown up on the north side, behind Beaver Dam Creek. The two corps of Sumner and Franklin were permanently established on the south side of the river, and only the Fifth Corps, of Fitz John Porter, remained on the north side.

On the 20 June the bridges had been completed, and the weather was fine. This was obviously McClellan's time to attack, if he ever intended to do so. He had received reinforcements which had brought his army up to an aggregate of 105,000 men, and there was no immediate prospect of a further increase in numbers. It was plain that the chances of success were better now than they would be after General Lee was strengthened by the arrival of Jackson's command from the Shenandoah. At this time Lee had only 68,000 men within the lines of Richmond, and McClellan outnumbered him by more than three to two. These odds, according to Napoleon, are sufficient, and if a general cannot discover from the attitude of his enemy what the odds are, he is unfitted for supreme command. McClellan was a man of undoubted ability, but his good qualities were accompanied by marked defects. Bold in conception, he was terribly slow in execution: his will was less powerful than his imagination.

Lee had served on the same staff with McClellan in the Mexican War, and had personal knowledge of his capacity and character: "he read him like an open book." McClellan, on the other hand, failed to draw a single correct inference. It is true that he was misled by his famous detective staff, and believed the garrison of Richmond to number at least 200,000 men. But he made no effort whatever to supplement or check up this information. It must be admitted that his cavalry, which numbered only 5000 sabres, was weak in proportion to his other arms, and also of inferior quality, but he scarcely employed it at all.

Lee, on the other hand, had found means to acquire ample information of the dispostion of his adversary's forces on the north bank of the Chickahominy, the point he had decided to attack. His cavalry, also, was below the usual proportion of one trooper to every six men of the other arms, numbering not more than 3000; but it was of superior quality, familiar with the country, and united under the command of J. E. B. Stuart, one of the ablest cavalry leaders developed during the Civil War.

Early on the 12 June, with 1200 horsemen, and a section of artillery, Stuart rode out on an enterprise of a kind which at that time was absolutely unique, and which will keep his memory green so long as cavalry is used in war. He encountered and defeated a small Federal force near Old Church, and reached Tunstall's Station on the York River railroad without further opposition. He had then accomplished the object of the expedition, which was to ascertain the nature of the region lying north of the Chickahominy, and the arrangements of McClellan to protect his line of supplies. Stuart now realized that it would be dangerous, if not impossible, to return to Richmond by the route by which he had come, so he determined to make a complete circuit of the Union army. This feat he successfully accomplished, crossing the Chickahominy fifteen miles below Bottom's Bridge, and reaching Richmond by way of the James River Road on the 15th. He had marched nearly 150 miles, in four days; captured many prisoners, and lost but one man.

On the whole, however, this brilliant raid cost the Confederates more than its results were worth. It seriously alarmed McClellan for his line of supplies, and he immediately gave orders to begin loading the transports, preparatory to a change of base to Harrison's Landing on the James River. If these preliminary arrangements had not been made, the results of the campaign would have been much more favorable to the Confederates.

At the same time, McClellan caused a survey to be made by his engineers of the region between the railroad and White Oak Swamp. From the data furnished by these officers, maps were prepared for use in case the movement to the James should be found advisable.

General Lee had also been largely reinforced during the month of June, and when joined by Jackson would dispose of 86,500 men.

He now decided to take the offensive, and made arrangements for the cooperation of Jackson, which was essential to the success of such a movement. At this time, the Federal troops in the Shenandoah had fallen back, and no further trouble from them was anticipated for the time being. Jackson was therefore ordered to leave a small force to guard the passes, and to join the main army as soon as possible, moving east to Ashland, on the Richmond and Fredericksburg Railroad.

Before issuing on the 24 June the orders for the battle of Gaines's Mill (General Orders No. 75), General Lee called a conference at his headquarters, of Jackson, Longstreet, A. P. Hill, and D. H. Hill, to arrange all details. When summoned to this meeting on Saturday, 21 June, Jackson was near Gordonsville. He started on a freight train bound to Richmond, but left the train before midnight that night at a station where he spent Sunday, attending church twice. At midnight he set out on horseback for the conference at Richmond some fifty miles away, arriving about three o'clock Monday afternoon. If he had kept on the train he would have reached Richmond early Sunday morning. His infantry followed by train, but the artillery and cavalry marched all the way. His brigades, on the march, also kept Sunday in camp, as usual.

At the conference, Longstreet asked Jackson to fix the date for the attack, and he named the 25 June, but on Longstreet's suggestion that he allow more time, the 26th was selected.

CHAPTER SIX

JUNE — JULY 1862

THE SEVEN DAYS

THE morning of Thursday, the 26 June, dawned clear and bright, giving promise that the day would be a brilliant one. For twenty-four hours, General Porter, in command of the Fifth Corps, on the north bank of the Chickahominy, had been expecting an attack from the enemy. At midnight on the 24th, General McClellan had telegraphed him that a deserter had given information that Jackson was in the immediate vicinity, ready to unite with Lee in an attack upon his command. In the far distant northern and western horizon, vast clouds of dust indicated the approach of Jackson's army.

A despatch on the 23 June, from McClellan's chief-of-staff, had stated to Porter: "If you are attacked … the troops on this side will be held ready either to support you directly or to attack the enemy in their front. If the force attacking you is large, the general would prefer the latter course, counting upon your skill and the admirable troops under your command to hold their own against superior numbers long enough for him to make the decisive movement which will determine the fate of Richmond." This was an admirable plan, if only McClellan had had the energy to carry it out!

The Federal position on Beaver Dam Creek was naturally very strong. The banks of the valley were steep, and forces advancing to the attack, on the adjacent plains, would present their flanks, as well as their front, to fire of both infantry and artillery, safely posted behind entrenchments. The stream was over waist-deep and bordered by swamps. Its passage was difficult for infantry at all points, and impracticable for artillery except at the bridge-crossing near Mechanicsville, and the one below, at Ellerson's Mill.

General Lee's plans for the initial operations were of a somewhat complicated nature. Magruder, who had so successfully imposed on McClellan at Yorktown, with 28,000 men was relied upon to hold Richmond until Porter was crushed. With the remainder of his army, 35,000 men all told, Lee would cross the Chickahominy and attack the front of the Federals, while the 18,500 troops under Jackson descended on their flank and rear.

Four bridges crossed the river on Lee's left, but only two of these could be used for the attack — Mechanicsville Bridge, and Meadow Bridge, about a mile and a half up stream. Five and a half miles above Mechanicsville, at the Half Sink, there is Winston's Bridge, where Branch, of A. P. Hill's division, was to cross; and three and a half miles below is New Bridge. With the exception of the passage at the Half Sink, the northern approaches to all these bridges were in possession of the Federals, so it was a difficult operation to transfer the Richmond troops from one bank of the Chickahominy to the other.

Lee's first object was to secure the two centre bridges, which he expected to achieve by the advance of the Valley army. Then, as soon as the Federals fell back, Longstreet and the two Hills would cross the river and strike Porter in front, while Jackson attacked his right. A victory would ensure the possession of New Bridge, and put the troops north of the river in close communication with Magruder.

We can now see how, in the hands of a skillful general, entrenchments may form a "pivot of operations," — the means whereby he covers his most vulnerable point, holds the enemy in front, and sets his main body free for offensive action. This is clearly exposed in Lee's report, and shows that he contemplated this action from the first. Yet it is very doubtful whether he would have taken such a desperate chance if he had not known McClellan as he did. "From Hannibal to Moltke," says Colonel Henderson, "there has been no great captain who has neglected to study the character of his opponent, and who did not trade on the knowledge thus acquired; and it was this knowledge which justified Lee's audacity."

Lee's plans all hinged upon the movements of the Valley army. On the morning of the 24 June, Jackson, with his infantry, was at Beaver Dam Station, on the Virginia Central road, about 18 miles from Ashland, and was expected to reach Ashland that night. The following night, the 25th, he was to halt near Merry Oaks Church, just west of the Virginia Central Railroad. At three o'clock on Thursday morning, the 26th, he was to advance on the road leading to Pole Green Church, and, bearing well to the left, turning Beaver Dam Creek, to proceed toward Cold Harbor.

At three o'clock on the morning of the 26th, however, Jackson was still at Ashland, and it was not until nine that he crossed the railroad. Branch, on hearing that the Valley army was at last advancing, crossed at Winston's Bridge and moved on Mechanicsville. Meanwhile, A. P. Hill was waiting near Meadow Bridge until the advance of Branch and Jackson should clear the way for his passage. At two o'clock, hearing nothing from his associates, and fearing that further delay might result in the failure of the whole plan, he gave orders to seize the bridge. The Federal pickets fell back, followed by Hill, who, after a short march of three miles, found himself under fire of Porter's artillery.

About two o'clock on the afternoon of the 26th, the boom of a single cannon, the signal agreed upon, announced to Porter that the enemy was crossing the Chickahominy. His divisions were promptly formed, and took the positions to which they had previously been assigned. An hour later, the Confederates, under Longstreet and the two Hills, crossed the two centre bridges in force, and pushed down the roads leading to Beaver Dam Creek, the Union outposts falling back across the creek, and destroying the bridges behind them.

A part of the Confederate forces took the road to the right to Ellerson's Mill, but the main body advanced directly into the valley of Beaver Dam Creek. Suddenly, when halfway down the valley, the Federals opened up with rapid volleys of artillery and infantry, which drove the attacking force back in hasty flight. Later in the afternoon they returned again to the attack, but were once more repulsed with terrible slaughter. The forces directed against Ellerson's Mill suffered an even more disastrous defeat. When night came on, they all fell back beyond gun-shot, and the contest was over. The Union loss was only 361, while the Confederates lost nearly 1500 out of some 10,000 attacking.

General McClellan came on the field at an early hour in the afternoon, and remained with Porter until about one o'clock the next morning. After his return to his headquarters, south of the river, he sent orders, about three o'clock, for Porter to withdraw to a well-selected and very strong position east of Gaines's Mill. These orders were immediately executed.

About 4:30 P.M., Jackson had reached Hundley's Corner, three miles north of the Federal position, but separated from it by a dense forest and the windings of the creek. Here, after establishing his outposts, he ordered his troops to bivouac. Although the cannonade was distinctly heard, he made no attempt to assist his comrades, who, not three miles away, were assaulting the Federal lines. The victor of the Valley campaign, on his first appearance in combination with the main army, had proved a failure, and wrecked General Lee's plans. His biographer, Colonel Henderson, offers many excuses for his lack of energy, but none is convincing. "To fix an hour so long in advance," he says, "was worse than useless, and Jackson cannot be blamed if he failed to comply with the exact letter of a foolish order." But Jackson himself had proposed a time twenty-four hours earlier!

The position selected for the final Federal stand was east of Powhite Creek, about six miles from Beaver Dam Creek. The line of battle was semicircular, the ends being in the valley of the Chickahominy, while the central part occupied the high grounds along the bank of a creek, and curved around past McGehee's to Elder Swamp. Part of the front was covered by the ravine of the creek, and, toward the east, by a series of boggy swamps, covered with dense brush. Near McGehee's, and beyond, the ground, elevated and drier, was broken by ravines swept by the Union fire. The high land at the centre was cleared, and the numerous fences and ditches afforded cover to both infantry and artillery.

The new line of battle was strong, but it was too extended to be held by Porter's forces, and he certainly had a right to expect that enough troops would be sent by McClellan to enable him to maintain his position during the day. But this obvious duty McClellan did not perform.

Porter's force consisted of three divisions of infantry, six regiments of cavalry, and twenty batteries of artillery — in all about 30,000 men. The men were well disciplined, and they were well commanded. Porter himself was a graduate of West Point, an officer of the Old Army, who had seen service in Mexico under Scott, and he was known to be a brave and skillful general.

The battle, which took its name from Gaines's Mill on the creek, began about two o'clock with a furious assault by A. P. Hill, who was finally repulsed with great loss. For several hours the efforts of the Confederates were absolutely fruitless, and General Lee began to imagine that he was confronted by the principal part of the Federal army. He continued, however, to press the attack, with Jackson and D. H. Hill on the north front, A. P. Hill and Longstreet on the west. When Slocum's division, from Franklin's corps, arrived to reinforce Porter, about four o'clock, the Union reserves were entirely exhausted. With these fresh troops, Porter held out for about two hours more, but toward evening the Confederates succeeded in breaking the centre of his line, and the Federals were forced to retreat. Their withdrawal was aided by the appearance on the field of two brigades of Sumner's corps. During the night all the Federal troops crossed to the south bank of the Chickahominy, destroying the bridges behind them. The Confederate loss in killed and wounded was about 9000. The Federal loss is reported as

Gaines Mill

The White Oak Swamp was a flat area densely grown up in trees and bushes, generally with good footing.

6837 men, killed, wounded, and missing, including some 2800 prisoners, of whom about 1200 were wounded, left in the hands of the victorious Confederates. There were also 22 guns abandoned on the field.

"No one can read the accounts of this action," says Mr. Ropes, "without coming to the conclusion that 10,000 or 15,000 more men sent to Porter would have enabled him to hold his own till nightfall, and then to have effected the withdrawal of his command with entire safety." General Alexander expresses the same opinion in even stronger terms. He writes: "Porter himself was perhaps the hardest opponent to fight in the Federal army.... Indeed, had McClellan reinforced Porter, as he should have done, with a whole corps, he might have won a great victory."

McClellan might also have relieved the pressure on Porter by an attack on Magruder, who himself believed that his lines might have been carried. But that prince of "bluff" maintained such a brisk demonstration against McClellan's front, that the Union commander, with his exaggerated estimate of the numbers opposed to him, postponed moving his reserves until it was too late. With 66,000 men on the south bank of the Chickahominy, McClellan was held in his entrenchments throughout the day by 28,000 Confederates. "Intent on saving his trains on securing his retreat to the river James, and utterly regardless of the chances which fortune offered, the 'Young Napoleon' had allowed his rear-guard to be overwhelmed."

As usual, McClellan was not seen on the field of battle which his devoted troops so well defended, but Porter was more than a sufficient substitute for the commander-in-chief.

General James Longstreet joined Jackson to turn the Federal's left at Manassas and secure victory for the Confederate Army. He would be wounded by friendly fire during the Wilderness campaign.

Porter's tactics were admirable; and, when his front was broken, he conducted the withdrawal in a masterly manner. The Federal retreat was favored by the absence of Stuart, who, in common with Lee and Jackson thought that the enemy would endeavor to reach the White House, and dashed in that direction with his 2000 horsemen. When he learned his error, darkness had already fallen, and it was too late to accomplish anything.

The Confederate tactics in the battle were poor, and nearly lost them the victory. The attack was made too late in the day, and then their energies were not concentrated or their assaults properly coordinated. This made the victory much more bloody than it need have been.

It is a curious fact that all the severe battles in this campaign began after noon, which, even in the long June days, caused the Confederates on many occasions to lose the precious hours of daylight necessary to gather the fruits of victory.

At Gaines's Mill, the French princes, who were volunteer aides on General McClellan's staff, served with General Porter, and displayed the greatest gallantry — exposing themselves to every danger.

On the night of the 28 June, the day after the battle of Gaines's Mill, the corps commanders were assembled at the Trent house, the headquarters of General McClellan. He then announced his intention to change his base to the James River, and handed each of the officers a map showing the route across the White Oak Swamp. It was a perilous undertaking, for he had only one narrow road to move by, a great swamp and a creek to cross, with his army encumbered by a train of 5000 wagons, and 2500 cattle. The bulk of the stores at White House was moved by water.

Porter, with the Fifth Corps, was sent ahead to occupy the strong position at Malvern Hill. He was followed by the Fourth Corps, under Keyes, who was ordered to take up a position south of the swamp, to cover the flank of the column on the side toward Richmond. The three other corps, of Sumner, Heintzelman, and Franklin, remained north of the swamp to cover the retreat.

Lee practically did nothing on the 28th, as he was still in the dark as to the intentions of the enemy. But by the morning of the 29th, he became convinced that McClellan was moving toward the James. He then ordered Magruder and Huger to push forward on the Williamsburg and Charles City roads; Longstreet and A. P. Hill, to cross by New Bridge and march to strike the Federal flank south of the swamp; Jackson and D. H. Hill, nearly 25,000 strong, to follow the shortest and most direct route, by the Grapevine Bridge, over which Porter had retreated across the Chickahominy.

Lee's orders were simple and obvious, but he would have done better to leave the pursuit of the Federal rear-guard to Huger and Magruder, while he himself, with Jackson, Longstreet, and A. P. Hill, moved swiftly to the right by good roads, and placed the bulk of his army across McClellan's path near Malvern Hill.

Magruder came upon Sumner, with his own and part of Franklin's corps, at Savage Station on the afternoon of the 29th, and immediately engaged the Federals. He was in momentary expectation of seeing Jackson fall upon the flank of the enemy from the direction of Grapevine Bridge, but he was left without aid; his attacks were repulsed, and at nightfall the Federals resumed their march.

The excuse of Jackson, which Lee accepted, was that he found the bridge destroyed, and spent the day in repairing it; although he might have crossed by the ford close at hand. The real explanation is given by General Alexander: "But this was Sunday, and Jackson gave it strict observance. The greater part of his troops remained in camp all day and until after midnight Sunday night. Then they made a start at, or before, 2:30 A.M."

The morning of the 30 June found the Army of the Potomac, with all of its artillery and trains, south of White Oak Swamp, and the bridge destroyed. Franklin remained to guard the crossing of the creek against the pursuit of the enemy. Five divisions took up a position near Glendale, where the Charles City, Darbytown, and New Market roads come together. The two corps of Keyes and Porter covered Malvern Hill.

The battle of Glendale or Frayser's Farm, on the 30 June, was the crisis of the "Seven Days." During the night, the entire Federal army had crossed the White Oak Swamp, and McClellan had accomplished one-half his retreat safely. He had only eight miles more to traverse; his trains were well on the way; and his army was concentrated to protect his flank. Whatever may have been McClellan's shortcomings on the field of battle, he had shown himself admirable in retreat, and the change of base had been handled most skillfully. With one day more, his flank would no longer be exposed, and his whole army would be united in the strong position of Malvern Hill, with the trains in safety.

On the 26th at Beaver Dam, on the 27th at Gaines's Mill, and on the 29th at Savage Station, the Federal army had been in danger of destruction, but had escaped through the poor tactics of the Confederates. At Glendale one more opportunity was offered, and every condition seemed favorable. Lee had in hand the forces of Holmes, Longstreet, A. P. Hill, Magruder, and Huger, a total of 24 brigades, or about 44,000 men, all ready for the attack.

At the same hour, Jackson, with his 14 brigades, 25,000 strong, was only four miles away in an air-line; he was expected to assault the enemy's rear-guard with the vigor he had displayed in the Valley, and make up for his lack of energy on the previous days. At last Fortune seemed about to smile on the Confederate cause.

In a field of broom-grass and small pines, Lee, with Longstreet and Hill, waited impatiently for the signal. He was so close to the rear of his line of battle that officers on his staff were wounded by random shots. Hour after hour passed, and nothing happened. Four o'clock came, and the day was drawing to a close, but not a shot had been fired. Lee had waited for either Huger or Jackson, or both, to begin, and neither had done anything.

Briefly, this is what had happened: Holmes, in command of the extreme right of the Confederate columns was marching along the river road, from New Market to Harrison's Landing, which passes under and around the south side of Malvern Heights, between them and the James River. The ground is low and flat, and when the advance reached a point about 1000 yards from Malvern, the Federal trains, passing over the heights, were in plain view. Holmes could not resist the temptation to order his guns to fire upon these wagons. But no sooner did his six guns open than they were answered by thirty of the heaviest rifles of the Federal Artillery Reserve, aided by the fire of the heavy guns on the gunboats in the river at Turkey Bend. The Confederate guns were quickly wrecked, and Holmes's whole division was thrown into confusion. There was nothing to do but to withdraw. Lee directed Magruder's six brigades, on the adjoining Central Road, to march to the support of Holmes, but there was nothing for them to attack or defend. Thus 18,000 men, who were to have supported Longstreet's right, were diverted from the real work of the day.

To turn next to Huger's division: This command, marching by the Charles City Road, which had been ob-structed by the Federals, made very slow progress, and did not get through in time to take part in the battle. "It seems incredible," remarks General Alexander, "that this division, within four miles of Lee, could have been allowed to spend the whole day in a mere contest of axemen, wherein the Federals, with the most axes, had only to cut down, and the Confederates, with the fewest, to cut up and remove."

It only remains to tell the story of Jackson's movements. He had always before acted alone and independently ; so Lee had shown his supreme confidence by giving him only very brief and general orders, and then going to the furthest flank, "as if generously to leave to Jackson the opportunity of the most brilliant victory of the war." But Jackson "did not try and fail, he simply made no effort." After spending the 29th (Sunday) in camp, in absolute disregard of Lee's instructions, he passed the 30th in equal idleness in White Oak Swamp. His 25,000 infantry practically did not fire a shot in the two days. For some unaccountable reason, he contented himself with simply shelling Franklin's position. He made little effort to cross at the bridge, and none whatever to use the five fords in the neighborhood. He held his own and D. H. Hill's troops all day north of the creek.

Longstreet and A. P. Hill, under Lee's immediate command, therefore fought the battle without assistance; and instead of making a simultaneous attack with their whole force, they let their brigades go into the battle piecemeal. The fight was desperate, and lasted until long after dark. The Federal line was broken once, but was soon reestablished by reinforcements. The Confederates gained no strategical advantage, nor did they inflict a greater loss of men than they suffered.

It must be admitted that in this action, Lee was badly served by two of his lieutenants — Huger and Jackson. The inactivity of the latter has been severely criticised by both friends and foes.

In Jackson's own account of the day he writes that he was "anxious to press forward, but the marshy character of the soil, the destruction of the bridge over the marsh and creek, and the strong position of the enemy for defending the passage, prevented my advancing until the following morning." Regarding this statement, General Alexander makes the caustic comment: "Considered as an excuse for Jackson's inaction during the whole day this report is simply farcical."

This formidable obstacle, which held up Jackson for a whole day, was a small creek, averaging 10 to 15 feet wide and six inches deep, with a sandy bottom. The White Oak Swamp was merely a flat area densely grown up in trees and bushes, more or less wet in places, but generally with firm footing. Small farms and settlements were scattered along its edges, and residents and cattle had many paths in and through it. The swamp was widest, and the country flatter, near its source, about five miles from Richmond, between the Williamsburg and the Charles City roads. Near the bridge the country was rolling, and the swamp narrower. Above the bridge, there were four good crossings known to the natives, and one below; but besides there were many less-known paths.

The battle of Glendale, says Mr. Ropes, closed the second act in the drama of the "Seven Days." For the second time, General Lee had failed in the attempt to strike his adversary a crushing blow during the change of base, and the critical period of the movement was over.

During the night of the 30 June, the Federal troops fell back from Glendale to Malvern Hill, where the Army of the Potomac was once more united on the morning of the first of July.

The position of Malvern Hill was one of great natural strength. The open plateau at the top, at a height of 150 feet above the surrounding country, was a mile and a half in length by half a mile in width. On the northerly side, the slopes, covered with wheat, standing or in shock, fell gradually to the edge of the woods, 800 to 1600 yards from the commanding crest. The base of the hill, except on the easterly side, was covered with dense forest; and within the woods, at the foot of the declivity, ran a winding and marshy stream. The right flank was partially protected by a long mill-dam. On the left, which was more open, there was an excellent artillery position, commanding a broad expanse of meadow-land, drained by a narrow stream and deep ditches, and flanked by the fire of the Federal gunboats. Only three approaches, the Quaker and the river roads and a track from the northwest, gave access to the heights.

The ground had been thoroughly examined by Fitz John Porter, who had been there for twenty-four hours; and General Hunt had had ample time to post the reserve artillery, which he had done with his usual skill. All the forenoon was spent in arranging the troops and guns, and resting.

General Fitz John Porter, the ablest of McClellan's corps commanders fought the two principal actions at Gaines's Mill and Malvern Hill without any personal direction from the commander-in-chief.

In his report, General D. H. Hill speaks of the formidable strength of the Federal position, on a commanding hill, guarded by swarms of infantry, securely sheltered by fences, ditches, and ravines, with all the approaches swept by artillery. Tier after tier of batteries were grimly visible on the heights, rising in the form of an amphitheatre. The Confederates could only reach the first line of batteries by crossing an open space of from 300 to

400 yards, exposed to a deadly fire of grape and canister from the artillery, and musketry from the infantry. If that first line were carried, another and another, still more difficult, remained in the rear.

General Lee appears to have hesitated as to ordering an assault upon the Federals, in this strong position, but late in the afternoon he decided to make the attack. He probably thought the Federal army was entirely demoralized, or he would not have taken such a desperate chance.

The battle was opened at four o'clock by an assault on the centre of the Union line by D. H. Hill, whose division was repulsed with heavy loss. Later, an attack on the Federal left was made by Huger, supported by Magruder, which also was a failure. There were also other isolated, useless, and unsuccessful attempts, each resulting in a bloody repulse. The failure was complete: absolutely no impression was made on the Federal lines.

The action lasted only three hours, but the Confederates lost over 5000 men, killed and wounded, while the Union casualties were not more than one-third of that number. General Hill states that more than half the Confederate casualties were from artillery fire — an unprecedented thing in warfare.

The following day, the 2 July, the Army of the Potomac fell back to Harrison's Landing on the James, where it fortified itself. A reconnaissance of the position convinced Lee of the uselessness of making another attack, and he withdrew his troops within the defences of Richmond.

At the beginning of the "Seven Days' Battles," McClellan had 105,000 men, and Lee, 86,500. The losses were as follows:

	Federals	*Confederates*
Killed	1,734	3,286
Wounded	8,062	15,909
Missing	6,053	940
Totals	15,849	20,135
	15%	23%

The Peninsula Campaign and the Seven Days have always been the subject of much controversy, both North and South.

The plans of General Lee were bold and excellent, but they fell short of success owing to the faults of his lieutenants — particularly Jackson.

It is difficult to explain the failure of Jackson during the Seven Days. As General Alexander says: "He nowhere, even distantly, approached his record as a soldier won in his every other battle, either before or afterward.... Nothing that he had to do was done with the vigor which marked all the rest of his career."

His brother-in-law, General D. H. Hill, writes: "Jackson's genius never shone when he was under the command of another. It seemed then to be shrouded or paralyzed.... This was the keynote to his whole character. The hooded falcon cannot strike the quarry."

The Army of the Potomac fell back to Harrison's Landing on the James on July 2. Here are the headquarters of Fitz John Porter.

But it is impossible to accept this explanation. Jackson was certainly under the command of Lee at Second Manassas and Chancellorsville, where he displayed all of his former activity and energy. During the Seven Days he was apparently suffering from the "mysterious malady" which attacked Napoleon on two or three occasions during his career, notably at Borodino and Dresden, and which was nothing less than absolute physical and mental prostration.

The criticisms of McClellan have been equally severe, and in most cases these were fully justified, although in some instances they were due to misapprehensions. The Federal position athwart the Chickahominy was not "chosen" by McClellan, but was forced upon him by orders from Washington at the time McDowell was expected to advance from Fredericksburg.

The change of base to the James had always been in his mind, but was precipitated by Lee's determination to break his communications with White House. Then his only mistake was the delay of twenty-four hours in giving the order to march, which necessitated the actions at Savage Station, Glendale, and Malvern Hill.

The movement was dictated by the absolute necessity of establishing a new base of supplies, and was not the result of the Confederate attacks. The marching away of the Federal army after each engagement was not because it had been beaten: it was simply continuing the movement to the James. To speak of "the pursuit" and "the escape" of the Union army is therefore scarcely correct. Yet, these views were generally held, both at the time, and for many years afterwards.

Two years later, General Grant, after losing 55,000 men, found himself literally driven into the position which McClellan reached voluntarily, with one quarter that loss. It was a position of rare strategic advantage, the key to Richmond, when properly utilized; and it seems strange that this was not realized in 1862. After his change of base, McClellan had nearly stumbled into this key-position, and he seems to have comprehended this fact, for his army was recalled to Washington against his violent protests and appeals. "Here is the true defence of Washington," he wrote; "it is here on the banks of the James that the fate of the Union should be decided." These words were prophetic!

Considering the many difficulties of the operation, the change of base was made in a masterly manner. The critic will have a hard task to find a flaw in either the strategy or the tactics of the movement.

Nevertheless, as Mr. Ropes points out, the moral and political effect of the campaign was entirely to the advantage of the Confederates. Two years later, the Administration and the public had had more experience, and Grant was supported, where McClellan had been condemned.

But, for this attitude of the public mind, McClellan himself was largely responsible. He was an accomplished soldier and a very able engineer; he had a very rare genius for organization and administration; but he was hardly equal at this time to the position of commander of a field army. He lacked vigor and activity and aggressiveness. He was too methodical and too cautious.

While it would be unjust to state that McClellan was lacking in physical courage, he was not a fighting general. "He had," says Mr. Ropes, "a constitutional aversion to the risks inseparable from all military operations. He shrank from the test of battle." In fact, on few occasions during the campaign did he order an attack made. He acted almost entirely on the defensive. Furthermore, he was usually absent from the field of battle, doing work which should have been delegated to a member of his staff. At Williamsburg he did not arrive on the field "until the action was practically over," having stayed at Yorktown to give his personal attention to the embarkation of some troops going up the York River. At Fair Oaks and Seven Pines, he did not appear on the ground until about two o'clock on the afternoon of the second day, and then he "gave no orders looking to an attack." At that time the Confederates were much demoralized from their severe losses, and the change of leaders, and many authorities are of the opinion that McClellan could have won an easy victory.

During the "Seven Days' Battles," McClellan was never at the front. The two principal actions, Gaines's Mill and Malvern Hill, were fought by Fitz John Porter, the ablest of his corps commanders, without any personal direction from the commander-in-chief. At Savage Station, "General McClellan was not on the ground, and the senior corps-commander, Sumner, who ought promptly to have assumed command in his absence, evidently did not do so." At the battle of Frayser's Farm, or Glendale, General Lee commanded in person, stationing himself where the fighting was going on, and where he could superintend the operations of Longstreet and A. P. Hill. "General McClellan, on the other hand, after giving in the morning certain directions to his corps-commanders, but apparently without handing over the command to any one of them, rode down to Malvern Hill, and even as far as Haxall's Landing, and conferred with Captain Rodgers of the navy in regard to the place where the army had better finally be stationed... . It is almost incredible that any intelligent man should have acted as General McClellan acted on this critical day."

In speaking of the actions of the 29 and 30 June, and 1 July, General Alexander also says: "Unknown to us, another circumstance was rarely in our favor... . McClellan, on each day, left his army without placing any one in command during his absence, while he did engineer's duty, examining the localities toward which he was marching. Had the Confederates accomplished their reasonable expectations, the criticism of McClellan would have been very severe."

One of the four conditions of the plan for the transfer of the Army of the Potomac to the Peninsula was:

"That the force to be left to cover Washington be such as to give an entire feeling of security for its safety from menace."

As to whether General McClellan had a just grievance against the Government because President Lincoln detained McDowell's corps in the vicinity of Washington, authorities have always differed. General Webb thinks that this action was not warranted, and "in fact did everything to insure disaster to the Peninsula Campaign." On the other hand, Mr. Ropes maintains that "the Government was perfectly right."

On the eve of the battle of Gaines's Mill, McClellan sent Stanton one of his characteristic communications. He telegraphed the Secretary that he thought Jackson was going to attack his right and rear; that the enemy's force was stated at 200,000 men; that he regretted his inferiority in numbers, but felt himself in no way to blame for it; and that, if a disaster should result, the responsibility could not be thrown on his shoulders, but "must rest where it belongs," that is to say — on the President and Secretary. To this insolent communication Mr. Stanton made no direct reply, but sent McClellan his best wishes.

After the battle, at 12:30 A.M. on the 28 June, McClellan sent a long telegram, in which he stated that his men were overwhelmed by vastly superior numbers even after he had brought his last reserves into action; that he had lost the battle because his force was too small; that the Government could not hold him responsible for the result; that the Government had not sustained his army; "if I save this army now, I tell you plainly that I owe no thanks to you or to any other person in Washington. You have done your best to sacrifice this army."

On reaching the James River, McClellan reported that he had saved the army, but would require reinforcement to the extent of 50,000 men — a number which he raised the next day to 100,000. In reply the President promised 31,000 men at once, and 10,000 more if possible.

In a very kind letter, under date of the 2 July, Mr. Lincoln wrote: "If you think you are not strong enough to take Richmond just now, I do not ask you to try." On the 5th, Mr. Stanton also wrote: "Be assured that you shall have the support of this Department and the Government as cordially and as faithfully as ever was rendered by man to man." The next day Mr. Stanton followed this by a personal letter, couched in still warmer terms. General McClellan's reply was cold and formal.

The President visited Harrison's Landing to inform himself personally regarding the situation. Then McClellan handed Mr. Lincoln his well-known letter "upon a civil and military policy."

This was the last straw. On the 11 July the President appointed General Halleck commander-in-chief of the army, and Halleck, after a visit to McClellan's camp, recommended the withdrawal of the army from the Peninsula, and its union with the forces of General Pope. The orders for the removal followed. "There was, to my mind," General Halleck says, "no alternative."

As we see it now, this was a great mistake, but under all the circumstances it is difficult to blame the Administration for its action.

"On the whole," says Major Steele, "the Peninsula Campaign was, on the part of the Confederates, a campaign of good plans and bad execution. . . . On the part of the Federals, it was a campaign of neglected opportunities."

CHAPTER SEVEN

JUNE — SEPTEMBER 1862

SECOND MANASSAS

ON the 26 June 1862 an order was issued by Mr. Lincoln consolidating the forces under Fremont, Banks, and McDowell, and the troops in Washington, into one army, to be called the Army of Virginia, and placing at its head Major-General John Pope. The victories of Stonewall Jackson over these separate commands in the Valley had convinced the President and Mr. Stanton that they made a mistake in the spring when they divided the territory east of the Alleghanies into four departments. All three of the superseded generals were seniors to Pope, and Fremont refused to serve under him. His corps, now called the First Corps of the Army of Virginia, was accordingly assigned to Sigel; Banks commanded the Second, and McDowell the Third Corps.

Pope was graduated from West Point in 1842, in the same class with Rosecrans, Sykes, and Doubleday, on the Union side, and Longstreet, D. H. Hill, and G. H. Smith, of the Confederate army. He was a handsome, dashing officer, and a splendid horseman. He saw but little service until the Civil War, when he gained some reputation by the capture of New Madrid and Island No. 10, on the Mississippi. When he assumed command in the East, he was in the prime of life, less than forty years old, and had lost little, if any, of the dash and grace of his youth.

The consolidation of the three armies was a wise measure, but the selection of Pope for the new command was a grave mistake; McDowell would have been a much better choice. For a brief period, Pope acted as military adviser to the President at Washington, but on the 11 July, General Halleck was appointed commander-in-chief of all the armies of the United States, and summoned to the capital. No selection for the supreme command could possibly have been more unfortunate, as Mr. Lincoln and the public were soon to find out.

General Pope's first official act, on taking command the 14 July, was to issue a bombastic address to his troops, in which he displayed an absolute lack of tact. Not content with extolling the prowess of the Western troops, he was bitterly sarcastic in his references to McClellan and his army. "I have come to you," he said, "from the West, where we have always seen the backs of our enemies — from an army ... whose policy has been attack and not defence... I hear constantly of taking strong positions and holding them — of lines of retreat and of bases of supplies. Let us discard such ideas.... Let us look before and not behind."

At the time that Pope assumed command, the forces of Banks and Fremont were still in the Shenandoah Valley, and two divisions of McDowell were at Manassas and Falmouth, respectively. The task laid out for him in the order constituting the new army was three-fold: (1) To cover the city of Washington from attack; (2) to assure the safety of the Shenandoah Valley; and (3), so to operate on the Confederate lines of communications in the direction of Gordonsville and Charlottesville as to draw off, if possible, a considerable force of the enemy from Richmond, and thus relieve the operations against that city of the Army of the Potomac.

General Pope thought that the first two of these objects could be accomplished best by withdrawing the corps of Sigel and Banks to the east side of the Blue Ridge. Accordingly these two commanders were ordered to cross the mountains and take position near Sperryville, about twenty-five miles west of Warrenton. At the same time McDowell was directed to send the division of Ricketts to Warrenton, but to leave King's division at Falmouth "to protect the crossing of the Rappahannock at that point, ... the railroad thence to Aquia Creek, and the public buildings which had been erected at the latter place." This was

John Pope, Commander of the Army of Virginia, June to September, 1862. Pope wore his men out with marching and destroyed what little confidence they had in him by his vacillating and contradictory orders.

contrary to General Pope's judgment, and he was undoubtedly correct in his position.

At this time the army of General Lee was still concentrated in the vicinity of Richmond, and his communications with the Valley, by the Virginia Central Railroad remained unbroken. The important junction of this line with the Orange and Alexandria at Gordonsville was defended, as was also Charlottesville, whence one line ran to Staunton in the upper Valley, and another to Lynchburg, where it met the East Tennessee and Georgia, the main line to Chattanooga. The Manassas Gap, and the Orange and Alexandria, which came together at Manassas Junction, served to connect the Union forces with the lower Valley, and with their base at Washington. The junctions at Manassas, Gordonsville, and Charlottesville, were therefore points of great strategic importance. The former place was in the hands of the Federals, and the second was exposed to capture, as the Union forces could advance upon it easily, and be supplied directly from Alexandria: its protection was therefore of special concern to Lee.

Between the regions occupied by the Army of Virginia and the Confederate forces, flowed in an easterly direction the Rappahannock River and its branch, the Rapidan. Both were crossed by several bridges, and in the dry season were fordable at many points, but none the less they were quite formidable military obstacles. North and west of Gordonsville, the country was mountainous, and the entire theatre was more or less thickly covered with forest. The Bull Run Mountains could be passed only at a few gaps. The highways were mainly dirt roads, fairly good in dry weather, but difficult after a storm. There were a few macadam roads, like the Warrenton Turnpike, and the Little River Turnpike through Aldie Gap.

The military position in the early days of July was as follows: At Harrison's Landing on the James River, McClellan with some 80,000 men was still threatening Richmond. Pope, with about 47,000 troops in all, was near Sperryville with the two corps of Sigel and Banks, while one division (King's) of McDowell's corps was at Fredericksburg, and the other (Ricketts's) at Warrenton.

As Lee's army at Richmond was between the two Federal forces, it was obviously out of the question for Pope to march to the aid of McClellan, or to be sent to him by water without leaving the Capital and the Valley exposed. His efforts were therefore necessarily confined to threatening Gordonsville and Charlottesville. Accordingly, on the 7 July, and again on the 12th, and 14th, Banks was ordered to despatch his cavalry under Hatch to seize Gordonsville and Charlottesville. Much to the annoyance of Pope, this movement failed because Hatch did not march with sufficient celerity. At that time Gordonsville was held by only 200 infantry and a few cavalry, and could easily have been captured.

To turn now to Lee: his first solicitude was to have McClellan's army recalled, and not reinforced, so that it could operate against Richmond from its new base. Knowing the inactivity of McClellan, he decided, with his usual audacity, to leave a small force within the defences of Richmond, and crush Pope before his army could be joined by that of McClellan. He had received prompt reports of the advance of Pope, and on the 13 July he ordered Jackson to Gordonsville, with the divisions of Winder and Ewell. The Confederate army was not organized into corps until the following autumn, and Jackson and Longstreet were still only major-generals commanding divisions; but each now usually commanded other divisions besides his own, called a wing. Thus, Jackson's old division became Winder's (afterwards Taliaferro's), and Longstreet's became Pickett's.

On his arrival at Gordonsville, Jackson was anxious to undertake some aggressive movement against Pope, but considered his force of 12,000 men too small; so he appealed to Lee for reinforcements. After some hesitation, on the 27 July Lee ordered A. P. Hill's division, about 12,000 strong, to Gordonsville.

On the 6 August, pursuant to orders from Halleck, Pope began an advance with his infantry, with the purpose of concentrating near Culpeper. The following day Jackson put his whole force in motion to fall upon Pope's army before it could be united. But the weather was very hot, and there were some blunders in the orders, so that it was three o'clock on the afternoon of the 9th before two of his divisions formed line in front of Banks's corps, which had been encountered at Cedar Mountain, some seven miles south of Culpeper. While awaiting the arrival of his other forces, Jackson brought up 26 rifled guns and opened fire on the enemy's lines. Banks at once attacked furiously, and routed the left of Jackson's line; but A. P. Hill arrived on the field with his division in time to save the day. Banks had begun the action without asking for reinforcements, and his unaided corps was "utterly overwhelmed and driven back with great loss." It was now dark, but Jackson pursued by moonlight until he came upon Ricketts's division of McDowell's corps in line of battle beyond Cedar Creek, and was checked.

Such, in brief, was the battle of Cedar Mountain. Banks had about 8000 men on the ground, and Jackson some 20,000 at the end. The Federal loss was nearly 2400, killed, wounded, and missing; the Confederate casualties were about 1300.

Both armies remained for two days in face of each other, and then Jackson wisely retired across the Rapidan toward Gordonsville. Pope followed as far as the river, but did not venture to cross, as he thought his "whole effective force was barely equal to that of the enemy." In this he was entirely mistaken, for he had in hand nearly 40,000 men, while Jackson had hardly 23,000. On the 15 August, Pope was reinforced by 8000 men under Reno, from Burnside's command. He had then not less than 45,000 men, exclusive of cavalry. But his force was not an army: it was an amalgamation of corps and divisions which had never fought together, and which had no confidence in each other or in their commander. This heterogeneous body was now to be attacked by a real army, under the command of the most accomplished soldier of the day, General Robert E. Lee.

McClellan's army abandoned its camp at Harrison's Landing on the 13 August, and the same day Longstreet was ordered to proceed to Gordonsville, where Lee himself took command on the 15th. Stuart's cavalry, and the remainder of the army quickly followed, with the exception of two brigades of infantry left to guard the capital against cavalry raids.

Lee now had about 55,000 seasoned troops; he occupied interior lines between Pope and McClellan, and he laid his plans to overwhelm the Army of Virginia before it could be joined by the Army of the Potomac. Pope's army, of about 45,000 men, had its centre at Cedar Mountain, with its right flank resting upon Robertson River to the west of the railway, and its left on the Rapidan to the east, the line being eight or ten miles long. Nearly opposite Pope's left flank, on the south side of the Rapidan, was a high wooded hill called Clark's Mountain, with spurs stretching down to the river at Sommerville Ford, about two miles above Raccoon Ford where the Union line rested on the Rapidan.

On Clark's Mountain Jackson had established a signal station from which there was an extensive view, covering a peaceful and pastoral district, which had not yet known the ravages of war, but whose rivers and villages were soon to become household words. Northward, beyond the green crest of Cedar Mountain, and the woods which hide the Rapidan, lie the wide and fertile plains of Culpeper. Just visible in the middle distance are the dim levels of Brandy Station, the scene of the great cavalry battle of the following June. On the horizon can be faintly traced the Bull Run Mountains, which mark the source of the creek, and the plateau of Manassas, the scene of the first battle of the war, and soon to be the field of an even more sanguinary conflict. To the east, as far as the eye can reach, is the great forest of Spottsylvania, where the armies of Grant and Lee were to meet in deadly combat; within whose gloomy depths the gallant Jackson was to receive his mortal wound on the field of Chancellorsville; and on the further edge of which Burnside was to wreck his brave army against the fieldworks of Fredericksburg.

On the 17 August, Lee had his army massed behind this mountain. His position gave him an excellent opportunity to cross at Sommerville Ford, fall upon Pope's left flank, and cut off his line of retreat. Probably at no time during the war was a finer chance put within his grasp.

Lee's orders were to have Stuart's cavalry cross at a ford further to the east, dash for Rappahannock Station, and destroy the bridge behind Pope's position. Failure on the part of Fitz Lee to understand, or to execute promptly, an order of Stuart, caused a delay of two days, and also led to the capture of a staff officer carrying a copy of Lee's order, which disclosed his plan. Pope immediately took alarm, and withdrew his army behind the Rappahannock. No such unfortunate *contretemps* had occurred in war since the capture of Napoleon's orders to Bernadotte saved the Russian army from destruction during the Campaign of Poland in 1807.

Lee now advanced to the Rappahannock, which he found low and easily fordable. He then spent five days in making feints to find a favorable opening to cross, and turn Pope's right. Meanwhile Stuart made a bold raid in rear of the Union army, and turned the tables by capturing Pope's headquarters, with his despatch-book containing much valuable information. Lee thus learned that the corps of Heintzelman and Porter, and Reynolds's division of Pennsylvania Reserves, 20,000 men in all, were within two days' march of Pope, and that the remainder of the Army of the Potomac was not more than a week behind. In this situation, Lee's only hope was in acting quickly, and he decided upon one of the most daring operations recorded in the annals of war. While he himself remained on the Rappahannock, with Longstreet's force of some 30,000 men, to occupy Pope's attention, he started Jackson, and Stuart's cavalry, about 24,000 men in all, to make a wide turning movement to the left, and strike at the Union line of communications.

Starting on the morning of the 25 August, Jackson marched that day to Salem, by way of Amissville and Orleans. The following day, without meeting any resistance, he pushed on through Thoroughfare Gap and Gainesville to Bristoe Station, on the Orange and Alexandria Railroad, where he arrived about sunset. That same night, Stuart's cavalry and two regiments of infantry captured Manassas Junction, a few miles to the north. The supplies of the Union army stored at Manassas "presented a sight to the ragged and half-starved Confederates, such as they had never before imagined." There were acres of warehouses filled to overflowing; two miles of side-tracks covered with loaded cars; and immense quantities of goods of every kind stacked in the open fields under tarpaulin covers. After his men had feasted, and supplied themselves with everything they could wear, or store in their haversacks, Jackson gave orders to apply the torch. When Pope looked upon the ashes the next day, he must have regretted his words: "Let us study the probable lines of retreat of our opponents, and leave our own to take care of themselves."

The movement of Jackson's column on the morning of the 25th was observed by the Federals, but they thought that it was going to the Valley, and no troops were sent to observe its march. Pope's army also made no move on the 26th, and that day Lee followed Jackson, with Longstreet's wing, which bivouacked at Orleans.

When Pope finally realized the situation, on the morning of the 27th, his first orders were very judicious. He directed on Gainesville the two corps of McDowell and Sigel, with the division of Reynolds, about 40,000 men. The occupation of this point with a strong force would place his troops directly between Jackson and Longstreet and prevent their junction: Gainesville was therefore the key to the whole position. In support of this movement, Heintzelman and Reno were sent to Greenwich, with three divisions; and Hooker was ordered to Bristoe, to attack Ewell, with Porter marching to support him. Banks remained in the rear to protect the trains.

McDowell and Heintzelman reached their destinations without opposition. At about two o'clock Hooker came in contact with Ewell at Bristoe, and attacked vigorously. Ewell was superior in numbers, but he had orders not to bring on a general engagement; so after an hour of resistance he retreated to Manassas.

Pope now made the first of his many blunders in this campaign. As yet he had no conception that Lee was marching "to throw himself into the lion's den by the side of Jackson." Instead of manoeuvring, therefore, in such a manner as to prevent their junction, his only idea was to "bag Jackson." Accordingly, at 1 A.M. on the 28th he ordered Porter and Heintzelman to march to Bristoe; Reno from Greenwich to Manassas; and McDowell, with his own and Sigel's corps, and Reynolds's division, from Gainesville to Manassas, "so as to intercept Jackson in case he attempted to retreat to the north." He thus deliberately threw away the advantages of his position at Gainesville, and made possible the easy junction of the two Confederate wings. Only McDowell had sense enough, on his own responsibility, to order Ricketts's division of his corps to take position in front of Thoroughfare Gap. It was this order for all of his troops to march on Manassas "at the very earliest blush of dawn," as Pope poetically expressed it, which lost him the campaign.

But Jackson did not wait at Manassas to be caught in a trap. On the night of the 27th he sent the Stonewall division northward by the Sudley Springs road to cross the turnpike and take position beyond Groveton. Early the following morning Ewell's division marched to the same place, crossing Bull Run at Blackburn's Ford, traversing the fields north of the stream, and recrossing to the right bank at the Stone Bridge. Later in the day, the division of A. P. Hill followed, marching north to Centreville, and thence westward on the Warrenton Pike. The divisions had been sent by these roundabout routes for the purpose of mystifying Pope.

When Pope himself reached Manassas about noon on the 28th he found Jackson gone, and could learn nothing definite as to his destination. Later, he heard that Hill's division had been seen at Centreville, and accordingly issued orders at 4:15 for all his troops to march to that place. Heintzelman and Reno went directly to Centreville; Sigel and Reynolds counter-marched to the turnpike, but did not cross Bull Run. King's division of McDowell's corps turned eastward on the pike toward Centreville, and about 5:30 was suddenly fired upon by Jackson's artillery. Immediately afterwards it was attacked by the divisions of Taliaferro and Ewell, and a fierce engagement ensued, which lasted until seven o'clock, with heavy losses on both sides. No advantage was gained by either party. Owing to the length of the Federal column, or the late hour of the day, only two of King's four brigades took any part in the action. Both Ewell and Taliaferro were severely wounded.

Jackson, about a mile from the road, might have remained hidden and allowed King to pass, but he feared that Pope would concentrate his entire army in an impregnable position

Second Manassas (1&2)

behind Bull Run, and the main object of the campaign be lost. He therefore attacked, even at the risk of drawing upon himself Pope's whole force.

News of this action soon reached Pope, at his headquarters near Manassas, and he jumped to the conclusion that Jackson was in full retreat from Centreville for Thoroughfare Gap. He therefore at once issued orders for the assembling of his troops on the Warrenton Pike. In his orders he wrote: "General McDowell has intercepted the retreat of the enemy, and is now in his front... . Unless he can escape by by-paths leading to the north tonight, he must be captured." Pope was entirely mistaken in his conjecture; and, in fact, he failed to draw a single correct inference during the course of this campaign. Not only was he in the dark regarding the intentions of his adversary, but he was also ignorant of the positions of his own corps. Therefore, instead of directing Hooker, who bivouacked south of Bull Run, to join Sigel by marching up the Sudley Springs road, he sent him by way of Centreville; and Porter, who was at Bristoe Station, was also ordered to make this wholly unnecessary detour.

In the meantime the head of Longstreet's column had reached Thoroughfare Gap, about three o'clock on this same day, the 28 August. This gap is the outlet by which the Manassas Gap Railroad, passing from the Shenandoah, penetrates the last mountainous obstruction on its way to tide-water. It is a rough pass in the Bull Run Mountains, at some points not more than a hundred yards wide. A turbid stream rushes over its rugged bottom, on both sides of which the mountain rises several hundred feet. On the north the face of the gap is almost perpendicular. The south face is less precipitous, but is covered with tangled mountain ivy and projecting boulders, forming an impregnable position when occupied by even a small force of infantry and artillery.

At the eastern end of this gap, the Confederates encountered resistance from Ricketts's division, which, it will be remembered, McDowell had wisely ordered there, to postpone as long as possible the union of the two wings of Lee's army. Finding the position too strong to assail, Longstreet turned it by sending a force through Hopewell Gap, a few miles to the north. At nightfall, therefore, Ricketts retired to Gainesville, whence a short march would have united his division to that of King. Connecting with King on the right was the division of Reynolds ; and on his right was the corps of Sigel. These forces were strong enough to hold their own until Pope could reinforce them in the morning. Nevertheless, King decided at 1 A.M. on the 29th to retire to Manassas; and this naturally induced Ricketts to fall back from Gainesville to Bristoe. Unfortunately McDowell was absent the whole evening, trying to find Pope, and was unable to rejoin his command until the next day.

The morning of the 29 August, therefore, found the Union army badly scattered. The only troops in front of Jackson at Groveton were the corps of Sigel and Reynolds's division. Banks, Porter, and Ricketts's division of McDowell's corps, were at Bristoe; King's division of McDowell's corps, and Hooker's division of Heintzelman's corps, were at Manassas; the other division of Heintzelman (Kearny's) and Reno's two divisions were near Centreville.

It was hardly possible to unite all these forces for battle on that day; and there was nothing to prevent Longstreet from joining Jackson. The Union troops were much exhausted from their long and useless marches; rations were also scarce on account of the destruction of the depot at Manassas, and the fact that the trains under General Banks were so far in the rear. Under the circumstances, it would have been wiser for General Pope to withdraw his entire army behind Bull Run, for rest and refreshment, in a practically impregnable position, where he would be reinforced in a day or two by the corps of Sumner and Franklin from the Army of the Potomac.

"At the same time," writes Mr. Ropes, "notwithstanding all these facts, it was probably possible to inflict a severe blow on the corps of Jackson before it could be joined by that of Longstreet; but to effect this, it was necessary that General Pope should have a clear idea in his mind of what he proposed to do, and that no time should be lost by mistakes or delays, or by changes of purpose on his part."

Longstreet had indeed cleared the gap, and the Federals who defended it had retired; but the main body of the Confederate army was still twelve miles away, and Jackson was confronted by vastly superior numbers. His forces had been reduced to about 23,000 effectives by the affair at Groveton. Less than two miles away, on the plateau of Manassas, were encamped 20,000 Federals, with the same number at the Junction; seven miles to the east, at Centreville, there were 18,000; and, at Bristoe Station, about the same distance, 11,000 — an aggregate of 69,000 men.

"Although it would have been sounder strategy, on the part of the Federal commander," writes Colonel Henderson, "to have concentrated toward Centreville, and have there awaited reinforcements," Pope decided to hurl his superior forces against Jackson before Lee could come up. Many motives may have influenced him to take this course — ambition, anxiety to retrieve his blemished reputation, fear that he might be superseded by McClellan — all urged him forward.

On the morning of the 29 August, the Confederate outlook was far from bright. Jackson did not yet know whether Longstreet had broken through, or even whether he *could* break through. In any event, his three divisions, worn with long marching and the fierce combat of the previous evening, would have to hold their own for several hours unaided.

The position chosen by Jackson was a very strong one. The long, flat-topped ridge, north of the Warrenton Turnpike, commands the approaches from the east and south. Some five hundred yards below the crest ran the line of an unfinished railroad, and behind the deep cuttings and high embankments the Confederate fightingline was strongly placed. The left, slightly thrown back, rested on a rocky spur, near Bull Run, commanding Sudley Springs Ford, and the road to Aldie Gap, his line of retreat. The front extended southwest for a mile and three-quarters. Early, with two brigades and a battery, occupied a wooded knoll, where the unfinished railroad crossed the pike, protecting the right rear, and stretching a hand to Longstreet.

Before the right and right centre the open green pastures sloped gradually for a distance of 1300 yards to Young's Branch. The left centre and left were shut in by a belt of timber which obstructed the field of fire, but also screened the defenders from the enemy's artillery. Within the position there was ample cover for the reserves. Jackson's numbers were sufficient for the defence of the position, which was not only strong by nature, but strongly held. To every yard of the line, 3000 yards in length, there were more than five muskets, so that half the force could be retained in reserve.

As Jackson was forming his lines at sunrise, the columns of Sigel and Reynolds were visible, nearly two miles away, deploying for the assault. They numbered only 19,000 men, so the attack was no stronger than the defence; and as the fire of the Federal artillery was restricted by the woods there could be little doubt of the result. The assault failed, and the Federals retreated across the fields.

But now Reno and Kearny, from Centreville, were coming on the field; and Sigel, calling on Reno for reinforcements, again made a desperate attack, which nearly broke the enemy's line. Jackson called up Branch's brigade from Hill's reserves; the wood was again cleared, and Sigel's division was put *hors de combat*. At this hour, about noon, Pope arrived on the field from Centreville. He immediately organized a fresh attack with the three divisions of Kearny, Hooker, and Reno. This assault was made about one o'clock, and portions of the attacking columns actually crossed the railroad, where a fierce hand-to-hand combat ensued. Jackson called up Pender's brigade from his reserves, and the Federals were at last driven back. Pender incautiously followed, and was forced to retire under the hot fire of the Federal artillery. Seeing his retreat, Grover's brigade of Hooker's division, which was in reserve, was sent forward for a counter-stroke. Grover broke through the Confederate line, and, if promptly and fully supported, had victory within his grasp.

By this time, Longstreet's troops had begun to form on Jackson's right, relieving the brigades of Early and Forno, which were placed in reserve in the rear of the centre. These fresh troops, and other reserves, were sent in against Grover, who was driven back across the pike, with a loss of one-fourth his command.

The battle had now been going on for nine hours; four determined assaults had been made; and at least 4000 Federals had fallen. None of the attacks had had any chance of success, because made with too few men, and without proper support. Ignorant of Longstreet's arrival, and with fresh troops at hand, Pope was not yet willing to give up the effort, while the sun was still high above the horizon. The three brigades of Kearny, and the two of Reno were in good condition; and the corps of Porter and McDowell had not yet been in action.

In connection with Porter, there is much interesting history, which can only be briefly summarized here.

Pursuant to the 3 A.M. orders of Pope, on the morning of the 29th Porter was marching his corps from Bristoe to Groveton by way of Centreville (an unnecessary detour of ten miles), and had passed Manassas Junction, when he was met by a staff-officer of General Pope's, who gave him the purport of a written order (which was afterwards confirmed), to the effect that he (Porter) was to take King's division (of McDowell's corps) and move to Gainesville. His column at once faced about, and proceeded toward Gainesville through the Junction, where, about 11 A.M., he was joined by McDowell. An hour later he received a third order, addressed to McDowell as well as himself, known subsequently as the "Joint Order."

From this order two things are plain: (1) That Pope believed that Jackson had retreated, and that they must not follow him even so far as Gainesville, because the army must be brought back at night to Centreville for needed supplies; (2) that if, contrary to his expectation, Jackson had not retreated, he would have to deal only with Jackson, and not with the whole of Lee's army united.

The battlefield of the Second Manassas. The battle fought here was scarcely surpassed for desperation on either side during the war.

The two generals soon discovered that the situation was very different from that indicated in the Joint Order: Jackson had *not* retreated, and they had to deal with *the whole* of Lee's army. About 11:30, at a little stream called Dawkin's Branch, three and a half miles from Gainesville, they encountered the van of Longstreet's army, which had left Thoroughfare Gap that morning. At the same time it was evident from the clouds of dust in the direction of Gainesville that large bodies of troops were following.

The order in question contained a clause reading: "If any considerable advantages are to be gained by departing from this order, it will not be strictly carried out." After consultation, the two generals decided to avail themselves of this latitude. McDowell accordingly departed with King's division, leaving Porter where he was.

Porter, with only 9000 or 10,000 men, was thus left isolated. His plain task was simply to observe, or contain, the troops in his front, and this task he fully performed. Pope did not know that Longstreet had arrived, and when, at the close of the afternoon, he gave Porter a positive written order to attack Jackson's right flank, which he supposed to be "in the air," he could not understand Porter's failure to act. As ascertained later, the facts were, that when Porter arrived on the crest of the hills which descend to Dawkin's Branch, he encountered the advance of Longstreet's four divisions of 25,000 men; that Lee himself was on the field two or three hours before Pope in person arrived; and that "Porter with his two divisions saved the Army of Virginia that day from disaster due to the enemy's earlier preparation for battle." Furthermore, Porter's right was not in connection or communication with Reynolds, who held the left of the main line; and he was separated by Longstreet's entire corps from Jackson's right flank which he was ordered by Pope to attack.

Late in the afternoon, about five o'clock, Pope again assaulted the Confederate left, with the two divisions of Kearny and Reno. In a very gallant and persistent attack, Hill's troops were forced back fully 300 yards, but at the critical moment Jackson once more called on his reserves, and the Federals were finally compelled to retire in disorder.

We must now return to Longstreet's corps, to explain the sixth and last combat of the day. On his arrival, Longstreet had formed his line, not in prolongation of Jackson's, but inclining forward, in a large obtuse angle. Lee's intention was to engage at once, but he finally yielded to Longstreet's request that he first be allowed to make a personal reconnaissance. This took an hour, and then the day was so nearly gone, it was decided to make only a reconnaissance in force, reserving the attack until early the next morning. Meanwhile McDowell had brought King's division on the field, and Pope had given orders for it to advance down the pike and fall upon Jackson's right, where, too, he was looking for Porter's attack. It thus happened that when King's division went forward to the attack, instead of finding Jackson in retreat, it met Longstreet advancing. King's weary troops were defeated in a fierce combat, which lasted until after nine o'clock.

After the repulse and pursuit of King, Longstreet withdrew his men to the line from which they had advanced, and Jackson ordered his men back from the railroad cut, their line during the day, to the crest a few hundred yards in the rear. It thus happened that the Federals were left with a deserted battlefield in their front. Had this been a deliberate ruse, says General Alexander, it would have been a masterpiece. To Pope, it proved to be a fatal delusion and a snare. At daybreak he telegraphed Halleck that, after a terrible battle, with combined forces of the enemy, lasting from daylight until dark, the enemy was driven from the field which he then occupied. He concluded: "The news has just reached me from the front that the enemy is retreating toward the mountains."

This was Pope's last and greatest blunder, which made him the aggressor on the second day, and cost him the battle.

On the morning of the 30 August, Pope had united his entire army except the corps of Banks, which, not yet recovered from the affair of Cedar Mountain, was in charge of the trains near Bristoe. Before daybreak Porter had been withdrawn from his isolated position on the left, and brought around to the centre. Pope now had on the field 65,000 men and 28 batteries. Besides, the corps of Sumner and Franklin, and the divisions of Cox and Sturgis, about 42,000 troops in all, had landed at Alexandria, and were only twenty-five miles away.

Lee had in hand the force of Jackson, reduced to about 17,000, the troops of Longstreet, 30,000, and some 2500 cavalry, an aggregate of nearly 50,000 men. He also had about 20,000 reinforcements coming up, and already at the Rappahannock River.

Pope spent several hours in forming his troops, and setting his army in battle array, with a view of avoiding the isolated attacks of the previous day, and pressing the "retreating" Confederates along the whole line.

The Union line was short and strong. From its right on Bull Run, in front of Jackson's left, to its left across the turnpike near Groveton, was less than three miles. About 20,000 infantry were deployed in the front line, with 40,000 more massed behind. Lee's line covered at least four miles. Jackson still held the left, in the strong position behind the railroad cut. Except for a battery of 18 guns, under Colonel S. D. Lee, which was placed on his right flank, he had received no reinforcements. Longstreet's line, as already stated, was not prolongation of Jackson's, but bent forward at an obtuse angle; and it considerably overlapped the Union left.

Pope, from his headquarters on Buck Hill near his centre, could see only a few Confederate batteries, supported by a strong line of skirmishers, and he could not be convinced by his officers that the enemy was not in full retreat. About noon the Federals attacked in force, and met a reception for which Pope was not prepared. The battle which followed was scarcely surpassed for desperation on either side during the war.

The whole weight of the assault fell upon Jackson, who called for assistance. The Federals, in their attack, had advanced into the angle between Jackson and Longstreet, so that their line could be enfiladed. Longstreet sent several batteries into position, and opened upon the Union flank with a fire which nothing could withstand. In vain Pope sent in his reserves to stem the tide of retreat. Jackson ordered forward two brigades, in a counter-stroke, and Pope's battle was lost.

Seeing the effect of Longstreet's fire, about four o'clock Lee ordered a general advance. The objective point aimed at by Longstreet was the Henry House plateau, where Jackson's brigade, "standing like a stone wall," had made his name immortal thirteen months before. The capture of this position would have cut off the Federal retreat across Bull Run by the Stone Bridge, and here Pope made a desperate stand. Fortunately for the Federals the hour

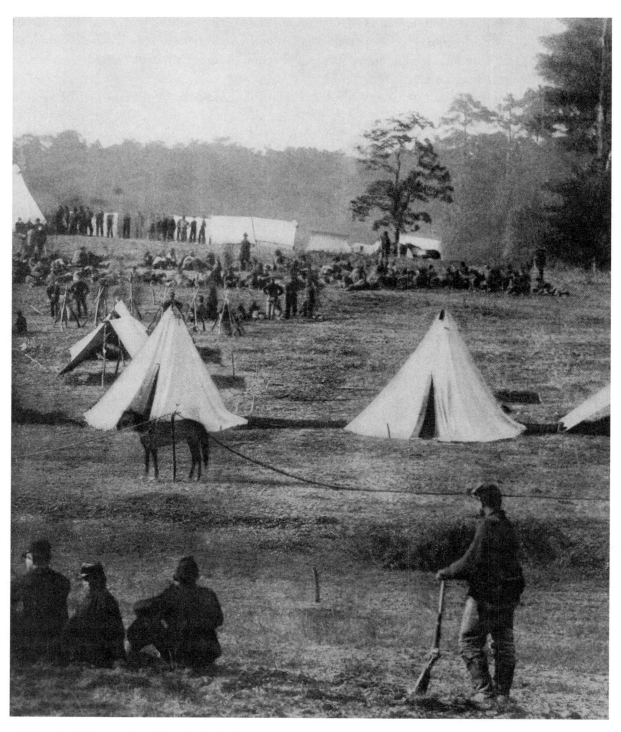

At the end of the campaign, the Federals had 14,462 killed, wounded, or missing. The Confederates totals were at 9,112. The latter collected over 20,000 small arms from the field of battle. Above: Union prisoners. Facing page: Confederate prisoners.

was too late for Lee to gather the full fruits of his victory; the daylight was also shortened by heavy clouds, and a rain set in about dusk which continued during the night and much of the next day.

The Federal troops, in great disorder, poured across the bridge and through the fords toward Centreville. Here the whole army was concentrated on the corps of Franklin, which had arrived about six o'clock, only a few hours too late to reach the field and save the day.

As the Federal position at Centreville was very strong, Lee decided to turn it. On the morning of the 31st, Jackson's corps, preceded by Stuart's cavalry, was ordered to cross Bull Run at Sudley, and march by the Little River Turnpike on Fairfax Court House. Longstreet was to collect the spoils on the battlefield, and then to follow Jackson. Progress was slow on account of the rain and mud.

Pope, although still claiming a victory, ordered Banks to destroy the trains at Bristoe, and join him by a night march. With Franklin, Banks, and Sumner, who arrived on the 31st, he now had 30,000 fresh troops, but he remained at Centreville only a single day. The whole army was withdrawn to Fairfax, where it was too close to its fortified lines to be flanked again out of position.

On the first day of September there was a small affair at Chantilly, in which Stevens, who commanded a division of Reno's corps, was shot through the head; and Kearny, who had ridden into the Confederate lines in the dusk, was killed in trying to escape. They both were prominent and distinguished officers. Stevens had graduated at the head of Halleck's class at West Point in 1839; and at the time of his death the Government was considering his appointment to the command of the now united armies of Pope and McClellan.

The losses of the two armies for the entire campaign are summarized as follows:

	Federals	Confederates
Killed	1,747	1,468
Wounded	8,452	7,563
Missing	4,263	81
Totals	14,462	9,112

The Confederates collected 30 guns and over 20,000 small-arms from the fields of battle.

The results of the campaign are very ably summed up by General Alexander in two brief paragraphs:

"While Lee had fallen short of destroying his greatly superior adversaries, he could yet look back with pride upon the record he had made within the ninety days since taking command on the first of June. He had had the use of about 85,000 men, and the enemy had had the use, in all, of fully 200,000.

"At the beginning, the enemy had been within six miles of Richmond. He was now driven within the fortifications of Washington, with a loss in the two campaigns of about 33,000 men, 82 guns, and 58,000 small-arms. Lee's own losses had been about 31,000 men and two guns."

In his comments on the campaign, Mr. Ropes writes: "General Lee's operations had indeed been successful, but we must point out that his successes were due much more to the ability with which he improved the mistakes of his antagonist, than to any advantages which he procured for himself by the hazardous strategy which he employed.... Of these mistakes Lee took prompt advantage, and thus won his victory."

These remarks, from a critic of the standing of Mr. Ropes, are surprising.

It is true that Napoleon, in his *Maxims,* warns against the division of an army into two columns unable to communicate; and especially against the strategy which places the point of junction in the very presence of a concentrated enemy. Both of these maxims Lee violated: *the first because he knew Jackson, the last because he knew Pope.* It is rare indeed that such strategy succeeds, and it has been remarked that, after Jackson's death, Lee never again attempted those great turning movements which had achieved his most brilliant victories.

"History," says Colonel Henderson, "often unconsciously injures the reputation of great soldiers. The more detailed the narrative, the less brilliant seems success, the less excusable defeat."

"If," said Frederick the Great, "we had exact information of our enemy's dispositions, we should beat him every time."

"It is too often overlooked, by those who study the history of campaigns," says Colonel Henderson again, "that war is the province of uncertainty. The reader has the whole theatre of war displayed before him. He notes the exact disposition of the opposing forces at each hour of the campaign, and with this in his mind's eye he condemns or approves the action of the commanders. In the action of the defeated general he often sees much to blame; in the action of the successful general but little to admire. But his judgment is not based on a true foundation. He has ignored the fact that the information at his disposal was not at the disposal of those he criticises; and until he realizes that both generals, to a greater or less degree, must have been groping in the dark, he will neither make just allowance for the errors of the one, nor appreciate the genius of the other."

As a tactician, Pope was incapable. As a strategist, he lacked imagination, except in his despatches. Lee, with his extraordinary insight into character, played on Pope as he had played on McClellan, and his strategy was justified by success. If, as Moltke states, the junction of two armies on the field of battle is the highest achievement of military genius, the campaign against Pope has seldom been surpassed. Lee's strategy was certainly hazardous, but against an antagonist of different calibre he would never have attempted such manoeuvres. To condemn them is therefore short-sighted criticism.

"How often," says Napier, "have we not heard the genius of Bonaparte slighted, and his victories talked of as destitute of merit, because, at the point of attack, he was superior in numbers to his enemies. This very fact … constitutes his greatest and truest praise." It is often forgotten that Napoleon, in nearly all of his campaigns, was outnumbered in the whole theatre of war — not only in Italy, but in the campaigns of Ulm, Austerlitz, Eckmuhl, Dresden, Leipzig, France (1814), and Waterloo. He never waited for his adversary to become fully prepared, but struck him the first blow. The first principle of war is to concentrate superior force at the decisive point, that is, upon the field of battle. But this principle can never be observed by standing still and permitting the enemy to concentrate. True generalship is, therefore, "to make up in activity for lack of strength"; to strike the enemy in detail, and overthrow his columns in succession. To claim therefore that Lee's victory was due, less to his strategy, than to his ability to improve the mistakes of his antagonist, is absurd.

Another of Napoleon's maxims says: "The first qualification in a general-in-chief is a cool head — that is, a head which receives just impressions, and estimates things and objects at their real value." This, General Pope certainly did not have. He never made a correct inference during the whole campaign, and consequently committed one blunder after another. With each new report he changed his mind regarding the situation and issued new orders. He wore his men out with marching and countermarching, and destroyed what little confidence they already had in him by his vacillating and contradictory orders.

After he knew of the arrival of Lee's army, he should not have renewed his attack on the 30th, but have remained on the defensive, or withdrawn his army across Bull Run, to await the arrival of the other corps of the Army of the Potomac. But again he drew a false conclusion: he thought that Lee had begun to retreat, and accordingly gave orders to pursue.

It is difficult, moreover, to agree with the statement of Mr. Ropes, adopted by Major Steele, that the Union army, though "beaten and badly beaten; still ... was not forced from the field"; and that it was only Pope's retreat on the night of the 30th which "stamped the whole campaign as a failure."

Pope, indeed, "with an audacity which disaster was powerless to tame," reported to Halleck that the enemy was "badly whipped." But these statements do not agree with the descriptions of the utter confusion and disorder of the Federal retreat as recorded by other writers.

At the beginning of the campaign Pope handled his cavalry very well. They "were employed with a boldness which had not hitherto been seen." Led by two able young generals, Buford and Bayard, they did far better service than McClellan's detectives. There were frequent reconnaissances, and outposts were maintained twenty miles in advance of the army. But at the end they were utterly broken down, — "worn out by courier and escort service"; so that at Centreville Pope had to send out a brigade of infantry on reconnaissance, because "there was absolutely no cavalry fit for service."

The work of the Confederate cavalry, as usual, was excellent. While the armies were facing each other on the Rappahannock, Stuart rode around Pope's flank, and captured his headquarters, with much valuable information. During Jackson's famous march, Stuart's cavalry was in the van, and covering the flanks. On the morning of the 31 August, Stuart reported to Lee before eight o'clock that the Federal army was at Centreville. Again, when Jackson moved out on the Little River Turnpike, Stuart led the way. If Pope had used his cavalry as well as Lee, there might have been a very different outcome to the campaign.

CHAPTER EIGHT

SEPTEMBER 1862

ANTIETAM

ON the morning of the 2 September, as soon as he knew that Pope had found shelter within the defences of Washington, Lee ordered Jackson to cross the Potomac, and form the vanguard of an invasion of the North. Hitherto, the Confederates had been content to play the role of defenders, and they had played it to perfection. Although they had awaited the attack within their own frontiers, their tactics had been essentially offensive: it was by strategical and tactical counter-strokes that the recent victories had been won. Like Napoleon, Lee and Jackson believed that the best defence lies not in strong positions, but in the concentration of superior numbers on the field of battle. But if the best defence lies in a vigorous offensive, to make victory complete it is necessary to carry the war into hostile territory. The Great War has proved conclusively that even if a nation is brought to the point of making terms by the defeat of its armies beyond its own frontiers, it is never really conquered unless its capital is occupied, and the hideous sufferings of war are brought directly home to the mass of the population. "A single victory on Northern soil ... was far more likely to bring about the independence of the South than even a succession of victories in Virginia."

Such were the ideas, advocated by General Lee, and accepted by President Davis, which led to the invasion of Maryland. Nevertheless, Lee himself had no great expectations of decisive results. He wrote Mr. Davis: "The army is not properly equipped for an invasion of the enemy's territory. It lacks much of the material of war, is feeble in transportation, the animals being much reduced; the men are poorly provided with clothes, and in thousands of instances are destitute of shoes.... What concerns me most is the fear of getting out of ammunition." At a later date (12 September), Lee wrote the President that the 1650 pairs of shoes obtained at Frederick, Williamsport, and Hagerstown, would "not be sufficient to cover the bare feet of the army."

The captures made in the Peninsula, and especially at Manassas, had proved of the greatest value. Old muskets had been exchanged for new, smooth-bore cannon for rifled guns, tattered blankets for good overcoats. Their well-supplied foes had furnished the impoverished Confederates with tents, medicines, ambulances, ammunition wagons, and war material of every kind. Many of the soldiers were clad in Federal uniforms, and even the wagons at Lee's headquarters were marked with the initials U. S. A.

Campaigns of Gettysburg and Antietam

Antietam

Lee had been joined by the three divisions of D. H. Hill, McLaws, and Walker, and by Hampton's cavalry, and he should have had at this time about 65,000 effectives, but there were thousands of stragglers.

When Lee began his invasion of Maryland there were about 14,000 Union troops in the lower Shenandoah Valley: 3000 infantry and artillery at Winchester; 3000 cavalry at Martinsburg, and a garrison of 8000 at Harper's Ferry. Lee was aware of the presence of these forces, but he thought that they would all be withdrawn as soon as it was known that he had crossed the Potomac. If it had depended on McClellan this would have been done; but Halleck gave orders for the commander at Harper's Ferry to hold that position.

Lee thus found his situation suddenly complicated. His line of communications, which ran from Manassas by Leesburg to Frederick, was too near to Washington, and in danger of being cut at any moment by the Federal cavalry. Arrangements had already been made, therefore, to transfer the line to the Valley; but this line also would be exposed so long as Harper's Ferry was garrisoned by the enemy. It was manifestly out of the question for Lee, with his small forces, to mask this post, and nothing remained but to capture it by a *coup de main*. Jackson, with 25,000 men, nearly half the Confederate army, was detailed for the expedition, and he was ordered to march at daybreak on the 10 September. Meanwhile, the remainder of the army was to move northwest to Hagerstown, twenty-five miles from Frederick, where it would threaten Pennsylvania with invasion, and be protected from McClellan by the parallel ranges of the Catoctin and South mountains.

When the army under Pope retreated within the lines of Washington, there was great alarm at the capital, and both the President and General Halleck feared that "it was impossible to save the city." At an early hour on the morning of the 2 September they called together on General McClellan, who had come up from Alexandria the previous day. The President stated, writes McClellan, that "the army was entirely defeated and falling back to Washington in confusion. He then said that he regarded Washington as lost, and asked me if I would, under the circumstances, consent to accept command of all the forces." McClellan at once accepted, and this verbal order of the President was the only one by which he was reinstated in command.

Making a virtue of necessity, Pope asked to be relieved, and was sent to a distant post in the Northwest where there were some Indian disturbances.

The reinstatement of McClellan was very popular with the army, and did much to restore the morale of the troops. On his first appearance he was greeted with "frantic cheers of welcome that extended for miles along the column." Yet neither the President nor Halleck had any confidence in him, and the appointment was made with great reluctance. General McClellan himself says that he fought the campaign with a "halter around his neck," and if the Army of the Potomac had been defeated, he would have been condemned like General Porter, and perhaps executed. This feeling undoubtedly influenced McClellan's actions during the campaign, and was most unfortunate.

The army which McClellan led from Washington was made up of the First Corps under Hooker; the Second under Sumner; of one division of the Fourth Corps under Couch; of the

Sixth under Franklin; of the Ninth under Reno; and the Twelfth under Mansfield. Couch's division was attached to the Sixth Corps, and Cox's (Kanawha) division was at this time incorporated in the Ninth Corps.

The First and Ninth corps formed the right, under General Burnside; the Second and Twelfth, the centre, under General Sumner; and the Sixth Corps, with the division of Couch, constituted the left, under General Franklin.

General Banks was assigned to the "command or the defences of the capital," and had under him the Third Corps (Heintzelman), the Fifth (Porter), and the Seventh (Sigel).

At the time it left Washington, the army numbered on paper 84,000 men — in reality less than 70,000. About the same number (72,000) was left under Banks; but on the 12 September, at the urgent request of McClellan, Porter was sent to him, with the two divisions of Morrell and Sykes, about 13,000 men, thus raising his forces nominally to an aggregate of 97,000.

On the 7 September the corps of the Army of the Potomac occupied the following positions: Hooker and Burnside were at Leesboro; Sumner and Mansfield were in front of Rockville; Franklin was at Rockville: and Couch was at Offutt's Cross Roads. The Union cavalry under Pleasanton, was well in front, and in contact with Stuart, who formed a screen for Lee's army. From the 6th to the 15th, when Stuart finally retired behind the Antietam, there were daily engagements between the two cavalry forces.

Lee's army had crossed the Potomac by the fords near Leesburg on the 4th to the 6th, and on the 7 September was concentrated near Frederick. Here, on the 9th, he issued his famous order, known as "Special Orders No. 191," for the movement on Harper's Ferry. Jackson with his corps (except D. H. Hill's division) was ordered via Williamsport to drive the Federals from Martinsburg into Harper's Ferry, which he would then attack from the south. Walker's division was to cross the Potomac below Harper's Ferry and occupy Loudoun Heights. McLaws, with his own division and Anderson's, was to march by the most direct route, and take possession of Maryland Heights, which command Harper's Ferry.

Harper's Ferry, at the junction of the Shenandoah with the Potomac, is nearly fifty miles northwest of Washington, in a straight line. Loudoun Heights, at the northern end of the Blue Ridge, are thirty miles from Washington, between Harper's Ferry and Leesburg where Lee crossed the Potomac. Maryland Heights, on the north side of the river, opposite Harper's Ferry, are the hills at the southern end of Elk Ridge, the range next west of South Mountain. Frederick is in Maryland forty miles north by west of Washington.

The Union army had moved very slowly, on account of the "fears of the authorities at Washington, and the necessity of reorganization." On the 9th, Couch's division, the extreme left, touched the Potomac, at the mouth of Seneca Creek. Franklin's corps was at Darnestown. The Second and Twelfth corps, constituting the centre, were at Middlebrook, and the First and Ninth, forming the right, were at Brookeville. Thus the army was still within twenty miles of the capital, on a front stretching from left to right of about twenty-five miles.

On the night of the 13th, having advanced only about twenty miles in four days, the army was concentrated near Frederick. In the meantime, Lee had crossed the mountains, and was at Hagerstown.

Ruins of the Bridge at Harper's Ferry, Virginia where the Federal garrison of 12,500 was outnumbered and surrendered on Sept. 15 after two days. Jackson then rejoined Lee in Maryland just in time to stem the tide at Antietam.

On his arrival at Frederick, on the 13th, an official copy of Lee's order No. 191, addressed to D. H. Hill, fell into McClellan's hands, and gave him an opportunity rarely presented to a general. This order told McClellan two things, both of great importance:

First, that Lee had divided his army, and sent Jackson to capture Harper's Ferry.

Second, where the remainder of the Confederate army was to march and to halt, and where the detached commands were to rejoin the main body.

This information placed the Army of Northern Virginia absolutely at the mercy of McClellan, provided he acted with the greatest celerity. If he despatched his left column through Crampton's Gap, it would fall directly upon the rear of McLaws at Maryland Heights. If he advanced his right, through Turner's Gap, he would interpose between Hill and Longstreet on the one hand, and Jackson's command on the other. These two Federal columns had less than twenty miles to march; the gaps were not held in any force before the morning of the 14th, and Harper's Ferry was not surrendered until 8 A.M. on the 15th. It must be admitted that, for him, McClellan acted with considerable energy: he almost grasped the opportunity, but not entirely.

Lee's movements, which were earlier in point of time, will be described first. Jackson left Frederick early on the 10th, and marched rapidly twenty-five miles through Middletown and Boonsboro, to Williamsport, where he crossed the Potomac the next morning. Hearing of the Confederate movement, the Union forces at Martinsburg abandoned that town on the night of the 11th and retreated to Harper's Ferry. Jackson followed, and on the 12th went into camp near Halltown, about two miles from the Union position on Bolivar Heights.

On the 10th, McLaws also moved, by way of Pleasant Valley, which separates South Mountain on the east from Elk Ridge on the west. The southern extremity of the ridge, Maryland Heights, completely commands Harper's Ferry on the opposite bank of the Potomac. McLaws easily drove the small Union force from the heights, and gained full possession on the afternoon of the 13th. He at once placed his artillery in position, and opened fire at two o'clock the following afternoon.

The third Confederate column, under Walker, crossed the Potomac at Point of Rocks, on the night of the 10th, and on the 13th occupied Loudoun Heights, where he arranged his forces so as to prevent the escape of the garrison of Harper's Ferry down the right bank of the Potomac.

Harper's Ferry was now completely surrounded, and at the mercy of the enemy. At daybreak on the 15th, the Confederate guns opened fire, and at eight o'clock the Federal commander displayed the white flag. As the results of the expedition, Jackson captured over 12,000 men, with 73 pieces of artillery, many small-arms, and other stores.

The first part of Lee's program had been carried out successfully, although not quite as expeditiously as he had hoped, and the delay nearly proved fatal to him.

Leaving Hill to receive the surrender of the Federal troops and property, Jackson started at once to rejoin Lee in Maryland. By a severe night march of seventeen miles he reached Sharpsburg on the morning of the 16th. Walker's division followed closely, and also reported to General Lee the same morning.

To return now to General McClellan, whom we left at Frederick, on the 13th, with Lee's order in his hands. He decided not to move his left by the most direct road, through Jefferson and Knoxville, and thence up the river to Harper's Ferry, but by Burkittsville to Crampton's Gap, while the centre and right marched by Middletown to Turner's Gap. The Union left would thus debouch in rear of McLaws at Maryland Heights, and the remainder of the army between Longstreet and Hill on the right and Jackson's corps on the left.

The Blue Ridge Mountains cross Maryland from north to south in two distinct ranges six or eight miles apart, with a fertile valley between them. These ranges are known as the Catoctin and South mountains. The latter is a formidable obstacle, and can be crossed by an army only at two gaps, Turner's and Crampton's. There were several turnpikes in the region, of which the best known was the Old National Road, which passed westward through Frederick and crossed South Mountain at Turner's Gap. About a mile to the south, at Fox's Gap, the summit is passed by another route, known as the Old Sharpsburg, or Braddock, road, because it was used by General Braddock's army, in 1755. At about an equal distance to the north, still another road, the Old Hagerstown Road, finds a passage over the ridge. The National Road, because of easier grades and better engineering, was then, as now, the principal route, the others having remained rough country roads. The mountain crests are from 1000 to 1300 feet above the valley, and the gaps are 200 to 300 feet below the summits. There were other dirt roads in every direction, and all of them were in good condition at this season of the year. There were many small towns and villages, of which the most considerable was Frederick. It was on the whole a thickly settled farming country; the mountains were generally covered with woods; as also the valleys, except where cleared for cultivation.

General Lee's original plan had been for the main part of his army, under Longstreet, to halt at Boonsboro, with all the trains, and there await the return of Jackson, and the other detachments, while D. H. Hill's division formed the rear guard, and Stuart's cavalry covered the route. Learning, however, that a body of Pennsylvania militia had been collected at Chambersburg, Lee sent Longstreet forward to Hagerstown.

Looking down onto the Antietam.

On the night of the 13th, Lee heard that a copy of his field order was in the hands of McClellan, and that the advance of the Union army was at the eastern end of Turner's Gap. He immediately ordered Longstreet, who was thirteen miles away, to return; and directed D. H. Hill, two of whose brigades were already at the gap, to proceed there with the remainder of his division.

The battle of South Mountain was opened on the morning of the 14th by the Union cavalry, under Pleasanton. About nine o'clock, Cox arrived with the Kanawha division, and took command of the attack. Three hours later the remainder of the Ninth Corps came up, under Reno, who was killed during the action. Later still, Hooker arrived with the First Corps, and all of the right wing was then on the field, under the immediate command of Burnside. The First Corps assaulted the Confederate left, and the Ninth attacked the right, at Fox's Gap, on the Braddock Road. The combat lasted until 10 P.M.; and at midnight the Confederates withdrew. The battle hardly admits of precise description, as it was a succession of sharp skirmishes rather than one connected action. The general result was a Confederate defeat.

Franklin had been ordered to move the same day with the left wing by Crampton's Gap, to relieve the garrison at Harper's Ferry. As the distance from Turner's Gap is about six miles in a straight line, and the country between is very rugged, the action there was entirely disconnected from the other. Beginning about noon, after a spirited engagement of three hours Franklin, with his superior forces, easily carried the crest, and established his line in Pleasant Valley. On hearing of this, McLaws formed his troops in a strong defensive position across the valley, and made such a show of strength that Franklin believed he was outnumbered "two to one." After the surrender of Harper's Ferry, during the afternoon of the 15th McLaws skillfully and without molestation withdrew his command across the river to the town.

After his failure to hold the passes of South Mountain, Lee, who had only 19,000 men with him, decided to retreat to the south side of the Potomac. About noon on the 15th, when his forces were on the way to the ford, he received at Sharpsburg a despatch stating that Harper's Ferry had fallen, and Jackson was on his way to rejoin him. He at once recalled his troops from the ford, established a line of battle on the heights overlooking the Antietam, and ordered the batteries into position. By nightfall the divisions of Hood, D. H. Hill, and Jones, were in line of battle. After a hard night-march, Jackson arrived on the morning of the 16th, and McLaws, with his own division and Anderson's, twenty-four hours later. Lee's whole army was therefore reunited on the morning of the 17th, except the division of A. P. Hill, which Jackson had left behind to complete the arrangements for the surrender of Harper's Ferry.

Mr. Ropes speaks of Lee's decision to stand and fight at Sharpsburg as one of the "boldest and most hazardous" in his career, and is "bewildered that he should even have thought seriously of making it."

General Alexander also expresses his amazement at the "audacity" of Lee in accepting battle "in the open field, without a yard of earthworks, against a better-equipped army of double his force, and with a river close behind him, to be crossed by a single ford, peculiarly bad and exposed, in case he had to retreat."

The Dunker church of Antietam marks the center of the bloodiest single day's fighting in the Civil War. The dead and wounded numbered some 23,500 with another 15,500 counted as missing.

General Longstreet was also of the opinion that the army should have recrossed the Potomac at once. But Jackson, when he reached Sharpsburg on the morning of the 16th, heartily approved of Lee's decision. Colonel Henderson, as usual, agrees with his hero. He thinks that "the Army of Northern Virginia was so superior to the Army of the Potomac that Lee and Jackson" were warranted in believing that "they might fight a defensive battle, outnumbered as they were, with the hope of annihilating their' enemy.... By retreating across the Potomac, in accordance with General Longstreet's suggestion, Lee would certainly have avoided all chances of disaster; but, at the same time, he would have abandoned a good hope of ending the war."

McClellan's own words are the strongest justification of the views held by the Southern leaders. He says that the Army of the Potomac was so "thoroughly exhausted and depleted" by the last two campaigns; and its trains, administrative services and supplies, so disorganized, that "nothing but sheer necessity justified the advance ... to South Mountain and Antietam."

And in his official report he says: "One battle lost and almost all would have been lost. Lee's army might have marched as it pleased on Washington, Baltimore, Philadelphia, or New York; ... nowhere east of the Alleghanies was there another organized force to avert its march." This apprehension goes far to explain, and to excuse McClellan's excessive caution during the campaign.

It is a curious fact that many battles of the Civil War bear double names. The Confederates generally named them for the town or place near the field of action: the Federals, for some natural object adjoining the scene of the conflict. Thus we have Manassas and Bull Run; Shiloh and Pittsburg Landing; Murfreesboro and Stones River; Sharpsburg and Antietam.

The village of Sharpsburg is in the midst of a very irregular plateau which is almost enclosed by the Potomac River and the Antietam Creek. The Potomac bounds it on the south and west, and the Antietam on the east. In general outline, the plateau may be considered a parallelogram, four miles in length from north to south, and two and a half miles in width inside the bends of the river. From the village the ground descends in all directions, though a continuous ridge runs northward, on which is the Hagerstown Pike. The Boonsboro Turnpike crossed the Antietam on a stone bridge; entered the village from the northeast, and, continuing through Sharpsburg, ran southwest to the ford of the Potomac at Shepherdstown. The Hagerstown road entered the town from the north, passing the Dunker Church a mile out, and ran nearly due south, crossing the Antietam at its mouth, and continuing down the Potomac toward Harper's Ferry.

The Antietam is a deep creek, with few fords at an ordinary stage of water, and the principal roads, at the time of the battle, crossed it on solid stone bridges, which Lee did not have the time or the means to destroy. Within the field of battle there were three of these bridges: the upper one in front of Keedysville; the middle one upon the Boonsboro road; and the lower one, since known as Burnside's Bridge, on the road to Rohrersville.

Between Mercersville on the north and the mouth of the Antietam on the south, the Potomac flows in a series of remarkable curves, but its general course is such that a line of battle less than six miles long can be drawn from near Mercersville to a point just above the mouth of the Antietam, so as to rest both its flanks on the Potomac, to cover the town and the ford across the river, and to have its front covered by the creek.

Today, the National Cemetery is situated upon the crest of a hill to the eastward of the town, and just beyond the houses. If one enters the cemetery and takes his position on the highest point, at the base of the flagstaff, he will be within the concave of the Confederate line as it stood at the beginning of the battle. Near this spot, on a small mass of limestone, which commands an extensive view, it is said that Lee stood to direct the battle. On the left, looking westward, is the town of Sharpsburg, with the road to Hagerstown partially in sight. In the border of a patch of woods, at the distance of about a mile, and in plain view, stood the famous Dunker Church. At the church two roads met the turnpike, almost forming a right angle with each other. To the west, northwest, and north of the church, were the so-called West Woods; and the woods to the east of the pike, separated from it by open ground, were called the East Woods. These two patches of timber, with the fields between, were the scene of the most desperate fighting of the 17 September.

To the northeast, at a distance of about two miles, on the further side of the Antietam, could be seen a large brick building: this was the Pry house, the headquarters of McClellan during the battle. The creek itself cannot be seen, because of the depth of the ravine which forms its bed, but its course can easily be traced by the line of trees along its banks.

Further to the right, at the base of some hills, but concealed from view, is the Burnside Bridge, about a mile away. Practically the whole battlefield may be seen from this single point. To complete the description, it is to be added that the famous "sunken road" was almost directly opposite the centre of the Union position, looking west. It branched off from the northern side of the Boonsboro Pike, about halfway from the creek to Sharpsburg, and ran in zigzag fashion to the Hagerstown Pike, which it joined about mid-distance from the village to the Dunker Church, but nearer the latter.

If troops moved on the field as chessmen are moved on the board; if corps and divisions went into action as complete wholes, the story of a battle could be told with more precision; but this is very far from being the case. "The combinations of a battlefield," writes General Palfrey, "are almost as varying, and far less distinctly visible and separable than those of a kaleidoscope." A great battle cannot be described in detail except at immense length, and even then imperfectly. Napoleon once said that no attempt should ever be made to narrate the events of a battle in smaller terms than army corps. If lesser units are used — "it is impossible to see the forest for the trees."

The Confederate position at Sharpsburg was in many respects a strong one, and could have been made even stronger with entrenchments, but these were not used, although there was ample time to dig them. The flanks were reasonably secure. The right rested on the Antietam. The left was more open, but beyond the West Woods a low ridge gave room for several batteries, while the Potomac was so close that there was but little space available for attack.

Confederate dead on the Hagerstown Pike. Tactically, Antietam was a drawn battle; but the prestige of victory rested with McClellan. Lee's invasion had terminated in failure.

Jackson held the left, with Hood in second line. Next in order came D. H. Hill. Longstreet held the centre and right, with Walker in reserve. On the left flank, Stuart with Fitz Lee's brigade and his four guns, were between the West Woods and the river. On the right, Munford's two regiments of cavalry, with a battery, held the bridge at the Antietam Iron Works, and kept open the road to Harper's Ferry.

For the occupation of this front, of about three miles, Lee had at first only 23,500 men; and, even after the arrival of the absent divisions, no more than 35,000 infantry, 4000 cavalry, and 194 guns would be in line.

On paper, McClellan's forces were far superior:

	Men	*Guns*
First Corps — Hooker	15,000	40
Second Corps — Sumner	19,000	42
Fifth Corps — Porter	13,000	70
Sixth Corps — Franklin	12,000	36

Ninth Corps— BURNSIDE 14,000		35
Twelfth Corps— MANSFIELD.............................. 10,000		36
	83,000	259
Cavalry — PLEASANTON 4,000		16
TOTALS 87,000		275

The morning of Monday the 15 September found the Confederates retreating from South Mountain. It was only seven miles to Antietam Creek; the weather was fine; the roads were excellent and unobstructed. By noon the mass of McClellan's army might have been in contact with the enemy. With the First, Second, Fifth, and Twelfth corps, and the cavalry, in hand, he had over 60,000 men to the 25,500 of Lee. But McClellan never appreciated the value of time, and nothing was done that day. "Instead of making his reconnaissance at three in the afternoon of Monday," writes General Cox, "it might have been made at ten in the morning, and the battle could have been fought before night.... Or if McClellan had pushed boldly for the bridge at the mouth of the Antietam, nothing but a precipitate retreat by Lee could have prevented the interposition of the whole National army between the separated wings of the Confederates." Nothing was done, however, either on Monday or Tuesday, except reconnoitring, while Lee was straining every nerve to concentrate his forces.

On the afternoon of the 16th, McClellan completed his preparations for the battle which he proposed to deliver the next day. Sumner, with his own corps and that of Mansfield, was on the right, and Hooker, who had been removed from Burnside's command, was beyond Sumner, on the extreme right. The centre was occupied by the Fifth Corps, under Porter, and the left by the Ninth Corps, under Burnside. Franklin, who had been sent to watch McLaws, had been recalled on the night of the 16th, and on his arrival with the Sixth Corps McClellan proposed to place his troops in reserve.

McClellan's plan of battle, as stated by himself in his final and elaborate report, was to attack Lee's left with the corps of Hooker and Mansfield, supported by Sumner, and, if necessary, Franklin. Then, "as soon as matters looked favorably there," to carry the heights of Sharpsburg with Burnside's Ninth Corps. In case of success, with either or both these assaults, he proposed to advance his centre.

Whatever McClellan's plans may have been, his execution of them was very bad. It seems almost inconceivable that a commander of any military ability should have left a corps of four divisions idle for hours on his left, while he attacked on the right with three corps *in succession* held the centre with a fifth corps, his cavalry and horse-artillery, and had another corps hastening up to the rear of his line. Yet this is precisely what he did do.

The three corps ordered to attack the Confederate left should have been under one commander, and should have moved together. The assault on Lee's right, which was the vulnerable part of his line, should have been made at the same time. If this had been done, it is hard to see how Lee's army could have escaped destruction.

As the first step in the execution of McClellan's plan, Hooker crossed the Antietam on the afternoon of the 16th and came in contact with Hood on the Confederate left. The action was sharp while it lasted, but the firing ceased at dark. About nine a light rain began to fall, and continued most of the night. When all was quiet, Hood's brigades were withdrawn to cook rations, and their position was filled by Lawton's division.

The morning of Wednesday, the 17th, broke crisp and clear. At early dawn the fight was renewed, and Hooker's three fine divisions advanced in columns of brigades in line: Doubleday on the right, Ricketts on the left, and Meade in reserve close behind. The attack fell principally upon Lawton, and the fighting was very severe. Hooker, in his report, says that he never witnessed a more bloody, dismal battlefield. Part of the Confederate line was exposed to the fire of the Union rifle batteries across the Antietam, at a range of about 3000 yards. Hooker handled his troops well, and conducted the attack with all the dash and energy which had earned him the soubriquet of "Fighting Joe." The Confederate resistance was desperate, and the losses great on both sides. Lawton was borne off wounded, and his brigades were put out of action for the day. He called on Hood for support, and the latter sent in his two brigades, about 2000 strong. Hooker was wounded, and his men driven back so far that they were forced to abandon some of their guns.

By this time the Twelfth Corps, under Mansfield, was coming on the field. He had crossed the Antietam during the night, and bivouacked more than a mile north of the First Corps. At daybreak he started to Hooker's support, but was so slow in deploying his troops that it was seven-thirty before he took any part in the action. His corps arrived just in time to save the First Corps from being routed by Hood's counter-stroke. Hooker's corps had lost 2500 out of the 9000 men who went into action, and Meade, who had succeeded to the command, withdrew from the field to a strong position about a mile in the rear. This ended the first phase of the battle.

The attack of Mansfield, which now followed, can scarcely be described in detail. Mansfield was killed at the start, and Williams took command of the corps. For two hours, the lines wavered backward and forward. Finally the Federals broke the Confederate line, and Greene's division was in possession of the Dunker Church, as well as a portion of the woods near it. By this time the Twelfth Corps had lost all of its *élan*, and for a period the firing ceased entirely. The casualties amounted to 1746 out of some 7000 men engaged. Here may be said to end in a draw the second phase of the battle.

But this truce was of short duration. The head of the Second Corps was now approaching. At 7:20 A.M., Sumner had at last received his needlessly delayed orders to advance. He immediately crossed the creek, and arrived upon the field about nine o'clock. "If his nine brigades of veterans," says General Alexander, "had been put into action along with Mansfield's five, they would have made decisive work upon Lee's left flank, and opened the road to Porter's corps to attack his centre. Here McClellan threw away another one of his many chances for a decisive victory, though it was by no means his last."

Sumner reports that he found affairs in a "desperate state." The First Corps had been repulsed and forced to retire, and the Twelfth was barely holding its own. Sumner's corps had not fought at the Second Manassas, and consequently it was large, numbering on paper about 19,000 men, of whom some 15,000 were brought on to the field. Impatient at the three hours' delay imposed on his corps, Sumner ordered Sedgwick's division, with which he rode, to assault in close column of brigade front. He did not wait for his two other divisions, under French and Richardson, to come up or stop to reconnoitre, or to inquire as to the enemy's position. Sedgwick advanced out of the East Woods, passed on his left the Dunker Church, where the remains of Greene's division were lying down, and traversed the West Woods. His brigades were only between twenty and thirty yards apart — in too close order to be brought safely under fire.

Meanwhile, Lee had sent to the front his last reserves — the divisions of McLaws and Anderson, which after a weary night's march from Harper's Ferry had arrived about sunrise. Anderson's six brigades, about 3600 strong, were sent to D. H. Hill's division. McLaws's four brigades, some 3000 men, were directed to the woods behind the Dunker Church, under the guidance of Hood, who was familiar with the ground.

In his march, Sedgwick passed, without being aware of it, Early's brigade upon his right, with the remnants of Jones's division; and on his left, he passed what was left of Walker's two brigades, who were holding in front of Greene's troops about the church. Early, unseen behind the ridge, moved parallel to Sedgwick's march, and opened fire on the flank of the Federal column as soon as it issued from the woods. At the same moment the column found itself presenting its left front angle to McLaws's division, which fired at close range. "Sedgwick had practically marched into an ambuscade." Exposed to this deadly flank fire, "which it was impossible for the troops to return," Sedgwick's division lost over 2200 men "in a very few minutes." Sedgwick himself received three wounds, and his division was driven off the field. At the same time, Greene was forced to retire from the church, and the Confederate line rested where it had stood at the beginning of the battle, although very feebly held. This finished the third affair of the day.

The fourth, and last, assault upon this part of the field was made by the two remaining divisions of the Second Corps, under French and Richardson. Their combined strength amounted to about 10,000 muskets; and they were opposed by some 7000 Confederates "in good order and condition," besides three brigades "broken and much demoralized" by previ- ous' fighting. This struggle, the most terrible of the day, took place on new ground to the east of the scene of the previous combats. The field was open and moderately rolling, with but one good feature for defence. This was the famous "sunken road," — an excellent thing under certain conditions, but a dangerous trap when enfiladed by the enemy.

After the second affair of the day, three of D. H. Hill's brigades had remained in posi- tion, holding advanced ground about the Roulette house, a few hundred yards in front of this sunken road. Here they were attacked by French, and after a stubborn resistance were driven back to the sunken road. In this position Hill received the united attacks of both French and Richardson. He was aided by Anderson's division of some 3000 or 4000 men, which had formed in his rear. After a brisk engagement of perhaps an hour, the Federals reached a position from which they could enfilade a portion of the sunken road. The road was soon filled with the dead and wounded, and has since borne the name of the "Bloody Lane."

When the Confederates finally gave way and fled in confusion, leaving the Federals in possession of this part of the field, "Lee's army was ruined and the end of the Confederacy was in sight." The rout was in plain sight of McClellan's headquarters at the Pry house, but he gave no orders to follow on the victory.

Franklin was now on the field, with his fine corps of 12,000 men, and was about to attack, when Sumner, his ranking officer, refused his consent. About the same time, McClellan came up, "on a visit to his right flank," and conferred with Sumner and Franklin. The latter urged a renewal of the attack, but Sumner advised against it, and McClellan ordered Franklin simply to stand on the defensive.

This ended the battle on the left and centre of Lee's line. There was not a single fresh regiment in reserve: one more vigorous assault would have crushed Lee's army, but no attack was made. Yet, at that moment, McClellan had available the corps of Franklin and Porter — 25,000 men who had not fired a shot. All the morning, too, the Federal cavalry had stood idle. These fresh troops were almost equal to the forces that Lee had on the field at first.

It only remains to speak of the attack by the Ninth Corps on the Confederate right. At about nine in the morning, Burnside received an order to carry the bridge, since known by his name, and assault the Confederate lines posted on the bluffs above. There has been considerable controversy over the exact time at which this order was issued, but General Cox claims that it was not received until ten o'clock.

The task of carrying this bridge was a difficult one, as the hills were higher than at other points, and the roads, on both sides of the creek, could not go up at right angles to the bank. The bluffs on the west side were wooded to the water's edge, while the assailants on the east side had no cover from the enemy. The first two efforts to carry the bridge failed, but a third attempt, at one o'clock, was successful. The Confederates, under Tombs, withdrew to the right of the main line on the heights three-quarters of a mile from the bridge. Cox took command of the Union troops who had crossed the creek, and formed them to assault the enemy's line, which was held by four brigades of the division of D. R. Jones. The Confederates, only 2000 strong, were driven back up Cemetery Hill into the edge of the town. This success, if properly followed up, would have cut off Lee's retreat, and insured the destruction of his army. But once more Fortune favored the side of the weakest battalions and the greatest brains. A. P. Hill, after a forced march from Harper's Ferry, came on the field, and threw his division against the left flank of the victorious Federals. Cox was driven back to the bridge, in some disorder, and there his troops bivouacked for the night. This ended the battle.

On the 18th, the hostile armies faced each other all day, but McClellan refused to attack. That night Lee crossed the Potomac, unmolested, and the invasion of Maryland was over.

It is not easy to determine the exact numbers engaged on either side at the battle of Antietam. As stated above, Colonel Henderson estimates Lee's total, after the arrival of all his troops, at about 40,000. McClellan had over 87,000 men (nominally) on the field, but used less than 60,000. The odds against Lee were therefore about three to two, if we accept these figures.

Mr. Ropes makes the Confederate total 39,200 men; and he states that the First, Second, Ninth, and Twelfth corps, the only troops put in by McClellan, actually numbered only 46,000 men.

These figures agree substantially with those given by General Palfrey, who says that the nominal totals of the four corps used by McClellan, about 58,000 men, should be reduced by 20 per cent., say 12,000, to ascertain the strength of these corps on the day of the battle.

Mr. Ropes states further that, based upon the official statement of the strength of the Confederate army on the 22 September 1862, five days after the battle, and allowing for losses in the battle, as well as the return of stragglers, he arrives at a total of 58,000 men present for duty on the morning of the 17 September." But Longstreet says that the stragglers at Sharpsburg "reached nearly 20,000."

In explanation of the discrepancies between the Confederate and Federal reports of men "present for duty," it may be stated that the former generally included *only* the combatants, while the latter included also all men on detached duty, such as, camp, depot, and train guards, and escorts; besides non-combatants, such as, cooks, servants, orderlies, and extra-duty men in various staff departments. To make an exact comparison, therefore, of the number of men, on either side, available for combat, the Federal figures should always be reduced by one-fifth. An equal allowance should also generally be made, on both sides, for straggling, which had reached enormous proportions.

"The battle of Sharpsburg, or of the Antietam," says Mr. Ropes, "was one of the bloodiest battles of the war, and it is likely that more men were killed and wounded on the 17 September than on any single day in the whole war. The Confederate loss probably amounted to 8000 men or more; that of the Union army is given at 12,410 men. Each side lost about one quarter of the troops engaged."

McClellan reported his losses for the 16th and 17th as, 2010 killed, 9416 wounded, and 1043 missing, a total of 12,469. He also stated that 2700 Confederate dead were buried by his officers. From these figures it is probable that their losses at least equalled those of the Federals.

For the whole Maryland Campaign, General Alexander gives the losses as follows:

	Federals	*Confederates*
Killed	3,273	1,924
Wounded	11,756	9,381
Missing	13,338	2,304
Totals	28,367	13,609

Tactically, Antietam was a drawn battle; but the prestige of victory rested with McClellan. Lee's invasion had terminated in failure — failure which could not but be admitted by the authorities and people of the South. Even Colonel Henderson concedes that the Confederates had not "drawn much profit from the invasion of Maryland." He claims, however, that the stake was well worth the hazard.

"Of McClellan's conduct of the battle," writes General Palfrey, "there is little to be said in the way of praise beyond the fact that he did fight it voluntarily, without having it forced upon him."

Colonel Henderson is very severe in his comments. "The Federal attack," he says, "was badly designed and badly executed." There was nothing like close concert and aggressive energy; the principle of mutual support was utterly ignored; the army corps attacked, not simultaneously, but in succession, and in succession they were defeated. McClellan fought three separate battles: from dawn to 10 A.M. against Lee's left; from 10 A.M. to 1 P.M. against his centre; from 1 to 4 P.M. against his right. Only two-thirds of his army was engaged — 25,000 men hardly fired a shot; and from first to last there was not the slightest attempt at cooperation. "He had still to grasp the elementary rule that the combination of superior numbers and of all arms against a single point is necessary to win battles."

Lee undoubtedly made a mistake in fighting at Sharpsburg. Considering the great superiority of the Federals in numbers, and particularly in their artillery arm, a victory could have had no decisive results. On the other hand, owing to his dangerous position, a defeat would have involved the absolute destruction of his army. No commander is ever justified in voluntarily taking such chances. *C'est magnifique, mais ce n'est pas la guerre!*

In his comments on the battle, General Palfrey says: "If Lee had been in McClellan's place on the 17 September, and had sent Jackson to conduct the right attack and Longstreet to force the passage of the lower bridge and turn the Confederate right, the Army of Northern Virginia, though commanded by a second Lee, a second Jackson, and a second Longstreet, would have ceased to exist that day."

The Confederate leaders on this day, almost without exception, were men who made great names in the Civil War, while the Federal commanders were generally men who never became conspicuous, except through failure. Hooker was brave, handsome, vain, insubordinate, untrustworthy; and he failed dismally when made commander-in-chief. Sumner was an old man, though still active and vigorous. He was a graduate of West Point, and had been a colonel of cavalry. His training in this arm seems to have done him positive harm as a leader of infantry. Of the unfortunate Porter it is unnecessary to add anything to what has already been said. Franklin had graduated at West Point at the head of his class in 1839, and was a brave and capable, but unfortunate, soldier. Burnside was also a graduate of the Military Academy, but he had been out of the service seven years when the war began. His large, fine eyes, his winning smile and cordial manners, won him friends on every side. Few men have ever risen so high as he on so slight a foundation. As commander of the army, he failed disastrously. Most of the men who later attained distinction, like Hancock, Humphreys, Griffin, Warren, and Barlow, in September 1862 were brigade or regimental commanders.

The strategical employment of cavalry, on both sides, was excellent in this campaign during the preliminary operations. But, during the battle, McClellan put his cavalry in the centre of his line, instead of on the flanks. This was all the more remarkable, because he had every reason to expect that Lee would be reinforced by A. P. Hill's division from Harper's Ferry, of whose approach the cavalry could have given notice, at least, even if it could not have held back the Confederates.

Major Steele sums up his comments on the battle in the words: "From beginning to end of the campaign the Confederate commander's conduct was characterized by boldness, resolution, and quickness; the Federal commander's, by timidity, irresolution, and slowness."

CHAPTER NINE

SEPTEMBER 1862 —JANUARY 1863

FREDERICKSBURG

AFTER crossing the Potomac on the night of the 18 September, Lee placed his army in camps in the fertile valley of Opequon Creek, near Winchester, where he could observe the movements of the Federals, while his men were recuperating from the late campaign.

On the 2 October, at the suggestion of General Lee, the Army of Northern Virginia was organized into two army corps, to the command of which President Davis appointed Longstreet and Jackson, with the rank of lieutenant-general. At the same time, major-generals and brigadiers were promoted to command the divisions and brigades into which the corps were divided.

It was while his army was resting near Winchester that Lee sent Stuart with about 1800 men across the Potomac, ostensibly "to ascertain the positions and designs of the enemy." The cavalry crossed the Potomac above Williamsport on the 10 October, went to Chambersburg, where some stores and horses were picked up, and forded the river on their return just above Poolesville. In a sense the raid was a success, but Stuart did his adversaries no harm, with the exception of wearing out the Union cavalry sent to chase him, and he secured no information of value to Lee.

Lee's army gained rapidly in strength and efficiency. On the first day of November, the First Corps (Longstreet) reported a total of officers and men "present for duty" of 31,925, and the Second Corps (Jackson), of 31,794, while Stuart's cavalry numbered 71765 making an aggregate of 70,895.

Meanwhile, McClellan in his camp in Maryland was preparing for a winter campaign. He was determined not to make any movement until his ranks were recruited, his cavalry remounted, his army properly equipped, and his administrative service reorganized. "His obstinacy," says General Cox, "was of a feminine sort. He avoided open antagonism which would have been a challenge of strength, but found constantly fresh obstacles in the way of doing what he was determined from the first not to do." '

The first of October, Mr. Lincoln visited the camp at Sharpsburg and remained two or three days. He rode over the battlefield with McClellan, visited the Dunker Church, and returned by way of the Bloody Lane. He was very cordial in his praise of McClellan, and avoided any criticism of the campaign. But he showed plainly his apprehension that the delays of 1861 were to be repeated, and the fine October weather wasted. That General McClellan was aware of the President's anxiety is shown in his letters: "I incline to think,"

President Abraham Lincoln visited McClellan at his headquarters two weeks after Antietam and told the commander that his greatest fault was excess of caution. McClellan was a great organizer and admired by his troops. Many debate his talents on the field, but his removal after Antietam prolonged the war for many months.

he wrote home, "that the real purpose of his visit is to push me into a premature advance into Virginia."

The official correspondence proves conclusively that Mr. Lincoln returned to Washington fully determined to take drastic action if forced to do so. McClellan's private letters, at the same period, show that he was not ignorant of the situation, for he wrote that it was not improbable that he would be relieved from command.

During his visit Mr. Lincoln told McClellan plainly that his greatest fault was excess of caution; and he intimated that he should insist on an early advance. On his return to Washington, the President directed Halleck to send McClellan a peremptory order to cross the Potomac. This order, dated the 6 October, reads:

The President directs that you cross the Potomac and give battle to the enemy or drive him south. Your army must move now while the roads are good. If you cross the river between the enemy and Washington, and cover the latter by your line of operations, you can be reinforced with 30,000 men. If you move up the valley of the Shenandoah, not more than 12,000 or 15,000 can be sent to you. The President advises the interior line between Washington and the enemy, but does not order it.

McClellan replied on the 7th that he would adopt the exterior line, because it would cover Maryland from a return of Lee's army, and indicated that he would move in three days. At the end of that time, he complained of lacking clothing; then, of horses for his cavalry; and so the discussion ran on until the 21st.

In a remarkable letter to McClellan on the 13th, Mr. Lincoln showed a grasp of the military situation and its strategic possibilities which place him "head and shoulders above both his military subordinates." He argued in favor of the interior line, and pointed out its many advantages. The decisive vigor of this plan dismayed McClellan, but he finally adopted it as the means of getting larger reinforcements.

The advance began in the last days of October, the Sixth Corps, which was in the rear, crossing the Potomac on the 2 November. Lee, who had been closely following the movements of the Federal army, marched the same day from Winchester toward Culpeper, leaving Jackson in the Valley.

On the 7 November, the Army of the Potomac was concentrated in the vicinity of Warrenton. Late that evening, as McClellan sat in his tent near Salem, a special messenger from the War Department presented himself and handed the general a sealed envelope. It contained an order from the President relieving McClellan from the command of the Army of the Potomac, and appointing Burnside in his stead.

"McClellan ought not to have been removed," writes Mr. Ropes, "unless the Government were prepared to put in his place some officer whom they knew to be at least his equal in military capacity. This, assuredly, was not the case at this moment. No one, in or out of the service, had ever considered Burnside as able a man as McClellan."

In the event of McClellan's removal, it was naturally to be expected that the selection of a new commander-in-chief would be made from the four senior corps-commanders — Burnside, Hooker, Sumner, and Franklin. The latter would have been decidedly the best appointment which the Government could have made, but the opposition to him on political grounds was too strong.

McClellan and Burnside had been classmates at West Point, and had always kept up the intimacy which began at the Academy. They were "Mac" and "Burn" to each other, and their friendship was much closer than that with Fitz John Porter, Reno, and Hancock, who were in the same class. After Burnside had secured his first success in the Roanoke expedition, he was offered the command of the Army of the Potomac, but he refused it, and urged that his friend should be reinforced and allowed to continue his campaign against Richmond.

Before the Maryland campaign began, Mr. Lincoln again urged Burnside to accept the command, but he once more declined, and warmly advocated the reinstatement of McClellan.

These favors from his friend seem to have been too much for the vanity of McClellan, and during the Sharpsburg campaign every one noticed a marked coldness between the two former comrades. Hooker, who was under Burnside's command, was ordered to the right of the army at Antietam, and given an independent position, while Burnside was assigned to the left of the line. Although he did not waver in his loyal friendship to McClellan, Burnside was deeply grieved at many things which occurred during this campaign. There is the strongest evidence of his real unwillingness to supersede McClellan when the final order came in November. He was also sincere in feeling that he was not equal to the command; and the chief reason for his acceptance was his reluctance to see it go to Hooker, who would have been the next choice.

Regarding none of the leading generals of the Civil War has there been such a difference of opinion as in the case of General McClellan; and after the lapse of three score years the controversy is not yet settled. As Cicero said of Julius Caesar, "coming generations will dispute over him." To some, McClellan is the "prince of egoists, the grand procrastinator, the timid and doubting captain"; to others, he is a "military genius of the first order," who was "thwarted by an incapable administration and the intrigue of politicians."

The character and abilities of General McClellan have been so freely commented on in the course of this narrative that it is unnecessary to repeat those criticisms here. His capacity and energy as an organizer are universally acknowledged. "Had McClellan never done anything else but organize the Army of the Potomac, and bring order out of chaos after the battle of Bull Run," writes Dr. Macartney, "his service to the nation would have been not far behind that of any of the Union generals. The weapon which Grant finally used to strike down the Confederacy was the finely tempered sword of McClellan, the Army of the Potomac."

McClellan was a good strategist, and in many respects an excellent soldier. He was a courteous gentleman, and his private character was above reproach. No orgies disgraced headquarters while he was in command.

It is manifestly unfair to judge McClellan, as so many writers seem inclined to do, by his *Own Story*. This work, printed after his death, "is one of the most lamentable publications that family piety ever produced, and has made it exceedingly difficult to treat McClellan with fairness."

Notwithstanding all of the faults of McClellan's military operations, General Palfrey expresses the opinion that "he was the best commander that the Army of the Potomac ever had."

This opinion is endorsed by so great an authority as General Lee. "His failure to accomplish more," adds General Palfrey, "was partly his misfortune and not altogether his fault."

McClellan, as a general, was certainly far superior to Pope, or Burnside, or Hooker; and, in many respects, to Meade or Grant. No commander since Napoleon has ever aroused such enthusiasm among his soldiers, or inspired them with such personal devotion.

Major-General Ambrose Everett Burnside. Appointed to the command of the Army of the Potomac and succeeded General George B. McClellan on November 8, 1862.

Colonel Henderson, one of the ablest military critics of our times, says: "McClellan was not a general of the first order; but he was the only officer in the United States who had experience of handling large masses of troops, and he was improving every day. Stuart had taught him the use of cavalry, and Lee the value of the initiative. He was by no means deficient in resolution, as his march with an army of recently defeated men against Lee in Maryland conclusively proves; and although he had never won a decisive victory, he possessed, to a degree which was never attained by any of his successors, the confidence and affection of his troops."

Few students of the war today will deny that the withdrawal of McClellan's army from the Peninsula was a great blunder — the first of the many errors for which Halleck was to be responsible. McClellan's protest was not heeded at Washington, and he was condemned where, two years later, Grant was supported.

That McClellan's apprehensions regarding his fate, if he had failed in the Antietam campaign, were not groundless is proved by the *Diary* of Secretary Welles. "It was evident," he writes, "that there was a fixed determination to remove, and, if possible, to disgrace McClellan. Chase frankly stated that he deserved it; that he deliberately believed that McClellan ought to be shot, and should, were he President, be brought to summary punishment."

The restoration of McClellan to command, in September 1862, in the face of the almost unanimous opposition of the Cabinet and Congress, was "one of the most important and patriotic acts of Lincoln's administration of the war." It was the only step which could have restored the shattered morale of the army, after its defeat under Pope, and it enabled the Army of the Potomac to repel Lee's invasion of the North. Blair states that Stanton and Chase "actually declared that they would prefer the loss of the capital to the restoration of McClellan to command;" and Welles describes the meeting of the Cabinet as "the most agitated and despondent ever held." But the splendid reception which the army gave McClellan when he returned to take command proved that Lincoln was right and his Cabinet wrong.

However, if the reinstatement of General McClellan was one of the finest acts of President Lincoln's administration, his removal after Antietam was perhaps the most unfortunate and inexcusable. It certainly prolonged the war for many months.

At the same time that McClellan was removed, Fitz John Porter, the gallant soldier of Gaines's Mill and Malvern Hill, "probably the best officer in the Army of the Potomac," was ordered to resign command of the Fifth Corps, and to appear before a court-martial on charges growing out of the Second Manassas, already mentioned.

On the 7 November, Lee was at Culpeper with Longstreet's corps, the reserve artillery, and two brigades of cavalry under Stuart, about 45,000 men; while Jackson's corps, some 40,000 strong, was near Millwood in the Valley.

On this date the Federal army was distributed as follows: the First, Second, and Fifth corps, with the reserve artillery, were at Warrenton; the Ninth Corps at Waterloo; the Sixth at New Baltimore; the Eleventh en route for the same place; and one division of the Third Corps was between Manassas and Warrenton Junction. Pleasanton with two brigades of cavalry was at Amissville and Jefferson, and the front and flanks of the army were covered by cavalry pickets and patrols. The Twelfth Corps was at Harper's Ferry, and General Morrell with a division of infantry was on the upper Potomac.

The Federal army concentrated about Warrenton was therefore within twenty miles of Longstreet's corps, and still nearer the direct road to Millwood in the Valley, where Jackson was stationed, at a distance from Lee of forty miles in a direct line. There was never a better opportunity for the Federal army to attack and defeat the Confederates in detail, or force them to concentrate as far back as Gordonsville, which had been McClellan's plan. But this was not to be. McClellan was removed and Burnside adopted an entirely different plan. The day he took command, the 9 November, he forwarded a letter to Halleck explaining his project. This, in brief, was to abandon his line of communications by the Orange and Alexandria Railroad, and transfer his base to Aquia Creek; to "impress upon the enemy the belief that he was to attack Culpeper or Gordonsville; ... then to make a rapid move of the whole force to Fredericksburg, with a view to a movement upon Richmond from that point."

This was poor strategy, as it made Richmond, instead of Lee's army, his objective; and it was not until the 14th that President Lincoln gave his reluctant assent to Burnside's plan.

A feature of Burnside's plan, which was not made very prominent in his statement, was that pontoon trains enough to span the Rappahannock with two tracks should be sent at once to Falmouth. To Halleck's delay in complying promptly with this request, Burnside attributed his failure at Fredericksburg.

Burnside's first step on assuming command, on the 9 November, was to reorganize the Army of the Potomac into three Grand Divisions and a Reserve Corps.

The Right Grand Division, under General Sumner, was formed of the Second Corps (Couch) and the Ninth (Willcox).

The Centre Grand Division, under General Hooker, comprised the Third Corps (Stoneman) and the Fifth (Butterfield).

The Left Grand Division, under General Franklin, was made up of the First Corps (Reynolds) and the Sixth (W. F. Smith).

The Reserve Corps, under General Sigel, was composed of his own corps, the Eleventh, and the Twelfth, under General Slocum. These two corps did not arrive at Fredericksburg until after the battle.

It will be noticed that nearly all of the corps had new commanders. Among the division commanders were many officers who subsequently gained great distinction.

In sending Mr. Lincoln's approval of Burnside's plan, General Halleck wrote: "He thinks that it will succeed, if you move very rapidly; otherwise not." Burnside, however, made no unnecessary delay. Sumner marched on the morning of the 15th, and reached Falmouth on the 17th. Hooker and Franklin followed, and arrived a day or two later. But the pontoons were not there, and in fact did not come until the 25th. Sumner wanted to cross by the fords, and seize the heights opposite, but Burnside would not consent, as he feared that any troops sent over to the south side might be overwhelmed before they could be reinforced or withdrawn. At that time the Confederate forces holding Fredericksburg were so weak that they could have offered but feeble resistance to Sumner's Grand Division. But on the 18th, as soon as he learned of

Fredericksburg

Burnside's movement, Lee sent McLaws's division to Fredericksburg, and the remainder of Longstreet's corps followed immediately, arriving on the 21st, or a day or two later.

Lee had not definitely decided, however, to stand at Fredericksburg. On the 19th, he wrote Jackson from Culpeper that he did not anticipate making a determined stand above the North Anna River. This explains his reason for leaving so small a garrison in the city, and his delay in ordering Jackson to join him. Even after his arrival at Fredericksburg, on the 23rd, Lee still abstained from giving the commander of the Second Corps any order. When it became apparent, however, a few days later, that the Federals were preparing to cross the river, Lee finally decided to fight at Fredericksburg, and wrote Jackson to join him at once, as he feared the roads might become bad later. Jackson accordingly joined the main army on the 30 November.

The two armies now confronting each other across the Rappahannock were very unequal in point of numbers, the Union forces consisting of about 122,000 officers and men of all arms of the service, while Lee had only about 78,500 men. But the strength of the Confederate position went far to equalize the discrepancy in numbers.

The river at Fredericksburg is about 400 feet wide and unfordable. The hills on the north side, known as Stafford Heights, are closer to the river, and higher, than those on the opposite bank, which they command. On the south bank nestles the little city of Fredericksburg, surrounded by fertile fields. At a point just above the town, a range of hills begins, and extends around the valley somewhat in the form of a crescent, at a distance of about a mile from the river. The first elevation on the west was known as Taylor's Hill; the next, Marye's Hill; then came the highest point, called Telegraph Hill, but later known as Lee's Hill, as General Lee had his headquarters there during the battle. Beyond this was a ravine, through which ran Deep Run Creek; and then the gentle elevations at Hamilton's Crossing, not dignified with a name, where Jackson massed his corps during the battle. The range of heights is broken by ravines and small streams, and covered in parts with woods.

The gently sloping ground between the city and the heights was crossed by a ditch that carried off the waste water from a canal. The railroad crossed the river at Fredericksburg, and followed down it for about four miles to Hamilton's Crossing, where it turned south. Another line, unfinished, led out of the town and through the hills by Hazel Run Valley. There were numerous roads running out from the town, of which the most notable were the Plank Road and the Telegraph Road. At the base of Marye's Hill there was a sunken road, with a stone retaining wall, about breast-high, on either side. This was to play a very important role in the battle.

The left of the Confederate line was held by Longstreet's corps: Anderson's division was on Taylor's Hill, near the river; Ransom's and McLaws's divisions, on Marye's Hill; Pickett's, on Lee's Hill; and Hood's, about Deep Run Creek.

On the hill occupied by Jackson's corps, at the right of the line, were the divisions of A. P. Hill, Early, and Taliaferro, that of D. H. Hill being in reserve on the extreme right.

After some tentative movements at places down the river, which resulted in nothing, Burnside decided to force a crossing in front of the Confederate position. On the night of the 10 December arrangements were made to span the river with five pontoon bridges, three opposite Fredericksburg, and two just below the mouth of Deep Run. Sumner was to cross by the upper, and Franklin by the lower bridges. Hooker was to remain in reserve on the left bank.

The two lower bridges were thrown across without much trouble, but the construction of those opposite the town was impeded for a time by Confederate sharpshooters in the houses along the bank of the river. Finally, a call was made for volunteers, who crossed the river in boats and dislodged the enemy. Then the bridges were soon completed. Franklin's troops had already crossed by the lower bridges; Sumner's men now went over, and occupied the town.

The Federal left wing, under Franklin, was opposite Jackson's position at Hamilton's Crossing. Its only line of supply and retreat was over the bridges which had been laid south of Deep Run, behind the extreme right of his line. Jackson's front, which did not rest on any natural obstacle, had been protected by earthworks and abattis, and Franklin thought that the

Aquia Creek Landing, Virginia, February, 1863. This point became the base of supplies for the Army of the Potomac..

best chance of success lay in a strong attack on the extreme Confederate right. As Hamilton's Crossing was two miles below the bridges, this operation called for important changes in the disposition of the Union troops.

General Franklin says that he strongly advised General Burnside to make this attack upon the enemy's right with a column of at least 30,000 men, and that it be supported by two divisions of General Hooker's command, which were on the north side near the two bridges he had crossed. He urged also that the orders should be issued as early as possible, so that he might arrange his troops before daylight.

The orders, promised by Burnside before midnight at the latest, finally came at seven-thirty in the morning; but they were as far as possible from the plan suggested by Franklin. They directed him: (1) To keep his whole command in position for a rapid movement down the Old Richmond Road; and (2), to send out at once a division, at least, to pass below Smith-field, to seize, if possible, the height near Captain Hamilton's, on this side of the Massaponax, taking care to keep it well supported and its line of retreat open.

Attention should be called to the word *seize*, which in a military sense is used to refer to an unguarded position, or one weakly held, to be taken by a sudden rush. When a point is to be gained by hard fighting, the word *carry* is generally used. The peculiar wording of this order shows conclusively the state of Burnside's mind. "One rises," says Mr. Ropes, "from the perusal of this famous order with a feeling of hopeless amazement that such a wild and absurd plan of battle should ever have been entertained by any one."

Burnside's one chance of winning a victory was to recognize the impregnable character of Lee's left, and to attack Jackson on the right with more than half the Federal army, as advised by Franklin. This he did not do; and it only remains to sketch the events of the day.

Meade, who commanded a division of Reynolds's corps, was entrusted with the task which Burnside's order directed should be performed by "a division, at least, well supported," namely, that of "seizing "the height near Captain Hamilton's; and he was supported by the division of Gibbon on his right, and that of Doubleday on his left and rear. Meade succeeded in penetrating the enemy's lines at a weak point, and capturing several hundred prisoners. Gibbon was also successful, but not to the same degree. But the Confederates soon rallied, and were reinforced; the Union divisions were driven back in confusion, with heavy loss; and the pursuit was only checked by the resistance of other Federal troops. Franklin's loss amounted to nearly 5000 men.

Burnside states in his Report that he did not intend to move Sumner until he had "learned that Franklin was about to gain the heights near Hamilton's," and it would have been wiser if he had adhered to this plan. But about eleven o'clock, "feeling the importance of haste," he ordered Sumner to begin his attack.

The Federal attack on the right had but little chance of success. As the corps of Couch issued from the town, the troops found themselves in an open plain, with the Confederate works in their front only 600 or 700 yards distant. From the hills on their right the Confederate artillery poured upon them an enfilading fire. At the foot of Marye's Hill, the stone wall, already described, made an entrenchment which was practically impregnable. On the summit above were other lines of infantry, and powerful batteries. The Union troops advanced in column, until they passed the ditch or canal, which could only be crossed by the bridges, and then deployed for the assault, at a distance of only 300 yards from the enemy's front line. They advanced to the attack in the most gallant fashion, but the fire was too strong for them. Two other divisions, under Hancock and Howard, were ordered up to support French, who had led the attack, but all in vain. The sunken road could not be carried. After suffering terrible losses, the men were withdrawn.

This failure ought to have satisfied General Burnside that the Confederate position was too strong to be carried, but he insisted on several more efforts. The division of Sturgis, with one brigade of Getty's division from the Ninth Corps, and the divisions of Griffin and Humphreys of the Fifth Corps, were sent in. These troops were also repulsed with terrible slaughter before they could reach the stone wall. The Federal losses at this point were nearly 8 000 men.

The total losses, on both sides, were reported as follows:

	Federals	*Confederates*
Killed	1,284	608
Wounded	9,600	4,116
Missing	1,769	653
Totals	12,653	5,377

General Burnside wished to renew the battle the next day, and even proposed to lead his old Ninth Corps in column of regiments to the assault of the stone wall; but he was dissuaded by the unanimous remonstrance of his officers. The two armies remained facing each other for two days, but there was no more fighting. On the morning of the 15th, Burnside admitted his defeat by sending a flag of truce with a request that he might be allowed to bury his dead, and remove the wounded, who for forty-eight hours had been lying untended between the hostile lines.

The same night a fierce storm swept the valley of the Rappahannock; under cover of the elements the Army of the Potomac recrossed the river and returned to its old camps at Falmouth. The retreat was effected with a skill which did much credit to the Federal staff. Within fourteen hours 100,000 troops with all their trains passed the river without attracting the observation of the Confederate patrols.

No attempt was made by Lee to follow the Federals across the Rappahannock. The upper fords were open, but the river was rising fast, and the Army of the Potomac, closely concentrated, was too strong to be attacked. Burnside's escape, says Colonel Henderson, demonstrated the fallacy of one of the so-called rules of war. The great river which lay behind his army at the battle of Fredericksburg had proved his salvation, instead of his ruin, as theoretically it should have done. The five bridges across the river provided more lines of retreat than is usually the case when only roads are available; these lines of retreat also were protected by the river from the Confederate cavalry, and from the infantry and artillery by the powerful batteries on Stafford Heights. The result might have been very different if the battle had been fought on the North Anna, thirty-six miles from Fredericksburg.

There was a striking resemblance between the situation of Lee at Fredericksburg and that of Napoleon at Austerlitz in December 1805. Napoleon wanted a decisive victory, and not "only an *ordinary* battle," as he expressed it. With this object in view, he allowed the Allies to seize without opposition the commanding heights of the Pratzen, which almost any other general would have held in force. Then, on the day of battle, he rested on the defensive until the Allies had weakened their centre, in the endeavor to turn his right flank and cut off his line of retreat. As soon as the turning movement was fully developed, he easily pierced the enemy's centre, and then destroyed his wings in detail.

The Confederate position at Fredericksburg possessed two of the requirements for an ideal battlefield, but it lacked two others. It afforded (1) good cover to the troops, and a good field of fire; and (2) was not so strong as to deter the enemy from attacking; but (3) it gave no facilities for a counter-stroke, or (4) any opening for a pursuit in case of victory.

For the two reasons last named, Jackson, on his arrival, objected to the position, and thought that the army should retire behind the North Anna. This was also Lee's design in the first instance, but he yielded to the wishes of President Davis, who was almost as poor a strategist as General Halleck. The Confederate authorities objected to allowing the Army of the Potomac to approach any nearer to Richmond, and were also unwilling to open more of their country than necessary to depredation.

For these inconclusive reasons, Lee accepted battle at Fredericksburg, and, at the loss of 5000 valuable lives, gained a victory which was absolutely barren of any decisive results.

After the battle General Lee went to Richmond to suggest further operations, "but was assured that the war was virtually over." On the news of Fredericksburg gold had advanced in New York to 200, and the Confederate authorities were confident that peace would be proclaimed within thirty or forty days. General Lee was far from sharing this belief.

"In reviewing this bloody defeat of the Army of the Potomac," writes Mr. Ropes, "one is moved to wonder at the fact that General Burnside made the attempt at all. He had practically no chance of success in assaulting the Confederate left; and even if he had given Franklin *carte blanche* as respects the attack on the Confederate right, and had that able officer done what he told Burnside he proposed to do … the issue of the battle would have been far from certain… . Nothing short of a complete rout of Jackson's extreme right — which was hardly to be expected — would have answered Franklin's needs."

Undeterred by his defeat, Burnside immediately decided on another forward movement, to be made the latter part of December, but was checked by a telegram from President Lincoln enjoining him not to take any further steps without first informing him. Burnside then went to Washington, where he had a conference with the President, General Halleck, and the Secretary of War, Mr. Stanton. He was informed that certain general officers were of the opinion that his movement would end in disaster; and it was formally disapproved by the authorities.

Burnside finally resolved to act on his own responsibility: on the 20 January 1863 he moved up the river, and was preparing to cross in force when the whole operation was stopped by a storm of unusual violence. The army returned from this "Mud March "to its camps at Falmouth, tired, discouraged, and absolutely convinced of the incompetency of Burnside for his high command.

Burnside went directly to Washington and made the issue boldly with the Government. He gave Mr. Lincoln the choice of accepting his resignation, or approving an order, which he had prepared, relieving from further duty with the army, Hooker, Franklin, and other high officers. Mr. Lincoln met the situation by relieving Burnside himself from command, and appointing in his place "Fighting Joe" Hooker, who had gained much popularity in the army and with the public by his dashing bearing and frank manners. At the same time Mr. Lincoln declined to accept Burnside's resignation from the service, and gave him a leave of absence for his home in Providence. In March 1863, Burnside was appointed to the command of the Department of the Ohio, where he relieved General Wright.

The order of the 25 January 1863, appointing General Hooker to the command of the Army of the Potomac, relieved Sumner and Franklin from further duty with that organization. The reasons for this action are not clear. Sumner was old for active service, but apparently hale and hearty, although he died within the year. There was dissatisfaction with Franklin's conduct at Fredericksburg, and a general feeling that, with the large force under his command, he did not accomplish what might have been expected. He "had contributed the only valuable suggestion for winning the battle;" and his failure to accomplish anything under Burnside's ridiculous orders in no way justified "the removal from the service of so intelligent and capable an officer." This is also the opinion of General Palfrey, who says: "General Franklin was practically ruined as a soldier by the battle of Fredericksburg, and his connection with it, but so far as the accessible evidence enables one to judge, he was most unjustly blamed."

It is a sad reflection upon the Administration of Mr. Lincoln that, from one cause or another, the Union lost, long before the close of the war, the services of four of its ablest officers — Buell, McClellan, Porter, and Franklin. With the exception of President Davis's unjust treatment of General Joseph E. Johnston, the Confederacy made few, if any, mistakes of this kind. It does not make the matter any better that several of these removals were made by Mr. Lincoln mainly for political reasons, and largely growing out of the Emancipation Proclamation, which he issued just after the battle of Antietam.

In commenting on the Fredericksburg Campaign, General Longstreet says: "Burnside made a mistake from the first. He should have gone from Warrenton to Chester Gap. He might then have held Jackson and fought me, or have held me and fought Jackson, thus taking us in detail. ... By interposing between the corps of Lee's army, he would have secured strong ground and advantage of position. With skill equal to the occasion, he should have had success. This was the move about which we felt serious apprehension."

Other critics, however, think that the movement to Fredericksburg was right, and that it failed, through no fault of Burnside's, on account of Halleck's neglect to send the pontoons in time. In that event, General Longstreet states that the Confederates would have concentrated behind the North Anna, in a much stronger position. In either position, the Union army would probably have been defeated under a commander as incompetent as General Burnside, and at the North Anna might have met with a greater disaster. As in previous campaigns, the best of Lee's strategy appears to have been his comprehension of the character of the Federal commander, and the use he made of it.

MURFREESBORO

ON the 11 April 1862, four days after the battle of Shiloh, General Halleck arrived at Pittsburg Landing and took command in person of the Union forces. On the 21st, he was joined there by General Pope, who had successfully terminated on the 8 April his operations against New Madrid and Island No. 10 on the Mississippi River. He brought with him some 30,000 troops, and other reinforcements soon raised Halleck's army to about 120,000 men.

After the battle, the Confederate army, under General Beauregard, had retired to Corinth, where it was joined about the first of May by General Van Dorn with upwards of 15,000 men. Beauregard's forces were then estimated at about 70,000, but in reality they were much smaller, and the men were demoralized from their recent defeat.

The last of April, Halleck began a slow and cautious advance toward Corinth. His army was organized into a right wing, commanded by Thomas; centre, under Buell; left, under Pope; and a reserve, under McClernand. Grant was second in command — a position more honorable than useful, as no specific duties were assigned to him.

General Grant says in his *Memoirs* that, "the movement was a siege from the start to the close." The army would construct corduroy roads, move forward a mile or two, then halt and entrench. Nearly a month was consumed in covering the twenty miles from Pittsburg Landing to Corinth! Finally, on the 30 May, Beauregard evacuated the place. He withdrew with 52,000 men, carrying off all his artillery, and the greater part of his stores. The army retired to Tupelo in Mississippi, a place about fifty miles south of Corinth, which Beauregard had selected as possessing healthful surroundings and a good water supply. In a very short time the Confederate army was as large and formidable as ever.

On the 30 May, the Federal army reached Corinth, and took possession of the town almost without bloodshed. Although the Confederate army had been allowed to escape intact, the occupation of Corinth was nevertheless an event of great importance. It gave the Federals possession of the only railroad which directly connected the Mississippi with the Atlantic seaboard. It turned the Confederate positions at Fort Pillow and Memphis, which were occupied a week later, thus opening the river as far down as Vicksburg.

Instead of pursuing the Confederate army, which should have been his first objective, Halleck now made the terrible mistake of dispersing his army of over 100,000 men. While he himself remained at Corinth, and undertook the impracticable task of repairing the

Union soldiers under General Halleck.

railroads, he sent Wallace's division to Curtis in Arkansas, and ordered Buell to proceed to Chattanooga. Buell, who had resumed command of the Army of the Ohio, now about 31,000 strong, began his march on the 10 June. He was instructed by Halleck, as he proceeded toward Chattanooga, to repair and rebuild the Memphis and Charleston Railroad, on which he was to depend for his supplies. Nothing could more distinctly show Halleck's military incapacity than this order. This line, which ran on the boundary between the territory just conquered, and the hostile region to the south, was everywhere exposed to interruption by the Confederate troopers. Buell protested against this order, but Halleck for several weeks insisted upon it.

The reminder of Halleck's army, about 65,000 strong, was stationed at various points between Memphis and Decatur. It consisted of the Army of the Tennessee, once more under the command of Grant, and the Army of the Mississippi, commanded by Pope until he was ordered East, and then by Rosecrans. Halleck remained at Corinth until early in July, when he too was ordered to Washington to assume the position of commander-in-chief. Grant then took the command of the two armies of the Tennessee and the Mississippi. The force left with him by Halleck was not large enough to undertake an offensive campaign against the Confederates at Tupelo, and his army was practically useless during the entire summer.

In his movement on Chattanooga, Buell had with him the four divisions of McCook, Nelson, Crittenden, and Wood. His first division, under Thomas, was not allowed to join him until the end of July. In the opinion of General Grant, if Buell had had his whole army at the outset, and been allowed to move on Chattanooga with all despatch, he would have had a good chance of success. But the delay, occasioned by the repairs to the railway, gave the enemy notice of his intentions, and ample time to thwart his plans.

On the 27 June, Beauregard, whose health had broken down, was succeeded in command by Braxton Bragg, who immediately sent McCown's division to Chattanooga, for the defence of that post. On the 21 July, Bragg started for the same place with the greater part of his forces, sending his infantry by rail by way of Mobile. The remainder of his army was left in Mississippi under Price and Van Dorn. The force thus assembled at Chattanooga numbered about 30,000. At the same time there was another Confederate army of 18,000 men under General Kirby Smith at Knoxville in eastern Tennessee.

The last of June, Buell finally secured Halleck's consent to abandon the effort to keep open the Memphis and Charleston in his rear, and he adopted for his line of communications the Louisville and Nashville, and Nashville and Chattanooga railroads, with Louisville as his primary base, and Nashville as his secondary base of supplies. But on the 13 July, Forrest, with some 1400 troopers, captured the Union garrison of over 1000 men at Murfreesboro, and broke up the railway so thoroughly that it was not repaired until the 28th. Buell's march was thereby brought to a full stop for over two weeks. Later, he was again halted by the destruction of a tunnel on the Louisville and Nashville at Gallatin, Tennessee, by another Confederate cavalry raid under John Morgan.

"Cavalry-raids like these," says Mr. Ropes, "made in a friendly country, upon the communications of a hostile army which has advanced far into this country, are justifiable on the plainest principles of warfare, and ought always to be distinguished from those cavalry-raids which are made in a hostile territory, and are intended either to intimidate and harass its inhabitants, or cut the communications of a hostile army operating in its own country." Chattanooga was one of the most important strategic points in the Confederacy. If it were lost, the direct line of communication between the Atlantic and the Mississippi would be cut, and there would be no connection between the sections east and west of the Alleghanies except by a long detour by way of Atlanta. General Kirby Smith, who commanded the Department of East Tennessee, seems to have had a clear and comprehensive view of the whole situation.

Braxton Bragg succeeded General Beauregard on June 27 due to the latter's ill health. He retreated to Louisville after the campaign to secure supplies and reinforcements.

He urged Bragg in several letters to bring the main body of his army to East Tennessee, and undertake an offensive campaign, offering cheerfully to serve under him. He pointed out that there was yet time for a brilliant summer campaign, with a chance of regaining middle Tennessee, and perhaps Kentucky.

Bragg, as we have seen, issued orders for the movement; and he came to Chattanooga the last of July for a conference with Smith, at which their plans were arranged. His infantry arrived by rail early in August, but his cavalry and artillery, being compelled to march over the hilly country of northern Alabama and Georgia, did not get there until later.

The plan proposed that Kirby Smith, with his 18,000 men, should turn the Union position at Cumberland Gap, held by a Federal force under General Morgan, while Bragg, with the main column of some 30,000 troops, should move directly on Munfordville, where he would be squarely on Buell's line of communications. The two forces were to unite in Kentucky.

On the 6 August, Buell's headquarters were at Huntsville, Alabama, where he wrote Halleck that he was preparing to concentrate his divisions for an advance on Chattanooga. He had learned of the arrival of Bragg, with some of his troops, and expected to find the place occupied in force. The next day, in a fuller letter to Halleck, he gave his strength, exclusive of garrisons and railway-guards, as about 35,000 men, and the forces under Kirby Smith and Bragg at about 15,000 and 30,000 respectively. These estimates were substantially correct. In this letter he reiterated his intention of marching at once on Chattanooga, unless he learned that "the enemy's strength rendered it imprudent;" and on the 12th he asked General Grant to send him the two divisions for which General Halleck had authorized him to call in case of emergency.

But, before Buell could concentrate his forces, the destruction of the tunnel at Gallatin effectually broke his line of communications, and compelled him to modify his plans. Toward the last of August he renounced his project of an advance on Chattanooga, and hurried back to repel the invasion of his Department by the enemy.

It was late in August before Bragg could complete all his arrangements for the movement. He sent Smith at Knoxville McCown's division and some other troops, thereby increasing Smith's forces to 20,000 men. Bragg's original intention had been to operate only in Tennessee, but he was later influenced to change his plans, by Smith's views of the political results of an invasion of Kentucky; and he "ended by practically subordinating the military management of his campaign to political projects."

There were no railroads or rivers running in the direction of the proposed Confederate advance, and the roads, over which their stores must be transported in wagon trains, were mountainous and generally poor. The distance from Chattanooga to Munfordville, in a straight line, was about 160 miles. Very little forage and subsistence could be obtained in the country; and Bragg's march presented many other peculiarly trying features. He had to cross the river Tennessee; traverse Walden Ridge, some 1200 feet above the level of the sea; descend into the valley of the Sequatchie River; and then ascend the plateau of the Cumberland Mountains, somewhere about 2200 feet above the sea level, before he could possibly concentrate his army for the invasion proper.

William Starke Rosencrans. His decisive victory at Corinth established the reputation of one of the Union's finest generals.

Kirby Smith crossed the mountains about the middle of August, and cut Morgan's line of communications. Leaving one of his divisions to watch the Federals, he pressed on to Lexington, where he arrived on the 2 September, and established his headquarters. He met no opposition en route, except at Richmond, where he routed a small Union force on the 30 August.

Bragg began his advance the first of September, and arrived at Sparta on the 5th. Up to this time his movements had been screened by the Cumberland Mountains, and Buell could not obtain any definite information regarding them. That same day Buell concentrated his army at Murfreesboro, where he could cover Nashville, and could easily be joined by the reinforcements he was expecting from Grant. Here he heard of Smith's victory at Richmond, and concluded that Bragg was intending to effect a junction with him. So he left a sufficient force to protect Nashville, and marched north with the remainder of his army.

On the 14th, Buell was at Bowling Green, and Bragg at Glasgow. On the 17th the Federal commander at Munfordville surrendered to Bragg, with 4000 men. Bragg, who was now squarely across Buell's line of communications, remained at Munfordville several days, hoping that Buell would attack him. He then started for Bardstown to connect with Kirby Smith, and Buell marched to Louisville, where he arrived on the 25th.

Members of the Washington Artillery from New Orleans destined to fight the guns at Murfreesboro, also known as Stones River.

Buell remained only a week at Louisville, where his army was largely reinforced. On the 30 September, as he was ready to move against the enemy, there came an order from Halleck removing him from command, and appointing Thomas in his place. But Thomas was magnanimous enough to protest against this injustice, and the order was revoked.

The first day of October, Buell began his advance. Bragg's forces were at Bardstown, and Smith's at Lexington, where the two generals were amusing themselves with inaugurating a Confederate governor. Both Bragg and Smith were deceived as to Buell's movements, and thought he was advancing toward Frankfort. They therefore moved to Harrodsburg and Versailles in order to cover the large depot of stores collected at Lexington. These manoeuvres brought on an engagement at Perryville between Bragg's left wing, under Hardee, and the Federal left under McCook. The Federals were driven back in disorder, and lost some fifteen guns. Later in the day they rallied, and drove back the enemy. In the counter-attack, a young Union brigadier showed brilliant leadership, and the name of Philip H. Sheridan first became known to fame. Although the Federal centre and right were hardly three miles away, through some strange atmospheric condition the cannon were not heard, and the remainder of Buell's army was not aware of the combat. The Union losses were 845 killed, 2851 wounded; Confederate, 510 killed, 2635 wounded.

The battle of Perryville, on the 8 October, was a tactical success for the Confederates, but for all practical purposes it was a drawn battle. At night Bragg's forces retired to Harrodsburg, where, on the 10th, they were joined by Kirby Smith's.

Bragg waited a day or two, to see if Buell would attack him; then passed through Cumberland Gap, and returned to Chattanooga. After following the Confederates as far as the mountains, Buell gave up the pursuit, and stationed his troops at Bowling Green and Glasgow, with the intention later on of moving to some point on the railroad to Chattanooga, as a base for a new campaign. But on the 30 October he was relieved from command and succeeded by Rosecrans.

Rosecrans, as already stated, had served under Grant in western Tennessee; and he had recently fought two bloody actions against the forces under Van Dorn and Price. The battle at Iuka, on the 19 September, was not a brilliant success, although the Confederates retired after it. The second action, fought at Corinth on the 3 and 4 October, was a decisive victory, and established Rosecrans's reputation as a hard fighter and an able officer.

Don Carlos Buell was a graduate of West Point; he was an excellent soldier, brave, able, and accomplished. Mr. Ropes considers him "as able a general as any in the service." He also expresses the rather extravagant opinion that if Buell had been placed in chief command in the West in November 1861, "it is not too much to say that the Confederate army of the West would have ceased to exist before June 1, 1862, and that thereafter a regiment of Union troops could have marched without opposition from Nashville to Chattanooga and Knoxville."

In several respects Buell much resembled McClellan. He was a good organizer, and to him the Army of the Cumberland owed its efficiency. He had the same dislike of moving until he was entirely prepared. He was equally lacking in political tact, and his removal was due partly to his having gained the enmity of the war governors of Illinois, Indiana, and Ohio, and partly to his failure to carry out Mr. Lincoln's impracticable plans for the occupation of East Tennessee.

As a strategist, Buell was superior to McClellan, and he handled his men better in the field; but he was entirely devoid of the personal magnetism which made McClellan so popular with his troops. He, too, was unfortunate in being placed prematurely in a position of extraordinary responsibility and difficulty. His retirement was a distinct loss to the Union cause.

By the end of November, Rosecrans had concentrated his entire army at Nashville. From this point he refused to move, in spite of urgent and even threatening letters from Halleck, until he had collected two million rations, to make him independent of the railroad back to Louisville. The wisdom of this course was proved by the fact that his communications were broken by Morgan's cavalry on the 26 December.

In the meantime, Bragg had advanced from Chattanooga to Murfreesboro, a station on the railroad thirty miles southeast of Nashville, and on the morning of the 26 December, Rosecrans set out to meet him. The Union army marched in three columns, designated as the Right Wing, Centre, and Left Wing, commanded respectively by McCook, Thomas, and Crittenden. As soon as the army left Nashville, it encountered Wheeler's cavalry, which reported the movement to Bragg, and opposed it at every step. Aided by fogs and heavy rains, the cavalry so impeded the progress of the Federals that it took them four days to cover the thirty miles from Nashville to Murfreesboro. The Union cavalry seems to have accompanied the infantry on the march, and not to have taken its place in front of the columns until the 29th. Rosecrans was kept so poorly informed by his cavalry concerning the position of the Confederate army that he ordered Crittenden, whose wing was in advance, "to occupy Murfreesboro with one of his divisions on the night of the 29th, and encamp the other two miles outside." But Bragg's army at that time was drawn up in front of the town!

The battlefield of Murfreesboro, or Stones River as it is generally called by the Federals, is situated west of the river, about two miles from the town. The river, which flows in a winding course slightly west of north, at the time of the battle was spanned by several bridges, and was fordable in various places; hence it was not a serious military obstacle. The turnpike and railway from Nashville traversed the northern part of the field, and, after intersecting at an acute angle, passed the river by separate bridges. The centre of the field was crossed from east to west by the Wilkinson Turnpike, and the southern part by the road to Franklin. The country was generally flat, with occasional hills which afforded good artillery positions. There were a number of farmhouses, in the midst of cultivated fields; and many patches of cedar woods, which could be traversed easily by infantry, but formed an obstacle to artillery. The thickets were dense enough to conceal troops within them.

The Confederate army was drawn up in line of battle nearly parallel to the general course of the river and mostly to the west of it. The left wing under Hardee and the centre under Polk were west of the river, while on the east side was the right wing, composed of Breckinridge's division of Hardee's corps, separated from its fellows. The general direction of the line west of the river was north and south, with the left wing somewhat advanced toward the west. Breckinridge's division was refused to the northeast, to ward off any flank attack upon the town. If Murfreesboro had been located in hostile territory, Bragg would probably have

Ruined bridge over the Tennessee River

taken up a position on the east side of Stones River, in front of the town, but he wished, so far as possible, to protect the place. Under the circumstances, but little fault can be found with his arrangements.

The Union army was drawn up in a somewhat irregular line, but generally parallel to the enemy's front. The right under McCook stretched from the Franklin to the Wilkinson road. It consisted of three divisions, commanded by Johnson, Davis, and Sheridan. The centre under Thomas comprised the two divisions of Negley and Rousseau, but in the plan of battle Palmer's division of the left wing practically formed part of the centre. The remainder of the left wing under Crittenden, made up of the divisions of Wood and Van Cleve, reached from the Nashville Pike across the railroad, and rested its left on the river. The two lines, Union and Confederate, were each about three miles in length, and the two armies were practically equal in numbers, aggregating about 40,000 each.

By a curious coincidence, as at the first Manassas, the two plans of battle were exactly the same. At Manassas, both McDowell and Beauregard had proposed to turn the enemy's left flank at Murfreesboro, also, Rosecrans and Bragg had planned to turn their adversary's left. On both occasions, the course of the battle was determined by the party who secured the initiative: at Manassas, by the Federals, and at Murfreesboro by the Confederates.

Rosecrans's plan of attack was bold and brilliant. It was, to throw the two divisions of Wood and Van Cleve across the river, crush the single division of Breckinridge, and place their artillery upon a commanding ridge from which the entire Confederate line could be enfiladed. Aided by this galling fire, Rosecrans then expected to break the Confederate centre with the three divisions under Thomas, while his right under McCook would carry Murfreesboro, occupy the Franklin road, and cut off the enemy's retreat. It was for this purpose that Rosecrans massed his troops so heavily on his left, where he had nearly two-thirds of his forces. But for the success of this plan it was essential that the Federal right should be so strong, and so well placed, that it could hold Bragg while the attack on his right was carried out. In this particular, Rosecrans failed; and his error not only spoiled his plan of battle, but nearly resulted in the defeat of the Union army. McCook's line was too long and too thin, and faced too much to the east. It should have been refused nearly to the Wilkinson road, so as to face more to the south. In this position, the enemy would have had to move farther to attack it, and it could have been more easily reinforced from the centre. Rosecrans had realized this weakness, and called McCook's attention to it. But McCook, who was over-confident, stated that he could hold out for three hours, and Rosecrans did not press the matter, as he should have done.

As above stated, Bragg's plan of battle was practically identical. He had massed his troops on the left, and proposed to overlap and crush the Union right; then, swinging to the north, with Polk's right as the pivot, he would take the Union centre in reverse, fold it back against the river, seize the Nashville road, and cut off the Federal line of retreat. The position favored Bragg's plan, as there was no natural obstacle in the way, and the woods on the Union right formed a screen for his movement. On the other hand, Rosecrans had to throw his two divisions across the river, which, although easily fordable, would cause considerable delay.

Soon after dawn on the morning of the 31 December, Hardee with nearly half the Confederate infantry attacked the Federal right, which was at once thrown upon the defensive. Johnson, who commanded the First Division, was at his headquarters a mile and a half in the rear, with one of his brigade commanders, and there was no one at the front to direct the troops. The Confederate attack, led by Patrick Cleburne, the ablest division-commander in the West, was absolutely irresistible, and Johnson's whole division was forced to flee in wild disorder toward the Wilkinson road. This disaster uncovered the right of Davis's division which was immediately refused, forming with Sheridan's line a salient to the enemy. Here, two assaults of the Confederates were repulsed, but a third was more successful, and Davis was forced back. This left Sheridan's right exposed, but he ordered his left brigade to charge the Confederates, and thus gained time to form a new line facing south, parallel to the Nashville Pike, and forming a right angle with Negley's division. At the same time, Rousseau's division, which had been held in reserve, formed on Sheridan's right. The new Federal front, held by the divisions of Rousseau, Sheridan, Negley, and Palmer, arranged in order from right to left, was now assaulted by the entire Confederate force west of the river. The attacks at first were repulsed, but finally Sheridan's ammunition was exhausted, and he was forced to fall back. This necessitated the withdrawal of Rousseau and Negley, also of Palmer's right; but his left, under Hazen, stood fast, and was the only part of the original Union line to hold its ground. The entire right, centre, and right of the left wing, had been forced back about this point as a pivot, "like a knife blade half-shut."

Early in the morning, pursuant to his original plan, Rosecrans had sent Van Cleve's division across the river, and these troops were actually deployed in front of Breckinridge's position before Rosecrans realized the extent of the disaster on his right. He then recalled the division to reinforce his line west of the river. It arrived just in time to hold the Confederates after Rousseau and Negley were driven back.

By noon, Rosecrans had formed a strong new line on high ground along the Nashville Turnpike, and here for four hours he resisted the continued assaults of the Confederates. The offensive movement against Bragg's right, although a failure, had nevertheless a decided effect upon the result of the battle, as it prevented Breckinridge from obeying Bragg's first order to send assistance to Hardee, which might have enabled him to break the Union line.

The final Confederate assaults had been repulsed with great slaughter, and "at four o'clock it became evident to the Confederate commander that his only hope of success lay in a charge upon the Union left, which, by its overpowering weight, should carry everything before it." But there were no fresh troops left except those of Breckinridge, and he was again ordered to send them across the river. As soon as the first two brigades arrived, Polk hurled them against the Union left, where Hazen had been strongly reinforced. The attack failed, as did another made later when the other Confederate brigades had arrived. This ended the day's battle.

The two hostile armies bivouacked on the field within musket-range of each other. There was no fighting on the following day; in the afternoon Crittenden moved a division across the river, and formed line of battle in front of Breckinridge, who had returned to his former position.

On the 2 January, Bragg was disappointed to find the Federal army still in front of him. He ordered Breckinridge to dislodge the enemy from his position east of the river. The Union troops were driven back at first, but were soon reinforced, and recovered the position, which they entrenched.

There was some fighting on the 3rd, but of little consequence, and that night Bragg began his retreat to Tullahoma. Rosecrans occupied Murfreesboro, but made no pursuit of the Confederates. Like Antietam, Murfreesboro was practically a drawn battle; but the Federals remained in possession of the field of battle, in both cases.

The total losses during the campaign were as follows:

	Federals	Confederates
Killed	1,730	1,294
Wounded	7,802	7,945
Missing	3,717	1,027
Totals	13,249	10,266

The outcome of the campaign in Kentucky was a distinct disappointment both to the North and to the South. The Government at Washington thought that Buell should not have allowed Bragg to escape, and he was removed from command. Mr. Davis felt that Bragg should have fought Buell and defeated him, instead of allowing him to retreat to Louisville, where he secured supplies and reinforcements for his army.

After the battle of Murfreesboro, Bragg's corps-commanders scarcely concealed their lack of confidence in him, and General Polk wrote Mr. Davis that another commander should be appointed. The feeling against Bragg finally became so strong, both inside and outside the army, that Mr. Davis sent General Joseph E. Johnston to Chattanooga, with authority to relieve General Bragg from command. After a full investigation of the conditions, however, General Johnston decided not to remove Bragg, and returned to Mobile.

The excellence of the work of the Confederate cavalry during the campaign has already been noticed. In Forrest, Morgan, and Wheeler, Bragg possessed three of the best cavalry commanders of the time. As Major Steele says: "It would be hard to find in the annals of modern warfare any better cavalry work."

On the other hand, the Federal cavalry was so lacking in numbers and efficiency that both Buell and Rosecrans were at a great disadvantage. Buell had again and again urged the Government to remedy his deficiency in this respect, but in vain.

The tactics were good on both sides, at Murfreesboro. "Few battles have been fought," says Mr. Ropes, "which have better exhibited the soldierly virtues. The Confederate assaults were conducted with the utmost gallantry and with untiring energy. They were met with great coolness and resolution.... The Confederates had a right to claim a victory, for they had taken 28 guns and about 3700 prisoners. Still, the Federal army was, for all practical purposes, as strong as ever. The truth is, the Confederates were not numerous enough to complete their victory."

Army of the Potomac.
Federal

Ist. Corps.   Reynolds
IInd. Corps.   Couch
IIIrd. Corps. Sickles
Vth. Corps.   Meade
VIth. Corps.   Sedgwick
XIth. Corps.   Howard
XIIth. Corps. Slocum

By J. Hotchkiss. Top. Eng. 2nd. Corps A.N.V.
From Actual Surveys made immediately
after the Battle, by order of Gen. R.E. LEE.

Chancellorsville

THE BATTLEFIELDS OF
CHANCELLORSVILLE, SALEM CHURCH
AND FREDERICKSBURG,
May 1st., 2nd., 3rd., 4th., 5th. 1862.
showing
the positions at 5.30. p.m. on Saturday May 2nd.

Scale of Miles

....Confederate
....Federal

CHAPTER ELEVEN

JANUARY — MAY 1863

CHANCELLORSVILLE

AFTER the disaster of Fredericksburg, the Union army went into winter quarters on the north bank of the Rappahannock. The new commander, General Hooker, was a man of fine presence, of great personal magnetism, and had the reputation of being one of the most efficient and successful of the corps commanders. He at once instituted some excellent reforms, which did much to restore the badly shaken morale of the troops. He adopted a system of furloughs, which remedied to a great extent the evil of desertion, which had assumed enormous proportions. He abolished the clumsy grand divisions of Burnside, and reorganized the army corps. He consolidated the scattered squadrons of cavalry into a corps, under General Stoneman. The Cavalry Corps comprised three divisions, under Pleasanton, Averell, and Gregg, and a reserve brigade of regulars under Buford.

The infantry now consisted of seven corps: First (Reynolds), Second (Couch), Third (Sickles), Fifth (Meade), Sixth (Sedgwick), Eleventh (Howard), and Twelfth (Slocum). Burnside's old corps, the Ninth, was sent to Newport News.

By the end of April 1863, Hooker had the largest, the best organized and equipped army ever assembled on the continent. It numbered on paper about 120,000 infantry and artillery, with more than 400 cannon, and nearly 12,000 cavalry. From these aggregates, the usual deductions should be made, so that it is doubtful if Hooker had over 105,000 men for combat.

On the opposite side of the river, the Army of Northern Virginia, under General Lee, numbered about 60,000 men, including 3000 cavalry. Although so near Richmond, the army was poorly clothed, shod, and fed, in spite of Lee's earnest efforts. The corps occupied approximately the same positions as at the time of the battle of Fredericksburg — Longstreet's on the left and Jackson's on the right. Lee's headquarters were in a camp near Hamilton's Crossing; Jackson's at Moss Neck, eleven miles below Fredericksburg.

The great need of rations for the coming campaign had led the Confederate War Department to send Longstreet with two divisions for a campaign toward Suffolk, to collect provisions and forage from the territory near the Union lines. This had reduced Lee's available forces by about a quarter, and was poor policy. At the opening of the campaign, therefore, Lee had only the two divisions of Anderson and McLaws, of Longstreet's corps; and those of A. P. Hill, Rodes, Early, and Colston, of Jackson's corps.

Hooker's plan of campaign was to force Lee to come out from behind his breastworks and fight in the open. To turn his right was very difficult, owing to the width of the

General Joseph Hooker, known as "Fighting Joe."

Rappahannock toward its mouth, the swampy character of the country, and the practical impossibility of concealing the movement. Hooker therefore decided to turn Lee's left. Stoneman was to start upon a raid against the Confederate line of communications with all the cavalry except Pleasanton's small brigade. Sedgwick, with his own corps and that of Reynolds, was to cross the river below Fredericksburg and make a demonstration against Lee's right. The three corps of Meade, Howard, and Slocum, under the personal command of Hooker, would cross the Rappahannock at Kelly's Ford; then the Rapidan at Germanna and Ely's fords, march down the river, and reopen Banks's Ford, thus reuniting the two wings of the army. Sickles was to remain on Stafford Heights, ready to reinforce either wing. Couch was to leave one division of his corps on outpost at Falmouth, and place two divisions on the north bank of the river opposite Banks's Ford.

This plan was simple, and should have been successful : the only error was in sending away so large a proportion of the Union cavalry. Stoneman was detained two weeks by a heavy storm, which made the river unfordable, and did not get across until the 28 April. The result was that he did little harm to Lee's communications, and his absence from the battlefield made possible Jackson's turning movement which defeated the Union army.

Hooker felt no apprehension in thus dividing his army in the face of the enemy, as either wing was practically equal to the whole Confederate force. Sedgwick would have about 40,000 men, with the Third Corps (Sickles), about 19,000, on Stafford Heights, and one division of the Second Corps (Couch) at Falmouth. The main turning force under Hooker would also be about 40,000 strong, with two divisions of the Second Corps, say 10,000 men, at Banks's Ford. If Lee detached any considerable part of his force toward Chancellorsville, Sedgwick was ordered to carry the Fredericksburg works at all hazards, and establish his force on the Telegraph Road. The right wing, if not strongly resisted, was to advance far enough to uncover Banks's Ford; but, in case the Confederates were found in force, it was to

The wooded terrain at Chancellorsville.

select a strong position and await attack, while Sedgwick, coming up from Fredericksburg, would assail the enemy in flank and rear. It thus appears that Hooker's ambitious program aimed at nothing short of surrounding Lee and forcing him to surrender! Let us now see how it was carried out.

After making several demonstrations at various points, with a view of confusing the enemy, Hooker began his grand movement on the 27 April. The Fifth, Eleventh, and Twelfth corps started for Kelly's Ford under the command of Slocum. The small Confederate guard at the ford was easily dispersed, and by the morning of the 29th the three corps had crossed the Rappahannock on pontoon bridges. On the afternoon of the 30th, they reached Chancellorsville, the Fifth Corps having crossed the Rapidan by way of Ely's Ford, and the two other corps by Germanna Ford. As soon as these troops had crossed the Rapidan, the two divisions of the Second Corps joined them at Chancellorsville, by way of United States Ford. Hooker himself arrived at Chancellorsville on the night of the 30th. Meanwhile the Fifth and Sixth corps, under Sedgwick, had laid four pontoon bridges below Fredericksburg, and crossed the river there on the 29th.

No resistance, except that of picket forces, had been encountered anywhere, and the first part of Hooker's program had been carried out successfully. In three days and a half, he had covered forty-five miles, crossing two rivers, and established a force of 45,000 men on Lee's flank at Chancellorsville. Hooker was naturally elated at his success, and issued a congratulatory order to his troops, in which he said that, "the enemy must ingloriously fly, or come out from behind his defences and give us battle on our own ground, where certain destruction awaits him."

But Lee had no idea even of a "strategic retreat." Manoeuvre was to be met by manoeuvre, blow by counterblow! At first he had been in doubt as to the meaning of Hooker's movement, and even suspected that it was an advance against Gordonsville and the Virginia Central Railroad. It was not until the evening of the 29th that he received word from Stuart that the Federals had crossed the Rapidan at two fords that afternoon. Anderson's division was at once despatched to Chancellorsville.

During the morning of the 30th, Lee learned that Hooker had divided his army, and that one-half of it was at Chancellorsville, while most of the remainder was in his front. He at once resolved to attack one of the wings. As his army was concentrated in front of Sedgwick, Jackson at first favored a movement against the Federal left; but, after a careful reconnaissance, he came to the same conclusion as Lee, that the position was impregnable. A force of 10,000 men under Early was left, therefore, to hold the Fredericksburg lines, and contain Sedgwick; the rest of the army was ordered to march to Chancellorsville. Jackson's three divisions, under Hill, Rodes, and Colston, numbered about 25,000; Anderson's division of Longstreet's corps about 8000, and McLaws's three brigades of the same corps about 6000. Thus Lee had in hand less than 40,000 troops, to meet Hooker's 72,000 men. To any general but Lee the outlook would have seemed hopeless.

The field upon which the battle of Chancellorsville was to be fought was in the midst of a forest of second-growth pine and black oak, the original forest having been cut for charcoal many years before. This tract, well named the "Wilderness," was about fourteen miles long from east to west, toward the Rapidan, by some ten miles wide from north to south. It was drained by many crooked brooks, with marshy borders; the soil was poor, farms were scarce, and the few clearings were not more than a rifle-shot in width. A terrain less suitable for the manoeuvring of a large army would be hard to find. Infantry could move only with difficulty, and cavalry nowhere, except along the roads. There were few good positions for artillery, and there was no range for the guns.

Lieutenant -General Stonewall Jackson two weeks before his mortal wound.

Chancellorsville was merely a brick mansion, situated at an important junction of roads, on high ground, about a mile back from the eastern edge of the Wilderness, with a considerable clearing to the westward. From the house, three roads ran toward Fredericksburg: the Plank Road to the right; the more direct Old Turnpike in the centre — these two roads joining about midway to the city near the Tabernacle Church; and, to the left, the roundabout River Road, which passed near Banks's Ford.

East of the Wilderness, the country was more open, and it was there that Hooker expected to fight his battle. Accordingly he ordered his columns to move forward on the morning of the first day of May. Slocum, followed by Howard, took the Plank Road on the right. Sykes's division of Meade's corps, followed by Hancock's division of Couch's corps, went by the Turnpike in the centre. The two other divisions of Meade's corps, under Griffin and Humphreys, took the River Road. French's division of Couch's corps was ordered to march to Todd's Tavern.

Before the advance began, Sickles came up with the Third Corps, and was left at Chancellorsville as a general reserve, with one brigade guarding United States Ford, and another at Dowdall's Tavern, watching the approaches in that quarter.

Hooker's line of battle ran about two miles in a northeasterly direction from Chancellorsville to the river, covering United States Ford. To the west, it covered the Plank Road for about three miles, ending in a short offset to the north. The front was protected by entrenchments, hastily constructed.

Anderson, on his arrival the previous day, had taken a strong position at Tabernacle Church. When Jackson, marching since midnight, arrived about eight o'clock on the morning of the first, he found that Anderson had entrenched his whole front, from near Duerson's Mill on the right, to the unfinished railway on the left, about three miles. The position effectually blocked all of the roads by which the Federals would have to advance beyond the forest, and there were 40,000 Confederates to hold it, with 100 guns, and Fitz Lee's brigade of cavalry.

But Lee could not afford to rest on the defensive: only Early's small force of 10,000 men was in the lines at Fredericksburg to keep the Federal left wing under Sedgwick from falling upon the Confederate rear at Tabernacle Church. Therefore, at the same hour that Hooker began his advance, Lee's army also moved forward. Anderson was in advance, with one brigade on the Turnpike, and two on the Plank Road; his two other brigades and McLaws's division followed on the Turnpike; and Jackson's corps of three divisions marched on the Plank Road.

The fronts of the two armies soon came in contact on both roads. The Federals, says Doubleday, were almost out of the thickets, and the general line, on the whole, was a good one, for there were large open spaces where the artillery could move and manoeuvre. Sykes, however, had been directed to advance only to the first ridge beyond the forest; and there he maintained his line until ordered to withdraw to his original position. Slocum's corps had not become seriously engaged, when he, too, was directed to fall back. Griffin and Humphreys had advanced nearly five miles along the River Road, entirely unopposed, and were within sight of Banks's Ford when the orders for the countermarch reached them.

"Up to the moment of the withdrawal of his troops," says General Alexander, "Hooker's campaign had been well planned and well managed, and its culmination was now at hand in the open field — as he had desired.... . By all the rules of the game a victory was now within his grasp." Yet, at this early stage of the engagement, "Fighting Joe" seems for once to have lost his nerve; and, in spite of the protests of his amazed and indignant corps-commanders, he ordered his forces to withdraw to Chancellorsville. For this Hooker has been very severely blamed, and it is not too much to say that these orders lost him the campaign.

The Confederates felt that there was something mysterious about so easy a victory, and pursued with great caution, fearing a trap. At length, late in the afternoon, Hooker's tactics became clear: it was evident that he was standing fast on the defensive, in a position of great natural strength. As the nature of the country rendered a night attack hazardous, Lee halted his troops, and formed line of battle in front of Chancellorsville, at right angles to the Plank Road, extending on the right to the Mine Road, and to the left in the direction of Catherine Furnace.

Hooker's position at Chancellorsville was about five miles in length, reaching from Scott's Dam on the Rappahannock to Talley's farm on the Turnpike. The left of the line was held by Meade; then, at an angle, and facing more nearly east, came Couch's corps, — French's division covering the junction of the roads at Chancellorsville, and Hancock's division in an advanced position several hundred yards in front. Next came the Twelfth Corps (Slocum), formed around the crest of Fairview Hill, and facing south. Then there was a gap in the line of about 800 yards, beyond which Howard's corps, *en échelon* along the Plank Road, held the right of the line. The Third Corps (Sickles) was kept in reserve back of the mansion. On the morning of the 2nd, two brigades of Birney's division of this corps, and two batteries, were placed in the gap between Slocum and Howard, with a strong line of skirmishers thrown out in front. The 8th Pennsylvania cavalry picketed the roads and kept the enemy in sight.

Although the Federal position was very strong in some respects, it had several marked defects: the almost impenetrable thickets made manoeuvring difficult, and gave little scope to the artillery; besides, and most important of all, the right of Howard's line was "in the air," that is, it rested on no obstacle. Hooker was aware of this weakness, and sent one brigade of the Third Corps, with a battery, to strengthen the line; but Howard declined this assistance, as being a reflection on the bravery of his troops, or on his own military skill. As Howard had recently been appointed to the command of the Eleventh Corps, Hooker did not like to offend him, by any action which might imply lack of confidence, so the order was countermanded.

During the night of the 1st, a council of war was held at Hooker's headquarters. Some of the generals favored an early assault; others, a strictly defensive attitude. Hooker himself wished to contract, and thus strengthen, his lines, but was deterred by Howard's opinion that his position was impregnable against any assault: "he would send his compliments to the whole rebel army, if they lay in front of him, and invite them to attack him."

Three miles down the Plank Road, under a grove of oak and pine, Lee and Jackson, for the fourth and last time, laid their plans for the overthrow of their enemy. If Hooker was still in position in the morning, he was to be attacked: the situation admitted of no other course. The Federal army was divided, the right wing involved in a difficult country, and so favorable an opportunity might never occur again.

News had come from Fitz Lee, who commanded the cavalry on the extreme Confederate left, that Hooker's right wing was in the air. Lee's only chance was to cross the enemy's front and get in the rear of this exposed flank. The attempt would be both difficult and hazardous, and failure meant absolute destruction: if defeated, retreat would be impossible. "But no risks appalled the heart of Lee, either of odds, or position, or of both combined. His supreme faith in his army was only equalled by the faith of his army in him."

The decision once made, immediate preparations were begun for the movement. Wilcox was sent with his brigade to hold Banks's Ford. This was a wise precaution, for after midnight on the first Hooker ordered Reynolds to leave Sedgwick and march with his corps to Chancellorsville. It will be remembered that the divisions of Griffin and Humphreys, after arriving within sight of Banks's Ford, on the afternoon of the first, had been recalled. Therefore, Reynolds, on reaching the ford after sunrise on the 2nd, found Wilcox's brigade occupying the trenches, and was forced to continue his march to United States Ford, where he crossed.

The four remaining brigades of Anderson, and the three of McLaws, of Longstreet's corps, were ordered to entrench during the night. The turning movement was to be made by Jackson, with his three divisions, his own artillery, and Alexander's battalion of Longstreet's corps. Fitz Lee, with his cavalry, was to precede the infantry and cover the flank. Lee himself was to remain with Anderson's and McLaws's troops, and contain the enemy while the long march of fourteen miles was made.

Two hours after sunrise, Lee, standing by the roadside, watched the head of the column march by, and exchanged with Jackson the last few words ever to pass between them. The division of Rodes led the column, Colston followed, and A. P. Hill brought up the rear.

The sun rose on this day, the 1 May, about five o'clock, and set a little before seven. There was a full moon that night. Moving in a southwesterly direction, Jackson struck the Brock Road, a narrow track which runs nearly due north, and crosses both the Plank Road and the Pike about two miles west of Howard's position. The Brock Road, which would have been strongly held by the Union cavalry if Stoneman had been present, was free and unobstructed. Couriers brought word that the trains in the rear had been attacked and forced off the

The firing of guns was not heard at Chancellorsville and Hooker believed that Lee was in full retreat.

direct road; that some of Hill's brigades had turned back to save them, and that the enemy in great strength had poured into the gap between the two Confederate wings, but still Jackson pressed on, without a look behind him.

About two o'clock, just as the rear brigades, after checking Sickles's attack on the trains, were leaving the Welford house, six miles distant, Jackson himself reached the Plank Road, where he purposed to turn eastward against the Federal flank. Here he was met by Fitz Lee with the important information that by attacking down the Turnpike, instead of the Plank

Road, he could take the Union line in reverse. Having satisfied himself by a personal reconnaissance that this was correct, Jackson at once changed his plans. The cavalry, supported by the Stonewall Brigade, was sent a short distance down the Plank Road, to mask the march of the column. At four o'clock, Rodes was on the Pike, where he was joined by Jackson. Marching down the road about a mile, in the direction of the enemy, the troops were ordered to halt and deploy for battle. Meanwhile, seated on a stump near the Brock Road, Jackson wrote his last despatch to General Lee:

Near 3 p.m., May 2, 1863

GENERAL — The enemy has made a stand at Chancellor's [Dowdall's Tavern], which is about two miles from Chancellorsville. I hope as soon as practicable to attack. I trust that an ever-kind Providence will bless us with great success.

Respectfully
T. J. Jackson,
Lieutenant-General

The leading division is up, and the next two appear to be well closed.

T. J. J.

GENERAL R. E. LEE

Without their presence being suspected by a soul in the Federal army, 25,000 Confederates were now deploying in the forest directly in the rear of the Union lines, and overlapping them both to north and south.

At Chancellorsville, the day had passed quietly. Early in the morning, Hooker had ridden around his lines. Expecting to be attacked only in front, he was well satisfied with their location and construction. To Howard, he exclaimed, "How strong! how strong!" When he heard about ten o'clock that a large Confederate column had been seen marching westward past Catherine Furnace, he was uncertain as to the meaning of the movement. As the hours went by, however, and there was no further news, he became convinced that Lee was retreating on Gordonsville. At four o'clock he sent orders to Sedgwick to "capture Fredericksburg with everything in it, and vigorously pursue the enemy." He added, "We know that the enemy is fleeting, trying to save his trains." At this very moment, the Confederate avalanche was about to descend on his unprotected flank and rear!

Howard, in charge of the Union right, seems to have been as blind as Hooker. During the morning some slight preparations were made to defend the Pike to the westward, but even when his only reserve, Barlow's brigade, was sent to reinforce Sickles's attack on Jackson's trains, no change was made in the disposition of the other troops. Every one was convinced that Lee was retreating. No attention was paid to the reports of the pickets that the enemy was massing in the forest, and no attempt was made by a reconnaissance in force to ascertain what was actually going on in the thickets.

This neglect was the more remarkable because Howard's position was very weak. He had twenty regiments of infantry, and six batteries, but his force was completely isolated.

Devens's division was along the Pike on the right, with two regiments facing west and the balance south. Next came the division of Schurz, deployed along the Pike, and to its north. At Dowdall's Tavern, one brigade of Steinwehr's German division held a line of rifle-pits at right angles to the Pike. There were batteries in the road and near the Wilderness Church.

It was now six o'clock, and less than two hours of daylight remained. Jackson sat on his horse, watch in hand, awaiting the formation of his lines.

"Are you ready, General Rodes? "he asked.

"Yes, sir," Rodes replied.

"You can go forward, sir."

The signal for the advance was given by a bugle, taken up and repeated for each brigade by bugles to the right and left through the woods. But no mention is made in the Federal reports of these sounds, which seem to have been deadened in the forest. The first warning to the Union troops came from the wild rabbits, foxes, and deer, which ran scuttling through their lines. Then came shots from the pickets, followed by the onrush of the Confederate line, which charged with the famous rebel yell. For the second time in the Civil War, the Federals were taken completely by surprise. They were not "bayoneted in their beds," as at Shiloh, but the soldiers, "scattered in small groups, laughing, cooking, smoking, sleeping, and playing cards," with "their arms stacked in the rear," were taken entirely unawares. Devens's division, struck in flank, was driven back against that of Schurz, before the latter had time to deploy, and the whole mass ran pell-mell toward Chancellorsville, where they streamed in wild disorder past Hooker's headquarters.

"Much undeserved obloquy," says General Alexander, "was heaped upon the Eleventh Corps for their enforced retreat. No troops could have acted differently."

The pursuit was kept up for some distance, but was finally ended by the fading daylight. The Confederate troops were much fatigued and entirely disorganized. The loss of the Federals was 1438 killed and wounded, 974 missing — the total of 2412 being only about 20 per cent, of Howard's corps. This loss would certainly have been much larger but for the fact that only one-third of Jackson's force took part in the attack and pursuit. Five brigades did not reach the field in time, and four of A. P. Hill's brigades were not in line until after six o'clock.

Owing to some peculiar state of the atmosphere, as happened at Perryville, the firing was not heard at Chancellorsville, only two miles away. At half-past six, Hooker was sitting on the veranda of the mansion in entire confidence that Lee was in full retreat, when an aide, looking down the road with his glass, exclaimed, "My God! here they come!" All sprang to their horses, and, riding down the road, soon met the fugitives from Howard's corps. If the hour had not been so late, Hooker's situation would have been desperate, as he had only two divisions at hand to confront Lee and Jackson, who were then only two miles apart. But, as so often happened in the Peninsula, darkness robbed the Confederates of the full fruits of their victory. Hooker acted promptly and on the whole judiciously, and the night restored nearly all the advantages lost during the day. Even with the moon at its full, offensive operations could not be continued by night in such a wooded country.

Sickles was recalled, and reached the field with his corps at ten o'clock. The artillery of the Twelfth Corps (Slocum) was placed in a commanding position, known as Fairview, along the western brow of the plateau south of the Plank Road, and this now became the key point of the Union line. In front of it the open ground extended about 600 yards to the edge of the forest, and a small stream at the foot of the plateau offered shelter for a strong body of infantry in front of the guns. During the night parapets were constructed, and a powerful battery of 34 guns was established. The forest in front offered no single position for a Confederate gun.

About eight o'clock in the evening, Jackson was at Dowdall's Tavern. There was a lull in the battle, and he was planning a further advance, to cut Hooker off from United States Ford. After issuing his orders, about 8:45 he rode forward to join his advanced line. He was followed by several staff officers and couriers. The party rode slowly forward upon an old mountain road, now almost obliterated by the forest, which ran toward Chancellorsville, parallel to, and about 80 yards distant from the Plank Road. After advancing some 100 or 200 yards, they halted and listened awhile to the axes of the Federals, who were cutting abattis in the woods beyond. Suddenly firing began between the skirmishers of both armies,

Union soldiers in deserted Confederate camp.

and spread rapidly along the lines. Jackson was slowly retracing his way back to his line, when Major Barry of the 18 th North Carolina ordered his men to fire on the group of horsemen, whom he took to be a squadron of Federal cavalry. Two of the party were killed, and Jackson received three wounds, one of which proved fatal. During the night it was found necessary to amputate his left arm, which had been shattered between shoulder and elbow. The next day he was taken in an ambulance via Spottsylvania to a small house called Chandler's, near Guinea Station. For several days his recovery was expected, but pneumonia set in, and he died on the 10 May.

As A. P. Hill, the next in rank, was soon afterwards wounded, Stuart took command of Jackson's corps.

At dawn on Sunday, the 3rd, Stuart renewed the attack. Hooker had made the mistake of withdrawing Sickles from the heights of Hazel Grove, which were seized by the enemy. Here, Stuart placed thirty guns, which enfiladed a part of the Union line, and reached the space around the mansion.

During the night Hooker had readjusted his line. Howard's corps had been sent to the left to reorganize; the right was held by Couch, Sickles, and Slocum. The Union line, about a mile and a quarter long, extending northward from Fairview to beyond the Plank Road, was held by some 25,000 men — about as many as Stuart had. The position was strongly entrenched. The roads toward Fredericksburg were covered by Hancock's division of the Second Corps, and a part of the Twelfth Corps (Slocum). Meade was near Howard, on the left, on the road to United States Ford; and Reynolds, in the rear, covered the road to Ely's Ford.

After several hours of hard fighting, Stuart forced the Federals back, and occupied Fairview Hill, to which he moved his batteries. At the same time, Anderson and McLaws were assaulting the centre and left of the Union line, which were also compelled to fall back. Finally the flanks of Stuart's and Anderson's forces came together at Fairview. At ten o'clock Lee had possession of the mansion, now only a smoking ruin.

Just before this Hooker had been knocked down and disabled by a brick torn by a shell from one of the columns of the front porch of the house. Couch succeeded temporarily to the command, and directed the withdrawal of the Union forces to a new line in the rear, which had been selected and prepared by the engineers. The right rested on the Rapidan and the left on the Rappahannock, the position covering the line of retreat by United States Ford.

Lee was preparing to assault the new position when he was forced to turn his attention to the Federal movement on his rear.

At nine o'clock on the evening of the 2nd, Hooker had sent Sedgwick an order to carry the works at Fredericksburg; then move on Chancellorsville, and attack Lee from the rear. As Reynolds was gone, Sedgwick now had only his own corps, of about 22,000 men. The works were held by Early's division, of some 10,000 men, but he was soon reinforced by Wilcox, who brought his brigade from Banks's Ford.

Sedgwick reached Fredericksburg about three o'clock on the morning of the 3rd, and attacked at daybreak. During the morning three separate assaults were repulsed, and an effort to turn Marye's Hill failed. But a fourth attack carried the strong position in the sunken road, and the Federals soon reached the crest of the hill. Early's troops retreated by the Telegraph Road, leaving the roads to Chancellorsville protected only by Wilcox's single brigade.

This was the news which reached Lee just as he was preparing for a final attack. He at once sent four brigades under McLaws to meet Sedgwick. Wilcox formed his brigade across the Plank Road, and fell back slowly to Salem Church, where he was joined by McLaws, about three o'clock. When Sedgwick came up, about an hour later, a desperate combat ensued, which lasted until dark. Sedgwick could make no further progress; since morning, he had lost nearly a fourth of his force.

Finding that Hooker did not attack the next morning, the 4th, Lee sent Anderson's division to join McLaws, leaving only what remained of Jackson's old corps in front of Hooker. Meanwhile Early had retaken Marye's Hill, and then advanced on the rear of Sedgwick, who found himself surrounded on three sides, with only the road to Banks's Ford open. Fortunately for the Federals, it was six o'clock before the Confederates were ready to make a vigorous attack, and Sedgwick was able to reach the river at Banks's Ford, where he crossed during the night on a pontoon bridge which had been laid after the departure of Wilcox the previous day.

Tuesday morning, the 5th, Lee concentrated all his forces in front of Hooker, and prepared to assault the Union lines at daybreak on the 6th. When morning came, however, it was found that, during the night, the Army of the Potomac had retreated across the river, leaving behind the killed and wounded; fourteen guns, and twenty thousand stand of arms.

The losses on both sides during the few days of the campaign were:

	Federals	Confederates
Killed	1,606	1,649
Wounded	9,762	9,106
Missing	5,919	1,708
Totals	17,287	12,463

According to the official returns of the 30 April, Hooker had about 130,000 men, including 11,000 cavalry, most of which was not present at the battle. Lee's army was some 60,000 strong.

After the disaster of Fredericksburg, there was a strong demand from the army for the recall of McClellan, but the authorities at Washington seemed to fear that a military dictatorship might result from the return of the "young Napoleon." General Halleck and Secretary Stanton favored the transfer of Rosecrans; but at this time it was thought unwise to put another Western man in command. The choice being narrowed to the Army of the Potomac, a process of elimination began. Franklin was under a cloud owing to his alleged misconduct at Fredericksburg; Sumner was considered too old and too feeble; Couch was a possible second choice. Finally the selection was found to be restricted to Reynolds, Meade, and Hooker. The latter had strong popular and political support, but his appointment was violently opposed by Halleck and Stanton, who thought that he was unfit for a position of such responsibility. Reynolds, when sounded on the subject, refused to accept the command unless given complete liberty of action, which at that time the Administration was not willing to grant. Finally, as the result of an obscure political intrigue, connected with the aspirations of Secretary Chase to be elevated to the Presidency at the end of Mr. Lincoln's term, the President overruled Halleck and Stanton, and directed the appointment of Hooker.

In making the announcement of his selection, Mr. Lincoln wrote Hooker a most remarkable letter, in which he said, among other things: "I have heard, in such a way as to believe it, of your recently saying that both the army and the Government needed a Dictator. Of course it was not for this, but in spite of it, that I have given you the command. Only those generals who gain successes can set up dictators. What I now ask of you is military success, and I will risk the dictatorship.... And now beware of rashness. Beware of rashness, but with energy and sleepless vigilance go forward and give us victories."

During a visit to Hooker's camp, in April, Mr. Lincoln gave him another bit of good advice: "I want to impress upon you in your next fight — *put in all of your men!*"

The Campaign of Chancellorsville began with the crossing of the Rappahannock on the 28 April, and ended with the return of the Union army to the north side of the river on the night of the 5 May. It will be hard to find in the annals of the Civil War a greater series of blunders than those made by the Federal commander during this brief period of eight days!

Hooker's first mistake was in sending Stoneman with 10,000 sabres against Lee's communications, while he retained with his army only Pleasanton's small brigade of 1500 men. It would have been better if the arrangement had been exactly reversed. Nearly all of the successful cavalry raids during the war were made with comparatively small bodies of men. During this same month of April, Grierson rode the whole length of the State of Mississippi with only a thousand troopers, and destroyed an immense amount of Confederate property. Stuart's brilliant rides around the Union army were generally made with less than two thousand horsemen.

It was an essential part of Hooker's plan that the cavalry should begin operations two weeks before the infantry. Stoneman started on the 13 April, but a heavy storm made the river unfordable until the 28th. Although this delay had entirely altered conditions, Hooker was too impatient to wait longer, and all — infantry, artillery, and cavalry — were sent over together. The result was that the battle was fought before Stoneman had time to carry out the plan of cutting Lee's communications.

If Stoneman's 10,000 men had been on the Union right, where they should have been, on the 2 May, Jackson's famous turning movement would not have been made; or, if attempted, it would have been a disastrous failure, instead of a brilliant success.

Another great mistake was made by Hooker in withdrawing his troops on the afternoon of the 1st. "The position thus abandoned," says General Couch, "was high ground, more or less open in front, over which an army might move and artillery be used advantageously; moreover, were it left in the hands of an enemy, his batteries, established on its crest and slopes, would command the position at Chancellorsville."

It was also of the utmost importance to secure Banks's Ford, then almost within the grasp of the Federals, which would have greatly shortened the distance between the two wings of the army.

When the order to retire was received, the Union officers at the front — Couch, Hancock, Sykes, Warren, and others — agreed that the ground should not be abandoned. An aide was sent to General Hooker, to protest against the withdrawal; but he returned in half an hour with positive orders to fall back. Even so loyal an officer as General Warren suggested that they should disobey; and he then rode back to see the general. Later, about two o'clock, when nearly all the regiments had been withdrawn, there came a third order from Hooker: "Hold on until five o'clock." Disgusted at the general's vacillation, General Couch sent back the rather impertinent reply: "Tell General Hooker he is too late, the enemy is already on my right and rear. I am in full retreat."

The Army of the Potomac was in no sense defeated by the disaster to Howard's corps. By a vigorous combined assault, Lee might still have been driven off the field. Hooker failed to comply with Lincoln's order, "to put in all his men." He employed little more than half his force. The two corps of Reynolds and Meade — over 30,000 strong — were not allowed to go into action, though the generals were eager to do so. In the opinion of General Alexander, Hooker's decision to retreat, on the night of the 5th, was "the mistake of his life." He then had his whole united army, upwards of 90,000 men, behind "probably the strongest field-entrenchment ever built in Virginia." Lee was preparing to attack this position with only 35,000 men, worn out with seven days' marching and fighting! Hooker's retreat saved Lee from a disastrous repulse.

General Couch alludes to the "charge that the battle was lost because the general was intoxicated." By implication, he denies this, but insinuates that it might have been better for the Union army if the charge had been true! He says that Hooker "probably abstained from the use of ardent spirits when it would have been far better for him to have continued in his usual habit in that respect."

Howard was principally responsible for the disaster to the Union right on the 2nd, and should have been cashiered, but he got off with a mild censure. The whole blame was laid on the Germans, who did not deserve it.

In spite of all his precautions, Jackson's column was seen to pass over a bare hill about a mile and a half from Birney's front, and the number was almost exactly estimated. Birney immediately reported this important fact to headquarters, and at 9:30 a.m., General Hooker issued an order, addressed to Slocum and Howard, warning them to guard their flanks, and be prepared for the enemy "in whatever direction he advances."

Notwithstanding this order to Howard, *he took no precautions against the impending danger.* His apathy and indifference can only be explained on the supposition that he really believed Jackson was retreating to Gordonsville, although on what grounds, it is difficult to imagine. During the eight hours, from 10 A.M., when Hooker's order was received, to 6 P.M., when the assault came, Howard had ample time to render his line impregnable, but he did nothing. The few precautions taken were due entirely to the initiative of two of his division commanders — Schurz and Devens.

All the blame for the rout was thrown upon the Germans, but it is only fair to state that when a force, not deployed, is struck suddenly and violently on the flank, resistance is impossible. Napoleon's Old Guard, the best and bravest troops that ever existed, could not have held together in such a case.

Howard scouted the reports which came in all day long, and fairly insulted the informants, saying that their stories were the result of their imaginations or their fears. Apparently nothing could vanquish his incredulity; he could not be made to believe that there was any force of the enemy near him. In his official report the pious Howard writes as though he believed that his corps was overwhelmed by the act of God!

The two greatest commanders of modern times — Frederick and Napoleon — both played a good game of chess, and every student in the Army War College should be taught the game; for it is *the* game, above all others, in which one must constantly play his opponent's hand as well as his own, in order to achieve success. Otherwise, he will continually find that his most brilliant combinations fail, because his adversary is not considerate enough to make the moves that he desires or expects.

In the first Italian campaign of 1796, the Austrian commanders — Beaulieu, Alvinzy, and Wurmser — all complained bitterly that the young Bonaparte did not play the game according to the rules of war! Lee and Jackson had the same disagreeable habit. According to all precedents, when Lee found himself outnumbered two to one at Fredericksburg, with the Federal hosts massed on both his flanks, and Stoneman's 10,000 horsemen riding against his communications, he should have retreated precipitately. But Lee did nothing of the sort. In defiance of all the rules of war, he left Early with 10,000 men behind the breastworks of Fredericksburg, to hold back Sedgwick's two corps of 40,000 troops, and with the balance of his forces marched to Chancellorsville to meet Hooker. Then he had the even greater audacity to divide his army once more, and remain with 25,000 men in front of Hooker while he sent Jackson with the other half of his available forces by a roundabout march of fourteen miles to fall upon the Federal flank and rear!

The power of striking like a "bolt from the blue," says Colonel Henderson, is of the very greatest value in war. Surprise was the foundation of almost all the grand strategical combinations of the past, as it will be of the future. Success is seldom to be won without incurring risks. "The very course which appeared to ordinary minds so beset by difficulties and dangers as to be outside the pale of practical strategy has, over and over again, been that which led to decisive victory."

"The battle of Chancellorsville," says Colonel Livermore, "although faulty in respect to the flank march of Jackson, is nevertheless one of the most instructive to the military student of any in ancient or modern times, from the succession of kaleidoscopic changes of position from day to day and from hour to hour, in which superior tactical skill on the part of one or more of the commanders on either side might have changed the fate of the campaign; and this faulty move, which did in fact partially succeed through the stupendous blunders of Hooker and especially through the persistent negligence and blind credulity of Howard, gave rise to situations of great dramatic interest, in one of which the picturesque and noble Jackson was stricken down at the moment when he thought that all Hooker's army would soon be within his grasp."

CHAPTER TWELVE

JUNE — JULY 1863

GETTYSBURG

AFTER the battle of Chancellorsville the two armies resumed their former positions on the opposite sides of the Rappahannock. The morale of the Union army had suffered from another defeat, while the Confederate *hopes*, in the words of General Alexander, reached the highest point attained during the war. Under the system of obligatory service, Lee's army was at once increased by a large force of conscripts. He was also rejoined by Longstreet with his two divisions which had been absent during the Chancellorsville campaign. On the 31 May, Lee had an army of over 76,000 men, and 272 guns. At the same date, the Army of the Potomac was reduced by loss in battle and by expiration of the terms of service to less than 105,000 effectives.

Although there were few men then endowed with the foresight to realize the fact, the next five weeks were to mark the turning point of the war; and the fate of the Confederacy was to be decided by the policy adopted by the Southern leaders at this time. Grant, with 75,000 men, had Pemberton, with 30,000, securely invested at Vicksburg, while Johnston, with less than 25,000, was at Canton, powerless to raise the siege. Unless Johnston could be heavily reinforced, or some measure taken to force the Washington Government to recall a part of Grant's army, Vicksburg was doomed, and the Mississippi would be lost to the Confederacy.

On the 15 May, Beauregard suggested to Johnston a plan to submit to the War Department for a "brilliant" summer campaign; and about the same date, Longstreet, when passing through Richmond on his way to rejoin Lee, outlined to Mr. Seddon, the Secretary of War, a very similar project. This plan, in brief, was to take advantage of the interior lines of the Confederacy to transfer Longstreet's two veteran divisions, 13,000 strong, via Lynchburg, Knoxville, and Chattanooga, to Murfreesboro, Tennessee, where Bragg, with some 45,000 Confederates, confronted Rosecrans with about 60,000 Federals; to send Johnston's 25,000 from Mississippi, and Buckner's 5000 from Knoxville to the same point; then for Lee to go West, take command in person, defeat Rosecrans, and march on Louisville and Cincinnati. "If anything could have caused Grant's recall from Vicksburg," says General Alexander, "it would have been this. Surely the chances of success were greater, and of disaster less, than those involved in our crossing the bridgeless Potomac, into the heart of the enemy's country, where ammunition and supplies must come by wagons from Staunton, nearly 200 miles, over roads exposed to the raids of the enemy from either the east or the west. In

Lee excelled in surprise and audacity, but Gettysburg proved he was not invincible.

General G.E. Pickett. Pickett's charge, ordered by Lee on the last day of Gettysburg, sent 5,000 men across an open plain where they were fired upon by the Union resulting in a losses of up to sixty percent.

this position, a drawn battle, or even a victory, would still leave us compelled soon to find our way back across the Potomac."

But foreign intervention was the ruling idea with President Davis, and he declined to entertain the proposition. After reporting to General Lee, Longstreet made him the same suggestion. "He reflected over the matter several days," says Longstreet, "and then fell upon the plan of invading the Northern soil, and so threatening Washington as to bring about the same hoped-for result."

What might have been the result of the acceptance of this plan, which was strategically sound, is a problem of great interest; but it is doubtful whether the result for the Confederacy would have been any more satisfactory than the campaign which Lee actually conducted in the East. At that time Mr. Davis was very sanguine that a victory on Northern soil would bring about foreign recognition; and Lee himself was averse to leaving Virginia, — also to any division of his army. Ever since the failure of the invasion of Maryland, both Lee and Jackson had longed to try it once more, and during the winter and spring, the latter had had prepared a remarkable large-scale map of the country from Winchester to the Susquehanna, on which even the farm-houses were noted, with the names of the owners.

In preparation for the coming campaign, Lee decided to reorganize his army, making three corps, instead of two. General James Longstreet, a native of South Carolina, remained in command of the First Corps. He had the unbounded confidence of his troops, who called him "Old Pete," and was considered the hardest fighter in the Confederate service. Jackson's old corps, the Second, was assigned to General Ewell, who was entitled to the command by reason of his rank, services, and ability. Lee wished to place the new third corps under the command of a Virginian, although this made it necessary to disregard the claims of two officers who had been very efficient. He accordingly selected for the command of the Third Corps, General Ambrose P. Hill, passing over the two generals next in rank, D. H. Hill, a native of North Carolina, and McLaws, a Georgian, against whom there was no objection, except that they were not Virginians. General Longstreet thinks that this reorganization somewhat impaired the morale of the troops. General Alexander also states that D. H. Hill had strong claims for promotion, and that Stuart would have made a more active and efficient corps-commander than Ewell.

Each corps consisted of three divisions, and each division of four brigades, except Anderson's and Rodes's, which had five each, and Pickett's, which had three at Gettysburg, — in all thirty-seven infantry brigades.

The cavalry, which comprised the select troops of the Confederacy, were now organized as a division, consisting of six brigades, under Stuart.

At this time, the general artillery reserve, commanded by Pendleton, was broken up, chiefly due to the lack of guns, and was never reestablished. Pendleton, however, was retained as chief of artillery. The new artillery organization, of a few batteries with each division, and a reserve with each corps, but with no general reserve for the army, was the first of the kind ever adopted, and it was subsequently copied by all the principal nations of Europe. But General Alexander thinks

General George Gordon Meade, Commander of the Army of the Potomac at Gettysburg, in the Wilderness campaign and at the siege of Petersburg.

that the fine service of the Federal reserve of 110 guns, under Hunt, at Gettysburg demonstrates the advantage of such an organization in every large army.

The three Confederate army corps, of from 21,000 to 23,000 men, approximated in numbers what is to-day considered the proper strength of an army corps, that is 30,000 men; and each corps only lacked a complement of cavalry to make it a complete little army in itself, which is also the approved organization of today.

Lee was a full general; his corps were commanded by lieutenant-generals, his divisions by major-generals, and all but two of his forty-two infantry and cavalry brigades by brigadier-generals. Nearly all of these officers were veterans of proved ability, and many had served in the Mexican War.

In the Army of the Potomac, on the other hand, the average strength of the army corps and divisions was about half that of the Confederates. At the battle of Gettysburg the seven army corps consisted of nineteen infantry divisions, of which seven had two brigades, eleven had three, and one had four — in all fifty-one brigades. The army and the corps were commanded by major-generals, the divisions by three major-generals and sixteen brigadiers, the infantry brigades by twenty-two brigadiers and twenty-nine colonels. It is impossible to understand or explain the aversion of the Congress to bestowing proper rank upon the general

Meade's headquarters on Cemetery Ridge.

officers in the United States Army. Since the Revolutionary War, there have been only four full generals in our service — Grant, Sherman, Sheridan, and Pershing. Washington was only a lieutenant-general, and Scott, until after his retirement, held the same rank only by brevet. During the four short years of the existence of the Confederacy, eight full generals, and twenty-three lieutenant-generals were commissioned: their armies were always commanded by full generals, and their army corps by lieutenant-generals.

"It will be perceived by comparison," says General Hunt, "that the organization of the Army of the Potomac was at this period in every way inferior to that of its adversary. The army corps and divisions were too numerous and too weak. They required too many commanders and staffs, and this imposed unnecessary burdens on the general-in-chief, who was often compelled to place several army corps under the commander of one of them, thus reproducing the much abused 'grand divisions' of Burnside, under every possible disadvantage. Had the number of infantry corps been reduced to four at most, and the divisions to twelve, the army would have been more manageable and better commanded; and the artillery, without any loss, but rather a gain of efficiency, would have been reduced by a dozen or fifteen batteries."

Lee's movement began on the 5 June, and on the 8th the corps of Longstreet and Ewell were concentrated at Culpeper. Hill remained at Fredericksburg to watch Hooker, and keep him quiet as long as possible. On the 5th, Hooker wrote the President that he thought Lee was contemplating another invasion of the North, and asked instructions. In their replies both Mr. Lincoln and General Halleck advised Hooker to attack Lee's column on the north side of the river, and by no means to cross the Rappahannock to assault his entrenchments. In the President's letter he uses the famous illustration of the "risk of being entangled upon the river, like an ox jumped half over a fence and liable to be torn by dogs front and rear, without a fair chance to gore one way or kick the other."

As a matter of fact, the Army of the Potomac, under a competent commander, stood in no danger of being caught "half over the fence," and could have attacked Lee's movable column, or assaulted his entrenchments, with equal impunity. But the Administration had lost all confidence in Hooker since the battle of Chancellorsville.

Since Lee took command of the Army of Northern Virginia in June 1862, his career had been one of almost uninterrupted success. His victories on his own soil had been extraordinary, and he had become convinced, like nearly all of his officers and men, that he and his army were invincible. Over and over again — in the Peninsula, at Second Manassas, at Chancellorsville — he had showed contempt of his foe. In his second invasion of the North he displayed the same contempt. No other construction can be placed on the stretching of his line from Fredericksburg to Winchester in the face of an opponent who greatly outnumbered him. On the 14 June, President Lincoln wrote Hooker: "If the head of Lee's army is at Martinsburg and the tail of it on the plank road between Fredericksburg and Chancellorsville, the animal must be very slim somewhere. Could you not break him? "

"War," says Colonel Henderson, "is more a struggle between two human intelligences than between two masses or armed men." The great general does not give his first attention to numbers or position, but puts himself in his opponent's place, and observes the situation with that commander's eyes, taking into consideration his weakness, tactical, strategical, and political; detecting the points for the security of which he is most apprehensive; divining what his action will be if attacked here or threatened there. Looking at things thus from his enemy's point of view, he decides whether or not apparent risks can be taken with impunity.

It was through his knowledge of the character and position of Mr. Lincoln, the Commander-in-Chief of the Armies of the United States, that General Lee well knew that a threat against Washington was morally certain to result in the recall of Hooker's army for the protection of the capital, and that there was little danger of an attack on Hill. This is why he ventured to distribute his army corps along so wide a front."

In order to obtain information as to the enemy's position and proposed movements, Hooker ordered Pleasanton, who was now in command of the cavalry, to beat up Stuart's camps at Culpeper, and gave him two small brigades of infantry, 3000 men, which raised his total force to about 11,000. These troops were in echelon along the railroad, which crosses the river at Rappahannock Station, and runs thence ten miles to Culpeper. About midway is Brandy Station, and here the two cavalry forces came in contact on the 9 June. After an indecisive battle, lasting all day, Pleasanton withdrew, but not until he had secured sufficient information to report to Hooker that two-thirds of the enemy were at Culpeper preparing to move on Washington. The affair was of importance chiefly from the fact that it was the first true cavalry battle fought during the war, and that "it enabled the Federals to dispute the superiority hitherto claimed by, and conceded to, the Confederate cavalry."

On the 10 June, Ewell left Culpeper for Winchester, where he arrived on the 13th. He then pushed on to the Potomac, crossed the river, and occupied Hagerstown and Sharpsburg. The Union forces in the Valley withdrew before the enemy's advance, the garrison at Harper's Ferry being the last to cross the river, to Maryland Heights; and on the 17th the Shenandoah Valley was cleared of Federal troops.

On the night of the 13th, Hooker started for Manassas Junction, on his way to the Potomac, which he expected to cross near Leesburg. A. P. Hill's corps immediately followed toward the Valley, crossed the mountains to the south of Longstreet, who had left Culpeper on the 15th; then marched down the Shenandoah, and reached Shepherdstown on the 23rd. Longstreet marched along the east side of the Blue Ridge, to cover the passes; but finally crossed to the Valley, and followed Hill to the Potomac. Their columns united at Hagerstown on the 25th. These movements were all screened by the cavalry thrown out on the flanks of the two armies, so that it was impossible for either commander to obtain much information.

Hooker crossed the Potomac at Edwards Ferry on the 25th and 26th. On the 27th, the First and Eleventh corps, under Reynolds, occupied Middletown and the South Mountain passes; the Twelfth Corps was near Harper's Ferry, and the four other corps were at Frederick.

Lee's objective was Harrisburg, and Ewell, continuing his march, reached Carlisle and York on the 28th. The same day, Hooker ordered Slocum, with the Twelfth Corps, to march to Harper's Ferry, there unite with the force at Maryland Heights, cut Lee's communications, and, in conjunction with Reynolds, operate on his rear.

In a council held after the battle of Chancellorsville, Mr. Lincoln, Stanton, and Halleck had decided that Hooker should not be entrusted with the conduct of another battle. He could not be removed immediately, however, as he still had the strong support of the Chase faction, who refused

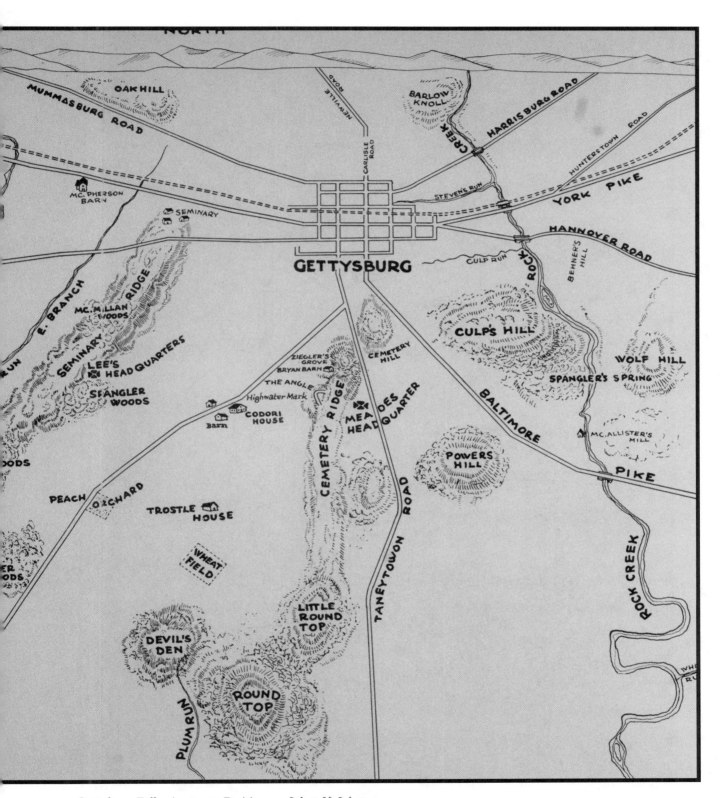

Gettysburg. Following pages: Positions on July 2 & July 3.

Little Round Top was key to the Federal left. The Union line was about 4 miles long.

to consent to a change in the command of the Army of the Potomac unless Hooker should *voluntarily resign.*

Halleck now interposed and refused to allow the withdrawal of the troops from Maryland Heights, although Hooker pointed out that the position was of no possible importance. Hooker appealed in vain to the President and Secretary Stanton. Finding that he had lost the support of the Government, and that he was "not to be allowed to manoeuvre his own army in the presence of the enemy," on the 27 June Hooker tendered his resignation. This was just what Stanton and Halleck had been scheming to bring about, and his request to be relieved was immediately granted. Major-General George G. Meade was appointed in his place, and took command at Frederick on the 28th. Meade was an excellent corps-commander, and a safe choice, but he was too lacking in aggressiveness to make a good general-in-chief. He had a disagreeable disposition, and was not popular with his fellow-officers. Meade was succeeded in the command of the Fifth Corps by Major-General George Sykes, a veteran of the Mexican War and a distinguished soldier.

The Union army was now organized as follows: First Corps, Reynolds; Second, Hancock; Third, Sickles; Fifth, Sykes; Sixth, Sedgwick; Eleventh, Howard; and Twelfth, Slocum. The seven corps averaged about 12,000 men, making a total of 84,000 infantry; there were about 5000 in the artillery, and 15,000 cavalry — an aggregate of 104,000.

Lee had about 66,000 infantry, divided almost equally between the three corps of Longstreet, Ewell, and Hill; and about 10,000 cavalry, under Stuart, who were not present at the opening of the battle of Gettysburg.

With the consent of Lee, on the 24 June, Stuart had started on another of his famous rides around the Union army; but this time his raid was a total failure, and his absence probably lost Lee a victory at Gettysburg. He finally rejoined the army on the second day of the battle, with his horses worn out and his men utterly exhausted.

At the time Meade assumed command the situation was briefly as follows: The advance of Lee's army, under Ewell, was at Carlisle and York, threatening Harrisburg; Longstreet's corps was at Chambersburg, and Hill's between that place and Cashtown. Meade's army was in and around Frederick.

Owing to the absence of Stuart, and the failure of his "scouts" to report, Lee did not yet know that the Federal army was across the Potomac. But about midnight on the 28th, the famous spy, Harrison, appeared at headquarters, with the news that Hooker had crossed the Potomac, and had been superseded by Meade. He was able also to give the approximate positions of five of the seven Federal corps.

This news caused an immediate change in Lee's plans. On the 29th, orders were sent recalling Ewell, and directing a concentration of the three corps at Cashtown, eight miles west of Gettysburg, where he hoped the enemy would be forced to attack him. At the same time, Meade was laying out a line behind Pipe Creek, in northern Maryland, where he, too, hoped to fight on the defensive.

The Administration at Washington at last seemed to have learned some wisdom from experience. Halleck wrote Meade that he would "not be hampered by any minute instructions from these headquarters"; and that he was "intrusted with all the power and authority" which the Government could confer on him. Accordingly, as soon as Meade took command, he had abandoned Hooker's plan of operating against Lee's rear, and selected the line Emmitsburg-Hanover for the front of his army, with Westminster as his base, in order to force Lee to battle before he could cross the Susquehanna. This line covered both Baltimore and Washington.

On the 30 June, the Union troops occupied the following positions: Buford's cavalry division was at Gettysburg; Reynolds was at Marsh Run; Sickles at Bridgeport; Slocum at Littlestown; Howard, behind Reynolds, at Emmitsburg. These troops, with Kilpatrick's cavalry division at Hanover, composed the first line. In second line were Hancock at Uniontown, Sykes at Union Mills, and Sedgwick at Manchester, with Gregg's cavalry division covering the rear at Westminster.

On the same day, Lee's army was thus situated: two of Ewell's divisions were at Heidlersburg, and the third at Greenwood; two of Longstreet's were at Fayetteville, and the third (Pickett) at Chambersburg, guarding the trains; one of Hill's divisions (Anderson) was back at the mountain pass on the Chambersburg Road, and the two others had reached Cashtown and Mummasburg.

On the 30 June, Heth, in command of one of Hill's divisions, heard that shoes could be obtained at Gettysburg, and ordered Pettigrew's brigade to go there and get them. But on approaching Gettysburg, Pettigrew found Buford's cavalry just occupying the town, so he withdrew about five miles and bivouacked. This chance collision suddenly precipitated a battle, unforeseen and undesired by either party.

Buford realized the importance of Gettysburg as a strategic centre, and made his dispositions to hold it if possible. He established his outposts to the west and north of the town, and sent word to Reynolds and Meade.

The town of Gettysburg lies in a small valley surrounded by low hills. From the town twelve roads run to every point of the compass. Ten miles to the west the horizon is bounded by the South Mountains, through which lay Lee's line of retreat in case of defeat. About a half mile west of the town is an elevation called Seminary Ridge, from the Lutheran Seminary standing on it. This ridge begins at a commanding knoll, nearly a mile and a half north of the Seminary, called Oak Hill; from this point the ridge runs in a southerly direction, and is covered with open woods. The Chambersburg Pike and the Hagerstown Road pass over the ridge, and meet at an acute angle at the end of one of the streets on the western edge of the town. Parallel to the Pike, and 200 yards north of it, was an unfinished railway.

Directly north of the town the country is low and flat, and is traversed by Rock Creek. About a half mile south of the town, facing Seminary Ridge, is Cemetery Hill, rising 80 feet above the level of the valley below. The position which was occupied by the Union army on the second and third days of the battle is shaped like a fishhook. The shank is formed by Cemetery Ridge, which connects the Round Tops on the south with Cemetery Hill on the north. The line then curves to the east and again to the south to Culp's Hill, which corresponds to the point of the hook. The total length is about three miles, and the distance from Seminary Ridge is from 1400 to 1600 yards. Round Top rises about 330 feet, and Little Round Top about 220 feet above the bed of Plum Run on the west, Culp's Hill about 170 feet above Rock Creek on the east. Both of the extremities of the line were strong, and capable of defence against superior numbers. Cemetery Ridge is not high, and the slopes are gentle. The distance of the point of the hook from the shank was little more than a mile, so that any point attacked could be readily reinforced. Troops could move from one part of the line to another out of view of the enemy; and the reserves were sheltered by the rocks and hills. So long as Culp's Hill on the north and the Round Tops on the south were held, the position could not be outflanked. The weak point of the position was Cemetery Hill, which presented a salient where the line could be enfiladed, and the enemy could approach from the north and west under shelter to within a few hundred yards of the entrenchments. Of this part of the line General Alexander says: "Briefly, the one weak point of the enemy's line, and the one advantage possessed by ours, were never apprehended." This salient *"offered the only hopeful point of attack upon the enemy's entire line. ... It would not be too much to say that an attack here on the morning of the 2 July would have succeeded."*

Some 500 yards west of Seminary Ridge the land rises gradually to another ridge, which is wider, smoother, and lower than Seminary Ridge, and which also begins at Oak Hill. Beyond this second ridge, Willoughby Run flows south to Marsh Creek. The roads to Chambersburg and Hagerstown cross the run about a mile apart.

About five o'clock on the morning of the 1st, Hill, with the divisions of Heth and Pender, started from Cashtown for Gettysburg, eight miles distant. At dawn, Buford had made arrangements to "entertain" the enemy until General Reynolds could reach the scene. He dismounted his two cavalry brigades, 3100 men, and deployed them beyond the second ridge along Willoughby Run. About ten o'clock Heth advanced to the attack, with Pender close behind. Although greatly outnumbered, Buford kept the Confederates back for half an hour, until Reynolds arrived on the ground, with Wadsworth's division, of his corps, which was immediately deployed along the ridge; the cavalry then took post on the flanks. Almost at the beginning of the engagement, Reynolds was shot through the head and instantly killed. "The death of this splendid officer," writes Fitz Lee, "was regretted by friend and foe"; and, borrowing the words of another, he adds, "No man died on that field with more glory than he; yet many died, and there was much glory!"

About eleven o'clock, the two other divisions of the First Corps came up, with four more batteries. Rowley's division and the guns were placed in the line, which was thus extended to the right along Seminary Ridge. The third division (Robinson) was posted in reserve at the Seminary.

Howard arrived at noon, ahead of his corps, and assumed command by virtue of his rank. When the Eleventh Corps came up, an hour later, Schurz, who was in temporary command, was ordered to prolong the line of the First Corps to the north on Seminary Ridge with his own division and that of Barlow, and place the third division (Steinwehr) at Cemetery Hill in reserve.

Before these arrangements were completed, Buford's cavalry brought word that Ewell's Confederate corps was approaching by the Heidlersburg Road, directly on the right flank and rear of the Federal position. Thereupon, Howard ordered the Eleventh Corps to change front to the right, and take up a line across the valley to the north of the town, in order to hold back the enemy. At the same time he called for aid from Slocum and Sickles, whose corps were between Gettysburg and Emmitsburg, from five to ten miles away.

Up to this time, the Federals had been quite successful, as they were superior in numbers at the actual points of contact. "Whether from discipline, or the inspiration of home," writes General Alexander, "the fighting done by the Federal brigades was of the best type." Archer was captured, with several hundred of his men, and two regiments of Davis's brigade were cut off and made prisoners.

Ewell's two leading divisions were soon at hand, and he deployed his troops facing south on a line about two miles and a half long, from the Hunterstown Road on his left to the Mummasburg Road on his right. He had been directed by Lee not to bring on an engagement, if the enemy was in force at Gettysburg, until the remainder of the Confederate army was up.

Fallen Confederate sharpshooters in the Devil's Den.

Howard's dispositions were bad, as he attempted to hold a line too long for his small forces, and his right was in the air. Ewell placed a battalion of artillery on Oak Hill, which opened fire on both angles of the Union line, enfilading the left wing, and forcing the right end back to Seminary Ridge. The reserve of the First Corps, Robinson's division, was ordered to reinforce this part of the line, one brigade facing west and the other north.

By this time, Hill's corps was coming up on the Chambersburg Road, and attacking the Union left, while Ewell was assailing their right with overwhelming numbers. Schurz called on his reserve (Steinwehr) for assistance, and tried to cover the town; but the Confederate attack was overpowering. About three o'clock the whole Union right gave way, and the troops were driven back to Cemetery Hill, with the loss of some 5000 prisoners. This retreat uncovered the Federal left, and made its position untenable. Doubleday accordingly gave the command for the First Corps to fall back to Cemetery Hill. Wadsworth's division went to Culp's Hill, and the two other divisions were posted on the left of Steinwehr, whose position became the rallying point of the Union troops. The two other divisions (Schurz and Barlow) of the Eleventh Corps were placed at the right of Steinwehr. Barlow himself had been severely wounded, and fallen into the hands of the Confederates.

About three o'clock, Hancock arrived on the scene, and took command, under orders from General Meade. He at once gave orders to establish a line of battle on Cemetery Hill.

Soon after two o'clock General Lee arrived on Seminary Ridge. Seeing the flight of the Federals through the town, he sent a staff-officer to Ewell with orders to press the pursuit, and "if possible" secure possession of the heights; but he took no steps to see that the order was obeyed. Sunset was about 7:30; twilight was long, and the moon was full; but Ewell, for some unknown reason, failed to continue the pursuit, and made no attempt to carry the heights. As General Alexander remarks: this was another striking illustration of the danger of giving conditional orders, and then failing to follow them up. If the Confederates had been prompt, they might have carried Cemetery Ridge, before the Federals were able to occupy it in force. Nevertheless the battle of the first day at Gettysburg was a Confederate success.

About one o'clock, Meade at Taneytown, hearing that Reynolds was killed or badly wounded, ordered Hancock to go in person to the front, assume command of the First (Reynolds) and Eleventh (Howard) corps, and of the Third (Sickles), then at Emmitsburg; also, if he thought the position better than Pipe Creek to fight a battle, so to advise him (Meade), and he would order up all the troops.

General Warren, the chief engineer on Meade's staff, arrived soon after Hancock, and, going over the ground together, they came to the conclusion that if the position could be held until night, it would be the best place for the army to accept battle if attacked. The Twelfth Corps (Slocum) arrived between four and five o'clock, and was placed in line with the other troops already on the ground. Hancock then sent an aide to Meade to say that he could hold the position until night. He added that, "the position at Gettysburg was a very strong one," and he left it to Meade to decide whether the battle should be fought there or at Pipe Creek. Between five and six, Slocum himself arrived, and Hancock, after transferring the command to him, returned to Taneytown.

During the afternoon, Longstreet had joined Lee on Seminary Ridge, and surveyed the Union position. He said to Lee: "We could not call the enemy to a position better suited to our plans. We have only to file around his left and secure good ground between him and his capital." To his surprise, Lee replied: "If he is there tomorrow, I shall attack him." Longstreet answered: "If he is there tomorrow, it will be because he wants you to attack him."

Late in the afternoon, Lee had a long conference with Ewell, Early, and Rodes. Ewell obtained permission to send Johnson's division to occupy Culp's Hill, a half-mile to the east of the town. But Johnson found the Federals in possession of the hill, and was not strong enough to attack this almost impregnable position. Nevertheless, says General Alexander, *"the division was allowed to remain until the end of the battle, and, as long as it remained absent, the task before the remainder of the army was beyond its strength."*

The field of the second and third days of battle at Gettysburg has already been described. The key-points of the strong defensive position occupied by the Union army were Culp's Hill, Cemetery Ridge, and the two Round Tops. The line as finally occupied was about four miles long. Its convex form gave it the advantage of interior lines of operation. The only weak point was the salient, already mentioned, where the apex of the line rested on Cemetery Hill, which was exposed to an enfilading fire from the town and its flanks and suburbs.

Meade arrived in person about one o'clock on the morning of the 2nd, and at daybreak rode over the field, assigning his troops to position. By noon, all of his army was on the field except the Sixth Corps (Sedgwick), which arrived during the afternoon, nearly exhausted after a continuous march of thirty-four miles from Manchester.

As finally arranged the Union line was formed as follows: One division (Wadsworth) of the First Corps held Culp's Hill, with the Twelfth Corps (Slocum) to the right; along Cemetery Ridge were the Eleventh Corps (Howard), the two other divisions of the First Corps (Reynolds — now commanded by Newton), the Second (Hancock) and the Third (Sickles), which prolonged the line to the Round Top on the left. The Fifth Corps (Sykes) was in reserve near the point where the Baltimore Pike crossed Rock Creek. On its arrival the Sixth Corps (Sedgwick) was also held in reserve back of the Round Tops. The artillery reserve and the ammunition trains were parked in a central position from which roads radiated to various sections of the line. The right flank was covered by the cavalry divisions of Gregg and Kilpatrick, and the left by Buford. But on the morning of the 2nd, Buford was sent to Westminster to escort the trains, and the left of the line, through some error, remained uncovered until Kilpatrick was sent over from the right the next morning.

At the base of the steep western slopes of the Round Tops flows a small marshy stream, Plum Run, beyond which, at a distance of some 500 yards, rises another wild and steep hill, known as the Devil's Den. From Cemetery Hill, the Emmitsburg Road runs southwest along a low ridge past the Peach Orchard, which lies just at the foot of the slope from Devil's Den, about a half-mile west of the lowest part of Cemetery Ridge.

Sickles, on finding the part of the line assigned him, just north of Little Round Top, to be lower than the ground in front of it at the Peach Orchard, asked leave to move his corps forward to the higher position. While General Hunt was examining the forward position, Sickles, without awaiting an answer to his request, took the grave responsibility of ordering his line to advance to the Emmitsburg Road. He placed Humphrey's division along the road, with its left at the Peach Orchard, and Birney's division on the ridge from the orchard to Devil's Den. No troops were posted on the Round Tops.

On the afternoon of the 2 July, the forces were practically all up on both sides, and the two armies faced each other across the valley between Cemetery Hill and Seminary Ridge. Meade had nearly 90,000 men and Lee about 70,000. "Except in equipment," writes General Alexander, "I think a better army ... never marched upon a battlefield." "With such soldiers," says Mr. Rhodes, "if Lee had been as great a general as Napoleon, Gettysburg had been an Austerlitz; Washington and the Union had fallen."

It was Lee's intention to attack the enemy as early as practicable on the morning of the 2nd, but much time was consumed in reconnoitring the Union position, and it was eleven o'clock before his orders were issued: "Anderson's division of Hill's corps was directed to extend Hill's line upon Seminary Ridge to the right, while Longstreet with Hood's and McLaws's

General Winfield Scott Hancock, "the Superb," (seated) took part in Pickett's charge and was wounded in the effort.

divisions should make a flank march to the right and pass the enemy's flank, which seemed to extend along the Emmitsburg Road. Forming then at right angles to the road, the attack was to sweep down the enemy's line from their left, being taken up successively by the brigades of Anderson's division as they were reached. Ewell's corps, holding the extreme left, was to attack on hearing Longstreet's guns."

Pickett's division was still at a distance, but Longstreet's other divisions (Hood and McLaws), with the exception of one brigade (Law) had bivouacked only four miles from the field. Longstreet set his men in motion at daybreak, but they halted on the way, and lost time in trying to find a route out of sight of the Union Signal Corps on Little Round Top, also in waiting for Law to come up. These incidents caused the loss of two or three hours, and "it was about 3 P.M. when Hood's division, in the advance, crossed the Emmitsburg Road about 1000 yards south of the Peach Orchard."

The centre of Lee's line was held by Hill's corps, with Anderson at the right, Pender on the left, and Heth in the rear, acting as a general reserve. Ewell's corps was on the left: Rodes's division in the town, Early's between the town and Rock Creek, and Johnson's east of the creek, under Culp's Hill.

Stuart was still absent, and Lee had only a few squadrons of cavalry, on the extreme left.

Union artillerymen who repulsed Pickett's charge.

The Confederate artillery opened fire at three o'clock against the two sides of the angle at the Peach Orchard, but it was after four o'clock when Hood advanced to the attack. The fault of Sickles's position was now obvious. No force can hold its ground when attacked on both sides of a right angle; Sickles's force had both its lines enfiladed by batteries, to the south and west, and had to yield: each side of the angle was taken in flank, and the position was untenable.

About this time Warren, who was inspecting the Union left, discovered that there were no troops on Little Round Top, the key of the position. He sent a request to Meade for a division to hold that point, and also asked Sykes, whose corps was moving to the support of Sickles, to detach two brigades and a battery to Little Round Top. The two brigades arrived just in time to drive back the right of Hood's line, which, after seizing Round Top, was on the point of occupying the other elevation.

A fierce combat now ensued for the possession of the Peach Orchard. Hood was wounded, and Law, who took command of the division, finally got possession of Devil's Den. Longstreet and Meade both hurried up reinforcements; the Federals were driven back with severe loss, and followed across the Wheat Field up the slopes of Little Round Top. Then other forces, sent by Meade, came to the rescue of the imperiled Union line, and the enemy was slowly driven back. Several other Confederate attacks were repulsed, although one brigade

(Wright) actually gained the crest of Cemetery Ridge, before it was forced to retire from lack of prompt support. This ended the battle of the second day on the right end of the Confederate line.

The faulty salient of Sickles at the Peach Orchard had been crushed in, and the defenders driven back to the main Federal line, which was still intact. Only eleven Confederate brigades — eight of Longstreet's and three of Hill's — had been engaged, while Meade had sent twenty brigades to reinforce that part of his line. Hill and Ewell, although ordered to cooperate with Longstreet's attack, had confined themselves mainly to an ineffective long-distance cannonading of the Federal entrenchments in their front. Johnson made a demonstration against Culp's Hill, but refrained from attacking; two brigades of Early's division carried a part of the Union line on Cemetery Hill, but were not supported, and were soon forced to withdraw.

The result of the day is accurately summed up by Lee: "We attempted to dislodge the enemy, and, although we gained some ground, we were unable to gain possession of his position." At 8 P.M., Meade telegraphed Halleck: "The enemy attacked me about 4 P.M. this day, and, after one of the severest contests of the war, was repulsed at all points." In brief, the small success of the Confederates was due to a succession of tardy, isolated, unsupported attacks, which showed very poor management on the part of Lee and his three corps-commanders. On the Union side, Warren and Humphreys distinguished themselves. Sickles was struck by a cannon ball that caused the loss of a leg, and was borne from the field.

General Alexander finishes his account of the day with the words: "Thus ended the second day, and one is tempted to say that thus ended the battle of Gettysburg. For of the third day it must be said, as was said of the charge of the Six Hundred at Balaklava, 'Magnificent, but not War!' "

Nevertheless, in the Union camp that night the feeling was one of gloom. On the first day, the First and Eleventh corps had been badly shattered; on the second day, the Third, the Fifth, and part of the Second, had been used up and were not in good condition to fight; only the Sixth and Twelfth corps were fresh. The army had lost nearly 20,000 men.

Soon after the fighting had ceased, Meade called a council of war, and put the question in writing, "Should the army remain in its present position or take up some other?" All voted to remain and await another attack. As the council broke up, Meade said to Gibbon, who was in temporary command of the Second Corps: "If Lee attacks tomorrow it will be on your front; because, he has made attacks on both our flanks and failed, and if he concludes to try it again, it will be on our centre." Meade has been very unjustly criticised for directing his chief-of-staff to prepare orders for retiring to Pipe Creek in case it should become necessary.

About midnight, Geary's division of the Twelfth Corps, which had been withdrawn from the extreme right of the line, returned to its former position, and was surprised to find its trenches occupied by a part of Johnson's Confederate division. This position enabled the Confederates to take the Federal line in reverse. Before dawn, Ewell reinforced Johnson with one of Early's brigades and two of Rodes's. Some other changes were made on both sides during the course of the night, but on the whole the two armies occupied about the same positions as at the close of the battle on the second day. Longstreet held the rocks and woods of the Devil's Den, the bases of the Round Tops, and the Wheat Field; and had possession of the Emmitsburg Road, at this point.

Lee believed that, with proper concert of action, and with the increased support that the artillery could give the columns from the positions gained on the right, ultimate success was possible. He accordingly decided to continue the attack. The general plan was unchanged. Longstreet, reinforced by Pickett's three brigades, was to assault the Union centre, while Ewell was to attack the right at the same time.

General Lee was aware that Cemetery Ridge was strongly held from one end to the other, but, after a careful reconnaissance of the enemy's position, he concluded that the weakest point of the line was at the angle where it approached nearest to the Emmitsburg Road, about half a mile south of the intersection of that road with the Taneytown Road. If the Confederate assaulting column could pierce the Union line at this point, it would take the entire right of the position in reverse: owing to the convexity of their line there, the Federals could not support the position by a cross artillery-fire either from the right or the left, and their troops could not fire into the backs of the victorious Confederates without endangering their comrades on the right as much as their foes. So Lee decided to make his assault at this point, and directed Longstreet to carry it out.

Longstreet, who had not been in full accord with Lee since the opening of the campaign, protested against this plan of a frontal attack. He said that, "the column would have to march a mile under concentrating battery fire, and a thousand yards under long range musketry; ... that the 15,000 men who could make successful assault over that field had never been arrayed for battle." But Lee was "impatient of listening and tired of talking," so nothing remained but to obey orders.

Before telling the story of the celebrated assault, known as "Pickett's charge," which was the event of the last day at Gettysburg, it may be well, however, to give here briefly the outcome of Johnson's battle. The effect of sending him the three brigades from Rodes and Early, says General Alexander, was "to emasculate the centre of our line and to concentrate seven brigades where they were utterly useless." Johnson had been ordered to attack at daylight, but was himself attacked by the Federals at that hour. He repulsed the assault, and attempted to follow up his success, but was in turn driven back. Heavy firing was kept up until noon, when he retired to the foot of the hill; in this position, he remained unmolested until night, and was then recalled to the west of the town. He lost 1873 men, which shows the severity of the fighting.

The formation of the infantry lines for Pickett's assault consumed a long time, and then the arrangement was one not suited for such a heavy task. For the attack, in addition to Pickett's three brigades, Lee assigned to Longstreet six brigades of Hill's corps; and one more, Wilcox of Anderson's division, was added later, making ten brigades in all. None of these brigades, except Wilcox's, had taken part in the battle of the previous day. The brigades of Garnett and Kemper formed Pickett's first line, with Armistead in second line. In the first line, on the left of Pickett's men (from right to left), were the four brigades of Archer, Pettigrew, Davis, and Brockenbrough, of Heth's division, which was commanded by Pettigrew. Behind the right of these four brigades were Scales and Lane, in second line. The six brigades in the first line comprised about 10,000 men; the three in second line about 4000, and the third line about 1000 — or 15,000 men in all. There was a distance of about 200 yards between the first and second lines. The brigade of Wilcox, which alone formed the third line, was posted in the rear of the right of the column; it was not put in motion until twenty minutes after the rest of the column — too late to be of any assistance whatever. "Both flanks of the assaulting column were in the air, and the left without any support in the rear: it was sure to crumble away under fire."

The arrangement may be represented thus: —

Brockenbrough Davis Pettigrew Archer Garnett Kemper Lane Scales Armistead

Wilcox

The front line was more than a mile long; its right was near the Peach Orchard, and its left near the southern end of an old sunken road leading out of the southwestern angle of the town.

The charge was preceded by a heavy cannonading by 115 guns on the Confederate side, replied to by 80 guns of the Federals, whose convex line did not admit of bringing into action a large part of their artillery. At the end of an hour and a half of this bombardment, which did little harm on either side, Hunt, the Union chief-of-artillery, gave the order to cease firing, as his ammunition was running low.

In the morning, Longstreet had taken Pickett to the crest of Seminary Ridge, and pointed out to him what was to be done. Alexander, in charge of the Confederate artillery, was directed to note carefully the effect of his fire, and when the favorable moment came, to give Pickett the order to advance. When the Federal fire ceased, Alexander sent word to Pickett: "For God's sake come quick, ... or my ammunition will not let me support you properly." The note reached Pickett in Longstreet's presence. He read it, and handed it to Longstreet, who read it without comment.

"General, shall I advance?" said Pickett.

Longstreet was unwilling to give the order; he turned in his saddle, and looked away.

"I am going to move forward, sir," said Pickett, as he saluted, and galloped off.

It was now about two o'clock, and Longstreet, leaving his staff, rode over to join Alexander. "I do not want to make this charge," he said, slowly and with great emotion. "I do not see how it can succeed. I would not make it now but that General Lee has ordered it and is expecting it." Alexander felt that on a word of acquiescence from him, Longstreet, even then, would have countermanded the order, but he was too conscious of his youth and inexperience to express an opinion not directly asked.

At this moment Pickett at the head of his troops rode over the crest of Seminary Ridge and descended down the slope. "As he passed me," writes Longstreet, "he rode gracefully, with his jaunty cap raked well over on his right ear, and his auburn locks, nicely dressed, hanging almost to his shoulders. He seemed a holiday soldier."

Meade still held the line of the "fishhook": Slocum at Culp's Hill; Howard at Cemetery Hill; Hancock, and Newton now commanding the First Corps, along Cemetery Ridge; Sykes and Sedgwick at the Round Tops; Birney, with Sickles's corps, in reserve behind Hancock and Sykes.

The point of attack, marked by a clump of trees which has since become famous, was held by Hancock's corps. From a point on the Emmitsburg Road about half a mile from the outskirts of Gettysburg, his line extended about 500 yards along Hay's front, the southern half along a stone wall, which continued westward 100 yards, and then ran south again, along Gibbon's front, forming the "bloody angle." Here the wall was lower, and surmounted by a country rail-fence for about 100 yards to a point directly in front of the clump of trees; south of this there was an ordinary rail-fence, which had been thrown down to form the revetment of a shallow shelter-trench.

Pickett's men had nearly a mile to go to cross the valley. They moved at a walk, keeping their lines accurately, as though on parade. Midway, they halted for a short rest in a ravine, which gave some shelter from the enemy's fire, and then moved on.

The infantry had no sooner debouched on the plain than all the Federal batteries opened fire. As the troops drew nearer, they were exposed to the front and slant fire of the Union infantry and artillery, as well as the enfilade fire of the batteries from Cemetery Hill to the Round Tops. Both flanks of the advancing line were shot to pieces, but the survivors crowded in toward the centre, and continued to advance. The groans from the battlefield were heard amidst the storm of combat. The slaughter was terrible, but still they pressed on. Stannard's brigade of the First Corps wheeled to the right and attacked the Confederates in flank and rear, adding to the confusion. Armistead leaped the stone wall, waved his sword with his hat on it, shouted, "Give them the cold steel, boys!" and laid his hand upon a gun. A hundred of his men followed; the Confederate battle-flags were planted on the crest among the cannon they had captured and for the moment held. Armistead was shot down; Garnett was killed; and their men lay literally in heaps beside them.

"A thousand fell where Kemper led;
A thousand died where Garnett bled; In blinding flame and strangling smoke, The remnant through the batteries broke,
And crossed the works with Armistead."

When Armistead fell, the wavering troops "seemed appalled, broke their ranks, and retired." The Federals attacked them on all sides, and drove the remnants back on the Confederate lines. "The conflict," writes General Alexander, "hardly seemed to last five minutes before they were melted away, and only disorganized stragglers ... were coming back."

One of Pickett's brigade commanders, Kemper, was desperately wounded, and two others were killed. Eleven field officers were slain, nine wounded, and only one escaped. Pickett himself was not injured, and no member of his staff was killed or wounded. Although he set forth so bravely at the head of his troops, he stopped part way, and never reached the Union lines.

Twenty colors were captured within a space one hundred yards square, and nearly 2000 prisoners were taken. Out of 5000 men who went into action, Pickett's division lost nearly 1400 killed and wounded, and 1500 prisoners — the total loss being about sixty per cent. The casualties in the seven other brigades were not reported separately, but were probably nearly as large.

Hancock displayed the same reckless courage as the Confederate brigadiers, and seemed to be everywhere, directing and encouraging his men, until he was struck by a ball and fell from his horse. Lying on the ground, he shouted, "Go in, Colonel, and give it to them on the flank!"

"It is a popular belief," says Colonel Livermore, "that if the gap where Armistead entered had not been closed, Meade's line would have been shattered and the battle lost. But this is far from probable. About 30,000 men were closing around the 3000 of Pickett's shattered division. ... If they had forced their way into the mass of troops that was awaiting them, what could they do? Where could they go? ... Penetrating a hostile line like that on Cemetery Ridge was like entering the jaws of a monster."

While Wilcox's brigade was making its charge, General Lee, entirely alone, rode up to Alexander's position near the Emmitsburg Road, and remained about an hour. After the charge, he seemed apprehensive of a counter-stroke by the Federals, and endeavored to rally the fugitives. He spoke to nearly every man who passed, using such words as: *Don't be discouraged. It was my fault this time. Form your ranks again when you get under cover. All good men must hold together now.*

While this great battle was raging on the field of Gettysburg, there was a fight between the horsemen of the two armies about two miles and a half east of the town. Stuart with four brigades of cavalry and four horse-batteries endeavored to reach the rear of the Union line, between the York and the Hanover roads. Here he was met by the Federal cavalry, and a combat ensued which "swayed from side to side "about the Rummel farm. Afterwards the hostile batteries engaged in an indecisive duel, "and at nightfall each side held substantially its original ground."

About an hour after this fight, Kilpatrick ordered Farnsworth, with two regiments of cavalry, to charge the rear of Longstreet's line on the slopes of Round Top. The men rode, as best they could, over rocks and creeks, stone walls and rail fences, and were shot down helplessly by the Confederate infantry. Farnsworth was killed, and a large part of his brigade was sacrificed in what has been termed a "hopeless and useless" struggle, which, however, may have prevented Longstreet from supporting Pickett's charge. As soon as the Pickett assault was repulsed, Meade went to the left of the Union line with the determination to attack the enemy. Under his orders three brigades dashed across the Wheat Field, cleared the woods in front, and captured many prisoners. Longstreet's right fell back to Seminary

Among the fallen on the field of Gettysburg.

Ridge. It was then so late in the evening that Meade abandoned the attack which he had contemplated.

The next day, which was the Fourth of July, Lee concentrated his army on Seminary Ridge in a position nearly parallel to Meade's centre and left. Slocum's corps advanced, and Howard occupied Gettysburg. It rained very heavily during portions of this day, "so violently," says Meade, "as to interrupt any very active operations if I had designed making them." During the night he learned that the enemy had retreated through the Fairfield and Cashtown passes.

The losses on both sides at Gettysburg were very heavy:

	Federals	*Confederates*
Killed	3,072	2,592
Wounded	14,497	12,709
Missing	5,434	5,150
Totals	23,003	20,451

No complete returns were ever made of the Confederate losses. Comte de Paris estimates them at 22,728, and Livermore at the much higher figure of 28,063.

Meade probably had about 85,000 combat troops on the field; and Lee some 70,000 men of all arms, after making all allowances.

On the night of the 3rd, Lee decided that he could save his army only by a retreat across the Potomac. His ammunition was nearly exhausted, no supplies of food or forage could be obtained where he was, and there was danger of his line of retreat being cut off by the enemy. On the 4th, he started his ambulances by the Chambersburg Pike under escort of a brigade of cavalry. At dark the other trains set out by the Hagerstown Road, guarded by Hill's corps. Longstreet started next, and Ewell formed the rear-guard. The withdrawal was delayed by the heavy storm, and the wounded suffered terribly.

As soon as Meade was sure that Lee had begun his retreat, on the 5th, he started Gregg's cavalry brigade in pursuit by the Pike, and Sedgwick's corps by the Hagerstown Road. The next day, the other corps marched by the Emmitsburg Road. Finding the Confederate rear-guard entrenched in the Fairfield pass, Meade gave up the direct pursuit, and moved toward the lower passes.

On the 8th, Lee's army was near Hagerstown, and the Union forces were between Frederick and Boonsboro.

On his arrival at Williamsport, Lee found that the pontoon bridge had been destroyed by Federal cavalry, and the river was so high from the recent rains as to be impassable. He therefore took up a strong position, and began to build a bridge with what material he could find, while waiting for the river to fall. He was in daily expectation of being attacked by Meade.

On the 13th, the Union army was in front of Lee's position, but Meade spent the day in reconnoitring, instead of attacking. That night Lee's army crossed the river, partly by fording, partly by the new bridge. The second invasion of the North had ended in failure, and Lee had again escaped through excess of caution on the part of the Union commander. It is difficult to see how he could have avoided capture if he had been vigorously pursued and attacked by his adversary.

Meade's excessive caution after the battle, for which he has been so severely criticised, is perhaps explained by these words of Colonel Livermore: "In the dread silence which followed the result of the great charge," he writes, "it was hard for the men of the Army of the Potomac to realize that some fearful ordeal was not awaiting them. The memory of Fredericksburg and Chancellorsville was fresh in their minds; the great captain had at times been checked before, but never defeated in so great a battle. ... A false move on Meade's part ... might turn his victory into defeat."

If Lee had been victorious, the result might have been, the capture of Baltimore and Washington, foreign intervention, the recognition of the independence of the Confederate States. Meade stood in such awe of Lee, even in defeat, that he was unwilling to take any chances. By remaining on the defensive, and forcing Lee to strike again, or to retreat, he insured the safety of the North.

There are many striking points of resemblance between the battlefields of Gettysburg and of Waterloo. On both fields the hostile armies were drawn up on two parallel ridges, separated by a shallow valley, about three-quarters of a mile wide. The Federal salient at the Peach Orchard, occupied by Sickles on the second day, corresponds to the farm of Hougomont, held by the British at Waterloo. The Codori buildings, near the centre of the field, are similar to the farm of La Haie-Sainte.

The chief point of dissimilarity is, that the main highway at Waterloo ran perpendicular to the two lines of battle, while at Gettysburg the Emmitsburg Road was nearly parallel to the lines. This road was bordered on either side by a five-bar rail fence which proved almost as formidable an obstacle to the charge of Pickett's men as did the famous "sunken road" at Waterloo to the assaults of Napoleon's Old Guard. When the Confederates reached these fences, they tried to knock them down with the butts of their muskets, but the construction was too solid, and they were forced to climb over, under a heavy short-range musketry fire, before continuing their advance.

Pickett and his staff rode through the gates into the Codori barnyard on the easterly side of the road, and there they remained until the troops came back in defeat twenty or thirty minutes later. This point was not over 200 or 300 yards from the front of the Union line at the "bloody angle."

It will always be a mooted question whether Lee was right in deciding to attack the front of the Union position, instead of outflanking it by a move to his right as advocated by Longstreet. General Maurice, in his recent biography of General Lee, expresses the opinion that Lee was correct in rejecting Longstreet's plan. But there are many reasons for thinking that Sir Frederick is wrong.

The most vulnerable point of the Union position was not the angle which Lee selected for his assault on the third day, but the Round Tops, at the extreme left of the line. There were no Federal troops on Little Round Top until after four o'clock on the afternoon of the second day, and none on Round Top until the following morning. Moreover, Buford's cavalry division, which had been posted near Round Top, to guard the left flank, had been ordered on the morning of the 2nd to Westminster, to escort the trains, and had not been replaced by Gregg's division "as General Meade had understood." The left of the line was therefore entirely uncovered. If Lee had gained possession of the Round Tops on the morning of the 2nd, as he might easily have done, he would have won a great victory. Not only would the Union position on Cemetery Ridge have been untenable, but the Confederates would have commanded the roads to Taneytown and Littlestown by which the Federals would have to retreat in order to cover Washington and Baltimore. The Taneytown Road runs at the very foot of the Round Tops, and the Baltimore Pike only a short distance to the east. The only routes available for withdrawal would then have been the roads to Hanover and York, running to the east and northeast.

Lee's decision to make a frontal attack was all the more remarkable because his two greatest victories — Second Manassas and Chancellorsville— had been won by turning movements; but on both of these occasions he had owed his success largely to the energy and skill of his great lieutenant, Jackson; and he had lost his "right arm" at Chancellorsville. It has often been remarked that after the death of Jackson, Lee never again employed these tactics. If Stonewall Jackson had been in command of the right wing at Gettysburg, instead of Longstreet, the result might have been very different. "Had I had Stonewall Jackson at Gettysburg," Lee said to his nephew, "I should have won a great victory." "In war," said Napoleon, "*men* are nothing, *a man* is everything."

The victory of Gettysburg demonstrated two things: First, that the previous defeats of the Army of the Potomac were due to its leaders, and not to its troops; Second, that the great commander who had so often beaten it was not invincible. As a military genius, Meade cannot be compared with Lee; but his success in this campaign was due mainly to his fine generalship. Lee's repeated victories had led him to believe that he could take great risks in dealing with the Army of the Potomac, and his defeat may be attributed largely to overconfidence. "With that wonderful magnanimity which Lee so fully possessed," writes his nephew, "he took all the responsibility on his own broad shoulders."

Wellington is reported to have said that the best general is not the one who makes fewest mistakes, but the one who takes most advantage of the mistakes of his opponent. Like Napoleon, Lee made some mistakes in his campaigns, but no commanders, in ancient or modern times, were more prompt than these two to take advantage of the errors of their adversaries. During the first parts of their military careers they were therefore almost invariably successful; but, later, when their opponents had profited by experience, their success was not so marked.

At Gettysburg, Lee seems to have been below his usual form: his military genius was under an eclipse. His plan of battle appears to have been dictated by chance, rather than due to mature reflection. Ewell's corps had arrived by the northerly roads, from Carlisle and York, and it was left during the battle in and around the town, where it was of little use in deciding the issue of the conflict. Hill and Longstreet, who came up by the Chambersburg Road, were placed on Seminary Ridge. Lee's line, concave in form, was fully six or seven miles long, and was held by only 70,000 men; whereas the Union line, convex in shape, was manned by 90,000, and was only about half as long.

Then, as stated by Colonel Henderson, Lee's conduct of the battle "presents a picture of mismanagement that is almost without parallel," in the career of this great commander. On the first day, he gave Ewell an order to carry Cemetery Hill "if possible," and then failed to see that his command was obeyed. If the Confederates had gained this strong position before it was held in force by the Federals, there would have been no second and third days at Gettysburg: Meade would have retired to his Pipe Creek line, and the decisive battle would have been fought there.

When Lee decided to attack the Union army in its strong position on Cemetery Ridge, he should have concentrated all of his forces on Seminary Ridge, instead of leaving Ewell in the town, and giving Johnson seven brigades to assault the impregnable Union position on Culp's Hill. As General Alexander well says: in the absence of these troops, "the task before the remainder of the army was beyond its strength."

On the second day, too much time was wasted in reconnoitring, and getting the troops into position. Then the attacks which followed were isolated, and were not properly supported. While Meade sent twenty brigades to reinforce the menaced end of his line, only eleven Confederate brigades were engaged. The three divisions of Heth, Pender, and Rodes, and four brigades, scarcely fired a shot. Nothing was really accomplished except the destruction of the faulty Federal salient at the Peach Orchard, leaving the main Union line intact.

The famous assault on the third day, known as "Pickett's charge," was certainly a mistake, as Lee himself admitted later: it had little chance of success, in any event, and none at all as made, without proper formation, and with no support. After this useless sacrifice of ten thousand of his best men, Lee had no alternative except to retreat, to save his army from destruction: his ammunition was nearly exhausted, and no supplies of food or forage could be obtained where he was.

The Federal cavalry performed excellent service during this campaign. It constantly covered its own army, and kept in touch with the Confederates, until the two forces joined battle at Gettysburg. On the first day of the battle, it held back the enemy at Willoughby Run until the infantry came up. In the opinion of Major Steele, "This was the most valuable day's work done by the cavalry in the Civil War."

On the third day, a part of the Union cavalry defeated Stuart on the right, and prevented him from molesting the Federal rear; while on the left, another part so menaced Longstreet's flank and rear as to prevent him "from assailing Round Top with vigor, or detaching a force to aid Pickett."

After the battle, the cavalry led the pursuit; it destroyed the bridge over the Potomac, and thus delayed Lee's crossing six days; it captured wagon-trains, and hindered the retreat; and two divisions attacked the Confederate rear-guard just before it passed the river, killing General Pettigrew, and capturing about 1000 prisoners.

On the other hand, the Confederate cavalry was allowed, if not ordered, by Lee, to make a useless raid around the Union army. Leaving two brigades to guard the gaps of the Blue Ridge Mountains, Stuart started on the night of the 24 June with the three brigades of Fitz Lee, Hampton, and W. H. F. Lee. He expected to make the circuit and rejoin General Lee in Maryland, but the movements of the Federal army forced him so far east that he was obliged to ford the Potomac within twenty miles of Washington on the night of the 27th. Marching northward to Rockville, where he captured a wagon-train, he pushed on to Westminster. Finding that the Union cavalry was still between him and Lee, he proceeded across country on the 30th to Hanover, where he had an engagement with Kilpatrick.

Encumbered by a useless wagon-train, with his men and horses nearly worn out, Stuart was now in a perilous position. He made a night march to York, only to learn that Early had left the previous day; then he pushed on to Carlisle, to find once more that Early had gone, and that the town was held by a force of Pennsylvania militia. That night he learned that Lee's army was concentrating at Gettysburg, and he set out for that place the next morning (2 July).

Thus ended a useless raid, which probably cost the Confederates a victory at Gettysburg. Deprived of "the eyes of his army," Lee had been groping in the dark from the time that he started for the Potomac. He told Colonel Long that Stuart's absence "had materially hampered the movements, and disorganized the plans of the campaign."

During the retreat, however, the cavalry did good work, in guarding the flank and rear of the Confederate army, and protecting its trains.

CHAPTER THIRTEEN

SEPTEMBER 1862 — JULY 1863

VICKSBURG

IN September 1862, the situation in the West was as follows: After capturing Corinth, and dispersing his army, Halleck had gone to Washington to assume the position of general-in-chief, leaving Grant in command of the troops in the vicinity of Memphis and Corinth. Grant's forces had been reduced to 42,000 men, to reinforce Buell, who was on his way to Kentucky to oppose Bragg's invasion. He was required by Halleck to guard the railway from Memphis to Decatur, 200 miles in length, and keep communications open with Buell This, for a time, constrained him to adopt a passive attitude.

Opposed to him in Mississippi were two independent commands, each about 16,000 strong. One, under Van Dorn, scattered from Holly Springs to Vicksburg, was charged with the defence of the river; the other, under Price, near Tupelo, was to guard the Mobile and Ohio south of Corinth. Learning that Rosecrans was to be detached from Grant's army, to join Buell, Bragg asked Price to attack Rosecrans, and prevent this movement. Price accordingly moved on the 14 September to Iuka, where he expected to be joined by Van Dorn for an advance to Corinth. Grant resolved to attack Price before the Confederate forces were united, and ordered Rosecrans and Ord to march on Iuka. The troops advanced by two different roads, and the movement was not well coordinated. The result was that Rosecrans attacked alone. Darkness ended the battle, and during the night Price escaped.

Rosecrans and Ord then returned to Corinth. On the 28 September, Van Dorn and Price joined forces at Ripley, and the former took command by virtue of his rank. The Confederates advanced to Corinth, where they attacked Rosecrans on the morning of the 3 October. By sunset they had driven the Federals into the works at the edge of the town. Van Dorn renewed the assault the next morning, but by noon was defeated, after a furious combat, and forced to retreat. Rosecrans made no pursuit until the next day, and the Confederates retired to Holly Springs. General Pemberton was then sent to take the general command of the Confederate forces in Mississippi, and General Rosecrans relieved Buell of the command of the Army of the Ohio.

General Grant was now reinforced, and toward the end of October he felt strong enough to attempt the advance on Vicksburg, which he had long had in mind. His headquarters were then at Jackson, Tennessee. His right wing at Memphis, under Sherman, consisted of 7000 men; his centre at Bolivar, under Hurlbut, of 19,000; his left at Corinth, under Hamilton, of 17,500; with about 5000 more at Columbus, his base, under Dodge — a total of 48,500 men.

View of Vicksburg from an old postcard.

Pemberton had made his headquarters at Jackson, Mississippi, where he had 2000 troops; Van Dorn, at Holly Springs, had some 24,000 men, in two divisions under Price and Lovell; Vicksburg was garrisoned by 6000, and Port Hudson by 5500 — in all 37,500 men.

Grant's plan was to abandon Corinth, after destroying the railroads around it; concentrate his forces at Grand Junction, and move upon Vicksburg by way of the Mississippi Central Railroad. But his letter of 26 October to Halleck remained unanswered, and it was a full month before he got started.

Unknown to Grant, McClernand was then in Washington working out a secret scheme with the President, and the Secretary of War, to raise a volunteer army in Indiana, Illinois, and Iowa, and lead it down the Mississippi to capture Vicksburg. Although he had had no military training, McClernand had handled his division very creditably at Donelson and Shiloh. As an Illinois politician, he had long been known to Mr. Lincoln, and he succeeded in winning the President and Mr. Stanton to his plan. To the credit of General Halleck, it must be said that he was not in favor of this scheme. As a professional soldier he realized the defects of a plan which proposed an advance against the same point by two independent expeditions: it was contrary to military principles, ruinous to discipline, and full of the seeds of disaster. To make matters worse, Grant was kept ignorant of the whole scheme, and was so puzzled by Halleck's brief enigmatical telegrams that his own movements were embarrassed.

The Mississippi is the most crooked of all the great rivers of the world. In many places it is necessary for a boat to traverse thirty miles to reach a point ten miles distant from its starting place. The river flows through a soft alluvial soil, in which it cuts new channels to the right or left on meeting the slightest obstacle to its direct course. It is lined by natural dikes, created by the deposits of sediment along the banks, and by artificial "levees" constructed by the people who live along the stream. For twenty miles on either side of the great river the land is

Confederate forts on the heights at Port Hudson.

intersected by a network of "bayous," or sluggish streams as crooked as the Mississippi itself. The river basin is covered with dense forests of cypress and other trees. In such a country it is manifest that armies could not operate, and that, upon these low, flat shores, fortifications could not be erected.

But to this rule there were a few notable exceptions. At points like Columbus, Memphis, Vicksburg, Grand Gulf, and Port Hudson, there are bluffs rising from 80 to 200 feet sheer above the turbid stream. Fortifications erected at such points were unassailable from the river. A ship's guns could not be elevated sufficiently to inflict any damage, and the vessels were subjected to a destructive plunging fire.

Of all these points along the river, Vicksburg was the strongest. To a fleet it was inaccessible, and to an army nearly so. The city crowns the bluffs at a height of 200 feet above the river, which washes the cliffs for a distance of eleven miles below the place. Grand Gulf is 60 miles, and Port Hudson 250 miles further down the river, but much nearer in a direct line.

Between Vicksburg and Port Hudson, the Mississippi was joined on the west by the Red River, the great highway by which the states of Texas, Louisiana, and Arkansas were connected with the central and eastern sections of the Confederacy. Vicksburg and its outpost Port Hudson were therefore places of the highest strategical importance. Their capture would cut off the great granary from which the Confederacy was largely supplied with food, and destroy nearly half its power of resistance.

The Mississippi between these two points was entirely in the hands of the enemy. The Federal fleet at New Orleans could not pass above Port Hudson, nor the one at Helena go below Vicksburg. No Union army could land on the eastern bank of the river between these two fortresses without being cut off from its source of supplies.

Above the city the bluffs swerve in a northeasterly direction, and away from the Mississippi, but near to its tributary, the Yazoo. Here, twelve miles above Vicksburg, the Yazoo washes the base of Haynes's Bluff, which commands all the river approaches. This position, which had been strongly fortified by the Confederates, rendered the city inaccessible from the north.

Vicksburg, therefore, could only be assailed from the rear; and here, too, the rugged country, broken by deep ravines, presented formidable obstacles to an enemy. No more arduous task had ever confronted a general than the reduction of this "Gibraltar" of the Confederacy.

By the 5 November, Grant had reached Oxford, and Van Dorn, under orders from Pemberton, had fallen back to Grenada. As Grant's line of communications, by a single-track railway back to Columbus, Kentucky, was now more than 200 miles long, he established a secondary base at Holly Springs.

The first movement of Grant against Vicksburg was a continuation of the same strategy which had been so effective in the previous campaigns in the West. By moving south on a line parallel to the Mississippi, the river had been conquered all the way from Cairo to Vicksburg. One after another, the series of Confederate strongholds, at Columbus, Island No. 10, Fort Pillow, and Memphis, had become untenable, and had been abandoned. But now the conditions were different, for reasons which will be explained presently, and the length of the line of communications made a further advance almost impossible.

As Napoleon once said, every army, like a serpent, moves on its belly. In the densely populated centres of Europe an army can often live off the country, but this was seldom the case in the South. The food, forage, and ammunition, had to be brought to the armies. While the lines were near the great rivers — the Mississippi, the Tennessee, and the Cumberland — the problem was a very easy one, but the insecurity of the railroads rapidly increased with the length from the base, as it was impossible to guard them from the raids of the enemy's cavalry. The weight of food, ammunition, and other supplies, required by each soldier, averaged four pounds daily. The animals necessary for the cavalry, artillery, and trains, consumed twenty-five pounds of forage. In the present century, the problem of keeping an army supplied has been much simplified by the use of motors, but in December 1862, it required 1900 wagons, drawn by 11,000 animals, to keep Grant's army supplied at three days' march from its base. The army could not travel more than three days without shifting its base along the line of some river or railroad; and this base must be securely connected by river or rail with some permanent base established in a region entirely under Federal control.

After considerable correspondence, it was finally arranged with Halleck that Sherman should return with one division to Memphis; there pick up the newly arrived troops, and organize an expedition to move down the river to Haynes's Bluff, under escort of Porter's gunboats, while Grant marched his army along the left bank of the Yazoo to the same objective point. Sherman arrived at Memphis on the 12 December, and started down the river on the 20th.

But Grant was prevented from carrying out his part of the program. Forrest's cavalry tore up sixty miles of the railway north of Jackson, Tennessee, and another mounted force captured the Union garrison at Holly Springs and destroyed all the Union supplies at that base.

Grant's initial attempt to take Vicksburg was unsuccessful. Here is pictured the Courthouse in Oxford, Mississippi where his advance was halted.

Grant was forced to place his army on short rations, and fall back along the railway to a point where he could open communications with Memphis.

In the meantime Sherman had descended the river with his force of 32,000 men, and landed at Milliken's Bend, twenty-five miles above Vicksburg. On the 29th he assaulted the Confederate works at Haynes's Bluff, but was repulsed with heavy loss. The position was held by 12,000 troops sent there by Pemberton, and was too strong to be carried. On the 2 January, Sherman reembarked his men, and returned to the mouth of the Yazoo. Here he was met by McClernand, with an order assigning that general to the command of the expedition. Thus ended in failure Grant's first movement against Vicksburg.

Upon assuming command of the Union force near Vicksburg, which he called the "Army of the Mississippi," McClernand divided it into two corps, under Morgan and Sherman. He then moved his army about fifty miles up the Arkansas River, and attacked Fort Hindman, which surrendered on the 11 January, with 5000 prisoners. There he was contemplating what General Grant called a "wild-goose chase" further into Arkansas, when he was recalled by a peremptory order from Grant. Halleck, when informed of McClernand's operation, authorized Grant to relieve McClernand, and supersede him by the next in rank, or to take command of the Vicksburg expedition in person. Grant thought that the easiest way of solving the problem was to assume the command himself, which he did on the 30 January. He then reorganized the expeditionary force in four corps, under the command of McClernand, Sherman, Hurlbut, and McPherson. McClernand protested bitterly over his removal from the command of the Vicksburg movement, but the Washington authorities paid no attention to his complaints.

We do not propose to relate here in minute detail the history of Grant's work during February and March. His plans were foredoomed to failure, and except as showing the tenacity of the man — his grim determination to succeed in the face of the most appalling difficulties — the story possesses but few points of interest.

A little below the mouth of the Yazoo, the Mississippi turns sharply to the northeast, and after flowing five miles in that direction, it makes another equally abrupt bend to the southwest, enclosing a peninsula less than two miles in width, nearly opposite Vicksburg. McClernand and Sherman were ordered to set their men to digging a canal across this narrow neck of land. By this passage Grant hoped to transfer his army south of Vicksburg, there cross the river, and attack the town from the rear.

This plan was the simplest, and apparently the most promising of all. The distance was not much over a mile, but as the canal was designed to admit vessels of sixty feet beam and nine feet draught, considerable excavation was required. The chief problem, however, was to keep the water out during the progress of the work. After six weeks of hard labor, success seemed assured, when, on the 8 March, a sudden rise in the river broke the dam, and flooded not only the bed of the canal but also the surrounding country. From the first, Grant had but little confidence in this plan, as he had observed that the lower end of the canal would enter the river just opposite the bluffs at Warrenton, a few miles below Vicksburg. Indeed, just before the break occurred, the enemy planted batteries on these heights, which completely commanded the southern end of the canal, so that even if finished it would have been of little use.

Grant's second experiment was carried on simultaneously with the canal work. About seventy miles above Vicksburg, on the west side of the river, there is a remnant of one of the numerous deserted beds of the stream, known as Lake Providence. This lake connected with the Red River, by a tortuous system of waters, navigable almost the entire distance. By this roundabout route of 400 miles, the ships could avoid the guns of Vicksburg, and bring supplies and reinforcements to the army below the city. McPherson's men were ordered to clear a passage through Bayou Macon, the only point at which the channel was obstructed. As soon as this work was completed, it was proposed to break the levees east of the lake, and let in the waters of the Mississippi; but all the obstacles had not been overcome when Grant abandoned the plan for the one which finally proved successful.

The third plan was, to find a passage for the army down the east side of the river, so as to turn the enemy's strong position at Bluff. Just south of Helena, about 150 miles above Vicksburg in a straight line, there is a winding bayou, some 80 feet wide by 30 feet deep, known as the Yazoo Pass. This route, in former times, had been used by vessels plying between Vicksburg and Memphis. Later, it had been closed by a strong levee, 18 feet high and 100 feet thick, because the waters from the river overflowed so much land that they became a nuisance. On the 2 February this levee was destroyed by a mine, and the river let in to its old channel. But this route was obstructed by the enemy, who felled large trees across the stream, so as to make a formidable barricade. Before this obstacle could be removed, the Confederates constructed a strong earthwork, called Fort Pemberton, in a commanding position on a peninsula where two rivers unite to form the Yazoo. Here they mounted several heavy guns, and completely barred the descent of the river. So this experiment also failed.

One more attempt was made, on the east side of the river, to outflank Haynes's Bluff by utilizing the Big Sunflower River, which empties into the Yazoo 100 miles below Fort Pemberton. But the stream was obstructed by the Confederates, and the transports were attacked by a considerable force. The situation became so perilous that Sherman was obliged to back out.

Almost any other commander, except Grant, would have been entirely disheartened by these repeated fiascos, and have abandoned further efforts. The press was calling for his removal, and he had to do something. Only three plans seemed feasible: (1) To assault the Confederate batteries at Vicksburg, which would have been suicidal; (2) to return to Memphis and renew his attempt along the line of the railway, which presented no greater promise of success than before; or (3), to find some way of transporting his army to a point below Vicksburg, cross the river there, and attack the town from the rear, without any base of supplies. He chose the third plan.

The idea of Grant's final plan was suggested by the success of the gunboats, on several occasions in February and March, in running by the dreaded batteries at Vicksburg and Port Hudson. On the 2 February Porter sent a ram down; and ten days later a gunboat also made the passage without any damage. On the 14 March, Farragut, in his flagship the *Hartford*, with one consort, succeeded in passing the batteries at Port Hudson, although four other vessels were disabled and one destroyed. From this time forth, the Federals were able to close the mouth of the Red River.

Having decided upon his course, Grant went ahead regardless of the opinions of his generals. Every one of them, including even the sanguine Sherman, thought that it was sheer madness to cross south of Vicksburg. Having concentrated his army at Milliken's Bend, on the 29 March McClernand's corps was ordered to lead the way to New Carthage, twenty-seven miles below. By constructing corduroy roads Grant was able to move his troops and a large part of his supplies by land. On the night of the 16 April, ten shiploads of rations and forage, under convoy of the gunboats, made the passage of the forts without serious damage. Ten days later another squadron ran the gauntlet successfully; and now at last Grant was ready to cross the river.

Vicksburg

The point selected for crossing was Grand Gulf, opposite the hamlet of Hard Times where the army was concentrated. The fortress of Grand Gulf, on a bluff twenty-five miles below Vicksburg, formed the extreme left of the defences of the city. On the 29 April, the works were bombarded for five hours by Porter's fleet, but no impression was made. It was therefore necessary to select another point for the crossing. During the night the fleet, convoying the

The battlefield at Champion's Hill.

transports and supply ships, ran by the batteries, and the army marched farther down the right bank.

Grant was now informed by a slave that there was a good road from Bruinsburg, six miles below Grand Gulf, to Port Gibson twelve miles inland. The next day McClernand's corps was ferried over on the transports, and McPherson's corps immediately followed. In the meantime the attention of the enemy was completely absorbed by a demonstration made by Sherman in front of Haynes's Bluff. He now received orders from Grant to follow the other troops and cross at Bruinsburg.

Before continuing the story of the Vicksburg campaign, let us see what the Confederates were doing at this time. At the end of March, Pemberton had in Mississippi about 50,000 troops, scattered at different points. The line from Haynes's Bluff to Grand Gulf was held by 22,000; Port Hudson had a garrison of about 16,000; at Fort Pemberton and neighboring points there were some 7000; and in the northern part of the state perhaps 5000 more. All the cavalry had been sent to Bragg, and there was none in the state.

On the 17 April, Grierson left Lagrange, on his famous raid, and reached the Union camp at Baton Rouge on the 2 May. With 1000 men he rode the entire length of the state of Mississippi, covering 600 miles in 16 days, and destroying many miles of railway and telegraph lines, besides much other property. The Confederates were kept in a wild state of alarm, and, far more important than this, their attention was distracted at the most critical moment of the campaign — while Grant was crossing the river. "In its strategic effect," says Major Steele, "this was perhaps the most successful cavalry raid of the Civil War."

As soon as Pemberton, who was at Jackson, heard of the attack on Grand Gulf, he ordered reinforcements sent there from Vicksburg. By night two brigades had arrived, and one of these marched on toward Port Gibson. By daybreak on the first of May, this brigade, with one other which McClernand had encountered on his march, was in position in front of the Union corps. The combat opened at dawn. McClernand's whole corps, of 18,000 men, was soon on the ground, but the country was so difficult to manoeuvre on, that it was not easy to beat the Confederates, although they were outnumbered three to one. They finally gave way about five o'clock, and retreated to Grand Gulf, by two different routes, burning all the bridges behind them.

Pemberton hastened to Vicksburg, where he spent the following day in sending telegrams in every direction to collect his scattered forces. The Confederates, fleeing from the field of Port Gibson, stopped at Grand Gulf long enough to blow up the magazines and dismount the guns, and then started for Vicksburg by way of Hankinson's Ferry. At the ferry they met three brigades sent to their assistance, and were also joined by some troops from Jackson. The whole body then marched to Vicksburg, which the soldiers reached in a more or less demoralized condition.

Grant occupied Grand Gulf on the day after the battle, and established his base there. McPherson followed the retreating Confederates to the ferry, and halted there; McClernand bivouacked at Willow Spring. The two corps remained in these positions for three days, awaiting the arrival of ammunition and rations. Sherman crossed at Grand Gulf on the 7th, and Grant then had his entire force of 43,000 men concentrated on the east side of the river.

As previously stated, the forces of Pemberton were very badly dispersed. About 15,000 men were at Port Hudson, a place almost as important to hold as Vicksburg. Over 20,000 men were posted at Vicksburg, and this left only about 15,000 troops available to oppose Grant in the field.

Halleck had notified Grant that he was expected to cooperate with Banks in the reduction of Port Hudson and Vicksburg, but that officer was then absent from his headquarters at Baton Rouge in an expedition against the Confederates on the Red River. After crossing the river Grant received a letter from Banks, stating that he could not get back before the 10 May. Under all the circumstances, Grant decided that he could not wait. He resolved to advance at once against the railway from Vicksburg to Jackson, so as to place his army between the

Confederate garrison in the fortress, and the army which it was rumored that the enemy was assembling at the state capital. This was the critical moment in Grant's career, upon which his whole future turned. "To face the difficulties in the way of such a movement," says Mr. Fiske, "required the stoutest of hearts and the coolest of heads."

Grant was ignorant of the numbers and the exact positions of his adversaries. Unlike many Union commanders, he was apt to underrate, rather than to overestimate, the enemy's strength, but he assumed that there were about 30,000 men at Jackson. He had heard that Joseph E. Johnston was on his way from Chattanooga to take command in person, and he anticipated that troops would be rushed from every point to oppose him. His plan was to beat the two hostile forces in detail: first driving Johnston eastward, then turning upon Pemberton, defeating him, and pushing him back into Vicksburg. In order to do this, he must keep his army together; he could not spare any forces to guard his line of communications, and must cut loose from his base altogether, relying for supplies only upon what the men could carry with them or what they could find in the country. No general ever adopted a more daring scheme: there was no precedent for it in modern warfare. It seemed like defying Fortune outright. None of his generals approved of the plan, and Halleck forbade it as soon as the news reached Washington; but Grant was fortunately beyond the reach of the telegraph, and the order did not reach him until success was achieved.

Grant began his advance on the 7 May, as soon as Sherman arrived. His force consisted of the three corps of McClernand, McPherson, and Sherman — about 43,000 men. He had a train of 120 wagons, and the men carried five days' rations. Foraging parties were sent out every night to scour the country for food and forage.

Grant's movements were admirably calculated to mask his purpose. Small detachments were sent west of the Big Black to threaten Vicksburg and keep Pemberton in the city. The left wing under McClernand marched up the eastern bank of the Big Black toward Edwards's Station on the Vicksburg and Jackson railway, about midway between the two cities. The right wing under McPherson was directed toward Jackson by way of Bolton, and, after destroying the railroad and public stores, was to rejoin the main army. Sherman was to follow in the rear of McClernand, or midway between him and McPherson if he could find a road, and within supporting distance of the two wings. It was Napoleon's favorite movement of two wings with a central reserve column.

On the 12 May, McPherson encountered about 5000 Confederates in a strong position at Raymond and routed them after a sharp fight of about two hours. He then continued his advance on Jackson, supported by Sherman.

On the 9 May, Johnston had received orders at Tullahoma to proceed at once to Jackson, and take command of the forces in Mississippi. On his arrival there four days later, he found the brigades of Gregg and Walker. Two more brigades, Gist's and Maxey's, were expected to arrive on the 14th. This would give him 15,000 men, but Grant was too quick for him.

On the morning of the 14th, Sherman and McPherson were before Jackson. The flank of Gregg's brigade was enveloped by Sherman, and it was forced to retreat. Walker occupied a very strong position, and made more of a fight; but he could not resist the charge of McPherson's troops, and his brigade was soon driven from its trenches. The Confederates escaped by the Canton Road, and Sherman and McPherson entered Jackson between three and four o'clock in the afternoon. That night Grant slept in the house which Johnston had occupied the night before.

On receiving Pemberton's telegram, stating that Grant had crossed the river, Johnston replied: "Unite all your troops to beat him — success will give you back what was abandoned to win it." Pemberton should have advanced to Clinton, and attacked Grant in the rear; but he thought that sound strategy required him to seize Grant's line of communications to Grand Gulf. It never entered his head that Grant had done anything so rash as to abandon his base! Accordingly, he wasted his time in marching down toward Raymond.

Grant did not tarry long at Jackson. He faced his army to the westward, and started for Vicksburg, leaving Sherman to burn the bridges, factories, and arsenals at Jackson, and destroy the railroads for twenty miles in every direction. Johnston had retreated to Canton thirty miles north of the capital. From that place he telegraphed Pemberton, on the 16th, to march to Clinton, where he expected to unite all his forces. But Grant's army was already at Bolton, ten miles west of Clinton, and it was impossible for Pemberton to comply with the order.

On the 15th, Grant marched by the different convergent roads on Edwards's Station, where Pemberton was posted with three divisions, about 23,000 men; his two remaining divisions were at Vicksburg. On the night of the 15th the lines of the two armies were only about four miles apart, but neither commander seems to have been aware of the nearness of the other.

On the morning of the 16 May, the Confederates were found in line of battle in a strong position a little south of the railway, about three miles west of Bolton. Their left wing occupied the crest of an elevation some 70 feet in height, known as Champion's Hill. The knoll was steep and rugged and covered with timber on the northern side, but gentler and partly cleared on the eastern and southern slopes. The bald crest was covered with artillery. Pemberton had about 18,000 men to hold his line, which stretched for two miles south of the hill. Grant had the two corps of McClernand and McPherson. The fighting was almost all done by McPherson's corps and one division (Hovey's) of McClernand's, on the Union right, directed by Grant in person. The possession of the hill was stubbornly contested: it was taken and retaken several times. It required eight hours of severe fighting to dislodge the Confederates. McClernand, on the Union left, practically did nothing. If he had attacked as vigorously as McPherson, the defeated Confederates would have been cut off from the ford over Baker's Creek, on the Raymond road, and been captured.

Grant lost about 2500 men. The Confederate losses were 1400 killed and wounded, 2500 prisoners, and all their artillery; while one division of 4000 men, cut off from the rest of the army, fled to the southeast many miles beyond Jackson. Practically half of Pemberton's army had been destroyed, and the rest retreated in disorder toward Vicksburg. That evening Grant received Halleck's telegram! He had staked everything, but he had won: Vicksburg was doomed.

Sherman arrived at Bolton on the night of the battle. Grant took up the pursuit with his entire army at daylight on the 17th. The railway crossing was in a deep bend of the Big Black, and this point was defended by about 5000 of the retreating Confederates. The head of Grant's column came up about eight o'clock, and drove the enemy from this position after a fight of less than an hour. The Confederates abandoned 18 pieces of artillery, and 1750 men were captured. They succeeded however in burning the bridge, which delayed the Federals for a whole day.

Next day, the 18th, while the two other corps marched directly on Vicksburg, Sherman occupied the Benton Road, in the rear of Haynes's Bluff, thus rendering that stronghold untenable. It was immediately abandoned by the Confederates, with all its guns and stores, and Sherman had the satisfaction of occupying this fortress which had defied him only a few months before.

On the 18th, Pemberton received an order from Johnston to evacuate Vicksburg, if not too late, and save his army. Pemberton called a council of war, which decided that it was too late to withdraw, thus exemplifying Napoleon's maxim that these meetings always "terminate in the adoption of the worst course, which in war is ever the most timid." Pemberton therefore made no effort to obey Johnston's order.

Before two o'clock on the afternoon of the 19th, Grant's three corps were in position in front of the city— Sherman's on the right, McPherson's in the centre, and McClernand's on the left. Grant thought that the works might be carried by a vigorous assault, before the Confederates had recovered from their demoralization; he therefore ordered an immediate attack, but it failed all along the line.

Anxious to avoid the long and dreary work of a siege, Grant ordered another assault on the 22nd, which also was repulsed. The attack was continued after Grant was satisfied that it could not succeed, because of McClernand's mendacious reports of success on his part of the line. Grant lost over 3000 men, due largely to these misleading reports of McClernand's.

It was now plain that Vicksburg could only be taken by a regular siege, and preparations were begun at once. The ground about the city is much cut up by ravines and small streams, and is admirable for defence. The line of the enemy was about seven miles long; that of Grant, more than fifteen miles, extending around the city from Haynes's Bluff on the north to Warrenton on the south. He also had a second line to the east, as a defence against attacks by Johnston in the rear. He had not troops enough at first to man all these works, but Halleck forwarded reinforcements at once.

Grant had no siege-guns except six 32-pounders, but Admiral Porter supplied him with a battery of navy-guns of large calibre, and with these, and the field-artillery, the siege began. Within a short time, Grant had 248 guns in his line, and about 75,000 men in his investing force. Approaches were dug, and mines and counter-mines set off. On the first of July the approaches were all within a few yards of the enemy's works. Orders were issued for a final assault on the 6th. But this was not to be: on the 4 July Pemberton capitulated, after a siege of forty-seven days.

Grant at first demanded his usual terms of "unconditional surrender," but, for reasons stated in his *Memoirs* later agreed to release the Confederates under parole, and also granted them the privilege of marching out with flying colors to stack arms.

With the single exception of Napoleon's capture of the Austrian army at Ulm in 1805, where he took 23,000 men and 60 cannon, there had been no such surrender in modern history.

Over 29,000 men laid down their arms, and 172 cannon were taken. Sedan and Metz were in the future.

To find a parallel to this campaign, we must go back to Napoleon's first campaign in Italy in 1796. In eighteen days Grant marched 200 miles, and with a loss of 4000 men defeated two armies in five engagements, taking nearly 100 cannon, and destroying or capturing 12,000 of the enemy. Including the capture of Vicksburg, he put *hors de combat* 40,000 Confederates, and took nearly 300 cannon. This achievement by itself is sufficient to put Grant in the foremost rank of the second-rate captains of history, in the same class with Turenne, Marlborough, Wellington, and the Archduke Charles.

The capture of Vicksburg, with the simultaneous victory at Gettysburg, marked the turning-point of the Civil War. There were still many gloomy days to come, but the final outcome was no longer in doubt. Port Hudson surrendered to Banks five days later, and on the 16th a merchant vessel tied up to the wharf at New Orleans after an eight days' run from St. Louis. In the striking words of President Lincoln, "the Father of Waters rolled unvexed to the sea."

At the end of June, Johnston, who had finally succeeded in collecting an army of 25,000 men, advanced as far as Edwards's Station. But on the night of the 4 July, on hearing of Pemberton's surrender, he retreated rapidly to Jackson, with Sherman in hot pursuit. Sherman, who had about 30,000 men, refused to attack, but prepared for a siege. Johnston was not to be caught in a trap like Pemberton; on the night of the 16th he skillfully made his escape, and went into camp midway between Jackson and Meridian.

"Not a mistake of strategy can be pointed out in Grant's operations," says Major Steele, "and scarcely a mistake of tactics was made by his subordinate commanders." Grant was fortunate in having two such able corps-commanders as Sherman and McPherson. During the siege of Vicksburg, McClernand issued a congratulatory address to his corps, full of inuendoes against the other troops and their commanders. It was published in the Illinois papers, and was evidently intended for political effect. In flat defiance of army regulations, no copy was sent to headquarters, and for this act of insubordination, Grant sent him home to Illinois, appointing Ord to succeed him. So ended the stormy military career of McClernand.

Grant's effective forces during the campaign ranged from 43,000 at the beginning to 75,000 at the close.

According to Johnston's reports, his forces at no time exceeded 24,000. Pemberton's greatest available force probably numbered over 40,000.

The losses on both sides during the last two months of the campaign were as follows:

	Federals	*Confederates*
Killed	1,514	1,260
Wounded	7,395	3,572
Missing	453	4,227
Totals	9,362	9,059

According to the parole-lists on file at the War Department the number surrendered at Vicksburg was 29,491.

CHAPTER FOURTEEN

JANUARY — SEPTEMBER 1863

CHICKAMAUGA

AFTER the battle of Murfreesboro, during the first days of January 1863 Rosecrans occupied the town, and kept his headquarters there until the last week in June. During the same period, Bragg was strongly fortified at Shelbyville and Tullahoma, with his headquarters at the latter place. His cavalry was thrown well north of Duck River, and extended from Spring Hill on the west to McMinnville on the east. Polk's corps was at Shelbyville; Hardee's headquarters were at Wartrace, and his infantry held Hoovers, Liberty, and Bellbuckle gaps, passes in a range of rough rocky hills which covered his front toward Murfreesboro.

Although the two armies remained practically immobile during this half-year, the cavalry on both sides were very active. Each general was striving to cut the other's communications, and the cavalry operations almost assumed the proportions of campaigns. In January, an attempt of the Confederates to capture Fort Donelson was repulsed, and their cavalry lost 1000 men. In April, a Union force penetrated far into Georgia, and burned the important Round Mountain Ironworks, but the whole force of 1500 men was finally captured by Forrest.

The Union cavalry was greatly outnumbered by the squadrons of Forrest, Morgan, and Wheeler, and Rosecrans appealed, but in vain, to the War Department for an adequate force. He finally mounted Wilder's infantry brigade on captured horses, and it did good work during the campaign. The efficiency of the Confederate cavalry is shown by the report of the Louisville and Nashville Railroad for the year ending 30 June 1863. During this period, there were but seven months and twelve days when trains could run over the whole length of the road. Every bridge had been destroyed and rebuilt within the year — many of them several times. The tunnel at Gallatin was choked with rubbish for a distance of 800 feet, and could not be used for days. At times the Federal troops were on half rations; vegetables could not be had in quantity sufficient to keep off scurvy; and forage was scarce.

Although possessed of many amiable traits, Rosecrans was very irascible, and was constantly wrangling with Lincoln, Stanton, and Halleck. They were continually urging him to move against Bragg, and drive him out of Tennessee, but he always complained that something was wrong which should be righted at Washington.

In the spring Halleck hit on a new device for hastening matters. He wrote Grant and Rosecrans offering the rank of major-general in the regular army as a prize to the first commander who should win an important success. Grant treated the offer with a quiet disdain

The hotel at Stevenson, Alabama during the Union advance that ended in Chickamauga. The hotel was the temporary headquarters of the Army of the Cumberland.

which was more eloquent than words; but the fiery Rosecrans replied that he felt "degraded at such an auctioneering of honors," and thereby incurred the enmity of the incompetent Halleck, as well as of the despotic and passionate Stanton.

Meanwhile, by orders of the War Department, the Army of the Cumberland had been organized into three corps: the Fourteenth under Thomas, the Twentieth under McCook, and the Twenty-first under Crittenden, comprising practically the same divisions which had made up the Centre, Right Wing, and Left Wing, during the Murfreesboro Campaign. In addition Rosecrans formed a Reserve Corps of three brigades under General Gordon Granger. The army numbered some 60,000 men, while Bragg had about 43,000. At the same time, East Tennessee was occupied by a Confederate corps under Buckner; and Burnside, at Cincinnati, was organizing the Army of the Ohio, for an advance into East Tennessee from Kentucky by way of Cumberland Gap.

The last week in June the general situation in both theatres of the war was as follows:
In the East, Lee was on his way to Gettysburg; in the West, Grant had Pemberton's army
invested at Vicksburg, Burnside was advancing on Cumberland Gap, and Rosecrans at last
was ready to move.

On the 23 June Rosecrans issued his orders for the advance. As the Confederate position
at Shelbyville was nearly impregnable in front, Rosecrans made only a feint against this point
with Granger's Reserve Corps and most of his cavalry, while he massed his three main corps
against Bragg's right at Wartrace. There was some fighting at the gaps, but the Confederate

Vicinity of Chattanooga

right was forced back from one position to another, and the left had to retire to keep from being cut off. On the 30 June the Union army was concentrated at Manchester, and Bragg was
forced to abandon his position at Tullahoma. By the end of the first week in July the Confederate army was back in Chattanooga.

In a period of nine days of continuous rain, by brilliant strategy, with the loss of only
583 men, Rosecrans had manoeuvred the Confederate army out of its natural and artificial
strongholds, and forced it across the Tennessee. Up to this time there had been no strategic
campaign so brilliant in plan and execution, and General Rosecrans was warmly congratulated by all his corps-commanders, under the lead of General Thomas.

At the end of the short Tullahoma campaign the two armies occupied nearly the same positions as the previous year, when the Army of the Cumberland, then under Buell, was preparing for an aggressive campaign against Chattanooga. The Union army was encamped along the western base of the Cumberland Mountains from Winchester to McMinnville, a distance of forty miles. As usual, there was soon a feeling at Washington of irrational impatience over what seemed to be the lack of energy on the part of the Union commander. But time was needed to accumulate the supplies of every kind necessary for the campaign; also to acquire information regarding the mountain passes by which the army must move. The railroad by which supplies reached the army also had to be repaired, and this work was not completed until the last week in July. On the 14 August the advance began.

The most direct approach to Chattanooga was by the left over Walden Ridge, a spur of the Cumberland Mountains. The principal objection to that route was that it would necessitate a long line of communications over steep and narrow roads. The only other feasible route was by the right through Bridgeport and Stevenson, and over the mountains of northern Alabama and Georgia. This was finally adopted, because it would keep the army near the railway and its base of supplies, although there stood in the way a number of mountain ranges, hard to climb, and passable only at a few narrow defiles.

After crossing the Cumberland range west of the Tennessee, and the river itself, there is a series of mountain ridges, valleys, and streams, generally parallel to the river, on the eastern side. First, there is Raccoon Mountain, which ends in a mass of rough ridges and gorges, enclosed in a deep bend of the Tennessee, about four miles west of Chattanooga. Next comes Lookout Valley, beyond which is Lookout Mountain, which ends abruptly four miles south of Chattanooga in a commanding point of rock, rising from the edge of the river. From the summit of its steep palisades, 1400 feet above the swift current of the Tennessee, on a clear day parts of seven states can be seen, spread out in a magnificent panorama. Below, on the easterly side, is the valley of Chattanooga, through which flows Chattanooga Creek. Near the mouth of the creek stands the city, superbly situated in the midst of a great amphitheatre of hills. On the further side the valley is enclosed by Missionary Ridge, which also extends up to the river. Four miles south of the town this ridge is traversed by Rossville and McFarland's gaps, beyond which lies Chickamauga Valley, the scene of the battle.

At their upper or southern ends the valleys of Chattanooga and Chickamauga unite in a single valley known as McLemore's Cove. Beyond Pigeon Mountain and Taylor's Ridge, to the east, are the towns of Ringgold and Dalton, stations on the railroad from Chattanooga to Atlanta, where Bragg had his base of supplies.

The valleys were generally covered with timber, but there were some farms, and a few villages. There were no turnpikes, but good country roads through the valleys and the gaps in the mountains. The theatre was somewhat similar to that of Tullahoma, but different from any other in which a campaign had been carried on in this war.

The plan finally adopted by Rosecrans was to move his army directly across these formidable mountain barriers, and aim straight at Dalton, where he would be squarely on Bragg's line of communications. This would compel the enemy to evacuate Chattanooga or stand a siege there. The more effectually to mask his movements, Rosecrans kept his left wing under

Pine Mountain where General Lieutenant Leonidas Polk was killed. Polk was the nephew of President Polk and an Episcopal bishop in Louisiana before joining the Confederate army.

Crittenden thrown out so as to menace Chattanooga from the north. While still keeping up this demonstration, between the 29 August and the 4 September, he moved the remainder of his army across the Tennessee, and began his march over Raccoon Mountain. The left under Crittenden took position at Wauhatchie in Lookout Valley; the centre, under Thomas, went to Trenton; the right, under McCook, crossed from Stevenson and Bellefonte to Valley Head, whence cavalry demonstrations were made as far south as Alpine.

Meanwhile, the advance of Burnside on Knoxville had caused Bragg to order Buckner to Chattanooga; and he was also reinforced by Walker's corps from Mississippi. At the same time Lee sent him two divisions of Longstreet's corps, and Alexander's battalion of artillery, from the Army of Northern Virginia. Owing to Burnside's occupation of Knoxville, these troops had to make a long detour by way of Atlanta, and some of them did not arrive until after the battle. Hardee was detached about this time, and D. H. Hill was sent from Virginia to command his corps.

At first Bragg had been deceived by Rosecrans's feints, and was convinced that he intended to cross Walden Ridge, so as to join hands with Burnside. When the Federal plan was finally disclosed, Bragg evacuated Chattanooga on the 9 September and marched twenty-five miles south to Lafayette. But he had no idea of retreating, although he took great pains to give the impression that his army was fleeing in utter demoralization. His object was to cover his communications, and defeat the Union corps in detail as they debouched from the mountain passes.

Rosecrans, in turn, was absolutely deceived. He ordered Crittenden to leave a brigade in Chattanooga to garrison the town, and to pursue by the road to Ringgold. Thomas was directed to advance from Trenton on Lafayette, and McCook from Valley Head to Alpine and Summerville. These orders were issued on the 9th, and it was three days before Rosecrans realized his terrible mistake. The two wings of the Union army were then nearly sixty miles apart, and Bragg was concentrated opposite the centre under Thomas.

Bragg was aware of the isolated positions of the Federal corps, and made some efforts to cut them off, but his plans were frustrated by the neglect or incompetency of his subordinates. As already stated, his relations with his officers had not been very cordial since the battle of Murfreesboro.

As soon as he understood the situation, Rosecrans acted very promptly. Crittenden was moved from Ringgold to Lee and Gordon's Mill in Chickamauga Valley. Here he was joined by Thomas, who had withdrawn with great skill from the enemy's front, marched along the west side of Missionary Ridge, and passed through Cooper's Gap. McCook, however, was deceived by local guides, who assured him that there was no direct road practicable for his troops to McLemore's Cove; so he retraced his steps over Lookout Mountain to Valley Head, and did not reach the field until the 18th, after a tiresome march of five days. If it had not been for this delay of McCook's, Rosecrans would have withdrawn to Chattanooga instead of making a stand at Chickamauga. The delay also gave time for one of Longstreet's divisions to arrive. Therefore Rosecrans was forced to fight, not only in the wrong place, but also against larger numbers.

On the 18 September the Union corps were finally united along the west bank of Chickamauga Creek. The same day Hood's division of Longstreet's corps arrived, and Bragg was informed that McLaws was following closely. He accordingly issued his orders for an attack on the 19th.

The order of battle was of the progressive or *échelon* type, and prescribed that the attack should be begun by Hood on the right, who was to cross at Reed's Bridge, turn to the left oblique, sweep up the creek, and be joined as he proceeded by Walker and Buckner, who were to cross by Alexander's Bridge and Tedford's Ford. Hill was to cover the left flank; but to cross and attack the enemy's right if he attempted to reinforce his centre. The cavalry was to protect the flanks, Wheeler on the left and Forrest on the right.

The order contemplated turning the left of the Federals, and cutting off their retreat to Chattanooga; with this end in view, it was simple and well conceived, but it was based on wrong premises. Bragg thought that the Union centre was at Lee and Gordon's Mill, while in fact it was much further north, opposite Alexander's Bridge; and the left, under Thomas, greatly overlapped the Confederate right. The execution of the order therefore departed widely from the course prescribed, as will appear later.

Four miles south of Chattanooga the highway passes Missionary Ridge at Rossville Gap, where it forks, one branch running east to Ringgold, the other south to Lafayette. About three miles south of Rossville, the ridge is crossed by another gap, McFarland's. The battlefield of Chickamauga is an irregular parallelogram, bounded on the west by Missionary Ridge and on the east by Chickamauga Creek. From the Ringgold Road on the north to Crawfish Spring on the south the distance is about seven miles in a straight line; from McFarland's Gap on the west to Alexander's Bridge on the east is approximately four miles. The road to Lafayette traverses the field from north to south, and crosses the creek at Lee and Gordon's Mill. This road is intersected, at a point just north of the Union left, by the road from McFarland's Gap, which crosses the creek at Alexander's Bridge. The country is rolling, with some considerable elevations, and at the time of the battle was thickly wooded. There were no villages, but a number of farmhouses. The creek, which runs from south to north, is very winding in its course. Opposite the Federal position there were three bridges, Reed's, Alexander's, and Lee and Gordon's, and there were numerous fords. About three miles north of the Union left wing, the road to Ringgold crossed the creek at still another bridge, which did not figure in the battle.

On the evening of the 18 September, Colonel McCook, of Granger's Reserve Corps, made a reconnaissance as far as Reed's Bridge, which he burned. Meeting Thomas the next morning, he reported that there was an isolated brigade of the enemy on the west side of the creek, which might be cut off and captured. Thomas accordingly ordered Brannan to reconnoitre the road to Reed's Bridge in search of this brigade. Baird, under orders from Thomas, threw forward his right wing, so as to get in line with Brannan, and a part of Palmer's division, which came up a little later, was placed in position on the right of Baird. Thomas, who occupied the critical point of the line, on the left, had been ordered to hold the road to Rossville at all hazards, and had been assured by Rosecrans that he would be reinforced, if necessary, by the entire army.

Under Bragg's orders, Walker's corps forded the creek, on the morning of the 19th, a little below Alexander's Bridge, and then moved up the creek opposite this point. At the same time, Johnson, of Buckner's corps, crossed at Reed's Bridge, and marched up the stream some three miles. About ten o'clock, Brannan's advance movement encountered the enemy, being the cavalry of Forrest and two brigades of infantry, and drove them about half a mile, when it met with obstinate resistance. This reconnaissance of Brannan, therefore, developed the relative positions of the hostile forces, which had previously been unknown to the two commanders. Realizing for the first time that his right was greatly overlapped, and his flank in danger of being turned by the Federals, Bragg halted Walker on his march, and ordered him to retrace his steps. This movement brought on the battle of Chickamauga, before Bragg had his troops in position.

Under orders from Thomas, the two divisions of Brannan and Baird now attacked the enemy in their front and drove him back with great loss, taking many prisoners. Here the Union line was halted and readjusted; but, before this was completed, Walker assaulted in overwhelming numbers, and drove the Federals back in disorder.

Early on the morning of the 19th, McCook was in position at Crawfish Spring beyond the extreme left of the Confederate army. A little after ten o'clock, he was ordered by Rosecrans to send the two divisions of Johnson and Davis to Thomas. On Baird being driven back, Thomas ordered Reynolds's division of his own corps, and Johnson's division — both of which had opportunely arrived at the same time — to advance and repel the enemy. Walker's corps was attacked on the flank with great vigor, by these troops, and driven back to its first position, while Brannan also advanced in front and recaptured the artillery lost when Baird was forced back.

Bragg then sent Cheatham to the assistance of Walker, and the two united commands, charging with the "rebel yell," seemed on the point of sweeping everything before them. But, at the critical moment, Davis reported with his division, and, assisted by Wood, checked the Confederate advance. The Union line was reformed, and the divisions of Wood and Davis, reinforced by Sheridan, who came up from the right, then drove the Confederates back again to their first line.

Finding that Rosecrans was massing his troops on his left, to hold the road to Rossville and Chattanooga, Bragg placed Polk in command of his right, and ordered up Hill from Lee and Gordon's Mill.

At about half-past two o'clock, the Confederates made another furious assault on the Union line, which pierced the right centre and gained the Lafay-

George Henry Thomas, commander of the Army of the Cumberland in the Tennessee and Georgia campaigns, including Murfreesboro, Chickamauga, Chattanooga, and Atlanta. He became known as the Rock of Chickamauga.

ette Road, opposite the Widow Glenn house, three-quarters of a mile west of the road, where Rosecrans had his headquarters. At this moment, Negley's division came up from the right, and was sent into the fight, with Brannan from Thomas's left. Advancing with loud cheers, these two divisions hurled back Hood and Johnson, and pursued them until darkness ended the combat, the Union troops reoccupying their old positions.

After dusk, Thomas prepared to reform his lines for the engagement to be renewed on the morrow, and placed the divisions of Baird and Johnson on his left, with Palmer and Reynolds next, and Brannan to the rear and right of Reynolds as reserve. While these arrangements were being made, the Confederates assaulted with tremendous force, but were repulsed, with heavy losses on both sides. Minty's cavalry was now ordered to report to Granger, who with his reserve corps protected the road toward Rossville, and guarded the left flank.

When the fighting finally ceased, some time after dark, the troops slept on their arms, awaiting the more terrible conflict of the morrow. On the 19th, only Hood with three of Longstreet's veteran brigades had reached the field, but a little before midnight Longstreet himself arrived, closely followed by two more brigades, in time to take part in the second day's battle. The four remaining brigades, of McLaws, and Alexander with the reserve artillery, were just behind, but did not reach the field in time to turn the evenly balanced scale of the battle.

Bragg ordered the battle renewed at daybreak, but under a different organization. The army was now divided into two wings, the right under Polk, and the left under Long-street. To Polk was assigned Cheatham's division of his corps, and the corps of Hill and Walker, with Forrest's cavalry on the right. Longstreet had under him the division of Hindman of Polk's corps, Johnson's division, Buckner's corps, and the five brigades of Hood and McLaws, with Wheeler's cavalry on the left. This arrangement was adopted to avoid changing the positions of the troops, but it led to a delay of some hours in opening the battle.

Chickamauga

Bragg's plan of battle was the same as on the previous day: the whole army was to wheel on Longstreet's left as a pivot, to crush the Federal left, and gain possession of the road to Chattanooga.

During the night the Union troops threw up temporary breastworks of logs and rails. At daybreak Rosecrans rode along his lines and spent some time in rearranging his troops, particularly in strengthening Thomas on the left. A heavy fog hung over the battlefield during the early morning.

Bragg was also up at sunrise, and took position with his staff just in the rear of the centre of his line, where he waited impatiently for the attack to begin. Owing to unavoidable delays, two hours were consumed in getting the troops even approximately into position, and the first assault was not made until half-past nine o'clock.

For the second day's battle, on Sunday the 20 September, the lines of the two armies were arranged as follows:

Baird's division, of Thomas's left wing, extended around the northeast corner of Kelly Field, his left refused. Bordering this field on the east, next came the divisions of Johnson, Palmer, and Reynolds, the right brigade of the latter being in echelon, west of the Lafayette Road, its right reaching the Poe Field. Brannan's front covered the latter field at its western edge. Next came Negley, along the western line of the Brotherton Field; then Davis and Sheridan, in front of the Widow Glenn house, with Wood and Van Cleve in reserve, the latter reaching to Vittetoe's.

During the night, however, Thomas received word from Baird on his extreme left that his line did not extend to the road to Reed's Bridge, as had been anticipated; so Rosecrans, at Thomas's request, hurried Negley over to the extreme left, and sent Wood's division to occupy the position thus vacated. As will appear later, this change led to the catastrophe which overwhelmed the Federals.

The Confederate line was wholly east of the Lafayette Road, the right and centre being in close contact with the Union line. In order from right to left it was arranged as follows: Breckinridge confronted Baird, extending beyond his left; then in succession in the front line came the divisions of Cleburne, Stewart, Johnson, Hindman, and Preston. In reserve, in rear of Breckinridge, were the two divisions of Walker's corps; in rear of Cleburne and Stewart, the five brigades of Cheatham; and in column just behind Johnson, opposite Brotherton's, the divisions of Hood and Kershaw. The divisions of Hindman and Preston prolonged the line beyond the right of the Federals, who were thus overlapped on both flanks. Bragg had therefore five divisions, fifteen brigades, of infantry in reserve; besides two divisions of cavalry, who were between the Union left and Granger's reserve corps at McAfee Church. Rosecrans had in reserve only Wilder's brigade, and two brigades of Van Cleve.

The first Confederate assault, made by the divisions of Breckinridge and Cleburne, fell on Negley and Baird at the extreme Union left, and was delivered with tremendous force. Thomas hurried up reinforcements from the right of his line, which checked the assault and finally drove the enemy back. The attack on Baird was followed by assaults which successively struck Johnson, Palmer, and Reynolds, with equal fierceness, but all were gallantly repulsed. At last Bragg abandoned the attempt, and his troops fell back to their first positions.

About eleven o'clock, Longstreet appealed to Bragg for permission to attack with his entire wing, and, consent being given, prepared for a general advance. At nearly this same hour, an aide on Thomas's staff, who had been riding the lines, reported that there was a long gap in the line between Reynolds and Wood. This was not correct, as Brannan's division, although not in front line, was still in position, retired a short distance back, and concealed by the thick woods. This information was sent to Rosecrans, who dictated a message to Wood: *"The general commanding directs that you close up on Reynolds as fast as possible and support him."*

The order to Wood was dictated by General Rosecrans to Bond of his staff, and handed to Colonel Starling, Crittenden's chief of staff, for transmission. That officer, in his own words, "hesitated, not understanding the object of the order, when General Garfield called out that the object of the order was that *General Wood should occupy the vacancy made by the removal of Brannan's division, Brannan having been ordered to Thomas's left."*

If Garfield had written the order, he would, after his almost invariable custom, have included the explanatory phrase, but, as it was, the order was absolutely peremptory.

Wood could not understand this order, which it was impossible for him to execute literally, but he did not ask for any explanations, and undertook, in spite of the staff-officer's protest, to carry it out as well as he could. The withdrawal of his command from the front left a gap of two brigades in the line of battle. Into this gap, which he would have sacrificed a division to create, Longstreet poured the divisions of Stewart, Johnson, Hindman, Hood, Kershaw, with Preston's large division in support. The Union right, already depleted to sustain Thomas, was almost annihilated. Several thousand prisoners were lost, with forty guns, and a large number of wagon-trains. Davis, overpowered by numbers, was compelled to retire to save his command. One of Van Cleve's and two of Sheridan's brigades had already been sent to Thomas, but five brigades on the right were entirely cut off.

Davis returned to the field at sundown. Sheridan rallied part of his command, moved by way of McFarland's Gap to Rossville, and thence marched back toward the battlefield. As Rosecrans, McCook, and Crittenden were caught in the break of the right, and went to Chattanooga, Thomas was left in command on the field.

A part of the remnants of the Union right rallied at Snodgrass Hill, which should more properly be designated as "Horseshoe Ridge." It is not a single hill, but a ridge composed of three distinct hills, jutting out eastward from Missionary Ridge, and lying athwart the valley of the Chickamauga, with the concavity of its crescent-shaped curve opening directly toward the south. It is situated west of the Lafayette Road, about two-thirds of a mile from Kelly Field, and just south of the present military post of Fort Oglethorpe in Chickamauga Park. The distance from the Horseshoe to McFarland's Gap is about two miles and a half, and by this gap to Rossville nearly six miles.

About one o'clock, Brannan withdrew his line to this position, and Stanley's brigade, of Negley, rallied on his left, these two commands occupying the two westerly hills of the Horseshoe Ridge. Harker's brigade, of Wood, after repulsing part of Longstreet's column which was moving toward the ridge, finally took position on the easterly hill in front of the Snodgrass house, on Stanley's left.

Soon after one o'clock, Longstreet began his assaults on the Horseshoe with the brigades of Anderson (Hindman) and Kershaw (McLaws). By two o'clock the Confederates had passed over the hill on Brannan's right and gained the valley in his rear.

Three miles away, near Rossville Gap, Gordon Granger was stationed with three brigades of the reserve corps. He had listened all the morning to the heavy firing to the south, which seemed to increase in intensity as the day wore on. Judging that Thomas was being hard pressed, he now decided, against orders, "to march to the sound of the cannon." Placing Dan McCook's brigade at the McAfee Church to protect the Ringgold road, he started for the front with his two remaining brigades. Marching at double-quick, Granger arrived about two o'clock, at the most critical hour of the day, when Longstreet was forming the divisions of Hindman and Johnson in heavy columns for an assault on the right flank and rear of the Union position. Granger promptly hurled his two brigades, under Whitaker and Mitchell, against the threatening force. After a terrific conflict, which lasted only about twenty minutes, the Confederates were put to flight. The victory was won at fearful cost, but the army was saved.

The enemy was driven from Brannan's right and rear, and the Union line was extended south three-quarters of a mile to the heights overlooking Vittetoe's. Immediately after, Van Derveer's brigade of Brannan's division came up from the Kelly Field and strengthened his right, and Hazen's brigade, brought from Palmer's line, took position on Harker's left.

General James A. Garfield served as Chief-of-Staff under Rosencrans. He was elected president in 1880, but assassinated after serving only four months in office.

The Kelly Field line, where the four divisions still stood fast, now formed Thomas's left; the Horseshoe, with five brigades and some remnants of regiments, his right. Dan McCook's brigade, left by Granger, was on the high ground northwest of and overlooking Baird's left. On his way to the Horseshoe, Steedman, in command of Whitaker's and Mitchell's brigades of the reserve corps, had retaken the Union hospital at Cloud's Spring, captured about noon by Forrest's cavalry.

Longstreet had eleven brigades for his assaults on the Horseshoe. The final charges covered a period of nearly two hours. At three o'clock, he asked Bragg "for some troops of the right wing, but was informed by him that they had been beaten back so badly that they could be of no service."

In the meantime, Bragg had personally superintended the preparations for another assault on the Kelly Field line, in even greater force. This attack, which was made with Walker's corps and the divisions of Breckinridge and Cleburne, was repulsed by the divisions of Baird, Johnson, and Palmer. But later in the afternoon Bragg succeeded in reaching the Lafayette Road at McDonald's, in the rear of the Union army.

In the debacle of the right, two brigades of Davis's division, one of Van Cleve's, and two of Sheridan's, were cut off from any communication with Thomas except by a long detour by way of the Dry Valley Road to Rossville, and thence back by the Lafayette Road. A part of these troops tried to join Thomas, and were placed along the road from Rossville to the battlefield.

When Longstreet's men poured through the gap in the Union line, Rosecrans was on the right, near the rear of Davis. He was swept away with the tide of defeat, and finally reached Rossville with Garfield, his chief of staff. There, after a consultation with Garfield, he decided to send the latter back to Thomas, while he went himself to Chattanooga to make preparations for his troops as they came back in rout. This act practically ruined the fine reputation of Rosecrans. In this campaign, from Tullahoma to Chickamauga, Rosecrans had shown great ability, and but for the unfortunate order given to Wood during the battle he would doubtless have defeated Bragg, and won undying fame. It was a sad ending to a glorious career.

During the whole afternoon there was a gap of nearly half a mile between Thomas's right on the Horseshoe and his left at Kelly's Field, which was a constant anxiety to him and his generals. Longstreet, who was directing the Confederate assaults from his headquarters in the Dyer Field, entirely neglected this opportunity to move directly forward along the Lafayette Road and cut the Union line in two. His object seems to have been, not so much to drive an entering wedge between the two wings, as to prevent the Federal left at the Kelly Field from reinforcing that part of the army posted on the Horseshoe Ridge.

During the afternoon of the second day, three important despatches were sent, which have excited much controversy. These are given below in their chronological order: —

Garfield to Rosecrans

GENERAL THOMAS'S HEADQUARTERS

BATTLE-FIELD, FIVE MILES SOUTH OF ROSSVILLE

September 20, 1863, 3:45 PM.

GENERAL ROSECRANS: —

I arrived here ten minutes ago, via Rossville. ... I hope General Thomas will be able to hold on here till night, and will not need to fall back farther than Rossville; perhaps not any. ...

This despatch was sent from the headquarters of General Thomas near the Snodgrass house on Horseshoe Ridge.

At about 4:30 p.m., Thomas received the *first* order from Rosecrans to withdraw his troops. Up to that time, as the ranking general on the field, he had resolutely maintained his position.

This order, which was received "soon after Garfield had reported," read as follows: —

Rosecrans to Thomas

HEADQUARTERS DEPT. OF THE CUMBERLAND

CHATTANOOGA,

September 20, 1863, 12:15 P.M.

MAJOR-GENERAL THOMAS: —

Assume command of all the forces, and with Crittenden and McCook take a strong position and assume a threatening attitude at Rossville.

W. S. ROSECRANS, *Major-General*

When General Thomas was preparing his Official Report of the 30 September, he called the attention of General Rosecrans to the alleged sending-time of this order (*12:15* p.m.), and the latter said that it was an error, that he "did not leave the battlefield until after that hour, nor reach Chattanooga before 3:40 p.m."

We know that Rosecrans was on the battlefield until after midday. He then rode to Chattanooga, over ten miles, stopping en route at Rossville for a long conference with Garfield. It would therefore seem physically impossible for him to have reached Chattanooga before three-thirty or four o'clock. He afterwards stated that the despatch "must have been written as late as 4:15 p.m." This hour, however, seems too late, as Thomas began his withdrawal about 4:30.

Rosecrans's second despatch, of the same purport, was addressed to Garfield, and read as follows: —

Rosecrans to Garfield

CHATTANOOGA,

September 20, 1863

BRIGADIER-GENERAL GARFIELD: —

See General McCook and other general officers. Ascertain extent of disaster as nearly as you can and report. Tell General Granger to contest the enemy's advance stubbornly, making them advance with caution. Should General Thomas be retiring in order, tell him to resist the enemy's advance, retiring on Rossville to-night.

According to Thomas's Report, this second despatch was given him by Garfield at a point beyond the Ridge Road (which runs from the battlefield to McFarland's Gap) on his way from the field, whence he "proceeded to Rossville, accompanied by Generals Garfield and Gordon Granger." From other Reports it seems certain that the exact point was the Cloud house, near the Lafayette Road, about two miles from the Snodgrass house, and the time "a little after sunset," that is to say, soon after six o'clock.

Soon after Thomas received Rosecrans's *first* despatch, addressed to himself, ordering withdrawal, he sent an aide to Reynolds to direct the beginning of the movement. At the same time orders were despatched to the other left wing division commanders for their withdrawal successively.

Reynolds, who was in danger of being cut off, had already begun to retire before receiving Thomas's order. He was joined on the Lafayette Road by Thomas, who had left the Snodgrass house a little before five. Thomas then took personal charge of the movement, and directed the troops to withdraw by way of McFarland's Gap.

Misunderstanding Thomas's order, Reynolds marched directly along the Lafayette Road toward Rossville Gap, until checked at Cloud Church by Forrest's cavalry, while Thomas, separating King's brigade from the rest of the division, wheeled to the left near McDonald's and took the Ridge Road to McFarland's Gap. Here he halted and sent orders for the withdrawal of the troops on the Horseshoe, who, however, had been driven from their positions before the order arrived.

The most direct line of retreat would have been by Rossville Gap, but Thomas obeyed literally the order of Rosecrans, and withdrew via McFarland's, in order to join his forces "with Crittenden and McCook," whose troops were in that vicinity. As directed, he also "assumed a threatening attitude," by forming a line from the gap to the Lafayette Road, to protect the withdrawal and check pursuit. This alignment was completed about 5:30, and shortly thereafter he received Rosecrans's *second* despatch ordering him to retire on Rossville.

The assaults by Anderson and Kershaw ceased about four o'clock, and Preston's two brigades of Buckner's corps made their final and successful attacks about five. An hour later, the whole of the Horseshoe was in the possession of the Confederates — the last Federal stand being, not on the main ridge, but over 300 yards north of it, on the bare hill near the Snodgrass house. "At the end of the battle, at the hour of sunset [6. p.m.]," says General Buckner, "the enemy was retreating hastily from every part of the field."

About six o'clock, General Longstreet, in command of the Confederate left wing, halted the pursuit. A few minutes later, the sun went down, and the moon rose; it was a bright moonlight night.

After nightfall, Thomas skillfully withdrew his command to Rossville, where ammunition and rations were sent him by Rosecrans from the city. Some attempts by the Confederates to interfere with this movement were repulsed without serious difficulty. So quietly was the army withdrawn that Bragg did not discover the retirement until the next morning.

There was no object to be gained in holding the line at Rossville Gap beyond securing time to make the final arrangements for the withdrawal of the troops to Chattanooga, which was accomplished on the 21st. The following morning found the Army of the Cumberland in position before the city, and too strong to be attacked by the enemy with any chance of success.

The name "Chickamauga" in the Indian tongue is said to mean "Valley of Death," and the place had now fairly earned that sombre epithet. Chickamauga was the most bloody battle of the Civil War, and also, with few exceptions, of modern times. The losses, as given by General Alexander, were as follows:

	Federals	*Confederates*
Killed	1,657	2,074
Wounded	9,754	12,797
Missing	4,753	1,328
Totals	16,164	16,199

It is hard to determine the exact numbers engaged on each side. Cist says: "The largest number of troops Rosecrans had of all arms on the field during the two days' fighting was 55,000 effective men"; and that "Bragg, during the battle, when his entire five corps were engaged, had about 70,000 effective troops in line."

The figures given in *Battles and Leaders* are substantially the same: Federals, 56,965 of all arms; Confederates, 71,551 of all arms.

Livermore estimates the Union effectives at 58,000, and the Confederates at 66,000.

General Alexander gives the following figures:

Federals, 55,799 infantry and artillery, and 9842 cavalry; total 65,641; Confederates, 47,520 infantry and artillery, and 14,260 cavalry; total 61,780.

There were probably about 125,000 men, on both sides, engaged in the battle, and the total losses, in killed, wounded, and missing, were about 32,000. If we deduct from the total forces the 24,000 cavalry, in which the casualties were very light, we find that the losses in the two other arms were about 32 per cent., or nearly one-third of those engaged. If we exclude prisoners, the losses in killed and wounded were about 27 per cent.

To paint a battle, says Victor Hugo, would require one of those powerful artists who has chaos in his brush. The historian narrates the features which strike him in this *péle-méle*. The line of battle floats and twists like a rope stretched across a swift current; the fronts of the armies move forward and back; regiments advancing or retiring make promontories or indentations. There always arrives a certain moment when a battle degenerates into a combat, becomes particularized, and is resolved into innumerable details, which, to borrow the expression of Napoleon, "belong rather to the biography of regiments than to the history of the army." In this case, the historian evidently has the right to give a résumé. He can seize only the outstanding features of the combat: no narrator, however conscientious, has the gift to fix absolutely the form of that horrible haze which we call a battle. This, which is true of all great combats, is applicable particularly to Chickamauga.

"Chickamauga," says Judge Tourgee, "was a battle almost unparalleled in modern times. Volumes have been written to prove how those who fought were marshalled. Such efforts are mostly vain. ... Confusion grows more confounded with each attempt to reduce order out of impenetrable chaos."

Other authors have also had to confess the impossibility of making up a clear and true account from the published material. But, although the details of the battle are very complicated, the salient points are not difficult to understand. The trouble has been that nearly all of the earlier histories were based, not upon official authority, but upon unreliable newspaper stories, and that until recently no true and complete account of the battle has been written. None of the histories published prior to 1889 was based on official facts, as the Official Records had not then been published. The reports written by 215 Federal and 199 Confederate officers have since been printed, and fill nearly four volumes of about 1000 pages each.

The misinformation began in the "complimentary orders" issued to his troops by General Rosecrans on the 2 October 1863. He wrote:

When the day closed you held the field, from which you withdrew in the face of overpowering numbers, to occupy the point for which you set out — Chattanooga.

Here are recorded three statements of alleged fact, not one of which is supported by the records.

(1) "When the day closed," the field was abandoned by the Federals.
(2) The records show that Rosecrans had about 60,000 men in the battle, and Bragg about 65,000.
(3) The battle was *not* fought to gain possession of Chattanooga, which Rosecrans might have occupied on the 9 September without opposition.

The facts are more correctly stated in Rosecrans's telegram to President Lincoln from Chattanooga at 9 a.m. on Monday the 21 September: —

After two days of the severest fighting I ever witnessed our right and centre were beaten. The left wing held its position until sunset [six o'clock]… We have no certainty of holding our position here.

Thomas received about 4:30 the order from Rosecrans to withdraw his troops from the battlefield. He was then holding the Horseshoe with some remnants from the right wing, and the Kelly Field with the divisions of Reynolds, Palmer, Johnson, Baird, and Barnes's brigade, of Van Cleve. He began the movement at once by despatching orders to Reynolds and his other left wing division commanders for their withdrawal successively from right to left. Thus General Thomas "quit when ordered and because he was ordered."

Through a misunderstanding of Thomas's orders, as stated above, Reynolds moved straight along the Lafayette Road toward Rossville, while the other divisions took the Ridge Road, as intended, toward McFarland's Gap.

Thomas formed his divisions to resist pursuit in a line from the head of McFarland's Gap to the Lafayette Road and the Cloud house, nearly to Rossville Gap. This formation was completed about 5:30. *At that hour the Horseshoe Ridge was in the possession of the enemy.*

At this same hour, in the vicinity of the Cloud house, Sheridan reported his arrival on Thomas's left. This brave general had accomplished a feat almost unique in the annals of war. After the dispersal of his division by the onslaught of Longstreet on the Union right, and the loss of thirty per cent of his command, he had gathered and rallied together in the woods more than half of the scattered remnants, about 1500 men, and brought them into line again at the extreme left flank, ready for action, before sunset.

It thus appears that there is little or no truth in the three popular fallacies regarding Thomas's connection with the battle, which may be specified as follows: —

(1) That the troops who remained with him were all members of his own Fourteenth Corps.

(2) That he used his own discretion, and did not immediately withdraw his men on receiving Rosecrans's order.

(3) That he held Horseshoe Ridge until nightfall (7:30), and then marched his men from the battlefield in perfect order.

The facts, as conclusively proved by the Official Records, are: —

(1) That the troops under Thomas's orders, who held the Kelly Field and the Horseshoe, were composed of all the different corps of the Army of the Cumberland.

(2) That on the receipt of Rosecrans's order, about 4:30, Thomas immediately issued his orders for the withdrawal.

(3) That his troops were so much "disorganized" he considered it futile to attempt to make a stand in front of the two gaps.

What is said above is not meant in any sense as a criticism of General Thomas. He did his full duty; he inspired his men with courage and confidence, and his conduct deserves only words of praise. He was in no way responsible for the Federal defeat, and was powerless to avert the disaster. He took no steps to withdraw his men until he received direct orders from the commander-in-chief to retire. Although he did not retreat to the famous Horseshoe Ridge, and there stand at bay "for six weary hours," while with "25,000 men "he "hurled back again and again the furious onset of 60,000 rebels mad with desire to clutch the prize they had so nearly won," he none the less deserved his title of the "Rock of Chickamauga." He could not prevent the Federal defeat, but he saved the army from destruction.

General Cist says that the campaign of Chickamauga, taking everything into consideration, was "the most brilliant one of the war." Up to the time of Bragg's withdrawal from Chattanooga, Rosecrans's manoeuvres were masterly, but then he was utterly deceived. Bragg never intended his retirement to be permanent: all the indications he left behind him proved that. No bridges were destroyed; all hospitals, storehouses, and other buildings used by his army were left standing. Yet Rosecrans was duped by one of the oldest and most common *ruses de guerre*, and believed the tales of "deserters "that the Confederate army was retreating in utter demoralization. His first mistake was in scattering his army in pursuit before this fact was definitely determined, and the difficulty in again concentrating his troops forced him to fight at Chickamauga. Had Bragg received his promised reinforcements at the date he expected them, the Union army would have been completely crushed in detail.

While the Confederates gained some slight advantages in the battle of the 19th, there was nothing to indicate that they could finally defeat the Federals. Their victory on the second day was due mainly to Rosecrans's order to Wood, given under a misapprehension, and which so experienced a soldier should never have executed without question. General Wood was a graduate of West Point, had been in the army all his life, and knew the full meaning of all technical terms used to describe military movements. He must have realized that there was some error in the order to "close up on Reynolds," for he carefully put away the order in his note-book, with the remark that he "was glad the order was in writing, as it was a good thing to have for future reference." He was apparently irritated over a reprimand received from Rosecrans earlier in the day, and undertook the execution of an impossible order rather than ask an explanation of it from the general in command. To this extent he was responsible for the disaster which overwhelmed the Union army. In justice to General Wood, however, it should be added that after he reported to Thomas "there was no more splendid fighting done ... than was done by Thomas J. Wood and his division. To the last he aided Thomas in holding Horseshoe Ridge, and his was one of the last divisions to retire."

Rosecrans's final error was in not returning personally to the battlefield, instead of sending Garfield. As at Murfreesboro, he might have done much to restore the morale of his troops, and pluck victory from defeat. Thomas was a stubborn fighter, but he lacked the personal magnetism of Rosecrans. "That was the turning-point," says Cist, "and his hour had arrived."

The hero of Chickamauga was George H. Thomas, and well was it for the Army of the Cumberland that he was in command of the left on that day. Carefully posting his troops, he stood at bay, "with his back to the wall," and refused to be driven from the field. Here he stayed, repulsing every attack until ordered to withdraw. He fully earned his glorious title of the Rock of Chickamauga!

CHAPTER FIFTEEN

SEPTEMBER — DECEMBER 1863

CHATTANOOGA

HAVING retired to Chattanooga after the battle of Chickamauga, the Union army formed a line in front of the town from the river above to the river below. The troops occupied as salients the strong unfinished works left by the Confederates, which they connected by rifle-pits. Within two days the position was made practically impregnable.

In the meantime the Confederates had advanced from Chickamauga and taken up position in front of the Federals. Their line began on the right at a point near the railway tunnel east of the town, ran along the western side of Missionary Ridge to a point about two miles south of Orchard Knob, then turned westward across the valley to Lookout Mountain.

At Chattanooga the course of the Tennessee River is due west; after passing the town it flows south to the foot of Lookout Mountain, and then makes a great bend to the north, enclosing a peninsula some three miles in length by less than a mile in width, known as Moccasin Point. Crossing the river at the town, a road leads southwest across this point to Brown's Ferry, and thence continues in a southerly direction along a deep gorge between a narrow range of hills, close by the water's edge, and the base of Raccoon Mountain until, as it enters Lookout Valley, it curves westward and passes over a depression in the mountain to Kelly's Ferry. The railroad from Chattanooga to Bridgeport runs along the south side of the river, passes close under the point of Lookout Mountain, and crosses Raccoon Mountain by this same depression, as does also the wagon-road from Wauhatchie in the valley to Bridgeport. At the extreme northern angle of the bend in the river, the water rushes through the mountains with such velocity that steamers in high water cannot stem the current. This necessitated the landing of supplies at Kelly's Ferry, and then hauling them overland across the bridge at Brown's Ferry to Chattanooga.

On retiring to Chattanooga, Rosecrans withdrew a small force which had been stationed on the point of Lookout Mountain, as he did not think it practicable to keep up communication between this force and his army in the town. Bragg immediately occupied the mountain, and placed batteries commanding the railroad and the river. He also sent Longstreet's corps into Lookout Valley, and the Confederate sharp-shooters stationed along the river prevented the use of the wagon-road to Bridgeport. From water to water the Union army was invested in a semicircle. The only route by which supplies could come was a narrow and winding wagon-road from Bridgeport through Jasper and over Walden Ridge, a distance of sixty miles. Bragg sent Wheeler's cavalry to cut this line also, and sat down to await the starvation of the Union army. Longstreet, indeed, advocated the bolder course of crossing the river above Chattanooga, so as to cut off Rosecrans's line of retreat and compel him to come out and fight at a disadvantage, but Bragg felt that he would make sure of his prey by simply waiting.

Rosecrans had placed his cavalry on the northern side of the river to protect his trains; but they were eluded by Wheeler, who struck the line at Anderson's Cross-Roads in the Sequatchie Valley, where he burned 300 wagons and captured 1800 mules. He was closely pursued, however, by the Federal cavalry, and finally driven across the Tennessee into Alabama in a very shattered condition.

Then, early in October, heavy rains set in, and proved a worse foe than the Confederate troopers. The roads became almost impassable; the remaining mules were pressed beyond endurance; each successive trip from Bridgeport was made with fewer wagons and lighter loads. The artillery horses died by the score from starvation, and finally it was impossible to move the guns for lack of animals. It began to look as if the Union army would be starved into surrender, or forced to retreat with great peril, and certain loss of all *matériél*. But the Government at Washington had become thoroughly aroused concerning the dangerous situation of the army at Chattanooga, and prompt measures were taken for its relief. Hooker was sent West with the Eleventh and Twelfth corps, under Howard and Slocum, from the Army of the Potomac; and General Grant, at Vicksburg, was ordered to despatch large reinforcements to Rosecrans.

Grant himself was directed to go to Louisville, and was met en route at Indianapolis on the 17 October, by Mr. Stanton. The secretary handed him two orders, identical in all but one particular, and told him that he might take his choice. Both gave him the command of all the territory between the Alleghanies and the Mississippi River, but one left the department commanders as they were, while the other assigned Thomas to the command of the Army of the Cumberland in place of Rosecrans. Grant accepted the latter, and a copy was telegraphed to Rosecrans.

While Grant and Stanton were at Louisville, a telegram was received from Charles A. Dana, a representative of the War Department then at Chattanooga, saying that Rosecrans was preparing to retreat. This information was incorrect, but Grant telegraphed Thomas, now in command, that he "must hold Chattanooga at all hazards;" and that brave soldier replied, "We will hold the town till we starve."

Meanwhile, there had been several important changes in the organizations of the two hostile armies. McCook and Crittenden had been relieved, and ordered before a Court of Inquiry for their conduct at the battle of Chickamauga; and their two corps, the Twentieth and Twenty-first, had been consolidated into a single corps, numbered the Fourth, which was placed under the command of Gordon Granger. In the Confederate army, Polk had been relieved, under charges for failure to open the battle of the 20 September at daybreak; Hill and Buckner were gone, but Hardee had returned. The army was now organized in three corps, under Longstreet, Hardee, and Breckinridge.

The right of the Confederate line was held by Hardee, the centre by Breckinridge, and the left by Longstreet, whose line extended from Chattanooga Creek to Mount Lookout. Although the outposts of the two armies were so close together that the sentinels could "swap

Headquarters of General Thomas at Chattanooga.

yarns and tobacco," there was practically no fighting. Occasionally the Confederates threw a few shells into the town, but they did no harm.

On the 3 October, Hooker arrived at Stevenson. On the 21st, after dark, Grant reached the same place on his way to Chattanooga. Rosecrans, who was there on his way north, saw Grant, and they had a "brief interview in which he [Rosecrans] described very clearly the situation at Chattanooga, and made some excellent suggestions as to what should be done." Grant adds, very sarcastically, "My only wonder was that he had not carried them out." This slur was absolutely uncalled for, as Grant, when he reached Chattanooga two days later, had nothing to do beyond approving the plan proposed by General Smith, for reopening the line of communications to Bridgeport, which Rosecrans had accepted, and Thomas was arranging to carry out. It is necessary to make this point clear, because some writers have shown a disposition to give all the credit to Grant.

There was universal regret among the troops when they learned that Rosecrans had been relieved. Every soldier in the army felt that he had a friend in "Old Rosy." Although Rosecrans was frequently irascible with his superiors, to his subordinates he was one of the most genial of men. He was one of the finest strategists of the Civil War, and the Union cause suffered a great loss when he went to join so many other able generals in retirement.

On the 24 October, the morning after his arrival, General Grant ordered pushed to completion the admirable plan conceived by the chief engineer of the Army of the Cumberland, General William F. Smith — familiarly known to the soldiers as "Baldy "Smith. This plan was to throw a pontoon bridge across the river at Brown's Ferry; get control of the country south of the Tennessee and west of Lookout Mountain; then reopen the line of communications by the wagon-road to Kelly's Ferry, and by boat from there to Bridgeport. As Hooker's troops were not required in Chattanooga, they had been kept near Bridgeport since their arrival on the 3 October, until arrangements could be made for their cooperation. Hooker was now ordered to cross the river with the Eleventh Corps and one division of the Twelfth, and march up via Wauhatchie to Brown's Ferry. Palmer, with a division of the Fourteenth Corps, was ordered to move down the river on the north side, by a back road, until opposite Whiteside's, then cross and hold the road in Hooker's rear, after he had passed. At the same time 4000 men were detailed to act directly under Smith from Chattanooga: 1800 of these troops, under General Hazen, were to float down the river in pontoon boats to Brown's Ferry, under cover of night, land on the south side, and capture or drive away the enemy's pickets. Smith was to march with the remainder of his force, also by night, by the north bank to Brown's Ferry, taking with him all the material for laying the bridge as soon as the crossing was secured.

This project was carried out exactly as planned: the Confederate pickets were driven off, up the valley; the bridge was promptly laid; the position entrenched, and held until the arrival of Hooker's troops the next day.

Hooker marched into Lookout Valley by the road along the base of Raccoon Mountain. Howard's corps, which was in the lead, met a part of Law's brigade, which was supporting the Confederate sharp-shooters along the river, and drove it up the valley. This detachment, in its retreat, destroyed the railway bridge over Lookout Creek. Geary's division was left at Wauhatchie to guard the road to Kelly's Ferry, and at six o'clock Howard halted for the night within two miles of Brown's Ferry. Bragg, at first, could not credit the report of his signal officers, but hurried to Lookout Mountain with Longstreet, and from the summit watched the Federal column "marching quietly along the valley toward Brown's Ferry." Longstreet continues: "Presently the rear guard came in sight and made a bivouac immediately in front of the point where we stood." This was Geary's division at Wauhatchie.

It was arranged to make a night attack upon Geary with four brigades, but the Confederates were repulsed, with heavy casualties on both sides. General Alexander terms this night attack "one of the most foolhardy adventures of the war."

No further attempts were made by Bragg to molest the "cracker line," as the soldiers called it, and the supply problem was solved. The siege of Chattanooga was raised, and the reinforcements from the Army of the Potomac made Grant's strength equal to that of Bragg. A Richmond paper said: "The admirably conceived and perfectly executed coup at

The view from Lookout Mountain.

Brown's Ferry ...has robbed the Confederacy of all its dearly earned advantages gained at Chickamauga."

It seems almost inconceivable that Bragg should have chosen this moment to weaken his forces by sending Longstreet, his ablest corps-commander, with one-third his army, to attack Burnside at Knoxville. He apparently underrated the energy of his opponent, and thought that Longstreet could chase Burnside out of East Tennessee and return before Grant was ready to assume the offensive. Bragg has been very severely criticised for his action. "It ought to have been clear to him," says Professor Fiske, "that if he won the battle Knoxville would be at his mercy, while if he lost it, Knoxville would be relieved."

But Bragg was no fool. He knew the deplorable condition of the Army of the Cumberland at this time. When Grant suggested to Thomas an assault on Missionary Ridge, in the hope of causing Bragg to recall Longstreet, Thomas reminded him that the artillery horses were all dead, and the cannon could not be moved.

Immediately after the defeat at Chickamauga, Halleck had ordered Sherman to start for Chattanooga. Sherman accordingly left Vicksburg on the 27 September, with his command in steamboats, and reached Memphis, 400 miles up the river, five days later. With his usual fatuity, Halleck had directed Sherman to repair the railroad as he advanced toward Chattanooga. Thus hampered, it was nearly a month before Sherman could reach Iuka, still 200 miles distant from Chattanooga. As soon as Grant arrived at Chattanooga he telegraphed Sherman to "drop everything," and hurry to Stevenson with his entire force. The result was that Sherman got his army up to Stevenson and Bridgeport by the 14 November, and the following day reported in person to Grant at Chattanooga. With his arrival, and the army again well supplied with everything necessary, Grant was at last ready to strike. His plan of battle was as follows:

Sherman with his four divisions was to cross to the north bank at Brown's Ferry, march east behind the hills, out of view of the Confederates, and take a position under cover of the woods opposite the mouth of Chickamauga Creek. Here he was to recross the river by a pontoon bridge, and seize the north end of Missionary Ridge before the enemy could occupy it in force. As soon as he was astride the ridge at the tunnel, Thomas was to move the Army of the Cumberland to the left and connect with Sherman; then their united forces were to move southward, driving the Confederates up the valley of Chattanooga Creek and away from their base of supplies at Chickamauga Station. Howard's corps was to be in reserve on the north bank, ready to aid Sherman or Thomas as circumstances might require. Hooker, with Cruft's division of Granger's corps, sent him from Chattanooga, was to hold Lookout Valley. This plan, as will appear later, was modified in its execution.

Sherman's movement was much delayed by heavy rains which raised the river, and he did not cross east of the town until the morning of the 24 November. Even then, a break in the bridge at Brown's Ferry prevented Osterhaus's division from joining him, and it was ordered to report to Hooker.

Bragg was completely deceived by Sherman's movements, and thought that he was going to the relief of Burnside at Knoxville. He, therefore, on the very eve of the battle, despatched two more divisions to reinforce Longstreet, and was able to get only one of them back in time to be of service.

On the 20th Bragg sent Grant a most extraordinary letter, which it is not easy to understand. "As there may still be some non-combatants in Chattanooga," he wrote, "I deem it proper to notify you that prudence would dictate their early withdrawal." This may have been intended to deter Grant from detaching any more troops to aid Burnside, but Grant was more inclined to regard it as a ruse to prevent him from attacking before the enemy had time to withdraw. Accordingly, on the afternoon of the 23rd, he ordered Thomas to make a demonstration in force. His line, in the centre, facing Missionary Ridge, was made up of the corps of Granger and Palmer, of the Army of the Cumberland, and Howard's corps, of the Army of the Potomac, about 30,000 men in all. After advancing a short distance with such deliberation that the enemy thought they were on parade, these troops made a sudden rush and

Chattanooga

Pickets were the eyes of the army. Their task was to observe all movement made by the enemy. In general, pickets upon the outer lines were not allowed fires of any kind.

captured Orchard Knob, a prominent knoll about a mile in front of the western base of Missionary Ridge.

The results of this demonstration were three-fold: It was developed that Bragg's army was present in force, and meant to stay; it gained an excellent position, when strengthened by artillery, from which to make the final assault two days later; and it caused Bragg to weaken his left on Lookout Mountain by transferring Walker's strong division to his right. This division took position on Missionary Ridge, half a mile south of the tunnel, and was the first Confederate detachment to occupy the crest. This withdrawal greatly lightened Hooker's task of assaulting and carrying Lookout the following day.

Grant's original plan was only for Hooker to hold Lookout Valley and guard the line of communications with Bridgeport. But the addition of Osterhaus's division gave him a force of some 10,000 men, and Grant thought that he was strong enough to do more. Hooker was therefore ordered to try to take the point of Lookout Mountain. This position was almost impregnable by nature, but since the withdrawal of Walker's division it was held only by three weak brigades: one on the slope where Hooker made his assault, and two at the summit — about 1700 men in all.

The side of Lookout Mountain rises from the valley below in a natural slope, covered with a scrubby growth of wood, and of boulders of all sizes which have fallen from the cliffs. Beyond this slope, a precipice, of solid, bare, jagged rock, rises several hundred feet straight to the plateau of the mountain, 1400 feet above the waters of the Tennessee. At the northern end of the mountain, however, beyond the foot of the precipice, was the Craven farm, a comparatively smooth piece of land under cultivation. Between the farm and the base of the palisades there were wooded and rocky slopes; as also on the river side, where they ended in another cliff which drops straight to the railway track at the water's edge. The narrow road from Chattanooga to Lookout Valley passes over the nose of the mountain just above this cliff. Another road from the town ran up the eastern face of the mountain to Summertown on the plateau. The military road, winding up the north face of Lookout, was built by Hooker after the battle. The Summertown road was then the only way by which troops on the plateau could reach the slopes of the mountains or the valley below. The Confederates had entrenchments at the Craven farm; also near the base of the western slope, covering the railway and wagon bridges over Lookout Creek, and down the northern slope, so arranged as to meet attacks from either Lookout or Chattanooga valleys.

On the morning of the 24 November there was a mist over the mountain, which later settled down into a dense fog. At eight o'clock, Geary's division of the Twelfth Corps crossed Lookout Creek from Wauhatchie; it was joined on the left in the valley by Osterhaus's division of the Fifteenth Corps, and Cruft's division of the Fourth Corps. These troops, supported by artillery placed in commanding positions on the left bank of the creek, drove the enemy out of his entrenchments at the bridges, and crossed near that point. Aided by the fire of batteries on Moccasin Point, the Union forces pushed up the rocky slope, driving the Confederates from one position after another. By noon Hooker had possession of the Craven farm. Here the Confederate brigade which had defended the slope was joined by the two brigades from the plateau, and a stand was made about 400 yards beyond the Craven house. This line was held until midnight, when the Confederates withdrew from the mountain. On account of the fog, and the exhaustion of his ammunition, Hooker halted his line and entrenched.

Late in the afternoon, a supply of ammunition was brought from Chattanooga by Carlin's brigade, which took post on the right of the line. Early the next morning, the 25th, some men from the 8th Kentucky scaled the heights and hoisted the Stars and Stripes on the summit, where, at sunrise, the flag floated in full view of the Union and Confederate troops in the lines below.

While the "battle above the clouds "was taking place, Sherman, at the other end of the line, was endeavoring to carry out his part of the program. His pontoons had been concealed in North Chickamauga Creek, which enters the Tennessee on the north side two miles above the mouth of the Chickamauga on the opposite side. During the night of the 23rd, these were quietly floated down the stream, and by daybreak 8000 men had crossed. Little opposition was encountered, and the troops immediately threw up a bridge-head. As soon as the bridge was finished, at one o'clock Sherman crossed with his three divisions, and Davis's division of the Fourteenth Corps which had been sent him to take the place of Osterhaus's. At four o'clock, Sherman seized the north end of Missionary Ridge, which was occupied only by Confederate outposts. Then, to his surprise, he found that the ridge was not continuous, but was separated by a wide depression from Tunnel Hill, his objective on the south. Viewed from below and at a distance this break in the crest of Missionary Ridge was not apparent. Sherman also found Cleburne's division in position at Tunnel Hill, and strongly entrenched. He therefore made no attempt to carry the hill that afternoon.

During the night of the 24th, Bragg drew in all his troops from Lookout Mountain and Chattanooga Valley, and formed his line along Missionary Ridge from Tunnel Hill to Rossville Gap, a distance of over six miles. Hardee commanded the right wing, and Breckinridge the left.

On the morning of the 25th, Grant stationed his headquarters at Orchard Knob, from which the whole field was in full view. The day was clear and bright, and Bragg's headquarters on the ridge could be plainly seen — with the staff officers coming and going constantly.

Grant's orders for the day were as follows: "Sherman was directed to attack at daylight. Hooker was ordered to move at the same hour, and endeavor to intercept the enemy's retreat if he still remained; if he had gone, then to move directly to Rossville and operate against the left and rear of the force on Missionary Ridge. Thomas was not to move until Hooker had reached Missionary Ridge."

Sherman's assault, the main attack, was a complete failure. Although he had six divisions against Cleburne's one, the position was too strong to be carried by frontal assault, and all his attacks were repulsed with heavy losses. "Such is the strength of field-works against frontal assault; and Sherman does not appear to have tried to outflank Cleburne's position."

On the right, Hooker had marched at daybreak, but he found the bridge over Chattanooga Creek destroyed and the roads obstructed; he was thus delayed four or five hours. From his central position at Orchard Knob, Grant watched in vain "to see Hooker crossing the ridge in the neighborhood of Rossville." He saw that Sherman's assault had failed, and judged incorrectly, from some movements of the Confederate troops, that Bragg was weakening his centre to reinforce Cleburne on his right. So, to relieve Sherman, he ordered Thomas to move out the four divisions he held at the centre, assault the first line of the enemy's rifle-pits in front, and there to halt and await orders. Baird was on the left, Wood next, then Sheridan, with Johnson on the extreme right — in all eleven brigades and four field-batteries, on a front two miles and a half long. The men had been under arms all day, and when the order to attack came at three-thirty, they advanced with a rush, eager to redeem their defeat at Chickamauga. Three lines of entrenchments were in front of them, one at the foot of the ridge, another near the middle of the slope, the third and strongest at the crest. Through an error of the Confederate engineers, the upper line of works had been placed on the natural instead of the "military "crest, which "left numerous approaches up ravines and swales entirely covered from the fire of the breastworks." Bragg had also made the fatal mistake of dividing his forces, already too small, putting one-half in their skirmish line at the bottom of the hill, and the other half at the top. Private instructions were given the superior officers, if attacked by more than a single line of battle, to await the enemy's approach within 200 yards, then to deliver their fire, and retire to the works above.

The ridge here was some 200 feet high, with steep slopes broken by many ravines and swales, and obstructed at the time by the stumps of recently felled timber. The line was held by four Confederate divisions — eleven and a half brigades, and sixteen batteries.

The Federals charged at double-quick, and carried the first line at the point of the bayonet, killing and capturing large numbers of the defenders, and putting the rest to flight. Here the troops halted as ordered; but, finding themselves exposed to a galling fire from the enemy, by an almost spontaneous impulse the line resumed its advance up the ridge, which was carried in six places at the same moment. Wood and Sheridan both claimed the credit of reaching the top first.

Bragg's centre was broken, and his troops, after a feeble resistance, gave way and fled from the field in a panic. Thirty-seven guns and 2000 prisoners were taken. Bragg, with his entire staff, narrowly escaped capture. Sheridan and Wood followed the fleeing enemy for a short distance, but the hour was too late for a general pursuit.

Meanwhile Hooker had reached Rossville and driven into the Confederate left. He then advanced northward, with one division on top the ridge, and one on either side, until he connected about sunset with Thomas's right. During the night Cleburne withdrew from the position he had so valiantly held in front of Sherman.

The following morning, Sherman, Hooker, and Palmer, took up the pursuit and pressed it as far as Ringgold, where the enemy made a stand on the 27th. Bragg then withdrew to Dalton, where a few days later he was relieved of the command, at his own request. He was called to Richmond by President Davis, and given the position of chief-of-staff, his duties being to control military operations under the direction of the President. He did not see any more active service until the final days of the war. He was a good strategist and tactician, with great powers of organization and discipline. Grant considered him a man of the highest character, and Sherman also speaks well of him. But he had a most irritable temper, due largely to ill health, and was disliked by his officers and men. His failure to crush Rosecrans at Chickamauga was caused mainly by the disaffection of his subordinates.

Owing to various reasons, Longstreet was not ready to attack Burnside at Knoxville until the 29th, and then he was repulsed with a loss of over 800 men. He was about to renew the assault when he heard of Bragg's defeat, and of the approach of large Federal reinforcements. On the 4 December he raised the siege, and returned to Virginia.

In the battles around Chattanooga Grant had about 60,000 men and Bragg 40,000. The losses were not heavy:

	Federals	Confederates
Killed	752	361
Wounded	4,713	2,180
Missing	350	4,146
Totals	5,815	6,687

Both Bragg and Alexander attribute the sudden panic, which seized the veteran Confederate troops, to the sight of the "enemy marshalling his immense forces in plain view." General Alexander says: "The sight was a grand and impressive one, the like of which had never been seen before by any one who witnessed it." This was the only battle of the Civil War in which the topographical conditions were such that the defenders, in a position "which ought to have been held by a line of skirmishers against any assaulting column," could look down upon the hosts of the enemy forming for the attack, and it was too much for the nerve of the Confederate soldiers, who were as brave as any on earth.

Among the great battles of the Civil War, Chattanooga was unique in many respects: First, it was a series of three distinct actions, fought by the Union troops at different points on a line thirteen miles in length. Second, for the first time, corps of the three great armies, of the Potomac, the Cumberland, and the Tennessee, fought together under one commander. Third, it was the only battle of the war in which the four most famous Union generals — Grant, Sherman, Sheridan, and Thomas — were all engaged. Fourth, unlike most of the battles, the fighting was nearly all in full view of both armies. Finally, the immense length of the line, the grandeur of the scenery, the dizzy heights scaled, all combined to make it a wonderful spectacle.

Owing to unforeseen obstacles, the attack of Sherman on the left was almost a complete failure; but Hooker's "battle above the clouds," and the assault of Missionary Ridge by the Army of the Cumberland, were both brilliant victories, owing to the irresistable elan of the soldiers rather than the plans of the commander-in-chief. It is therefore absurd for Grant to claim that the battle effectually carried out his orders. Grant's orders to Thomas on the 25th were only to make another "demonstration "in behalf of Sherman, so that he could take the tunnel in accordance with the original plan. When the soldiers of the Army of the Cumberland, who were "so demoralized that they would not fight," pressed on up the ridge, without orders and even against orders, Grant was very angry, and told Thomas that "some one would suffer "if the movement failed. But it won for General Grant the battle of Missionary Ridge! In his official report, after narrating the events of the 23-25 November, General Thomas quietly says: "It will be seen by the above report that the original plan of operations was somewhat modified to meet and take the best advantage of emergencies which necessitated material modifications of that plan." And Professor Fiske remarks: "Now if anything in this world can be said to be clear, it is that the battle of Chattanooga was not fought as Grant had planned it."

In many respects Chattanooga was the most brilliant victory of the war: remarkable not only for its picturesque features and interesting tactics, but also for its strategic importance. The Confederate line of communications between the Atlantic seaboard and the Mississippi was severed at the centre, and there was no longer any connection between the sections east and west of the Alleghanies except by a long detour by way of Atlanta. It completed the recovery of the valley of the Mississippi, begun by the capture of New Orleans and Vicksburg. With the exception of Hood's rash advance to Nashville at the end of the following year, the remaining campaigns of the war were fought within the limits of the original thirteen states of the Union.

The exultation at the North, after the great victories of Gettysburg and Vicksburg in July, had been changed almost to despair by the terrible reverse at Chickamauga. Now, when the people sat down to their dinners on this Thanksgiving Day, as Halleck said in his telegram of congratulations, Grant had indeed given them cause for thanksgiving!

It is a general rule of modern warfare that an army which allows itself to be shut up within fortifications is lost. But the Army of the Cumberland was never entirely invested, although for a time its line of supplies was over a long and difficult road. Nevertheless, the army would ultimately have been starved into surrender, or have been forced to retreat, with the loss of most of its artillery and equipage, if means had not been found to open the short piece of road, about five miles long, from Brown's Ferry across Raccoon Mountain to Kelly's Ferry. Neither Bragg, nor Longstreet who commanded the Confederate left, appears to have appreciated the great strategic importance of this road. It was guarded only by a small brigade, which was sent around the toe of Lookout Mountain for the purpose. "A full division at least," says General Alexander, "should have guarded so important a point, and one so exposed." Bragg lost his campaign primarily when he allowed the enemy to reopen the short line of his communications.

CHAPTER SIXTEEN

JULY 1863 — MAY 1864

THE WILDERNESS

TEN days after the battle of Gettysburg, on the night of the 13 July 1863, Lee crossed the Potomac, and then continued his retreat slowly up the Shenandoah Valley. The last week in July, Meade also passed the river, and marched south along the east side of the Blue Ridge. Lee thereupon left the Valley and took position near Culpeper. Meade continued his advance, and placed his army on the north side of the Rappahannock.

The end of July, Lee withdrew across the Rapidan to Orange Court House, where he could receive supplies by rail. At this time Longstreet again called attention to the plan suggested by him the previous May, of taking advantage of the interior lines of the Confederacy to transfer troops to the West. About the 23 August, Lee was called to Richmond, and was detained there by President Davis for nearly two weeks. During this time, it was decided to send Longstreet, with the divisions of Hood and McLaws, to reinforce Bragg at Chattanooga.

As soon as Lee withdrew behind the Rapidan, Meade again advanced, and posted his army along the north bank of the river. Learning of the departure of Longstreet, the authorities at Washington detached the Eleventh and Twelfth corps from the Army of the Potomac, and sent them West, under the command of Hooker, to reinforce Rosecrans. This reduced Meade to the defensive; and there then ensued a "campaign of manoeuvres," marked by much marching and strategy, but little fighting or tactics. Meade was gradually forced back until he took a strong position on the heights of Centreville, almost in sight of the defences of Washington, behind which he could retire within a few hours. As Lee was now a long way from his base, he fell back again to his former position at Culpeper. Meade immediately followed, crossing the Rappahannock at Kelly's Ford on the 7 November, and turning the Confederate right; thereupon Lee retired once more to the south side of the Rapidan.

The last week in November, Meade crossed the river at Germanna Ford, with the object of surprising the Confederates in their extended winter quarters, but Lee was warned of the movement by his cavalry, and Meade found him so strongly entrenched along Mine Run that he did not deem it prudent to attack. He quietly recrossed the river, and both armies resumed their quarters along the Rapidan. Here Meade and Lee were content to watch each other across the river until the following May.

In February 1864, Congress revived the grade of lieutenant-general which had first been conferred on Washington in 1798. President Lincoln, as was generally expected, immediately appointed Grant to the office, and made him general-in-chief of all the armies of the United States. Grant was personally assured by the President that he would be allowed full freedom of action, and be supported by all the resources of the Government.

Grant states that it was his first intention to remain in the West, but he soon realized that this was not practicable. He accordingly recommended the appointment of Sherman to

In the Fall of 1863, the headquarters of the Army of the Potomac were pitched at Castle Murray near Auburn, Virginia.

his former command. Early in March, Grant visited Meade at his headquarters at Brandy Station, and at that time requested him to remain in command of the Army of the Potomac. This proved to be a cumbersome arrangement, as it made it necessary to transmit all orders through Meade, instead of giving them direct to the corps commanders, and was often embarrassing to Grant.

At this time the South had left in the field only two considerable forces: Lee's Army of Northern Virginia, and the two western armies of Tennessee and Mississippi, now under

General Joseph E. Johnston, at Dalton, Georgia. For the first time since the beginning of the Civil War, a definite plan was now adopted by the Union Government for a simultaneous and concentrated movement of all the Federal forces toward a single objective — the destruction of these two remaining organized bodies of Confederate troops.

Before this time the various Union armies had acted separately and independently of each other, giving the enemy an opportunity often of depleting one command not pressed, to reinforce another more actively engaged. Grant was determined to stop this. He regarded the Union forces as one large army, of which the Army of the Potomac was the centre, Sherman's army the right wing, and the Army of the James, under Butler, the left wing.

There was to be a "simultaneous movement all along the line." Sherman was to move from Chattanooga; Crook, in West Virginia, was to move against the Virginia and Tennessee Railroad; Sigel was to advance up the Shenandoah Valley; Butler was to move by the James River on Petersburg and Richmond.

So far as the main armies under Grant and Sherman were concerned, this plan was carried out successfully, but some of the details did not work out as expected. Butler allowed his army to be "bottled up "by Beauregard, and Sigel did nothing but retreat.

Grant established his headquarters at Culpeper on the 26 March. The First and Third corps had been suppressed, and their divisions transferred to the Second, Fifth, and Sixth corps, which were retained. Upon the reorganization of the army, General Hancock, who had been absent, owing to wounds received at Gettysburg, resumed command of the Second Corps; General Warren was appointed to the command of the Fifth Corps; General Sedgwick continued at the head of the Sixth Corps; and General Sheridan was brought on from the West to command the Cavalry Corps.

The Ninth Corps, under General Burnside, joined the army on the 6 May, but was not formally incorporated in the Army of the Potomac until the 24 May.

Longstreet had rejoined Lee with his two divisions which took part in the Chickamauga campaign, and the Confederate army was still organized the same as at Gettysburg, except that Pickett was absent.

The organizations of the two armies at the beginning of the campaign were as follows:

Army of the Potomac

Second Corp, HANCOCK	27,000
Fifth Corp, WARREN	24,000
Sixth Corp, SEDGWICK	23,000
Ninth Corp, BURNSIDE	19,000
Cavalry Corp, SHERIDAN	12,000
Total	105,000

Army of Northern Virginia

First Corp, LONGSTREET	15,000
Second Corp, EWELL	17,000
Third Corp, HILL	22,000

Cavalry Corp, Stuart	8,500
Artillery and Miscellaneous	6,500
Total	69,000

Pickett's division of 5000 men did not join Lee until the last of May; he therefore had only 64,000 men at the beginning of the campaign.

The Union army had 15 divisions, 40 brigades, of Infantry; 3 divisions, 6 brigades, of Cavalry; and 242 guns.

The Confederate army had 9 divisions, 40 brigades, of Infantry; 3 divisions, 7 brigades, of Cavalry; and 224 guns.

That part of the Union army not engaged in guarding the lines of communication was on the northern bank of the Rapidan. It was confronted, on the opposite side of the river, by the Confederate forces in a strongly entrenched position, which was almost impregnable against direct attack. The country back to the James River was cut up with many streams, generally narrow, deep, and difficult to cross except where bridged. The region was heavily timbered, the roads narrow, and almost impassable after the least rain. It would be hard to find a country more difficult for manoeuvring and supplying a large army.

As already stated, Grant's main objective was Lee's army, and, as it was practically unassailable in front, he decided to turn its right flank. He hoped by concealment and celerity to cross the Rapidan and traverse the Wilderness on the south side before Lee could discover his movement, or at least before Lee could have time to oppose it.

On the second day of May 1864, General Lee, surrounded by his corps and division commanders, stood at the Confederate signal station on Clark's Mountain, south of the Rapidan, and examined through his field-glass the position of the Federal army across the river. Although several demonstrations had been made in the direction of the upper fords, General Lee expressed the opinion that the Union army would cross at Germanna or Ely's. Thirty-six hours later the Army of the Potomac began its march to the fords indicated by him.

Grant issued his orders for the movement on the 2 May, and the troops began their march at midnight on the 3rd. Sheridan with two of his cavalry divisions led the way, and the third was left to cover the rear. Two pontoon bridges had been laid at Germanna, and two more at Ely's ford, where Hooker crossed twelve months before, and a fifth was laid between, at Culpeper Mine Ford. Hancock's corps, preceded by Gregg's cavalry division, after crossing the river, took the road from Ely's Ford to Chancellorsville, where it arrived at nine o'clock on the morning of the 4th, followed by the reserve artillery. The corps remained there all day, waiting for the trains to come up, and bivouacked that night on the old battlefield. The cavalry pushed on to Piney Branch Church, and from there threw out patrols on all the roads.

Warren's corps, preceded by Wilson's cavalry division, marched by way of Germanna Ford, and bivouacked the night of the 4th at the Old Wilderness Tavern, at the junction of the road from the ford with the Turnpike, just about a mile west of the point where Jackson's turning-column struck the pike on the afternoon of the 2 May the previous year. Sedgwick's corps followed the same route, and passed that night along the road, just south of the ford. The cavalry moved on to Parker's Store, throwing out patrols on all the roads from that point.

Up to this time the movement had been carried out successfully: the three corps were all south of the Rapidan, and no opposition had been encountered. But for the great train of 5000 wagons, the army might have moved further south, and been out of the Wilderness on the morning of the 5th. Although the baggage had been cut down to the smallest limit, the ammunition, ten days' rations, and three days' forage, filled a train which, in Grant's words, "would have extended from the Rapidan to Richmond, stretched along in single file." The army could not move on until the trains were up, and they did not finish crossing at Culpeper Mine and Ely's fords until after five o'clock on the afternoon of the 5th. Thus a whole precious day was lost, and Grant, much against his will, was forced to fight a battle in the Wilderness.

Union troops crossing the Rapidan River before the battle.

As already stated, Lee had not been deceived by the feints made on his left, and had anticipated Grant's movement. As usual, he took no steps to prevent the passage of the river, but made his plans to strike the Union army in flank before it could get out of the Wilderness.

Lee's headquarters were two miles northeast of Orange Court House; Ewell's corps was on and near the Rapidan; Hill's, higher up the river on the left; and Longstreet's, in the rear, near Gordonsville. Two roads led from Lee's position down the Rapidan toward Fredericksburg, both following the general direction of the river, and almost parallel to each other: the Old Turnpike, nearest the stream, and the Plank Road, a short distance south of it. The route of the Federal army lay directly across these two roads, along the western borders of the famous Wilderness.

About noon on the 4 May, Ewell's corps was put in motion along the Turnpike, while Hill with two divisions started by the Plank Road. The two divisions of Longstreet's corps, at Gordonsville, were ordered to march rapidly across country and follow Hill on the Plank Road.

As Ewell's corps advanced along the Turnpike on the morning of the 5th, a Federal column was seen crossing it from the direction of Germanna Ford. Ewell promptly deployed his troops across the Turnpike, and sent word to Lee, who was with Hill on the Plank Road. Lee ordered him to avoid bringing on a general engagement until Longstreet could come up, and to regulate his movements by the head of Hill's column, whose progress he could tell by the firing in its front. But his position was so near the flank of the Federal column that a collision soon occurred which opened the campaign in earnest.

Warren, whose corps was passing when Ewell came up, halted, formed line of battle, and vigorously attacked Johnson's division, posted across the Turnpike. The Confederates were driven back; but Rodes's division was thrown in on Johnson's right, south of the road, and the Federal attack was finally repulsed. The fighting was severe while it lasted, and the losses quite heavy.

Ewell's entire corps was now up, and Sedgwick soon joined Warren, on his right. Early's division was sent to meet Sedgwick, while the two other divisions continued to confront Warren. The Federals kept up their attacks until nightfall, but could not drive off the enemy.

Although the heads of the two Confederate columns had bivouacked on the night of the 4th within five miles of the Union camps, Grant does not seem to have been aware of the nearness of the enemy. When Warren was attacked the next morning, Meade is said to have remarked, "They have left a division to fool us here, while they concentrate and prepare a position on the North Anna."

If General Meade had any such idea, he must soon have been undeceived by Hill's attack along the Plank Road, which struck the Federal outposts at Parker's Store soon after Ewell became engaged on the Turnpike. The Union patrols were driven in, and followed up to their line of battle, which covered the junction of the Plank Road with the Stevensburg and Brock roads, by which the Federals were marching. The fight began between Heth's division, at the head of Hill's column, and Getty's division of the Sixth Corps. Hancock's corps, which was already two miles beyond Todd's Tavern, was recalled, and was ordered to drive Hill "out of the Wilderness."

The character of the Wilderness has already been described in connection with the Chancellorsville campaign. For more than one hundred years iron mines had been worked within it, and the great trees of the primaeval forest had been cut as fuel for the furnaces. The land was now covered with a dense second-growth of cedar, pine, and black oak. In his report Hancock says that the forest was "almost impenetrable by troops in line of battle," and "manoeuvring was an operation of extreme difficulty and uncertainty. The under-growth was so heavy that it was scarcely possible to see more than one hundred paces in any direction. The movements of the enemy could not be observed until the lines were almost in collision."

General Law writes: "It was a battle of brigades and regiments rather than of corps and divisions. Officers could not see the whole length of their commands, and could tell whether the troops on their right and left were driving or being driven only by the sound of the fir-ing. It was a fight at close quarters, too, for as night came on, in these tangled thickets ... the approach of the opposing lines could be discerned only by the noise of their passage through the underbrush or the flashing of their guns."

At two o'clock the head of Hancock's column reached the Plank Road. As his divisions came up they were formed on Getty's left, in front of and along the Brock Road, by which Jackson had made his turning movement the year before. Instead of engaging the enemy at once, as ordered, Hancock spent about an hour in completing the entrenchments begun by Getty, which gave Hill time to select and prepare his ground.

At a quarter past four, Getty advanced to the attack. He met with such stubborn resis-tance that Hancock sent two divisions to his assistance. The lines were very close, and a most desperate combat now ensued. Another Federal division was sent in, but Heth had been reinforced by Wilcox, and the Confederate line held fast. The fighting did not cease until after dark.

Late in the afternoon Grant sent Wadsworth's division of the Fifth Corps to Hancock's assistance, but it was so much delayed by the tangled underbrush that night fell before it got in position. As soon as the fighting ended on the night of the 5th, Grant issued orders to renew the battle at five o'clock the next morning.

It was near midday on the 4th, says General Alexander, when Longstreet, at his camp six miles south of Gordonsville, received news that Grant was crossing the Rapidan, and orders from General Lee to march to Todd's Tavern on the Brock Road. He was directed to march all night, only stopping to feed and water. At four o'clock he was on the way, and kept it up until near sundown the next day, when his corps bivouacked near Craig's Church, on the Carthapin Road, having marched about 36 miles. Longstreet at this time had with him only Hood's old division, under the command of Field, and McLaws's division, under Kershaw, about 10,000 men. Pickett's division, of 5000 men, was with Beauregard, and did not return until the last of May. The troops were ordered to rest until 1 a.m. before resuming their march; but, before starting, orders came from Lee to cross over to Parker's Store on the Plank Road, about six miles. It was after sunrise on the 6th before Longstreet reached this position, three miles in the rear of Hill's front line.

During the night both armies strengthened their field-works, and made preparations for the coming struggle. All day long, on the 5th, there had been a wide gap between the two wings of the line of battle — between Warren and Hancock on the Union side, and between Ewell and Hill on the Confederate side. In fact two distinct battles had been fought on fields more than a mile apart. Early in the afternoon of the 4th Grant had telegraphed Burnside at Brandy Station to make a forced march to Germanna Ford, and by the night of the 5th three of his four divisions were across the river. He was now ordered to place two of his divisions (Potter and Willcox) in the gap between Warren and Hancock, and to be in position to advance at five o'clock in the morning with the rest of the army. The third division of his corps (Stevenson), then south of the river, was to remain in reserve at the Wilderness Tavern.

At dawn on the 6th Hancock's troops advanced to the attack. The blow fell with greatest force on Wilcox's division south of the Plank Road. The whole Confederate line was "rolled up "from the right, and the troops fell back in disorder along the Plank Road until they reached the position of Poague's artillery, which now opened on the attacking force. The Federals pressed on, until abreast of the battery, and their musketry-fire reached the guns, where General Lee himself stood. Matters looked very serious for the Confederates, but Lee sent messengers to hurry the movement of Longstreet's corps, which soon appeared swinging down the Plank Road at double-quick. Kershaw's division took the right of the road and moved obliquely south to meet the Federal left, which had pivoted toward the north. The Union advance was checked, and the troops driven back to their breast-works, which were soon carried by the Confederate rush.

At the same time, Field's division deployed along the left side of the road, and advanced to the attack. As they passed General Lee, the men gave a rousing cheer for "Marse Robert," who spurred his horse forward to take part in the charge. As soon as the troops realized that he was "going in "with them, there was a general cry of, "We won't go on unless you go back! "One of the men seized the bridle and turned the general's horse around, and he reluctantly rode over to join General Longstreet on the Plank Road.

Field's troops struck the right of Hancock's line, and after a bloody combat finally succeeded in carrying the entrenchments. Here the storm of battle swept to and fro for more than two hours, and the works were taken and retaken several times. General Wadsworth was killed as he rode up close to the front of his line on the Plank Road.

About ten o'clock, Longstreet ascertained that the Union left south of the Plank Road was in the air, and sent Mahone with his own and three other brigades to make a turning movement. The Federal line, attacked in flank and rear, and in front, at the same time, was rolled up in confusion toward the Plank Road, and then back upon the Brock Road.

Mahone's turning column was now in position facing north on the south side of the Plank Road, and parallel to it. General Longstreet prepared to press his advantage, and ordered Jenkins's fresh brigade, supported by Kershaw's division, to move forward on the Plank Road and renew the attack. As Longstreet rode forward with Jenkins and Kershaw along the road, a sudden volley from Mahone's men killed Jenkins, and wounded Longstreet in the neck. The Confederates had failed to recognize their friends through the intervening thickets, and this unfortunate volley practically lost them the fruits of the success they had just won. It was almost an exact repetition of the killing of Jackson on this same field the year before.

Lee came up in a few minutes, and took personal charge of the attack. But, although Longstreet explained to him the situation and his plans, Lee "did not care to handle broken lines, and ordered a formation for parallel battle." This delayed the attack until after four

Ulysses S. Grant during the Wilderness Campaign, 1864, when he lost an army but saved a nation.

o'clock. Then a part of Hancock's front line was carried; but by five o'clock the Confederates had been repulsed, and driven back with heavy loss.

Meanwhile Burnside's corps had taken but small part in the battle. The divisions of Willcox and Potter, which were ordered to enter the gap between Ewell and Hill, did not get into position before two o'clock; by that time Heth and Wilcox had closed the gap, and the Union attack was repulsed.

Late in the afternoon, under the personal direction of General Lee, Ewell made an attack on the Union right, similar to that by which Longstreet had rolled up Hancock's left in the morning. Two brigades, under General Gordon, took the Federal line in reverse, and Sedgwick's corps was driven from a large portion of its works, with the loss of 600 prisoners — including Generals Seymour and Shaler. Night closed the combat, and the battle of the Wilderness was over.

The losses on both sides were as follows:

	Federals	*Confederates*
Killed	2,246	2,000
Wounded	12,037	6,000
Missing	3,383	3,400
Totals	17,666	11,400

Livermore estimates the numbers engaged as 102,000 Federals, 61,000 Confederates.

Grant's main objective in this campaign was Lee's army and not Richmond. In its entrenchments behind the Rapidan this army was unassailable in front, and it was necessary to turn one or the other of its flanks. To accomplish this object, three plans were possible: (1) To transport the Union army by water to the near vicinity of Richmond; (2) To move by the Federal right against Lee's left flank; (3) To move by the Federal left against the enemy's right flank. The latter plan was adopted. In his *Memoirs*, Grant states his reasons as follows:

"At this time I was not entirely decided as to whether I should move the Army of the Potomac by the right flank of the enemy, or by his left. Each plan presented advantages. If by his right — my left — the Potomac, Chesapeake Bay and tributaries, would furnish us an easy line over which to bring all supplies to within easy hauling distance of every position the army could occupy from the Rapidan to the James River. But Lee could, if he chose, detach or move his whole army north on a line rather interior to the one I would have to take in following. A movement by his left — our right — would obviate this; but all that was done would have to be done with the supplies and ammunition we started with. All idea of adopting this latter plan was abandoned when the limited quantity of supplies possible to take with us was considered. The country over which we would have to pass was so exhausted of all food or forage that we would be obliged to carry everything with us."

From the above it is evident that Grant did not even consider McClellan's plan, of moving his troops by water to the neighborhood of Richmond. The reason for this may have been political, rather than military. "Many of us thought," writes Mr. Everett P. Wheeler, "that politics had something to do with the plan that was adopted. McClellan had been removed from command and was at his home in Trenton, subject to order but receiving none. He was a conspicuous figure in the political debates, and many at the North still believed in him. Naturally the leaders of the Democratic party looked to him as an available candidate in the Presidential election of 1864. Many felt that McClellan's plan of assaulting Richmond from the south, on the line of the James River, was the true plan; and that the nature of the country between Washington and Richmond was such that the Confederates could not be defeated if assailed on that line. Therefore, when Grant undertook to march directly across that rugged and broken country, which was aptly called the Wilderness, and to attack Lee in the front, many thought that the wiser plan of campaign had been given up because to adopt it would have been to reflect credit upon the discarded leader. Certain it is that Grant's frontal attacks on Lee were bloody and unsuccessful."

On this same point General Humphreys says: "The question has been asked why the Army of the Potomac was not …moved by water to the near vicinity of Richmond, where, by taking possession of the lines of supply of that great military depot, the force defending it would be obliged to assume the offensive and attack the enveloping army in its entrenchments. But it is not to be supposed that Lee would have withdrawn to and remained within the carefully prepared fortifications enclosing Richmond while this transfer was being made, but that … he would have advanced beyond the city; …and that by his entrenching and continuing to extend and entrench, the Army of the Potomac would have been forced to attack constantly in order to gain possession of those lines of supply at a suitable distance from

The Wilderness and Spottsylvania

Richmond, and while extending its enveloping lines would have been subject to attack on the extending flank under unfavorable circumstances."

As this is exactly what finally occurred, it is difficult to see much point to this argument.

The overland route to Richmond had been tried five times — by McDowell in 1861, by Pope and Burnside in 1862, by Hooker and Meade in 1863 — and had proved a failure every time. Under Grant in 1864, it again proved a failure. At every turn he found Lee across his path, and was unable to drive him off. Finally, after six weeks of the hardest fighting in the Civil War, and the loss of 55,000 men — a number nearly equal to Lee's whole army — Grant was to find himself on the James River, with Fortress Monroe as his base, where his fleet might have landed him at the beginning, and without losing a man. "Here at last," says General Alexander, "literally driven into the location in front of Petersburg, Grant found himself in a position of rare strategic advantage: certain to give him possession of Richmond if properly utilized." This position was literally "the key to Richmond. For it would force Lee to hold an exterior line of such enormous length — nearly 30 miles — that it could not be long maintained."

A move by Grant's right flank had the apparent advantages that the rivers were smaller and more easily passed in that quarter, and the country was more open and better suited for the manoeuvring of large forces. But he would have been operating on a front parallel to his line of communications, the Orange and Alexandria Railway, which would require a large force for its protection; while Lee would have operated on a front perpendicular to his communications with Richmond.

On the other hand, in moving by his left flank, Grant had short lines of supply, entirely protected, to navigable waters connected with his main depots. The only drawback was the unfavorable character of the country for the distance of ten or fifteen miles south of the Rapidan; but Grant hoped, by concealing his movements, to cross the river, and traverse the Wilderness, before Lee had time to attack. In this expectation he was disappointed, owing to the necessity of waiting for his trains to come up, and it is difficult to understand why he had any such hopes. "It was well known," writes General Humphreys, chief-of-staff of the Army of the Potomac, "that daylight would divulge our movement to Lee's signal officers on Clark's Mountain, …and it was believed that he would at once move by the Orange and Fredericksburg pike and plank roads to oppose us."

"No poorer cavalry work was done in the Civil War," says Major Steele, "than that done by the cavalry of Sheridan and Stuart in the afternoon and evening of the 4 May and the early morning of the 5 May 1864."

In excuse of Stuart, however, it should be explained that Lee had sent him over to Fredericksburg to obtain forage for his lean horses, and he did not rejoin the army until the 5th. For Sheridan, and two of his division commanders, Torbert and Wilson, it may be said that they had had practically no cavalry experience before they were given their high commands in the Army of the Potomac. Wilson was an engineer officer, and the service of Sheridan and Torbert had been with the infantry. Later, both Sheridan and Wilson learned their lesson, and performed most efficient service.

Lee again showed his sublime audacity in attacking a Union army of twice his strength. His only error was in not calling up Longstreet sooner: he had 42 miles to march, while Hill had 28, and Ewell only 18. If Longstreet had been close behind Hill on the Plank Road on the morning of the 5th, Hancock's corps might have been cut off and overwhelmed.

The bad tactics of the Wilderness can be attributed to the difficult character of the country. There was no plan of battle on either side — no simultaneous, concerted effort either to turn the enemy's flank or pierce his centre. The first day, there were two distinct battles — one on the Plank Road and the other on the Turnpike. On the second day, the Confederates turned the left of the Federals in the morning and their right in the evening. Either of these flank attacks might have given decisive results; but the first failed on account of the wounding of Longstreet, and the second was made so late in the day that there was no time to gather the fruits of the victory.

The Wilderness is unique among battles as presenting the novel spectacle of an army of 60,000 men enveloping both flanks of an army of 100,000.

CHAPTER SEVENTEEN

SPOTTSYLVANIA AND COLD HARBOR

AFTER the bloody, but indecisive, battle of the Wilderness, Lee expected that Grant would retreat, as his predecessors in command of the Army of the Potomac — Pope, Burnside, and Hooker — had invariably done under similar circumstances; and probably this expectation was shared by every man in the Union army. But when Grant arose at dawn the next morning, thoroughly refreshed after a sound sleep, the first thing he did, at 6:30 a.m. on the 7 May, was to issue his orders for a night march of the entire army toward Spottsylvania Court House, on the direct road to Richmond.

The Federal situation is well summed up by Colonel Henderson in these words:

"Now, here was Grant, a stranger to his troops, face to face with the hero of the war, the man before whom so many generals had gone down. He had fought him for two days in the Wilderness, and if he had escaped defeat he had lost a great many more men than Lee, and the fighting all through had certainly not been in the Federal favor. The morning after the battle they brought in a list of losses — 15,000 men — and the enemy was still there: still there, and not retreating! Grant had to decide what to do; it was little use attacking the enemy in his entrenchments ; there seemed no hope of success, and the army would not have been surprised had he followed the example of his predecessors and retreated. But despite his losses, despite the demoralization of his troops, despite the fact that he had not won one inch of ground, he determined to move forward, to follow out his original plan, and, if possible, to cut Lee off from Richmond, or at all events to force him to battle in a less impregnable position than the one he now held. This was the turning point in the campaign."

As a commander, Grant cannot be compared with General Lee, "undoubtedly one of the greatest soldiers, if not the greatest, who ever spoke the English tongue," but he possessed the determination, the perseverance, the fixed resolve to conquer, which enabled him to triumph over obstacles before which men of weaker fibre would have turned aside. He was endowed with that almost indefinable force which Napoleon declared was three times more effective than physical means, that is, than numbers, armament, and position. In other words, Grant relied far more on the moral effect of his manoeuvres than on the mere fighting qualities of his troops, and it was this which finally brought him success. It was perhaps to this that Napoleon referred when he said that reading and meditating on the wars of the greatest captains is the only way of learning the science of war.

In order to appreciate fully Grant's difficulties, and his strength of character, we must remember that, with strange troops, who had far more dread of Lee than confidence in himself, he was to continue his campaign against that formidable adversary, in a most difficult country, which was far better known to Lee and his officers than to any one in the Union army. The few maps available were not reliable. The theatre of war was covered with primaeval forest, and very thinly populated. There were immense tracts of swamp and jungle which were terra incognita to all but a few farmers and their negro slaves. The roads were as scarce and as indifferent as the maps. There were many unfordable streams, crossed by few bridges, at long intervals. The country produced but little food or forage, and the invaders had to carry both their supplies and their ammunition.

Under Grant's orders, Hancock's corps, on the left of the line, was to remain in position until the trains and the other army corps marched by his rear. The trains were started in the afternoon of the 7th, and the troops moved at eight-thirty. Warren marched by the Brock Road; Sedgwick, followed by Burnside, moved by way of Chancellorsville, Aldrich's, and Piney Branch Church. Hancock was ordered to follow Warren to Todd's Tavern. The cavalry preceded the infantry columns, and covered the flanks and rear.

The troops began their march in a state of great discouragement, under the impression that they were to retire once more behind the Rapidan. But when they came to the cross-roads, the command was, "Column right!"

"Soon after dark," writes General Porter, "Generals Grant and Meade, accompanied by their staffs, ...rode along the Brock Road toward Hancock's headquarters, with the intention of waiting there till Warren's troops should reach that point." Then occurred an unexpected demonstration which was one of the most memorable scenes of the campaign. In spite of the darkness, Grant was recognized. The men then understood that the watchword was to be, "On to Richmond!" "Wild cheers echoed through the forest, and glad shouts of triumph rent the air.... The night march had become a triumphal procession for the new commander." Grant sent his staff-officers along the line to urge the men to keep quiet so as not to attract the enemy's attention.

On the afternoon of the 7th, Lee was informed by Stuart of the movement of the Federal trains, and he was convinced that Grant's objective was Spottsylvania Court House. He at once ordered Anderson, now commanding Longstreet's corps, to make a night march for the same point, and sent Stuart's cavalry to retard the Federals as much as possible, in order to enable Anderson to reach Spottsylvania first and take up position.

In the race for the Court House, Grant had a little the worse of the luck. His route was somewhat the longer of the two, but his troops started at 8:30 p.m. on the 7th, while the Confederate corps was not to march until 3 a.m. on the 8th. Luckily for Lee, however, Anderson took the responsibility of starting at an hour before midnight, in order to escape from the blazing woods, which had been set on fire by the battle. This enabled Anderson to win the race.

The Confederate cavalry felled trees across the Brock Road, and disputed every foot of ground, so that the progress of Warren's column was much delayed. It was half-after eight the next morning before the leading division (Robinson) emerged from the woods into open ground at Alsop's, about two miles and a half from the Court House. As the division advanced across the clearing, toward a dense pine thicket on the further side, it was met by a staggering musketry and artillery fire from the Confederate breast-works, and driven back to the shelter of the woods in the rear.

Robinson was badly wounded; Griffin came up on his right, but was also forced back, until the two other divisions (Crawford, and Wadsworth now under Cutler) of the Fifth Corps arrived and took part in the engagement. Warren then advanced, and entrenched a position from 200 to 400 yards in front of the Confederate line.

Several roads came together at the Court House, from Chancellorsville, and Fredericksburg, now the Union base, as well as from the east and south. This gave the place a strategic value, and made it the field of the battle.

The troops on both sides now came up rapidly. Sedgwick joined Warren, and in the afternoon his corps vigorously assaulted Anderson's right wing, which, assisted by the timely arrival of Ewell's corps, repulsed the attack with great slaughter. Hill's corps, now under the command of General Early, did not arrive until the next morning, the 9th.

General Lee's line now covered the Court House, with its left, Longstreet's corps, resting on a small stream called the Po River; Ewell's corps was in the centre, north of the Court House, and Hill's on the right, covering the Fredericksburg Road. These positions were generally maintained during the battle, although troops were frequently shifted from one point of the line to another.

The sketches show how skillfully Lee had made his dispositions. Like Napoleon, he had an extraordinary eye for ground, and relied largely on natural features in his defensive tactics. Throughout this campaign — in the midst of woods, jungle, and streams — with very little time at his disposal, he always seems to have selected positions of great strength. His eye for ground had much to do with his successful resistance to Grant's overwhelming numbers.

At Spottsylvania, Lee's front, between the Po and the Ny, was well adapted to his smaller forces, and his line was far stronger than that held in the Wilderness. In order to turn his position Grant would have to cross one of the streams, and so divide his army, giving Lee an opportunity of dealing with him in detail. The country was thickly wooded, and the Federals still had the same difficulty of finding out where the enemy was and in what direction his entrenchments ran.

On the 9 May began what is called the battle of Spottsylvania — which was really a series of engagements lasting about nine days. The first two days were occupied mainly in reconnoitring. This work is usually done by cavalry, but they were of no use at all in such a country, and reconnaissances in force by brigades of infantry were therefore the only means by which Grant could find out anything about the enemy.

SPOTTSYLVANIA
May 9th. & 10th.
POSITIONS OF ARMY CORPS
Confederates shaded
Scale of Miles

SPOTTSYLVANIA
May 14th.

General Philip H. Sheridan

The skirmishers and sharp-shooters were very active on both sides during the day, and General Sedgwick was killed close to the entrenchments to the right of his line. General Wright then took command of the Sixth Corps.

By this time it had been ascertained that the Confederate line ran from the Po, at a point 600 yards above the crossing of the Shady Grove Church Road, to a point half a mile south of the Fredericksburg Road, a distance of more than four miles. It enclosed the Court House on the northwest, north, and east, and covered the roads southward toward Richmond. The most marked feature of the line was a salient at the centre — a sort of loop a half-mile wide from east to west, having a sharp apex upon a high open point a quarter of a mile north by east from the McCool house. At the salient, the line turned southeast, for about 600 or 700 yards, with the woods about the McCool house behind it, and fairly open ground in front; then it ran in a southerly direction for a mile and a half, with the ground in front partly broken and wooded and partly open.

From left to right, the line was held in the following order: Longstreet's corps, under Anderson; Ewell's, around the loop in the centre; Hill's, except Anderson's old division, now under Mahone, which was on the extreme left overlooking the Po. Early's old division, now under Gordon, which was in reserve, was employed in digging a trench at the base of the salient about 400 yards south of the McCool house.

Hancock occupied the right of the Union line in an entrenchment overlooking the Po; Warren was next, in front of Anderson; Wright was on the left. Burnside, with the Ninth Corps, was still near the Ny River on the Fredericksburg Road. On arriving, Burnside had encountered a small force of dismounted Confederate cavalry, which he mistook for infantry. This led Grant to believe that Lee was about to move against his line of communications with Fredericksburg, and he ordered Hancock to cross the Po and reconnoitre Lee's left.

By nine o'clock Hancock had passed the river with the three divisions of Barlow, Gibbon, and Birney; his fourth division (Mott), which came up late, had been sent to the left to Wright's corps. During the night he had three bridges built across the Po, to secure his retreat, and pushed on to the bridge of Shady Grove Road known as the Blockhouse, because of a house near it, built of squared logs. Here he found the Confederate line too strong to attack. About 10 a.m. on the 10th, Hancock received an order to leave one of his divisions to threaten the Confederate left, and return, with his two other divisions, to command an attack to be made at five o'clock with his own corps, and the corps of Warren and Wright.

After his departure, Barlow's division, which he left behind, was attacked by the Confederates, and finally driven back over the river. The enemy then prolonged his lines a mile upon the high ground, thus covering the approach by the Shady Grove Church Road.

During the day, Warren and Wright had been feeling out the lines in their front, and the former reported the opportunity was so favorable that he was ordered to attack at once, without awaiting Hancock's return. The assault was made about four o'clock by the Fifth and Sixth corps, and two divisions (Mott and Gibbon) of the Second. The troops reached the Confederate lines, but were all driven back with heavy loss.

At seven o'clock, Hancock made a second attack with Birney's and Gibbon's divisions, supported by part of the Fifth Corps, but this also was repulsed with heavy loss.

General Alexander thinks that Burnside's mistake, mentioned above, was most fortunate for Lee, as it led to Grant's sending Hancock prematurely across the Po and then withdrawing him. If he had remained upon that flank, and been reinforced by Warren, "it is hard to see how he could have failed ...completely to turn Lee's flank, and get upon his communications which now ran to Louisa C. H."

While these affairs were going on upon the Confederate left, Grant was preparing for an assault upon the weakest point of their line — the salient at the centre. The attack was made at five o'clock by three brigades under Colonel Upton. The works were carried, but the Federals were finally driven back, with a loss of about 1000 men, or 20 per cent, of the attacking column. The total Federal losses for the day were over 4000.

Upton's attack was to have been supported by Mott, but the division, when it attempted to advance, was broken up by a severe artillery fire, and fell back.

The next day, the 11th, was rainy and disagreeable, and no serious fighting took place. Grant thought that Upton's failure was due to lack of support, and he made his plans for a much more formidable assault on the salient by the whole of the Second and Ninth corps. The point of attack was to be the apex of the loop, afterwards known as the "Bloody Angle."

General R.S. Ewell was assigned Stonewall Jackson's old corps.

Spottsylvania Court House. This photo was taken a few months after the two armies swarmed the area. Lee's army was entrenched on a ridge surrounding the area shown here.

Ruins of the bridge over the North Anna which was destroyed by Union troops.

Owing to misleading reports of a Federal movement on his left, Lee believed that Grant was preparing for another flank march. He therefore ordered all of the guns withdrawn at sundown from the parts of his line nearest the enemy, so as to be ready to move quickly. Consequently, when the attack came, the guns had all been removed from the salient, which was untenable without artillery. This was a fatal mistake, as will soon appear.

There was no moon, and heavy rain was falling when the Federals began their movement. Hancock's arrangement is interesting, but it failed from errors in formation. As given by General Alexander it was as follows:

BARLOW

BROOKS   MILES   BIRNEY

SMYTH   BROWN   MOTT

GIBBON

(Advanced later)

Barlow's division was formed in two columns of two brigades each; Birney's, in two lines, and Mott's in one. Gibbon's division was deployed in the rear. The columns were 10 ranks (or 20 men) deep. All officers were dismounted, and the division and brigade commanders with their staffs marched in the centre between the lines. In Barlow's division there was so little distance between the ranks that soon after the advance began it was a solid mass.

The assault, which had been ordered for 4 a.m., was delayed 25 minutes by the fog. The distance to the Confederate works was about 1200 yards. Urgent calls had been sent for the return of the 22 Confederate guns, but only two arrived in time, and these only fired three rounds before they were captured with the rest. If these guns had been in place, the charge could not have succeeded. On no other occasion during the Civil War was such a target presented to so large a force of artillery. The Federals came with such a rush that the Confederates were overwhelmed before they had a chance to fire more than two or three scattered volleys. Johnson was captured, with one of his brigadiers; in all, 4000 prisoners were taken, with 30 colors, and 20 guns.

The first assault had been a great success, but no further advantage was gained. Lee hurried up reinforcements from the right and left, and put in all his reserves. The Confederate line was reformed behind the trench at the south end of the salient. The Federals

NORTH ANNA
May 23rd.

Scale of Miles

NORTH ANNA
May 24th. & 25th.

Scale of Miles

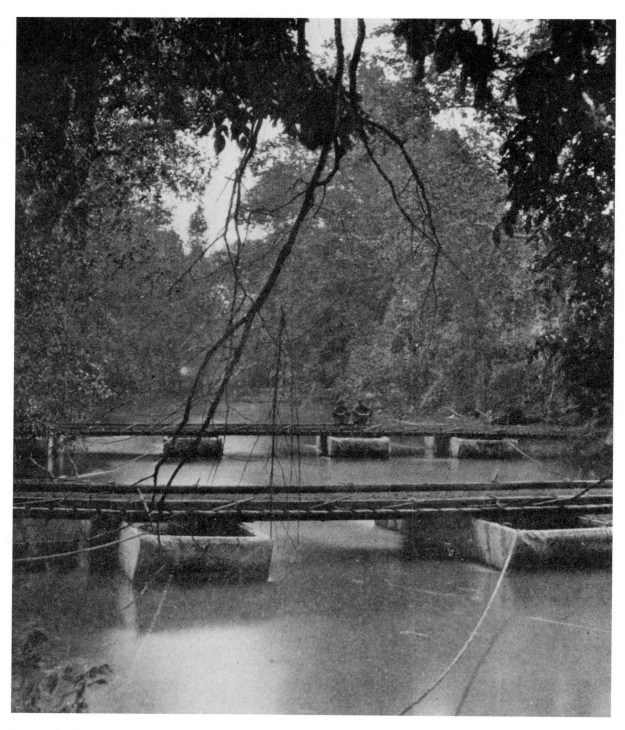

Pontoon bridges created to facilitate the rapid crossing of the North Anna by Hancock's Corps on May 24.

were much disorganized by their victory, and it was difficult to reform their lines within the salient.

It was reported to Grant that Hancock had been checked, and at eight o'clock eight brigades from the Sixth Corps were sent to his assistance. In the confined space, these reinforcements only added to the confusion.

In the meantime, at 5 a.m., Potter's division of the Ninth Corps had attacked the extreme right of the Confederate line, carried the works, and captured two guns; but the Federals were soon driven back and the guns retaken.

The Federals were finally driven out of the salient, but the combat there lasted all day, and till after midnight: it was perhaps the most desperate and the most sanguinary conflict of the whole war. At one time 24 Union brigades were engaged in assaulting a few hundred yards of the entrenchments. The men stood from twenty to forty deep outside the parapet. One tree, twenty-two inches in diameter, was literally cut down by the bullets.

There was some fighting during the day by Warren on the right, and Burnside on the left of the Union line, but little was accomplished beyond preventing Lee from sending more reinforcements to his centre.

The Union losses in killed and wounded on the 12 May were about 6800; the Confederate casualties, between 4000 and 5000. Hancock suffered the most, his corps losing about 2500 men. The Federal generals Wright and Webb were wounded. On the Confederate side, two general officers were killed, four severely wounded, and two captured.

On the 11 May, General Grant sent his famous despatch, that he would "fight it out on this line if it takes all summer." On the 12th came the famous assault on the Bloody Angle, which failed because of over-concentration, as the charge of Pickett's division at Gettysburg had miscarried because of too light formation. "The military lesson to be learned from the failure of Hancock's assault," says General Alexander, "... is, that there is a maximum limit to the force which can be advantageously used in any locality, and a superfluity may paralyze all efforts."

As explained by Colonel Henderson, however, the failure was not due so much to a superfluity of force, as to its unwise employment. "The principle is," he says, "that you mass opposite one point a great wedge which you intend to drive into the enemy's line, and that this wedge is composed of several lines one behind the other at such distance as may best suit the ground and the situation.... But it is a great point to remember that you should have a force behind this wedge in order to confirm success when you have broken in, for whatever may be the discipline of the troops it is impossible that confusion and intermingling of units can be avoided."

In this case the distance between the lines should have been very much increased, and the second and third lines should not have closed in until they were needed to reinforce the first. This great attack was almost a complete success, "and the cause of its ultimate defeat was that in the excitement of the attack the second and third lines, instead of keeping their respective distances, closed in upon the first."

The 13 May was comparatively a day of rest. Although the great assault had failed, it had come so near success that Grant was determined to make another effort. A movement by his left promised an opportunity of attacking Lee's right before it could be reinforced or its entrenchments extended.

The moon was young, the night foggy, rainy, and intensely dark. Warren and Wright were ordered to march by country roads, passing in the rear of Hancock and Burnside, cross the Ny, move through fields to the Fredericksburg Road, on it recross the Ny, form on Burnside's left, and attack the Confederate right flank at 4 a.m. on the 14th. Hancock and Burnside were to be ready, when ordered, to join in the attack.

Again Grant had the worst of luck. During the night the rain fell in torrents; the bonfires, and the torches of the signal men, were put out; and the troops, over roads knee-deep in mud, struggled wearily along at a very slow pace and with many halts. When day broke, only Warren with 4000 men had arrived at the appointed place. The other columns were so strung out in the rear and so scattered, the men so exhausted, that the attack had to be abandoned. "We doubtless had a narrow escape from serious trouble," writes General Alexander. "With ordinary weather the distance was not great, and both the Fifth and Sixth corps could have surprised our flank at dawn in the morning. Our entrenchments on that flank did not then extend much beyond the Court House."

During the next three days, Grant remained in position opposite Lee's right, resting his men and receiving reinforcements. He ordered strong defensive lines built, which could be held by a reduced force, with the idea of concentrating again for another effort to carry the Confederate line at the salient where he had been checked on the 12th.

By the 17th, the works were strong enough to be held by Warren with the Fifth Corps; that night, Hancock and Wright were ordered to pass around Burnside, and the Second, Sixth, and Ninth corps to attack in conjunction at dawn, while the Fifth Corps (Warren) cooperated on the left.

The plan seemed to promise well, but the attack was an entire failure. The infantry was slow in finding its way through the woods, and it was eight o'clock before the troops came in sight of the Confederate lines. The divisions of Gibbon and Barlow, which had taken part in the assault on the 12th, led the way in lines of brigades, a much more effective formation than that employed before. This time the Confederate guns were in position, and their fire was concentrated on the infantry. Only a few men reached the enemy's line and none penetrated it. About ten o'clock, Meade ordered the attack discontinued, and the men withdrawn.

At noon on the 19th, Grant issued orders for Hancock to move that night on the road to Richmond. Lee had anticipated this movement, and had ordered Ewell to make a reconnaissance in force. By a circuitous route, Ewell took his men far around the enemy's flank, and got his entire corps of 6000 troops in the rear of the Federals. Here he occupied a very critical position. He succeeded, however, in holding off the enemy until darkness covered his withdrawal. In this venture he lost 900 men, or about 15 per cent. of his force.

This ended the battle of Spottsylvania, in which the losses on both sides were very heavy. Grant's casualties were 2725 killed and 13,416 wounded, a total of 16,141. His total loss since the beginning of the campaign had been in excess of 33,000. The Confederate losses, from the Wilderness to the close of the war, can never be accurately known, as few reports were made. Livermore estimates their losses for these two battles at 17,250, the missing not included.

Grant now tried a new manoeuvre. On the night of the 20 May he started Hancock for Guinea Station, about ten miles east of Spottsylvania, with orders to march from that point south toward Hanover Court House. He hoped that Lee would move against this corps with the bulk of his army, and thus afford a chance of striking the Confederates in the open country before they had time to entrench.

At this time Sheridan was absent with most of the Union cavalry. After the battle of the Wilderness, Grant had sent him on a raid around the left of the Confederate army, with orders to attack Lee's cavalry, cut the Virginia Central and Fredericksburg railways, and do all the damage he could. Stuart followed him, as Grant had expected, and finally succeeded in placing his command across Sheridan's path at Yellow Tavern, only six miles north of Richmond. In the severe combat which followed, Stuart was mortally wounded, and his command defeated. Sheridan then passed close to the city, but was not strong enough to attack the works. He had a narrow escape from capture, but finally reached the James River, where he secured rations and forage from Butler. He then returned by way of White House, and rejoined the army on the 24 May, near Chesterfield, having ridden entirely around Lee's army.

This was only one more of those useless and perilous cavalry raids, so common during the Civil War. It had no material effect on the campaign, and deprived Grant of the eyes and ears of his army at a critical moment.

All of the cavalry that was left with the army was sent with Hancock under the command of Torbert. The Union movement was observed and hindered by the Confederate horsemen under Wade Hampton.

On the morning of the 21st, Warren started by the same route taken by Hancock, and was followed later by Burnside and Wright. Lee did not feel strong enough to assume the offensive, and therefore failed to fall into Grant's trap. As soon as he learned of the Federal movement he ordered Ewell to march directly for Hanover Junction, and followed with his whole army. Although Hancock had a start of twelve hours, on account of his long detour he did not arrive until after Lee. He found the Confederates drawn up behind the North Anna River, covering Richmond and the Virginia Central Railway. There were two bridges opposite their right, a ford in front of their centre, and another ford two and a half miles distant, beyond their left.

The line first held by Lee was dangerously extended, but he now executed a peculiar manoeuvre; he shut up his line as one closes an umbrella. The line originally had been almost straight: it now assumed a triangular form, with the apex on the river. His whole army was then massed in a space not more than two and a half miles broad. He could reinforce any point attacked in much shorter time than Grant could concentrate at the same point.

At this time Lee was rejoined by Pickett's division, some 5000 strong, and he received other reinforcements aggregating about 4000 more, or a total of 9000 fresh troops.

Grant formed his line in front of Lee's position, with the Fifth and Sixth corps on the right, the Second and part of the Ninth on the left. The two wings were unable to communicate without crossing the river twice. Lee's position was so strong that it defeated its object, as Grant did not venture to attack. Lee was anxious to take advantage of his reinforcements to strike a blow, but the Federal entrenchments were very strong, and the flat, open country gave full play to their artillery. Besides, Lee, at this time, was confined to his tent by a temporary illness, so neither side made any serious attack. On the night of the 26th, Grant removed the temptation, ere Lee had recovered, by moving for the Pamunkey.

After dark on the 26th, Grant set his army in motion for Hanover Town, near which he crossed the Pamunkey River. Sheridan's cavalry, which had just rejoined the army, led the way. At Haw's Shop, south of the river, it defeated the Confederate cavalry, under Wade Hampton, in a fierce combat which lasted all day.

As soon as Lee discovered, on the morning of the 27th, that the Federals had vanished, he marched by way of Half Sink to the Totopotomoy, which he reached the next day, in time to see the Union army just arriving on the opposite bank. As he moved by interior lines, about six miles shorter than the route taken by Grant, he won the race as usual. The Confederates immediately entrenched their position so strongly that Grant decided not to assault.

After leaving Spottsylvania Court House, the armies found themselves in a rich farming country, entirely different from the Wilderness. The farther south and east they marched, the broader and deeper they found the streams, the lower, flatter, and more marshy the land.

Grant once more moved by the left flank, Lee followed, and the two armies found themselves at Cold Harbor. In order to understand the strategic importance of this point, it is necessary to give a brief description of the country near it. Hanover Town, where the Union army was concentrated south of the Pamunkey, is about seventeen miles in a straight line northeast of Richmond. The theatre is traversed by two rivers, Totopotomoy Creek, running easterly into the Pamunkey, and the Chickahominy River, flowing southeasterly to the James. Between these, there are a number of smaller streams, with low banks, their borders swampy and covered with woods and thickets.

From Hanover Town three main roads lead to Richmond: the Shady Grove; the Mechanicsville; and the Cold Harbor, which runs via Old and New Cold Harbor, and Gaines's Mill. New Cold Harbor was little more than the intersection of cross-roads but Old Cold Harbor, a mile and a half east, and about midway between Hanover Town and Richmond, was an important strategic point, because it commanded the roads running south toward the James, and northeast toward White House, the present Union base.

At Cold Harbor, Grant was joined by W. F. Smith with about 10,000 men of the Tenth and Eighteenth corps from Butler's army, and Lee was further reinforced by Hoke's division of 5000 men from Drewry's Bluff.

Lee immediately began to work southward, by extending his right flank, so as to secure Old Cold Harbor, and command the roads above described. On the 31 May, this important strategic point was seized by Sheridan's cavalry, which entrenched, and held the position until relieved by Wright's corps. Several desperate attacks by the Confederates on the following day were all successfully repelled. The Union losses were nearly 2000, and the enemy probably suffered to about the same extent.

On the 3 June, Grant assaulted Lee's strongly entrenched position, and in one hour lost nearly 6000 men, killed and wounded. On this occasion, Grant seems to have lost his head, and he regretted this useless slaughter to the last day of his life. There was no manoeuvring as there had been at Spottsylvania; there was no massing against any particular point. The order was given for the whole line to attack, and the army moved straight against the enemy's front.

Swinton is responsible for the statement, repeated by many other historians, that Grant ordered the attack renewed, but the men refused to advance: they knew that the position could not be taken. This is absolutely denied by General Alexander, who was present at the battle. He says, "No such silent defiance of orders occurred, or anything like it."

Cold Harbor was only six miles from the outer works around Richmond, and the right of Lee's line was within three miles of those works. If Grant could have broken the Confederate centre at Cold Harbor, he might have destroyed Lee's army, captured Richmond, and ended the war at one stroke.

As early as the 26 May, Grant had taken steps to be prepared to cross the James, with a view of attacking Richmond and Petersburg from the south side. He ordered his engineers to collect material for making bridges, and telegraphed Halleck at Washington to forward to City Point all the pontoons on hand.

The Union army remained in front of Lee's position until the night of the 12 June, when Grant set his troops in motion to cross the James River. This ended the great campaign of the Wilderness.

The Union losses during the first twelve days of June totalled 1905 killed, and 10,570 wounded — in all 12,475. The Confederate losses are not known, but were certainly smaller. Grant began the campaign with 105,000 men, and received over 45,000 reinforcements. During the campaign he lost 55,000 men. Lee began with 62,000, and received about 14,000 reinforcements. His losses, as already stated, are unknown, but were probably under 20,000.

The student will look in vain for anything brilliant in the way of strategy or tactics in Grant's campaign from the Rapidan to the James. His successive turning operations all failed of their object — to get between Lee's army and Richmond, and cut his communications. At every move he found Lee entrenched across his path. At the end of six weeks, he found himself on the James, where he might have transported his army in the first place, without losing a man.

Nor were his tactics any better. He seems to have had no plan of attack in any of his battles. At Spottsylvania he assaulted first one part of the Confederate lines and then another. He wore his troops out in marches and countermarches. Orders were issued and countermanded; corps were sent to places only to be recalled. The one outstanding feature of the campaign is Grant's tenacity of purpose — his determination "to fight it out on this line if it takes all summer." He never seemed to know when he was getting the worse of it. The tenor of all his despatches was to the effect that the enemy was suffering more than his own army. To a deputation of influential politicians who recommended Grant's removal from command, President Lincoln replied, "I like that man — he fights!"

"If, as the mediaeval chroniclers tell us," writes General Law, "Charles Martel [the Hammer] gained that title by a seven days' continuous battle with the Saracens at Tours, General Grant certainly entitled himself to a like distinction by his thirty days' campaign from the Wilderness to Cold Harbor."

In these words of General Law, we find outlined the great distinction between generals of the two definite types of McClellan and Grant: the former never could make up his mind to fight; the latter well deserved his appellation of "the hammerer ": like Napoleon, he never hesitated to make sacrifices, if necessary, in order to achieve victory.

Reference has already been made in these pages to the analogy between war and chess. Some commanders, like some chess-masters, never attain great success because, having too great a regard for their materiel, they refuse to part with it. It should always be remembered that men are only the pieces in the game, the means to an end, and as such they should be made subservient to the purpose in view, namely, victory; therefore, the great general, like the chess-master, must ever be prepared for sacrifices.

Napoleon is reported to have said, "What are a million men to me! "This remark, if ever made, was not so brutal as it sounds. All that he meant to convey was that, to achieve victory, he never hesitated to press home his attack, no matter how great his losses.

"The *ardent desire* for the fight," writes Colonel Vachée, "*was a new and characteristic trait* of his genius, for how many generals-in-chief hesitate the moment they enter upon that terrible drama which is played at the cost of so many human lives, and on which there so often depends the fate of empires and nations! "

At Saint Helena, Napoleon also remarked that it was rare to find generals who were in a hurry to give battle. They carefully took up their positions, and thought out their combinations, but they could not make up their minds to attack.

The campaign was marked by the number of turning movements; the frequent night marches; and the changes of the base of supplies. As the army advanced, the base was shifted from the Orange and Alexandria Railway to Aquia Creek; then to Port Royal; next, to White House; and finally to the James River.

The most marked feature of the Wilderness Campaign, however, was the general use of entrenchments. As soon as the troops were halted, the men threw up shelter without waiting for the officers to give the order. In this wooded country it was an easy matter to construct entrenchments, and they were strong enough for the purpose. There were a great many expert axe-men in both armies, and trees were soon felled, or the fallen timber gathered. A pile of logs and branches made a good foundation, over these the men threw a little earth, and a breastwork was soon constructed that was bullet-proof at least. General Alexander says that the Confederate equipment with entrenching tools was very poor; the men habitually loosened the ground with bayonets, and scooped it up with tin cups. Their line was generally laid out by those who built it. The Federals, on the other hand, had a force of perhaps 2500 men, of engineer troops and heavy artillery regiments, habitually employed for this work under the direction of engineer officers.

This use of entrenchments was copied by both the hostile armies during the Great War, and carried to an extent never before known.

In summing up his interesting and valuable study of the Wilderness Campaign, Colonel Henderson says:

"For those who care to study the campaign closely, it is worth while noting with what skill Lee's positions were selected. His flanks at Spottsylvania, at the North Anna, and at Cold Harbor, were so secured by streams that it was very difficult indeed for his opponent to manoeuvre without crossing one of these streams, and so dividing his army. It was not only the entrenchments, but the natural features of the ground also on which Lee relied in his defensive tactics. His eye for ground must have been extraordinary."

CHAPTER EIGHTEEN

MAY — SEPTEMBER 1864

ATLANTA

THE Confederates were not actively pursued after the battle of Chattanooga. Bragg therefore halted at Dalton, only twenty-five miles from the field of his defeat, and entrenched his army. He was then relieved of the command, at his own request; but President Davis showed continued confidence in his ability by calling him to Richmond as chief-of-staff. He was ordered to turn over the command to the senior lieutenant-general, Hardee, who might have retained the position if he had not shrunk from the responsibility.

At this time there were but five officers of the full rank of general in the Confederate service, of whom the only two available were Johnston and Beauregard. General Lee suggested the name of the latter for the chief command in the West, but Mr. Davis did not take kindly to the idea. While the matter was under discussion, General Polk wrote the President a strong letter urging the appointment of Joseph E. Johnston. Mr. Davis, who was not on very friendly terms with either Beauregard or Johnston, was placed in a very embarrassing position, but finally decided to appoint the latter. On the 16 December, Johnston was ordered to turn over the command of the Army of the Mississippi to Polk, and proceed to Dalton to take command of the Army of the Tennessee.

The Richmond authorities were in favor of a prompt renewal of the aggressive, with a view to the recovery of Tennessee. Both Mr. Seddon, the Secretary of War, and President Davis wrote Johnston, the last of December, urging him to assume the offensive as soon as the condition of his army would allow it.

In his reply, on the 2 January, Johnston presented the difficulties in the way of action. "I can see no other mode of taking the offensive here," he wrote Mr. Davis, "than to beat the enemy when he advances, and then move forward." The correspondence continued throughout the winter, and Mr. Davis, by making it personal, evinced a desire to overlook former differences. But General Johnston's tone remained that of cold formality, and he showed no disposition to meet the views of the President. Finally, about the first of March, Mr. Davis dropped the correspondence, turning it over to General Bragg.

The situation was one which called for prompt action. During the winter, the Federal forces in the West were much dispersed, and a quick blow at Thomas, at Chattanooga, would have found him isolated. Schofield was at Knoxville, over 100 miles to the northeast; Logan, with part of Sherman's forces, was near Huntsville, an equal distance to the southwest; and the rest of Sherman's command was on the Meridian expedition or returning to Vicksburg.

Jefferson Davis, the President of the Confederacy, hailed from Mississippi and was Secretary of War under Franklin Pierce.

To wait for spring was to wait for the Federals to concentrate their now scattered armies, and be fully prepared for the campaign. It is no wonder that the Richmond Government lost patience with Johnston's attitude.

Lee, who had been in Richmond, was in full accord with this plan, and wrote Longstreet, who had not yet rejoined him after the Chattanooga Campaign, urging him to cooperate in influencing Johnston to adopt it. "If you and Johnston could unite and move into Middle Tennessee," he said, "it would cut the armies of Chattanooga and Knoxville in two, and draw them from those points, where either portion could be struck at as occasion offered."

It cannot be denied, as General Cox states, that this plan was based on sound strategy. Both Grant and Sherman were glad that they were allowed to complete their preparations, and were not called upon to meet the enemy before they were ready. Johnston's abilities are undoubted, and later he conducted his defensive campaign with great skill, but he lacked the audacity of Lee and Stonewall Jackson, which so often won victories for the Confederates.

Hood, who had been assigned to a corps in Johnston's army, wrote Mr. Davis on the 7 March that the army was well prepared, in high spirits, and anxious for battle. He strongly supported the plan of moving before Grant could concentrate.

As requested by Lee, Longstreet wrote Johnston on the 5 March, to the effect that he was ready to join in the movement. A week later, Bragg wrote from Richmond, outlining the plan of campaign mentioned above, and saying that on receiving the assurance of its immediate execution Johnston would be reinforced so as to have an army of at least 75,000 men. In his replies Johnston pronounced the plan impracticable, and again argued that it was better to let the enemy's forces advance, and fight them far from their base and near his own. There were certainly very sound arguments in favor of his position.

The principal Union depot for operations in Alabama and Georgia was Nashville, centrally located as the capital of Tennessee, but 186 miles by rail south of the Ohio River. It was directly connected with Chattanooga by 150 miles of railroad, and indirectly by a line 35 miles longer by way of Decatur and Stevenson. It had the further advantage of water connection with the Ohio by the Cumberland River. A railroad had also recently been completed, some 70 miles in length, from Nashville to Johnsonville on the Tennessee, a much larger river, nearly parallel to the Cumberland in this part of its course. With these great lines of communication, the problem of supplying the army seemed to be solved.

So much trouble had been experienced, however, in earlier campaigns, from the interruption of railway service by Confederate raids, that special means had been devised to protect the lines. Every wooden bridge across a stream was a vulnerable point, and a system of block-houses had been developed to guard all the bridges.

Ten tons made a load for the small freight cars of that day, and, with the iron rails and light locomotives, 20 to 30 cars made a full train. As Sherman estimated that he must receive at the front 150 car-loads daily, it is easy to understand the difficulty of supplying an army far from its base.

The work of the railways had also to be supplemented by the wagon-trains necessary in the field to carry the baggage of the army, its ammunition, and a few days' rations. The amount of food and forage required by a large army has already been referred to in connection with Grant's first advance on Vicksburg. It makes in the aggregate a bulk and weight astonishing to those who are not familiar with the subject. Great droves of beef cattle also accompanied the army, and the driving, feeding, and distributing of these, made, of itself, no small task.

After some further correspondence, the subject of the Confederate offensive in the West was dropped by the Richmond Government. It was now known that Grant would not personally lead the Western army, but would turn over his command to Sherman. Concentration on both sides was the order of the day, and Longstreet was directed to rejoin Lee. As Johnston had not accepted the aggressive plan suggested, he was notified that he could not expect the reinforcement promised him on that condition. Polk was ordered to join him, and he also received about 4000 men from Mobile. All the troops that Beauregard could spare, and that could be withdrawn from the Atlantic coast, were sent to Lee.

"The very unsatisfactory relations between Mr. Davis and General Johnston," says General Cox, "cannot be overlooked if we would judge intelligently the events of the Atlanta campaign." Johnston may have been right in thinking a winter campaign impracticable, but he should have carried out the wishes of his government, or resigned in time to let another undertake the task.

Little had been done by the Federal forces in the West during the winter. Grant remained in command until March, when he went East to assume his position of lieutenant-general, and commander-in-chief of all the armies. He was succeeded by General Sherman in Tennessee.

It was impossible for Sherman to assume the offensive against Johnston before the first of May, due to the bad condition of the roads in the early spring, the necessity of accumulating supplies, and the depletion of his ranks through the so-called "veteran act."

General William Tecumseh Sherman on horseback.

Prior to the opening of the campaign some changes were made in the organization of Sherman's army. The Twentieth Corps was formed by the consolidation of the Eleventh and

Twelfth, and placed under the command of Hooker; and Howard replaced Gordon Granger in command of the Fourth Corps. The Army of the Tennessee, consisting of the Fifteenth, Seventeenth, and part of the Sixteenth corps, was assigned to McPherson. Burnside was succeeded by Schofield in command of the Army of the Ohio, consisting only of the Twenty-third Corps. Thomas remained in command of the Army of the Cumberland, made up of the Fourth, Fourteenth, and Twentieth corps. As will appear later, several changes were made in these commands during the campaign.

The returns for the 30 April 1864 show Sherman's strength to have been about 110,000 men. After making all deductions for the garrisons of Nashville and Chattanooga, and the numerous small posts and blockhouses, he was able to take the field with nearly 100,000 troops. At the opening of the campaign, his forces were distributed as follows:

Army of the Ohio, Schofield, near Red Clay, on the railway thirteen miles north of Dalton, 13,559.

Army of the Tennessee, McPherson, at Lee and Gordon's Mill, twenty miles northwest of Dalton, 24,465.

Army of the Cumberland, Thomas, near Ringgold, on the railway twelve miles northwest of Dalton, 60,773.

The front from Red Clay to Lee and Gordon's Mill in Chickamauga Valley was twenty miles long.

Similar returns for Johnston's army at the end of April show that he had actually present at Dalton about 53,000 men. He was soon reinforced by Polk with 14,000, and a few detachments amounting to some 5000 more, giving him an aggregate of 75,000 men soon after the opening of the campaign.

Grant's instructions to Sherman, given in his confidential letter of the 4 April, were, to move against Johnston's army, to break it up, and to get into the interior of the enemy's country as far as he could, inflicting all the damage possible against their war resources.

Sherman's first objective therefore was Johnston's army, and the second, his base at Atlanta, 85 miles from Dalton. In his *Memoirs*, General Sherman says, "Atlanta was known as the Gate-City of the South, was full of foundries, arsenals, and machine-shops, and I knew that its capture would be the death-knell of the Southern Confederacy." It was a large town, of great strategic importance, the junction of railways leading to Chattanooga, Richmond, the Atlantic coast, and Montgomery, Alabama.

The country between Chattanooga and Atlanta was generally rugged and hilly, and covered with forests. Johnston's position at Dalton was protected in front by a ridge running north and south, some thirty miles long, which could be crossed by an army at two places only — the gap traversed by the railway, and Snake Creek Gap, fourteen miles farther south.

Sherman's advance began on the 7 May. Finding Johnston's position too strong to attack in front, Sherman sent McPherson to turn it by way of Villanow and Snake Creek Gap. Thomas was ordered to support him by making a strong demonstration against Johnston's front.

McPherson encountered a Confederate cavalry brigade on its way to occupy Snake Creek Gap, and routed it. On the afternoon of the 9th he was in front of Resaca, but considered the position too strong to assault; he therefore returned to the southern end of the gap, and there took up a strong position.

Leaving Howard, with Stoneman's cavalry division, to guard his line of communications, Sherman now moved the rest of his army to Snake Creek Gap, where, on the 12th, he concentrated his forces at McPherson's position.

As Sherman's first objective was Johnston's army, he did not undertake these flanking movements merely to compel the enemy to retreat and yield more territory. His constant desire was to force conclusions as near his own base as possible; but, unlike Grant, he was too wise to wreck his army in frontal attacks against impregnable positions. "It was with an unwillingness growing at times into impatience that he found himself compelled to follow Johnston's slow and skillful retreat. It was not till the change of the Confederate commanders that aggressive tactics on the part of the enemy gave the opportunity for severe punishment and led to the speedy destruction of the hostile army. Herein lies the key of the whole campaign."

On the morning of the 13 May, Johnston withdrew his army to Resaca, where he was joined by Polk's corps. He took up a strong position behind entrenchments on an irregular curve, covering the town, the bridges, and the railway. His right and left flanks were protected by the two rivers.

On the morning of the 14th, Sherman's advance was renewed, guided as before by the Army of the Tennessee on the right, and continuing the wheeling movement toward the east. The army was deployed in front of Resaca, and demonstrations were made against the enemy's front and right. At the same time, Sherman sent a division of infantry and Kilpatrick's cavalry to cross the Oostanaula by pontoon bridge at Lay's Ferry, five miles southwest of Resaca; and Garrard's cavalry division was despatched from Villanow by way of Rome to destroy the railroad between Calhoun and Kingston. These operations forced Johnston to withdraw from Resaca. Burning the railway bridge behind him, on the night of the 15th he began his retreat to Adairsville, where he arrived on the 17th. Here he was joined by a force of 3700 cavalry under W. H. Jackson.

On the 16th, Sherman took up the pursuit. The right under McPherson advanced by way of Lay's Ferry; Thomas, in the centre, followed the railway; the left, under Schofield, crossed the river a few miles east of Resaca. One division (Davis's) of the Fourteenth Corps was sent to the support of Garrard's cavalry in the capture of Rome. This town was important on account of the Confederate ironworks and machine-shops, as well as the large stores collected there.

The Union army was now in the most open district of northern Georgia, and Sherman was eager to bring the enemy to battle in this territory where his superior numbers would have a better chance of winning a decisive victory. He therefore pressed the advance of his columns.

On the afternoon of the 17th, Johnston selected a position for battle just north of Adairsville. Orders were given for the cavalry, strongly supported by infantry, to hold back Sherman's advance-guard until the deployment should be completed. The Confederate line was to be extended across the valley in which the railway ran, with the flanks upon the heights on either side. But, upon testing the position by a partial deployment, Johnston concluded that his army was not large enough to fill it, and he resumed his retreat on Cassville and Kingston. These two places were about seven miles apart. Johnston took the Kingston road with Hardee's corps, and the corps of Polk and Hood followed the route to Cassville. Johnston hoped that Sherman's columns would be so separated that he could concentrate upon one of them, and so fight his adversary in detail. The two hostile armies were now marching with wider fronts than at any time before, but the Federal flanks were farther apart than those of the Confederates.

The position on the hills behind the village of Cassville was so strong that Johnston decided to make a stand there and accept battle. He announced his purpose in an unusually formal manner by issuing a brief but stirring address to his troops. His plan was to have Polk's corps make a stand on the Cassville road, while Hardee guarded the flank toward Kingston, and Hood fell upon the left of Schofield, as the latter deployed to attack Polk. But when the Union left crossed Two Run Creek, and partly turned the right of the Confederate position, Hood and Polk became so uneasy that they protested against accepting battle there, and persuaded Johnston to continue his retreat through Cartersville across the Etowah River. Johnston always felt that he lost a great opportunity, and never ceased to regret it.

The relations of General Johnston with the Richmond Government had been strained since the beginning of the campaign, and his continued retreat had brought matters almost to the breaking point. Even a defeat at this time would have been better than a sudden withdrawal in the night, after he had so loudly proclaimed his intention of leading his men to battle. "Either the order had been an error," says General Cox, "or the retreat was one." Nothing is more destructive of the moral of an army than vacillation.

On the 20 May, Johnston took up a position at Allatoona Pass, which Sherman decided not to attempt to assail in front. After giving his army three days of rest, Sherman therefore set out on the 23rd to turn the position. As the army would be separated from the railway, supplies for twenty days were carried in the wagons. Three cavalry divisions covered the two flanks and the rear of the army, and the fourth cleared the front for the Union centre.

Sherman's general plan was to advance in several columns on Dallas, and from there on Marietta. Finding that his position at Allatoona was about to be turned, Johnston at once put his army in motion. His left under Hardee marched to Dallas, and took position south of the town, covering the main road to Atlanta and extending northeast toward New Hope Church. Hood held the right at the church, and Polk was in the centre upon the main road from Allatoona. Sherman's advance-column under Hooker vigorously attacked Hood's corps at New Hope Church, and the fighting lasted from about four o'clock in the afternoon until ended by the fall of night.

The Union army was now shifted to the left, and on the 6 June was again across the railroad at Acworth. In the new line the order of the armies was reversed, Schofield holding the right, and McPherson the left, with Thomas still in the centre. The base was moved to Allatoona.

In the meantime, Johnston had extended his line to the right until it reached from Lost Mountain to Brush Mountain, a distance of about twelve miles. Pine Mountain, an isolated hill in front of this line, was also occupied at first. Hardee's corps was still on the left, Polk's in the centre, and Hood's on the right. The cavalry, under Wheeler and Jackson, guarded the two flanks. The position covered Marietta, the railway back to Atlanta, and the bridges on Johnston's line of retreat.

On the 11th, the Union line was advanced close to that of the Confederates, and on the 14th Thomas deployed before Pine Mountain. On that day, while General Johnston, with Polk and Hardee, was reconnoitring on the mountain, Polk was struck and instantly killed by a shell from a Union battery. Loring succeeded to the command of his corps. That night the Confederate line was withdrawn from Pine Mountain.

Between the 16th and the 19th the Federals continued to press the Confederate lines, and Johnston drew in his forces nearer to Marietta. His line now extended along the crest of Kenesaw Mountain from end to end, and the Federals were close up to the Confederate trenches.

Since the first of June, it had rained continuously, and the whole country was a quagmire. There were only dirt roads in this region, and these were soon destroyed by the heavy army wagons. This greatly hindered the operations.

During the next few days there was considerable skirmishing between the two hostile lines, without any decisive result. Finally, on the 27 June, Sherman departed for the first time from his fixed policy and ordered an assault on Johnston's position on Kenesaw Mountain. The dense forest made any artillery preparation almost impossible, and the attack was one of infantry against unshaken earthworks. The assault was easily repulsed, with a Confederate loss of less than 500, while the Federal casualties are given as 2164 in the official reports.

The affairs at New Hope Church and Kenesaw Mountain convinced Sherman that it was impracticable to bring all his force to bear in this difficult country. He therefore resumed his advance by the tedious flanking movements, in the hope that the time would come when the enemy could no longer afford to retreat, and must resort to aggressive tactics.

Johnston continued to adhere to his patient and steady policy of defence, although he knew that his constant retreat was giving great dissatisfaction to the authorities at Richmond. He withdrew from one position to another, until he finally took up a line behind Peachtree Creek, to make a last stand for the defence of Atlanta. Meanwhile his relations with President Davis had reached a crisis, and on the evening of the 17 July he received a telegram from Richmond directing him to turn over the command of his army to Hood.

This step was taken by President Davis with great reluctance, and under strong popular and political pressure. It was claimed that Johnston intended to surrender Atlanta without giving battle. General Bragg was therefore sent from Richmond to interview him, and after spending two days at Atlanta telegraphed: "He has not sought my advice, and it was not volunteered. I cannot learn that he has any more plan in the future than he has had in the past."

Mr. Davis then telegraphed Johnston a direct inquiry: "I wish to hear from you as to present situation, and your plan of operations, so specifically as will enable me to anticipate events."

This was sent on the 16 July, and Johnston replied the same day as follows:

Confederate earthworks before Atlanta.

... As the enemy has double our numbers, we must be on the defensive. My plan of operations must therefore depend upon that of the enemy. It is mainly to watch for an opportunity to fight to advantage. We are trying to put Atlanta into condition to be held for a day or two by the Georgia militia, that army movements may be freer and wider.

This reply was certainly not specific, and was considered evasive. On the 17th, Adjutant-General Cooper telegraphed Johnston:

Sherman's men in the Atlanta trenches.

I am directed by the Secretary of War to inform you that as you have failed to arrest the advance of the enemy to the vicinity of Atlanta, far in the interior of Georgia, and express no confidence that you can defeat or repel him, you are hereby relieved from the command of the Army and the Department of the Tennessee, which you will immediately turn over to General Hood.

To this Johnston replied that the order had been received and obeyed, and added:

As to the alleged cause of my removal, I assert that Sherman's army is much stronger, compared with that of Tennessee, than Grant's compared with that of Northern Virginia. Yet the enemy has been compelled to advance much more slowly to the vicinity of Atlanta than to that of Richmond and Petersburg, and penetrated much deeper into Virginia than into Georgia. Confident language by a military commander is not usually regarded as evidence of competence.

It must be admitted that there was much truth in his statement, but it did not go to the heart of the matter. Between Lee and his government there was always a perfect frankness and a cordial understanding; so that in case of misfortune it was felt that he had done the best he could under the circumstances. Johnston's advice to Hood showed that he only needed to be equally frank with the Richmond authorities. Had he been so, it is quite safe to say that he would not have been removed.

The removal of General Johnston at this time has been generally condemned, and the result was certainly disastrous to the Confederate cause. A more favorable view of the action of President Davis, however, is expressed by General Cox. "It cannot be denied," he says, "that there was a certain justification for Mr. Davis's conclusion that the circumstances foreboded the yielding of Atlanta without the desperate struggle which the importance of the position demanded. Had Johnston expressed any hopefulness, or said, what was the fact, that he was himself coming to the determination to try the effect of a bold attack whilst Sherman's army was in motion, he would probably have been left in command."

Loring had already been succeeded by A. P. Stewart in command of Polk's old corps, and Cheatham now took the place of Hood.

John B. Hood, a native of Kentucky, was just entering upon his thirty-fourth year. After graduating at West Point in 1853, the same class with McPherson, Schofield, and Sheridan, he had seen active service fighting the Indians on the frontier, after which he was for some time a cavalry instructor at the Military Academy. He entered the Confederate army at the outbreak of the Civil War, and fought in most of the Virginia battles during the first two years. He was severely wounded at Gettysburg, losing the use of one arm. Going West with Longstreet, he fought bravely at Chickamauga, where he lost a leg. From Dalton to Atlanta he commanded a corps with the rank of lieutenant-general, and now, on his promotion to the command of the army, he received the provisional grade of a full general. In his *Memoirs*, General Sherman says that "Hood, though not deemed much of a scholar, or of great mental capacity, was undoubtedly a brave, determined, and rash man."

On the evening of the 19 July, the Union right under Thomas, and the centre under Schofield, were in the act of crossing Peachtree Creek at two different points, while the left under McPherson was near Decatur. The flanks of the army were fully ten miles apart, and there was a wide interval between Thomas and Schofield.

Johnston had expected to attack Sherman's army while it was divided in crossing this difficult stream, and he magnanimously explained his plans to Hood. In reading his statement, one cannot help thinking how unfortunate for him it was that he did not state his plans to Mr. Davis as fully as he gave them to Hood!

Pursuant to this plan, on the afternoon of the 20th Hood attacked Thomas in flank, while Cheatham held off Schofield and McPherson. The Confederate movement was well concealed by the dense woods up to the moment of the onset; but the assault was repulsed by Thomas. This was the battle of Peachtree Creek.

On the 22nd, the second part of Johnston's plan was tried. While Cheatham advanced from the Atlanta lines and resumed the assaults upon McPherson and Schofield, Hardee's corps made a long night march to a position south of Decatur, and fell upon McPherson's flank. A great battle was fought along a front of five miles, but the Confederates were repulsed at every point, and forced to retire within the defences of the city. The brave McPherson was killed on this day, and Howard succeeded him in command of the Army of the Tennessee.

On the 28th, as Howard was marching from the left wing to the right, to extend the Union lines southward on the west side of Atlanta, Hood fiercely attacked the Federal flank at Ezra Church, but was again repulsed.

In these three battles around Atlanta the Confederate losses were about 15,000, while the Federal casualities were only 6000. It was only a week since Johnston had been relieved, and the Confederate troops were so discouraged that for the first time in the Civil War they refused to continue the assaults. It was generally understood on both sides that a change of commanders meant the adoption of an aggressive policy on the part of the Confederates, but no one expected that it would so soon result in the ruin of their cause. At the time of his succession to the command Hood claimed that his army numbered less than 50,000 effectives; thus, in less than ten days, his tactics had resulted in the loss of thirty per cent, of his command.

At this time there were several more changes in the general officers of both armies. On the 26 July, Stephen D. Lee succeeded Cheatham in command of Hood's old corps. Hooker, who ranked Howard, resigned in disgust when the latter was promoted to succeed McPherson; and Slocum was assigned to the Twentieth Corps. Palmer also, a little later, took offense at being ordered to serve under Schofield, whom he claimed to rank, and gave up the command of the Fourteenth Corps. He was succeeded by Jeff. C. Davis.

At the end of July, Sherman was awaiting the result of several attempts with his cavalry to cut Hood's communications. These operations all failed, and he states in his *Memoirs*: "I now became satisfied that ...nothing would suffice but for us to reach it [the railroad below Atlanta] with the main army."

In furtherance of this plan, during the first three weeks of August the Union line was extended to the west and south of Atlanta. In the meantime Wheeler had raided the Union communications as far back as Dalton, and done considerable damage. Taking advantage of Wheeler's absence, Sherman sent Kilpatrick to try once more to cut Hood's communications. The Union cavalry made a complete circuit of Atlanta, took some prisoners, and destroyed a few miles of railway, but in a day or two the damage was all repaired. Sherman therefore returned to his plan of a movement with his whole army.

Accordingly, rations for fifteen days were issued to the army, and the movement began on the 25 August. On the 31st, Hardee, with about half the Confederate army, made a fierce attack on the Union lines, but was repulsed. The following day, Hood evacuated Atlanta, and concentrated his army at Lovejoy Station. Sherman then occupied the city, to rest and prepare for further operations. Thomas was stationed at Atlanta, Howard at East Point, and Schofield at Decatur. The cavalry covered the flanks and rear from Roswell to Sandtown. The Atlanta campaign was at an end.

According to the return of his army for the 30 April 1864, on file in the War Department, General Johnston had "present for duty "about 53,000 men. Between that date and the 10 June he received reinforcements to the number of 32,000 men. His army reached its maximum strength at New Hope Church, where he had about 75,000 troops in line. At that same time General Sherman's army numbered about 93,000 men of all arms. The odds against Johnston, therefore, were not so great as frequently stated.

The destruction of the Atlanta railroad depot. Sherman was intent on burning every building in Atlanta.

The losses on both sides during the campaign were approximately:

	Federals	*Confederates*
Killed	4,423	3,044
Wounded	22,822	18,952
Missing	4,442	12,983
Totals	31,687	34,979

"High as was the National estimate of the importance of Sherman's campaign," says General Cox, "Southern men rated it and its consequences quite as high as we did…. When the city fell, the whole South as well as the North knew that a decisive step had been taken toward the defeat of the rebellion."

The campaign began on the 7 May, and ended with Hood's evacuation of Atlanta. In less than four months, almost entirely by skillful manoeuvres, Sherman had forced the Confederate army back about ninety miles, and reached his goal. In the same length of time, Grant had forced Lee back from the Rapidan to the lines in front of Petersburg, but he did not capture Richmond until the following April. In both campaigns the opposing forces were practically the same — 100,000 Federals and 60,000 Confederates. The difference between Grant's tactics of "hammering," and Sherman's of manoeuvring, is shown by the list of casualties — Grant had lost over 50,000 men, while Sherman had lost less than 30,000. Both campaigns were made in very difficult country.

Sherman's campaign has been highly praised by both American and European critics, and little fault can be found with his strategy. His greatest mistake was the unnecessary and costly assault of Kenesaw Mountain. His excuse was, that the army was tired of marching over the muddy roads, and wanted to fight. The assault was tactically well made, but the position proved too strong.

Sherman seems to have missed a good opportunity to strike the Confederate army a decisive blow during Hood's withdrawal from Atlanta, when he had to make a flank march by the heads of the three Union armies. Hood himself expressed surprise that he was allowed to do so unmolested.

If Johnston had not been relieved of command he might have held Atlanta for as many months as Lee kept Grant at bay in front of Petersburg. But Hood, both by his natural disposition and the force of circumstances, was committed from the first to an aggressive policy, which speedily proved ruinous. He blamed his failure in the attacks of the 20th and 22nd to one of his corps commanders, General Hardee. But General Alexander states that it was due largely to his own neglect "to supervise the execution of important orders — a sort of failure from which even the most eminent commanders have never been exempt."

As in many other campaigns, the use of the cavalry in "raids" proved an amusement that was very costly to both sides. General Cox well remarks that, "the game was never worth the candle."

Both armies in this campaign made constant use of field-works. "Except in attacking the Kenesaw Mountain," says Hamley, "the character of Sherman's operations was, throughout, the same. To protect his main line from a counter-attack, he left a force entrenched across it. He then reinforced his flanking wing to a strength sufficient to cope with the whole army of the enemy, and directed it, by a circuit off the main line, upon the Confederate rear. In every case the operation was successful, obliging Johnston forthwith to abandon his strongest positions, and to retreat."

"No officer or soldier who ever served under me," writes General Sherman," will question the generalship of Joseph E. Johnston. His retreats were timely, in good order, and he left nothing behind."

CHAPTER NINETEEN

SEPTEMBER 1864 — APRIL 1865

NASHVILLE

FOLLOWING the occupation of Atlanta, there were no further military, operations for a period of several weeks. Logan and Blair went home to look after politics, and many of the regiments claimed the discharge to which they were entitled by reason of the expiration of their terms of service. The whole army, officers and men alike, seemed to relax more or less, and desire a rest after the fatigue of the four months' campaign.

Although Sherman had attained his goal, in taking Atlanta, he "had not accomplished all, for Hood's army, the chief objective, had escaped." The "real trouble "had only begun. The Confederate army, composed of veterans inured to war, and still 40,000 strong, was only thirty miles away, at Lovejoy Station, on the railroad to Savannah. On the 21 September, Hood shifted his position to Palmetto Station, twenty-five miles southwest of Atlanta, and began preparations for an active campaign against Sherman's line of communications, to compel him to abandon Atlanta. At this time, Hood was visited by President Davis, who made his celebrated speech in which he predicted that his army would make Sherman's retreat more disastrous than that of Napoleon from Moscow. Forewarned, Sherman took immediate steps to thwart Hood's plans. Newton's division of the Fourth Corps, and Morgan's of the Fourteenth, were sent back to Tennessee ; and Corse's division of the Seventeenth Corps was ordered to Rome. Thomas was despatched to his headquarters at Nashville, and Schofield to his at Knoxville, while Sherman remained at Atlanta to await Hood's next move. Orders were given the Union commanders at Nashville, Decatur, and Chattanooga to take active measures to protect the railway.

At this time, Grant had Lee's army invested at Petersburg; Canby at New Orleans was preparing for an expedition against Mobile, in conjunction with Farragut's fleet; and a combined land and naval expedition was contemplated against Fort Fisher at the mouth of Cape Fear River, in North Carolina. On the 12 September, General Grant wrote that he was in doubt as to the best plan for the use of the forces under Sherman's command. On the 20th, Sherman replied: "I should keep Hood employed, and put my army in fine order for a march on Augusta, Columbia, and Charleston; and start as soon as Wilmington is sealed to commerce, and the city of Savannah is in our possession."

At this stage of the correspondence, Hood simplified the situation by taking the offensive, and threatening Sherman's long line of communications. On the 5 October he attacked the Union base at Allatoona, but was repulsed with heavy loss. Leaving one corps under

Slocum to defend Atlanta, Sherman at once moved against Hood. A week later, Sherman was at Rome, while the Confederates captured Dalton, with its garrison of 1000 men. On the 15th, Sherman was back at Snake Creek Gap, where he had begun his campaign in May, and Hood was a few miles south of Lafayette. Here Hood intended to select a position, and give battle, but he was deterred by his corps-commanders who advised against it. Therefore, after resting two days at Cross Roads, he directed his march on Gadsden, where he concentrated his army on the 22 October.

In the meantime, General Beauregard had been placed in command of the Military Division of the West, which included Hood's army, and Cheatham had been assigned to the old corps of Hardee, whom Hood blamed for his defeats around Atlanta. Hood's far-reaching plans at this time, according to his own account, were to capture Nashville, and make it a base for a victorious campaign in Kentucky; then to

John B. Hood lost the use of an arm at Gettysburg and lost a leg at Chickamauga. He was given the command of Johnston's army. Under his command the Confederate army in the West was virtually annihilated at Nashville.

move east, through some of the gaps in the Cumberland Mountains, and fall upon Grant's rear at Petersburg. After this, his army, combined with Lee's, might turn and rend Sherman, or march north and capture Washington.

Sherman followed Hood as far as Gaylesville, where he halted to see what the Confederates would do next. After a short pause, Hood crossed the mountains to Decatur, which he avoided attacking, as it was well defended, and finally halted at Tuscumbia, opposite Florence, Alabama, on the Tennessee River.

Sherman then sent two of his six corps by rail to Thomas at Nashville, and began his preparations for the march to the coast. Repairing the broken railroads, he collected at Atlanta all the supplies necessary for his expedition. On the 4 November, he had assembled four infantry corps, one cavalry division, and 65 field-guns, an aggregate of about 60,000 men.

While at Gadsden, Hood received a visit from Beauregard, to whom he unfolded his plan of campaign, which was formally approved. Beauregard stipulated, however, that Wheeler's cavalry should be detached, to hang on Sherman's rear, but promised to send an order to

Rushing a federal battery out to Nashville to help Thomas fight the impending battle with Hood.

Forrest to join Hood's army as soon as it crossed the Tennessee. Hood was detained three weeks at Tuscumbia, waiting for supplies, and for Forrest to come up. The cavalry was much impeded in its march by muddy roads and high water, and did not join Hood until the 18 November. This delay proved to be the salvation of Nashville.

Notwithstanding all the efforts of the Union authorities to reinforce Thomas, there were only about 30,000 Federal troops within the whole District, when Hood reached the Tennessee River, the last of October. The Union forces were scattered in detachments all the way from Chattanooga to the Ohio River, guarding the lines of communication. As the success of Sherman's movement was bound up with Thomas's ability to defeat Hood's plans, it would have been more prudent to send another corps to Nashville, and make the march to the sea with a smaller force.

The forces which Sherman left behind for Thomas comprised the Fourth Corps under Stanley, the Twenty-third under Schofield, and about 5000 cavalry under General Wilson, whom Grant had sent West from the Army of the Potomac, with the message, "I believe he will add fifty per cent, to the effectiveness of your cavalry."

Thomas's force, of 22,000 infantry and 5000 cavalry, was entirely inadequate to cope with Hood's veteran army of 35,000 infantry, and 5000 cavalry led by the redoubtable Forrest, whose maxim was that "success lies in getting there first with the most men." But Sherman had sent to Missouri for an additional corps of 14,000 men, commanded by General Andrew J. Smith, an able officer. It was hoped that Smith could leave St. Louis by the 10 November, but he was busy driving Sterling Price out of the state, and this caused a delay of two weeks. He did not reach St. Louis until the 24th, and it was the last day of the month when he finally joined Thomas at Nashville. At the same time some 5000 men, belonging to different organizations, who had been belated in rejoining, were sent from Chattanooga, and formed into a provisional division under General Steedman. Other reinforcements from different points also joined about the first of December, so that on that date Thomas found himself at the head of a motley array of between 50,000 and 55,000 men.

Hood's long delay at Tuscumbia — an accident upon which no one could have calculated — gave time for Thomas to concentrate his army, and saved the situation. This would seem to prove that Sherman was unwarranted in taking so large a part of his army for his "military promenade," and leaving so slender a force to oppose Hood. Everything finally turned out all right, but Thomas had an anxious four weeks at Nashville after Sherman cut loose from Atlanta.

Having finally obtained his supplies, and been joined by the larger part of his cavalry, on the 19 November Hood crossed the river at Florence and began his northward march. Thomas was at Nashville, occupied with hurrying up his reinforcements, and the main body of the Union army, the Fourth and Twenty-third corps, was at Pulaski, under the command of Schofield.

Hood's army marched in three columns, Stewart's corps by the Lawrenceburg road, Cheatham's by the Waynesboro road, and Lee's by an intermediate road. Hood hoped to out-flank Schofield's position at Pulaski, and cut off his retreat by seizing the bridge across Duck River at Columbia.

On the 22nd, Stewart was at Lawrenceburg, sixteen miles west of Pulaski. Schofield now realized that he had no time to lose, and at once set his troops in motion. By a forced march he reached Columbia just in time to prevent Forrest from seizing the bridge, and cutting off his line of retreat. As fast as the troops arrived they were ordered to throw up earthworks to cover the approaches to the town from the south; the trains were sent across the river. There was a terrible storm of rain, turning to sleet and snow, and the roads were in such condition that Hood's army could make no more than ten miles a day. The last of his forces, therefore, did not arrive in front of Columbia until the 26th.

At Columbia, Schofield was joined by one brigade of infantry, and Wilson came forward from Nashville and took command of the cavalry, which had now been strengthened to 7000 horsemen. Wilson placed his force along the north bank of the river to observe the enemy's movements either to the right or the left.

As Thomas was anxious to preserve the railway bridge at Columbia for further use, he urged Schofield to hold his ground there. But Schofield became convinced that Hood intended to cross the river above the town and turn his position, so he withdrew his army to the north bank on the night of the 27th. The following night Forrest's cavalry forded the river; and early on the morning of the 29th, the corps of Cheatham and Stewart crossed by a pontoon bridge three miles above the town, and marched to Spring Hill on the Franklin Pike, twelve miles in Schofield's rear. Lee's corps was left behind, with orders to make a strong demonstration in front of the Union position.

Information of these movements reached Schofield the morning of the 29th, and he immediately started Stanley for Spring Hill with two of his divisions, the trains and reserve artillery. When Hood's force of about 18,000 men reached Spring Hill at 3 p.m., the place was held only by one Union division, 4000 strong. Hood took Cheatham, with Cleburne, one of his division commanders, within sight of the pike, along which the enemy could now be seen retreating at double-quick, with wagons in a trot, and gave orders to attack at once and seize the pike. Similar orders were given to Stewart, and further commands were sent later by staff-officers. But no attack was made, and the Confederate troops bivouacked within gunshot of the pike, without making any effort to occupy it. After nightfall the Federal infantry all passed by, unmolested except for some random shots to which they made no reply.

This failure to destroy the Union army has never been satisfactorily explained. In his book, Hood calls the opportunity "the best move in my career as a soldier." Nevertheless, as General Alexander says, it proved the death-blow to Hood's army. "A single Confederate brigade ...planted squarely across the pike, either north or south of Spring Hill, would have effectually prevented Schofield's retreat, and daylight would have found his whole force cut off from every avenue of escape by more than twice its numbers, to assault whom would have been madness, and to avoid whom would have been impossible." General Alexander states that Cheatham and Stewart were both absent from their troops that evening, and the former subsequently frankly admitted his delinquency. In view of the distinguished records of the two officers, Hood magnanimously overlooked their failure.

Schofield had realized his dangerous position, and fully expected to find his route blocked, at least at Thompson's Station, three miles north of Spring Hill. He hoped that the corps of A. J. Smith might have reached Franklin, and despatched one of his staff-officers to hurry it forward. He also telegraphed General Thomas that he regarded his situation as extremely perilous. But he found the way clear, and his army reached Franklin without being seriously molested.

The river there was unfordable after the recent rains; the old wagon bridge was in bad condition, and the pontoon-train had been destroyed at Columbia, to prevent it from falling into the hands of the Confederates. As soon as Schofield arrived, therefore, his first care was to repair the wagon bridge, and plank the railway bridge. By noon this work was completed. In the meantime preparations were made to hold the south side of the river until the trains could be got across.

The little town of Franklin was located on the southern bank of the Harpeth River in a bend less than a mile across at its widest part. As fast as the troops came up, they entrenched a line upon rising ground, convex in shape, with both flanks resting upon the river, and completely covering the town.

The two main highways left the town by the same street, but forked at the southern edge, the Columbia Pike running south, and Carter's Creek Pike southwest. The railway ran near the river, parallel to the road to Columbia. Just south of the town, and a quarter of a mile west of the river, the Carter house stood upon a low hill. To the east of the town, on the other side of the river, there was an earthwork, Fort Granger, where Federal batteries were placed, which commanded the open ground to the south and west.

The entire line of entrenchments was about a mile and a half long. The space between the river and the Columbia Pike, near the Carter house, was held by Cox's division; Ruger's division was between the two pikes; and Kimball's division carried the line to the river on the right. Wood was sent across to the north bank to protect the trains, and Wilson's cavalry was also on that side to guard against any turning movement of the enemy.

The Federal position was very strong, but it had one weak point which nearly proved fatal. On the arrival of Wagner's division of the Fourth Corps, which had served as rear-guard, the first brigade (Opdycke) took position within the lines, just west of the Columbia Pike, as a reserve; but the two other brigades (Lane and Conrad) made a halt on a knoll 500 yards in front of the lines. They were not entrenched, as there was no intention to have them remain in this position. Wagner had been ordered to occupy the point "in observation only till Hood should show a disposition to advance in force, and then to retire within the lines to Opdycke's position to act as a general reserve."

The head of Hood's column arrived between two and three o'clock on the afternoon of the 30th. Stewart's corps deployed to the east of the Columbia Pike, and Cheatham's to the west, with Cleburne's division on the right, partly astride the pike, Brown's next, and Bate's on the extreme left. Only Johnson's division of Lee's corps had come up, and it was held in reserve.

The impetuous Hood, anxious to make up for the opportunity that he had lost the previous night, ordered Cheatham to attack at once. The two divisions of Cleburne and Brown, charging at double-quick, fell like an avalanche upon Wagner's two brigades in their isolated position, and drove the men back in headlong flight. The Federal troops in the main line were obliged to withhold their fire in order to avoid killing their comrades, and the Confederates swept over the Union entrenchments on the heels of the fugitives. Over a thousand prisoners were taken, and a wide rent was made in the very centre of the Union line of battle.

Standing guard on the Cumberland

For a moment it looked as though the day were lost, but Opdycke hurried up his brigade from its position in reserve, and he was supported by two regiments of Cox's division. In the hand-to-hand struggle which ensued the Confederates were finally driven out of the works. Just before nightfall Johnson's division went to Cheatham's support, but the Union line held fast. Simultaneous attacks were made by Stewart on the right, and Bate on the opposite flank, but no impression was made on the Federal lines. Though many of the Confederates succeeded in reaching the ditches, none crossed the parapets.

Franklin was one of the most fiercely fought battles of the Civil War, and the Confederates "went down to defeat in a blaze of glory." Over 10 per cent. of the force engaged were killed on the field, over 20 per cent. were severely wounded, and as many more were slightly wounded or captured. Their loss of general officers was unparalleled on either side in any action of the war: five were killed, five were wounded, and one was captured. Of the regimental commanders, fifty-three were killed, wounded, or captured. Among the slain was Patrick Cleburne, the most brilliant Confederate division-commander in the West. He began his military career as corporal in the 41st Foot, and he himself attributed his rapid rise to the habits of efficiency he had acquired in the ranks of his old regiments in the British army.

General Alexander attributes the Confederate failure to three causes: —

(1) Hood did not prepare his assault with any severe cannonade, because the village of Franklin was just in the rear of the Union line.

(2) The action did not begin until 4 p.m.; the sun set at 4:50, and there was no moon. Darkness therefore prevented Hood from getting in two of Lee's divisions.

(3) The presence on the field of Casement's Federal brigade with magazine breech-loaders, which did terrible execution.

The battle continued with violence until 9 p.m., and firing was kept up until 3 a.m., when the Federals withdrew from the field, leaving their dead and wounded.

During the night the Union army continued its retreat to Nashville, taking with it the wagon-trains, more than 1000 prisoners, and 33 flags captured from the enemy.

The forces of Schofield reached Nashville on the morning of the first of December, and took their place in the works. Wilson's cavalry, which had covered the flanks and rear of the retreating army, was sent to Edgefield on the north bank of the Cumberland.

Hood followed, and arrived the next day. He immediately took position in front of the Union works, and threw up entrenchments. Lee's corps occupied the centre of the line, astride the road to Franklin; Cheatham's the right, and Stewart's the left. Most of the Confederate cavalry was stationed on the left, between Stewart and the river. Hood's army was now reduced to about 25,000 men, and he did not feel strong enough to assault the Union works. He hoped that Thomas would attack, and meet with a bloody repulse.

By this time, A. J. Smith's veteran Sixteenth Corps, 12,000 strong, had reached Nashville, and other reinforcements had brought Thomas's army up to about 55,000, including 12,000 cavalry.

The Union works ran on a line of hills around Nashville, extending from the river above to the river below the city. Steedman's division was on the left; next, the Twenty-third Corps under Schofield; then the Fourth Corps, now commanded by Wood, and Smith's troops on the right.

Having finally assembled an army, of good, though rather mixed elements, Thomas did not propose to fight an indecisive battle, like Shiloh or Gettysburg. He meant to make his victory a Waterloo, which should wipe the defeated army out of existence. He had a large force of cavalry, under a very able commander, and he intended to have it play an important part in the coming contest. He therefore proposed to give Wilson time to procure horses to replace the large number worn out during the campaign. He also needed time to prepare his trains and pontoons for a vigorous pursuit after the battle.

As usual, Mr. Stanton became impatient at once, and telegraphed General Grant that Thomas's course looked like "the McClellan and Rosecrans strategy of doing nothing." With Grant's own large experience of unavoidable delays, one would suppose that he would have shown a better appreciation of the situation, but he began bombarding Thomas with despatch after despatch, in which he displayed unusual anxiety and some irritation. On the 6th, he ordered Thomas to "attack Hood at once." But, in spite of this order, Thomas decided to give Wilson two days more.

On the 8 December, Thomas was entirely ready. Then there came a storm of sleet and snow which covered the ground with a sheet of ice, and made any movement impossible for several days. At last, on the 14th, a warm rain cleared the ice away, and orders were issued for an attack the next day.

In the meantime, Grant had prepared an order, which was never sent, appointing Schofield in place of Thomas; and on the 13th he directed Logan, who was still absent from his corps, to proceed to Nashville, and relieve Thomas. On the 15th, Grant himself reached Washington on his way to Nashville. Here he received news which satisfied him that neither he nor Logan was needed at Nashville.

Nearly the entire space occupied by the Union army was inclosed by two small streams, Richland and Brown's creeks, rising near each other in the high Brentwood Hills, four or five miles south of Nashville, and flowing in divergent courses to the Cumberland. The Granny White Turnpike ran southward on the high ridge between the two creeks, and eight other pikes radiated southward from the city. The ground was broken and hilly, with knolls and ridges rising 200 to 300 feet above the river; but it was mostly open, with timber here and there.

Hood's main line, which was more than five miles long, stretched along a series of hills from the Chattanooga Railroad on the east to the Franklin Pike; thence it crossed the valley of Brown's Creek, passed over the ridge on which ran the Granny White Pike, and reached a high knoll near the Hillsboro Pike, where it made a sharp turn to the south, following a stone wall along the pike for about 1000 yards. In advance of the main line, a body of skirmishers was strongly posted on Montgomery Hill, at the Hillsboro Pike.

Strong batteries were placed on three commanding points, and redoubts crowned two detached hills about a mile to the southwest, beyond a fork of Richland Creek. Hood's position was strong, but the line was too long to hold securely with his forces. The concave form was also an element of weakness.

Thomas's plan of battle was for Smith and Wood, supported by Wilson's cavalry on their right flank, to make the main attack on Hood's left wing. At the same time, Steedman was to make a vigorous demonstration against Cheatham, on the Confederate right. Schofield was to be kept in reserve.

The movement began at dawn on the 15 December. The early morning was foggy, but a hot sun burned off the mists before nine o'clock. The mud resulting from the thaw made the operations very slow. Wood's corps marched by the right flank until its left rested on the salient at Laurens Hill, which was the pivot upon which Wood and Smith were to wheel to the left. Smith formed on Wood's right, and Wilson's cavalry moved out to clear the Charlotte and Harden pikes of the enemy on the right.

Smith's corps and the cavalry advanced steadily, capturing the Confederate detached works one after another, until by noon they were well up to Hood's main line on the Hillsboro Pike. Wilson was then ordered to make a circuit to the right, with a view of gaining the Confederate rear, and Schofield was sent forward to take his place on Smith's right.

In the meantime, at eight o'clock, Steedman had advanced along the Murfreesboro Pike, and vigorously attacked Cheatham on the Confederate right. This demonstration not only occupied Cheatham all day, but it also neutralized Lee's corps and made it useless. Lee did not dare to send assistance either to Cheatham on his right, or Stewart on his left, for fear that the Federals would charge straight down the Franklin Pike and pierce the thin Confederate centre.

In the afternoon, Smith continued his advance against the Confederate left, and drove away the defenders behind the stone wall on the Hillsboro Pike. A division of the Fourth Corps had already taken the strong Confederate outpost position on Montgomery Hill, and Thomas now ordered Wood to carry the salient on the hill in front of his line. This was done in brilliant fashion, and the whole Confederate left was now shattered and falling back. The broken line did not rally until it had withdrawn behind the Granny White Pike. Here darkness ended the fighting.

After nightfall, Hood formed a new line about two miles farther south, and entrenched it. He also changed the arrangement of his corps: Cheatham was moved over to the left flank, Stewart was placed in the centre, and Lee, who had taken little part in the action, was stationed on the right. The line, which was about two miles long, covered the two main roads to the south. The right rested on Overton Hill, just east of the Franklin Pike; the left, on two hills west of the Granny White Pike; the centre was on lower ground which was broken by several branches of Brown's Creek. The cavalry, under Chalmers, was on the extreme left of the new line.

Forrest's cavalry, except Chalmers's division, was absent during the battle. A detachment of some 8000 Federals had been stationed at Murfreesboro to guard the Nashville and Chattanooga Railroad. On the 2 December Hood sent Bate's division, reinforced by two infantry brigades, to cooperate with Forrest in a raid against the railway and Rousseau's command at Murfreesboro. The expedition was successful in capturing a railway train and destroying several bridges and blockhouses, but Bate was defeated by Rousseau, and then recalled. The absence of Forrest, as General Cox states, "made the opportunity which resulted so gloriously for our arms."

On the morning of the 16th, the Federals advanced against the new Confederate line. The alignment was practically the same as on the previous day: Steedman on the extreme left; Wood next; then Smith and Schofield, with Wilson's cavalry on the extreme right.

After a preliminary reconnaissance in force, to feel out the Confederate line, soon after noon Wood's corps, supported by Steedman's division, assaulted the right of the enemy's position, but was repulsed with severe loss. Meanwhile Wilson's cavalry had reached a position in the rear of the Confederate left. About four o'clock Schofield and Smith attacked this part of the line in front and flank, while Wilson's dismounted troopers assailed it from the rear. Under the fire of artillery, which prevented the Confederates from raising their heads above the breastworks, the Federals made a sudden and gallant charge up to and over the entrenchments. The line, thus pierced, gave way, and soon afterward broke at all points. General Hood says: "I beheld for the first and only time a Confederate army abandon the field in confusion." All hope of rallying the troops proved vain.

Wilson's dismounted men, when the break came, were widely separated from their horses. This delayed their pursuit, which was also impeded by a drenching rain which set in after nightfall. Two miles from the battlefield they found Chalmers's cavalry division strongly posted across the Granny White Pike behind a barricade of fence-rails. This checked the Federal cavalry long enough to enable the fleeing Confederate infantry to pass the danger point, organize a rear-guard, and make good their escape the next day.

On the morning of the 17th, Smith and Schofield were ordered to follow Wilson along the Granny White Pike, while Wood's corps pursued the mass of the fugitives, who took the Franklin Pike. The cavalry caught up with Hood's rear-guard four miles north of Franklin, and captured 400 prisoners. Forrest rejoined the army at Columbia, and covered the retreat to the Tennessee River. There the pursuit was abandoned. On the 10 January 1865, the remnant of the Confederate army was at Tupelo, Mississippi. Three days later, Hood asked to be relieved from his command.

It is difficult to give an exact statement of the numbers and losses during the Nashville Campaign. At Franklin, Schofield had about 30,000 men of all arms; and at Nashville, Thomas had some 55,000. The Union losses at Franklin are reported as 2326, and at Nashville, as 3057, or less than 6000 for the whole campaign.

At the end of the Atlanta Campaign, Hood had about 35,000 infantry, and he was joined at Tuscumbia by Forrest with perhaps 5000 horsemen. He states that he lost 7500 men at Franklin, and that his effective strength at Nashville was only 23,000. As he had sent Forrest, with part of his cavalry, and Bate, with his division, reinforced by two infantry brigades, or an expedition against Murfreesboro, this estimate is probably correct. Van Home puts his losses at Franklin at 5252, Livermore at 6252, and Alexander at 7550. Hood made no estimate of his losses at Nashville, except to state that they were "very small." Thomas reported 4462 prisoners, and Hood puts his "missing" at about 4500. At Tupelo, after the campaign, the Confederate army was reduced to about 18,000 men of all arms.

At Nashville, the Confederate army in the West was virtually annihilated. It was the most decisive victory gained by either side during the Civil War, and one of the most brilliant.

The campaign of Franklin and Nashville is one of the most interesting and instructive of the war. Hood's operations during the first month, from the time he left Lovejoy on the 20 September until he arrived at Gadsden, were bold in conception and brilliant in execution. He drew Sherman with his army all the way back to Resaca, seventy miles, and from there to Gaylesville, over forty miles farther, and away from his line of communications. At this point, however, Sherman occupied a very, strong strategic position, which left no course open to Hood except to cross the Tennessee at a point beyond Sherman's reach, and move northward. This is precisely what Hood did.

Major Steele thinks that General Thomas ought to have stopped Hood's army south of Duck River, and General Cox says that Thomas's right policy was to concentrate all his available forces promptly and meet Hood as near the Tennessee River as practicable. But with all

On his March to the Sea, Sherman cut his army loose from its base and communications in order to destroy civil commerce and resources that could fund the Confederacy's war efforts.

deference to these authorities, it is doubtful whether the final outcome of the campaign would have been so decisive if Thomas had advanced from Nashville.

Hood really lost the campaign through his stay of three weeks at Florence, while awaiting his supplies and the arrival of Forrest. This gave time for Sherman to transfer the Fourth and Twenty-third corps from Georgia to Tennessee; for Smith to bring the Sixteenth Corps from Missouri; for Thomas to concentrate the scattered Federal detachments; and finally, for Wilson to mount his cavalry. Up to about the 10 November, Stanley's corps and a few regiments of cavalry were the only Union troops between Hood's army and Nashville.

Hood's delay at Florence, however, came near turning out a strategic advantage for him, as it afforded an opportunity of outflanking Schofield at Pulaski. Later, at Spring Hill, he failed to cut off and destroy the Union army only through the negligence of two of his corps commanders, which has never been satisfactorily explained. With victory almost in his grasp, like Hooker at Chancellorsville, Hood let the opportunity slip away. Although Cheatham was primarily to blame, Hood was on the ground, and cannot shift the responsibility.

After his failure at Franklin, Hood's advance to Nashville was a great mistake: it simply invited disaster. His final blunder was sending Forrest on a raid toward Murfreesboro. The absence of the bulk of the Confederate horsemen made possible the turning movement of the Federals which gained the victory on the second day. It was only one more instance of the general misuse of the cavalry during the Civil War.

Although Thomas was very slow in getting ready to attack Hood, his final operations were nearly perfect in plan and execution. His cavalry did more actual fighting than was done on any other battlefield of the Civil War, but it fought dismounted. "Considering the disorder and rout in which Hood's beaten army quitted the battlefield," says Major Steele, "it might seem that they ought to have been cut off and blocked by Wilson's horsemen, 12,000 strong, and captured or destroyed by the pursuing infantry. But the earthen by-roads over which the cavalry had to march were in such deplorable condition, the streams with their bridges destroyed were so high, and forage for animals was so scarce in the country, that Wilson, in spite of great exertion, was unable to check the fugitive column before it was safe across the Tennessee River."

On the 2 November Sherman finally secured Grant's permission to undertake the "March to the Sea," on the understanding that Thomas was to be left strong enough to deal with Hood. Sherman began his preparations by burning every building in Atlanta — "not a single one was spared, not even a church." This was excused on the ground that "War is Hell." As General Alexander tersely remarks: "It depends somewhat upon the warrior. The conduct of Lee's army in Pennsylvania presents a pleasing contrast."

On the 15th Sherman started, taking with him four infantry corps, 63,000 strong, besides 5000 cavalry under Kilpatrick. The wagon-trains carried rations for twenty days, but he proposed to have his army live largely off the country. The Confederate authorities had hoped that the Georgia militia, aided by the few troops which could be gathered in the state, and by thirteen brigades of cavalry under Wheeler, might impede the march, but such expectations proved vain.

The march is notable mainly as an example of an army's cutting loose from its base and communications. The main purpose was to destroy the resources of the Confederacy, and this was done over a wide area. "There is no question," says General Alexander, "that the moral effect of this march, upon the country at large, both at the North and at the South, and also upon foreign nations, was greater than would have been the most decided victory."

The march through Georgia met with no serious opposition. On the 10 December, Sherman was in front of the works about Savannah; on the 20th, Hardee evacuated the city, and withdrew to Charleston with the garrison of 18,000 men. On the 23rd, Sherman occupied the place, and sent President Lincoln a telegram stating that he made Uncle Sam a Christmas present of the city, with 150 heavy guns, and 25,000 bales of cotton.

From this point began the far more arduous march northward through the Carolinas. Fort Fisher was captured by General Terry about the middle of January 1865, and toward the end of that month Sherman started by way of Columbia, South Carolina, to join General Grant in front of Petersburg.

In February the Confederate Government made Lee general-in-chief, and he appointed Johnston to the command of such forces as could be assembled to oppose Sherman. Only about 30,000 men could be found to contend against the Union army of 90,000 veterans.

There was an action at Averysboro on the 16 March, and engagements from the 19th to the 21st at Bentonville. The Confederates were defeated at both places. Sherman then concentrated his army at Goldsboro for a further movement to the north.

On the 14 April, near Raleigh, North Carolina, General Sherman received from General Johnston a message requesting a cessation of hostilities with a view of negotiating terms of surrender. Arrangements were at once made for a personal interview on the 17th. As Sherman was starting for the meeting, he received a despatch from Secretary Stanton, announcing the assassination of President Lincoln by John Wilkes Booth at Ford's Theatre in Washington on the night of Friday, the 14th. After an interview with Johnston, another meeting was arranged for the following day, the 18 April, when a conditional treaty was signed, subject to the ratification of President Johnson. The terms were not approved by the President, as they covered matters of a political nature, and on the 26 April General Johnston surrendered his army upon the same terms that General Lee had received. There was never the slightest justification for the criticisms showered upon Sherman for his course in this matter.

CHAPTER TWENTY

JUNE 1864 —APRIL 1865

PETERSBURG

AT no other period during the Civil War was there such depression in all circles throughout the North as after Grant's bloody repulse at Cold Harbor. The expenses of the war were nearly four million dollars a day. Gold was at a high premium and advancing rapidly: it went from 168 in May 1864 to 285 in July. The terrible casualty lists of the Wilderness Campaign had brought mourning to every hamlet in the country. Although stimulated by enormous bounties, enlistment had almost ceased. It was under these circumstances that Grant, after a week of indecision, decided to transfer his army to the south side of the James, and thence move directly upon Petersburg. It was the supreme Crisis of the War!

Grant's movement, says General Alexander, "involved the performance of a feat in transportation which had never been equalled, and might well be considered impossible, without days of delay." His object was to capture Petersburg, then to turn Beauregard's entrenchments in front of Butler at Bermuda Hundred, and move on Richmond. The capture of Petersburg would cut off Lee's lines of supply by the Weldon and the Southside (Lynchburg) railways, and would leave no unbroken line entering the capital except the Richmond and Danville. This road Grant purposed seizing later, thus compelling Lee to abandon Richmond and retreat toward Danville or Lynchburg to avoid investment.

Grant's movement was accomplished without mishap, and in such incredibly short time that Lee for three days refused to believe it. During this period, from the 15 to the 17 June, Grant's whole army crossed the James, and assaulted Petersburg, which at first was defended only by Beauregard with 2500 men. In the meantime, Lee, with the corps of Longstreet and Hill, lay idle in the woods on the north side of the James.

On Saturday, 11 June, the Fifth Corps (Warren) was moved down the Chickahominy about ten miles, to the vicinity of Bottom's Bridge. The next night it crossed on two pontoon bridges, and took position east of Riddle's Shop, where it entrenched to cover the passage of the other corps. The Second Corps (Hancock) crossed on the same bridge; the Sixth (Wright) and the Ninth (Burnside), at Jones's Bridge; and all marched to Wilcox's Landing on the James. The Eighteenth Corps (Smith) was sent back to White House, where it took transports for City Point, and was landed there the night of the 14th. Here it was joined by Kautz's cavalry, 2400 strong, and Hink's colored division, 3700, making in all about 16,000 men. This force was ordered to move at dawn on the 15th, and attack Petersburg, which was only eight miles distant. Here we shall leave them for the moment.

Hancock reached the James on the night of the 13th, and the three other corps during the course of the following day. Pending the construction of the bridge, on the 14th Hancock's corps was ferried across the river by the transports which had brought Smith to City Point. By the morning of the 15th the whole corps was across, and at 10:30 set out for Petersburg to join Smith, who had marched at sunrise. Hancock had 20,000 men, and only sixteen miles to go. All the complicated details of this movement had been thought out with remarkable care, and fully covered in the orders and instructions — *with a single exception*, and this oversight postponed the fall of Petersburg for over nine months!

The whole trouble came from the supposed "political necessity" of keeping Butler in command of the Army of the James. As Smith's corps was a part of that army, it was necessary to have his orders issued from headquarters, and on the 14th Grant visited Butler for that purpose. On his return Grant neglected to notify Meade of the details of the orders to Smith, and Meade, of course, could not inform Hancock. It thus resulted that Hancock did not march until 10:30, when he could just as well have started five hours earlier, and, furthermore, he was not directed by the shortest route. He therefore arrived in front of Petersburg after dark — too late to assist in Smith's attack.

Meanwhile the three other corps of the Army of the Potomac awaited on the north side of the James the construction of the "greatest bridge which the world has seen since the days of Xerxes." At the point selected, the river was 700 yards wide, ninety feet deep, and had a rise and fall of tide of four feet, causing very strong currents. The construction was begun simultaneously at both ends at four o'clock on the afternoon of the 14 June, and finished at midnight. The artillery and trains immediately began to cross, and the Ninth, Fifth, and Sixth corps followed in the order named. At midnight of the 16th, Grant's entire army was south of the James. Considering the size of the river, it was as great a feat as Napoleon's passage of the Danube in the face of the enemy with his army of 150,000 men in July 1809.

To return now to Smith's column of 16,000 men, which began its march on Petersburg at sunrise on the 15 June. Beauregard, who was in command there, to gain time, sent forward a battery, and a regiment of cavalry, which delayed the march of the Federals for about three hours. But about nine o'clock the head of Smith's column came in sight of the Confederate works. The lines of Petersburg, then some ten miles in length, encircled the city, about two miles out, from the river above to the river below. The entrenchments consisted only of a small outside ditch and a parapet, with platforms and embrasures for guns at suitable intervals. There were no obstructions in front, but the forest had been felled within the zone of fire.

Beauregard had a good supply of guns and ammunition, which he used freely, to delay the placing of the Federal batteries and the deployment of their troops. Smith took time for a long and careful reconnaissance of the Confederate position, which convinced him that the entrenchments were held only by a very thin line of infantry. He therefore decided to attack, not with a column, but with clouds of skirmishers. It was now five o'clock, and another hour was taken to form the troops. When all was ready, it was found that the artillery horses had been sent to water, and it took another hour to get them back. That hour saved Petersburg. "By such small and accidental happenings does Fate decide battles!"

At seven o'clock, the Union guns opened fire, and the cloud of skirmishers advanced to the attack. They carried about a mile and a half of the entrenchments, capturing twenty guns, and taking many prisoners. About nine o'clock Hancock came up with his corps, and relieved Smith's troops. Smith had heard of the arrival of Confederate reinforcements, and he thought it wiser to hold what he had gained, rather than to venture more and risk disaster.

During the night, Beauregard's engineer laid out, and began work on, a better located permanent line about a half-mile in the rear. At the same time, he was reinforced by the arrival of Hoke's division from Drewry's Bluff, and by part of Johnson's division, which gave him in the morning about 14,000 infantry. Before the arrival of these troops the whole force at Petersburg consisted of one brigade of infantry, not more than 1200 strong; two small regiments of cavalry, and a few artillery men.

On the 16th, the Ninth Corps arrived, and Hancock, who was now in command, had about 48,000 men. He attacked each flank of the broken Confederate line, and during the day succeeded

General P.G.T. Beauregard delivered the demand for the surrender of Fort Sumter in 1861 and was with Lee at the surrender of the Confederate Army.

in capturing one redan on the left, and three on the right.

On the 17th, the fighting began at 3 a.m. and was continued until 11 p.m. The first attack, made by Potter's division of the Ninth Corps, was a complete surprise to the exhausted Confederates. Another redan was captured, with four guns, and 600 prisoners; but no advantage was gained elsewhere. In a final assault, late in the afternoon, the Federals obtained temporary possession of one more redan, but were driven out, with the loss of over 1000 prisoners. After the fighting ceased, the Confederate troops were withdrawn to the new line which had been prepared.

At 4 a.m. on the 18th, a general assault was made by the Second, Fifth, and Ninth corps, with the Sixth and Eighteenth in reserve. Information had been obtained from the prisoners and a few deserters that the Confederate lines were held by a very slim force, and the corps commanders were ordered to press the attack. The whole Union army was now at hand, and no further Confederate reinforcements had arrived, but practically nothing was accomplished during the whole day. This, as General Alexander remarks, "is striking evidence of the condition to which the Federal army had now been reduced."

General Lee did not discover until the morning of the 13th that the enemy was gone, and then, for several days, he was completely deceived regarding Grant's plans. Thinking that it was Grant's intention to advance on the north side of the James, so as to draw nearer to Butler, he moved his army across the Chickahominy and took position between White Oak Swamp and Malvern Hill. Hoke's division alone went on to Drewry's Bluff, and later was sent to Peters- burg, as we have seen. No other change was made in Lee's position until the morning of the 16th, when Pickett's and Field's divisions of Longstreet's corps were sent to the lines at Bermuda Hun- dred to take the place of Johnson's divi- sion, withdrawn by Beauregard the night of the 15th for the defence of Pe- tersburg. Kershaw's division followed only as far as Dre- wry's Bluff, and was halted there. Meanwhile Beauregard had re- peatedly reported to Lee the arrival of Grant's army, in front of Petersburg, and begged for reinforcements. Lee replied on the morning of the 16th that he did not know the position of Grant's army, and could not strip the north bank of troops. At noon on the 17th he again said, "Until I can get more definite information of Grant's movements, I do not think it prudent to draw more troops to this side of the river."

These Confederate abattis were placed in position to deter Grant's attack at Petersburg.

At 6:40 p.m. on the 17th, Beauregard telegraphed Lee that unless reinforced he might be compelled to evacuate the city very shortly. Upon receipt of this despatch, Kershaw's division was started for Petersburg. As soon as the fighting ceased, at about midnight, Beauregard took more radical measures to convince Lee of the situation. During the night, within two hours, he sent three members of his staff, one after another, to report to Lee. The first officer, who arrived about 2 a.m. on the 18th, could not convince Lee, and the second was not allowed to see him, as he was sleeping. The third, who came at 3 a.m., insisted on an interview, and succeeded in convincing Lee, from the statements of prisoners, that Grant's entire army had been across the James for over forty-eight hours. Lee immediately set his army in motion for Petersburg.

As a part of his general plan of operations, on the 5 June Grant had started Sheridan westward with his cavalry to break up the Virginia Central and Fredericksburg railways.

Sheridan also had orders to form a junction at Charlottesville with Hunter, who had succeeded Sigel in command in the Shenandoah Valley. Hunter had defeated the Confederates in that region, and was then moving toward Lynchburg. This part of his task Sheridan was unable to carry out, as he found the Confederate cavalry under Wade Hampton across his path, and could not shake them off. He therefore returned to White House on the 21 June. This expedition, known as Sheridan's Trevilian Raid, thus ended in failure, like so many others.

In the meantime an even more famous raid was in progress. On account of ill health, Ewell had been succeeded in command of the Second Corps by Early, who was sent by Lee on the 13 June to the Shenandoah. He drove Hunter over the mountains into West Virginia, then marched down the Valley, crossed the Potomac, and on the 11 July reached the outskirts of Washington. There was great alarm throughout the North, and Grant sent Wright from Virginia with two divisions of the Sixth Corps. He arrived on the 12th, at the same time as General Emory, from New Orleans, with part of the Nineteenth Corps. There were enough troops in Washington to defend the city, but these reinforcements made the situation doubly sure. Early, pursued by Wright, retreated to Virginia.

As a result of this last Confederate invasion of the North, Grant sent Sheridan to command the Union forces in the Shenandoah. He expelled Early from the Valley, and so thoroughly devastated that granary of the Confederacy that, to use his own words, "a crow would have had to carry its rations if it had flown across the Valley."

On the 7 August 1864, Sheridan assumed command of the forces for the protection of the Valley, subsequently known as the Army of the Shenandoah. His appointment was opposed by Secretary Stanton, who thought that Sheridan was too young for such important responsibility. Grant had decided that the Valley must be rendered useless to the Confederacy for future aggressive operations, and Sheridan was ordered to devastate it in a way as little injurious to the people as possible.

On the morning of the 10 August Sheridan, who had massed his army at Halltown, in front of Harper's Ferry, moved against Early's line of communications. On the 12th, his cavalry came up with the enemy's rear-guard at Cedar Creek. Here Early was reinforced, and Sheridan made preparations to retire to a position better suited for defence. After an engagement at Winchester, he fell back to Halltown.

Then the pressure of Grant's army at Petersburg caused the recall of Early's reinforcements, and Sheridan moved forward once more. About this time Grant visited the Valley, and found everything to his satisfaction.

At 2 a.m. on the 19 September, Sheridan's army advanced to attack Early in front of Winchester. After a hot engagement, which lasted all day, the enemy was driven in disorder from the field, and only darkness saved Early's army from capture.

The Federals pursued the following day, and found the enemy in a strong position at Fisher's Hill. After a careful reconnaissance, Sheridan decided to turn the Confederate position. The movement was entirely successful, and the enemy was driven from the field in confusion. Early refused to fight again, and retired up the Valley to Port Republic. Staunton was captured by the Union cavalry, and all the army stores destroyed. Kershaw, who was at Culpeper on his march to Lee, was ordered to rejoin Early.

Grant, with his staff in 1864, sitting with his characteristic indifferent attitude. He had begun the investment of Petersburg when this photograph was taken.

Sheridan was opposed to the Government plan of operating against Central Virginia from his base in the Valley, on account of the difficulty of protecting his long line of communications; and he was finally, ordered to withdraw, destroying on his return march everything which could be of value to the enemy. It was a severe measure, but excused, like Sherman's burning of Atlanta, as a necessity of war.

Sheridan placed his army on Cedar Creek, north of the Shenandoah. On the 15 October, he was called to Washington for a consultation with Secretary Stanton and General Halleck. During his absence, at early dawn on the 19th, Early surprised the Union troops in their beds, and the left and centre, under Crook and Emory, were driven from their positions. Wright's men, who were in reserve, made only a short resistance. The whole army fled in disorder toward Winchester.

Stopping over night at Winchester on the 18th, on his return from Washington, Sheridan heard the noise of battle the following morning, and hurried to the field. His coming restored confidence; he readjusted the lines, and then ordered an advance. It took less time to drive the enemy from the field than it had required for him to gain it. Night ended the pursuit at Fisher's Hill. Early lost three battle-flags, and almost all his artillery and trains.

The battle of Cedar Creek has been immortalized in song and story. It was one of the most spectacular victories of the Civil War.

This practically ended the operations in the Valley. Sheridan's command passed the winter at Kernstown. Toward spring, most of the infantry, and all of the cavalry, rejoined Grant's army in front of Petersburg.

Union veterans before Petersburg.

Sheridan had about 43,000 men in the Valley, and his total losses were 17,000. Early never had over 20,000; his losses are unknown.

Grant did not renew his assaults on Petersburg on the 19 June. Orders were given to entrench the positions gained by the several corps, and the two opposing lines in this part of the ground remained practically unchanged until the end of the siege.

The Federal losses from the 13 to the 18 June were over 10,000 men, killed, wounded, and missing. Since the opening of the campaign, on the 5 May, the casualties had been in excess of 62,000. No returns exist for Beauregard's losses at Petersburg, but they have been

Petersburg. This map joins Map 2 by a similar diagonal line on the northeast corner.

estimated at a total of 4700. The losses of general officers on both sides were very severe: Federals, 6 killed, 8 wounded, 2 captured, total 16; Confederates, 8 killed, 15 wounded, 2 captured, total 25.

The most interesting episode in the long and tedious siege of Petersburg was the affair of the Mine. This promised to be a great success, but through the neglect and cowardice of some of the principal actors it turned out a dismal failure.

Running approximately parallel to the general line of the Confederate works was the deep valley of Poor Creek, the western edge of which was only 400 feet from a point in their front called Elliott's Salient. The salient was held by Pegram's battery, and Elliott's brigade occupied the adjacent lines. By the assaults of the 17 and 18 June, the Ninth Corps (Burnside) had gained an advanced position in front of the salient. Along the farther edge of the valley the Union troops built strong rifle-pits, with elaborate head-logs and loopholes, from which a constant fire was kept up on the enemy's works. In the valley behind, there was ample room to collect and mass a large force, out of view of the Confederates.

Lieutenant-Colonel Pleasants, who had been a mining engineer and who belonged to the 48th Pennsylvania, composed for the most part of miners from the upper Schuylkill coal region, suggested to his division commander, General Robert Potter, the possibility of running a mine under the salient in front of this point. The plan was approved by General Burnside,

Petersburg. This map joins Map 1 by a similar diagonal line on the southwest corner.

and work was begun on the 25 June. A gallery was successfully extended over 500 feet, with two branches at the end, to the right and left, each 37 feet long. These branch galleries were charged with gunpowder in eight parcels of 1000 pounds each, connected by open troughs of powder to be fired by safety fuses coming through the tamping and along the gallery. All the preparations were finished on the 28 July.

The last of June, General Alexander became convinced that the enemy was preparing to mine the position at the salient, and warned General Lee, who ordered his engineers to start countermines. The shafts, however, were located on the right and left flanks of the battery, and the countermines did not meet the Federal gallery, which was so silently built that the Confederates did not know of its proximity.

The morning of the 30 July was chosen for the explosion of the mine, and all preliminary arrangements were made, such as massing the troops, removing parapets and abattis to make passage for the assaulting columns, and so on. No possible precaution was overlooked by General Meade, and very explicit orders were issued.

On the morning of the 30th, Lee had in the lines about Petersburg only the three divisions of Hoke, Johnson, and Mahone, about 18,000 men, most of the balance of his army being twenty miles away. Three of the Union corps, and parts of two others, with two divisions of Sheridan's cavalry, 16 divisions in all, some 60,000 men, were concentrated to follow up the surprise to be given by the explosion.

Everything had been so carefully prepared, that it is difficult to explain how the attack failed so completely. One cause was the same which on the 12 May nullified the Federal surprise at the Bloody Angle at Spottsylvania— too many troops had been concentrated, and they were in each other's way. The main reasons, however, were the cowardice of two of the Union division-commanders, Ledlie and Ferrero, and the negligence of one of the corps-commanders, Burnside. These three officers, with two others, Willcox and Bliss, were subsequently censured by a Military Court, and Burnside resigned from the service.

The assault was to be led by Ledlie's division of the Ninth Corps, followed by the colored division under Ferrero, but both these commanders took shelter in a bombproof, where they remained during the entire action.

The mine was fired at 4:40, ten minutes before sunrise, and the explosion made a crater 150 feet long, 97 feet wide, and 30 feet deep. The parapets were partially destroyed and largely buried by the falling earth. Two guns, 22 cannoneers, and perhaps 250 infantry were carried up in the air.

The assaulting columns literally swarmed into this crater, until it was packed so full the men could hardly move. Considering the surprise, and the novelty of the occasion, the Confederates rallied very quickly. The decided lack of energy on the part of the assailants permitted the defenders to form barricades, which were successfully held to the last. The attacking column, instead of spreading out, remained massed in the crater, and made no further advance; the reinforcements in the rear were prevented from coming up. Finally Meade ordered all offensive operations to cease, and the men were withdrawn. The Federal casualties for the day were in excess of 4000, while the Confederates lost less than 1500 men.

Between this period and the month of March 1865 several movements of the Union armies were made to the left and the right, which resulted in the extension of the entrenchments in both directions, and a corresponding prolongation of the Confederate lines. As these operations possess but little interest, no attempt will be made to narrate them in detail.

Each of Grant's movements, at the time, had some special object beyond extending his lines. Toward the end of July, for example, Hancock was sent to the north bank of the James with his own corps (Second) and the Tenth (Birney). Grant's thought was to prevent Lee from sending more reinforcements to Early in the Valley. Hancock remained there until the 20 August, when he was recalled.

On the 18 August, Warren was sent on an expedition against the Weldon Railway with the same object in view: to force Lee to withdraw some of his troops from the Shenandoah. While he was tearing up the track, Warren was attacked by Hill, and lost nearly 3000 men. He then withdrew to open ground about a mile back and entrenched. No further attacks were made, and the Union lines were then extended by the Ninth Corps from the Jerusalem Plank Road to connect with Warren's lines on the Weldon Railway.

The last week in October, Grant made another movement to the left with the view of turning Lee's right, and seizing the Southside Railway. The operation was not a success, and the Union troops were withdrawn to their former positions.

In December, Warren was again sent on an expedition against the Weldon Railway, and destroyed some twenty miles of track. This increased the difficulty of supplying the Confederate army.

At the beginning of February another ineffectual attempt was made to turn the Confederate right and seize the Southside Railway. This movement, made by the Second and Fifth corps, was met by Lee's right, and checkmated. The Union line had now been extended to Hatcher's Run near the crossing of the Vaughan Road, and the Confederate entrenchments reached across the Run at the Crow farm, and from Burgess's Mill along White Oak Road, and west of the Claiborne Road.

The winter was unusually severe, and the Confederate troops, with their insufficient clothing and meagre food, suffered terribly. They had no coffee or tea or sugar, except in the hospitals, and only a little meat, mostly imported from abroad. The condition of affairs throughout the South was truly deplorable. The loss to the army by desertion averaged a hundred men a day, the soldiers leaving in response to frantic appeals from their families at home.

In March 1865 the Confederate lines were so extended that it was thirty-seven miles by the shortest route from the extreme left on White Oak Swamp below Richmond to the extreme right beyond Petersburg. At this time Lee's army was reduced to about 50,000 men, and Grant had 124,000.

Early in March, Sherman had advanced into North Carolina, where he was confronted by General Joseph E. Johnston, who had been placed in command of a small Confederate force composed of the garrisons of Savannah and Charleston, and the remnants of Hood's army which had been brought over from Tupelo, Mississippi. It was evident that Lee would soon be forced to abandon Richmond and Petersburg, and endeavor to join Johnston, to crush Sherman before he could unite with Grant. But prior to undertaking this "almost impossible task," General Lee "determined upon one last effort to break up Grant in his immediate front." On the 25 March, he gave orders to Gordon, now in command of Early's corps, which had rejoined, to assault Fort Stedman, which was only 200 yards in front of his line. The Union troops were taken by surprise, and the fort captured, but the assailants were soon driven out, with very heavy losses.

Fearing that the object of Lee's assault was to induce him to transfer troops from his left to his right, which would make it easier for Lee to withdraw his army, and begin his retreat, Grant decided to take the initiative at once, and move around Lee's right flank. Leaving only one division (Devens) north of the James, and two divisions under Weitzel in the Bermuda

Hundred lines, Grant began to transfer all the rest of his infantry, about 90,000 men, and all of his cavalry, to his extreme left.

On this occasion, Grant narrowly avoided the mistake made by Hooker in May 1863, by Lee in June 1863, and by himself in May 1864, of sending his cavalry off on a raid against the railways. He countermanded such an order, issued on the 28th, and kept his cavalry with the infantry.

On the 31 March, Lee sent the two divisions of Pickett and Johnson, about 6600 strong, and two of Fitz Lee's divisions of cavalry, 5800 men, on an expedition against Sheridan, who was driven back in much confusion nearly to Dinwiddie Court House. During the night, Pickett, who was far in advance, was nearly cut off by Warren's corps; but he succeeded in withdrawing to Five Forks, four miles from Lee's right flank. Here he made the mistake of halting and entrenching, assuming that he would be reinforced. The following morning he was attacked by Sheridan's cavalry, and Warren's corps, and routed; 3244 of his men were captured, with eleven colors, and four guns, while the Federals lost only 634 men. The whole action was fought in the absence of Pickett and Fitz Lee, who were only a mile away, but heard no sound of the battle, owing to the same peculiar conditions of the atmosphere noted at Perryville and Chancellorsville.

After the action was over, Sheridan removed Warren from the command of the Fifth Corps, under charges of which he was afterwards fully acquitted by a Court of Inquiry.

On the 2 April, Grant renewed his attacks on the Confederate right, breaking their line, and forcing it back. The Federals then gained possession of the Southside Railroad, and pursued the enemy toward Petersburg, until stopped by the fire of Fort Gregg. In this last day's battle, General A. P. Hill was killed. He had borne a conspicuous part in every action fought by the Army of Northern Virginia, except Spottsylvania, where he was ill.

That night Lee abandoned Richmond and Petersburg, and started his army westward, in the hope of reaching either Danville or Lynchburg ahead of Grant. He had expected to find rations at Amelia Court House, but by some blunder the supplies had gone on to Richmond. This caused a delay of twenty-four hours, to collect supplies from the country.

In the last phase of the campaign, Grant, for the first time, used his cavalry to the best possible advantage. Instead of sending Sheridan off on some useless raid, he kept the cavalry with the main army, and it did most effective work. But for the Union horsemen, Lee might have reached the mountains of Virginia, and prolonged the struggle for several months.

After the evacuation of Petersburg and Richmond, Grant followed Lee on the south side of the Appomattox River. Weitzel was sent to take possession of Richmond, which surrendered at 8:15 the following morning.

Sheridan's cavalry and the Second and Sixth corps led in the pursuit. Both armies were trying to reach the junction at Burke's Station, and the Federals won in the race. At Sailor's Creek, on the 6 April, Ewell's corps, which formed the rear-guard, was cut off, surrounded, and captured, some 8000 men, with six general officers, including Ewell himself, and Kershaw.

After sundown on the 7th, Lee received the first letter from Grant, proposing a surrender:—

April 7, 1865.

GENERAL: The result of the last week must convince you of the hopelessness of further resistance on the part of the Army of Northern Virginia in this struggle. I feel that it is so, and regard it as my duty to shift from myself the responsibility of any further effusion of blood, by asking of you the surrender of that portion of the Confederate army known as the Army of Northern Virginia.

U. S. GRANT, *Lieutenant-General.*

Within an hour, General Lee sent back the following reply: —

April 7, 1865.

GENERAL: I have received your note of this date. Though not entertaining the opinion you express on the hopelessness of further resistance on the part of the Army of Northern Virginia, I reciprocate your desire to avoid useless effusion of blood, and therefore, before considering your proposition, ask the terms you will offer on condition of its surrender.

R. E. LEE, *General.*

During the afternoon of the 8th Lee received Grant's reply to his inquiry as to the terms proposed. Grant said that, peace being his great desire, there was but one condition upon which he should insist, namely, "that the officers and men surrendered shall be disqualified from taking up arms again against the government of the United States until properly exchanged." He concluded by saying that he was ready to meet Lee for the purpose of arranging the terms.

Lee immediately prepared his answer, and sent it to Grant the same evening. He said that he did not intend, in his previous note, to propose the surrender of his army, but to ask Grant's terms. He added: "I cannot therefore meet you with a view to surrender the Army of Northern Virginia, but as far as your proposal may affect the Confederate States' forces under my command, and tend to the restoration of peace, I should be pleased to meet you at 10 a.m. tomorrow on the stage road to Richmond between the picket-lines of the two armies."

Some time before the fall of Richmond, Grant had received a letter from Mr. Lincoln prohibiting him from embracing anything of a political nature in any negotiations that he might have with General Lee. As Lee's letter seemed to imply such a discussion, Grant decided to avoid the proposed meeting. He accordingly replied, on the morning of the 9th, that he had no authority to treat on the subject, and that the proposed meeting could do no good.

Meanwhile the Confederate army had arrived within two miles of Appomattox Court House, only to find the road barred by Sheridan and Ord. Lee sent orders to Gordon and Fitz Lee to clear the way, but they could make no progress against the large forces already, in their front. On receiving Gordon's report, General Lee exclaimed, "Then there is nothing left me but to go and see General Grant, and I would rather die a thousand deaths!"

Lee accordingly wrote Grant, asking an interview in accordance with the offer contained in his letter of the 8th, and rode to the rear, hoping soon to meet Grant and be able to make the surrender.

That morning Meade had taken the responsibility of granting a truce, pending the negotiations for a surrender. When this was arranged, Lee returned to his front and stopped in an apple orchard a hundred yards or so in advance of the line, where General Alexander had some fence-rails piled under a tree to make him a seat. Within two days this tree was cut down for souvenirs by the Confederate and Federal soldiers.

Here, while talking with General Longstreet, Lee received Grant's final letter, sent by Colonel Babcock of his staff. It read: —

April 9, 1865.

GENERAL R. E. LEE, Commanding C. S. A.: —

Your note of this date is but this moment, 11:50 a.m., received. ... I am at this writing four miles west of Walker's Church, and will push forward for the purpose of meeting you....

Very respectfully,
Your obedient servant,
U. S. GRANT
Lieutenant-General.

The meeting, by a strange coincidence, took place in the house of Major Wilmer McLean, who had owned the farm on Bull Run on which had occurred the first collision between the two armies at Blackburn's Ford on the 18 July 1861. His house there was used for a time as the headquarters of General Beauregard. To avoid the active theatre of the war he moved to the quiet village of Appomattox. Thus the first and the last scenes of the war in Virginia took place upon his property.

The house was a plain two-story wooden structure, standing a little distance back from the street, with a yard in front. A wooden porch, reached by seven steps, ran the length of the house. On each side of the hall, there was a single square room, entered by two doors, and having two windows, one in front and one in rear.

General Lee was accompanied only by his military secretary, Colonel Marshall, and a single courier, who held the horses during the meeting. Lee reached the house first, and entered the room on the left to await the arrival of General Grant, who came about one-thirty. It was Sunday, the 9 April 1865.

General Grant had in his party Generals Sheridan, Ord, and Ingalls, and nine members of his staff, including General (then Colonel) Horace Porter, who has given us a very interesting account of the interview.

General Grant sat at a marble-topped table in the centre of the room; Lee, at a small oval table near the front window, and facing Grant. Some of the party found seats on the sofa and the few chairs in the room, but most of them stood.

"The contrast between the two commanders," says General Porter, "was striking and could not fail to attract marked attention." Grant, then nearly forty-three years of age, was five feet eight inches in height, with shoulders slightly stooped. His hair and full beard were a nut-brown, without a trace of gray in them. He wore a plain blouse of dark-blue flannel, an ordinary pair of top-boots, with his trousers inside, and was without spurs. His boots and

Lee just after surrender. He had fought seven great campaigns against six picked generals of the Union.

uniform were spattered with mud. He had no sword; and, apart from the shoulder-straps which designated his rank, his uniform was that of a private soldier.

Lee, on the other hand, was fully six feet in height, and erect for one of his age, for he was Grant's senior by sixteen years. His thick hair and full beard were a silver gray. He wore a new uniform of Confederate gray, and carried at his side a long sword of very fine workmanship, the hilt studded with jewels. He wore top-boots, with handsome spurs. Like his uniform, his boots were remarkably clean. A felt hat, the color of his uniform, and a pair of long buckskin gauntlets, lay beside him on the table.

After a few words of general conversation, General Lee suggested that Grant should put his terms in writing. Whereupon Grant called for his manifold order-book, and wrote his well-known letter, which he handed to General Lee to read. Lee laid it on the table beside him while he drew from his pocket a pair of steel-rimmed spectacles and wiped the glasses carefully, with his handkerchief. Then he adjusted the spectacles very deliberately, and read the letter carefully. When he came to the sentence about the officers being allowed to retain their side-arms, horses, and baggage, he said, with considerable warmth of manner, "This will have a very happy effect upon my army."

In answer to a question from Grant, as to whether he had any suggestions to make regarding the terms, Lee said, after a little hesitation, that the men in his cavalry and artillery owned their own horses. Grant replied that the subject was new to him; then he added that, without altering the draft as written, he would instruct the officers appointed to receive the paroles "to let all the men who claim to own a horse or mule take the animals home with them to work their little farms." Lee showed a very lively appreciation of this concession, which, he said, would have the best possible effect upon the men, and would do much toward conciliating his people.

Grant then ordered one of his staff to copy his letter in ink, and while this was being done, Lee had Colonel Marshall draw up for his signature a letter of acceptance of the terms of surrender.

After the letters had been copied and signed, Lee spoke of his lack of provisions for his men, and Grant offered to send him at once 25,000 rations.

At a little before four o'clock General Lee shook hands with General Grant, bowed to the other officers, and with Colonel Marshall left the room. As soon as the horses were saddled, he mounted, saluted the Union officers by raising his hat, and rode slowly away. General Grant and his staff then mounted and started for the headquarters camp, which was now pitched near by. Firing of salutes had already begun, but Grant ordered these stopped at once, saying that the war was over, and the rebels fellow-countrymen once more.

On his way to headquarters, Grant was reminded that he had not yet announced the important event to the Government. He dismounted, sat down on a large stone by the roadside, and wrote the following despatch to Secretary Stanton, dated 4:30 p.m.: —

General Lee surrendered the Army of Northern Virginia this afternoon on terms proposed by myself. The accompanying additional correspondence will show the conditions fully.

U. S. GRANT, LIEUT. GENERAL

Lee was appointed to the command of the Army of Northern Virginia on the first day of June 1862. In the brief period of two years, ten months, and nine days, with an army always inferior in numbers, poorly equipped, and badly supplied with food and clothing, he had fought seven great campaigns, against six picked generals of the Union. With a force which never exceeded 80,000 men, he had put *hors de combat* 262,000 Federals. There is no parallel in history to this record except Napoleon's twelve major campaigns, covering a period of nineteen years.

The effective strength of the Union army at the beginning of the final operations was 120,000, and the losses up to the day of the surrender were 10,515. Grant's entire losses since crossing the Rapidan were 124,000 — a number about double the maximum strength of Lee's army. At the time Lee evacuated Richmond, he had about 50,000 men; his losses during the retreat are unknown. There were 28,231 men paroled at Appomattox; but Lee had lost large numbers by capture or desertion since leaving Petersburg.

Grant did not enter the Confederate lines after the surrender. He designated General Joshua Chamberlain to command the parade on the day that the Confederate soldiers marched out to lay down their arms and colors.

On the morning after the surrender, the 10 April, General Grant rode out about nine o'clock, and had a final interview with General Lee between the lines of the two armies. Their conversation was entirely private; but, as afterwards reported by Grant, it was mainly on the subject of peace, and reconciliation between the two Sections. Grant urged Lee to use his great influence to bring about this happy result. Lee, however, was averse to stepping beyond his duties as a soldier, and said the authorities would doubtless soon arrive at the same conclusion without his interference. There is no foundation for the statement that Grant asked Lee to see President Lincoln regarding the terms of reconstruction.

After this interview, which lasted about half an hour, Lee rode back to his camp to take a final farewell of his men, and Grant returned to the McLean house to await the hour of his departure. Some of his officers, who had been visiting the enemy's camp, now returned, with Wilcox, who had been groomsman when he was married; Longstreet, who had also been at his wedding; Heth, who had been with him in Mexico; Gordon, Pickett, and several others.

At noon, Grant mounted his horse, and with his staff started for the station to take the train for Washington. Lee set out for Richmond, the same day.

For the first time in four long, bloody years, the Army of the Potomac and the Army of Northern Virginia turned their backs upon each other!

"Grant's movement from Cold Harbor to the south bank of the James," says Major Steele, "belongs to a class of strategical operations which are considered among the most hazardous and difficult in warfare. It was a flank movement involving the crossing of close and wooded country by narrow roads, and the passage of two difficult streams, the Chickahominy and the James, over which pontoon bridges had to be laid."

Grant, and his efficient staff, are entitled to great credit for the skill with which the operation was carried out. The Union army had over fifty miles to march; Lee held nearly all the bridges across the Chickahominy, and had better roads, as well as fuller knowledge of the country, to aid him in attacking the right flank of Grant's columns. The Union army was withdrawn from a position only "a few hundred yards from the enemy in the widest place"; and the movement was so effectively screened that Lee was kept in ignorance of Grant's plans from the time he started, the night of the 12 June, until the morning of the 18th, when Grant had his army concentrated in front of Petersburg. Taken as a whole, the operation must be considered one of the finest achievements of strategy in military history.

Then came the fatal mistake of the campaign —Hancock's waiting for his rations on the morning of the 15 June. This delay of six hours probably prolonged the life of the Confederacy nine months. Yet no blame attaches to Hancock's fine record; the fault was entirely General Grant's, and the explanation of it is very plainly intimated by General Alexander, although he attributes the neglect to give Hancock proper orders mainly to "the political necessity of placing Butler in command of the Army of the James," which was really only a secondary cause.

As the primary object of Grant's campaign in front of Petersburg was to get possession of the two railways leading into Richmond from the south and southwest, it is not easy to understand why he could not succeed in less than nine months. Major Steele's explanation is, that Lee's army was never really invested; that he was so favored by the relative positions of Richmond and Petersburg, and the conformation of the two rivers, that Grant could not leave a small force in front of Petersburg, to detain Lee, while he moved with his main army against the railways, without thereby giving Lee an opportunity to seize the Union base on the James.

"Knowing as much as we do now about trench warfare," writes General Maurice, "it is easy to see that, without a far greater preponderance of artillery than he possessed, Grant had at no time much chance of carrying the Confederate lines. The rifles of 1864 were precise enough and could be fired sufficiently rapidly to make assault a dangerous expedient unless the defences had been flattened out and the defenders driven from them by accurate bombardment, or unless the attack could be made in overwhelming numbers and regardless of loss. Throughout the siege Grant's superiority in numbers was rarely more and often less than two to one, while Lee's watchfulness was such, and his handling of his reserves so masterly, that, though Grant was always free to choose his point of attack on a very lengthy front of defence, he was never able to accumulate sufficient strength to crash through the defences. The battle of the ' Crater' ended in a similar failure to that of the ' Bloody Angle' of Spottsylvania and for much the same reasons. Grant would indeed have been much better advised to have avoided a direct attack and relied earlier upon the policy into which he was forced by events of continually extending his left and so gradually cutting off Lee's lines of supply. But his plan of keeping Lee tied to the defences of Richmond and Petersburg, while elsewhere the Federal forces steadily reduced the area from which the troops in those defences could draw men, food, and munitions, was the best possible. Lee's great weapon was manoeuvre, and Grant had taken it from him; events proved that no plan was better calculated to undermine the moral of the people of the South."

In further explanation of Grant's inability to accomplish his object, we give below the official returns of the two armies for the seven months from June to December 1864.

	Federals	Confederates
June	107,000	55,000
July	77,000	57,000
August	59,000	35,000
September	77,000	35,000
October	85,000	47,000
November	87,000	56,000
December	110,000	67,000

In the five months, June to October inclusive, Grant's casualties were over 47,000, and his forces were further reduced by detachments sent to Washington and the Shenandoah, so that he was not strong enough, compared to Lee, to assume a more aggressive policy.

CHAPTER TWENTY-ONE

1861 — 1865

CONCLUSION

THE story that John B. Floyd, while Secretary of War in the cabinet of Mr. Buchanan, transferred guns from Northern to Southern arsenals, in order to arm the South for the Civil War, has been told and retold so often that it is still believed by many Northerners. It is not so generally known that this charge was investigated by a committee of Congress, which, in February 1861, made a report showing it to be groundless. The chairman of that committee was Mr. Stanton, afterwards Secretary of War, who was one of the most prominent Republicans in the House.

The facts are, that in 1859 the Armory at Springfield, Massachusetts, had become so crowded that it was necessary to remove some of the arms stored there. Accordingly, in December 1859, nearly a year before the election of Mr. Lincoln, the War Department ordered about one-fifth of the guns at Springfield distributed among five Southern arsenals. The total number of arms thus transferred was 125,000, of which all were obsolete patterns except 10,000 rifled muskets. About 400,000 of the old guns, and all of the new and improved ones, were kept in the North.

In reality, the South, at the outbreak of the Civil War, was poorly supplied with arms and ammunition. According to Mr. Davis, in the *Rise and Fall of the Confederate Government*, the six arsenals in the South, which were only storehouses, contained just 15,000 rifles, and 120,000 muskets, the latter mostly of antiquated patterns. Another authority states that the South had about 150,000 small-arms, of which only about 20,000 were modern rifles.

In a memorandum to Mr. Davis, General Gorgas, chief of ordnance of the Confederate army, writes: "We began in April 1861 without arsenal, or laboratory, or powder-mill of any capacity, and with no foundry or rolling-mill except in Richmond; and before the close of 1863 ...we supplied them." With no stock on hand even of such necessary articles as copper, leather, and iron, in that short period, the South created, almost literally out of the ground, foundries and rolling-mills at Richmond, Selma, Atlanta, and Macon; smelting works at Petersburg; chemical works at Charlotte; a powder-mill at Augusta, equal to any in the United States; and a chain of arsenals, armories, and laboratories stretching from Virginia to Alabama.

Without any previous industrial organization; shut off by the blockade from the commerce of the world; crippled by a depreciated currency; obliged to send nearly every able-bodied man to the field; unable to use slave labor except in the most unskilled departments of

In 1864, when Grant was appointed to the command of the Union armies, Lincoln said: "I neither ask nor desire to know anything of your plans. Take the responsibility and act, and call on me for assistance."

production, such an achievement of industrial organization has never been surpassed in the history of the world.

At the outbreak of the war, General Rains, of North Carolina, who had been professor of chemistry at West Point, left a prosperous engineering business at New York to enter the service of the Confederacy. He was almost at once put in charge of the proposed powder-mill at Augusta. He immediately set parties at work to explore the caves of the mountains of Virginia and Tennessee for saltpetre; cellars and old tobacco works were searched for nitre, and immense beds were developed at Columbia, Charleston, Savannah, Augusta, and Mobile. All the material obtained in this way was sent to Augusta, where, under the direction of General Rains, the powder-mill became the most famous example of Southern industrial efficiency.

When the Union troops evacuated Harper's Ferry, after setting fire to the arsenal, civilians rushed in, and saved a large part of the machinery. By the end of 1861, this machinery, set up at Richmond and Fayetteville, was turning out thousands of muskets, and firearms of every description. Prior to that time, the Southern arsenals had hardly a machine above the complexity of a foot-lathe.

The South had no skilled laborers to speak of; but a few men, like Ball, who literally died of over-work, trained the hundreds who were willing.

Lead at the rate of nearly 80,000 pounds a month came in from the mines near Wytheville, Virginia, to be smelted in the new plant at Petersburg. Every Confederate victory brought large supplies of arms and ammunition; the battlefields were literally combed for guns and bullets, with excellent results.

Within the Southern Confederacy, at the outbreak of the war, there were no arsenals at which guns were manufactured, except a small plant at Fayetteville, and the United States Arsenal at Harper's Ferry. The story of how the South armed its soldiers is an interesting one; and the way in which the emergency was met is a matter of which all Americans today may be proud.

There were but six sources of supply:

(1) The weapons already on hand.
(2) Conversion of old sporting arms to military use.
(3) Manufacture of new arms.
(4) Purchase in the North.
(5) Purchase in Europe.
(6) Capture from the enemy.

The first has already been mentioned; and the supplies obtained from the next three sources were so small as almost to be negligible. At first, every gunsmith in the South was kept busy altering and repairing private arms, but the results were not satisfactory. There was not much more success with the manufacture of new arms. The machinery for making the long rifled musket, saved at Harper's Ferry, was set up at Richmond, but the output never exceeded 1000 guns a month. The machinery for making the short Harper's Ferry rifles was sent to Fayetteville, where, in April 1862, it began to turn out about 400 rifles a month. There were also a number of private gun factories in the Confederacy, but it is difficult to obtain definite data about them, and their output seems to have been small.

At the beginning of the war, the South found little difficulty in making contracts with a number of Northern manufacturers to supply arms, but this matter became such a scandal that the Government put a stop to it by a strict embargo on all shipments to the South.

When the Confederacy found the factories of the North closed to it, the authorities turned to Europe. In May 1861, Major Huse was sent to England, where he succeeded in buying 12,000 Enfield rifles. He also contracted for a lot of 100,000 Austrian rifles from the Imperial Arsenal at Vienna. There was little trouble in running these guns through the blockade. In February 1863, General Gorgas reported that Major Huse had shipped over 131,000 guns, of which about 81,000 were long and short Enfield rifles, and carbines. At the same date, 23,000 rifles at London, and 30,000 at Vienna, were awaiting shipment. The long Enfield rifle, a splendidly made weapon, was the official arm of the British infantry, and proved the most popular gun with the Confederate army. It was about the same size and weight as the Springfield rifle, used by the Union troops, and would take the same cartridge.

It has already been stated that the South armed and equipped itself at the expense of the enemy, and it is certain that a large proportion of the arms used by the Confederates was captured from the Federals. General Gorgas reports that during the four years of the war 320,000 small-arms were issued from the main arsenal at Richmond. Probably one-half of these were captured guns. Richmond was the great arms clearing-house for the East, and guns gathered on the Virginia battlefields were sent there to be put in order and reissued. Many of the finest patterns, however, like the Spencer carbines, were useless, because the Confederates could not get the cartridges. During the last months of the war, a machine was devised for turning out the cartridges, but it was too late to be of service.

The beginning of the Civil War found the North almost as unprepared as the South. Of the 198 companies in the regular army, 183 were guarding 79 posts on the Western frontier, while the remaining 15 garrisoned the Canadian border, the Atlantic coast, and 23 arsenals. Few posts had even so much as a battalion, and in many cases a small company was split up into detachments. To hold in security three million square miles of territory, the United States had less than 13,000 men!

When South Carolina seceded there were few regular officers who had commanded as much as an assembled battalion. Their military life had been passed in the scattered forts along the Indian frontier, where, as expressed by General Ewell, a veteran of nearly twenty years' service, they "had learned all about commanding fifty United States dragoons and had forgotten everything else." The militia of the several States had had no training, in field-service, and were of little value for national defence.

A breech-loading rifle, the first of the successful repeaters, was invented this year (1860) by Christopher Spencer, and was destined to have considerable influence on some of the later battlefields of the war. Only a few of them, however, could be manufactured in time to be of service, and nearly all the troops were armed with old-fashioned muzzle-loading muskets.

The Springfield arsenal was the only service manufactory of small-arms in the United States, and its output did not exceed 2500 a month. As above stated, the Secretary of War, Mr. Floyd, had sent a part of the supply of small-arms to the Southern arsenals, which immediately fell into the hands of the seceding States. At first the Federal troops were so ill-provided that even flintlocks were issued. The markets of Europe were scoured by Federal agents, and every kind of weapon available was purchased at a high price. The calibres were as varied as during the Revolution, and few soldiers could use the ammunition of their comrades, even in the same company.

Although Parrott and Rodman had produced the best types of rifled cannon, none had been adopted by the Government; but there was an abundant supply on hand of smooth-bore guns of iron and brass of all calibres. Since the Government had no foundries of its own, the new cannon were hurriedly manufactured and poorly tested: the consequence was that many burst when they were first fired. The guns used were of many sizes and patterns, and on one battlefield of the war 36 different kinds of balls were picked up from the ground!

Immediately after the secession of the Southern States, nearly one-third of the 900 officers in the Old Army resigned their commissions, and 65 of the cadets at West Point resigned or were discharged. With the exception of 26 men, however, the rank and file remained in the service of the North.

No effort was made by the Union to utilize the experience of regular officers with the volunteers. The men of the local regiments were allowed to elect their officers. Many of the former officers who offered their services were ignored. Grant, who was in business, wrote the War Department, but was not even honored with a reply. Many graduates of West Point served throughout the war in minor capacities, while regiments were commanded by men with no military training or experience. The records show what the North lost by this remarkable procedure: 51 major-generals, 91 brigadiers, and 106 colonels came from the officers of the Old Army; but as against these 248, there were 308 former officers who were kept in subordinate positions.

The South, on the other hand, made early provision to accept the services of officers of the United States army, and to give them their original relative rank. Of the 250 who went with the South, 182 rose to the rank of general officer, including such men as Lee, Jackson, Longstreet, and the two Johnstons. In addition, as already stated, the Confederacy created ranks suitable to the units commanded; whereas, on the Union side, armies, corps, and divisions were commanded, indifferently, by major-generals.

The South organized early; it took the utmost advantage of every trained soldier among its adherents; it quickly concentrated in main armies; it gave confidence and stability to the troops by placing recruits beside old soldiers in the ranks; it clung to its leaders in the face of defeat and did not harass them; it built up morale in every possible way.

The primary organization of the North, on the other hand, was chaos. It did not seem to know how to make use of the few trained soldiers it had. It put excellent leaders in untenable positions, failed to support them properly, and promptly relieved them when they failed. By its ignorance of military affairs it destroyed the morale of as brave troops as ever marched.

The result was that the war was dragged out for four long years, with an inordinate loss of life and public treasure.

"I am of the opinion," writes Colonel Henderson, "that in order to discover the secret of the Confederate successes there is no need either to search for nice distinctions in races closely akin, or to appeal to the fact that Lee and his great lieutenant, Jackson, were a head and shoulders above any Union leaders who had as yet appeared. It was not only the genius of its commanders that won the laurels of the Virginia army. Many of its victories were achieved by sheer hard fighting: they were the work of the soldiers themselves; and that the Confederates were able to wrest success from opponents of equal vigor was due to their superior organization, more accurate shooting, and above all to their stronger discipline.

"As to the first, the Federal Government allowed the pernicious principle of the election of the officers by the rank and file to flourish without restraint; and, secondly, the strength of the army was kept up, not by a constant stream of recruits to the seasoned battalions, but by the formation of new regiments....

"The Southerners, on the other hand, early adopted the conscription; the superior officers were appointed by the Government, and the recruits sent to fill the vacancies in the ranks.... Few 'political regiments' existed in the South; men commanded because they were competent to command, and not because they could influence votes. Secondly, a great advantage in favor of the Confederate troops was their skill as marksmen....

"Lastly, as to discipline, ...the rich planter, possessing many slaves dependent on him ...acquired habits of command and organization highly useful to the officers of an army."

President Davis was a graduate of West Point; he had served with distinction in Mexico, and afterwards as Secretary of War. He had thus had many opportunities of learning the capabilities of the officers of the Old Army, and this knowledge he turned to good account. His selections for command were very judicious. All the regular officers who joined the Confederacy were given high commands, and no civilians were placed in positions of responsibility until they had demonstrated their fitness by handling troops in the field. Taught by military experience, Mr. Davis did not remove a commander because he had been unfortunate. Both his greatest generals, Lee and Jackson, met with reverses, but retained his confidence. He refused to accept the resignation which Lee tendered after Gettysburg. The only great mistake he made was in relieving Johnston in 1864.

In the North, on the other hand, the military policy was very different. Commander succeeded commander with startling rapidity. The Army of the Potomac was commanded by no less than six different officers, each one of whom except the last, Grant, was degraded for ill success. Neither President Lincoln, nor his Secretary of War, Mr. Stanton, had had any previous knowledge of military affairs; but, notwithstanding, they attempted to dictate to their generals in the field. Many of their selections for high command were unfortunate, and in too many cases were dictated by political, rather than military, considerations. The appointment, and the retention in positions of responsibility, of such men as Butler, Banks, Fremont, and Sigel, is hard to excuse. It was not until the last year of the war that the President and his advisers learned wisdom, and forbore to interfere with Grant and Sherman.

"It is a significant fact," says Colonel Henderson, "that, during the war of Secession, for the three years the control of the armies of the North remained in the hands of the Cabinet, the balance of success lay with the Confederates. But, in March 1864, Grant was appointed Commander-in-Chief; Lincoln abdicated his military functions in his favor, and the Secretary of War had nothing more to do than to comply with his requisitions. Then, for the first time, the enormous armies of the Union were manoeuvred in harmonious combination, and the superior force was exerted to its full effect."

"Lincoln, when the army he had so zealously toiled to organize, reeled back in confusion from Virginia, set himself to learn the art of war. He collected, says his biographer, a great library of military books; and, if it were not pathetic, it would be almost ludicrous, to read of the great President …poring night after night, while his capital was asleep, over the pages of Jomini and Clausewitz. And what was the result? In 1864, when Grant was appointed to the command of the Union armies, he said: I neither ask nor desire to know anything of your plans. Take the responsibility and act, and call on me for assistance.' He had learned at last that no man is a born strategist."

The first year of the war was one of unpreparedness; the second, of mismanagement; the third, of alternate success and failure. The fourth year marked the end of the political mismanagement of the forces: a trained soldier, for the first time, took full control of military operations. It had required three years of war to teach the Union authorities that trained professional soldiers should run armies, just as much as educated surgeons should manage hospitals.

"In war," said Napoleon, "men are nothing; it is the man who is everything. The general is the head, the whole of an army. It was not the Roman army that conquered Gaul, but Caesar; it was not the Carthaginian army that made Rome tremble in her gates, but Hannibal; it was not the Macedonian army that reached the Indus, but Alexander; it was not the French army that carried the war to the Weser and the Inn, but Turenne; it was not the Prussian army which, for seven years, defended Prussia against the three greatest Powers of Europe, but Frederick the Great."

"The history of famous armies," writes Henderson, "is the history of great generals; for no army has ever achieved great things unless it has been well commanded."

The history of the Army of the Potomac well illustrates this point. Between the soldiers of the North and the South there was little difference in martial qualities. Both were equally strong in defence, and displayed that stubborn resolve to maintain their ground which is characteristic of the Anglo-Saxon race. "My men," said Stonewall Jackson, "sometimes fail to drive the enemy from his position, but to hold one, never!" The Federal generals might have made the same assertion with equal truth.

But, if the armies were well matched in defence, it must be conceded that the Confederates were more vigorous in the attack. At Antietam, McClellan had twice as many men as Lee; at the Second Manassas, on the first day, Pope outnumbered Jackson two to one; yet on both occasions the smaller force was victorious. Except at Borodino, where he held his Old Guard in reserve, and probably wisely, Napoleon never hesitated to put in his last man. Just before the battle of Chancellorsville, Lincoln warned Hooker "to put in all his men";

The ruins of Richmond.

and the final defeat of the Union army was due mainly to the commander's failure to follow this advice. The Federal generals invariably kept large masses in reserve, and these masses were never used.

Again, the Federal soldiers in the East fought under the terrible disadvantage of having no confidence in their leaders. McClellan won the affection of his men, but it is doubtful whether they ever gave him credit for dash or resolution. The other commanders of the Army of the Potomac did not succeed in inspiring either love or confidence.

In the West, the Union armies were more successful, because they were better commanded, while the Confederates were led by men of inferior ability, as compared with Lee, Jackson,

A detail of the Twenty-sixth Michigan handing out paroles to surrendered Confederate troops. This was one of the last duties performed at Appomattox.

and Longstreet. Yet the Western armies of the Confederacy were fully as brave and as well disciplined as those of Virginia.

Without in any degree disparaging the high reputation of the Confederate soldiers, we may say, then, that it was not the Army of Northern Virginia which for three years kept the Federals at bay in front of Richmond, but Lee; not the Army of the Valley which paralyzed the Washington Government in 1862, but Jackson.

Strategy is defined as the art of bringing the enemy to battle, while *tactics* are the method by which a commander seeks to overwhelm him when battle is joined.

Grand tactics, the art of generalship, include those strategems, manoeuvres, and devices, by which victories are won, and concern only those officers who may find themselves in independent command. *Minor tactics* include the formation and disposition of the three arms for attack and defence, and concern officers of every rank.

Defeat is far more often due to bad strategy than to bad tactics. So the Confederates, despite their numerous successes, were beaten in the end through strategical faults: the failure to concentrate in sufficient numbers to reap the fruits of victory; the unnecessary dispersion of the troops; the deliberate disregard of the great end of strategy, namely, the annihilation of the enemy's fighting men, and the destruction of his material resources. To bring a stubborn enemy to his knees, the war, like that of Rome against Carthage, "must be carried into Africa."

Stonewall Jackson constantly advocated the invasion of the North, but in the councils of the South political expediency over-rode military considerations. Mr. Davis, always trusting that sooner or later the European Powers would intervene, chose *defence*, not *defiance*, as his motto.

Whenever he could seize the initiative, Napoleon never hesitated to invade the enemy's territory, even when he was inferior in strength to the mass of the opposing forces. The wisdom of an offensive policy is shown by the campaign of Gettysburg, where the Confederacy was "within a stone's throw of independence."

But the South, having deliberately chosen a defensive policy, made good use of its opportunities. Strategical points which lay at a distance from the main field of operations were garrisoned with the very smallest force compatible with security, while the two main armies, in Virginia and in the West, were always maintained at the greatest possible strength. There was one notable and fatal exception to this rule: after the loss of the Mississippi, by the fall of Vicksburg and Port Hudson, no less than 55,000 men were retained west of the river where they were absolutely useless to the Confederacy. These troops, transferred either to Virginia or to Tennessee, might have turned the almost evenly balanced scale. The explanation probably is that many of the Southern soldiers objected to serving outside their own States. The strong feeling of States' rights is shown by the fact that Lee always preferred Virginians, both officers and men, for his own army..

Throughout the war, the Confederates possessed the great advantage of interior lines, of which they availed themselves on many occasions. Thus, in 1863, after Gettysburg, Longstreet was sent West with 16,000 men from Lee's army, and enabled Bragg to gain the important victory of Chickamauga, which prolonged the life of the Confederacy for many months.

It must be said, however, that this shifting of strength from one wing to the other was made feasible by the errors of the Federals. It was not until Grant took command in 1864 that the Union forces operated in combination. Grant seems to have been the first to recognize the fact that the true objective of a campaign is the defeat of the enemy's main army. Before he took command, as Sherman well expressed it, "the trouble was that the commanders never went out to lick anybody, but always thought first of keeping from getting licked." Grant was always ready to force the fight, and his policy of constant "hammering," although terribly, and unnecessarily expensive, was in the end successful.

Some of the most remarkable victories in the war — such as the first and second Manassas, and Chancellorsville — were won by two distinct forces, approaching the field of battle from different directions, and crushing the enemy between them. Moltke has laid it down that the junction of two previously separated forces on the field of battle is the highest triumph of generalship; but Napoleon, although on more than one occasion he availed himself of the expedient, was never weary of pointing out the risk.

In all ages the power of intellect has asserted itself in war. It was not courage and experience only that made Hannibal, Alexander, and Caesar, the greatest names of antiquity. Napoleon, Wellington, and Archduke Charles, were certainly the best educated soldiers of their time; while Lee, Jackson, and Sherman, probably knew more of war before they waged it than any one else in the United States.

Surprise has been the foundation of almost all the grand strategical combinations of the past, as it will be of those to come. To what Federal soldier did it occur, on the morning of Chancellorsville, that Lee, confronted by 90,000 Federals, would detach the half of his own small force of 50,000 to attack the enemy in flank and rear? The heaven-born strategist "takes no counsel of his fears." Knowing that success is seldom to be won without incurring risks, he is always greatly daring; and by the skill with which he overcomes all obstacles he shows his superiority to the common herd.

The enlistments in the Union army during the Civil War aggregated 2,562,611. This does not include 105,000 seamen and marines, or some 230,000 militia and "emergency men," who served for short terms. Many of the enlistments, however, were for terms of only three to nine months, and the number, reduced to a term of three years, was 1,556,678.

It is not so easy to give exact figures for the Confederate army. Colonel Livermore says: "It is most disappointing that the mass of records published by the War Department contains no summary of the numbers who were under arms on the Confederate side. General Cooper, the adjutant-general of the Confederate army, stated soon after the war that no such summary existed. (7 *So. Hist. Society Papers*, 209)."

On the contrary, General Cooper stated (2 So. Hist. Society Papers, 20): "The files of this office which could best afford this information [as to numbers] were carefully boxed up and taken on our retreat from Richmond to Charlotte, N. C, where they were unfortunately captured, and, as I learn, are now in Washington."

There is no doubt as to the fact that the files referred to by General Cooper were in the archives of the War Department as late as 1867, and why they have never been published officially is a mystery.

The New York *Tribune* of the 26 June 1867 printed, from "Our Special Correspondent," an article on this subject which, for a long time, was supposed to have been the work of Swinton, but later was attributed to Whitelaw Reid. It read:

"Amongst the documents which fell into our hands at the downfall of the Confederacy are the returns, very nearly complete, of the Confederate armies from their organization in the summer of 1861 down to the spring of 1865. These returns have been carefully analyzed, and I am enabled to furnish the returns in every department and for almost every month, from these official sources. *We judge, in all, 600,000 different men were in the Confederate ranks during the war.*"

In the absence of official records, this is certainly good secondary evidence; and further confirmation is to be found in the fact that the *American Cyclopedia* (1875), edited by Charles A. Dana, late Assistant Secretary of War, quotes General Cooper's statement as to numbers, without comment.

Vice-President Stephens, Generals Cooper, Early, Wright, and Preston, Dr. Jones, and Dr. Bledsoe, — in fact, all of the Confederate authorities, who were familiar with the facts, agree that the total number of men in the army was about 600,000.

Their estimates are based upon the following figures:

Killed, or died of wounds		74,508
Deaths from all other causes		125,836
		200,344
Discharged	57,411	
Deserted	83,372	
Prisoners (1865)	90,000	
Surrendered (1865)	174,223	405,006
		605,350

A very instructive report to the Confederate Secretary of War, in January 1864, covering only six states east of the Mississippi, gives the following statistics regarding those not in the service:

Deducted for disloyalty	44,000
Unaccounted for (skulkers)	70,000
Exempt for all causes	96,000
Liable, but not enrolled	126,000
	336,000

Adding this total to the number of men actually enrolled (605,000) we have an aggregate of 941,000, which accounts for all but five per cent, of the men of military age in the Southern States, as shown by the Census of 1860.

During the first year of the war the Confederate ranks were filled entirely by volunteers. Then the act of the Confederate Congress of the 16 April 1862 authorized the President to call out for three years all white men resident in the Confederacy between the ages of 18 and 35. An act approved 27 September the same year enlarged the conscription to include all white males, not exempt, between 18 and 45; and the act of 17 February 1864 made all white males between 17 and 50 liable for service.

The only reliable basis, therefore, for estimating the potential military strength of the Confederacy is the United States Census of 1860. This gives in the eleven Confederate States a total of 984,475 white males between the ages of 18 and 45. It is thus demonstrated that the maximum possible strength of the Southern forces was less than a million men.

In the issue of *Current History* for August 1923, there is a labored article by A. B. Cassell- man, in which he endeavors to prove that there were 1,650,000 men in the Confederate army! This, by the way, is an increase of 10 per cent., or 150,000 men, from his previous estimate of 1,500,000 in *The Century* for March 1892.

Based upon the Census, Livermore estimates the number at 1,239,000; and based upon the average strength of regiments, at 1,228,000 to 1,406,000.

On the usual assumption that one in five of a total population is of age for military service, the Census of 1860, which showed in the Southern States a white population of about 5,500,000, would give an aggregate of 1,100,000 men of military age, but the actual figures were 984,000. Deducting the disloyal, the skulkers, the sick and unfit, and those legally exempt, we find that the actual military strength of the Confederacy could not have much exceeded 600,000 men.

The "estimates" of Colonel Livermore, and other Northern authorities, that there were from 1,200,000 to 1,650,000 men in the Confederate service are therefore manifestly absurd. The maximum manpower was less than a million, and no nation can possibly mobilize more than 60 per cent. of its entire male population. Granted that there were three and a half mil- lions of slaves, to do the domestic work, and furnish the manual labor, for raising the crops, and working on roads and fortifications, there must have been a large proportion of the adult white male population engaged in non-combatant work, such as making arms, ammunition, and supplies of every kind for the army, as well as employed in clerical and other positions.

In arriving at his figure of 1,239,000, for the number of men who came within the conscription acts, Colonel Livermore takes the census figures of 1860, then adds about 25 per cent. for the boys who reached the age of military service during the war, and assumes that *they were all in the ranks*! But this increase was fully counterbalanced by the number of men who passed the age of service; by deaths from natural causes, and by losses in battle. Moreover, fully 40 per cent. of the million adult white population of the Confederacy was in the four states of Tennessee, Arkansas, Louisiana, and Texas, from which comparatively few recruits were obtained during the last two years of the war.

In the letters of General Lee to his Government we find constant complaints of the unsatisfactory results from the conscription. For example, on the 11 February 1863, he writes the Secretary of War that only 421 new men have joined and 287 deserters returned, an aggregate of 708; while his losses by deaths, discharges, and desertions, amount to 1878. He begs the Secretary to use every means in his power to fill up the ranks.

Colonel Livermore, in another place, estimates the total Confederate levies, reduced to a three years' term of service, at 1,082,119, as compared with a similar figure of 1,556,678 for the Union army. This would give the Confederates about 70 per cent. of the Union strength; but a comparison of the Confederate and Union rolls, on the first days of January 1863, 1864, and 1865, gives them only 50 per cent. approximately of the Union totals. No adequate explanation of this discrepancy is offered.

The total number of men in the five main armies of the Union and the Confederacy, in service at any one period during the last year of the war, was approximately as follows:

	Federals	*Confederates*
Arkansas	30,000	20,000
Tennessee	70,000	40,000
Shenandoah	40,000	20,000
Carolinas	60,000	30,000
Virginia	100,000	60,000
	300,000	170,000

The same authority estimates the largest number of men in the Confederate army at any one time, the beginning of 1864, as 472,000; and, assuming that the deaths *prior to that date* were 250,000, arrives at an aggregate of over 700,000.

As the Confederate deaths, *during the entire war*, were about 200,000, these figures practically confirm the Confederate estimates.

The total deaths in the Union army during the Civil War, as shown by the Official Records, and in the Confederate army, as estimated by General Cooper, were:

	Federals	*Confederates*
Killed, or died of wounds	110,000	75,000
Deaths from other causes	250,000	125,000
	360,000	200,000

These statistics show that, in the Union army, 25 men died from disease to 11 who were killed or died from their wounds, while in the Confederate army the ratio was 25 to 15 — the average accepted ratio being 25 to 10. Taking into consideration the meagre hospital equipment of the South, the comparatively small proportion of deaths from disease is difficult to explain; but there is no doubt of the fact that the Southerners proved themselves able to withstand the strain of war better than their Northern opponents.

A whole volume might be written on the subject of numbers and losses, but we think that enough has been said to show that the Southern figures are substantially correct, and the Northern estimates grossly exaggerated.

The history of the Civil War conclusively proves the truth of Napoleon's adage, that Fortune always favors the heaviest battalions. There was but little difference in the fighting qualities of the two opposing armies. The South, on the whole, had abler commanders, a superior staff, and a more efficient intelligence department. The Confederate soldiers were better disciplined, more expert marksmen, finer horsemen, and more enduring marchers. Finally, the South had the enormous advantage of interior lines, and of acting generally on the defensive.

The North finally won, when it brought all its strength to bear, because it had far greater numbers, and enormous superiority in physical resources, such as arms, munitions of war, transportation, food, clothing, and hospital supplies. These advantages were, to a certain extent, counterbalanced by the fact that the Union armies were generally acting on the offensive, in the enemy's country, far from their base, thus making necessary large detachments to guard their lines of communication. Many Federal troops also were employed in non-combatant work, such as was done by negroes for the Southern army. Moreover, during the first three years of the war, the Union generals were constantly hampered by interference from their Government, and by lack of confidence on the part of their troops. "The success of our army," writes General Palfrey, "was undoubtedly greatly lessened by jealousy, distrust, and general want of *entente cordiale*." It is not necessary, therefore, to imagine that the South had twice as many soldiers as it really had, in order to explain why it took the North four long years to subdue a nation of a quarter its size.

Opinions have always differed, and probably always will, as to the reasons for the failure of the Southern States to achieve their independence. Northern writers generally assume that it was due to the larger population and greater resources of the Union; Southern authorities ascribe it to a want of perseverance, unanimity, and even of loyalty, on the part of the South.

The main cause, however, seems to have been the bad financial policy adopted by the Confederate Government. Mr. Davis and his Cabinet must have realized that a full treasury was necessary to defray the expenses of a great war; but they deliberately rejected the best means of raising money: the sale of the large and valuable cotton crop.

Statistics show that the cotton crop of 1860 amounted to nearly four million bales, and it is estimated that the South had on hand at the outbreak of the war about five million bales.

Appomattox after the end of hostilities.

During the war, "the price of cotton reached almost fabulous figures" in England. The mill-owners were finally forced to shut down entirely, and two million people were reduced to great distress. This cotton, if stored abroad at that time, could have been sold for at least $500,000,000, and probably for much more. The blockade of the Southern ports was proclaimed in May 1861, but it was not at all effective until the following spring. There was thus a period of nearly twelve months during which shipments could easily have been made. "The sum raised in that way," writes General Johnston, "would have enabled the War Department to procure at once arms enough for half a million of men, and after that expenditure the Confederate treasury would have been much richer than that of the United States."

Not only could the forces of the Confederacy have been completely armed and equipped, but the men could have been well fed, well paid, and the sick and wounded properly cared for. The Government, however, rejected this means of filling the treasury, and limited its financial efforts to printing bank-notes, which soon became practically worthless. During the last year of the war the monthly pay of a soldier would scarcely buy one meal for his family. Many men, thus compelled to choose between their loyalty to the State and their duties to their wives and children, left the army, or took every means to avoid military service, in order to support their families.

The proposition, that the Confederate Government should acquire all the cotton in the South, and ship it to Europe to be sold, was made when the problem of financing the war was seriously discussed at the outbreak of hostilities. The owners were ready to accept any fair terms that might be offered; and at that time, as above stated, there would have been no difficulty in putting the plan into operation. But this wise policy was rejected by Mr. Davis and his advisers, in the expectation that the distress caused by the lack of cotton in England and France would lead these two Powers to intervene, and force the United States to raise the blockade. Instead of relying on their own ample resources to win their independence, the Confederate States thus threw away their only means of financing the war. It was one of the worst political blunders in history, and it resulted in the loss of the struggle. With a full treasury, the success of the Confederacy would probably have been assured.

BIBLIOGRAPHY

THE principal source for the history of the Civil War is the *War of the Rebellion Official Records of the Union and Confederate Armies,* in 128 volumes, published by the Government, 1880-1901. In citing the Records the serial number only of the volume is given.

The list of books on the war is so long that it is possible to mention here only a few of the more important titles. For a fuller bibliography, see the *Cambridge Modern History,* vol. VII; also J. N. Larned, *Literature of American History,* in which about 300 of the more important works up to 1902 are considered. A guide to the thousands of articles published in magazines will be found in Poole's *Index.*

In addition to the special works listed below, the reader is referred to the general histories of McMaster, Rhodes, and Schouler.

WORKS CITED

ALEXANDER, GENERAL E. P. *Military Memoirs of a Confederate.* New York, 1907.

BATTLES AND LEADERS OF THE CIVIL WAR. 4 vols. New York, 1887.

BUCHAN, JOHN. *Two Ordeals of Democracy.* New York, 1925.

CAMPAIGNS OF THE CIVIL WAR. 12 vols. New York, 1882-1883.

1. NICOLAY. *The Outbreak of Rebellion.*
2. FORCE. *From Fort Henry to Corinth.*
3. WEBB. *The Peninsula.*
4. ROPES. *The Army Under Pope.*
5. PALFREY. *The Antietam and Fredericksburg.*
6. DOUBLEDAY. *Chancellorsville and Gettysburg.*
7. CIST. *The Army of the Cumberland.*
8. GREENE. *The Mississippi.*
9. COX. *Atlanta.*
10. COX. *Franklin and Nashville.*
11. POND. *The Shenandoah Valley.*
12. HUMPHREYS. *The Virginia Campaign of 1864 and 1865.*

CHANNING, EDWARD. *History of the United States.* Vol. VI. 1925.

COX, GENERAL J. D. *Military Reminiscences.* 2 vols. New York, 1900.

DAVIS, JEFFERSON. *Rise and Fall of the Confederate Government.* 2 vols. New York, 1881.

FISKE, JOHN. *The Mississippi Valley in the Civil War.* Boston, 1900.

GANOE, MAJOR WILLIAM A. *History of the United States Army*. New York, 1924.

GRACIE, ARCHIBALD. *The Truth about Chickamauga*. Boston, 1911.

GRANT, GENERAL U. S. *Personal Memoirs*. 2 vols. New York, 1885.

HENDERSON, COLONEL G. F. R. *Stonewall Jackson*. 2 vols. London, 1898. Also, *The Science of War*. London, 1919.

JOHNSTON, GENERAL J. E. *Narrative of Military Operations*. New York, 1874.

LIVERMORE, COLONEL T. L. *Numbers and Losses in the Civil War*. Boston, 1901.

LONG, A. L. *Memoirs of Robert E. Lee*. Philadelphia, 1887.

LONGSTREET, GENERAL JAMES. *From Manassas to Appomattox*. Philadelphia, 1896.

MACARTNEY, C. E. *Lincoln and His Generals*. Philadelphia, 1925.

MAURICE, SIR FREDERICK. *Robert E.Lee*. New York, 1925.

RHODES, JAMES F. *History of the Civil War*. New York, 1917.

ROPES, JOHN G. *Story of the Civil War*. 2 vols. New York, 1894–1898. Also the continuation by Colonel W. R. Livermore, 4 vols. New York, 1913.

SHERIDAN, GENERAL P. H. *Personal Memoirs*. 2 vols. New York, 1888.

SHERMAN, GENERAL W. T. *Memoirs*. 2 vols. New York, 1875.

SMITH, THEODORE C. *Life and Letters of James A. Garfield*. New Haven, 1925.

STEELE, MAJOR M. F. *American Campaigns*. 1 vol. and atlas. Washington, 1922.

UPTON, GENERAL EMORY. *Military Policy of the United States*. Washington, 1912.

VAN HORNE, THOMAS B. *History of the Army of the Cumberland*. 2 vols, and atlas. Cincinnati, 1875.